THE MILLER COLLECTION

ISBN: 978-0-9944968-6-7 (Print Collection)

Cover Design by Tugboat Design

Interior Formatting by Melissa Williams Design—based on initial design by Tugboat Design

Go to www.jasperwolfauthor.com
for more information on Jasper's latest releases

Become a subscriber and receive
chapter excerpts—pre-release special

CONTENTS

HUNTED..9

THE WAITING ROOM................................223

    PART ONE: *The Missing*.............................227
    PART TWO: *The Priest, the Cop and the Judge*............395
    PART THREE: *The Monster and The Spider's Nest*......463

PICTON...575

    Foreword...
    577

HUNTED

Jasper Wolf

HUNTED

"The world is full of monsters with friendly faces."

~ Heather Brewer

Dedicated to

DAVID

The best writer in the family, forever in my heart

Chapter 1

Friday Jan 24th 1992

Mason drove his brand-new white BMW along the Hume Highway at a steady speed, not obviously slow but making sure he kept below the 110-kilometre speed limit. As he neared the forest, his anxiety began to ease. Not far now.

Once he turned off the main road and down the long dirt road, he felt even more at ease. The gravel driveway, which was now overgrown, finally came into view. Seconds later, the cabin appeared behind a row of pine trees.

As a child, Mason had always enjoyed his time at the cabin. It was the only place where his innocence remained intact. Maybe it was because the rooms were too close to one another for his father to try anything. Or maybe it was the fact that his dad was enjoying his holiday and his mum was happy in her own way.

During those summers, he felt like a real child in a real family, and it was a good feeling. The cabin was his escape from the world. Even now, it was the only place where he felt safe.

Now, he was returning to his safe summer haven.

For the last two years, Mason had spent nearly every spare weekend at the cabin. He had turned the ramshackle cabin into a tri-level liveable weekend property. He now had it just the way he needed it. It offered a spacious lounge room, complete with stone fireplace. The hexagonal meals area and kitchen both overlooked the large 20-acre allotment. Finishing off the middle level was a quiet study nook.

The spiral staircase was located in a corner off the meals area. The stairs, leading up, led to three bedrooms and the communal bathroom, while the stairs leading down led to an enclosed garage-cum-cellar. It had originally been designed to keep as an open carport. It had seen better days and was in need of more than a lick of paint. Fitting it out was where Mason had concentrated most of his efforts. It had to be perfect.

The narrow winding driveway that had originally led directly to the front door had now been extended to provide access to the undercover cellar. It was enclosed by two large barn-style swinging doors.

By the time Mason was finished he was happy it would suit his purpose.

Today would be the first time it would be used.

His attention was broken when the prize in the boot of his car began stirring and making strange muffled noises.

He had arrived just in time!

* * *

Rebecca Carrington had been walking, as she had for the last eight months, from her doorstep in Amelia Avenue to the police academy situated at the top of Jells Road. The walk included a shortcut along the bike path through the wetlands.

The wetlands were surrounded by shrubs and reeds. Mason had lain in wait for her among the shrubs, kneeling on one knee. As soon as he caught sight of Rebecca turning the corner, her backpack slung over her right shoulder, he prepared himself. With the tall reeds blocking Rebecca's view of the bike path ahead, Mason lay himself down across the path, clutching his chest. As he had known she would, she knelt down beside him and asked, "Are you all right?"

"I'm fine but you're fucked!" he said, pressing an object into her side. Rebecca didn't see exactly what the object was; he was too fast. But as soon as she felt the pain, she knew what it was. The taser hurt like a thousand large needles and incapacitated her. Then he injected her with his prepared syringe of Benzodiapine, which only took a few seconds to render her unconscious.

Mason picked Rebecca up, together with her backpack, and carried her towards his vehicle, parked on the nearby side street.

Only one person saw him, a fit young jogger who looked as if he spent too much time in the gym. "Is she all right?" the jogger asked as he passed Mason, pausing as he awaited an answer. "She has diabetes," Mason quickly responded. "Needs her insulin," he added. The jogger, satisfied, continued on his way.

Mason approached the getaway vehicle in less than a minute. He had removed the key from his pocket ready to open the car. The boot popped and the indicator lights flashed twice. The inside of the boot was covered in plastic, top to bottom, front to back. Mason glanced around quickly before placing her into the boot. Then he calmly closed it, walked to the driver's side and got in.

Mason had taken every precaution possible to ensure his success. He had stolen two sets of plates and a second car, a white Holden. While it was only a short drive to his own vehicle, transferring the girl to his car was the most dangerous part of the plan. Hidden off a back track at the base of some parkland sat Mason's own BMW. While transferring Rebecca from one boot to the other had risks, Mason thought detection was a lot less likely on a secluded track than in a side street.

He knew he might have been seen in the side street. Yet with his disguise of red hair and beard and stolen car, should anyone have seen the abduction it could not be traced back to him.

* * *

Rebecca, who had regained consciousness shortly before, felt the vehicle slow down, followed by a few bumps before it came to a stop. She had no idea how long they had been travelling and with her hands tied firmly behind her back, there was no way she could see her watch. She knew only that she was in a car boot.

Rebecca began to rub her hands frantically against what she believed was a jack. She stopped when she heard the sound of the car door opening.

'I hope you're ready for a fight because I'm not going quietly,' she thought. Again, she began to rub her wrists, hoping it was doing some good, but the rope was holding tight.

By now, she was expecting the boot to pop at any second, but she was surprised when the footsteps on the gravel outside slowly moved away. She then heard what she thought were footsteps on wooden steps or flooring. When she heard a creaking sound, she thought it must be wooden steps.

Rebecca rested her hands for a moment before trying to pull them apart, but the rope held tight. She knew if she didn't get free, she would be dead.

Frantically moving her hands around, she couldn't find anything useful that might help her free them. Then her ears picked up the sound of footsteps on the gravel beside her. 'He must have missed the weak step,' she thought, as she hadn't heard it creak upon his return.

Shuffling her body around quickly, banging her head on the lid of the boot as she did so, Rebecca positioned herself ready for her own little surprise attack. She placed her feet straight at the lid of the boot, ready to kick up hard as soon as she saw it begin to open. Hopefully, she would be able to knock the lid up and clip the fucker right in the face and send him flying. All she needed was the right timing and a bit of luck.

Rebecca heard a small beep and moments later, a beam of light and a rush of fresh air entered the boot. Rebecca's reflexes were lightning fast. She kicked. The boot flew up. She heard a thump and then a cry of "Ahhh!" Mason's chin was collected by the lid of the boot. With the boot ajar, Rebecca scooted on her arse towards the daylight. Her legs were hanging out and her shoulders were holding up the lid. She couldn't see her assailant anywhere. She pushed all her weight forward, rolling her body out onto the hard, gravelly ground. Rebecca spun her head around but could still see no one. Staggering to her feet, she tried to run, still noticing the effects of the drugs. Her legs were heavy, as if she had just run a marathon.

"You looking for me?" said a voice from behind her. Spinning on her heels, Rebecca turned towards the voice. An object struck her on the right shoulder, sending a sharp burning pain down her arm. He had hit her with such force that it sent her back down to the gravel. She rolled over and looked up at a man standing over her with a shovel clasped in his hands. He didn't look like the same red-haired man who she thought had kidnapped her.

Blood was dripping from a cut just below his mouth where the boot had connected. Scooting away from the shovel-wielding man, she felt the gravel graze her butt and her palms as she dragged herself backwards.

"There's no point trying to get away," Mason said calmly, digging the shovel into the ground with his foot. "Look around. You're in the middle of nowhere. Where will you run?" he taunted her, approaching his prize who sat slumped on his driveway.

"Come and get me then, you sick fuck!" Rebecca sneered, not wanting to show him her fear. Mason removed the shovel from the ground and headed towards the five-foot-six blonde.

She knew what she was up against. But she also knew she had a lot of fight left in her and she wasn't giving up. As Mason approached, she waited to make her move. Once he was within reach, she would take her chance.

He took another step towards her, his shadow now over her. 'Now or never,' she thought, kicking out her right leg as hard as she could. The combination of the force of the kick and the loose gravel on the drive forced Mason to lose his balance and sent him crumbling to the ground before her.

Rebecca got to one knee and pressed her foot hard into the ground, ready for take-off, but before she could launch herself up, something connected with her leg and sent pain shooting up from her ankle. She cried out in pain and saw that the shovel was gouged into her heel.

Mason knew she was pinned and he was glad. The last thing he wanted in this heat was to chase some useless blonde through the woods.

Gathering himself, Mason got to his feet and removed the taser from his pocket.

* * *

Rebecca's hair was no longer tied neatly in a ponytail, as it had been when she'd begun her walk that morning. It was now clumped and smeared with dirt and blood. Her blue jeans were torn and stained.

Mason had leaned her against the balustrade at the top of the cellar stairs. When she awoke, she realised she was bound to the staircase by her hands and feet. She could see no way out.

"I told you not to run but you wouldn't listen, would you? Now your death will be more painful."

With her vision still blurry, she did not recognise the person speaking to her but she knew it was her captor. She blinked several times until she could see the man standing in front of her. He was holding something. She couldn't make it out at first, but then she saw exactly what it was. A sword, a samurai sword to be exact.

He began to wave it around in circles in front of her. Woosh! Woosh! The blade cut the air in front of her.

"What are you going to do to me?" Rebecca slurred, the taser still affecting her tongue and cheek muscles.

Mason offered no response. He simply began his work. Firstly, he sliced the two shoulder straps off her top. "Oops, I must have nicked you."

He laughed as blood began to flow down her shoulder onto her chest. "I'm new at this," he chuckled.

"Get the fuck away from me!" Rebecca began to shout. There was no hiding her fear now, which only grew as she saw the man in front of her change. It seemed as though the man behind the eyes had vacated the premises. His eyes were dark and she saw pure evil in them, which sent a shiver down her spine. She could smell death. Her death.

Mason firmly clasped the sword tightly in both hands and before Rebecca could absorb what was happening, he ran the sword through her stomach. Her mouth filled with blood and she gave a final, gurgling cry.

Then he raised the sword high over his head and brought it down hard, severing her head.

It was over.

Victorious, Mason had seen it happen in slow motion. It had been like watching himself in a movie. It was meant to have been perfect. The pressure gauge had been released a little but he still felt empty. No matter how much he looked at his handiwork, the satisfied feeling he was after remained absent.

Maybe when it was on display he would get the feeling he was looking for. He brought up a large jar from his cellar and unscrewed the lid. He picked up Rebecca's severed head by her hair and placed it in the jar, then filled it with formaldehyde. The last thing he wanted was for his work to go to ruin.

Mason placed the jar on the display shelf he had made specially for the cellar, stood back and admired his finished work. Finally, there was some excitement in his pants. Wasting no time, he began to masturbate.

Chapter 2

Monday September 15th 2003

"Now recruiting!" the TV blasted its high-spirited jingle for the Victorian Police advertisement. They had been recruiting heavily over the past few years, as many female officers had been murdered. Since the early 90s, the numbers joining the force had been in steady decline.

Female officers were clearly concerned about becoming the next victim of the madman who had been dubbed the 'East Side Slayer'. He was still out there and his love of killing was increasing. The Slayer's tally to date was six, with one still missing, suspected abducted and murdered.

The police didn't seem to have a clue as to his identity or how he was targeting his victims. The only common thread was that they were all policewomen.

I sat back in my leather chair staring at the TV mounted on my office wall. It was one of the latest LCD flat screens and it had cost me a small fortune, but it was a gift I had promised myself for my years of hard work.

I was now a qualified psychologist, majoring in criminal psychology. My major year had been my most enjoyable. I was able to secure a place for a four-week stay at the Quantico Behavioural Science Unit. It really lit the fire in my belly for criminology. While my practice paid the bills with the substantial number of normal cases, the criminal cases and requests for help from the police were more lucrative.

During my childhood, I had always wanted to be a police officer. Many of my friends wanted to be playing cricket for Australia or Aussie Rules, but not me. I always wanted to be a cop. My best friend was the same. Maybe that's what helped us stay such good friends. The only difference between Jake Miller and me was that he was fit and I was severely handicapped by the time I was 12. I had five major heart operations and after I turned 20, two more followed. It was before my last operation that Jake broke the news that he had made the cut at the academy. I was disappointed for myself, at first, but it was replaced with overwhelming pride for Jake's efforts. He knew how proud I was of him, but he also knew how hard it was for me.

It wasn't until after my last operation that Jake suggested I should pursue a psychology/criminology degree. Maybe I could fight crime that way. He was right. It would be the only way. I had trouble doing anything physical. I struggled to run any great distance. As unrealistic as my dream was, I still wanted to believe I could do it. After all, I was six foot four and I often wondered how big I would have grown had I not been afflicted by my heart condition. Although tall, I was slim with little muscle definition, due to a lack of oxygen over the years. I was a tall weed.

I sat in my office chair trying to have a quick break before starting my preparation for tomorrow. The leather was splitting a little along the stitching of the armrests. I sat tossing letters around my desk without opening them. I looked through the client's files I was working on for the next day. I knew I would have to make a start on them soon.

The blonde-haired newsreader on Seven Nightly News, Christine Hope, began her news report. "We have breaking news in the case of missing Constable Jan West. We will now cross to Mark Harrity on location."

"Thanks Christine. I'm on the shore of Rye Back Beach where earlier today, local surfers found a woman's remains. While they are yet to be identified, police believe they could be those of missing Constable Jan West. Police are seeking the public's help with this case and they stress that any information, no matter how small, could be vital in solving this series of terrible crimes!"

"Thanks Mark," Christine said, before the video cut off. "Moving on to other news."

I switched off the TV, threw the remote on the desk and stood in front of the window to take in the lovely view. The city looked beautiful at sunset. I caught the reflection of my bloodshot hazel eyes. My thoughts immediately returned to the Slayer murders. I stood there trying to imagine what type of person would be capable of such a thing.

When I was at Quantico, we'd spent many sessions studying profiling as a useful tool in narrowing the search for murderers. We had studied past killers like Bundy, Gacy and Sutcliffe. I had read all the books by John Douglas on criminal profiling techniques and while I was there, I was lucky enough to sit in on some of his classes. He was a quietly spoken but observant man. The interviews of past serial killers provided exceptional insight into why they acted the way they did.

Bundy, for example, killed in excess of 33 women. Many say he did it because he was insane, while others including me thought he did it so that he could finally be successful at something. But more importantly he killed because he liked it and once he got a taste for it, he was addicted. Addicted to the feeling of power he had over the women as they died.

I went back to my desk and sank back into the chair. Out of the matching filing cabinet, I withdrew the file I wanted and began to flick through it. I had kept all the newspaper clippings about the East Side Slayer and had created my own preliminary profile of him.

So far, I had compiled:

Late 20s-mid 30s
Professionally employed
Likely to have freedom in his job
Highly intelligent
Possibly a family man
Traumatic upbringing. Most likely a broken home.

If I had more information, I thought I might be able develop a more accurate profile. If I knew more about the killer's signature, for instance. Every killer had one, but the police had kept it out of the media for some reason.

I had also created two maps, one with locations where all the women had disappeared, the other of all the killer's dump sites. There was no pattern in either map.

The only pattern I could see was that this killer was evolving and becoming more confident. The cooling-off period between killings had decreased each time, the last two murders being only three months apart.

Chapter 3

September 15th 2003 (4.50pm)

Mason Belic stood in the park as twilight approached. He was dressed in blue jeans and a light brown knitted jumper. With the wind off the ocean beginning to pick up, he was glad he had brought the jumper.

His son Jamie laughed as he pushed him on the swing. "Higher Daddy," he called. Mason loved his son; he honestly believed that Jamie was the only person he ever could love, or feel attached to. He loved everything about him: his blond hair, his blue eyes, his contagious laugh. When he heard Jamie's laugh he felt almost human, a feeling he never had with anyone else. He often believed he was dead on the inside.

He loved being with his son although today he was not at the park for Jamie. Today he was there for his own reasons. He wanted to watch the police investigating the work he had done. He wanted to marvel in the glory of what he had created. The thought that he had caused this was the most fulfilling thing he had ever had. Soon, his whole plan would be laid out for all to see. Soon, very soon, he would feel the desire to kill again.

"Dad, keep pushing, come on, higher. Dad, more, you're slowing down."

"I'm sorry Jamie. I was daydreaming."

"You're being silly, Daddy," Jamie said as his father pushed him high into the air.

"Weeee!" he screamed, as he swung back towards his father. "You're being a silly billy," he sang. "You're a silly billy," he repeated several times between pushes. "Daddy, what are all the police doing? Why are there so many?" he asked, without waiting for the answer to his first question.

"I'm not sure, buddy," Mason replied, knowing exactly what they were doing across the road. He was the reason they were there.

"Dad, do you think they will take me for a ride in the car with the lights going?" His eyes were filled with excitement and he was grinning at the thought of riding in the police car. The only one more excited was the man pushing him on the swing. However, he showed no emotion at all.

"I think they might be too busy, I'm sure they have lots to do." Mason continued pushing Jamie. He had a real rhythm going now. Out of the corner of his eye, Mason could see a police officer approaching.

"Excuse me sir, I'm afraid you're going to have to clear the area, we have an investigation to conduct and we have to seal off the area. Sorry to spoil your day," the officer added as he removed a notepad and pen from his pocket.

"That's ok, Officer, we were about to leave anyhow." Mason bent over and grabbed Jamie off the swing.

"But Daddy, I want to play longer!" Jamie responded angrily, almost ready to throw a tantrum. Had the policeman not been standing there he was sure that Jamie would have been screaming at the top of his lungs.

"Before you go, may I just ask you a few questions? I also need your contact details in case we have any follow-up questions." The officer had his pen poised.

"Sure." Mason paused. "Do you mind if he plays a little while we talk?"

"Yes, no problem," the officer responded.

"How long have you been here?"

"I guess about 20 minutes, not too long," was Mason's quick reply.

"Have you noticed anyone or anything strange while you have been here?"

"No, I can't say I have. It's been really quiet. The only activity I noticed was a couple of people walking their dog but they looked like a retired couple on their afternoon stroll."

Jamie jumped off the swing and headed towards the merry-go-round, jumping up and down as he ran.

"May I just get your name and address?" the officer asked, surveying the area.

"Sure. It's Philip Andrews, 19 Chambers Road, Rye," Mason replied. The name and address were real, they just didn't belong to him. He even had the car registration and make in his head in case he was asked.

It was easy to get the information when you knew how. Mason had plenty of experience as a real estate agent. He'd learned a lot of ways to gain information. All he had to do was knock on the door of the home and tell them he had someone looking to relocate. Would they be interested in selling? In most cases, the owners said no, but when you mentioned that your clients were prepared to be very generous on the purchase price they seldom hesitated to give their name and contact numbers.

The policeman never asked for the registration or to see his licence. With very little information gained, he was finished with his brief series of questions. Little did he know he was standing just metres from the most wanted man in Melbourne.

As the officer headed back towards his colleagues, Mason began to laugh inside, or so he thought.

"What you laughing about, Daddy?" his son asked.

"I was laughing at you being a silly billy," he said. "Do you feel like a cheeseburger for dinner?" he asked as they walked out of the park together.

"I want a cheeby, I want a cheeby," Jamie sang and skipped all the way to the car.

Mason had parked two streets away. If the officer had asked him how they'd got to the park, he would have just said they'd walked from home.

"Daddy, can I get an ice cream too?" Jamie asked, as he hopped into his booster seat.

Mason thought his son must have been mustering up his courage all the way to the car. "Sure thing, buddy," Mason responded affectionately. It was fake affection and Mason knew it. Although he was pleased to see his son happy, his real happiness came from the scene of destruction he had caused.

Chapter 4

Friday 3rd October 2003 (1am)

Raindrops began falling on the windscreen. At first, the rain was light but after only a few seconds, it was almost hailing. "Shit Geoff, turn on the ignition so we can wind down the windows." Geoff leaned forward and turned the key into the accessory position.

Jake, who was sitting in the passenger seat, hit the window button. As the window slid down the water began to drip in, landing on the sleeve of his three-quarter length woollen black jacket. "We need to keep our eyes open here," Jake said, without offering a glance at the driver.

He sat with his right hand on his Beretta that was resting on his knee and his left hand around the door handle, his eyes fixed on the entrance to the Mobile service station.

It was their third night on watch. All three nights had been dead quiet so far. "It's not going to happen again tonight," Geoff said, sounding half-asleep and bored to tears. During the last five hours, every word spoken between them had occurred without either of them taking their gaze off the entrance.

"It will happen," Jake replied softly, as if willing it through some psychic force. It had to happen soon, he thought. After all, nine servos had been hit in 11 days and this was the only one that had been missed in the same area.

Every hit had been the same. Five guys. Two took the entrance, two hit the safes and one went after the register. The last one had been a BP station where the attendant had been shot and killed.

A lady in a black BMW X3 pulled up at pump six. In the back, a little blonde girl was asleep, her head slumped forward. From Jake's perception, she was probably a single mum who had been on a night out.

The mother finished pumping the petrol into the vehicle, replaced the cap, locked the car, and headed in to pay.

Jake wondered if parents understood the risks of leaving children in cars unsupervised. It could go so wrong so quickly. The mother exited the servo, got back in her vehicle and headed off.

* * *

Jake began thinking about his own childhood. He had been a big boy; six foot two at the age of 12 and he was the only year 7 student who could dunk a basketball, something that most year 12 students still couldn't do. He didn't grow much taller but he bulked up once he started hitting the gym.

When he went into the academy, he weighed 110 kilograms and was all muscle. He could not only move fast but also do a 15 on the beep test. Even as a boy, he had genuinely cared about people and wanted to see justice done. He was the type of kid who was good at all sports and yet could study little and still pass with high marks.

When he was in year 10, his desire to be a cop was confirmed and the notion of preserving justice really hit home. Karl, one of his classmates, was sitting innocently in his mum's car. It was nothing flashy but it was a new Holden commodore, valued at $30,000. He had been engrossed in the cricket. It was the final session on day 1 and Australia was 2/258. Dean Jones was nearing his hundred.

While Karl's mother was in the shop collecting groceries for the evening meal, a man came out of nowhere and drove off in the car. Karl and his kid sister Amanda were taken with the vehicle.

Police later found both Amanda and Karl dead on the side of a dirt track, shot at close range. The carjacker was a man named James Mitchell, on a three-day coke bender. He was caught trying to escape to Sydney. He was convicted of manslaughter and sentenced to only 20 years' jail, his lawyer successfully arguing that the drugs had affected him to such an extent that he did not know what he was doing, therefore he'd had no intent to kill.

The lenient sentence angered Jake and he promised himself to keep doing his job of getting criminals off the streets, while hoping the judges would start handing out sentences that reflected the severity of the crime.

* * *

Snapping out of his reflections, Jake took his left hand off the door handle and picked up the radio. "How are things going in there? I hope you've left some doughnuts for the customers?"

"I haven't served a hot chick in an hour," Bobby's voice crackled back.

"Now come on Bobby, you're supposed to be looking out for these guys, not searching for a future wife."

"Just trying to stay undercover. I thought I was supposed to pass for a dumb servo attendant and I bet all they do is perv."

"I'm sure you're right. Just try and stay alert in there, ok?" Jake tried not to laugh at his stupid remarks.

He placed the handset back in the cradle and reached into the back seat for the Thermos and the cups. It was coffee time. He was in the middle of undoing the lid when a group of five men, all wearing black Nike hoodies, turned the corner and entered the servo.

Jake's coffee time would have to wait. He threw the Thermos in the back. "Heads up, guys!" Bobby's voice said across the radio before gunfire rang out.

Jake was halfway out the door when he saw Bobby's head jerk backwards and his body disappear behind the counter.

"Stay here and call for backup!" Jake shouted to Geoff as he drew his second Beretta from its right shoulder holster. With Berettas in both hands, Jake headed towards the entrance. He could see all five men begin to disperse quickly throughout the store. The one who had shot Bobby was now behind the counter with one of his buddies, while two ethnic looking guys were heading to the back of the store. The last suspect was fat and slow and he was halfway down the chip aisle heading towards the ATM.

Jake opened fire.

He didn't even wait until he was inside the store before he unleashed the other Beretta. He fired at the slow one first, three quick shots. Two of them found their target, one destroyed a bag of Doritos. The big guy fell to his knees, paused and then flopped head first onto the floor.

Jake then showered the front counter with six more bullets. He didn't think any of them hit but the spray bought him enough time to dive through the doors and slide behind the ice-cream machine. It wasn't ideal, but it gave him enough cover to continue his fire at the counter and the door that the other two had disappeared behind.

Jake reloaded his Beretta. He had a feeling he would need every bullet.

He peered over the ice-cream machine to see what was happening at the front of the store. The man who had shot Bobby returned fire with a 12 gauge. It was loud and it packed a punch. The outer side of the metal machine was sprayed with pellets. Jake felt a pellet clip his ear.

A large Caucasian man slid across the counter. Jake estimated he was several centimetres taller than he was and probably 15 kilos heavier. He landed, pumped his shotgun and ran towards Jake.

Jake acted quickly, firing two shots from each gun. He hit the gunman three times, twice in the neck and once in the chest. The last bullet flew into the counter somewhere. The gunman hit the floor, dropping his gun and clasping at his chest.

The two ethnic guys returned from the back of the store looking to see what the fuck was going on. Both men stepped through the doorway and instantly began firing. Jake ducked for cover. They looked like brothers, maybe even twins. The two kept firing for what seemed like an eternity.

The door buzzer went and Jake heard two quick shots followed by a third and finally a fourth. Jake's attention immediately turned to Geoff.

"Let's get this fuck and get out of here!" one of the voices from the rear of the store said. He sounded like a Maori.

Jake looked around the left corner of the machine. They were no longer standing in the doorway; they had obviously split up.

Jake heard movement on his left but could see nothing. He knelt down lower and saw the ankles of one of the men. They were fat and wide and led to big feet and big shoes. Jake aimed and let fire a quick burst. He wasn't sure how many shots he fired. He purposely shot in a direct line from the ankle upwards.

Cries of pain filled the petrol station; Jake had hit him but he wasn't sure where or how many times.

His brother came running out of the middle aisle firing his weapon, a high calibre Magnum. The buzzer went again as someone exited. Jake stood and fired through the door. The brother, running backwards, returned fire, and glass went flying everywhere. Jake continued to fire with both pistols until there was nothing left to fire. The brother had almost made the pump before Jake's bullets stilled him.

It wasn't until the gunfight was over that he realised he had been hit. It might have been a ricocheted bullet; nonetheless, the damage was done. Jake sat behind the machine once again, his calf spurting blood. He removed his jacket and ripped off the sleeves from his shirt, folded them and placed them over the bullet wound. He used his tie to hold the self-made bandages and hoped it would stem the flow of blood.

Jake reloaded and hobbled out from behind the machine, checking the corners and covering himself in both directions as he went from aisle to aisle. He came to the other brother. He was still alive but Jake didn't think he would last long. He had been hit several times, including in the chest and side. There was a large pool of blood under him and blood had started to seep from his ears.

Jake slowly headed towards the counter that Bobby had occupied only minutes earlier.

He went around the cash register side and saw Bobby slumped against the wall. He had been shot in the head at close range with the 12 gauge and the damage was significant. The blood splatter was all across the wall. Jake was lucky not to dry retch.

Jake left Bobby where he lay and headed for Geoff. The assailant on the driveway was dead but there was no sign of the one who had fled. Geoff was sitting where he had left him, but there was a trail of blood leading back to the car. Geoff's breathing was shallow and weak. "Hold on buddy, help's on the way."

Geoff had obviously met the fleeing robber on the drive. Geoff looked like he'd got the worst of the exchange.

Jake knelt beside Geoff until help arrived and then Jake was loaded into the second ambulance to have the bullet removed from his calf.

Geoff succumbed to his injuries on the way to the hospital. His vital organs had been directly hit and the blood loss was just too great.

By the time backup arrived, there were two dead officers and four dead robbers.

One was still missing. His name was Tyrone, and he lay just metres away at the bottom of the dumpster where he was hiding and trying to figure out what to do next. He had taken a shot to the knee and had struggled to make it this far.

He had killed a cop. Fuck, he was in deep shit now.

He could hear the police outside surrounding him, his blood trail easy to follow.

Tyrone had made the decision he would not be going back to jail. His plan was 'death by cop'. It was his only way out of this shithole and he accepted that his time to check out had arrived.

Tyrone reloaded, stood up and opened fire. He only managed two shots in his last blaze of glory before he finally checked out.

Chapter 5

Friday 3rd October 2003 (6am)

I had arrived early to prepare for my clients that day. It was only early but the offices opposite me were already buzzing with life.

I wasn't looking forward to the day, as I had a sex addict client coming in. I was helping her understand that sex and love were very different, and sex was not the only way to feel needed.

I hated dealing with sex addicts and divorcees, because they often misread a sympathetic ear as a sign of affection.

In this case, the attraction was there, well, the physical aspect anyway. She was stunning and I was . . . how would you put it? Male, and single. However, she was my patient and that line would never be crossed.

I took out the notes of our last session, which I had taped, as always. They knew I was the only one who ever listened to them.

Halfway through the tape, I received the call I had always feared. It was Jake Miller's mum. My best friend had been shot in the line of duty.

He was the only survivor of a sting that had gone wrong. His mum quickly reassured me that he was all right and his injuries were only minor. Of course, that's the last thing you think when you hear the word 'shot'.

Jake had spent years in the police force moving up from traffic to desk jockey, before he made detective and then lead detective in vice. After that, he'd headed up the armed robbery taskforce for the servo bandits.

Even though his injuries were minor, I put down the files and left a message for my secretary to reschedule all my appointments for that day.

Jake looked like he was enjoying the time off when I walked into his room. He was sitting in bed with his left leg up, wrapped in bandages, watching television and eating some sort of cereal. "It's 8am and you're already eating?" I said without hesitating.

"I'm still groggy from theatre but the food is helping."

I knew what he meant. I had spent more hours in hospital than anyone should ever have to.

I'd only been there a few minutes when Jake's parents walked into the room. His mum had a newspaper under her arm and his dad was holding a

Styrofoam cup of coffee. "We got you a coffee and the newspaper, darl," his mum said.

"Thanks Mum," Jake mumbled with a mouth full of cereal.

The events of Jake's night had made the front page. The article, headed 'Two Police Dead in Servo Shootout', focused on the two dead police officer heroes rather than on the criminals. Below the heading were photos of Geoff and Bobby. There was also a separate two-page spread detailing the events.

Jake didn't read the article or speak of what had happened. He just lay there drinking his coffee. His parents left soon after, and he and I didn't speak much at first, until I asked him if he wanted to do the trivia in the paper. We used to do it quite often. He would usually win, but I was always up for the challenge.

After Jake again beat me at the trivia, I headed down to the hospital café for some food. I was starving and ordered an egg and bacon roll with a bottle of OJ. It was surprisingly good, or maybe I was just too hungry to notice it was average hospital food. On the way back, I passed the gift shop and bought Jake a book, getting a copy for myself at the same time. It was Stephen King's latest novel, 'Wolves of the Calla', the fifth book in his 'Dark Tower' series. We'd both started reading the series in the early 1990s. The last in the series, 'Wizard and Glass', was a cracker and we'd been eagerly awaiting the next instalment.

When I arrived back in Jake's room, he was watching some morning TV show about how to use a newly designed ladder.

"Looks like riveting stuff, maybe you'll find this more to your liking." I handed him the book. He smiled. I sat in the chair next to his bed and we both began reading the continuing saga of Roland, Eddie, Susanna, Jake, and Oy.

When a loud voice interrupted us, Jake didn't even have to look up to know the voice belonged to his boss, Richard Knight. "Sorry to interrupt your recovery. I just wanted to run a few things past you so you know what's going on.

"We're holding a state funeral for Geoff and Bobby next week. Their families are hoping you'll be able to make it. They're very appreciative of everything you did. They know you did your best."

"I didn't do enough." Jake turned his head and attention to the window.

"You know, Jake, we have people you can talk to. You've been through an extraordinary ordeal."

"I'll be fine, I just need some time." Jake's attention remained fixed on the window.

"I do have some good news for you. I had a call from the head of homicide this morning requesting you be transferred there. I said I'd speak to you about it. They want you to be the new lead detective of the Slayer taskforce, Eagle. You get to select your own team."

Jake didn't reply immediately, and Richard continued. "Have a think about it."

Jake looked at the captain. "I'll do it. Send me the files and I'll get started from here."

"It can wait a few days, Jake," Richard replied.

"Just send the files," Jake repeated. Richard nodded. He looked uncomfortable but he didn't seem ready to leave.

Jake returned his attention to his book.

"Are you ok?" I asked. He lifted his head and his eyes met mine. "Geoff and Bobby are dead because of me, I didn't do enough, Brodie, it's as simple as that." Tears welled in his eyes.

I offered no advice because there was nothing I could say that would help. We had been friends for years and he knew I understood his pain.

Jake put his bookmark in the book and put the book down beside him. "You know, if I'm heading up the Slayer taskforce, I'll need a criminologist. Interested?"

"Are you able to do that?"

"Of course. They'll need someone to have a fresh look and if I bring in fresh people, that will be even better. You're qualified, aren't you?

"Yes, of course I am, you know that. But I'm not a police officer. I can't just become one."

"I can get the commissioner to use his authority to make you one," Richard interrupted.

"Can he do that?" I asked, still unsure of the possibility.

"Believe it or not, section 27 of the Police Act allows for the commissioner to waive the prescribed requirements and appoint anyone as a police officer under special circumstances. I think seven unsolved police murders qualifies as special circumstances. Don't you think?" Richard asked.

"Well it's settled then," Jake said. "You're a qualified criminologist and I need to appoint one to my taskforce. And the chief will organise with the commissioner to make it official."

I sat there in shock. I couldn't believe that with this turn of events, something I'd dreamed of all my life was now a reality.

Jake pressed the buzzer for a nurse, who arrived shortly afterwards. I could tell he was taken aback by her looks. He tried to read her nametag without giving the impression he was staring at her breasts. I saw that it read 'Hayley'.

"What can I help you with, Detective?" Her voice was soft and sweet. Her curly blonde hair would have reached just below her shoulders had it not been in a ponytail. She was reasonably tall, about five foot eight.

Jake remained frozen before finally regaining his senses. "I was wondering if I could get a video recorder hooked up to my TV? I'm expecting some case information to come in. If not, I can arrange to have it done."

"No, that's ok. We have some around. I'll get it hooked up for you."

"No rush, I'm not expecting the information for a little while. Just when you get a chance."

Hayley checked his chart and then left the room.

"You were a bit speechless there, buddy. You ok?"

"She was amazing, don't you think?"

I nodded. "Female nurses and paramedics always seem to be hot." That had been my experience, anyway. "The best thing is, she's single."

Jake frowned and looked at me. "How do you know?"

"Firstly, no ring, and secondly, she was extremely well presented for a day at work. She's 'on the market'," I said, nodding. "But don't get too excited, you'll be competing with all the doctors and they earn more than you," I added.

Jake started to reply, then stopped, as if about to argue the point but then thinking better of it.

It took only about 20 minutes before the VCR was brought into the room and hooked up to the existing TV.

Jake knew if he didn't ask her out, he would never forgive himself. Maybe the events of the night before had affected him more than he knew. Subconsciously, life had suddenly become more precious than it had been just 24 hours before. "So, Hayley, what do you do when you're not working here?" Jake asked sheepishly.

"Is that a way to ask me out, without asking me out, Detective?"

My head was buried in my book and there was no way it was coming out until this little bit of banter was done with.

"Would you like to go out for dinner sometime?" Jake asked, still unsure of what her answer would be.

Hayley smiled, "I would love to, thank you. But we might have to wait until you're back on your feet." She continued smiling as she finished taking his obs and adding the details to his chart. "I'll come and see you again later. We can exchange numbers then." She turned and left his room. Her smile had not faded.

"I told you she was single," I said, keeping my head in my book. Stephen King had introduced me to a new word, 'roont', meaning ruined. He never let me down when it came to new ways of enhancing my imagination.

Jake raised his eyebrows and offered a quick, simple response. "That's why you're the profiler," he said with a slight smirk, going back to his book.

When a uniformed officer arrived carrying a filing box, Jake knew the information he was waiting for had arrived. He set his book aside. He was already ahead of me.

He asked the officer to place the box on the chair next to his bed.

I stood up from a chair on the other side of Jake's bed. "I'd better go and leave you to it."

Jake looked from the box to me. "After I've looked through this stuff, I'll get it sent over to your office," he said, removing the lid.

"No problem, I'll be in to see you again in the morning." I patted him on his good leg and left his room.

* * *

Jake removed the first manila folder from the box labelled 'Rebecca Carrington'. He opened the file clipped to the left-hand side protected by a clear A4 plastic folder that contained a set of crime scene photos.

On the right-hand side of the file was a stack of paperwork. The crime investigation report.

Rebecca had been on her way to work. It was only a short 15-minute walk from her house to the police academy. Her husband, Simon Carrington, said she always left at approximately 7.15am to ensure she was at the academy by 7.30am.

Simon had been ruled out as a suspect very early in the investigation. He had a solid alibi and when the second murder occurred, it was clear to investigators that they were dealing with someone far more dangerous than a possible jilted husband.

Rebecca was still considered a missing person despite the fact investigators believed she had already been murdered.

Jake leaned back against his pillows and placed the pen in his mouth, thinking.

Then he wrote a single note on a blank sheet of paper.

'First victim—mistakes made? Reason why she hasn't been dumped?'

Jake put the Carrington file to one side and withdrew the next file from the box, 'Karen Fitzgerald'. Karen had disappeared less than two years after Rebecca went missing. Although she was slightly younger, Karen's features were similar to Rebecca's. They were roughly the same height and had the same long blonde hair and hourglass figure.

Karen's disappearance was eerily similar to Rebecca's. Karen had been on her way home from the Prahran Police Station, and was last seen getting off the bus only 500 metres from her home. It seemed extremely likely that the same person was responsible for the disappearance of both women.

Two things concerned the investigators.

1. This offender seemed to have no geographical boundaries.
2. The offender was directly targeting female police officers.

Three weeks later, Karen's body was found floating in the Yarra River in the suburb of Warrenwood.

According to the coroner's report, her body showed marks most likely caused by an electrical current, from either a stun gun or a cattle prod. There were also traces of Benzodiazepine found in her system, a drug with sedative and muscle relaxant properties.

Cause of death was listed as multiple stab wounds—81 in all. Many of them had occurred post mortem. Overkill, as it was commonly known within police circles, often pointed to a sadistic killer where the act of killing was the reason for the killing.

The existence of overkill led Jake to believe that this person had had time on his side. He must have been in a place where he wouldn't be disturbed. You don't stab someone 81 times on the street.

Jake continued through the autopsy report and noted a second important piece of information. Karen had been dead for up to 19 days before she was found. This confirmed to Jake that the girls were being taken somewhere to be killed.

None of Karen's belongings had ever been found.

Jake wrote several more notes.

1. Using stun gun and sedative on victim.
2. Victims being moved after death.
3. Time taken with murder.
4. Offender non-geographical.
5. Overkill present.
6. No witnesses, no suspects.

Jake then examined the evidence register in the file.

It was blank except for one note at the bottom of the page. 'No trace evidence found due to victim being submerged prior to being found. Victim may also have been washed prior to being dumped.'

Jake placed the files and his notes on the side table, lay his head back and closed his eyes. It had been a long day and night. He was exhausted and his body desperately needed sleep but his mind was racing.

Soon enough sleep came.

Chapter 6

Monday 6th October 2003 (8am)

Jake had told me that he would send the files to my office, but I was surprised when lobby security advised me I had a delivery when I arrived first thing Monday morning.

Norm was far from the fittest security guard who worked in the North-brook office building. In fact, from what I had witnessed, he looked as if his lunch was usually a combination of hamburgers and coke with the odd guilty-occasion wrap and diet coke. His belt buckle was on the last hole and the shirt buttons looked as if they were about to pop and fly through the air at high velocity.

"I'll have one of the guys bring them up to your office on a trolley, Brodie." He tapped the top of the box.

I thanked Norm and headed up to my office to get a head start. My office consisted of a reception area with a medium sized room adjoining it, which I had converted into a waiting area. Then there were two offices, one tempo-rarily being used for filing until my business was big enough to put on a colleague. My office was by far the bigger of the two, with room for my desk, a bookcase, a couch, and plenty of space. Each office in the building was also equipped with a small kitchenette, although the bathrooms on each floor were communal.

Minutes after I'd arrived, a security guard who I had never met before arrived with a trolley carrying several boxes.

I picked out a file at random. I didn't need to start with the first murder. I knew that the first victim was still missing and that finding her would be the key.

Then I flicked through the other files. The cases were all similar to one another. I placed the victims' photos on the desk side by side. I wondered if there were similarities in the dump sites, or whether the bodies had been posed after death.

Apart from the method of decapitation, common to all the murders where the victims had been found, the sites were all different in style and location. Also, the bodies had been dumped, not posed.

One thing concerned me: whoever had done this was very confident.

Usually, serial killers were geographical, only killing and dumping where they were familiar with the area. This person had shown that he could abduct and dump all across the city.

Apart from letting me know that he was confident, it also led me to believe he knew his areas. Perhaps he had a job that involved a lot of driving?

I jotted down some professions that could give freedom of movement.

Truck driver
Salesperson
Retail merchandise supplier

Then my mind went to the victims themselves. Why police officers? Why these girls? The girls were from all over the state. All were blonde and had similar features.

He had a type. What did this tell us?

I sat back in my chair and pondered, then added to my notes.

Blonde women all similar in appearance.
Past police officer upset with the force, maybe a disgruntled ex-cop.
Suffered abuse as a child.
A hatred of police. Family involved in crime?
Maybe lost a family member at the hands of a police officer and look-ing for payback?

Any of these reasons could have been the initial trigger.

However, if my studies had taught me anything, he continued to kill because he enjoyed the power it gave him over the women. He liked to be in control. He enjoyed the thrill and the rush.

He was hooked.

His next victim fed the addiction but like any addiction it would become insatiable.

* * *

I spent the next two days in and out of the hospital visiting Jake. When I wasn't at his bedside reading our new book, I was looking at the case files hoping I would come up with something. Some miracle breakthrough: some vital clue everyone else had missed.

However, the few days I had spent on the case had so far revealed no such result.

Jake and I had agreed not to discuss the case until he was out of hospital and I had finished my review. A lunch would be good for both of us, we decided.

Chapter 7

Monday 12th October 2003 (12.30pm)

After a week's rest, Jake was still on crutches and I picked him up from his apartment in Docklands. His apartment was architecturally designed and elegant and its location was ideal, just a short stroll from the Telstra Dome, a place we both loved to visit when either of our teams played and time permitted.

Jake took it slowly coming down to the car, still getting used to his crutches. Our restaurant was only minutes from Jake's apartment and while it wasn't the cheapest place for a steak, you were guaranteed a great meal. I was sure Jake would be craving a good feed, as usual.

We hadn't even ordered our drinks before Jake started on the shop talk. "Before we start, congratulations are in order. You're officially a detective." He slid my badge across the table. It was majestic, I never thought I would hold one let alone be given one. "You don't get a gun until you've done the safety course and have spent time at the range. So, Detective, what do you think?"

I wasn't used to being called detective and it was something that would take time to get used to. Clearly, Jake had been chomping at the bit to discuss the case. I was just as keen to discuss my thoughts.

"I think you're correct in assuming your missing person Rebecca Carrington was in fact his first victim. I think the reason she hasn't yet been found is because something went wrong and maybe he worried he would have left evidence behind. He dumped the other women because he believes he got his method right. But be assured, the dumping of the women is not just to get rid of the bodies. He's dumping them to send us a message."

"There were no messages left with the bodies though. What message is he trying to send us?" Jake responded quizzically.

"He's not trying to communicate with us directly as some serial killers do, although that may yet happen. His message is simple. He's saying, "I'm in control. Look at what I've done.""

"Ok, so he's in control, why then is he cutting off their heads? I think he's saying 'I'm a fuckin' nut bag'."

"I think you'll find that the removal of the heads is also a control thing.

Jeffrey Dahmer kept parts of his victims. He didn't want them to leave. He even ate some of them so they'd be with him forever."

"You serious? Man, some people are fucked. You saying this guy could be eating the heads? You wouldn't want to look in the toilet bowl the next day. You might have an eyeball staring back at you."

Humour was a way Jake dealt with stress.

"I don't know if he eats them but I would think he's collecting them in some way. I also think he maybe visits the dump sites. I wouldn't be surprised if he enjoyed watching us fuss over his latest conquest."

The waitress arrived asking if we were ready to order. From his order, I think Jake had been ready days ago. His was goat's cheese tortellini for entree and a rib eye for main with chips and salad. I ordered the same for entree but went for the rack of lamb as the main. We both had soft drinks because of our various medications warning against mixing with alcohol.

"There are a few things that I think are particularly important to this case," I said. "One. Why is he choosing policewomen? Most serial killers choose victims like prostitutes or backpackers, easy targets who are usually not reported missing for days or weeks. But this guy picks girls who can defend themselves and yet will be reported missing immediately. There's a reason for his selection, although what that is, we may never know.

"Two. He is methodical. These are not opportunistic victims. Somehow, he's targeted them specifically. He washes the bodies clean and then dumps them at a predetermined location. He plans everything.

"Three. He loves what he's doing and he'll get better. The wounds on the victims show overkill, which means he enjoys the act of killing."

"I think it shows he had time with the victim, time to do what he wanted," Jake said.

I nodded in agreement.

"Four. The fact that our victims are not raped doesn't mean the killings aren't sexual. I'm sure he gets sexual pleasure out of every kill. Maybe that's why he keeps the heads to relive the fantasy."

"So how do we catch him then?" Jake asked.

"Unfortunately, unless we get lucky, we're going to have to hope he makes a mistake. But that means there'll be more victims."

Jake nodded and had another sip of his lemon squash.

I continued, "There are a few things I think we can do. Look at any ex-police officers and parolees incarcerated between February and October 2000 who are now doing a job that involves a lot of travel, especially driving."

"So what happened in 2000 that I'm missing?" Jake asked, as the waitress brought our entrees.

"Would you like another drink each?" she asked. She'd already removed my last drink without asking, and I hadn't even finished it. Nothing annoyed me more, but she looked young and probably didn't know any better.

"Great, thanks," Jake replied, digging into his pasta.

"Make sure your tip is a dollar less. You still had a quarter left." Jake had a way of knowing just what I was thinking.

"Back to 2000," I continued. "It was the only period over the past 10 years that there were no murders. Something happened that made him stop for a while. We need to look at that carefully."

"I thought you said he wasn't going to stop?" Jake said, as he scraped the last of his burnt butter sauce onto his fork.

"He didn't stop. He paused for a while. A cooling off period. Maybe he couldn't find anything that excited him. Maybe he was in custody."

"Ok, we'll look into the jail records see if any names on our radar appear." Jake wiped his mouth and pushed the plate to one side, then asked, "And why did you say he must have a job involving driving?"

"Because he only dumps bodies in areas he's familiar with. Based on the big distances between dump sites, he frequents a lot of areas."

We spent the next hour arguing about how people became serial killers. I believed they were a product of their environment, upbringing and circumstances. Jake believed that some people were just born evil, with all goodness missing from them.

That thought was just too simplistic for me. When our discussion became heated, we agreed to disagree. We were good like that. No matter how much we disagreed, we always put the friendship first.

With the serial killer discussion abandoned, conversation turned to Jake's stay in the hospital. More precisely, his upcoming date. "So, when is the date?" I asked as my main arrived, and it looked beyond delicious. The rack was set on a bed of mashed potato and minted peas and was served with a red wine jus. Not waiting for Jake to answer, I hoed in. When I looked up from my first mouthful, I realised Jake hadn't answered because his mouth was also full.

"Sorry bud, so looking forward to this. Next week, sometime, we haven't nailed anything down exactly yet. It will depend on how I feel."

I got the impression he wasn't too keen on discussing his potential date. Maybe he was worried he would jinx himself.

"So how are you enjoying 'Wolves of the Calla'?"

Jake was getting through his steak, answering with a mouth full of beef. "Awesome. Almost finished. It's going to be another cliff hanger," he added, cutting into his next piece of meat. "I have about a hundred pages to go and I'm hoping to knock it off tonight. It's getting exciting."

I scraped the last of my potato and lamb onto my fork. Nothing was going to waste. "I think I have two-fifty to go. I find it hard to stay focused with everything that's happened over the last few days."

"It's been crazy," Jake agreed.

We finished off our lunch with dessert and an in-depth analysis of who was favourite for the NBA title and which players would rise to stardom in the next few years. We both agreed that LeBron James would be a star, as number one picks should be. We both had doubts over the number two pick, Darko Milicic. I would have chosen Chris Bosh. Jake said he would have gone with Dwyane Wade.

"Only time will tell," I said.

"I'll be proven right," Jake said, always wanting to stir the pot a little.

On the drive home, Jake organised a meeting for the next day with the outgoing lead detectives of the Eagle taskforce. It was the official handover, but Jake used the word 'briefing' so as not to offend.

Chapter 8

Thursday 16th October 2003 (1pm)

Mason sat in his car just down from the police academy in Glen Waverley. It was the second Thursday he'd done this. Although he was facing south, he was looking north, in the rear-view mirror. The recruits were beginning to leave. Most left in cars, but some on foot. It seemed today there were more entering than leaving. He hadn't seen anything he liked. Nothing close to his type had triggered his dark desire. But she should be coming soon. Any minute now, he thought.

The academy had produced three of his six victims and his big concern was that it wasn't the best place for him to consider again, given the heat his endeavours had caused. But as he always told himself, high risk, high reward. As if on cue, out she walked. This one took his breath away and excited him like none before her. While the uniform and the blonde hair triggered his desire, it was the thrill of the kill that kept him looking for more.

Mason hoped she would follow the same routine as she had last time.

The hunting phase was the most enjoyable part, except for the end. Mason thought he liked the hunt the most because it gave him a god-like sense. As he sat there, he wondered what this girl's name was, what her hobbies were and what family she had.

Finally, Mason thought, 'it's funny how fate finds people.' Everything this girl had done in her life so far had led her to this point. Nothing but the intervention of God himself would stop him from adding her to his collection.

Mason waited until she was almost out of sight before he started his car and began to pull away slowly from the curb. He drove past her as she continued her walk. Mason turned his vehicle into the next side street and pulled over. He kept his vehicle running and leaned over to his passenger door and removed his Melway Street Directory, which sat neatly in its own leather-bound protective cover. He opened it to the Glen Waverley pages and began to pretend he was lost and checking his whereabouts.

Mason expected that he would soon see her turn into the street.

He was overwhelmed with joy. The thought of confirming where 'Blondie' lived was like winning the lottery. Even though he had seen her leave the police academy, it didn't mean she was enrolled there.

After all, receptionists, bookkeepers and other admin staff also worked there.

Mason removed his spiral-bound notebook and flicked through to the page with the folded corner. He paused, watching her, hoping she would enter a home soon. He was still pretending to be looking up an address as he watched her continue walking to the end of the street. Suddenly, she turned left and entered a property. It was in the distance, but Mason could make out a double-storey house with an orange, tiled roof. He would have to drive past to get the number. He waited a few more minutes to ensure she was inside.

Leaving his notepad open on the passenger seat, he started the ignition and headed towards the orange roof. The number '4' was written on the page and Mason simply ticked it.

*　*　*

Mason sat in his study while his son played and his wife cooked dinner. His family knew that once the doors of the study were closed, it meant he did not want to be disturbed.

Every piece of furniture in his study was opposite in style to the rest of the house, which was decorated in Edwardian style. His study was furnished in Georgian style. Mason's desk had been specially made to suit his needs. It had been crafted out of mahogany and it matched the green Chesterfield lounge suite in the corner of his office.

A large grandfather clock with a gold chime pendulum stood in the opposite corner. It chimed resoundingly every hour, on the hour. It had originally belonged to Mason's grandfather. On the wall behind his desk hung his estate agent's licence, the only item hanging on the wall of his study. Mason paused, remembering the day he'd graduated. Finally, the days of the fast bucks had begun.

His mother had wanted him to be a police officer, like his father and his two brothers. He couldn't think of anything worse; after all, it was the police force that had taken his father from him at the age of nine. Mason recalled that night as if it was yesterday.

But he remembered the two years leading up to his father's death more clearly. Maybe remembering them wasn't exactly correct. Maybe haunted by the two years leading up would be a better way of thinking about it, Mason thought, correcting his thoughts as he continued his stroll down memory lane.

He had just turned seven the first time he'd been woken in the middle of the night by his father sliding into bed next to him. It sent a shiver down his spine even as he thought of it now, all these years later.

He'd meant to ask his father what he was doing but he never got the chance. His father placed his hand over his mouth and began to remove his

Superman PJs. The rest was a painful blur that would be repeated many times before his father's death. Even though the first time didn't last long, it was long enough to scar him for life. Mason didn't understand what had happened exactly but he did know it was wrong.

His dad left his room that night with the only sentence spoken between them. "If you ever say anything, bad things will happen to your mother and you wouldn't want that, would you?" Mason shook his head, desperately clinging to his doona. "This is our secret," his father reinforced, as he closed the bedroom door behind him.

After the second incident, his father brought him home two Huskie pups. Mason knew the real reason behind the dogs. His mother just thought he was being a good dad.

The pups were beautiful. One was all white and Mason named him Snow, while the other was grey with touches of white. He named this one Storm. He loved those dogs and considered them the two best friends he'd ever had. He never had any real friends at school. He often spent school lunch times sitting by himself. He even had trouble connecting with his brothers, who chose to spend time with each other rather than with him. He was definitely the odd one out.

By the end of the second year of his father's midnight visits, Mason had decided enough was enough and despite his dad's threats, he was ready to tell his mum.

It was a Friday night, and he was happy that there was no school the next day. It was past midnight. Mason remembered seeing his clock radio showing 12 but he couldn't remember the rest of the display. Usually, Mason would pretend he was asleep and just think of his favourite things when his father began his routine. But on that Friday night there was to be no pretending: everything would be out in the open. As his father climbed into his bed, Mason rolled over to confront him. "Not tonight, Dad. Not any night ever again: it stops here." Mason's voice was weak and jittery but the words came out clearly enough.

"I think you've forgotten our deal, Mase," he replied quietly.

"Not at all, Dad. If you ever touch me again, I will not only tell Mum but your captain, and I know he's hanging out for any excuse to boot your drunken arse off the force. Imagine how happy he'll be to send you to jail." His voice was no longer weak or quivering, he was firm and confident. "Leave now and I'll never say anything to anyone."

Mason's father looked ready to speak but then, as if reconsidering his position, he paused for a moment, and then left his son's room.

Mason had the best sleep he'd had in years and it felt good.

Saturday morning was brighter than any of the Saturdays he could remember in a long time. He had a spring in his step and his secret was no longer his shadow. His father was sitting at the head of the table eating his eggs and reading the paper. Steam rose off his freshly made coffee. His mother was in her usual Saturday housework clothes and she was standing at the stove making porridge. "Morning hun. Would you like some porridge?" she asked in her happy Saturday voice.

Before Mason could reply, his father spoke, his head still buried in the morning paper. "Looks like someone tried to break into the shed last night. Storm must have disturbed him. He was cut up pretty bad, Mase. Unfortunately when I found him this morning, it was too late."

His mother turned from the stove. "Oh George! We need to call the police. That's horrible." She turned off the stove and headed over to hold Mason.

"I am the police, dear. It was most likely local kids trying to steal some tools. We'll never find them." His father was trying to put an end to the conversation.

Mason broke from his mother's grasp and headed towards the back door, tears welling in his eyes. The path to the door had become blurry.

George stood up and grabbed Mason by the arm before he reached the door, pulling him in for a consoling hug, or so it would seem to his mother.

"Don't threaten me again, nothing stops," he whispered, then released him.

Mason would never forget when he first saw Storm lying in the dirt, his fur smeared with mud and blood. His throat had been cut and his body had been punctured many times. It had been a painful death, Mason thought.

His father had left Storm's body for Mason to see and for Mason to bury. Only a monster, like George, would do this to his nine-year-old son.

Mason spent that sunny Saturday morning burying Storm. He knew the perfect spot, a quiet place on the farm that enjoyed the sunlight as well as the tranquil sounds of the stream. He had spent many days sitting on the grass by the stream playing fetch and enjoying the quiet. It was his spot and his alone and it was going to stay that way.

Mason expected his father to pay him a visit that Saturday night but when 2am had come and he was still alone, Mason decided he had to make sure his dad never visited again.

Mason removed the doona, put some track pants over his PJs and pulled an old windcheater over his singlet. As the floor creaked beneath him when he moved throughout the house, he was sure he would wake his parents or even his brothers, but no one woke. No one came to investigate the rumblings within the house.

It was cold and frosty out. Mason pulled up his hood and headed towards Snow.

He approached Snow quietly so he wouldn't be startled and begin a barking frenzy that would be sure to wake everyone in the house. "Here boy," he called softly, holding out a treat in his palm.

Snow approached excitedly. Mason put his hands around him and hugged him tightly, never wanting to let him go. Snow returned the love with a generous licking of the face and ears that seemed to be propelled by his wagging tail.

Mason took Snow by the collar and led him away from the house, to his spot by the stream. The same spot where he had finished laying Storm to rest only hours earlier.

Snow sat next to him panting. Mason sat on the damp frosty grass beside him and stroked his fur. He played with his ears and told him how much he loved him. His tears flowed for the second time that day. "I'm sorry, buddy," he whispered. Snow responded with another set of licks. Mason removed the knife from his sock, took Snow by the muzzle to muffle any sound, kissed him on his nose one last time. Mason took a deep breath then drove the knife deep into Snow's chest as hard as he could. Snow whimpered a few times before he fell limply into Mason's lap. It was the last time Mason ever cried.

Mason carried Snow back to his kennel and laid him in the mud where he had found Storm that morning. He removed the knife from his sock. To this day, he didn't remember decapitating Snow or slashing his dad's tyres, but he knew he must have done it.

Sunday morning it was Mason sitting at the table when his parents came out for breakfast. "Mum was right. We should have called the cops, those guys came back. They killed Snow this time and I think they slashed your tyres, Dad."

His father stood there, unemotional and silent. His mother had clasped her hand to her mouth as if to prevent herself from screaming.

His father's night visits stopped from then on.

Mason knew the events of that weekend had taken his soul. From that day forward, he'd felt removed from everything and everyone, as if he was in a constant dream. Nothing seemed real.

Less than a week later, death again entered his family.

It was a Friday night when his father was killed at work. His mum had told him there was an accident and his father had been killed.

The report said that George Mason and his new partner, Samantha Leirs, who had only recently graduated from the academy, were called out to Prahran on a suspected B&E. Upon arrival, they had surveyed the premises for any signs of unlawful entry. The back of the factory revealed an open roller door that was a quarter of the way up, enough for someone to slide under.

According to the report, George entered the building first, flashlight over pistol per standard police procedure. According to Samantha, they had only taken a few steps once she entered before they split. They were both making their way to the front of the factory, with Sam taking the left and George the right. There were pallets stacked floor to ceiling. There were no lights on in the factory but George could see light moving off to his left. He was hoping it was Sam's flashlight. George thought it best that he head over her way just in case she needed help. He turned off his flashlight and began to head towards the light to his left. A sudden burst of gunfire rang out, which was quickly answered by another short burst of gunfire.

The gunfire broke the eerie silence and almost pierced Samantha's eardrums. Before the echoing had stopped, Sam had taken cover, down on one knee, waiting for whoever had just fired at her to make themselves visible. George was also shocked by the sudden fire and noticed the lights he was following had disappeared. They had either killed Sam or they were now hunting her. George had immediately thought the worst and began to run towards where the light had been. His eyes had adjusted to the dark and despite his better judgement and police procedure, he left his flashlight off; the last thing he wanted was to be a walking lighthouse for some nut to pick off at ease.

With her knee resting on the cold cement floor and her back protected by the pallet behind her, a thought suddenly struck her. What if they weren't shooting at her? What if they had just killed George and he was lying in a pool of blood and they were coming for her? This question continued to run through her mind until the sound of running brought it to a sudden stop. The footsteps sounded quick and heavy. She thought it was only one set but then second-guessed herself. Then it appeared. It was distant but it was there and it was running towards her. She froze with fear, her mind blank. What was she supposed to do? She couldn't remember. The shadow moved closer, in fact it was running at her. Still she sat frozen to her spot. The shadow was holding something, a gun, it was definitely a gun. Soon the shadow would see her and she would be dead. She realised it was either shoot or die. She took a breath and pulled the trigger.

It could be George, she briefly thought as she squeezed but no sooner had it entered her head, than the explosion of her gun rang out. The shadow staggered. She fired again ignoring the nagging voice in her head. Her gun was empty. The shadow had finally dropped and was still. Her hands were shaking, heart pounding, chest tight, and she was struggling to regain her normal breathing. She placed her head in her hands and then it hit her.

It never occurred to George the shots he heard were aimed at him from his partner until the first bullet had hit him. Four more struck then struck in quick succession. He had heard a sixth shot but had not felt it hit him. By that time, he was beyond feeling anything.

Sam went into shock as soon as she saw George on the ground. She had killed him and nothing would undo it.

Several months later, an independent police enquiry cleared Sam. It was determined that George's decision to stray from following standard police procedure had significantly contributed to his own death.

While Sam was cleared, it was recommended that she be moved back to traffic for 12 months.

Hundreds of police were on parade at the funeral. His mum cried, even his brothers shed a tear, obviously their memories of night visits having begun to fade. Mason's were still too fresh to end in anything but hate. Mason had fantasised about putting his father in the ground himself, but now that opportunity was gone and they would all pay the price.

Everyone who spoke made out George to be a saint, a pillar of the community. Little did they know they were crying over someone who was roasting in Hell.

The only sad thought Mason had now was that there was no one to unleash his pain upon.

* * *

With the chime of Windows 2000 starting up, his memories faded.

"At last we have lift-off," Mason mumbled to himself.

He double clicked the Impact property logo and waited for it to boot. Impact was a perfect tool for his real estate career as well as for his side projects. It was like a reverse phone directory. He could type in the address and the program would show the owner's contact details, including all telephone numbers.

It would never have occurred to the programmers that the program might be used by a serial killer to find his victims. While it loaded, he looked at the two photos sitting on his desk. One was a photo of him on his honeymoon in 2000. He and his bride had spent almost a year touring the states. The other was a photo of the cabin after his renovations.

Mason typed the address into the search bar and a name and number appeared. Without hesitation, Mason picked up the receiver and began to dial.

"Hello?" a voice answered.

"Yes, I was after a Miss Janson?"

"Speaking," the voice replied.

"Miss Janson, you don't know me, my name is Bill Taylor. I'm from the Victorian Police. I'm just ringing our graduate classes to see if any of the students need any help or have any concerns."

"No, everything is fine, only a few weeks to go, so I'm really excited."

"Miss Janson . . ." Mason began again before she cut him off.

"Maggie, please call me Maggie," the soft voice on the other end of the phone said.

Finally, Mason thought, as he continued, "Sorry Maggie, I just have a few quick questions for you. As I'm with Human Resources here at the Victorian Police, I just wondered if you have any preference of station to begin your career?"

"No, I'm fine, I'll be happy anywhere."

"We have a lot of country positions available at the moment and we're always careful not to break up families. God knows this job is hard enough without being away from your partner." Mason paused, hoping she would butt in again. When she did, it was like magic, he thought.

Maggie replied, "No, I don't care where I go, I have no partner or kids, but I don't want to be too far from my parents if I can avoid it."

The smile on Mason's face had widened and he was becoming more excited with each word she spoke.

"It's tough for young people to be away from their parents, especially when they're still living at home."

"Oh God no. I moved out a year ago, but I see them all the time," Maggie replied.

"Well, thanks for the chat Maggie, I'll come and introduce myself at your graduation and I'll do my best to keep you local."

"Thank you, nice to speak to you, Bill."

Mason hung up the phone. He was excited. He was pretty sure she lived alone. There might be a housemate but unlikely, Mason thought. It would be worth the risk anyway.

He rocked back in his office chair, steepling his hands and holding them under his chin. Soon, Maggie, soon your path will cross mine and that's where it will end.

The golden handle of his office door turned and slowly opened. A cute face peeped in. "You busy, Daddy?" the little voice asked in a cautious tone so as not to upset his father.

"No Jamie, I've just finished," Mason answered.

"Good, come eat it before it goes cold, k?" There was no 'o' with Jamie, it was always just 'k'. Jamie opened the door a little further and stretched out his arm, motioning with his hand to come.

He had learned this gesture from his favourite TV WWF character 'The Rock'. Mason couldn't help but laugh. He was glad his wife was still cooking dinner. Had she known that he was allowing Jamie to watch wrestling, she would be upset. If she knew Jamie was copying the characters' moves, she would be furious.

Rising out of the chair, Mason picked up Jamie and headed to the table for dinner.

Chapter 9

Friday 17th October 2003 (8am)

Jake and I walked up the stairs of the St Kilda Road Police Station. It was where Jake was based and it would be the new home of the Eagle taskforce. We were there to meet the previous heads of the taskforce and revisit the current leads.

Senior Detective Warren James was the outgoing head of Eagle but he held no grudge about being replaced. He was a true professional, happy to help in any way he could.

Once we exited the lift, we headed towards what Jake called the control room. Jake led the way, through to a smaller boardroom. The room was full of laptops, whiteboards, notes, and pictures, clearly the information hub of the taskforce. The whiteboards contained names, dates and victims' details and then on a separate whiteboard were stuck two photos labelled 'suspect 1' and 'suspect 2'.

I peeled the tape from the whiteboard and took both photos with me into the adjoining boardroom.

I sat down at the boardroom table in the seat next to Jake. Warren sat opposite us with two men I had never met, one either side of him. His two colleagues looked a lot more put out about being replaced than their boss did.

After a general discussion, I posed the question regarding the two pictures. "What do you have on these two?" I asked.

"Well, suspect 1 is our best to date. However, he doesn't outdo the other guy by much. His name is Tony Donaldson. He's been in for three interviews and hasn't been unable to provide an alibi for any of the murders, although the medical examiner can't be exact on time of death, due to the substantial time some of the victims were exposed to the elements."

"What, not even for one of the days? He has no one who can vouch for him?"

"Correct," Warren replied, taking a sip of his coffee.

"The other reason he's our number one guy is that he has a previous record, did two years for rape 12 years ago and he's on the sexual offenders register. He was released just months before the first disappearance. We picked him up about six months ago. We had a call from his neighbour saying he was going out late at night, so we put a tail on him and found him trawling the streets. We grabbed him after he spent a night sitting in a bar for five hours. It was a police bar.

"While he hadn't committed any crime, his activity was unusual considering his past. Not many ex-cons visit known police bars. When we questioned him, he said it was simple, he was trying to find the killer. He wanted the reward money. He said the best way to catch a killer was to try and place himself in the killer's shoes. We asked him to partake in a polygraph but he refused and we don't have anything to get a warrant for one. We still have the tail on him, but our budget has limits."

"The other guy is Lance Silver. Again, he is a sexual predator who has done a stint in Port Philip for attempted kidnapping. Every time a victim has been taken, he's been out. Coincidentally, during the cooling-off periods in the disappearances, we discovered he'd been in the big house. He did two stints, one for six months for B&E and another of 12 months for stalking. Both times, there were no new disappearances that we believe are related to the case.

"Importantly, the person being stalked was an ex-girlfriend, who was also a police officer. She had no idea of his past."

Jake and I looked at each other as if we both suddenly knew this was our guy. However, we both knew that being a depraved sex offender didn't automatically make him a killer.

"We've raided both their homes and found some items of interest, but nothing that links either of them directly to any of the victims. We found what looks like kill kits in both homes, plus in Lance's home we found a lot of porn, mostly bondage. He also had a fascination with serial killers. Found a heap of material on Bundy, in particular."

I reached for the jug of cool water from the middle of the board table. As I poured the chilled water into the glass, something came to me. "You know, Bundy was well known for staging to catch his prey. He would pretend he had a broken arm and be struggling to get into his car at the college campus. Girls would come to help him any time he had his hands full and bang, he would strike. As they say, beware the man with a fake limp." Their talking stopped. "It could be his inspiration." I put the cool glass to my lips and the chilled water shocked my teeth.

Jake turned from me and requested Warren to continue his thoughts. "As I was saying, we have had them both under surveillance. It's up to you guys if you want to keep the surveillance going." Warren was interrupted by a young brunette who seemed very shy and timid. I gathered she was probably new to the job and maybe a little shocked by the aggressiveness of her boss.

"Just place the files on the table, Sophie. They can look at them after the meeting," Warren said.

"Yes sir," she replied, doing as instructed and then leaving.

"These are the files of our two suspects. Feel free to have a read." Warren stood up and offered his hand and his best wishes. We accepted the gesture and returned wishes for Warren's future.

Warren's two colleagues hadn't spoken during the whole meeting. Now, they stood and offered their hands in a thankyou gesture, still saying nothing.

Before I knew it, Jake and I were sitting at the table staring into space. As usual, not liking the silence, I opened my trap again. "Well that was weird. Obviously Bill and Ben didn't like us!"

Without even turning to face me, Jake replied, "They just got demoted, what did you expect?"

"I expected some courtesy and maybe a word or two, something, anything."

"What you said about Bundy was interesting. Do you think our guy is copying his method?" Jake asked.

"Maybe he also used fake injuries to lure his victims," I replied. "Bundy even used clumsiness against them."

"What do you mean clumsiness?" Jake asked.

"Often he'd pretend he was lost and ask for directions, or pretend that he couldn't read a map, things like that."

"Interesting," Jake replied. "So what do you think about our two suspects, Brodie?" Jake sipped the last of his cold coffee.

"I think they are both legitimate suspects. Maybe one of them is the killer, maybe it's someone else entirely. But out of the two, I think that Lance is more likely and I'll tell you why.

"One. Attempted kidnapping could have been his practice run. Two. Break and enter, robbery may not have been on his list. Maybe he was lying in wait. Without even looking at the case file, I would suggest the house was either owned or rented by a single girl. Three, and most importantly, he has heaps of material on Bundy and I would say he is using him as the example he wants to imitate."

"So you think it's him then. You think this is our guy?" Jake asked in an almost excited voice.

"I think he could be a killer, however, whether he is the Slayer or not, I'm not sure. You need to remember the person we're looking for is not the only serial predator walking our streets. One thing I do know is that our guy is showing likeminded nut bags it can be done. Look at all the press our guy gets. He'll spawn more killers, copycats, trying to get in on his fame."

Jake stared at me for a while and then asked, "So where do we start?"

I stood up and tucked my shirt into my trousers. "We start with the two leads we have, but the key to this case is Rebecca Carrington."

"Why her? Why is she so important?" Jake asked, confused.

"The first time is when they're most likely to make a mistake. She's the best chance we have of finding a clue. I don't want to have to wait until he makes his next mistake. Who knows what the body count could be by then!"

"I think we continue to watch both of them and organise a second search on their properties, if a judge will give us a search warrant," Jake said, taking the files from the desk as he finally stood up. "Come on, we can read these in the car. Let's have a look at these guys ourselves.

Chapter 10

Thursday 6th November 2003 (7am)

Mason doubled and triple checked Maggie's Thursday schedule for the last few weeks.

He had done this so many times he could not believe how precise his planning had become.

His alarm clock flashed 6.30am and as the radio came on, his wife stirred in her sleep beside him. He became excited as soon as he thought of his plans for the day.

By the time he had fed Jamie his Coco Pops and made his wife a coffee, it was 8.00am and he was ready to head off to work.

Mason was just leaving as his wife came down the stairs to watch Jamie. He kissed her as they passed. "I won't be home tonight, babe. I'm going straight from work to the airport. I have that conference and I won't be back till late Friday night.

"That's fine because I'm taking Jamie down to Mum's for the weekend and I might even stay until Monday. I just want to help Mum a bit. She's been struggling with Dad since the stroke. You don't mind, do you?"

"Not at all babe, I might do a bit of work on the cabin Sunday and maybe even Monday if I feel like taking a sickie."

"Take the day off, you've been working so hard," Sophie said.

"Have a good weekend. I'll call you. Say hi to your parents for me."

"Have a good weekend too, darling," Sophie replied, grabbing his arse as she gave him a passionate second kiss.

"See you later," Mason said, as he closed the door behind him.

Mason had been doing paperwork for about 45 minutes before the office had even opened. It was the only real estate work he would be doing today.

"I'll be out most of the day," he said to his receptionist as he was leaving the office. "I have some meetings with a couple of developers from Sydney."

"Ok, that's fine. I'll put all your calls through to your mobile," Vanessa replied.

"Could you just take messages, Nes? I don't want to be interrupted while I'm in these meetings."

"Sure," she said, as she wrote a note on a Post-it sticker to remind herself.

As Mason got in his car and plugged his mobile into the hands-free kit, he could still see Nes through the glass door, and he thought, 'that is one attractive receptionist'. She was the only attractive receptionist the company had hired in years. There had been many days when he thought she had caught him perving on her, but he didn't really care.

Mason pulled up outside the council offices and headed to the rates department. He placed his folder on the desk and buzzed for the attendant. A few seconds later, a rather plump woman arrived at the desk and stood there as if to say, 'why are you bothering me?'

"How may I help you, Sir?"

"I would like the address and names of the owners of this property," he said, sliding the paper across the desk.

She took the paper and looked up at Mason. "There's a six-dollar fee for that information, Sir."

"That's fine," Mason replied, smiling.

The plump lady turned side on and faced the computer and then typed in the address provided. Looking up from the screen, she said, "There you go," and passed the piece of paper back to him along with a printout of the information he'd requested.

Mason placed the six dollars on the counter and took the paper and printout. He noticed a big mole on her right cheek and thought immediately of the scene in 'Uncle Buck'. It made him almost laugh aloud. "Thanks," he said as he walked away. As he walked to the car, he looked down at the piece of paper clasped in his hand. A smile spread across his face as he read the printout.

Property address: 4 Ascot Close Glen Waverley
Owner: Mr and Mrs P Jackson.
13 Laslowe Road Wantirna.

No mention of the tenant Miss M. Janson.
"Just as I thought," he muttered to himself. "You're just a tenant, Maggie."

Chapter 11

Thursday 6th November 2003 (10.15am)

Lance stood at the bottom of the stairs to his garage. He was a tall man, standing just over six foot. Despite his hair thinning on top, he was still handsome.

He stood motionless in the dark, cold garage. He could feel it building up again, like it had the time he was in that house. It would have been perfect had she not brought a man home and ruined his plan.

This time though, it felt more intense. He felt more pressure. Finally, he would kill. Nothing was going to stop him this time.

He walked over to the workbench and caught a glimpse of his reflection in the side mirror of the old Holden Monaro he had attempted to restore in his younger years. Despite the steam that was building up inside him, his outward appearance was completely normal.

Jail had aged him, but it had done nothing to deter his fantasy. If anything, the only lesson he had learned was, don't get caught.

"No mistakes," Lance repeated to himself several times under his breath, as he made his way over to the workbench. He flicked the light on. He then walked over to the Monaro that took up almost half the garage, hopped in the driver's side, released the handbrake, and rolled the car back, almost flush against the door. On the garage floor was a large mat. It served the purpose of protecting the concrete from the oil, but more importantly, it hid his hidey-hole.

Lance rolled back the rug, removed the flick knife from his back pocket and used the tip to find the crack in the concrete. Then he used the knife to lever the door open. Inside the nook was a bag that had once housed a four-man tent. Now it hid the tools of a dark mind. Inside the dusty blue bag lay rope, a carving knife and duct tape. Next to the bag was a leather-bound note-book. Lance removed the items and headed back to the workbench. He placed them upon the dusty and cracked bench and then opened the book. Each page contained clippings from newspapers. All of them were about the Slayer's victims. Lance was proud of his book; he had kept every clipping, had placed perfectly in order every article on every victim. It was his inspiration.

'All I have to do is find myself a policewoman and I'll have articles written about my work,' Lance thought. After a couple of minutes of entertaining this daydream, he realised it was potentially only hours away from becoming a reality.

Lance replaced the book in its original hiding spot. He rolled the mat and the car back into position. With his hands filthy from the trapdoor and the car, he headed to the old trough in the corner of his workshop, which had seen its fair share of grease.

As he rubbed the soap bar across both hands, he began to mumble to himself, "I must be better than him. No mistakes, and then they'll be talking about me, not him. I can be better than him. I can be better than him, better than him."

Chapter 12

Thursday 6th November (2.25pm)

Mason was sitting two streets away from Maggie's address. He had found a nice spot for his car in a very quiet little cul-de-sac, parking outside a house at the end. It appeared to be the best house in the street and he assumed it would take a professional couple to pay for it.

He reached into the centre console and pulled out some business cards of colleagues in the industry. Flicking through them, he stopped when he found the one he wanted. 'Perfect,' he thought. Brent Samuels from Stevens and Co. No photo on the card and a local agent. Minutes later, Mason walked up the drive of 4 Ascot Close and approached the door. He knocked and then stepped away from the door as if to appear less confronting. Mason was now Brent Samuels, and he held out the business card ready to prove it.

A few seconds later, the door opened and Maggie appeared. "May I help you?" she asked softly.

"Yes, I'm Brent Samuels from Stevens and Co, Real Estate." Mason handed over Brent's card. "I'm here for the 2.30 appraisal for Mr and Mrs Jackson." He opened his diary to appear as if he was confirming the details.

"Well, no one told me, so you'll have to come back another time. I do have rights, you know." Maggie began to close the door.

"I am sorry, miss. I was under the impression that the owners were going to make an appointment with you. I could do it now? It will only take me five minutes, then I'll be out of your hair." Mason was using every ounce of charm he had.

He paused while Maggie considered his request. "Really, I'll be gone in two minutes." Mason smiled as if to say, 'come on, better now than later.'

Maggie stepped aside and let in her killer.

Mason opened his little briefcase, removed a piece of paper and began to write notes. Then he placed the paper and pen on the table and began sifting through his satchel. As if he was looking for something.

"So, you're in the police force then?" he asked. He lifted his head slightly to focus on the police cadet photo on the wall behind her. Maggie turned to see what Mason was looking at and as she did so, Mason struck swiftly and forcefully as soon as her back was turned to him, placing the stun gun on the back of her right kidney and his left arm around her throat. The stun gun took effect almost immediately and after the first initial convulsing of her body from the electrical current, Maggie lay limp in his arms.

Alive but ineffectual.

He quickly injected the usual Benzodiazepine.

Mason lay Maggie on the floor of her living room and pulled on the latex gloves that he had at the ready.

Once the gloves were on, he removed a little rag and wiped everything he'd touched, including the Stevens & Co card, which he removed from Maggie's hand.

Mason again reached into his case and removed his biohazard suit. He had stolen it off the clothesline while doing an inspection at a vendor's home. The owners had assumed that some kid had taken it as a prank.

Mason walked over to the kitchen drawer and removed some garbage bags. Then he walked back to the limp, unconscious body lying in the middle of the lounge room. He placed her feet into one bag, which came up to her waist, and pulled the drawstring tight, closing it around her waist. He then moved to the other end of her limp body and lifted her head.

He placed the garbage bag over her head, ripping air holes into the bag so she could breathe. He wanted her immobilised, not dead . . . well not yet, anyway.

It took Mason about three minutes to do a quick search of her house before finding her car keys on the bedside table.

Obvious place.

He walked to the family room that adjoined the garage and opened the internal access door. He loved this. No one would see him.

It was so easy.

He was so smart, he kept thinking to himself.

He carried Maggie into the boot of her own car.

He doubled back inside, checking he had left nothing behind.

As usual, all clear.

He placed his case on the passenger seat beside him and opened the garage door with the remote that hung from the key ring. He waited until the garage door was just above the car before he rolled out onto the driveway, closing the door as he left.

It would seem to anyone looking that she had just gone to the shops.

Mason parked Maggie's 1997 white Holden Commodore right beside his car and popped the boot. Then he pressed the button on his remote, unlocking the boot of his car. He picked Maggie up and placed her in the boot of his car, then closed the boots of both cars and left hers where he had parked it, just two streets away.

Within seconds, he was headed for his cabin to finish off his eighth victim. This time, it would be perfect.

Chapter 13

Thursday 6th November (1pm)

Jake and I stood in front of Justice Aaron pleading our case for a search warrant for Lance's property, for the second time. Considering we had very little to go on, getting the warrant wasn't going to be easy.

Justice Aaron looked up from our submission, removed his bifocals and looked directly at Jake. "I hope you have something else, Detectives?" he asked, almost pleading.

"No, your Honour," Jake responded quietly.

"I understand your need to search but unless I have some new evidence or a valid reason as to why you believe that in the next 72 hours Mr Silver will commit a crime, I don't know how you can meet the State's legal burden." Do you have such a reason or evidence, Detective Miller?"

"No, we can't say it's likely that an offence will be committed in the next 72 hours, your Honour. However, we would like to plead that this is an exceptional case that has resulted in many police officers' deaths."

After considering our plea, Justice Aaron continued, "Hypothetically, if I did give you the warrant and you found something, it is very likely that any decent lawyer worth his salt could have any evidence you found deemed inadmissible and thus any arrest or conviction that may occur as a result would be overturned. Therefore, despite my strong personal feelings, unfortunately I believe your submission fails to meet the requirements of the Crimes Act. Please bring me something new and you will have your warrant."

Jake and I stood and thanked him for his time and left his chambers. "What the hell are we going to do now?" Jake asked me as we left the courthouse.

"I think we need to try and get something more on him. Maybe we can keep an eye on him, see if he leads us anywhere. Hey, we might get lucky," I said.

"I don't think he's going to drop evidence in the street, Brodie."

"I'm not saying that, but he might lead us somewhere! What other choice do we have?"

Jake paused two steps ahead of me, then turned and nodded in agreement. "We might as well get started, but we should stop for snacks first." He removed his phone from his pocket.

By the time we reached the car, Jake had cancelled his date with his newfound love, Hayley. I could see he was stressed about having to let her down again. But work came first, especially now.

Chapter 14

Thursday 6th November 2003 (4pm)

We had parked the car on the opposite corner of the street from where Lance lived and had a clear view of the front door and the garage. We would see anyone entering or leaving.

Jake had arranged with two other senior members of Eagle, Steve and Darren, to watch the back. When we'd stopped for supplies, they had radioed in saying that they were about half an hour away. Within minutes of arriving at Lance's, Jake had got stuck into a bag of Cheesy Doritos. I sat there trying to take in the excitement of my first sting, anticipating something might happen at any moment.

Jake, on the other hand, looked as if he was not at all interested and continued to shovel in the Doritos.

That was the difference between us. He had done this before. I was a rookie and a nervous wreck; he was cool, calm and collected. "Where are they? Steve and Darren should be here by now," I said, without taking my eyes off the house.

"It hasn't even been half an hour yet, mate. Don't panic," Jake mumbled, his mouth half full of Doritos. It was a wonder he didn't choke on them.

Jake shuffled back in his seat, reached down and removed the bottle of OJ from the plastic bag provided by the kind service station attendant.

I couldn't believe how much Jake had consumed in such a short time, although I shouldn't have been surprised. It was 4.30 in the afternoon and Jake was just eating his lunch. He would have been starving again two hours after breakfast. He had always been that way even when we were kids in high school. He used to take lunch from home, always a couple of sandwiches, cake and drinks, plenty to keep him going for the day.

When I was about 14 and Jake was 12, we went to a Pizza Hut. It was all the go back then. Pizza Hut had just introduced the 'all you could eat' pizza for $5.95. They couldn't have known there were people who would eat as much as Jake. I sat opposite him and watched in amazement as he devoured 14 slices of pizza while I ate only four.

I looked over at Jake and began to snigger a little. Jake, who was finishing off the Doritos, looked at me with a 'what the fuck are you laughing at?'

expression. "What's so funny?" He looked down at his shirt to see if he had spilt anything.

"Nothing," I replied, "just that seeing you eat those Doritos reminded me of when you ate those 14 slices of pizza at Pizza Hut."

Jake began to laugh, almost spitting the half-chewed corn chips all over the car. "How was that waitress? She couldn't believe I'd eaten almost two family-size pizzas by myself. She was ready to stop serving us."

I focused back on Lance's house.

Still no movement.

Then, out of nowhere, the garage door began to roll up, revealing the old Ford Ute. The Ute reversed and headed north towards the city. I started the ignition and began to follow Lance's vehicle. Jake radioed Steve and Darren and gave them the plate and description. While they were close, they had two busy roads to navigate before they would meet up with us. Lance headed out of Hawthorn and up Toorak Road towards the outer edge of the city. We sat a few cars behind so as not to draw attention to ourselves. The traffic for this time of night was heavy and it was getting harder to stay far enough away to not arouse his suspicions yet remain in sight of his Ford. The traffic lights at peak hour were on their short cycle. If we didn't stay a little closer we would lose him.

"Keep up with him, buddy, stay close." Jake repeated the sentence a few seconds later. As the last words of the sentence came out of his mouth, we approached a tram, which Lance's Ford had already passed in the middle of Toorak Road. The stop sign popped out and I had no choice but to stop or run over the passengers exiting the tram. As the tram began to pull away again and the lights ahead of us changed, I could not see the Ford Ute beyond the lights. Our tail was broken.

The lights and siren were not an option if we wanted to keep our cover. We accelerated up the hill. When we reached the top, we knew we were in trouble and that finding Lance would not be easy. Six different roads led into and out of the city. We would only be guessing. There was no sign of the Ute.

We had lost him.

Jake looked over to me. "Don't worry, mate, we'll find him. Let's head into the city and call in that we've lost him. One of the divisional units might sight him."

Chapter 15

Thursday 6th November 2003 (4.38pm)

Mason had parked near the front door. Leaving the car running, he got out and opened the doors to the enclosed garage.

Then he returned to the car and unlocked his boot. Maggie had begun to stir, beginning to recover from the effects of his jab. As Mason picked her up to unload her, Maggie began to kick and struggle.

Mason walked in through the open doors and into his garage. Her body thudded in a puff of dust as he dropped her to the hard dirt floor. Mason grabbed Maggie by her feet and dragged her further inside his cellar, her head hitting each step on the way down. Her cries and screams rang throughout the empty cabin. After a few seconds, Maggie began to squirm in the dirt again and Mason just stood back and watched his prey. He was enjoying every moment of his little game but soon it would all end. Well, for Maggie, anyway.

"Maggie," Mason said, as he removed the bag off her head.

"What do you want with me?" she asked, still trying to recover from the hours in the bag.

Mason knelt down beside her and spoke softly. "Do you know who I am?"

"Some fucked-up psycho. Where am I? Let me go, you fuckin' sicko!" Maggie yelled, beginning to cry. "Just let me go, I'm a copper, you know. You're under arrest, you have the right to remain silent . . ." She began to sob louder as she continued to read Mason his rights.

"Listen, you little bitch, you're not in a positon to be reading anyone their rights, especially me. I'll tell you who I am. I'm the person you've dubbed the East Side Slayer and soon I'll be reading you your last rites."

Maggie's face froze with the knowledge that she was in the hands of a killer.

"Do you know why I'm doing this, Maggie? I'll tell you why. Because it's fun. I enjoy watching your eyes when you know you're going to die. I like having you pigs beg for your life and the best part is, your smart-arse cop friends don't have a clue who I am."

Mason walked over to a large covered tool cage hanging on the cellar wall with an array of swords and knives. "Let me show you something."

Mason grabbed her head and forced her to look. "Look!" he yelled, pulling Maggie's hair and pointing to the top shelf of the cabinet. "Show me some respect and look."

Maggie tried to worm away from Mason, shaking her head, the tears flowing.

"I said look, you bitch. Look at what you coppers have made me do."

Maggie again wriggled away and continued to shake her head.

"See what you people have caused."

Maggie could not avoid looking up at the top shelf. Then she began to dry-retch at the sight of seven heads floating in some concoction all staring back at her through glass jars. She guessed the liquid was to preserve the heads.

"You're next, Maggie. Soon you will join them. You will be number eight." Maggie vomited right down her front. "Don't worry about the clothes, Maggie, you won't be needing them much longer."

Maggie tried to move but Mason was far too strong.

He picked her up and slammed her against a steel pole. The back of her head took the biggest impact. Mason cuffed her right hand to a second pole and her left hand to the first pole. Then he pulled on a nearby cable, raising Maggie off the ground, leaving her hanging by her wrists.

Mason went back to the cabinet and removed a long sword and turned and smiled at Maggie. With that smile, Maggie knew her life would soon be over. She also knew the end would be excruciatingly painful.

Chapter 16

Thursday 6th November 2003 (6.23pm)

Lance parked his Ford in a secured parking lot a few blocks away from the Sweet Kandy adult club. The 'K' in the logo was a picture of a girl kicking a leg high in the air. Lance removed his tool kit from the pocket of his coat and placed it neatly under his seat. He could not get a lap dance with a carving knife in his pocket.

It was about a five-minute walk to the Sweet Kandy Club from the car park.

The unceasingly cold air bid Lance good evening and the wind rushed into his lungs, filling his chest with frost. Or so it felt. He began walking to the club. He had no idea how much his life would change in a short few hours.

Sweet Kandy was a well-known strip club. It had become very popular due to all the publicity it received when the owners applied for a licence. Many of the Melbourne City Council board members had tried vigorously to block it. However, it had received a majority vote and the operating hours had been passed. It was suggested by the media that some members of the council had been paid off. The publicity ensured that Sweet Kandy would be a success from the day it opened.

Some people went just once to see what all the fuss was about, while others like Lance were hooked by the beautiful girls on offer.

Lance had his favourite, Charlie. She was young and very pretty and possessed a very sexy body that looked amazing in a g-string.

Her dark black hair curved into her cleavage and she had a marvellous way of saying, "I want to fuck you", looking at you with her deep blue eyes. Of course, she said that to every guy in the place, to get them to pay her to dance. It was her job and it only paid well for the girls who knew how to sell it.

Lance knew that there was no way she would date him, but just having her perform for him was enough to get him off. Since he'd first had her dance for him, he had felt an extra special connection with her.

That connection was growing stronger within him, building up, pushing him to take his desires for her further.

He had felt the connection from the moment he'd laid eyes upon her, one wintry Friday night several months before.

A week later, he'd returned to the club just after dinner, only planning to stay an hour or so.

Charlie always worked Thursday, Friday and Saturday nights. Apparently, the tips were good. She was paying her way through uni and had no classes on Fridays.

He had just finished his first drink at the bar and was about to order his second when she approached him and whispered in his ear, "Would you like me to give you a lap dance?"

Lance was beginning to feel movement in his pants and he smiled and replied, "Anytime with you."

"It's good to see you again, cutie," Charlie answered. Lance wondered if she remembered him or if she just called everyone cutie.

She reached out and grabbed Lance's hand, walking him towards a booth where the private dances took place. She sat him down on the chair and began to dance. Charlie was wearing a bikini top, a short cheerleader skirt and a bright yellow g-string. Lance was a sucker for g-strings. He loved seeing women in them. When he spent his nights watching pornos, he was always excited to see a cute girl getting fucked in a g-string.

He was equally disappointed when the girls removed them.

He knew that his love for g-strings was becoming an obsession but he didn't care. He could have whatever fantasy he liked.

His thoughts were shocked back from his nights of porn when Charlie placed her ankle on his shoulder and thrust her pussy towards his face. Then she stepped back in time with the music and began to remove her bikini and push her breasts together.

She then lowered her head and as she moved closer to Lance, she began to tweak and lick her own nipples.

Then she grabbed Lance's head and moved it in between her breasts, rubbing the sides of his face with her breasts. His cock was now very hard.

The smell of her vanilla perfume kept him wanting more. He thought it must be some type of aphrodisiac. It was the club policy that the girls were allowed to touch the clients but under no circumstances were the clients allowed to touch the girls. The girls generally touched the customer's thigh and maybe gave them a kiss on the cheek at the end of the dance, but if they did more than that and the boss found out, they would no longer be employed by Sweet Kandy. Ricardo, the owner, did not want his girls exciting the guys so much that they became trouble and he didn't want his girls using his business as a hook-up place where they could prostitute themselves on the side. Charlie continued her dance, removing her skirt and beginning to wave her cute arse in front of him. The dance continued for four more songs due to the extra cash she had received at the start of the second song. When the third song began, Lance began to feel that little bit special. Charlie got down on her knees and rubbed his penis through his pants. Then, after looking around to see if anyone was watching, she unzipped him, pulled out Lance's dick and quickly placed it in her mouth, sucking it for just a few seconds then licking the top of it prior to placing it back in his pants. It was the quickest and best blowjob he had ever received.

Charlie again looked around, checking she was not being watched, lifted herself up off her knees, and kissed Lance's ear. At the same time, she rubbed her cheek against his and then slowly brushed Lance's lips with hers. As they met, Charlie's tongue softly entered Lance's mouth. "Don't tell anyone I did that. I'll lose my job. Let me know if you want any more dances today, ok?"

Charlie backed away, picked up her clothes and left the booth. Lance sat there for a few seconds, for two reasons. One, to give himself time to work out what the hell had happened and the other to give his boner time to go down. Nothing looked worse than walking out of a booth in a strip club with a rocket in your pocket.

Chapter 17

Thursday 6th November 2003 (7pm)

Lance sat nervously thinking about how to ask Charlie out.

In the end, he decided just to go ahead and ask her.

Charlie was leaning on the bar, still puffing after her aerobic shift on the main stage. Lance bought her a drink and flashed a hundred-dollar note. "After the drink, you got time for another dance?"

"Always for you, cutie," she replied in her excited voice, which Lance had begun to suspect was fake. He knew that tonight if he got her he would not be able to let her go.

The music pumped, Charlie began her dance and as she danced, Lance's desire increased. He wanted her and he wanted to be written about. He wanted to be hunted by the police.

Soon, he would replace the Slayer. Charlie was the perfect way to start his plans.

"Hey, Charlie, do you ever see any people from the club, outside the club, I mean?" he asked her, stuttering a little.

"Are you asking me out, sexy? Cos I'm not allowed to date guys I meet at the club, but if you don't say anything, I won't." She smiled and flicked her hair. "I don't get off until 12 so if you're not doing anything then, you could pick me up and we could go to my place for coffee if you like." She flashed that sexy smile and softly kissed his lips.

"That'd be cool, I'd love to, I'll meet you out the back then?" Lance had forgotten where he was for a second and as the words came out, he cringed at how juvenile they made him sound. How many 32-year-olds still used the word cool.

"Yeah, at 12, ok cutie," Charlie said, as she hurriedly redressed.

"Could I have another dance first?"

"I'd love to, cutie, but I'm due on stage. How about I make it up to you later?"

Charlie placed the hundred-dollar note in her garter, gave him a quick wink and left the booth.

Chapter 18

Thursday 6th November 2003 (7.33pm)

I sat there with my arm up against the glass of the driver's side window and my knee on the dash, waiting for a response from any patrol car that might have sighted Lance's car.

Our search had turned up jack shit. We had cruised the city for the last few hours without locating Lance's car. "Jake, I can't believe that no other police have spotted Lance's car either. Are they all fucking useless?" I asked.

"Easy, tiger," Jake replied, "we'll find him."

"Yeah, but I hope it's this year. Why are we just sitting here in the middle of King Street and not driving around looking for him?" I questioned.

My lack of police skills was showing.

"Mate, King Street has the most pubs and clubs. It's the heart of sleaze. More strip joints here than in the rest of Melbourne. If he's out on the town trawling, it's a good chance he'll be here. If his car is in one of those underground car parks, when he leaves, we'll see him."

"But there are heaps of other places he could be. There are other pubs and strip joints outside of this area as well. He could be anywhere."

"Yes, he could, Bruce," Jake acknowledged, "but here is our best chance."

Jake often called me Bruce. When he'd first started doing it, I'd wondered what the hell had happened to him.

Stroke maybe.

Then I thought I must have misheard. When he said it again, I asked, "Mate, why the hell you calling me Bruce?"

He smiled. "Mate, every Aussie has a best friend called Bruce, you're my best friend."

I thought it was both logical and stupid at the same time. That was why we were best friends.

I'd just let it ride ever since.

Chapter 19

Thursday 6th November 2003 (8.38pm)

The sun was almost set as Lance walked down the dark steps of the strip club and out into the bright lights of the city. He did not want to drive home and back before 12 so he thought it would be best to spend what was left of the evening in the city.

He was halfway down Collins Street when he stopped in the middle of the footpath and stared into the window of an adult shop. On display on the mannequin was what would make his night with Charlie perfect. He couldn't believe he hadn't thought of it until now. He looked up at the name of the shop. 'Adult Playground' was sign-written across a big pair of red lips, an eye-catching logo. Underneath the lips were the words, 'Making your play-time more exciting'.

Lance looked at the mannequin staring back at him through the window.

'Perfect,' he thought, entering the shop.

Lance walked in and stared at all the lingerie, toys and costumes.

"Can I help you?" the voice from behind the counter asked. After taking a few seconds to observe the cashier, Lance answered, "I was wondering how much the police costume in the window is?"

"It's actually on sale. It normally retails for $259 but it's only $199 at the moment. What size is the lucky lady?" the attendant asked in a friendly manner.

"I think she's a size eight or ten," Lance replied.

"Well, it comes in small, medium and large. Small will suit girls sized eight to twelve. The material is lycra and spandex so it stretches. A small should suit her then," she said, showing him one from the rack. "Would you like me to wrap one up for you?"

"That would be great. Do you take Visa?" Lance asked, hoping that they did as he had little cash left on him.

All his money was wrapped around a garter.

"Yes, we do, sir," the attendant replied. "Would you like the uniform in a gift box? They're only $5."

He nodded in acceptance. "Are the handcuffs that come with the uniform real or plastic?" Lance asked.

The attendant, who was now placing the item in the box, replied, "They're plastic, but we do have real ones on the back shelf. I think they're about $40.00."

Lance headed for the back shelf. Gazed at the wide selection that lay before him.

Most of the handcuffs on offer had a separate release tab that the prisoner could activate to let themselves out. He wasn't surprised, considering they were novelty handcuffs.

He had almost given up looking and then he saw them, second from the end. Real handcuffs with only a key to open them. Lance removed the box from the shelf and headed back to the counter.

"Take those as well?" the attendant asked, to double check before she scanned the attached tag and opened the gift box to place the handcuffs in.

"Yeah, that'd be great. All on the Visa, thanks," Lance replied, as he handed the attendant his card.

She put the gift box inside a black plastic bag.

Lance signed the receipt and thanked the attendant for her help.

A few minutes later, he was back out on the street. The sun was quickly fading on the city horizon. The air seemed colder now.

He continued to walk through the city. Seeing the casino in the distance, he decided that was the place to fill in the night until Charlie finished work.

The air had become incredibly cold and the wind pierced his lungs with each breath.

He passed the Crocodile Club with its unique green door glowing in the darkness, the usual line of drunken horny guys waiting on the footpath.

Lance looked over his shoulder and checked there was no traffic coming up behind him. He saw the lights of a small vehicle, waited for it to pass and then crossed. As it passed, a gust of wind generated by the passing vehicle blew a cold shivery chill up his back.

By 9.30, Lance had won over $500 on blackjack. Playing on would likely result in the loss of all his gains. He pocketed his chips and headed for the cashier. A meal and a bit of sport at the sports bar would be the perfect way to settle himself for the big night ahead.

Lance looked over at the bar attendant and as soon as he noticed her brown curly hair, the thought of spending tonight with Charlie came flooding into his brain and he suddenly felt hot and nervous at the same time. "Can I get you anything?" the young bar attendant asked, as she continued to remove empty beer and spirit glasses from the bar with her right hand and wiped the bar with the rag in her left.

"I'll have a Scotch and Coke on the rocks. Do you do counter meals?"

Lance asked as she placed ice in his glass. He placed his Visa on the bar to cover his tab.

"Sure, I'll grab you a menu," the girl replied.

"It's ok, I'll have a parma if you have that?" Lance asked, glancing back at a TV screen showing football.

"Sure do. I'll get you one, Sir," she said, taking his Visa and placing his drink on the coaster in front of him.

She then clipped a ticket to the service line.

He assumed it was his parma order.

Lance's mind was only on Charlie even though his eyes were flickering between the EPL and the cricket in the Caribbean. The attendant brought his parma, but that and the Scotch did little to settle his nerves and nothing to satisfy his hunger.

"Can I get you another?" the bar attendant asked, holding up his empty glass.

Lanced nodded.

She placed the drink in front of him and went to serve a young couple who had just blown in from the street, bringing with them a gust of cold night air.

Lance could not concentrate on the game.

His only thought was, 'tonight is my night.'

Soon he would be the new East Side Slayer.

Soon everyone would be talking about him.

Writing about him.

Finally, he would get the respect he deserved.

Chapter 20

Thursday 6th November 2003 (11.45pm)

Lance had just finished his fourth Scotch and Coke. The EPL had finished and he wasn't even sure who had won.

He picked up his wallet and his package from Adult Playground to prepare for the bitterly cold stroll back to the Sweet Kandy Club. In the alleyway behind the nightclub, he stood shivering, thinking how cold it must be even though he was wearing his long jacket. Perhaps he should have worn a warmer jumper as well.

It was 15 minutes past 12 by the time Charlie came out of the rear steel door of the club. It had been 15 minutes that Lance had spent thinking that she must have changed her mind.

That it was all a cruel joke.

A hoax.

As Charlie came outside, she was followed by a large security guard who looked as if he had spent too many years in the gym and most likely on steroids.

"You know this man, Charlie?" the security guard asked, standing close enough to act if Lance were some perverted fuck who was hiding in the dark alley lying in wait ready to rape or kidnap one of the dancers.

"Yeah, I'm fine, Gus, this is just an old friend I haven't seen in a while." Charlie turned to Gus and blew him a kiss as if to say, thanks for caring. Charlie took Lance's hand and began to walk with him towards the main street. As she neared the end of the alleyway, Charlie raised her left hand and yelled, "See ya tomorrow, Gus!" She knew he would still be at the rear door watching her leave.

As they entered the main street, Charlie removed her hand from Lance's and lowered it to his arse, giving a slight squeeze of his butt cheek. "We can walk to my place from here. It's two minutes at the most." Charlie began to drag on his arm to lead the way.

"Ok, ok, I'm coming, I just need to get my bag. I have my phone and stuff in my car. It'll only take me a sec then we can go to your place for some fun." Lance started to pull her towards the parking garage.

Within a few minutes, they were standing at Lance's car.

Lance was looking for the car key on his key ring so he could open the door to get his tool kit from under his seat.

He sat in the car, adding the contents to the black plastic bag from Adult Playground.

"What's in the bag?" Charlie asked, as she tried to get a sneak peek. "You didn't have that when you came into the club."

"It's a surprise and you'll just have to wait until we get to your house," Lance replied, pulling the bag away from her and moving it into his other hand so that she would not have a chance to glimpse the contents.

They walked hand in hand all the way to Charlie's home and when they arrived, Lance was surprised at how nice it appeared from the outside.

It was a modern townhouse, of the type that had been all the go in Melbourne for the last five years. Many developers had built them, making open-plan living one- and two-bedroom homes and then selling them to young couples and young corporate singles who worked in the city.

Charlie unlocked the downstairs security door and closed it behind them. She and all the other tenants had been told at the last body corporate meeting to make sure they did this. Apparently, too many tenants had been leaving it unlocked and there had been three burglaries recently.

"Here we are," Charlie said, as she swung the door open to her apartment. The furniture was sandstone, which suited the modern look of the home. The main wall of the lounge housed a gas log fire. Charlie opened up two double doors that stood at the end of the lounge, revealing her large king-sized jarrah bed.

The posts were carved, joined at the top by an inch-thick piece of timber. Attached to the timber was a soft lace netting that draped to the floor. The bed was decorated with at least 10 large cushions, all covered in silk or satin covers.

Charlie simply nodded her head as if to say, 'come here'. Then she said, "Are you going to stand there all night or are you coming in?" as she removed her dress, leaving it on the floor at the entrance to her bedroom. She parted the lace and crawled onto the bed.

'Remain calm,' he thought. 'Your time of infamy is just beginning. The Slayer wouldn't panic and neither must you.' Soon, his vision would be complete and he would never be forgotten. He had to ensure that this was only the beginning.

Not his first and last. After all, anyone could kill.

'Only the great ones are remembered,' he continued thinking, as he slowly approached the bedroom.

Chapter 21

Thursday 6th November 2003 (11.57pm)

"Mate, I think he's gone. We've spent over seven hours and there's been no sign of him," I said, struggling to keep awake.

Jake turned his head towards me while still trying to keep one eye on King Street. "Maybe we should go and stake out his house. He has to come back sooner or later."

"Yeah, we're just wasting our time here, but I need a coffee and some fresh air if I'm going to stay awake for the rest of the night." I started the car and headed towards the freeway.

"No Brucey, you're better off going towards Toorak Road. That way we can go down Chapel Street, get a coffee, have a walk, look for Lance."

"With the thought of a hot coffee and the possibility of finding our boy, how could I say no?"

It only took about 15 minutes at this time of night.

We were soon cruising down Chapel Street. All you can do in Chapel Street is cruise. There were so many teenyboppers looking for clubs, pubs and dance spots that the traffic was bumper to bumper. As we slowed to a crawl in our police issued 2000 VS Commodore, a 1995 dark green Ford pulled up beside us. The car was crammed with six guys, most likely late teens. Obviously out looking for some fun or trouble.

Maybe trouble was fun to them.

The driver and most of the passengers looked Greek or Italian. The driver had the radio blasting and he was bopping his head in time to the bopping of the mmcha, mmcha, mmcha of the techno music.

The passenger looked over at our car. He was obviously not impressed that I was staring at him and their car. "What the fuck are you looking at?" he said through his wound-down window. "What's your fucking problem?" he repeated. He turned his head and began to speak to the four guys in the back, as if to rally the troops. He turned back towards me and leaned out of the window, shouting. This time one of the backseat passengers, who had also wound down his window, decided to join in the fun.

"You're fucked," the front-seat passenger said, pointing his finger at me, and the guy in the back added some smart-arse comment that I didn't quite catch.

Jake leaned over, took the CB radio out of its holder and called in for a divvy van.

"What the hell are you doing?" I asked, puzzled, as he began to open his door. "Just stop the fucking car. These boys are going to hurt someone or themselves if we don't stop them. They have too many passengers in the car and they're drinking in public. That's enough to arrest them, plus they've just pissed me off."

Jake removed his seat belt. "You can either stay here or come with me and kick some arse, but don't forget your piece."

I had only limited training with my Glock and I wasn't looking forward to having to use it. I also didn't want some big guy taking it from me and then shooting me with it.

Jake was out of the car before I had pulled to a complete stop. "Did you have something to say to us?" I heard him say as he went in front of the bonnet and headed towards the Ford.

"Yeah! What the fuck if I did? Whatcha gunna do about it?" I heard the passenger say. I looked in the side mirror and saw all the passengers opening their doors. Although I had never been in a fight before, I knew that these numbers were bad even for Jake. I took a deep breath and opened my door, making sure the safety on my Glock was off.

As I stood at the side of the car, I saw the passenger in the Ford turn towards me. He was a lot shorter and fatter than I'd expected. His hair was a long and greasy tangle beneath his dark blue bandana.

He looked like a typical street punk, long tracksuit pants and replica American football jacket with 'Raiders' across the front. As he approached me, I heard Jake say, "Well, I have something to say to all of you."

"Fuck you, man," the driver said, tossing his jacket on the bonnet to prepare for the fight that he foresaw. Jake reached into his inside breast pocket and removed his badge. "I said, I have something to say." He flipped open the black leather top of his badge cover.

"You have the right to remain silent, the right . . ."

"What the fuck! What are you arresting us for, man?" the passenger said as he realised the fight he was so desperately trying to start was not going to happen.

Jake finished reading them their rights. "Hands on the car, guys, all of you, now!"

"Fuck you, pig," the short passenger said as he leaned on the car. "We haven't done anything wrong. You have nothing on us."

"I have you drinking in a public place and that's against the law, threatening two police officers, and illegal use of a motor vehicle. I think that's enough to have you in front of a magistrate. Plus, I'm sure my colleagues will find drugs in the car when they search it."

A minute later the divvy van arrived to take them away and impound their car. I couldn't believe that we had got out of that without having to even pull a gun.

"How did you do that?" I asked as we made our way back to the car.

"Just punks, Brodie. They were never going to fight once they knew we were cops. If we'd just been kids, then there would have been trouble, of that I have no doubt."

Jake and I jumped back in the car and continued our search for Lance.

About 300 metres down Chapel Street, we finally decided to pull over and grab a coffee.

After that, we would check out the inside of some of the clubs to see if we could find Lance hiding in a dark corner.

I sat down on the bench seat in the booth and immediately looked out the window at the throng of passing women, all of whom looked as if they had just come from a fashion parade. I never knew Melbourne had so many attractive women. I certainly never met any in my own social life.

I had obviously led a sheltered life, I thought.

Jake had sat down but instead of looking at the view outside the café, he was preoccupied with reading the menu.

"You can't possibly still be hungry after everything that you consumed tonight?" I asked, surprised.

"You know me, mate, I'm always hungry," Jake replied, his eyes still firmly fixed on the menu. "I think I'll have some pancakes with my coffee, Brodie," he said, as if to seek my approval.

Jake was finishing his last pancake, making sure it had as much maple syrup on it as possible. He quickly whisked it around the plate before devouring the last bite. I went to pay, and then returned to the booth and asked him, "Shall we hit the clubs now, Jake?"

He nodded. I gathered my jacket from the booth and said, pointing across the road, "I think we should start at the clubs here."

"If that fails, then we head back to Lance's," Jake suggested.

I nodded in agreement and followed Jake across the road.

Chapter 22

Friday 7th November 2003 (12.27am)

Charlie sat in the middle of the bed with her legs slightly apart, flopped back and exposing her full, voluptuous breasts. "You coming over here, cutie?"

"Would you mind putting this on? I hope you don't mind, but I got you something." Lance held out the gift box to Charlie.

"Sure hun, whatever gets you going." Charlie raised herself up from the bed, her cute arse showing in her g-string, and took the box from Lance's extended hand. She opened the ensuite door. "I'll be right back. Get yourself ready," she said as she closed the bathroom door behind her.

Lance began to undress. When he was down to his boxers, he grabbed the bag that still held the cuffs and his other items. He placed them under the bed, making sure they were within arm's reach.

Charlie reappeared from the ensuite and Lance was stunned. She looked amazing in the lycra police uniform. She had even gone to the trouble of putting on the badge and was swirling the plastic baton around as she walked towards him.

"You're under arrest, Sir. I think I'll need to frisk you," Charlie said, giggling as she knelt on the bed beside him.

Lance had planned not to take part in any sexual activity with Charlie. He knew that the DNA evidence would put him behind bars. Again. He knew he had to be careful, for this was just the start of his plan.

Charlie began to rub his thigh, moving her hand higher up his groin and at the same time, she slowly caressed his lips with her own. Lance began to feel more tempted with each kiss from Charlie. "Are you going to bend me over and fuck me?" Charlie softly whispered into his ear. It was those words and the rub of her butt against his groin that caused him to deviate from his plan.

Lance took Charlie by the hair and began to kiss her passionately. It wasn't long before they were both enjoying hot passionate sex. "Can I tie you up?" Lance asked.

"You like it, kinky, do you?"

Charlie moaned between thrusts as she ground down harder on Lance. Lance began to lift Charlie up and grab the sheets to tie her up in.

"Not yet honey, I'm almost there. Keep fucking me. Don't stop!" she yelled. She was grinding harder and faster, bringing herself to orgasm.

"Now tie me up, baby, and do what you want with me. Just make me orgasm again. You're so good!"

Charlie rolled on her back. Placed her hands against the carved headboard. Lance grabbed the cuffs from below the bed. "Ohh, kinky!" Charlie giggled. "Not too tight, cutie," she said, as she thrust her body back and forth waiting for Lance to start fucking her again.

"I don't want you to get away from me," Lance whispered, as he cuffed her hands around a groove in the woodwork.

Charlie was naked lying on her back, hands cuffed, waiting for more pleasure.

Lance bent down and grabbed his bag of goodies, removing the long knife. He rose to face Charlie, who was watching him with interest. "What you got there, cutie? Did you pick up some naughty toys from that store?" Charlie caught a glimpse of the knife as she finished speaking. She began to pull wildly on the cuffs that held her hands to the bedhead.

"What do you think you're doing! Let me go, you freak! Let me fucking go!" She began to scream as she again tried to pull herself free.

Without another word, Lance took the knife and slit Charlie's throat, spraying blood all across the bedhead and over her face. He then stabbed Charlie several times. From the reports in the papers, he knew the East Side Slayer stabbed his victims many times. Sitting on top of her, he stabbed her all over her upper torso. Once he was over his frenzy, he packed up his belongings, went out to the kitchen and wrote a quick note. 'Here is another victim for you. I will not stop. You will not catch me. East Side Slayer.'

Lance no longer wanted to copy the Slayer.

He wanted to become him.

Chapter 23

Friday 7th November 2003 (1am)

I sat at my desk in the corner of an old open office that was in need of a major renovation. It was obvious from my corner space that I wasn't thought of highly within the police system. The detectives had their own office with all the extras including timber Venetian blinds, laptops and in some cases, TVs and video players.

It didn't matter to me that I wasn't well respected, after all, my father always told me that respect should be earned, not expected. I was from the outside and had been brought in as an outside expert, and I hadn't done any of the hard yards. Most of the guys here had been through the academy together.

The one man I knew who respected me and believed in my abilities was sitting in his office (one of the good ones) with his head in his hands, his old oak desk submerged in papers, files and photos.

His body language said it all. He was under the pump. Losing Lance last night had not helped his cause. The chief had always believed in Jake and his abilities but had no option but to rake him over the coals after last night's stuff-up. Jake was hurting. My mistake had cut him deep: he had been embarrassed and I knew that if he had been with someone else, we would not have lost Lance. I had lost Lance, Jake knew I had lost Lance, yet he'd said nothing. It was just another sign of the true friend he was.

I turned my attention back to the old case reports on my desk. These were the initial reports made by friends or family members when they'd first noticed the victims were missing. I was looking for a pattern, some sort of similarity. It is commonly thought that 90 per cent of murders are carried out by someone known to the victim.

While this was the opposite in serial murders, I was certain that there was a pattern. He was targeting female police officers and I needed to look for a link in the way he took his victims.

There had to be something.

They all couldn't just be opportunistic killings.

There was no doubt in my mind we were dealing with a killer who planned everything meticulously. One who would keep killing until he was caught.

It was now a necessity for him to kill. It provided him with some kind of satisfaction, a release, almost like a sexual release.

The other fact that I was becoming more aware of was that the killer would become more daring and more violent the longer he was loose.

I finished highlighting the fourth statement: 'The victim reported missing after failing to return home from a night out with friends.'

There was no pattern. All the victims had gone missing in different ways, at different times and in different places. I knew he had used the police academy several times. As for the others, I was at a loss. I decided to head home for some desperately needed sleep.

Chapter 24

Friday 7th November 2003 (6.21am)

I was interrupted by the phone ringing on my bedside table. Before I could even say hello, Jake had started talking. "Get up, we have a report of another one! I'm two minutes away."

It was more than a coincidence on the morning after we had lost Lance that there was another possible murder. A possible Slayer murder. I prayed it wouldn't be the case, however, I knew one thing was for sure, I was about to see my first dead body.

My head was so full of thoughts that it wasn't until I saw the wet road from the passenger seat of the police cruiser that I realised we were passing many of the places we had searched just hours before. We even passed the Casino.

I looked over at Jake.

He just looked back and shook his head.

We had been so close and we both knew it.

I got out in the freezing cold, realising I had left my woollen jacket on the back of my chair in the office the night before.

The apartment block had been taped off and there were two uniformed officers standing guard. "What's the situation?" Jake asked.

"Apparently a house mate found her flatmate dead. Stabbed to death. There was a note left for us. The guys first on the scene are still up there."

"Do you think it could be the Slayer?" Jake asked me.

"Let's wait and see. The crime scene will tell us," I responded, removing a jar of Vicks VapoRub from my suit jacket and placing two blobs under my nose.

"What the hell are you doing?" Jake asked me.

"Hey, I hear dead people smell. I'd rather smell this stuff than decomposing flesh!"

When we arrived at the apartment floor, uniformed police met us at the elevator door. "It's room 3316. The flatmate is in the neighbour's apartment, 3314," one of the officers told us.

We walked down the dimly lit hall.

As we approached room 3314, I paused and saw the flatmate providing her statement to another uniformed officer. She was a short, slim, blonde-haired woman with shoulder-length hair.

She was sitting in a wooden chair at the neighbour's dining table with a cup held firmly in her hands and a shock blanket, given to her by the first police officers on the scene, wrapped around her shoulders and back.

She was shaking, and her hair and makeup were a mess. Her mascara had run and the foundation had smeared.

"Let's check out the body first. Give her some time to compose herself," Jake whispered into my ear, as he led us back to apartment 3316. It was a nice place, very modern, bright and open.

At one end was a bedroom. I could smell death from the entrance. What I had been told was true. It's an awful odour. Jake put his tie to his nose. "You have any of that stuff?" he asked, his mouth muffled by his tie. I handed him the jar and Jake followed my lead, putting a dab of Vicks under each nostril.

We entered the room, which held about 15 other people, including patrol officers, ambos and forensics. "Listen up!" I yelled. "I need everyone except forensics and Jake out of the room now!"

All the various officers stood stunned for a few moments and then began to vacate the room. I stopped the last officer by placing my hand in the middle of his chest. "Who was the first police officer here?" I asked.

"Me and my partner Vince," the officer replied hesitantly.

"What's your name?" I asked calmly.

"Constable Simon Davison," the officer answered.

"What I want you to do, Simon, is ask all the neighbours if they saw or heard anything. Get as much information as you can. The smallest thing may break this case wide open. Once you've got everything, you can come back and see me."

Simon began to leave and when he was in the doorway, I called him back. "Simon, next time you arrive at a murder scene, don't let anyone in the room. Do you understand? If you want to get ahead in the force, you need to think about things."

I closed the door behind Simon and turned back to the victim. For a moment, I was stunned by the amount of blood all over the bed and the room. "I was glad you said something. I was about to blow my top!" Jake said, waking me from my trance.

"Yeah, I didn't mean to override you or anything," I said apologetically.

"Let's just get to work," Jake said, passing me some surgical gloves.

Jake went straight to the body and began to examine the stab wounds on the victim. I was just finishing putting on the gloves when I saw the uniform on the floor. I picked up the top and noticed straightaway. This was no police officer; this was an imitation uniform.

"Do we know who this girl is yet?" I asked Jake, still holding the uniform in my right hand.

"You'll have to ask the officers, they should have an ID by now," Jake replied with a puzzled look on his face.

"Simon, come in here please?" I called, as I opened the bedroom door. Did the flatmate give you the victim's name I asked.

"Lucy Akin. Her stage name is Charlie. She worked as a stripper at the Sweet Kandy Club. Her flatmate also works there and hasn't seen her since Friday morning," Simon answered, reading from his notepad.

"So she is a stripper not a police officer," I said.

Simon looked at me, puzzled, and began to flick through his notepad again.

"That's fine, Simon," I was thinking aloud. "Go and see what else you can find out about her."

Simon placed his notebook back in his top pocket and left the room, closing the door behind him.

"This isn't the work of the Slayer," I said, as I turned in Jake's direction.

"What are you talking about?" Jake asked, looking up from the body.

"This isn't the work of our killer," I said, shaking my head.

"Are you blind, Brodie? She's been stabbed in a frenzy just like the others. This is our man all right," Jake said, looking at me as if to say, 'what drugs are you on?'

"Jake, she isn't a cop, she's a stripper. Our killer has a purpose, a reason, a plan. A stripper is not part of that plan. But most importantly, our killer forgot to take his trophy. She still has her head, mate!"

"Maybe that's why he dressed her up as a cop, to get off when he killed her; maybe he was in a hurry and didn't have time to remove the head, who knows. He's a fucking psycho. That's why he's killing people and we're chasing him," Jake said in a raised voice.

"He dumped every other victim. This one he just left here. It doesn't fit. It's all wrong. You hired me to give you an insight into who's doing this, and out of all the files I've seen, nothing suggests that he would change his MO midstream. Believe me when I tell you that this is not the Slayer's work."

Jake looked up at me with an accepting look as if to concede defeat on the point.

"Are you sure it's not him?" he asked, giving his argument one last shot.

"Positive," I replied, and nodded as if confirm my answer.

"This is a copycat." I placed the police uniform into a big plastic evidence bag.

"What have you guys found so far?" Jake asked the forensics team, pathologist Dr David Lewis and Grace Edils, his assistant.

I remember Jake telling me, in the pre-Hayley days, how there was a hot girl named Grace in forensics. He was right. While I knew this was not the appropriate time to be admiring her looks, I found myself struggling to focus for the first few seconds after meeting her.

"Your friend appears to be right," David said to Jake. "Come here. I'll show you something. See how there's torn flesh around the knife entry and exit wounds? This tells me it was a serrated knife, while all the others have had a straight edge. So it's a different weapon to start with. Secondly, as your friend mentioned, her head is still intact. I don't think this guy would have left such an important part of his ritual unfinished. Finally, based on what Grace's blue light is showing up, I would say our killer had sex with her and that is a first in these killings."

Jake glanced up at me as if to say sorry for not believing me.

"There is a different lack of overkill in this case. I think it's safe to say that it's unlikely to be the work of the same person." David paused. "Well, we're done here. I'll compare the evidence to past victims when we get back to the lab. I'll call you with the results."

As the forensics team left, Simon reappeared. "The coroner is here for the body. Are you finished?" he asked quietly.

"Yeah, we're finished. Send them in," Jake said, as he removed his other glove and we began to leave the room.

We returned to the neighbour's apartment and both sat down at the dining room table. It was nothing flash, just the type of table that you buy on a budget, at a store like Ikea.

Jake started the conversation by introducing himself and then me to the young lady who was still holding the now empty cup in her hands.

"I'm Jessica," she replied in a low voice, trying to hold back tears.

"I know that you've been through an ordeal and I know you've been very helpful to the officers, I just want to make sure that we've covered everything so we can catch the person responsible for this," Jake said. "I understand that you and Charlie both worked at the same club in Melbourne? I don't want to pry but I take it that you were both strippers?"

"Yeah, we were just trying to get ahead. It paid so well, I never thought it would be dangerous," Jessica replied, crying, wrecking what was left of her makeup.

"We don't know that she met the person who did this at your club, but it is a strong possibility. Do you know if she knew anybody who might want to hurt her? Any ex- or current boyfriends, special admirers, or a client that was perhaps upset with her?"

"Not that I know of. Her ex is back in WA and I don't know about any clients. You might have to ask Midget at the club. He takes care of the girls while they're at the club and when they leave. She would have told him if she had problems with a client." Jessica was now sobbing.

"Midget?" Jake repeated, as if not sure he had heard the name correctly.

"His name is Gus and we just call him Midget, cos of his size."

"Do you know the name of the ex-boyfriend in Perth?" I asked.

She sat thinking for a few seconds. "Josh, I think, but I'm not sure. Her parents will probably know," she mumbled.

"One final question, Jessica. Did Charlie have drug issues, or anyone chasing her for money who might have done this?"

"No," Jessica replied quickly, shaking her head. Her words became inaudible from the tears. "She wasn't into that stuff," she muttered a few seconds later, when the tears subsided.

"Have you got a place you can go and stay for a while? We're going to need to seal off this apartment at least for a week or two," Jake said.

Jessica responded with a little nod.

"Simon, make sure you take Jessica wherever she needs to go and organise a counsellor and whatever else she needs," Jake continued. "Ok, thanks for your help, Jessica. Try and take care. I know it's going to be hard. Here's my card if you need anything or remember anything else. Just let me know."

"Thank you, Detective," she muttered as the tears began to flow again.

We left the apartment, leaving the officers to take Jessica to her interim home.

"Where are we off to now?" I asked as we exited the apartment block. It was still freezing cold. "It feels like it's about to snow," I said as we quickly made our way to the car.

I was hoping that Jake had pressed the remote for the central locking so I could get in without having to wait. When I pulled the door handle, it felt freezing. It was ridiculously cold for November, the coldest weather in 42 years. It was meant to be spring but it felt like winter.

I realised my wish had not been answered. Jake walked slowly to the car in his nice warm jacket and began to laugh as he watched me shivering beside the passenger door. "Hurry the fuck up and press the button. I'm freezing out here."

The indicator lights flashed.

I was very glad to get into the vehicle and out of the icy wind. "So, are you going to answer my question?" I asked as I did up my seatbelt.

Jake started the car and looked at me, before pulling away from the curb. "I think our first port of call should be the Sweet Kandy Club," he replied as he turned to check the traffic. "I think we need to speak to Midget and see if he knows anything."

Jake merged into the traffic and we headed back through the city towards the club.

Chapter 25

Friday 7th November 2003 (7.35am)

Maggie was shivering, partly because of the cold but mainly in fear. Cuffed to some homemade torture contraption. She had been there all night.

A madman with a sword stood motionless in front of her.

She knew from the moment she had seen the heads in the jars that she needed a miracle to get out of this.

Mason was calming himself. It had to be perfect this time.

He wondered what Maggie would be thinking.

What thoughts run through your head when you know you're going to die?

Would they be of family?

Loved ones?

Would she beg? Most did.

Time to find out.

"Now Maggie, I'm sure by now you know why they call me the East Side Slayer?" Mason asked. He removed the sword from its cover, and pointed the shiny silver blade at Maggie's face. He pressed the tip of the blade onto her cheek.

The screams started as soon as the metal touched her skin.

"Please don't!" she screamed. "Please stop, please."

She begged just like the others, Mason thought.

Mason ignored her begging and went to work.

Her screams filled the room. Mason wondered if with all the screaming Maggie knew her left eye was now lying on his dirty cellar floor.

He assumed she did.

Maggie's good eye continued to weep tears, while the other flowed blood, and a considerable amount of it. Mason took the sword tip to the other eye, the screams continued, even after the other eye had joined its mate. Mason had never removed the eyes before but thought it wouldn't be too hard to stitch them back into the skull for preservation.

Her horrendous screams increased in pitch, thus increasing Mason's sexual desire and enjoyment.

Mason managed to remove her top with the sword without cutting any of her skin. He moved a little closer, and began to feel her right breast through the soft unpadded bra. He could even feel her nipple through the mesh.

Mason ripped at the bra, not showing any care, and grabbed the breast harshly in his hand. It was firm and ripe and he began playing with it like an overzealous teenage schoolboy.

Mason ripped off the rest of her bra and then removed her pants. Maggie wasn't wearing bloomers or a g-string, she had decided to go for the three-quarter boy legs, and what part of her arse Mason could see was impressive. It was as close as he would get sexually. No evidence, he reminded himself. No matter how much he wanted to, he couldn't get carried away with her.

Maggie stood in darkness, shaking with fear. As he touched her, she decided it was time to leave. While she couldn't leave physically, she could mentally. She began to think of all the good things in her life.

Happy times.

Her family.

Most of all her mum.

Even though he was still sexually aroused, Mason knew that what gave him the most pleasure was yet to happen. Mason savoured the final moment for a few seconds and then without further thought, he raised his sword.

With one quick strike, her head was rolling in the dirt at his feet.

Mason dropped the sword to the ground.

He stared at his handiwork and took in all the euphoria.

Then he went to work on his own body.

Ejaculation was his final act of pleasure.

Chapter 26

Friday 7th November 2003 (10.04am)

We pulled up outside the club. For a Friday morning, it was surprisingly busy. The patrons leaving were all in good spirits and had wide smiles, obviously impressed with the talent they had seen inside. The bouncers requested ID of any patrons who looked under age and refused entry to those who didn't abide by the dress code.

As we entered the darkened foyer, Jake asked the hostess sitting behind a large mahogany counter, "Where can we find Gus?"

"We don't have guys here. This is a girls' only bar, boys, $10 per head if you want to enter."

Jake just flashed his badge and the girl picked up the phone. "Can you come downstairs, Gus? There are two officers here to see you." She hung up the phone and smiled. "He'll be down in a second."

"$10 dollars to enter," she said to the next boys in the queue.

They gladly handed over the money. "Just upstairs, boys. Don't forget to tip well," she reminded them as they ascended the stairs.

"Have you heard from Charlie?" a voice from behind us said.

"Not yet, Gus," was the reply from the hostess as she pointed to us with her pen to indicate we were waiting for him.

"Damn that girl!" Gus said loudly, as he turned towards us. "You better make it quick, guys, because I've got a lot to do."

"We will take as long as we like, Sir," Jake replied with a smile. "Is there somewhere we can go to talk?"

"Yeah, follow me." His voice was deep and considering his size, I was not surprised. I estimated that Gus stood about six foot six and he was of very solid build. He was one person who I think Jake would have had trouble handling. Midget was obviously an ironic nickname. We went up the stairs and off to the left. To our right we could see two semi-naked women dancing and performing some sort of lesbian show. One was a brunette wearing a pink g-string with a big star on the front and the other was a blonde in a black g-string with a gold dollar sign on the front. It was only a quick glimpse but it looked like a very raunchy show.

We entered a room with a big banner hanging across that said 'Bucks Party'.

"This room isn't booked until midnight so we have plenty of time," Gus said as he took a seat in front of the round table with a long metal pole in the middle.

Jake and I positioned ourselves opposite Gus so we could both see his expressions as he answered our questions.

"Firstly, Gus, I'd like to introduce myself. I'm Detective Jake Miller. This is Detective Brodie Foxx," Jake said, pointing to me. "Charlie won't be coming into work. Gus, she was found deceased in her home earlier today. We know that you have worked with her for a while and we know that you were close. We are sorry for your loss," Jake said in a soft voice, and paused to give Gus time to take in the news of Charlie's death.

"If you don't mind, Gus, we have a few questions to ask you to try and piece together what happened," Jake continued.

"How did she die?" Gus asked, his face now ashen.

"We believe that she was murdered. We can't give too much information as this is an ongoing investigation. Can you tell us when you last saw her?" Jake had his notepad and pen ready.

"I saw her last night as she was leaving just after midnight. She was walking home with a male friend. I asked her if she knew him, and she said she did. I thought I had seen him around here getting lap dances. I can't be sure though; it's not the best lighting out the back."

"Could you describe the man with Charlie?" Jake asked, again poising his pen for the answers.

"Yeah sure." Gus described the guy. As Jake finished his notes, he turned to me.

"Do you know who this guy is?" Gus asked, puzzled.

"Not yet, but hopefully we will have him soon." Jake again paused. "Could you identify this man if you saw him again?"

"Yeah, I sure could, I'd know his slimy little face if I saw it," Gus said angrily.

"Apart from this guy, had Charlie said anything to you about anyone, an ex, an over-the-top patron perhaps, anyone who had been annoying her or stalking her?"

"No. She hadn't mentioned anyone to me. Usually the girls will tell me if they're having a problem. After all, that's why I'm here."

"Just a few more questions, Gus, then we'll be on our way," Jake said. "We have to ask, as we believe you were the last to see Charlie alive. Can you please tell us your whereabouts for the last 24 hours?"

"Yeah, after Charlie left I was here till 5am which is closing time. I escort the girls out as I do every shift. Then I went home with Vicki—she was the blonde girl on the stage when you first walked in, I'm sure you noticed her. I don't have to go into all the details of what we did when we got home, do I?" Gus asked with dirty smirk.

"No," Jake replied quickly.

"We woke up about midday and had some lunch at Donatellos on Lygon Street till we both started here at 3.00pm, and here I am."

"Thanks for your time, Gus. We just need to ask Vicki some questions now," Jake said, "can you send her in?"

"Sure," Gus replied, picking up the phone and hitting the intercom button. "Sal, could you send Vicki in to function room one? Well, if she's on stage, then get her off now!" Gus said, raising his voice.

Within seconds, the door opened and Vicki appeared, topless and in her black g-string.

"That's all we need from you Gus, you can leave now." Jake gestured for Vicki to take a seat.

Once Gus had left and closed the door behind him, Jake began to question Vicki. Again, he first went through the standard introductions, and then asked a simple but straightforward question. "Please tell us where you were last night?"

Although a little taken aback by the question, Vicki answered it in the same forthright manner as Gus had. "I worked till 5am then I went to Gus' house where he banged my brains out for the next two hours. He was good too. I bet you'd like to have a go at me for a couple of hours, wouldn't you, Copper?" she said, looking at me as if to say, I know you want me. She purposely licked her lips.

Jake just glanced at me with a smile. "You can go now, Vicki, thanks for your help."

"No problem," she replied, smiling, "I hope to see you later, Coppers, especially you," she said, pointing to me.

As she left, Gus returned to stand in the doorway, arms crossed and leaning on the door. "Is that all you guys need?"

"We're finished," Jake replied, as he gathered his things and headed out. "Oh yes, one more thing. All we need now is the video footage of the back laneway last night, if you have it?"

"Yeah, we should do. I'll get it for you on the way out," Gus said, leading the way.

We went down the stairs and headed back to the entrance. Gus stopped at the front counter and opened a drawer below the till, sifting through three rows of tapes that looked as if they were marked in date order and with 'Rear' or 'Front' written next to the date.

"There you go," Gus said, as he plucked out one of the tapes from the drawer and handed it to Jake.

"Do you have any of inside the club?" I asked.

"We only record this foyer, we don't record where the dancers are," Gus replied quickly.

"Can we have that too?"

Gus opened a second drawer and handed over a tape.

"We'll return them both as soon as we've finished with them," Jake said.

We were on our way back to the station when Jake's phone rang.

"Miller?" he answered. "Yeah, in 15 or 20. See ya then, Captain."

"The captain wants to catch up on everything we have," Jake said to me. "It'll give us an opportunity to look at that tape too."

Chapter 27

Friday 7th November 2003 (10.41am)

We were keen to get a look at the tape from the club and see what it revealed.

The captain was waiting for us when we arrived.

"Was it him?" he asked as we walked down the hall and headed towards the media room.

"Brodie doesn't think so. He thinks it's more likely a copycat, but we have a tape from where she went missing so we'll see what that gives us."

The captain turned to me. "What do you mean it wasn't him?"

"Her head wasn't missing."

"Different MO?"

I replied, quickly and firmly, "Yes, he wouldn't change such an important part of his ritual."

We continued down the hall until we reached the media room. Jake wasted no time in switching on the TV and placing the video in the machine.

"Maybe he was rushed," the captain continued.

Before I had a chance to answer, Jake stepped in. "Forensics agree with Brodie. They think there are too many inconsistencies between this murder and the others." He Jake bent down and pressed the play button.

The digital readout at the top right-hand side of the screen showed 10.03pm. Jake hit fast forward until the counter reached 11.57pm, and then slowed the tape down to normal speed. At 12.01am, a tall male figure made his way into the bottom corner of the screen. All that could be seen of him was his right shoulder and arm. At 12.13am, from the bottom left of the screen, a girl entered the picture. "That's our girl," Jake said, tapping the screen.

"It's a pity we can't see the guy," I said.

With the counter on 12.14am, a third figure appeared. From his bulk, there was no doubt that it was Midget.

By the time Midget had headed back where he had come from, only the backs of Charlie and her possible killer were visible, and then they walked out of view.

"Shit!" Jake screamed as he hit the top of the video set.

"Settle, Jake," I said. "Go back to where that guy came into view." Jake rewound the tape. "There, in his hand," I said, "it's a bag. It has some writing on it. Do you think we could get the lab to try and enhance the bag so we can read what it says?"

"We can give it a go," Jake replied, as he ejected the tape and we headed through the double doors.

Sitting behind the biggest computer I had ever seen was Jason, the lab technician.

"Jason, could you have a look at this for me?" Jake asked as he handed him the tape.

"Sure thing," Jason replied, spinning around in his chair. Jason looked like a typical high school nerd who'd spent all of his time in computer class, not to become smarter but to be away from the bullies in the school yard. He wore inch-thick glasses of the sort that everyone at school used to refer to as coke bottles, and I thought about what Mum always used to say. "If you sit too close to the screen, you'll go blind." 'Must be true,' I thought.

"What do you need me do with this, Jake?" Jason asked as he placed the tape into his wiz-bang super computer.

"The guy is holding a bag. Can you enlarge it so we can see what's written on it?"

Jason began to move his cursor across the screen until he had highlighted the bag. He then turned several knobs and dials on the computer and before our eyes, the words 'Adult Playground' appeared.

I looked at Jake. "Let's find out what the hell Adult Playground is. Probably one of those sleazy city adult shops."

Jake replied, smiling as if he was excited at the idea of being in a room full of toys and porn. "Thanks Jason," he said, slapping him on the back.

"Let's check the entrance tape, Jake," I said, "see if we can get a match."

After viewing the video, Jake and I realised two things.

1. Lance had been at the club that night wearing a similar jacket but without a bag.
2. There were four or five other guys similarly dressed and of similar build who could easily have been the man in the alleyway.

"We need to find who was at Adult Playground last night before we go any further," Jake said, heading back to his desk. Before he had even sat down, he had Google up on his screen. Within a few seconds, he was impatiently waiting for the printer to finish.

This time I made sure I had my jacket and waited for Jake to let me know if we were going back to the city.

"You were right. It's an all-night adult shop. So let's get going." Jake scooped up his keys with his left hand.

"Don't forget your coat," Jake remarked, allowing himself a dig at me.

Chapter 28

Friday 7th November 2003 (11.13am)

The wind seemed to have picked up a couple of knots and the air felt as though it was about to snow.

"You know, Jake, the guy who did this is just as dangerous as the East Side Slayer. He thinks he's the Slayer and he can't see the difference."

"So what you're saying is, he's also going to keep killing until we catch him. Is that what you're telling me?" Jake was trying to look at me and keep his eyes on the road at the same time.

"That's what I'm telling you, buddy. He won't stop until he's caught or killed. This guy probably sees his kill as a dare to the Slayer himself."

The door chime buzzed as we entered Adult Playground. Jake immediately made his way to the counter, while I spent a bit of time wandering around the shop looking for some of the items that I'd seen at the murder scene. In particular, the police uniform. I saw it displayed on a mannequin, everything from the lycra shorts to the police cap complete with its imitation badge. "Jake," I called, "over here. This is what we're looking for." I began to take the mannequin down. Jake and the shop assistant headed to the back of the store.

The assistant was about five foot eight and had long, flowing, shoulder-length blonde hair. She was wearing a pale pink top that showed off her stomach. Her belly button had been pierced and she had a diamond belly ring dangling down towards her low-cut Levis. She was obviously told to dress provocatively to entice the customers to purchase.

"We're looking for a customer who may have purchased this recently," I said, turning to the assistant for her response, when a shiny steel object on the other side of the store caught my eye. Jake didn't have a clue as to what I was doing. I pointed to the handcuffs hanging from the shelf and asked, "Have you had anyone purchase both these items at the same time?"

"I can get my manager Dianne to check the system for you. She's the owner. I can ring her now if you like?" She punched in a handful of numbers for a mobile.

"What's your name, Miss?" I asked as she waited patiently for Dianne to answer the call.

"I'm Leah," she said, pointing at the nametag pinned to her chest.

"That's a nice name," I replied in my standard dorky fashion. (It was no wonder I had trouble meeting women.)

When she hung up, Leah said, "Dianne said she remembers a fairly tall guy coming in last night and buying a uniform and he purchased the cuffs as a secondary thought, kind of on his way out. The police uniforms only came in last week."

"Can we view last night's video footage?" I asked.

"Sure, no problem, Officer," Leah replied, as she headed towards the back room, looking over her shoulder to see if I was following.

"You can call me Brodie," I said.

She again looked over her shoulder and smiled. "Ok Brodie." She muttered something after that but I couldn't quite make it out. My hearing wasn't what it used to be.

My hearing had cost me some opportunities for sex in my younger days. I had been on a Christmas holiday just after my eighteenth birthday and being older than Jake and the only one with a licence, I was given the task of driving down to the caravan park for our holiday. We had been there about two days when he sparked up a conversation with a couple of girls who were staying about two spots over. By the third night, we were spending all of our time with them, and me being a dorky 18-year-old, I did nothing. Made no attempt to even chat to the remaining girl whose friend had quickly abandoned her for Jake. It wasn't until Jake came to me and said that she liked me and suggested that I make a move that on the fourth night, while Jake and his newly acquired friend were playing handies under a blanket, I summoned enough courage to kiss the girl I only knew as Mindy. Then I placed my hand on her breast and cheekily slid it inside her loose-fitting top. Worried about the move I had just made, I asked her if she minded. For some reason, I didn't hear her response. To this day, I still don't know what the answer was. I was so afraid she had said something like "get your hand off" that I was too afraid to ask the question again so I simply removed my hand and went no further with any advances. The next day, she left.

Jake asked me why I hadn't gone any further and I said, "I couldn't hear what she said." Jake told me what he'd heard and the words, while music to my ears, left me feeling like an idiot. "She said you could put your hand anywhere you like!"

I followed Leah into the small tearoom at the back of the store, while Jake waited patiently at the cash register to keep an eye on the shop for her. "Ah, here it is," Leah said as she ran her finger along the front of the video cassettes on the shelf in numerical order, stopping on the Friday one. "You can watch it here if you like? We have the equipment," she said, pointing to the TV and video machine used for all the store cameras.

"That would be a great help," I replied, removing the cassette from its cover. Leah removed the one from the machine and took the other one from my hand, stroking my fingers lightly as she removed the cassette from my grip. The counter started at 10am.

Leah handed me the remote, "I'll leave it with you. Call me if you need me," she said as she left the room. This time there was no second look back over her shoulder.

Jake came in a few seconds later. "I think she likes you, Brucey," he said, as he looked up at the TV screen.

"What are you talking about?" I replied, with my finger still firmly pressed on the fast-forward button. The counter had reached 7.23pm when Jake interrupted again.

"She said your name was cute. She wouldn't say that if she didn't like you," Jake continued. Jake thought it was his responsibility to find my future wife.

"Maybe you should ask her out?" Jake suggested

I hit the fast-forward button again to skim through all the costumers until the counter reached 8.47pm, when a tall slim man walked in then disappeared to the back of the store. A few seconds later, he reappeared and placed an item on the counter. It was a police uniform. He then disappeared again towards the back of the shop, reappearing again a few seconds later holding a small shiny object.

"That's him," I said to Jake.

"That's Lance!" he replied immediately. I hit the pause button and moved closer to the TV screen. He was right. It was Lance, there was no doubt about it. Jake ejected the tape and headed briskly back into the store, with me following him. "We need to take this as evidence," he explained to Leah, holding up the cassette.

"That's fine," Leah responded. "Do you have a card for my boss in case she asks any questions?" she asked shyly.

"Brodie will leave his contact details and you or your boss can call him anytime," Jake replied without hesitation. Then he walked outside to the car, smiling.

"Hey Brodie, you have to give me your contact details. Your partner dobbed you in," she said, smiling.

I handed her my card that had been recently supplied by the Victorian Police Department.

"I'll call you if I need you," Leah said, still smiling, as I walked out of the store. Jake was leaning against the car. "Let's go get this sick fuck," Jake proposed as I approached the vehicle.

"I think that we need to think about this before we rush off to arrest him," I answered, as I got in the passenger side of the vehicle.

"What are you talking about? We have him cold," Jake said with a degree of anger in his voice.

"Hear me out. I know we have him cold but we don't have the Slayer. We could use this situation to our advantage. Lance doesn't know that his killing wasn't the same as the Slayer's and the Slayer doesn't know that someone is copying him."

"So what are you proposing?" Jake asked with an inquisitive frown.

"I think we release details of Lance being wanted as the East Side Slayer. The real Slayer will see this and be furious that someone else has taken his glory. He may slip up, make a mistake, by wanting to take back the glory that's been stolen from him."

"Sure, or the Slayer could kill someone else just to prove to us that we have the wrong guy." As Jake finished his sentence, it suddenly hit me.

"If we play this right and feed the right info to the media he could possibly hand himself in and then we could arrest them both!"

"Sounds easy, no problem, are you on crack? That is the most absurd thing I have ever heard. You can't be serious? Why would he do that? He has spent 10 years trying not to get caught, suddenly he will just give up?"

I knew Jake was pissed, but I was sure I could convince him that my plan had merit.

"Jake, he's addicted to killing, he won't stop. He loves the power it gives him. However, he also believes he's better than us because he's beaten us for 10 years. Suddenly someone else will get his credit. It might just persuade him. We need to take a risk if we want to catch this guy," I finished.

Jake sat in his seat pondering for several minutes, then he replied, "We need to talk to the chief about this.

Chapter 29

Friday 7th November (12.05pm)

By the time we got back to the station, it had been just over six hours since Charlie had been reported murdered. It had been one of the saddest, yet most exciting, 24 hours of my life. I had been running on adrenaline the whole time and now I felt the urge to sleep run through my body. A 15-minute power nap would do me good, but there wasn't even time for that.

The chief had come into the station at Jake's request. He had been at home sleeping and Jake said he'd sounded a little pissed.

"This better be good, Miller," were his first words as we entered his office. "You know I didn't get to sleep until 4am and then you woke me!"

Jake ignored his boss's comments and went straight to business.

"Brodie has a plan, Chief, and I think it's a good one."

Without speaking, the chief turned his attention to me and waited.

Nervous, I hesitated a little and my voice cracked as the first words came out. "My plan is simple. The girl killed yesterday was a stripper. She'd been dressed in a police uniform. This was no doubt a Slayer copycat killing. However, the true Slayer doesn't know he is being copied. If we arrest Lance now, he will admit to all the killings even though he didn't do them and the Slayer will continue, with us being no closer to his identity. My plan is this: while we wait for Lance's DNA to come back and forensics to search his car, which we will need to prove his guilt, we front the media and release the video footage of Lance at the store and in the alley, asking for anyone that knows this man to contact Crime Stoppers as a 'person of interest' in connection with the East Side slayings."

"What does that achieve?" the chief asked in a less-than-approving tone.

"Well, the real Slayer will hopefully be pissed that someone else is about to take his glory and turn himself in, or at the least, contact us. Many serial killers in the past have contacted police to prove that they are the killer. Quite often this leads to their downfall."

"That's your plan?" the chief asked me. He then turned to Jake. "What amazes me more is that you thought this was a good idea." He pointed his finger at Jake. "What if the Slayer instead of contacting us goes out and kills another girl to prove he's the Slayer?"

"He will do that anyway, if we don't stop him. We know that for sure," I interrupted.

"What if this causes Lance to go on a killing spree?" Richard questioned.

"Anything is possible with these nutters, as you know!" Jake said.

"We will have him under strict supervision. If he leaves his house we will arrest him, Chief," I added.

"Don't call me Chief, you haven't earned that right yet! Remember, your appointment to the force can be revoked as quickly as it was given. Don't forget that! If this goes bad we will never hear the end of it. I went to the commissioner to get you approved, don't put me in a position where I have to go back to him."

The chief was now standing, leaning across his desk.

Shocked at his outburst, I put my head down and also wondered what the hell I was doing in the middle of all this. Maybe he was right; maybe I didn't belong.

"Don't start going off your tree. This case has been going on for 10 years so maybe you should take a look in the mirror," Jake fired back. "At least Brodie has a plan, which is better than you and your previous taskforce have ever done."

The chief sat back in his chair and began to rub his eyes. "All right, Jake, it's your call and your arse if you do this, and if it goes horribly wrong, you're back on traffic duty. Do you understand? As for you, Brodie, well you know the consequences."

"You don't have to threaten us, Chief, we get it."

"Jake," I interrupted, "it's ok, I understand your boss's position." I was being careful not to use the word 'chief'. "This wasn't Jake's idea. It was mine and I offer you this. If we do what I have suggested and if we don't flush out the Slayer, I'll be your fall guy if you need one. I can't guarantee that we'll catch him but I can be fairly sure that this plan will get us closer to him."

The chief, who had now calmed down, looked at me and sighed.

"You better pray it flushes him out."

I followed Jake out of the office. He turned to me in the hall. "Are you sure you want to go ahead with this plan of yours? We have a lot of information we could sort through before we resort to this strategy."

"Charlie's murder won't remain quiet for long. If we arrest Lance now, we won't get another opportunity like this again," I said. "I think it's our best chance and I'd rather try and fail than not try at all."

Jake continued walking towards his office. "Let's do this then," he said, smiling slightly.

Chapter 30

Friday 7th November 2003 (6.43pm)

"Now Maggie, it's time for you to go where you can be found," Mason muttered to himself as he again went across to his workbench. He returned a short time later, holding a large piece of extra-thick plastic normally used for ground cover to prevent weeds coming through the mulch.

Mason laid the plastic along the dirt floor of the cabin cellar next to Maggie's lifeless body. He grabbed Maggie under the shoulders, dragging her headless body onto the plastic. Laying her on the plastic, he began to wash her with a bleach solution, then wrapped her up like a cigarette. He then began to cut several pieces of orange rope from the spindle he had retrieved from his bench. He cut each piece to a length of approximately three foot. He began to tie the end where Maggie's head would have been, ensuring there was enough plastic at the end so the ends would not come free during transportation. Mason then tied a second rope around Maggie's chest. It took five pieces to secure Maggie's body fully.

Mason went outside and drove his BMW down to the cellar. He drove in through the open doors and parked on the dusty cellar floor, swiftly closing the doors behind him. Then he loaded Maggie's body into the open boot.

Mason knew that if the police ever found this place there would be enough evidence from Maggie and all the other victims to convict him a hundred times over. However, the chance of finding this place was remote.

By the time Mason drove his car out of the cellar, it was well after 7pm. With the drive ahead of him, he would be dumping the body in the dark as planned.

Chapter 31

Friday 7th November 2003 (7.30pm)

"Are you all set for this conference?" I asked Jake. "You know what to say?"

Jake nodded. Then he was on.

"We have information about the East Side Slayer and we feel it is important to let the public know some of the facts that have come to hand," Jake began. "My name is Detective Jake Miller I am lead detective of the Eagle taskforce. We are looking for this man . . ." they rolled the surveillance footage, "in relation to the murder of Lucy Akin and the unsolved police officer murders. We encourage anyone with any knowledge of this man to contact Crime Stoppers immediately. We believe the community will be able to help us identify this man."

We had given the public the impression that we didn't know who Lance was, which was exactly what we wanted.

Jake finished up and headed back to us. "The conference doesn't hit the air at 7am tomorrow, I'll pick you up in the morning, say at 6.15?" Jake didn't wait for an answer.

We arrived at Lance's house about 6.40am and it was good to see that our night surveillance was still there and awake. "What's the status?" Jake asked into the handset.

There was a short pause before the answer returned, "He's been inside since 10.35 last night. Before that, he was at the Crazy Horse cinemas watching porn. I'd say he's been in there spanking the monkey ever since."

"Thanks for the detail, Chad, you guys can leave now," I replied.

"So we just sit and wait?" Jake asked, as Chad's vehicle left to return to the police station. "Yep, just be patient. Soon, both Lance and the Slayer will see the press conference and then we just wait for the Slayer to contact us or turn himself in to claim his glory." At least I hoped that was what would happen. My whole plan rested on my study of serial killers and their egos preventing them from allowing someone else to take the credit. Surely he would contact us.

Chapter 32

Friday 7th November 2003 (8.00pm)

As Mason drove back to Melbourne, he knew exactly where he would dump Maggie. While he knew the location, it was impossible to plan exactly. He never knew who might be floating around. After all, the last thing he wanted when he was taking a body out of the boot was someone seeing him.

A dead body wrapped in plastic was difficult to disguise.

Mason had prided himself on dumping the bodies in different locations. He knew that it would make it harder for police to track him. His plan was simple. He wanted the police to think that he was on the move all the time and that no one in the whole state was safe. For the last decade, it had worked. They had released several suspect profiles through the media. One had suggested it would most likely be a person who travelled in his job, who had a position that provided the freedom to commit these horrendous acts. The police media spokesperson had suggested that it was likely he was a truck driver or possibly a cabbie. Both of these theories pleased Mason a great deal.

He had figured that this body needed to be dumped somewhere remote, and miles away from the last one. He had sold a couple of properties back in the old 'multi-list' days out in a suburb called the Basin, which was an area of bush.

The outskirts of the suburb abutted a national park. Mason always liked dumping in the parks. There was an abundance of walking and riding tracks, increasing the chances of the body being found within a reasonable time. Yet, at night, the parks were practically deserted, giving Mason the privacy he needed.

Mason pulled his car into the turning circle at the top of Clairveness Avenue, the Basin, at almost 8.30. It was nearing dark. He had parked where the road met the beginning of the Basin National Reserve, as some moron at the council had decided to name it. While the turning circle didn't provide any cover for getting Maggie out of his boot, it did provide perfect and quick access to the park and the dense bushland, which would protect him while he was dumping her. All Mason had to do was time his run. Reaching under the dash, he pushed the boot release button. He heard the mechanical release and the boot popped open about half an inch. Mason took a final look in the rear vision mirror and saw no headlights approaching.

He got out of his car and stood at the boot, taking a final look down the road. He could see approximately 300 metres before the road curved and vision of any oncoming vehicles became impossible. Mason swung around and looked up the road for any approaching vehicles from the rear. There was about a 200-metre view in that direction.

Mason knew that if a car came from either way once he had removed the body, he would have no time to put it back before the car was well and truly upon him. After a couple of further glances, up and down the road, he opened the boot a little more, lifted his shirt up and placed the knife, still in its leather case, down the back of his jeans. It rested against the small of his back and at the top of his buttocks.

Mason always took his knife when he was dumping someone. He never knew when he might need to cut some brush.

Mason placed his arms in the boot and took hold of Maggie's body, still with the boot only ajar, allowing him enough space to reach in. He took his final look and then prepared himself for the lift and run into the park. In a single motion, he pushed the boot up with his biceps and lifted the body out.

Maggie's feet weren't even clear of the boot as Mason began his dash for the cover of the bush, clipping Maggie's foot on the corner of the boot and tearing the plastic as he went. He carried her almost at a run and was glad when he found himself in a secluded area away from the road in the scrub. Mason left the stony path, obviously provided for mountain bikers and walkers, and trudged through the bracken, ferns and fallen bark from nearby gums, which towered above Mason and his headless victim.

Mason began to struggle to carry the body once he left the dirt track. Fallen branches and potholes made the journey more difficult.

He almost dropped Maggie twice within the first five metres after leaving the track.

The third time, Mason was forced to drop his victim when he stepped into a concealed hole, causing him to lose his balance and roll his ankle. Had he not dropped Maggie, he probably would have broken his ankle.

That would have left him in a fine mess, sitting next to the victim and unable to walk.

He had a vision of himself crawling back to the car. How stupid that would look, not to mention a great way to attract attention.

Maggie's body rolled a few metres before coming to rest against the side of a fallen gum. It was here that Mason decided to leave her, not because he thought it was the best place for her but because his ankle was killing him and he knew he wouldn't be able to carry her any further.

Mason undid the rope from the plastic and unrolled Maggie, like a rolled-up sleeping bag in front of a blazing campfire.

He tore a few branches off a nearby fern and began laying them over the package of Maggie's sprawled body. Mason had only half covered the body when he felt something wet on his back.

He turned, half startled, to see the nose of a German Shepherd sniffing his back and leg and trying to sniff Maggie. What the hell was a dog doing out here at this time of night? Mason tried to get the dog away from him.

Chapter 33

Friday 7th November (8.43pm)

Alan was heading for home at the end of his jog. He had been doing this run for a little over six months now and winter had not stopped him. Even the dark didn't bother him. Jogging had become easier over the months and the rewards were now visible. He could see that his body was more toned. His main concern was finding his dog Rex, who had gone exploring.

He had started his jog a little later than usual this evening; work had been hectic. He had almost decided not to go because it was getting too late. But he knew Rex needed the run and he always took Rex on both his morning and evening jogs, more for exercise than company.

"Rex, Rex, where are you?" he called, slowing down and scanning each side of the path for Rex. Where had he gone? He had been running nearby.

Mason heard the distant calls for the dog, which was obviously the one sniffing around behind him. The calls were coming a lot closer.

Mason knew his time was limited so he quickly tried to cover the exposed parts of Maggie's body. As he grabbed more bracken and fern branches, he knew that his time had run out when he saw Rex's owner standing on the track.

He had obviously been jogging for a while. Mason could see he had well defined and toned thigh muscles. Mason guessed he must have been close to the end of his jog because sweat was running down his face.

Alan sighted Rex and cautiously observed the stranger with the large plastic tarp. He then noticed what appeared to be a leg protruding from beneath it.

Alan quickly comprehended what he had seen and decided to flee. He began to run away as fast as he could sprint. Mason knew that there was no way he would catch him: not with his ankle in its current condition.

Reaching around his back, Mason withdrew his knife from its holster, held it by the tip and began to focus. He knew that he only had one chance and if he missed, his killing days would soon be over. He aimed at the jogger's broad back.

His target was one of the lungs. He knew the best way to stop him would be to cut the oxygen supply and a knife through a lung could certainly do that.

Taking a deep breath, he swiftly threw the knife at the escaping witness.

The knife spun end over end, compass, tip, compass, tip, compass, tip, through the air, until it hit its target. Alan felt something hit him, but couldn't understand what it was. There was no pain at first. Then his breathing became spasmodic, wheezing and slow. Had he been shot by the man in the bushes? He hadn't heard anything. His running had slowed to a stagger.

Then the taste of blood. It wet his lips, and was quickly filling his mouth. Then the pain came. With every breath, the pain increased, sharp and excruciating and becoming increasingly shallow.

His adrenaline could carry him no longer. He was dying and he knew it.

The ground was wet and muddy in places from the winter rains and the mud clung to him as his knees hit the mossy ground. Still desperate to escape, he began to crawl along the track, trying not to think of the inevitable.

His hands and knees quickly became muddy and slippery. He could no longer continue on all fours. He fell, face first into the mud. He tasted the dirt mixed with blood. He rolled onto his side, hoping he could muster the strength to call and command Rex to attack. Maybe then his attacker would not be able to pursue him any further.

Alan's breathing was a real struggle now and more painful than ever.

He took the deepest breath possible, causing himself more pain than he could have thought possible.

Rex's ears pricked up at the cries from his owner. He turned his head away from the body he was sniffing on the ground, and towards his owner. At the sound of his second weaker cry of anguish, Rex jumped into action.

Mason heard the call coming from the jogger, but he never expected the dog to attack him from behind.

Mason was halfway to the collapsed jogger who was lying on his side in the mud and gravel with the knife still embedded in his back, when he was suddenly knocked to the ground. The large dog attacked him ferociously. First, he went for Mason's throat but Mason protected himself with his right forearm. Mason felt the dog's teeth pierce the skin then tear the flesh away. He knew that his arm could not protect him for much longer and that he had to do something.

Mason used all the power he could in his good foot and what little power he could muster from his sprained one and kicked as hard as he could, dazing the shepherd temporarily.

The kick didn't seem to do it any serious harm, but it was certainly enough to stun it.

Mason rolled onto his stomach and got to all fours and then to his feet. He had only taken a few steps when the shepherd was back at him, this time attacking his foot. Mason dropped to the ground for a second time.

Mason twisted his neck around to see if he could reach his knife embedded in the jogger's back, but it was still out of reach.

He had to get this dog off him and fast. The jogger was still alive and trying to crawl away, and the longer the dog was on him, the more injuries he would sustain.

A serious injury would be hard to explain. Not to mention the unfinished business and the chances of someone coming across what had become nothing short of a disaster.

Mason reached out both arms to ward off the dog as best he could, scanning the ground for any weapon he could use. Then he felt a rock. Rolling over, he wasted no time in grasping the rock and hitting the dog continually until finally, the rock connected with the shepherd's temple and it gave a loud yelp before falling silent.

After kicking the dog off him with his good foot, Mason got to his feet. There was no doubt the dog had done some damage but not enough to prevent him from hobbling out of this mess. Mason staggered towards the almost lifeless sprawled body of the jogger. "Your fucking dog had a lot of fight in him but I sent him on a little trip and now I'm sending you there with him." Placing his knee in the small of his back, Mason withdrew his knife from under his shoulder blade and flipped him over. He wanted to see his eyes. This wasn't his usual kill but he needed to see him go. Mason wasted no more time, slitting his throat and then beginning his frenzy of stabbing. He wrenched him up by the hair and stared into his eyes as he began to splutter and wheeze. He was almost gone. Then silence, as he passed. Mason used what energy he had left to remove his head. Finally, he rolled him off the walking track, wrapped the jogger's head inside his own jacket and returned to the safety of his vehicle.

Mason had always kept a spare bag of clothes in his car in case of an emergency such as this. He removed a garbage bag, placed the jacket and the head into it, and tied it tight. He removed his bloody pants behind the cover of his car. He added them to a separate garbage bag. Dressed in his spare clothes, he placed the bags in his boot and headed home.

He had left the jogger's body barely covered, but it would have to do. He was just hoping he hadn't left too much evidence behind.

He couldn't get home soon enough. Mason entered the home still hobbling and headed straight for the powder room and the medicine cabinet.

He was so lucky his wife had gone away. How could he have explained his injuries?

He washed his foot and forearm under the tap before applying the antiseptic and adding some gauze and Betadine, hoping it would do the job. The bites didn't look deep enough to require stitches, and that wouldn't be possible anyway without raising alarm bells. Especially when the police found the dog and the headless jogger. Mason wound the bandages tight, swallowed a couple of painkillers and headed upstairs, where he watched a movie in bed and fell asleep.

Chapter 34

Saturday 8th November 2003 (7am)

Despite his injuries, Mason rose early as he had always done on a Saturday morning. Saturdays were his open home days he had to be up and out early. He stood in front of the mirror with the shaver balanced delicately in his right hand. He no longer recognised the man looking back at him. Mason leaned forward and looked deep into his own eyes. Nothing there; nothing but darkness. It even scared him. It was eerie. What had he become?

Twenty minutes later, Mason sat down at the table ready to eat breakfast. The morning news was on in the background.

Before he had even consumed a mouthful of his cereal, he stopped, in a trance, staring at the vision on the television screen. Mason watched the police interview and listened intently as Jake introduced himself and the taskforce. His heart felt like it was about to burst out his chest. When CCTV footage appeared, his panic turned to anger. It wasn't him. The footage was of someone else. Some tall skinny bloke. Mason stood and threw his bowl from the table to the kitchen sink. It smashed on impact, sending pieces of the bowl across the room along with cereal and milk.

This was not right. All his hard work for someone else to take the glory, 'Uh ahh,' Mason thought. 'No way. It won't end like this.' He had to put a stop to it.

Mason didn't arrive at work for at least another 40 minutes. He had decided to put his open for inspection boards out early, giving him time to listen to the talkback stations, which were buzzing with excitement at the possibility of a suspect. They had even taken the unusual step of bringing in ex-profilers to prove that the police had been on the right track all along. How wrong they were.

Talkback callers suggested that the death penalty be brought back for the man found guilty of the murders. By the time he arrived at the office, the host had announced that News Limited had identified the 'man in the alley' as one Lance Silver of Kew and that his car was in the hands of forensics.

Mason was the first to arrive at the office, as was often the case. He unlocked the door, turned off the alarm and turned on the lights, immediately heading for his laptop. He had a good hour before his first appointment. His last open home finished at 2, so he would have plenty of time to act if need be.

Removing the notepad from the top pocket of his shirt, Mason entered the name into his reverse phone directory. 'Please don't be unlisted,' Mason thought. Then after what seemed like an eternity, the search brought up exactly what he needed: There were three on the list but only one 'L. Silver' in Kew. His phone number was unlisted. All Mason needed now was a plan to show everyone who the real Slayer was, once and for all.

Mason spent the next half hour doing a little research of his own. He typed into his Google search bar 'Jake Miller Eagle taskforce'. Several links came up. He clicked on the link 'Eagle taskforce restructured after 10 years'.

He read that Senior Detective Jake Miller would head up the revamped Eagle taskforce in an attempt to reinvigorate the much-maligned original taskforce. Upon his appointment, Miller had said he believed that the cases were solvable. The Victorian police would do everything in its power to ensure the killer was caught and brought to justice.

Yet, less than a week later, the taskforce had already come under fire for the appointment of criminal psychologist Brodie Foxx. Foxx's appointment was highly criticised by the state government who were now debating amending the Police Act to forbid any such future appointments.

"Can I see you in my office, Mason?" a distant but distinctive voice called out. Mason sighed. He wanted a plan and now his planning was being interrupted. Probably over something trivial.

Kurt had only been made the boss because it was his father's company, not because he was an outstanding salesperson. Kurt had tried to demand respect from the moment he'd taken the helm, without success. Mason thought the pressure of running his father's multi-million dollar business was taking its toll.

In the last two years, Kurt had gained a lot of weight and lost some hair. What little remained was now grey. He looked as if he was falling apart.

"Shut the door," Kurt said from his seat on the other side of his desk. Mason did as he was told and took a seat opposite his boss, surprised by his boss's request for a meeting. "What's going on with you lately? Is there a problem at home that I don't know about?" his boss asked, wasting no time in getting to the point.

Mason sat there, stunned. Then he replied with a stutter, "No, everything is fine." He was unsure where this conversation was heading.

"Well, it's just that your sales figures have dropped dramatically and you're never in the office any more," Kurt said, flicking through a sales result spreadsheet.

Without hesitation, Mason went on the attack. "Everything is fine. I'm just having a bad run, that's all. The reason I'm out of the office is because I'm trying to get business. Houses and land are out there, not in here. I have a lot on, that's all."

"Well, if your results don't improve by the end of the month, I'm going to have to consider letting you go."

Mason sat silently for a minute, looking at his boss's desk, still trying to come up with a plan. Then it appeared in front of him. It was sitting there staring back at him and it was brilliant. 'Opportunities always present themselves when needed,' he thought. "I understand; I'll work harder," Mason replied.

Mason stood and paused. "Is that photo new?" he asked, pointing to the photo of his boss's daughter on his desk. "Yes, she just graduated," Kurt replied abruptly, picking up his phone to dial his next call. "They grow up so fast," Mason said, as he left his boss's office and pretended to get back to work.

It would have to wait until tomorrow before it was revealed in all its glory, but it was simply perfect.

Mason spent the rest of the day doing the mundane tasks that he was required to do in order to keep his job for at least a little longer. It wasn't until around 1pm that he told his lovely receptionist that he was going to do a market appraisal after his open home, and that he might not be back that day.

Chapter 35

Saturday 8th November 2003 (10.30am)

We had spent Saturday morning sitting at the front of Lance's house. We had been there for almost four hours and thankfully, our shift was almost over. He was so stupid; he kept sticking his head out from behind the curtain to peek into the street.

We had his phone bugged and he had made two calls, both to his solicitor Dale Moreholm. His answering machine had answered both times. Obviously, it had taken the second call for Lance to realise it was a Saturday afternoon and the office was closed.

Both times Lance left the same message: 'The police have taken my car and I'm on the news. Please call me'.

We had issued strict instructions to the media that they were to stay away from here. The media had reported that police had confiscated his vehicle.

My plan wasn't going as I had hoped. I thought we would have at least heard from the Slayer by now. Maybe he was smarter than I thought. I kept hearing the chief's voice in my mind. "Don't make me have to go back to the commissioner!"

In the time we had been sitting, watching and waiting, Jake must have consumed more chocolate, chips and cola than most humans could do in a whole week. There was no argument; if Jake had a weakness, food was it.

We prepared to go back to the station to continue our investigation into other Slayer leads. Lance was a killer and as soon as we had enough evidence to gain a conviction for the murder of Charlie, he would be off the street. It was only because we were a few pieces shy of what the prosecution called 'overwhelming evidence' that he was still free.

We had spent most of our time on the other Slayer suspect leads. We needed to follow those leads just in case my plan didn't yield the desired result.

Chapter 36

Saturday 8th November 2003 (10.42am)

Chad's car pulled into the empty space behind us and he turned off the engine. He and his partner, Henry, had arrived a few minutes before their 10-hour shift was due to start. Josh and Leah had the 9pm to 7am graveyard shift. Henry had been off sick the previous night. I glanced at them in the side mirror. Chad, who was observant of his surroundings, as all good cops need to be, noticed me peering at him and made a gesture with his right index finger.

Henry looked as if he had vomited very recently or was full of the flu.

Forensics had matched the fingerprints found on a bottle of beer in Charlie's apartment to Lance, through a process known as 'fuming'. The bottle was put in an oven with super glue. When the oven reached the required temperature, the glue evaporated and stuck to the oil left behind from the human print. Once removed from the oven, the bottle was lightly dusted and the prints appeared.

It was proving difficult for the forensic team to locate blood, hair or fibre samples from Lance in Charlie's apartment. Proving that Lance had been in Charlie's apartment didn't prove he'd killed her. Even the video evidence from the club and the lingerie shop, and traces of his semen, didn't prove conclusively he'd killed her. This was all circumstantial evidence, which could easily be argued against by a good defence lawyer.

Chad told us that the lab had finished testing the vehicle and that the evidence brief would be lodged with the director of public prosecutions today. We would only have until Sunday noon to flush out the Slayer.

Finding the murder weapon had been crucial. Now our submission to the DPP had substance and would outline that Lance had killed Charlie and in returning to his car, had hidden the knife inside his vehicle. They say every murderer makes 25 mistakes while committing a crime. Lance's biggest one was not disposing of the weapon.

We headed back to the station to continue our search for the Slayer. I was calmer now that we knew for sure Lance was Charlie's killer. But I was still haunted by the thought that there was someone out there planning his next kill, selecting his next victim. Such thoughts had kept me up most nights, sifting through the files looking for more answers, more clues, or both. I had found nothing yet, but I was sure that I would continue to search until the early hours of Sunday morning. I don't think I had enjoyed a decent sleep since I'd started this case.

We were only minutes away from the station when dispatch called us on the CB. "Jake, come in," the familiar voice of Kim Reynolds requested. Jake picked up the CB and replied, "Jake here. Not far away, Kim. What's up?"

"I have someone here who says she has information regarding the Slayer case." Jake almost dropped the handset to the floor. Thankfully, I was driving, preventing any chance of an accident. He recovered and replied quickly and firmly, "Kim, we're on our way. Whatever you do, don't let her go! Make her a coffee. Just make sure that you keep her there!"

We drove to the station with the siren screaming and headed straight for the waiting area. Kim had done her job. Sitting on one of the plastic chairs with a steaming drink, our informant was waiting patiently.

Kim came out from behind the counter to introduce us. "Detective Jake Miller and Brodie Foxx, Esmeralda."

"I'm a psychic," she said immediately. "I came here because I see things. I can't control what I see or why I see it but this, I can't ignore."

Jake glanced my way as if to say, here we go, another nut.

"With all due respect," I said, "we've had many psychics offer assistance but it has always led us nowhere. So please forgive my partner's scepticism. Sometimes, it gets the better of him." I hoped she would start telling us what she knew.

"Of course," Esmeralda replied, "I understand and I don't want to waste your time."

Jake gestured towards the interview room at the end of the hall. I followed closely without saying anything more. I had heard stories and seen documentaries on psychics solving crimes, but like Jake, I had my doubts. Still, anything was possible and our luck had to change eventually.

In the interview room, we sat opposite Esmeralda, who was sitting where the criminals usually sat when being interviewed. Esmeralda didn't look how I expected a psychic to look. I had pictured a witch-like character, yet Esmeralda was a middle-aged, distinguished looking lady, someone you expected might live in Toorak or Beaumaris, and who might drive an Audi rather than ride a broomstick.

"It all started last night when I had a dream; well, it was more like a vision. It felt very real." Esmeralda paused and shuffled in her seat, clearly uncomfortable with the two sceptical officers staring at her. "In the vision, I saw a man being dragged. His head had been removed. Then, I saw another body being carried under a blue tarp. Whoever was carrying it dropped it. The head was missing too. I think the body was a woman but I can't be sure. One leg was hanging out from the tarp. Then suddenly I saw a wolf."

"What makes you think that this has anything to do with the Slayer case?" Jake asked seriously but calmly.

"It may not be connected, but some deep instinct tells me it is."

Jake looked at me and gestured towards the door.

We got up and stood in the hallway under a flickering fluorescent light. "What do you think, Brodie?" Jake asked with a lost look on his face.

"Well Jake, no one knows about the Slayer removing the heads. So how the hell could she know about that?"

"Yeah, but he's never killed a man before," Jake replied. "Well, let's see what else she knows," Jake continued. We entered the room again and took up our position opposite Esmeralda.

"Is there anything else you can tell us about the dream or vision?" I asked.

"Did you see the man at all?" Jake added as he removed his notepad.

"No. Sorry, that's all I have."

Jake stood up and reached over to take Esmeralda by the hand. He could see this vision had seriously scared her. "We believe you. We will look into it, ok?"

"Can you tell us more about this girl in a tarp? Is there anything else you remember seeing?" I asked, nodding at Jake to allow me to question her further.

"No, I can't even be sure it was a girl, I just felt that it was."

"The area he dropped her in. What did that look like?" I asked.

"It was light bush parkland with shrubs and trails. It wasn't familiar to me. I didn't know the place."

Jake and I looked at each other, knowing it could be anywhere, if it existed at all.

She could tell us nothing more and so before she left, Jake said, "Please, Esmeralda, if there is anything else that comes to you, please let us know, anything at all. Any information may be vital."

"Anything at all," I reiterated.

I asked Kim to notify us of any recent missing persons in the last day or two. Minutes later, Kim reported that as of Friday 8pm, no one had been listed as missing across the state.

Chapter 37

Saturday 8th November (2.30pm)

Half an hour after his last open home, Mason stood in the driveway of his next victim. He knew that what he was about to do might increase the possibility of him getting caught. But his options were limited. It was either this or let the skinny man take the credit for his work.

Wasting no time, Mason walked up to the door of his unsuspecting victim and calmly rang the bell. Silence. Mason again pressed the bell. Silence, then footsteps. 'Jackpot, she's home,' Mason thought. The door swung open. On the other side of the security door, she beamed and asked, "Can I help you?" drying her hands on a tea towel.

Mason began his usual door-knocking speech. "Hi, my name is Mason Belic from Greenside Real Estate. We have buyers."

"Is that you, Mason?" the woman on the other side of the door asked. The security door clicked open. "It's me, Tammy Green," the girl continued as she opened the door and invited Mason in with a wave of her hand, still clutching the tea towel. "I thought you knew I lived here?"

"I had no idea," Mason lied.

"I moved in just after last year's company awards. That would have been the last time I saw you."

Mason nodded and followed Tammy down the hallway to the kitchen. "I think I must have been a little drunk back then. I'm sorry I made a pass at you, combination of my thing for an older guy and too much champagne. I hope you don't have any bad feelings towards me?"

"Not at all. It's water under the bridge," Mason replied, as he sat on a stool at the breakfast bar. She didn't know how close Mason had come to accepting her invitation at the awards night. If her father hadn't been his boss, he was sure he would have. Damn, she'd looked great that night, Mason remembered. Hair done, silky red dress that showed off all of her gorgeous features along with most of her breasts.

Tammy removed two white cups from the overhead cupboard and began filling the kettle. "So how's Dad treating you? Ok, I hope?" Tammy asked, as she removed the coffee from the cupboard and placed it on the breakfast bar.

"You know your dad. Always wanting to get more out of his workers.

What boss wouldn't though?" Mason asked, not interested in an answer. "How are you going? Do you like it here?" Mason asked. This was the first real question he had asked.

All Mason had been thinking of was how he was going to kill her. But first, he might as well have a little fun.

"Well, I get lonely being here by myself, but apart from that I really like it. Do you take sugar?" Tammy asked, hand poised over the sugar bowl.

"No thanks," Mason replied. "You know, I would have said yes at the awards night. I wanted to go back to your room with you. I just thought you should know that the only reason I didn't was because you're my boss's daughter. I was worried your dad would find out and sack me."

"So that's why?" Tammy responded with her mouth open, blushing. She was stunned.

"Maybe I should go," Mason said, moving to stand up.

"Don't be silly," Tammy replied, grabbing his arm before he had a chance to leave. "Stay. Have your coffee."

Mason loved the smell of freshly percolating coffee. Tammy poured him a cup and placed it in front of him. "So what would your answer be now?" she asked.

"First, I would ask how old you are."

"Twenty-two," she replied. "You afraid you mightn't be able to keep up?" Tammy added, smiling as she sipped her coffee.

A little embarrassed, Mason could not help but laugh at Tammy's question. "I would say yes," Mason replied, as he sipped his steaming hot coffee and looked over the cup at her. Tammy moved around to the other side of the breakfast bar and pulled up a stool next to Mason. Although she wasn't dressed in that stunning red dress that she'd worn to the awards, she still looked sensational in casual jeans and a top. Her blonde hair looked amazing, even though it hadn't been done by a hairdresser as it had been on the night of the awards.

"So do I have to ask or can we just assume that I have asked?" Tammy said, as she leaned forward towards Mason.

"I don't know what you're referring to," Mason replied with a shrewd smile.

Tammy, enjoying the game playing, repeated the question of almost a year before on a crowded dance floor. His answer had crushed her heart, as rejection always did. This time there would be no such rejection. "Do you want to come to my bedroom?" she asked.

Mason simply nodded and made no resistance to Tammy, who leaned in further for a kiss. Before Mason could respond, he felt Tammy's tongue slide gently into his mouth. She took his hand and they walked back down the hallway to the front of the house. Mason hadn't seen things going this way when he'd pulled up in the driveway. He'd been expecting to get inside, stun her and get out but he thought it would be worth the small risk associated with sleeping with her.

As they walked through the bedroom doorway, Tammy lifted her arms, breaking the connection with Mason, and removed her top.

There was no bra, just firm round breasts, breasts the like of which he hadn't seen for many years.

Mason's shirt dropped to the floor as he returned the favour. His chest was still firm, but his stomach had let go a little. The remnants of his sculpted six-pack were still visible, despite a bit of flab. Tammy flicked her jeans through the air with her left foot, and they landed on the other side of the room. Her bum was round and firm and it was unlike anything he had ever experienced before, and he doubted he ever would again.

Tammy flopped onto the bed, naked, and gestured for Mason to join her.

Despite his obvious excitement, sex was the last thing on Mason's mind. He always kept his victims away from his normal life. He wanted no connection with them whatsoever. Stranger murders were always harder for police to solve. He couldn't believe he was about to break his number one rule.

Mason didn't want to admit it to Tammy but he soon realised that she was right. He did have trouble keeping up. She just kept going and going.

They were still lying on the bed when Mason decided there was no more time for fun. He had risked being here too long already.

Tammy jumped up from the bed after giving herself a few minutes to regain her breath and headed to the shower. Mason knew he had to act and act now. He began searching through the walk-in robe for a bag or suitcase. He found what appeared to be Tammy's gym bag on the top shelf. Listening out for the sound of the shower, Mason quickly began to strip the bed: sheets, pillowcases, the whole box and dice. He had risked too much already by sleeping with her and he didn't want compromise the situation any further by leaving behind his DNA.

He went out to the kitchen where he had left his jacket hanging over the bar stool and his briefcase sitting on the floor next to it. Mason removed the precious items from the inside pocket of his jacket. First, the gloves. There was no point leaving his fingerprints lying around. The second and third items were two pre-filled syringes and a 25-ml vanilla essence bottle filled with his ever-reliable Benzodiapine. This would be essential in providing him time to tidy up any trace evidence and get to his cabin. The fourth item, his favourite, he kept in its case. It was his taser, or as most people knew it, a stun gun. It was quiet and provided immediate control over the victim, giving him the necessary time required to inject his Benzodiapine..

He was glad Tammy had decided to take a shower. It would help remove any DNA evidence that he surely would have left behind. Mason knew hair and semen were the hardest to remove and while the shower would help, he would have to soak her in bleach before he dumped her body.

Mason walked back into the bedroom with his gloves on, and placed the drawstring garbage bag that he had found in the bottom kitchen drawer on the bedside table. The shower stopped and the ensuite door remained shut.

Mason opened it and placed his right hand behind his back with the stun gun firmly clenched in his hand.

Tammy had finished drying herself and was standing in front of the mirror, wearing only a pair of pink panties, her breasts free of a bra. She was just putting on foundation and lipstick. Mason moved up behind her, his right hand still hidden behind his back. "You ready for more?" she asked, pressing her lips together to ensure her lipstick was even.

Mason began to kiss her neck and caress her breasts with his left hand. She closed her eyes for a second. That was all Mason needed to strike.

Chapter 38

Saturday 8th November (5.17pm)

"Wake up, you slut!" Mason said as he slapped Tammy's face hard enough to bring her around.

"What are you doing?" she asked groggily.

Mason knelt down in front of her. "I want you to listen very carefully, do you understand?" Tammy nodded. "Now, I will explain why you're sitting naked in my bath, but firstly, you're going to wash yourself clean. I want you rid of all your filth and smuttiness. Then tomorrow you're coming with me door-knocking at some houses. The area will be surrounded by police and yet you will not try to escape. Do you understand?"

Tammy nodded.

"Just so we're clear: if you try to escape or fail to do what I've asked of you, your father will die. At precisely 11am tomorrow, if I don't make a call, he will be killed. Do you understand?"

Tammy nodded again, tears streaming down her cheeks at the thought of her father dying.

"I will let you and your father go once I have conducted my business. Do you understand?" he asked again. She nodded in agreement.

"Now, put some water in that bath. You're starting to shiver, you'll catch your death and we can't have that, can we?"

"No," she said simply. She turned on the taps to fill the bath.

"I've made up the spare room for you and here's your nightgown," Mason said, tapping the shelf in the bathroom where a red silk gown sat alongside a thick cream robe. "Tomorrow's clothes are on the bed. When you're finished, put your gown on and we'll have some food."

Mason left the bathroom. The cabin had seen so many deaths, but not tonight.

Mason knew very well that Tammy would not risk disobeying his instructions because of the fear of losing her father. Love can sometimes be one's best weapon.

He was certain his plan was perfect. After all, how would she know if her father was safe and well? Knowing him as Mason did, he guessed he would still be at the office.

For Mason, tomorrow could not come soon enough. Executing one of his plans always gave him the same feeling he'd had as a child when the next day he was going to the royal show. Pure excitement. Mason slept very little that night thinking of the day ahead.

Chapter 39

Sunday 9th November 2003 (6.30am)

It was Sunday morning. To me, that meant two things. One, I had to stake out Lance's house today with Jake and two, we were running out of time for my plan to work. There was no doubt that Lance would have to be arrested today and our chance of catching the Slayer would be gone.

I finished off my eggs and bacon accompanied by a glass of orange juice. It had been my standard Sunday morning breakfast ever since I was a child.

Over the past few weeks, I had become accustomed to picking Jake up from his unit in Hawthorn. Yet this morning, I would have to pick him up from Hayley's unit in Parkville. It appeared things had seriously progressed for him. I was glad. It had been a long time coming. I just wanted him to be happy and it appeared finally to be on the horizon.

The drive to Parkville was a lot busier than the one to Hawthorn; the closer I got to the city, the heavier the traffic became. My saving grace was that it was a Sunday and not a Monday. Despite the traffic, my mind was on autopilot. I searched for the reasons why my plan hadn't worked. Had I underestimated the Slayer? Had I overestimated my own ability? The last question was the one that rang the loudest through my head.

I pulled up at the address that Jake had given me over the phone and tooted the horn twice. In hindsight, it probably wasn't the smartest or the most considerate thing to do on a Sunday morning.

Within a few minutes, Jake was sitting in the seat beside me. "Morning, Bruce." It was a more spirited Jake than the one I had been working with over the last few weeks. I just looked at him, ready to ask the questions that all best friends do. However, his smile told me the answer and from the size of it, I knew all I wanted to know. "Let's go catch ourselves a killer," Jake said as he changed the radio from the AM band to FM. It was a constant struggle in our car; I always wanted to listen to the talkback and Jake always wanted to listen to his tunes. Flicking to the FM dial was only the start. It usually took Jake a few runs through to find a song he liked.

I waited until he stopped flicking. "Yes, we will."

Now engrossed in his song, Jake just nodded.

We were almost at Lance's when a call came in, one that sent a shivers down both of our spines.

It was Georgie. She worked the front desk in rotation with Kim and Stephanie. Georgie was by far the cutest; she had that intangible quality that attracted the other gender.

"We've just had a call from the Knox CIB. They reported a double homicide at the Basin nature reserve. They believe it may be related to the Slayer case, a missing person's report that matches a request you put in yesterday."

I looked at Jake and he looked back at me as if to say, 'oh my God'. It was chilling.

Jake radioed back to base to arrange someone to cover our shift and relieve Josh and Leah from their all-night-stint at Lance's.

Chapter 40

Sunday 9th November 2003 (7.00am)

The first sign of daybreak gave Mason a feeling that his plan would soon be realised, and that thought excited him.

Tammy had lain awake the entire night, too afraid to sleep. She had made herself a promise and a plan of her own. She knew that she could do nothing here. There was no help for her in this godforsaken place. In the morning, she would make her move; she just had to make sure her father was all right. She couldn't risk Mason not making the call and her father dying. Her plan was to go to the house that he wanted, wait for him to make his call, and then attempt to take him down. She knew enough karate and martial arts to take him down, as long as he wasn't behind her with a stun gun.

Mason instructed her to get up and put on the set of clothes he'd left for her on the bed. By the time she was dressed, Mason had made her toast and coffee.

Tammy wondered about the clothes, but dared not ask anything. Her outfit consisted of a long black dress that went all the way to her ankles, matching black shoes, a black woollen jumper, and a scarf to cover her head. He also made her wear a shiny silver cross around her neck. A large Bible finished Mason's handpicked outfit.

They headed out to the car. Both had very different plans for the day ahead.

* * *

We arrived at the crime scene about 25 minutes after Georgie had put the call to us across the radio.

A neatly dressed middle-aged man in a suit headed towards us and introduced himself as Detective Jacob Rein. He was tall and a lot fitter than most men his age. Even so, he looked as if he had been through a long night himself.

"A dog walker early this morning found his dog sniffing at a deceased body in the bush about 25 metres off the track to your right as you head up the hill. We believe the victim is Alan Simpson. His mother reported his disappearance to police late yesterday."

"So what makes you think this has anything to do with the Slayer case?" Jake asked.

"When investigating the crime scene, we found the body of a young female as well. Both victims had been decapitated."

Rein led us to the body of the male jogger.

"We organised a team to include uniformed officers, the SES and the dog squad," Rein explained, as he held up the police tape.

The body of the male jogger was lying off the side of the track, with little cover. My initial thoughts were that this had been rushed: it wasn't typical of the Slayer. Something had gone wrong.

"If this is what Esmeralda's vision was about, then where is the wolf?" Jake asked, still trying to throw doubt on the psychic's visions.

I was hunched down to study the scene. "It'll be here somewhere. I'm sure we'll find it soon."

I headed further up the track to where Rein had said they had found a deceased female. The track was wet and muddy. I stepped into a thick clump of mud that came halfway up my shoe. Then I stopped suddenly, realising there were other footprints close to me and I did not want to contaminate any vital evidence.

Bending down, I could see a few more shoe prints. They might be clear enough for forensics to take casts. I left the track and headed towards the broken bracken and the blue tarp. Under the trampled shrubs, I could see a large piece of plastic with a foot exposed.

Before I had a chance to call out to Jake, Jake yelled, "Dog! I've found the dog!" I stayed kneeling in position and called back, "Jake come here, you need to see this." It had to be the latest missing girl, Maggie, as all the other victims except the first had been found.

I called forensics and asked Rein to get an officer to go back to the car to collect my bag. It was designed to carry everything required to take evidence and protect that evidence until forensics arrived. The bag included tweezers, bottles, a variety of plastic bags of different sizes, test tubes, clean plastic sheets and body bags, camera, vacuum kit, torch, ultra violet light, tape measure, and of course, gloves.

David's forensics team arrived. He had worked on all of the Slayer victims and the copycat killing of poor Charlie.

"Good to see you again, David."

"This is becoming too common for my liking," he replied. "Another Slayer one?"

"That's for you to tell me, but we think there may be two here."

"Two? That's new for him." David looked sad at the possible escalation of violence.

"There's also a dog," I said. "I don't think the man with the dog was planned. I believe he was dumping one victim here—I think it's probably

Maggie—and the male jogger and dog just got in the way. Let's hope we find something to finally lead us to this bastard," I said.

"Let's get to work then," David said, waving the rest of his team over.

Chapter 41

Sunday 9th November (10.38am)

It was mid-morning and beginning to drizzle, but that mattered little to the two Mormons who strolled the streets knocking on doors trying to help people find God.

You could spot them from a mile away, thought Ryan, who was back on duty after what seemed like a very short break. He was on his own today, as his partner was off sick. Ryan had only recently been promoted to detective, but he knew he had what it took to be one of the best.

'Haven't they got anything better to do than door knocking on a Sunday morning?' Ryan thought as he watched the Bible bashers walk from house to house, offering guidance to those willing to listen.

It wasn't long before they had almost completed the street. The next house was Lance's home, and Ryan was sure they would not get a warm reception there. The two Bible bashers approached the door and knocked. After a few moments, the door cracked open and the male Bible basher passed through what appeared to be a brochure spreading the Lord's word, no doubt.

Ryan was beginning to wonder whether he should call this in. He was under strict instructions to call in any activity.

On the other hand, he was sure if he called in two Bible bashers, he would never hear the end of it from the boys at the station. He could hear them now. "Morning, Father," they would say when he arrived at work, "do you have time for a prayer session, Father?" He could imagine them joking and was sure they would hang it on him for a long time to come.

Ryan finally decided to let it play out and see what happened first before calling it in.

He calmed himself, leaned over and grabbed his Thermos, spun off the top, and poured himself a cup of coffee.

Chapter 42

Sunday 9th November (10.42am)

Lance had received a call from his solicitor early that morning. A solicitor calling on a Sunday was unheard of. What would that cost him? he'd wondered when he'd hung up. His solicitor had advised it was best to wait for the police to arrest him. The fact that they hadn't already done so showed they were lacking evidence.

When he heard the doorbell ring, he assumed it was the police or the media. Either way, Lance was not in the mood for visitors, although he knew he had to face the consequences of his night with Charlie.

How had he stuffed it up?

He had it planned so well.

He reluctantly opened the door, making sure the chain was still on. The man on the other side of the door said nothing, simply passed him a piece of paper through the crack.

It was a brochure on 'letting the Lord into your heart' but that was not what grabbed Lance's attention. It was a handwritten passage that Lance focused on.

'You tried to copy me. Let me in and I will help you!'

Lance opened the door and let them in, quickly closing it behind them.

Ryan reached for the radio. The thoughts of taunts from his fellow colleagues filled his head again.

He decided that waiting a few more minutes would not hurt.

"You like to copy me, do you?" Mason asked quietly as he entered. Lance offered no response except a mumbled, "I just want to be famous."

"I will make you famous, don't worry about that," Mason said, opening his case and removing a bag and a CD. He handed over a CD. "Put this on and turn it up."

Lance nodded and headed for the lounge room. Soon the house was loud with the sound of scripture interspersed with prayer music.

It wasn't the music that worried Tammy, it was the fact that she was now in a house with two men and there was still no sign of her father.

"Where is my dad?" Tammy asked the new man. Lance didn't have a reply for her, but the blank look he gave her said it all.

She had been duped. She knew her dad was fine, but she herself was in serious danger and she had to get outside, somehow.

Chapter 43

Sunday 9th November 2003 (10.45am)

They were in the lounge with all the lights off and the blinds drawn. What was going on here? Tammy wondered. It just didn't feel right.

How was she to get out of this? She kept thinking she needed to separate them and race for the door. Mason handed Lance a bag. "Put these on. Hurry, we don't have much time."

Lance left the room and headed to the back of the house. They had just separated themselves. Now was her chance and she had to take it. Leaning on the dining room chair, Tammy made sure she had a good grip of it and was ready to swing. As if she'd heard something, Tammy said, "Shh, you hear that? People outside?"

Concerned it might be the police ready to raid, Mason moved closer to the wall and to Tammy. He focused all his concentration on trying to hear the noise outside.

Tammy struck, swinging the chair right across Mason's head and kicking him as she ran past. She knew that he would not stay down for long, and she rushed for the front door.

Frantically grabbing the handle, she turned and pulled it, but nothing. It was deadlocked, and she needed a key to open it.

With this realisation came the fear that she would soon be dead. She slid down the front door with tears freely rolling down her face. Even with her eyes closed, Tammy could feel Mason's presence, feel his shadow cross her face.

Mason bent down and grabbed her by the throat.

"Who is she anyway?" Lance asked from behind him.

"She's the girl I will use to show you how to kill properly, unlike the bitch you killed in the city that's ended in this mess. Take her into the lounge." He handed Tammy to him by the throat.

Mason went back to his attaché case and removed a clear plastic coat and his favourite knife. The Wakizashi knife wasn't his usual method for removing someone's head but with the time constraints, he had no alternative. "Lay her on the floor and hold her down," he ordered. Without hesitation, Mason went to her head and without warning began his frenzied attack. The attack only finished with the removal of her head. It was short but ferocious, more horrifying than Lance could ever have imagined. Mason removed his coat and placed Tammy's head into a plastic bag and tied it to his shoulder. He then dipped his knuckles into Tammy's blood, flowing freely from her neck, being careful not to get any of the blood on his clothes. He then went across to the lounge room wall.

'Don't FUCK

with

Me!' he wrote across the wall.

Worried by now that the Mormons hadn't yet emerged from Lance's house, Ryan again reached for the radio, but as he picked it up, the music in the house stopped and the door opened. Two people emerged and as they stepped into the daylight, a van pulled in front of Ryan, blocking his line of sight. It began to reverse into the driveway of the house diagonally opposite Lance's property. By the time the truck had parked, the Mormons were out of sight.

He thought it would be best to call it in, just in case.

Chapter 44

Sunday 9th November 2003 (10.56am)

We had been studying the murder scene at the parkland for close to four hours. It was apparent that the killer had, for the first time, been forced to kill in haste for his own survival. It was this haste and his mistake that we hoped would give us a clue as to his identity.

It was a horrible way to get a lead but it could be our best chance to catch him.

David gestured me over to Maggie, where he had been examining her and taking samples. I walked over and thought what a sad sight it was. When you stepped out of the job and looked at it from a different perspective, this body only a short while ago had been full of life. Now it lay limp and discarded in a ditch of dirt, mud and ferns. It was a horrible thing to experience and I could never imagine the pain of the parents.

"It's the same guy all right. He took the head and like all the others, he took it pre-mortem. The stab pattern is also consistent with the other victims from what I can tell, although I'll need to do more tests back at the lab. Even the jogger's head was taken pre-mortem and while the knife doesn't match, the MO is the same. There are fibres and hairs but again, I need to do more analysis on them before I can give you any further information. It appears that like the last victim, Maggie had been washed prior to being dumped. That being the case, it's likely all the fibres are hers. I have found one unusual item, though." He held up a plastic bag with a two-centimetre splinter of wood.

"If you find the wood it came from, you'll know where she was murdered," David said. "It looks like the splinter entered her flesh when she was being dragged."

"What have the other guys found?" I asked David. We looked over at them.

"I was just about to find out. Come with me," David replied, heading off down the track.

David's assistant Grace had been examining the jogger and the dog.

"What information do you have for us, Grace?" David asked as he stumbled on some loose dirt at the side of the track.

"We have a Caucasian male, 28 to 32 years. The deceased died from decapitation, although the severe stab wounds to the chest, back and throat would suggest he was barely alive when the murderer took his head. The blood splatter indicates that his heart was still beating when his head was removed. I believe he was then dragged over here," Grace said, moving back up on to the walking track, "and then he was rolled into the ditch off the track. There was no real attempt to conceal him. The dog, on the other hand, was killed with a blunt instrument. We found a rock nearby, which we are having tested for blood and fingerprints. We also found blood on the dog's teeth, which suggests the dog bit someone. Our guess is that it was the assailant."

"If it's his blood, then we can get him," I said stupidly, regretting the statement as soon as it left my mouth.

"It's the strongest evidence we have, however, blood isn't much good unless we have a sample on file for comparison," David replied. "But it will go a long way towards the conviction, if you catch him. We're going to take all this back to the lab for further tests," David continued, as he and the crew began to pack up.

I stood there thinking, which was what I did best. I tried to turn myself into the killer and reconstruct the events as best I could. It was no easy task, but it was something they had trained us for at Quantico.

I walked down the track to the road, through bracken, weeds, ferns, and a whole heap of mud. I said to myself, "Here is where he would have parked the vehicle." I looked for tyre prints, but I was sure that the rain had washed them away by now. I retraced his steps as I thought it had happened.

He had carried her up the track, most likely over his shoulder, and then dumped her in the gully. But it was here where it had all gone wrong for him. I had no doubt that the jogger was killed only because he had seen something he shouldn't have. The dog had done a hell of a job protecting his owner. He'd fought and given his life to try and save him.

"Are you finished?" Jake called from the top of the hill. He seemed impatient.

"Yeah, all done," I called. I saw the coroner's team loading the bodies into those thick black plastic bags and I thought to myself, 'how lucky I am to be alive.'

Jake placed his arm around my shoulder, which broke me out of my trance.

"We have to go to Lance's house. Ryan from the surveillance team called. Apparently, Lance let some Mormons in this morning and Lance's ugly head hasn't been seen peering out the windows since."

"Fucking great, just fucking great," I replied.

Chapter 45

Sunday 9th November 2003 (11.06am)

Lance sat in the passenger's seat of Mason's car.

"So how do you want me to help you?" Lance asked Mason nervously.

"After that fuck-up you made in the hotel with the stripper, I realised that with a bit of training, you and I could be the best team of serial killers ever." Mason was playing to Lance's misguided illusions of himself.

Mason was not lying when he said he needed Lance's help. It could only be with his help that he would get the attention of the police, who were trying to offer Lance up as bait to catch him.

How stupid did they think he was?

"Where are we going?" Lance asked, as he began to remove the wig and dress Mason had given him.

"We are going to where I do all my work that you love so much. I'm going to give you a tour of my workshop and then we can select my next victim."

"You mean *our* next victim?" Lance replied, thoughts of killing again racing through his head.

"Yes, *our* next victim," Mason replied, almost letting out a laugh at the same time. He had already selected his next victim.

Mason had made good time, which surprised him considering it was a Sunday when the Volvo drivers were usually out in force, slowing down the traffic.

As Mason pulled his car into the drive of his cabin, he still wasn't sure as to what he would do with Lance. He had a rough idea, but no clear plan.

He led the way into the cabin, with Lance following closely behind him.

"I'll take those from you," Mason said, holding out to Lance a plastic shopping bag full of fresh male clothing he had placed on the couch in the lounge. "I'll show you around after you change."

Lance nodded in agreement and excitement, like a teenager being asked by his girlfriend if he would like to see her breasts.

Lance followed Mason through the lounge and down the spiral wooden staircase that had a wrought-iron rail. The stairs led down to the cellar. Lance felt much more like himself in the clothes Mason had provided him. He felt like a serial killer again. Mason opened the solid oak door, complete with an old castle-style handle.

The door creaked and moaned as it opened and Lance felt a cold eerie presence as he took the stairs down to the damp and foul smelling room. It was dark, with little natural light filtering through some cracks. He'd thought it would be a room that he would enjoy and thrive in, yet he hated it and wanted to leave straightaway. However, he knew that if he showed any weakness, he would not see the light of day ever again.

Lance took in all the equipment in this hellhole, as he now considered it. There were chains attached to posts, all types of saws and axes locked behind a clear mesh cage, and an old coiled spring bed with the remnants of a mattress.

All the Slayer's victims' heads were lined up on the shelf like a child would display his basketball trophies. Below them was a Samurai sword, also on display. From the second Lance saw the heads, he knew the police had played him, and his next thought was, was Mason playing him too?

"I need you to help me fix some of this equipment," Mason said, holding out the chains.

"What do you need me to do?" Lance asked, a little worried.

"You're not scared, are you, Lance? Isn't this what you wanted? To copy me and be me? Well, here's your chance! But we need to get the equipment right. I need you to put these on and pull as hard as you can and I'll tighten up the bolts. The last thing we want is our prize to escape."

Lance reluctantly put his wrists inside the cuffs and watched as Mason locked the cuffs with a key he had plucked from his pants pocket. Lance's heart was in his mouth and he was scared as hell. He tried to keep his mind focused on what was going on, but the disgusting smell in the cellar was beginning to get to him.

"Now, when I say pull, I want you to pull as hard as you can." Mason was now behind the post that held Lance. "Let's test these babies." Mason was becoming excited. "Pull!" Mason yelled, and as he pulled, Lance's worst fears were realised.

The harder Lance pulled, the tighter the cuffs became. With all his attention on his wrists, he had not noticed Mason had looped a piece of rope around his legs until Mason pulled the rope tight, and the rope burnt his ankle. Lance began to pull and kick his legs, but it was too late. He knew what his fate was going to be. The same as Charlie's. "Hey, where you going, you fuck?" he yelled as Mason left the cellar.

Chapter 46

Sunday 9th November 2003 (11.33am)

We pulled in behind Ryan's car, stopped and got in, Jake in the passenger seat and me in the back.

"What's the update?" Jake asked, as he lifted the binoculars to his eyes.

"Nothing! I haven't seen him since this morning, when he let the Mormons in."

"How long did the Mormons stay?"

"Fifteen or twenty minutes, then they left."

"How long ago was that?" I asked.

"Half an hour," Ryan confirmed after looking at his watch.

Jake leaned over the passenger seat. "What do you think?" he asked me.

"Sounds strange, if you ask me. Something isn't right. There's been no sign of anyone else?" I asked Ryan.

"No," he confirmed.

'My plan has failed,' I thought.

"Let's bring him in for Charlie's murder," I said, tapping Jake on the shoulder.

Jake and I left the car while Ryan stayed in it. Jake walked up to the front door, unclipped his gun and then knocked. There was no reply. "Lance, it's the police, let us in!" Jake repeated this three more times, then he said, "Ok Lance, we're coming in!" He gently tried the door handle.

Jake had learnt long ago to always test the door handle first before resorting to kicking the door in.

As soon as we entered, the smell of blood and death hit us and we knew we were in trouble. Jake immediately checked the corners and entered the house. The sight was the worst we had ever seen. There appeared to be a sea of blood, and a headless body was slumped on a chair in the corner. There was a message written on the wall, we assumed from the Slayer.

"How did he get the woman in here and where the hell is Lance?" I asked.

"I'll call for backup," Jake said, "and then we'll search the house. Lance has to be here somewhere."

But he wasn't. By the time we'd returned to the lounge, the forensics team and the chief had arrived. The chief was the last person I wanted to see right now and I knew that things were about to get worse.

"You! Get the fuck out," he yelled at me. "You're fired!" I got up from my crouched position in front of the body and headed for the door.

"If he goes, I go, Chief." Jake stood with his arms folded.

"Well that's your call, Jake, but he's going. I don't want to lose you but I have to let him go. Look at this mess," the chief said, as he held a handkerchief to his nose.

I put up my hand to indicate to Jake that it was ok, that I wanted him to stay. He knew what I meant. It was something we had done as kids, raise a hand to offer an apology. Jake looked at me and nodded, then went back to work.

One of the patrol officers drove me home. I would clear out my office the next day, Monday. There was no hurry. I felt I had unfinished business and it was killing me not to be a part of the investigation. But I had to acknowledge that the plan I had come up with had failed miserably, resulting in the death of another innocent young woman.

Several hours after my departure, Jake rang to ask my opinion about what we had seen at Lance's. They had no new information on the deceased girl, he said. She was carrying no ID, there was no car at Lance's that the police could go off, and no one had reported her missing.

They were going to place a news report on TV, asking for anyone with a family member recently missing to contact police. Jake also told me that forensics were doing comparisons on the weapons used in the murder at Lance's house and those used in Charlie's murder. They would compare stab wounds and angles, but they would not have the results until the next morning.

Jake finished the phone call by telling me to keep my head up. He said the fact that I wasn't sitting behind the desk didn't mean I was no longer a part of the case. He promised that he would keep me up to date, and that I still had an important role to play.

I thanked him and knew that he would do all he could to keep me involved.

But I also knew reality when it kicked me in the arse and that I was no longer a member of taskforce Eagle.

Chapter 47

Sunday 9th November 2003 (4.40pm)

Lance wasn't sure how many hours he had spent chained to the post. His estimate was at least two. Daylight was still visible through the few cracks in the wood. Lance had spent most of his time trying to ignore the smell and unbind his feet and hands.

The metal cuffs had cut into his hands and wrists, which were now bleeding. The rope burn had probably caused similar damage to his legs because although he could not see them, he could feel the blood dripping onto his feet.

The strange smell was getting to him, as was the presence of death that sat looking at him through the glass jars on the shelf. He had to get out. He had his own plans and fantasies to fulfil. His killing spree wasn't over, and it certainly wasn't meant to end like this.

As the sun faded, Lance was left in darkness and all alone, except for the lost souls he could feel all around him. Now that darkness was upon him, he could feel the creatures of the night crawling beneath his feet. He assumed that rats had been attracted by the dripping blood.

Lance could move enough to get the rats off his body but he wasn't sure how long they would be so easily startled once they had the taste of blood in their system.

He had managed to drift off to sleep, when the old cellar door opened. Once his eyes adjusted to the dark, he could see Mason standing in front of him.

"Let me go. We're the same. We have the same passion to kill those skanky whores. We can still kill the sluts together and it's not too late." Lance was almost begging. His voice was quivering.

"Oh, it's far too late for that, Lance. Let me tell you something: we are not the same. I don't kill for sexual pleasure like you. I don't kill whores or strippers. I kill for revenge, for a life that was taken from me. But enough about me, Lance," Mason said, pausing briefly. "Let's talk about you. If you hadn't tried to copy me, then you wouldn't be in this, shall we say, predicament. Enjoy the night. It will be your last." Mason left Lance with the darkness and the rats, locking the door behind him.

Chapter 48

Monday 10th November 2003 (7am)

The morning sunlight broke through the cracks and streamed across Lance's face. Once it hit his eyelids, he woke, and the first thought that went through his head was that this was going to be his last day on earth.

Lance guessed that first light meant it was about 6.30 in the morning, maybe 7. Then the door opened and Lance could clearly see Mason this time, unlike the night before.

He realised Mason had come ready to do what he had promised, and it didn't look pretty.

Mason was holding a sword in his right hand. Lance watched him approach slowly and with every step he took, Lance's heart fluttered. He wasn't usually a sook but the fear had taken hold and his eyes began to swell and the tears flow. By the time Mason was in front of him, his tears were running like a river.

"It will all be over soon." Mason said, stroking his face. "It will be painful, but by the end of the day, you will be at peace." Mason raised the sword and swung it quickly and accurately. It cut a large gash in Lance's right arm.

Lance screamed. Mason then made a big x into Lance's chest.

The pain was like nothing he had ever experienced. Mason then firmly hit him in the forehead with the handle of the sword, sending Lance into darkness.

When he awoke, the sun was bright in the sky above him. Where was he? he wondered. Certainly not in the dusty cellar. There was a lot of blood on his chest. He lifted his head. He was tied to a wooden picnic table. He could see the old cabin on the horizon above his toes. At least he had his legs, he thought. At least he could run, he thought. That thought was soon extinguished when he remembered the ropes binding him to the table.

A shadow eclipsed the sun from his eyes. "Let me go, please, just let me go," Lance begged.

"You're probably wondering what you're doing tied to a table, naked?" Mason asked rhetorically. You're here because I like to feed the kookaburras. Do you know what they like to eat?"

Lance offered no response. The only thing that Lance could think of was a passage from the Bible, which surprised him, as he was not a religious man at all. He hoped the passage was correct. *Even though I walk through the valley of the shadow of death . . .*

"Well, let me give you a quick nature lesson. I usually feed them fresh mincemeat but today, they're going to get a special treat. Today, they get to eat your flesh, and your intestines, not to forget your limp little cock that's dangling in this fine morning breeze."

Lance froze in horror as Mason removed a knife from his pocket. He placed Lance's hand down flat and quickly removed his index finger.

Lance's scream of agony was heard by no one but Mason.

As Mason held out Lance's clenched fist in front of him, he smiled, and said, "Goodbye." Then he opened his hand and sprinkled birdseed all over Lance's fresh wounds.

Lance had never seen so many birds fly from the trees at once. He closed his eyes and another Bible passage came to him: *Do unto others as you would have them do unto you.* 'Please forgive me for what I have done,' he thought, as he felt their pecking and their claws, before he again descended into blackness.

Mason watched as the birds enjoyed their meal en masse.

Mason scraped Lance's remains off the table with a shovel. By the time the birds had finished their breakfast, Mason the wheelbarrow was only half-full. He wheeled the barrow down towards the tree line, tipping the remains into a pre-dug hole.

Mason removed a bag of lime, emptied it into the hole and then spent the next 15 minutes filling it in.

Chapter 49

Monday 10th November 2003 (11.25am)

After burying what was left of Lance, Mason hosed his shovel and wheelbarrow, then sprayed each item with bleach and then hosed them down again. He burned the overalls he was wearing, went inside and had a nice hot shower.

He decided it was time to find out a bit more about the two officers who had been behind the Lance trap. Maybe it was time he stopped being the hunted and became the hunter.

Mason removed his laptop from its case and fired it up.

He needed to know more about Jake Miller and definitely more about this Mr Foxx. He must be good for the police to have used special authority to make him detective.

It was easy to find information on Foxx. Google was a great help. He found his profile and his qualifications as a criminal psychologist. He even found newspaper articles on him being appointed to the police force under the commissioner's powers. According to the article, Foxx had taken up studies due to a heart condition and had undergone several heart operations as a child.

Fate had spared him and led him to Mason.

The latest entry on the Google search result was a report from the morning paper. 'Eagle to undergo third revamp' was the heading. The article referred to unnamed police sources stating that "the Victorian Government has serious concerns about the abilities of the taskforce and suggested that the taskforce undergo a review.' Another source suggested that Brodie Foxx would soon be removed from Eagle.

'Well I will have to see to that,' Mason muttered to himself.

Very little came up when he Googled Jake Miller. There were several articles about a servo shooting he was involved in and now he was head of the Eagle taskforce. Mason needed to know more information.

There was only one way he could get it, up close and personal.

St Kilda Road was the best place to start.

He decided he best get home. He needed to get there before his wife if possible.

When Mason reached the town of Yea, he thought it best to stop and get something to eat, plus he had some mail to send.

Halfway down the street and two shops before the post office, he saw two boys sitting on the curb sharing some fries.

He stopped. "Could you do me a favour?" Mason asked the taller of the two boys.

"Sure, Mister," the boy said, standing up to see him better.

"I really need to post these packages today, but the lady who works in the post office is my ex-girlfriend and I really don't want to go in. Could you post them for me?" Mason asked. "I'll give you fifty dollars each and I won't tell anyone that you were playing hooky."

The boys looked at each other with excited smiles. To have $100 to spend on their day of leisure would mean they could swap an afternoon of riding for the movies and see 'Matrix Reloaded'.

"Sure," the taller boy replied.

The boys noted both packages were addressed to Brodie Foxx, Melbourne Police, St Kilda Road Melbourne. Mason gave the boy one of the $50 dollar notes and a separate $100 note to cover the cost of postage, and promised the other $50 when they brought back the postage receipt.

"Now, boys, make sure you tell the lady that your uncle has asked you to send them and that they need to be expressed to that address today. If anyone asks you, just tell them your uncle is sick and he asked you to do it for him."

A few minutes later, the boys returned with a red slip and $55 in change.

Mason not only kept his side of the bargain, he handed over the $55 in change, leaving the boys to enjoy their day.

Chapter 50

Tuesday 11th November 2003 (11.30am)

Even though I had slept until late, I had awoken several times through-out the night, many times in a cold sweat. It had been a night I'd rather forget. The dreams had been with me since I was a child, yet last night they had taken on a form of their own and they were more horrifying than ever.

I'd dreamt of the hospital's cold, alcohol-smelling hallways, light green walls and flickering fluorescent lights. They were memories of my past that I had hidden deep in my mind. However, some nights they found the door and let themselves out.

Last night was the worst I had ever experienced, even more terrifying than those I had suffered while I was in hospital undergoing the surgery itself. It was more vivid and real to me than anything I had ever dreamt before.

I was lying on a trolley being wheeled to the operating theatre, except there were no nurses walking beside me, no machines taking my vitals, no drip leading into my vein. Only a doctor in a white coat with a green mask. A doctor who did not speak or answer my cries as to what was happening to me.

He kept his head down and continued to wheel the trolley along the cold halls until we bashed through two large swinging doors where the sign above said 'Operating Theatre'.

My neck hurt as I tried to see the doctor who had been hovering over me, but all I could see were his cold lifeless eyes.

Then I found myself on the cold metal table of the operating theatre wear-ing only a surgical gown with the opening at the back. The cold metal pressed against my skin. Above, a bright operating light blurred my vision. There were other patients there too but no one was attending to them.

I turned to look at the other side of the operating theatre and when I turned back, I was no longer in the theatre but in a dark dusty room that had a horri-ble smell, a smell that filled my heart with fear.

It was the unmistakable smell of death.

I moved my hands around to try to untie my hideous gown. As I was removing it, my hand slipped onto my chest. It was wet.

I raised my fingers to my face and saw my own blood. I felt my chest again; there was an opening.

I could feel my ribs; I could put my hand inside my chest. I softly put my hand inside my chest, careful not to poke anything. There was no pain, only blood. I felt around more.

I could feel ribs.

I put my fingers through my ribs.

It was then I felt my heart, a heart that was no longer beating.

I was dead.

I wasn't in the operating theatre.

I wasn't even in a morgue. I was in a cold, damp, dirty cellar with chains dangling from the rafters above.

There was a wall full of saws, axes and swords. It was horrifying. I stood on the dirt floor with my chest open and blood dripping down my front. Then I saw them. They had surrounded me. "Help us! Help us!" they repeated. I was frozen. I felt something cold and metallic in my clenched hand and unclenched my fist. It was a key, a handcuff key, most likely to the cuff still attached to my wrist.

Chapter 51

Tuesday 11th November 2003 (1.00pm)

When I arrived at the station to pack up my desk, the place was buzzing.

Jake was in the meeting room with some new taskforce members. One of them I recognised immediately, Peter Brown. He was a well-respected criminal psychologist. He had been one of my guest lecturers during the final year of my doctorate in criminal psychology. He was an expert in his field, and I knew he was a good choice to replace me.

I went across to my desk and began emptying the drawers into a box I had brought from home. Jake had finished his meeting. "Don't pack up just yet, Brodie. I've convinced the chief to reconsider terminating you. He's agreed to keep you on as long as I agreed to bring in Peter Brown to help. I assumed you wouldn't mind?"

I was stunned. Ten minutes before, I was off the case and now, I was back on. I had almost packed up my whole desk. I began unpacking the box.

Chapter 52

Wednesday 12th November 2003 (10am)

I arrived at work on Wednesday morning. No new leads had come to hand on Lance's whereabouts. We had identified the victim in Lance's house as Tammy Green, who had recently graduated from the Glen Waverley Police Academy.

Two packages sat on my desk.

"Who are they from?" Jake asked.

I looked at him, bewildered. "I have no idea. There's no return address." I grabbed the scissors from the top of my box and was about to open them when Jake grabbed my wrist.

"Wait, we'd better call in the bomb squad."

"Why would I get a bomb!"

It took two hours after the bomb squad arrived to open the boxes without incident. When they were done, the hysteria in the department was worse than if it had been a bomb.

Still in full armour, Sam, the head of the bomb unit, came out to see us. "You guys had better come and look at this, right now. It's no bomb, but it's something you need to see."

We followed Sam back into the station from our kerbside evacuation point. The opened parcels were sitting on my desk. Jake and I looked at each other, unsure what we would find. Nothing could prepare me for the horrible sickness I felt when I saw the contents.

It was a severed finger in a plastic bag surrounded by Styrofoam.

The second box contained one photo and a yellow envelope. The photo showed Lance's lifeless face. I placed on my gloves.

Then we went to open the envelope.

The note was neither typed nor handwritten; it had been created from newspaper headlines. All different letters from different papers, I assumed.

It would have taken the person a long time to put it together. It read:

Brodie Foxx

Well, Brodie, congratulations on being the first cop to ever get close to me, except you're not a cop, are you? Maybe that's why you've done so well. If only you had been watching the house instead of that meathead, this could have all been over by now.

I know you would have been there if you could, I know that you were attending a crime scene, probably one of mine. The jogger one, I guess. Could you pass on an apology to his family for me? He wasn't in my plans. Just came along at a bad time.

Strange how fate works.

I read you may be getting replaced and I must say I don't approve. I would like you to pass on this message to your employer. Either you stay involved or one of the premier's family will be my next victim.

I expect to be able to reach you!

I hope I have made my point.

I'd better go. I have things to do, murders to plan. I look forward to meeting with you soon. To save you some time, the parts I sent you belong to the copycat idiot who didn't even have the brains to get it right.

He won't be attacking any more women I can tell you that. Sorry I couldn't send his head but as you know I collect them.

It looks good on display. Oh, before I go, tell Jake that I am glad he has finally found love. I approve of his choice.

I must say I bet you're still wondering why I am doing what I am doing? Or as you profilers would say what was the triggering event that caused me to begin my killings? I would tell you but it might give me away

The letter finished abruptly.

I didn't know why he wanted me on the case.

He was warning us by making Jake aware that he had been watching him as well, and his girl.

We believed that he had sent the message to tell us he had disposed of Lance and to taunt us, saying he knew more about us than we knew about him.

The overriding message, however, was that he hated the police with a passion. Something had caused this; something had triggered this hatred.

We sent all three items off to forensics and then asked one of the other task members to find out where the item had been posted.

Finally, Jake ordered a uniformed patrol be sent to guard Hayley and informed the premier about the latest threat.

Jake then rang Hayley on his mobile to let her know what had occurred. I could hear her panicked voice at the other end of the line. "Is he after me?" to which Jake replied, "We're sure he's just trying to scare us all," although I wasn't sure Jake was convinced of his answer, let alone Hayley.

Chapter 53

Wednesday 12th November 2003 (12 noon)

Mason had spent several hours following Jake over the previous two days, getting to know his routine. For a detective, he was not good at picking up the signs that he was being followed.

Maybe Mason had become good at following people and looking like he was an ordinary person, going about his ordinary day.

His surveillance had uncovered a lot of information.

Useful information.

Where they both lived and what cars they each drove.

He now knew he had a girlfriend, she was a nurse, she worked at the Alfred Hospital.

He thought it best to know a little about her too. You never knew when it might come in handy. He followed her to work, to ward 8 west, the post-operative ward. "Excuse me? I'm lost," Mason appealed to her, checking her nametag. "My mother came in for an operation and she's meant to be here to be picked up. Am I in the right place?"

Hayley smiled. "Was it day surgery?" she asked in her always-pleasant voice.

"Yes, she came in this morning, my sister dropped her off."

"Ok, then you need to go to the day surgery ward, second floor. Exit the lift and it's just on your left."

Mason now had all the information on Jake's girlfriend that he would need. It would be Jake's weak point.

Mason felt good again. His plan had gone off without a hitch and he was ready to show them who the real Slayer was once again.

He was smart. His confidence had risen. He was ready.

Chapter 54

Wednesday 12th November 2003 (2.17pm)

In light of the letter, we went to the home of the last Slayer's victim to see if we could find any leads that might shine some light on Tammy's killer. While Lance's house had yielded little evidence, we were hopeful that more would be found in her house. We believed she had been abducted from her home. It was her last known sighting.

When we arrived, the property had been sealed off with crime scene tape. We met her father, Kurt Green, out the front of the property. It was important that we have some inside knowledge on how Tammy's house should look.

The three of us entered the property. Her father was a tall man but not as fit as he must once have been. A liking of beer and chips must have got the better of his stomach. Once inside, we began the questions and the inspection of the residence.

"Thank you for meeting us here, Mr Green, I am so sorry for your loss," said Jake. "Anything you can tell us could help us catch this guy. Does anything seem unusual or out of place here? Do you know if Tammy had a boyfriend or if she was seeing someone?"

"No, not that I know about. She was very focused on her police training." He was struggling to keep it together as he stood in the hallway of his dead daughter's house.

"Do you know anyone who disliked her or who might have wanted to harm your daughter?"

"No, she was a lovely caring girl," he said, clasping his hands together.

"Let's have a wander through then, shall we?" Jake suggested.

I stopped and faced Mr Green. "If this gets too hard for you at any time, please tell us. It's understandable. Just let us know if you can't continue."

Mr Green nodded and we continued. The first room was the master bedroom. "This is where we believe the attack occurred," Jake said. "We found a little patch of blood in the ensuite. We believe she may have hit her head on the vanity when he grabbed her."

"She would not leave the bed unmade. She always made it. We taught her that when she was little. 'Keep your room tidy,' her mum would always say."

She was fastidious, Jake noted down, but he already knew that the sheets had probably been taken by the killer, possibly because she was bleeding and so he'd used them to wrap her in. We weren't sure yet. Mr Green pointed out that the gym bag he had bought her was also gone. "She usually keeps it in her wardrobe."

Jake noted down the missing items. "What colour was the bag?" Jake asked.

"Blue," Mr Green replied, "it was a Nike bag with the logo across the sides." As Mr Green walked into the ensuite, he noticed a vibrator on the bedside table. Clearly embarrassed, he asked, "Do you think that this scumbag raped my daughter?"

"We are not sure at this point and we won't be until the lab results are back," I responded.

We continued into the kitchen where we found one cup but two saucers, which meant that a cup had been taken. The only reason he would take a cup was if he had had a drink. It was the only logical conclusion. It also made me wonder if he had been known to his victim, and invited in.

This was very rare for a serial killer. I'd also considered the possibility that he might have had sex with her. That would explain why he'd removed the sheets and why there were adult toys in the bedroom. If she'd been expecting guests, she would have put them away.

Unless he was the guest, I thought.

When Mr Green saw his daughter's police academy photo on the fridge, he broke down and had to leave.

Once Jake knew Mr Green was out of the house, he asked me, "What do you think?"

"What I think scares me. It scares me a lot. Firstly, I think that our killer knew Tammy. How or why I don't know but he knew her. I think he had sex with her, most likely consensual sex. If you raped someone, you wouldn't have time to put porn on and use the toys. Then I think he took the sheets to cover his tracks and he probably put the stuff in the bag to dispose of it all."

"What makes you say he knew her? He didn't know any of the other victims," Jake said.

I picked up the saucer and held it up to him. "See this? It's a saucer without a cup."

Jake added quickly, "Yes, and you only get saucers out for guests you're trying to impress. You think it was him?" Jake asked. Then he continued, thinking he had found a loophole in my theory, "What if the guest was someone else and our serial killer came in just after the other person left?"

"Then why would he take a cup, Jake? If it wasn't his I can't see a reason for it."

Jake agreed that I was most probably right and the theory made sense. We both liked it when our theories made sense.

Chapter 55

Wednesday 12th November 2003 (4.00pm)

Stephen Sutton had spent all day on the couch with a phone and beeper beside him. He knew he was dying and there was nothing he could do about it. He would either die by the end of the month or have the transplant that would save his life.

Cardiomyopathy was what they called it, and for a 33-year-old guy who hadn't been sick a day in his life apart from the odd common cold, he was devastated when the doctors had told him his heart was diseased and failing.

The only treatment option left to him was a heart transplant.

His doctor was nice enough. They said he was the best in Australia, well, the best since Doctor Victor Chang had been brutally shot dead.

Stephen thought that Hanam was of Middle Eastern origin. He came across as very quiet and very smart. The only thing that he didn't like about Professor Hanam was his mumbling. Stephen had a great deal of trouble understanding what the hell the man was saying to him.

Two weeks before, Hanam had said to him, "This is not good. We won't be able to continue like this for much longer," as he removed the stethoscope.

"How long is not long?" Stephen asked, scared out of his wits.

"About a month, I am afraid," Hanam said, as he adjusted his comb-over with the palm of his hand. "But there is a lot that can change in a month. Just keep as fit as you can; it's important to be in good shape for the operation. I also suggest that you do the things you want to do now. Go out for dinner, go to the movies, do the things you enjoy, because if you haven't had the transplant within the next few weeks, you will be confined to your home or hospital with oxygen tanks and you won't be able to do much," Hanam said as he sat back at his desk.

"Let's hope I get a new heart before that happens," Stephen replied.

"Let's hope. Now I want to see you again in two weeks and remember, keep an eye on your weight. If you put on a couple of kilos within a day, call me straightaway."

"What does it mean if I put on weight quickly?" Stephen asked, trying to work it out.

"It means your heart is about to fail and the weight is all the fluid building up," Hanam responded.

Hanam had been right. Soon he would be confined to bed. All his energy was gone and had it not been for the oxygen tank, he assumed he would have been out of breath as well.

Stephen didn't know how much longer he could live like this. He guessed two more weeks, maybe three, but if he didn't get another heart then, he would be dead.

He often thought he should try praying, but he had never believed in God and didn't see why God would help him now after years of being ignored. God would consider him someone jumping on the bandwagon.

He had almost given up hope.

Cassie came in with his plate of hot chicken wings and barbeque sauce that she had kindly made for him. She was an amazing girl, full of positive spirit and cheerfully helpful. Stephen paused the movie he was watching. He had been trying to stay happy, so he was watching some of his favourite comedies. This one was 'Planes, Trains and Automobiles'. He loved anything with John Candy.

Cassie put down the plate of wings. "Do you know what you can have for dessert?" she asked him. Stephen shook his head.

Cassie lifted her top to reveal her breasts. "You can suck on these and I'll suck on something of yours," she replied, smiling. A rare smile crossed Stephen's face. That was another good thing about Cassie; she always knew ways to lift his spirits.

Sex was out of the question. Long past him. Even a BJ could be dangerous.

Best to pass, he thought.

Chapter 56

Thursday 13th November 2003 (11am)

My dream had been bothering me for two days now and I decided to call Esmeralda and run it past her. While I was telling her, she replied by saying she too had had a horrible dream. This concerned me a great deal, even more than my own dream. Two horrible dreams on the one night. We decided to meet at the Crown for lunch and discuss them further.

We met out the front of the Crown and decided on JJs Bar and Grill, a casual eatery with good food. We placed our orders and before our entrée arrived, we were already discussing the dreams.

I described mine to her first.

"They say premonitions come to us to tell us something, warn us in some way. From the dream you described, I think the key may actually be the key," Esmeralda said.

"So what are you saying? I'm confused," I said.

"Make sure you keep a handcuff key on you all the time for now. Will you do that for me, dear?" she asked, touching my hand from across the table.

Her request chilled me but I nodded.

Esmeralda began to describe her dream, then she stopped. "What's wrong?" I asked.

"I have to tell you something about Jake," she said, almost as if she was about to burst into tears. This time I offered my hand by way of comfort. Now I knew why she'd wanted to meet without Jake.

"I misled you, Brodie. I didn't have a dream. I thought it was best that I tell you this in person. I had another vision."

"Was the vision about Jake?" I asked calmly.

Our food arrived but neither of us even looked at it. She nodded and then spoke softly. "I am worried I have seen his death."

"What did you see?"

"I saw him being buried alive in the woods somewhere. There was a dam or a lake nearby. Jake was in a clear coffin but he couldn't get out. He was trapped. He had vomit all over his mouth and neck. He was struggling to breathe. I felt the tightness across his chest."

I sat there stunned and I must admit, very worried. After all, the vision of the jogger had been real. I took a deep breath. "We can't let that happen. Was there anything else in the vision that could help us prevent this? Do you know who did it?" I said, asking the second question before she had even had a chance to answer the first.

"I'll answer the second one first. I think it was the Slayer, but I can't be sure. The other thing I saw in the vision was an old cabin and a huge tree. It was an oak."

"Esmeralda, I know that you have experienced many visions, but have you ever had a vision from evidence? What I mean is, if I showed you items belonging to the victims, do you think this would help you have more visions that might lead us to this bastard?"

"I have never tried it, Brodie. I don't think any cop has taken me seriously enough to try it."

"Ok then," I replied, "let's keep the Jake thing between us and see if any of the evidence will give you some visions. I'm hoping that the reason for your visions is to help us in the future, not necessarily be of the future," I said, hoping for the best.

"It doesn't normally turn out that way," Esmeralda said with a little sigh.

Chapter 57

Thursday 13th November 2003 (6.30pm)

Mason had spent the remainder of the week working hard to make up for the days he had been away at his so-called conference. He arrived home to spend some time with Jamie, one eye scanning the Sky News channel for any updates. He enjoyed being at home with Jamie, who was his one and only true love in his pathetic existence.

They had spent the time just before dinner playing with his wooden Thomas the Tank Engine train set. Jamie loved the trains and he loved it even more when his dad did the voices of the trains and the Fat Controller. Between the trips around the track, Mason kept his eyes and ears firmly focused on the news.

It wasn't until the main news bulletin at 6pm that Jake's press conference aired around the country. Mason was pleased with the outcome. He was glad Brodie was still on board. The end was near and the final challenge excited him. The caption along the bottom of the screen read—'Taskforce Eagle add Forensic Psychologist Peter Brown.'

Jake went on to provide an update on the case. "We are still seeking the public's assistance in locating Mr Silver. We believe he has vital information regarding the East Side Slayer case. Should anyone know of Mr Silver's whereabouts, they are urged to call Crime Stoppers." Jake then introduced Dr Peter Brown.

"It is with great honour that I take on this position. I am hopeful that together with the other members of the taskforce we will soon have this case solved.

"Do you really think it will be solved? It's been over a decade and there doesn't seem to be an end in sight," a young reporter from the middle row asked.

"I believe we are on the right path, I believe all the work the police have done up until this point has been exceptional. While we may not publicly identify all persons of interest, that doesn't mean they don't exist. I can tell you we have hundreds of leads and several dozen persons of interest at this stage."

"Do you think the taskforce made a mistake putting Brodie Foxx on the case? Would you have been a better choice from the start?" an older journalist asked from the front.

"Let me say this, the taskforce is a team and we help each other. We are not here, I am certainly not here, to take over. It is common sense to have people in the same field helping each other. That's what I am doing with Mr Foxx. If it takes a hundred forensic psychologists to solve these murders, then that is what we will do."

With that answer, the interview ended.

Mason was very pleased to see both Jake and Brodie at the news conference.

It was time for him to kill again. His body was telling him it was time. The rage had built up again. The anger was crying to get out. Even though it was so soon after Tammy and Lance, the feeling was there stronger than ever. He was at boiling point again.

This time, it would be perfect.

Jamie sat with his mother on the couch after dinner while Mason headed to his study to begin planning. This time he had to plan for Brodie and Jake. He knew that they were close and with the letter he had sent, he knew they would be closing in soon.

Mason needed some insurance.

Chapter 58

Friday 14th November 2003 (9.30am)

With no new leads arising, the latest murders were starting to go cold. We had discussed at lunch that we needed to try something different.

I had decided to take Esmeralda with me to the latest crime scene to see if she could provide any new information, or at least confirm some of my original suspicions. Esmeralda walked into the master bedroom of Tammy's house. She stood in the doorway for a few seconds and then made her way around the hall. She touched the cup that was still sitting on the bench. No vision came to her this time; her mind remained blank.

Esmeralda returned to the master bedroom and then she went into the ensuite. It was only when she touched the basin that a vision came, except it was more than a vision. She could sense what the poor victim had felt. She felt a sharp shock to her right kidney.

"Ouch!" she cried, as I stood at the ensuite door.

"Are you ok?" I asked her.

She was clutching the basin with her left hand and her kidney with her right. "It was here," she said. "Here is where he took her and it was someone she knew. They had just had sex. She was happy, excited by the romance, until the shock at least."

"The shock?" I asked.

"I didn't have a vision this time, but I could feel a presence in the room. Her soul maybe, it was chilling whatever it was. She was having a fling with someone, and that someone is our killer, that someone came up from behind while she was doing her makeup or whatever and shocked her. I also felt a sharp pain in my neck."

"I think that the shock you felt to your kidney was most likely a stun gun he uses to subdue his victims. We believe he uses the stun gun in combination with an injection. We think that the shock gives him enough time for the injection to take effect."

Esmeralda watched me in the mirror as I explained.

"And I'm sure the pain in the neck you felt was the needle when he injected his sedative."

Esmeralda nodded as I finished.

"May I ask how you know that she had sex?"

"I can feel it when women have sex. There's a feeling that lasts after an orgasm. Just trust me; she had made love to her killer. I think you will find that's why the bed clothes have been removed. To remove the evidence, I would guess."

"Could you see who the man was?" I asked eagerly.

"I'm afraid not. I can only feel what she felt, not see him. But if you find him, you find the Slayer."

I had called Jake to let him know that Esmeralda had confirmed our suspicions and that we were on our way to Tammy's father's office to see if he could give us any of his daughter's possible acquaintances.

We only had to wait a few minutes before being met in the foyer by Mr Green. He led us into his office. "How can I help you today?" he asked, still visibly shaken by the loss of his daughter.

"We believe that your daughter may have known her attacker; we believe this may have been on an intimate level."

Taken aback by the news, Mr Green leaned forward and poured himself a glass of water.

"Are you saying my daughter was sleeping with this serial killer?"

"Yes, but to her, he may have just been a boyfriend or someone she met in a club. She would never have known what she was getting into, unfortunately."

Leaning over the desk, Mr Green looked at me in such a way that I knew immediately I had offended him. He let me know it too. "You may be a police officer but that doesn't give you the right to insult my daughter. I'll have you know that my daughter is not the type of girl to pick up a guy in a bar and then bring him back to her house. She was also a police officer."

"I did not mean to offend you, Mr Green."

"Can you think of anyone that she may have been with, an old boyfriend? Someone from here maybe? Anyone you know who she may have been willing to be intimate with?"

"She never talked to me about boyfriends. Since she'd been in the academy, she hadn't worried about boys. She was too focused on passing and becoming an officer. As far as I know, there was no one she was seeing. I'm sorry, but I can't help you with that. She may have confided in her best friend about that stuff. I can give you her number." Mr Green went through the contacts on his phone.

"Is this her graduation photo?" I asked picking up the photo from his desk.

"Yes, she gave it to me as a gift."

He took the photo from my hand, replacing it with a number written on a post-it note.

"That's great, thank you, and if anything comes of it, I'll let you know of course."

Chapter 59

Friday 14th November (10.44am)

Mason had just finished several back-to-back appointments. It had been a good start to the day. He had a buyer for the Lucas road property. No sooner had the buyers left than his mind turned back to his other life.

He wanted to visit his mum for morning tea, but he decided that he first better put in an appearance at the office. Firstly, he wanted to see his pig of a boss wallowing in misery, misery that Mason was sure he deserved. Secondly, he wanted to see if there was any office gossip about Tammy.

"Who are the people in the boss's office?" Mason asked the secretary, making out he had no idea. She was standing at the photocopier, running copies of the rental list.

"The police, asking him questions, I guess."

"It's so sad what happened to Tammy. I hope he's coping all right?" Mason said, trying to make out that he gave a shit.

"He seems to be struggling, to be honest. Who wouldn't though." She picked up the copies and raced off to answer the phone.

Inside, Mason was shaking.

Were they here for him?

Had they found something that had led them here? Had he made a mistake?

If they weren't here for him, he was certain they were getting closer.

Only one way to find out, he thought. Mason walked straight down the hall and opened his boss's office door, "Sorry, I didn't realise you were with people. I just needed to ask you a few questions about the Lucas Road file."

"I'll be with you in a few minutes, Mason," Mr Green responded.

Mason closed the door and headed back to his desk. He now knew they were not here for him. They were just doing their investigation, and it was good to see his letter had been taken seriously. Brodie was on the case all right, he was pleased to see. Mason was sure he would see Brodie on a more personal level before all this ended.

A few minutes later, Mason had a second meeting with the cops, except this time it was unexpected. They crossed paths in the car park as he was getting into his BMW. "How you going?" Mason spoke as they passed his open driver's door.

"Fine thanks," the older lady replied.

He wondered where Jake was and then thought, 'of course, looking after his girlfriend.' In the week since his threat, Mason had often visited Jake's home where he knew Hayley was receiving around-the-clock supervision. It usually came in the form of a patrol car sitting just outside either her or Jake's home. This week had been mostly Jake's. Shifts were usually four or six hours.

By his calculations, the next shift was due to end at 2pm and for his plan to work he had to be there by 1.30.

Chapter 60

Friday 14th November 2003 (11.15am)

"Something was strange about that agent. I got a very cold feeling when he came into the office," Esmeralda said as soon as we were in the privacy of the car.

"He's a real estate agent; what do you expect?" I joked. "Maybe that's just the way he is. Did you have a vision about him?" I asked.

"No, nothing like that, I just felt a cold presence around him. Can you run a check on him or something? I just have a feeling that I can't explain! It may lead you up the garden path, it may be totally unrelated to the case, but on the other hand, there may be something and if there is, it's worth following up."

Esmeralda's concerns with the agent bugged me all afternoon. I arrived back at the station and ran his name through the database. No criminal history existed; he was clean. I let it go but something kept nagging at me. I decided to ring Mr Green to see if there was anything to go on. "Excuse me, Mr Green, it's Brodie Foxx from the Victorian Police. Really sorry to bother you again but I'm just eliminating some suspects at the moment.

"Was Mason Belic working last weekend?" The phone was silent for a few seconds and then he replied, "Um, he was away Thursday and Friday at a conference in Brisbane and Saturday he was here but left early. He seemed lacking in interest that day. Sunday was his day off and Monday he was sick. But I would need to double check with HR."

"No need," I said. "Thank you. Can you send me his employment file please? Just so I can confirm a few things before I rule him out?"

"Sure, but I won't be back in until just after 2 and the files are locked in my office. Can it wait until then?"

"That's fine," I replied and hung up.

Something still nagged at me. I called Qantas to check for flights under Mason Belic to Gold Coast or Brisbane. "Sorry Sir, I have no bookings under that name. Maybe try Virgin."

I dialled Virgin and after a few seconds of typing, the voice came back to me. "I have a Mason Belic booked on flight VA663 Melbourne to Gold Coast. The 7.15 flight on Thursday 6th November."

That cleared him, was my first thought.

"Except he never boarded the flight," the voice at the other end said.

"When was he due to return?" I asked, thinking he might have caught another flight up for some reason.

"The return flight was VA459 Gold Coast to Melbourne 8pm Friday night. He also failed to board. We don't have him listed on either flight."

This had my mind ticking. Maybe I was getting somewhere. Things were starting to add up. This might just be our man.

I rang Corrections Victoria to see if they had any record of Mason Belic being incarcerated in 2000. Sometimes when updating the crime database, records occasionally fell through the cracks.

I rang Jake and explained that Mason had not boarded either of the two flights. I asked if he could organise a crosscheck on Mason. The purpose of the crosscheck was to verify where the suspect was at the time of each offence. Obviously, with so many abduction and murders, it would take some time. We needed to have more background on his movements before we could bring him in for questioning.

Jake told me he would be back just after 2pm as he was guarding Hayley until then, but he wasted no time in organising the taskforce to get the crosscheck underway.

Chapter 61

Friday 14th November (11.30am)

Soon after his second brush with the police, Mason arrived at his mother's house. She had purchased a simple, low maintenance unit recently. She had opted for a unit instead of a townhouse because her knees were shot and she didn't want a lot of garden to maintain or stairs to climb. She wasn't getting any younger, she said.

His mother, a grey-haired lady in her early 70s walking with a cane, answered the door. She was always delighted to see a child of hers but she was especially surprised and excited to see Mason. Friday had always been her day for shopping, the day after the pension arrived in her bank account. She had just returned home and was ready for some morning tea.

Mason spent the next half hour having tea and biscuits with his mother.

He had never told his mum the truth about his father. He knew it would destroy her, so he'd simply kept it to himself.

"Mum, I need to borrow Dad's uniform, if I can? I have a dress-up party on the weekend and I would feel privileged if you would let me wear it."

"You know how I feel about that uniform."

"Mum, it would be a great privilege. I will have it back early next week."

"I am sure your father would want you to wear it, but please look after it. Make sure you have it dry-cleaned before you return it." She dunked her biscuit into the remainder of her tea.

Mason left with the uniform folded over his arm, with an hour and a half to get home, change and be at Jake's in time for the shift changeover.

Chapter 62

Friday 14th November (1pm)

While I waited for the crosscheck to be done, I continued with the other leads.

I headed to see if David, who always seemed to be working, had come up with any results. David confirmed my suspicion that Tammy had slept with her attacker. "What did you find out?" I asked.

"Well, the case is building. I can tell you that we found a trace of semen in Tammy's vaginal cavity, despite the body having been recently thoroughly washed. I am hoping the sample will be enough to get a DNA profile. I've sent it to the lab and I've also sent the blood sample we found on the German Shepherd's teeth. If they match, we'll know that we at least have the same guy at two different murder scenes and you'll be able to test the sample against any future suspects."

He paused, sipped his coffee and continued.

"While I don't have the DNA yet, I can tell you his blood type is B-positive. I also got the toxicology results back on both Maggie and Tammy. They both had traces of Benzodiapine in their systems."

"Same as all the others," I said.

"There's enough evidence to suggest that Maggie was a victim of the Slayer. The stab pattern matches."

David dunked the doughnut into his coffee, bit off the soggy piece and continued.

"We've also done the cast of the tyre track recovered at Maggie's dump site as well as a partial sneaker cast. I've sent off a copy of the print to get an exact make of tyre. We know it's a medium size car by the diameter and width of the tyre." David finished off the doughnut and placed the empty cup on the desk next to him.

"When do you think that we will have the DNA results from Tammy Green? I was hoping for tonight," I said nervously.

David laughed as if to say, 'you're dreaming'.

"Those lab rats are slow, it may be a day or two. I'll see if I can give them the hurry-up."

I headed back to my desk to see if Jake had arrived. My conversation with

Esmeralda had really worried me. The thought of Jake being buried alive terrified me.

I feared that this case could kill us both if we didn't act with extreme caution.

Chapter 63

Friday 14th November 2003 (1.50pm)

Mason, who was now dressed in his father's police uniform, knew that this was going to be the hardest part of his plan. Yet once done, it would give him the upper hand.

Sitting in his car, Mason kept his head low, waiting for the patrol car to arrive. He knew that he would have to be quick and precise. One mistake and it would end here with his death. The thought of his own demise was quickly erased as a patrol car pulled into the curb on the other side of the street.

Mason got out of his car and casually walked over to the patrol car. He could see the officer leaning over, fumbling around in the back seat for his cap. Mason calmly tapped on the window. The officer was a little startled at first, yet when he saw the uniform, his fears subsided. The officer switched the engine back on and pressed the button for the electric window. By the time the window was halfway down, Mason's plan was almost complete. He fired three rapid shots from his silenced Beretta. It was the perfect weapon when a quick kill was required. All three bullets pierced the officer's chest, killing him almost instantly.

Mason quickly reached through the window and pushed him sideways to prevent his lifeless body from collapsing onto the horn and bringing unwanted attention. Then he leaned in and removed the nametag. 'Sergeant Slater', it read. 'Pleased to meet you,' he thought, as he pinned it on his shirt. Mason pressed the window button to wind it back up and removed the keys. Then he turned and headed for Jake's home, on the other side of the street.

Chapter 64

Friday 14th November 2003 (1.55pm)

Jake was sitting at the table drinking coffee with Hayley safely beside him drinking her cup of Milo. Ever since her early 20s, she had had migraines, and her doctor had suggested she cut down on her coffee intake. Since she couldn't stand 'that decaf crap' as she called it, Milo was her best alternative.

Although he was anxious to make sure Hayley was protected, Jake was also anxious to get back to the station and follow up on the only lead they had. While it was a long shot, or what an experienced detective would call playing a hunch, a hunch was a great lead when you had absolutely nothing else.

Jake kept running scenarios through his head, trying to imagine why the Slayer had suddenly struck so close to his domain. Why had he made his boss's daughter one of his victims?

"So do you think he will come for me?" Hayley asked softly, looking into the bottom of her empty mug.

Jake wasn't entirely sure yet but he thought Hayley might be 'the one'. "I don't think so. I think he just wanted to get Brodie back on the case. It was a stunt. He's playing games, but don't panic, I'm here. Once I leave, there'll be another officer here to protect you. You will be safe, I promise."

But Jake knew that this was not enough to ease Hayley's fears. Who was he to make such a promise? He tried to sound confident. "Babe, don't panic. We may have found him. We might have him soon."

Hayley smiled and reached for his hand.

Focused on his job, he knew that Brodie was onto something and that he needed to be there too. Impatient, he rang the chief. "Chief, where the hell is this guy who's supposed to be coming to guard Hayley?" he asked.

The chief was in his office with the phone resting on his shoulder, trying desperately to find the relieving officer's details. "He should be there soon. Traffic have sent, umm . . ." he fumbled through the notes on his desk, " . . . Sergeant Slater."

Jake was about to suggest that he ask Suzie to get traffic on the two-way to find out where the hell he was, when a knock came at the door. "It's all right. He's here," Jake said, ending the call.

Jake glanced through the opaque side window and saw the man in uniform standing there waiting patiently to be let in.

Jake opened the door and invited the officer in. "Hi. I'm Sergeant Slater. Traffic advised me to be on guard duty here. Is there anything I need to know?" Mason asked calmly.

"No, just watch her and ring me directly if anyone shows up. We think that this nutter was fucking with us. I don't think she's under any threat but as you know, we have to take every threat seriously."

Jake kissed Hayley goodbye and explained to her that the officer would watch her until he returned.

"I missed your first name?" Jake asked.

"Sorry, my mistake, Peter Slater," Mason replied, beginning to panic. He had no idea of the dead copper's first name, or if Jake was onto him. Peter was the first name that had popped into his head.

Jake picked up his jacket, holstered his gun and headed for the door. The guilt of leaving the safety of the only girl he had ever loved to a stranger, hit hard, but he swept the guilt aside and focused on the job ahead.

Chapter 65

Friday 14th November 2003 (2.07pm)

Mason watched Jake get into his car and speed off. He had been in such a rush that he hadn't even glanced at the squad car.

Mason turned his attention to Hayley. He was hopeful he could complete the rest of his plan without any hiccups. He wanted to take Hayley alive and without force if possible. If not, then force would be used.

As soon as Jake had left the property, Mason put his plan into action. He stepped into the kitchen and selected a ring tone on his phone, and then pretended to begin a conversation. "Yes, Jake, I can do that, and what time would you be there? Ok, uhh, huhh, really? The premier's daughter?" He walked back into the lounge to gauge Hayley's reaction. "This guy is sick. Do you want to speak to her? Ok, I'll let Hayley know."

With that, Mason pretended to hang up the call. Turning to Hayley, he said, "You might have guessed that was Jake. Someone apparently tried to abduct the premier's daughter from school. Jake wants me to take you to the police safe house where he'll collect you later tonight. Quick, come with me." Mason took Hayley by the hand and headed for the front door. He ushered her right past the squad car and escorted her into the front seat of his BMW.

"Why aren't we taking the squad car?" Hayley asked, as she tried to compose herself.

"We're undercover," Mason replied, as cool and as calm as usual.

"This doesn't seem right. I'm going to ring Jake." Hayley shuffled through her bag looking for her phone but before she could reach it, a sharp pain hit her in the kidney and she hit her head against the side window. Mason injected her without her even knowing.

Mason's plan was almost complete. Only one more stop to make before he headed back to the cabin.

Chapter 66

Friday 14th November 2003 (2.20pm)

As I waited for Jake to return, I couldn't believe how our investigation had taken on a new direction so quickly.

I had received a call from David, who had confirmed that the tyre cast had also come back as fitting a 1992 BMW.

I had received Mason's work records from Mr Green and at first glance, nothing had stood out. Then I turned to his absence roster. He had been away a lot, sometimes for days at a time. The other thing that stood out was that beside many of these multiple days, 'conference' was written beside them.

His police check with photo attached had come back all clear. He had no previous record.

I then flicked through his resume and stopped suddenly.

His vehicle was listed as a BMW.

I printed the email and added it to the file.

So far, it was all circumstantial evidence, but it was enough for us to detain Mason for questioning. Most likely, it would be enough to receive a court order for a compulsory DNA test.

Where the hell was Jake? I wanted to go and pick up this guy. I tried Jake's number again. No response: 'the number you have called is currently out of radio range, please try again later,' the automated voice said.

"Can you try Jake on the two-way?" I asked Suzie. "He's not responding to his mobile."

Jake picked up the two-way almost immediately. "I'm pulling into the car park right now," his voice crackled back.

I practically ambushed Jake as he entered the station. "Found a lot of circumstantial evidence on that guy that works for Mr Green." I handed him the file. "He has a BMW. David just verified it was a BMW that left the tyre cast taken from Maggie's dump site."

Jake nodded, trying to get his head around everything that I was telling him. Then as he was flicking through the pages, he suddenly stopped.

I was speaking at a million miles an hour about the conferences and his work history.

Jake's face turned ashen and his eyes began to well with tears.

"What's wrong?" I asked, as his look went from surprise to horror and then anger.

"I met him," Jake stuttered, lost for words, probably for the first time ever.

"You met him?" I asked.

"He came to my house, to guard Hayley. I left Hayley there with him."

"What the fuck are you on about?" I asked, totally confused.

Jake repeated what he'd said. While I was still trying to understand what he'd said, he ran out of the station back to his car, and I had to run to keep up. I only made it about halfway before Jake drove up and slowed down just long enough for me to get in.

"What the hell are you on about, Jake?"

We were travelling at high speed, weaving through the traffic, with what appeared to be a total disregard for our lives.

"He has her!" Jake replied sharply without taking his eyes off the road for a second.

"Mate, we're not going to be of any help to her if you kill us trying to get there."

Jake sailed through the third consecutive set of red lights. "If you want to jump out at the next lights, I'll stop." He said this without allowing the conversation to distract him from driving.

"I'm not fucking going anywhere, I'm here for the long haul, whatever that may be," I said, my grip tightening around the Jesus handle. I was holding on so tightly my knuckles were white.

Jake pulled the car over to the gutter outside his apartment building. He left the car half on the footpath and with the driver's door wide open, and sprinted up the stairs of his apartment two at a time.

Inside his apartment, there was no sign of a struggle or disturbance, no sign of anything unusual at all. "Where the fuck are they?" Jake screamed.

"For what it's worth, I think she's still alive. He'll have taken her as insurance. She's not a cop, she doesn't fit his profile."

"If he's not going to kill her, then why take her?" Jake groaned. He was on his knees with his head in his hands.

"We know who he is, now we just have to locate him," I said.

We were on our way back to the station when I told Jake to pull over. He pulled into the emergency lane on the freeway, looking at me with an expression of pure hopelessness.

"Keep your head up, mate. Hayley needs you focused. Now let's go through what we know. He works as a real estate agent in the burbs, he drives a white BMW. I assume you've already put out an APB for the vehicle?"

Jake nodded.

"He's married with one child, according to Mr Green. So why did he start killing policewomen? What triggered him?" I asked.

"Because he's a fucking nut bag and he finds this stuff sexually exciting."

Without replying to Jake, I flicked through the file looking for Mason Belic's address.

"Ok Jake, let's go there now." I punched the address into the sat nav system.

"Why are we going to his house? I don't think he's stupid enough to go home," Jake said.

"I agree. But we can find out something about his childhood, which may give us a clue as to where he might be headed."

Chapter 67

Friday 14th November 2003 (3.10pm)

Mason pulled into the drive of the woman he thought of as his final victim. The only photo he had of her was over 20 years old.

He left his car. Hayley was slumped in the passenger seat with her head against the window.

Mason rapped his knuckles on the security door. He knew that she would be home. He had rung her yesterday, pretending to be from the gas company and saying that they needed to check the meters in the area. Some of them had been reported as faulty, he'd explained.

Samantha came to the door soon after she heard the knocking.

"Excuse me, just wondering if I can ask you a few questions about the neighbours and the robbery last night?" Mason knew the fact that he was dressed in a police uniform would erase any fears Samantha might have.

Samantha unlocked her security door so she could answer his questions. In doing so, she sealed her fate. She was the final piece of his hatred. Finally, he would fill the void that he had been seeking to fill.

A void that all the others had failed to fill. Surely this time it would be perfect.

It had to be.

Samantha unlocked the latch. Mason pounced.

Stunning her in the kidney had the instant effect of dropping Samantha at the front door step.

Mason quickly injected his serum and dragged her inside, closing and locking the front door behind him. From the inside, Mason pressed the garage remote clipped to the holder on the inside wall and opened the garage. Then he went back to his BMW and parked alongside Samantha's blue 2002 Holden Commodore. Popping the trunk of Samantha's car, Mason began removing the contents from his BMW into her Holden. Then he dragged Hayley into the boot of the Commodore.

Mason spent only 10 minutes at Samantha's home. He dragged her bound body and laid her on the back seat. Then he drove out of Samantha's drive and headed for the cabin.

Finally, it would be perfect; he could feel it in his bones.

Chapter 68

Friday 14th November 2003 (3.17pm)

Jake commented that Belic's house didn't look like the type of home that a serial killer might reside in. However, it was everything I'd imagined. The lawn was well trimmed. The plants were perfectly nurtured and the drive was free of oil stains. The home was situated opposite a delightful lake, in the leafy suburb of Berwick. It reflected the personality of a neat, meticulous person. I had no doubt his car would be the same. It was no coincidence that the murders had all been well planned and meticulously carried out. One was a reflection of the other.

When we rang the doorbell, through the half-glass half-timber front door we saw a toddler approach.

A woman appeared and opened the door as far as the security chain allowed. She asked, "Can I help you?"

"Mrs Belic. It's the police. We would like to come in and ask you some questions about your husband." Jake showed the petite woman his police badge.

"Oh, ok, come in then," she replied, closing the door first to unlock the chain. "Is he all right?" she asked, as she sent her son off to play in his room.

I had told Jake on the drive to Mason's home to let me handle the questions.

We were sitting on the couch in the formal lounge.

"Mrs Belic, we believe that your husband may have some information on the East Side slayings. Do you know where he might be?"

"He would be at work, or you could get him on his cell phone. Sometimes he switches it off if he's in a meeting." Her reply was matter of fact.

"He hasn't been at work all day. Does he have a friend whose house he might go to, or a parent? Somewhere else he might go?" I asked.

She frowned, becoming more uncomfortable with each question.

"No one that I can think of," she replied, "why do you need to speak to him?"

"He may have information that's of use to our investigation, that's all," I replied, smiling and trying to ease her concern. "Does he have family close by?"

"We see his mother quite a bit but she lives in a townhouse in Melbourne."

"His father?"

"His dad died when he was about nine. He died in the line of duty and . . ."

"How did his dad die?" I asked.

"He was in the police force, he was shot by his partner. She was only young, a rookie, and, well, she thought he was a robber. That's the way Mason tells it anyhow. Mason didn't cope with the death of his father. He still gets upset about it sometimes, which I don't understand."

"Well, I'm sure the death of a parent must have been very hard to cope with, as a nine-year-old," I said sympathetically.

"I am not heartless, Officer, if that's what you're insinuating. I just don't understand how Mason cared so much for someone who sexually abused him and spent his spare time beating him. If it had been me, I'd have been glad not to have him come back home."

We tried to remain impassive as we heard Mason's likely motive being spelled out for us.

"Mrs Belic, is that your husband's study?" I asked, pointing to the room with the double doors.

She nodded.

"Do you mind if we have a look around?" I asked, hoping she would be cooperative. If she asked for a warrant, it was a waste of precious time, time we just didn't have.

"Of course you can. Why do you need to speak to Mason?" she asked again.

"We just need to ask him some questions." I didn't want to let on he was a wanted man.

"This picture, is that your holiday house?" I asked, picking up the photo from the desk.

"Far from it. I haven't been there for years. Mason goes up often. He's renovating it so we can sell it. It belonged to Mason's father." She seemed more and more concerned by our questioning.

I picked up the other photo of Mason and his wife at what looked like the Grand Canyon. "When was this?" I asked.

"It was back in 2000. We decided to go on holiday and tour the USA before we had children. My parents lived over there at the time so it was a family visit as well."

"Must have been fun. Have you seen them since?" I asked, placing the photo back in its original place.

"Oh, they live here now. So I see them all the time."

I had seen and heard all we needed. "Thanks for your help. If you see Mason, could you please ask him to call us?" Still smiling, I handed her one of Jake's cards.

It was lie, but a necessary one. The last thing I wanted was her thinking we were about to arrest him. I'd rather her thinking we were just making routine enquires. That way, if they did speak, she wouldn't be in a panic.

Chapter 69

Friday 14th November 2003 (3.30pm)

Back in the vehicle, I radioed Suzie.

"I want you to search for a policeman who was killed between 1975 and 1985. He had a female partner who survived, I believe his name was Belic."

She cut me off mid-sentence.

"I know that case. I studied it at the academy. He was killed during a robbery, accidentally shot by his junior partner. What do you need to know?"

"What was the young police officer's name and where does she live?"

"I'll do a search and get back to you."

"Suzie, I also need a title search done on Mr Belic. I need to know any properties he had or still has. You will need to ring the titles office. Tell them we need them urgently."

I placed the receiver down and leaned back in my seat.

"We're supposed to be finding Hayley!" Jake shouted at me.

"We will find her, I promise, but I think that the girl who killed Mason's dad is his real target. I think he's been killing these girls at the cabin in the photo. David found a piece of wood stuck under Maggie's finger. David believed it was from trying to grab a door or a veranda rail. What type of wood do you think that cabin is made out of?" I asked Jake.

He pondered. "Looked like cedar, or western red cedar."

"I agree. We sent the piece of wood off to a botanist and he said it was an old piece of cedar. Cedar isn't used to build houses today, but 50 years ago, cabins like that were made from the trees that grew in the area. "

Jake sat quietly. "He would have all the time in the world to spend with the girls up there."

"Exactly. We find that cabin, we find Hayley," I answered.

"Let's just get the address from Mrs Belic." Jake opened the car door.

I grabbed him by the jacket. "Wait, we don't want to alarm her. We don't want her to know that we know about the cabin. If she talks to him meantime, she'll tell him we've been asking questions and that'll tip him off."

Jake closed the door.

We waited in silence for Suzie to give us the address of the cabin. She also provided the name and address of the police colleague who had mistakenly killed Mason's father all those years ago.

Mason was most likely hunting her as we waited.

"The officer, her name is Samantha Bond. We sent a squad car around to her home. Front door was open, no one at home. She's gone. The officers found Belic's BMW parked in her garage. So we know Belic was there. Her car is a 2002 blue Holden Commodore. It's gone. Do you want me to put out an APB on it?"

I looked at Jake before responding, "Not yet, we don't want to scare him. He has Hayley and now Samantha. He will kill them if he sees a cop. Now that we know where he's headed, we'll call for backup when we get there. Thanks Suzie!" I said, placing the two-way back in its cradle.

Jake had already punched the cabin address into the sat nav.

"Where is that property?" I asked.

"Central Victoria," Jake replied.

"Before we go, we need to organise backup, we need SWAT to go in," I said.

Jake sat there in silence, then he said,. "I'm one for doing everything by the book but if we send SWAT and he catches even a glimpse of them, then the girls are dead. You said so yourself: if he sees a cop, he'll kill them."

I thought it over. "One thing is clear. He wants to finish this his way. He wants to take his time killing Samantha. That I am sure of. The death of his father was the trigger. The fact that he never had the opportunity to exact revenge on his father has led to his misguided belief that killing policewomen will give him the satisfaction he desires. He won't rush this one."

"I'm concerned that if we try to apprehend him now, or on the way to the cabin, he'll kill everyone he can, including Hayley. He'd have no reason not to," Jake said.

"I agree." I paused, contemplating whether to tell him about Esmeralda's vision. I decided it was best not to bring it up now, but I warned him about the dangers. "You know, if we go in alone, then we could all end up dead."

Jake nodded solemnly. "But he won't know we're coming. We'll have the element of surprise on our side. We can't allow it to become a hostage situation. Why don't we head up there, see if he's there first, then call for backup. No point sending SWAT if he isn't even there."

"I agree. Let's assess our next move when we get there."

Chapter 70

Friday 14th November 2003

Overnight, Stephen's condition had deteriorated rapidly and he was fighting for his life. His heart was rapidly giving in to the disease and his worst fears were being realised: he might soon be dead.

His heart had gone into systolic failure. It wasn't pumping hard enough and the beat had become slow and irregular.

By the time Stephen was wheeled through to the emergency ward at Alfred Hospital, his doctor was there waiting for him.

He was immediately sent to radiology for an MRI of his heart, then to cardiology for an echo. Cassie had ridden in the back of the ambulance with him and she now sat patiently awaiting Stephen's return to the cardiology ward. She tried to keep her mind occupied by reading the latest copies of 'Women's Day' and 'New Idea'.

"Cassie," a soft voice called from the door. "May I have a seat?" Doctor Hanam sat down beside her. "I am afraid that Stephen's condition has worsened quicker than I expected. Unfortunately, from the results of the MRI and the echo, I think we only have up to five days at the absolute outside before Stephen will require a heart transplant. We will need to keep him here until we find a heart."

Cassie burst into tears at the news of Stephen's predicament. Hanam held her hand.

"I have already told Stephen the news. He is coping quite well. He will be back in his room shortly. I have arranged with the nurses for you to stay. They will set up a bed in the room for you." Hanam clasped Cassie's hand tighter. "All you can do is hope. You have to have hope, Cassie." Hanam stood up, adjusted his comb-over and left the room.

Chapter 71

Friday 14th November 2002 (5.20pm)

By the time Mason reached his cabin, his excitement was at fever pitch. He had spoken to his wife, who had rung him in a panic.

"They were asking all sorts of strange questions. What's going on, Mase? They were even asking about the cabin, asked if I'd been there recently. What do you know? Why are they bothering us?" she asked him.

Mason as usual played it cool.

"I'm sure they're just investigating everyone who may have known Tammy," Mason replied. "It's just routine. I don't know anything, babe, I'll give them a call and clear it up."

He managed to put Sophie's mind at ease.

She read out the number that the police had left.

He guessed he was a good hour ahead of them.

He assumed Jake would be coming for Hayley, and he was ready.

Mason had already locked Hayley in a cage in the cellar, before he'd even attempted to move Samantha from the car, but now, he dragged Sam by the hair all the way from the car to the cellar. She only came to as she felt the cold cuffs around her wrists. She began to kick and scream and Mason cuffed her to two of the support beams.

Once in place, Samantha was hanging a foot off the ground with her hands and legs spread wide, held only by the chains, as if she was attached to an invisible cross.

"I'm glad to see you're now wide awake. I would hate for you to miss any of the fun," Mason said, in an almost jocular fashion. "Do you know why you're here, Samantha? Do you know why I chose you?" Mason asked, as he removed the Samurai sword from its place on the wall.

"I haven't done anything to you. I don't even know who you are!" Samantha screamed, spit flying from her mouth. "Let me go, please, just let me go before you do something you will regret." Samantha was trying to talk her way out of a bad situation.

"Look up at the shelf, Samantha. I have already done a lot of things. People like me don't feel regret."

Samantha looked up at the shelf and saw all the horrified lifeless faces looking back at her from their respective jars. She lost control of her emotions and continued screaming.

Mason raised the sword and cut away Samantha's clothes, cutting her skin several times. "Normally, I would apologise for cutting you. Under the circumstances, I am sure you would consider the apology insincere. I wouldn't want to be seen as fake." Mason picked up a clear bottle from the table next to him.

"Now, I will ask you again; tell me why you are here?"

"I don't know!" Samantha screamed.

"Maybe you should think a little harder before you answer next time, Samantha." He began pouring the clear liquid onto the cuts on Samantha's skin. "This is just good old-fashioned vinegar. It might sting a little, so hold on."

Again, Samantha screamed, louder than before. The pain was agonising. "Stop, please. I will think. Stop, please stop," Samantha begged, her tears flowing freely.

Mason stopped pouring and asked the question again.

Trying to compose herself and think of an answer, Samantha paused, thinking. 'What have I done? 'Why would he want me here?' Maybe it was just a trick question. She was now down to her bra and briefs. She mustered up all her courage to and said, "I am here because I was lucky and you chose me. Thank you."

"Wrong again," Mason answered, "and I don't care for you being a rude insincere little bitch either." Mason picked up the sword, this time cutting the bra straps from her shoulder and then down the middle, causing the bra to fall to the ground in tatters, leaving Samantha bare chested.

Mason spent a little time assessing the breasts. They were still nice and firm and held their shape well for a woman heading into her mid-40s. It was a shame he was going to have to disfigure them. Without another word, Mason raised the sword and made two quick strikes, cutting off the nipple from each breast. Samantha went into a screaming frenzy, the like of which he had never heard before, and Mason had heard more than his share.

"Leave her alone, you prick, leave her the fuck alone!" Hayley screamed from her cage.

"Don't worry, I will save some pain for you, my dear," Mason replied, showing her his overexcited smile. He placed his sword down on the bench and removed his gun. Then he turned and fired a bullet, which just grazed Hayley's right thigh. "Speak again and the next bullet will be between your eyes, you understand?" Mason still had the gun pointed at her.

Hayley nodded and moved to the back of the cage.

Mason returned his attention to Samantha. "Now, for the last fucking time, why the fuck did I pick you?" he screamed, at boiling point.

Without any delay this time, Samantha replied, "Because you're sick and twisted."

"Well, let me fill you in!" Mason shouted in his rage. "You killed my dad. Is it coming back to you now, you little bitch? You let him die! You didn't even fight to save him. What sort of cop were you?"

Samantha now realised who Mason was and why he was in a rage. "I'm so sorry," she sobbed, "I am so very sorry, I didn't mean for you to lose your dad."

"I didn't care that you let him die. He was a monster!"

"Why are you doing this to me then, if you wanted him dead anyway?" Samantha cried through her pain.

"It was my duty, my right, my revenge that you took away from me that night. Do you have any idea what he did to me? What punishment he deserved? Your stupid actions freed him from that punishment and now you will suffer his fate for him."

In silence, he raised his sword and in one quick motion, removed Samantha's head. It flew from her shoulders and landed on the dusty floor of his cellar, eyes peering directly at Hayley. Hayley screamed and would have moved away further if she'd had anywhere to go. Mason stood motionless with his sword still tightly grasped in both hands, with the tip touching the ground.

Hayley realised that Mason was in a place void of all that is decent in a human being, a place that didn't exist in ordinary people, a place that terrified her.

Motionless, Mason watched as the blood sprayed out of the neck. Only when it became a dribble did he awake from his trance. He picked up her head and placed it on the bench next to him. As Hayley watched him, she knew there would be no negotiating with this man.

Chapter 72

Friday 14th November 2003 (7.30pm)

Jake pulled the car into a track well off the road. It was hidden from the road in the undergrowth and in a heavily forested area.

The GPS showed the cabin to be off to our right about 500 metres. We guessed it was around a five-minute walk through the bush.

Jake grabbed my arm before I had a chance to exit the car. "This is a walkie-talkie radio. You place this part in your ear no one else will be able to hear us and you clip the microphone on your shirt so when you talk I will hear you and you will hear me, get it?" Jake demonstrated. "This doesn't connect to the station so if you need help and I'm dead, then it'll be useless. If you get into trouble or manage to bring the girls back here, call SWAT from the car. Leave that fucker for me, you understand?"

I nodded and went to get out of the car, but Jake held me back again. "On second thoughts, if you do see the fucker, shoot him; don't hesitate." Before I had a chance to tell Jake I didn't have a gun, he handed me a black pistol, butt first. "It's a Glock. Holds 10 shots, just pull the trigger. It does the rest. It's exactly the same as the gun you used at the range. Now, I'll take the front. What I want you to do is just go to the back of the cabin. Stay well hidden. Tell me what you see. I want you to be my eyes from the back as I come in the front. That way I have less chance of getting ambushed," Jake said.

"Can you give me a cuff key please? In case I need to unlock the girls."

Jake handed over a key, which I placed in my right pants pocket. "Be careful, mate," I said.

We left the car simultaneously. Jake headed east while I headed south. Night hadn't fallen as yet; it was overcast and the sun was low in the sky. Even though it wasn't pitch black it was already getting dark and seeing ahead was becoming difficult. There were no street lights out here. Our torches were off to keep our presence hidden. The only lights we could see were from the cabin.

I turned once, to get a visual on Jake's location, but he was already gone. I headed further south past the cabin. I could see it on the horizon but I wanted to head towards it, through the bush, rather than straight at it from the road. "Make sure you keep an eye out for snakes here, Jake," I said into the walkie-talkie, but I felt as if I was talking to myself. The thought had only just entered my head when Jake responded, "Do you really think there would be snakes out here, mate? I fucking hate snakes."

"Just watch where you walk. You'll be fine. They go down their holes at night." I was trying to calm Jake's nerves. In hindsight, it would have been better if I hadn't opened my fat mouth at all.

My eyes took a little while to adjust to the dark. "Ok Jake, I'm 20 or 30 metres from the back door. The cabin looks like a double storey, with a big garage or cellar underneath. It has large double doors that lead out the back. There's a broad clearing beyond the house before you hit the state forest." In the clearing, I noticed a big oak tree. It didn't belong here, a sole oak where all the other trees were pines. That was when I remembered Esmeralda's dream. "Hey Jake, out the back there are a few old cars. I can't see any lights on downstairs, but it looks like someone is upstairs."

"Ok, thanks mate, I'm only metres from going in. There's a blue Commodore in the drive. I would guess it's Samantha's. Brodie, try and get a bit closer so that when I go in, you can look for the girls," Jake's voice crackled back.

"Sure thing," I replied, although I was not keen on going in without Jake.

I headed a little closer, hiding behind a clump of bushes and some heavy bracken. My heart rate, if not high already, increased significantly when I saw the cellar light come on. "He's in the cellar," I radioed through to Jake, who replied with, "I'm going in the front. You wait there for my call."

I moved a few steps closer, still under the cover of large trees, when I noticed a red glow flash in the cellar. 'What's he doing?' I wondered, and saw another red flash.

Chapter 73

Friday 14th November 2003 (7.52pm)

The red light in the cellar was triggered by a sensor at the front of the cabin. Mason now knew he had company. No doubt, the guests he had been expecting. He was prepared. He retrieved his two pistols, both with laser sightings. He then removed a pair of goggles from the workbench. "Now the real games begin. Say goodbye to your boyfriend," he said as he passed the cage in which Hayley lay bleeding.

With his goggles on, Mason flicked off the power to the cabin. Then he headed for one of several trapdoors he had specially created. This one led from the cellar to the first floor.

Mason could hear whoever was in the cabin stumbling around. Obviously, the person's eyes had not yet adjusted to the darkness. The person's steps were slow. Mason assumed whoever it was would have a torch and that was the reason for the delay in the movement. He also assumed that the person in his cabin was Jake. He doubted that Brodie would be in the house. It was more likely that he was on lookout duty.

Mason waited patiently for the footsteps to move past his head. Slowly he lifted the door, aimed at the leg and fired. Seconds later, he heard Jake—he assumed it was Jake—fall to the floor. It was a lot quicker than Mason had anticipated and he was scared he had overloaded the tranquiliser. He had wanted to bring him down quickly but he didn't want him dead, not yet anyway.

Mason opened the trapdoor again to see Jake sprawled out on the floor with his gun and torch a short distance from each hand. Mason could see him breathing so he was confident his plan was still on track.

Mason dropped back down to the cellar and fired his other pistol, twice. The shots rang through the cabin and out into the darkness.

Chapter 74

Friday 14th November 2003 (7.55pm)

The shots made me jump and for the first time, I was truly scared. "Jake, are you there?" I asked into the walkie-talkie, but there was only silence. "Jake," I tried again, "are you there?"

He had told me to go for help, to call for backup if everything went bad, but I couldn't leave him in there possibly dying. I had to go in. I got up slowly and then sprinted for the cellar doors.

I had my torch and my gun hand over fist, just as Jake had taught me. I gently pushed the door open with my left foot and slowly moved the torch around the cellar floor.

Immediately, the strong smell of death hit me. We were at the right house. As I moved the torch from each corner of the cellar to the other, I was more horrified with each sight. My heart was beating very fast now. I saw the jars sitting on the shelf proudly displayed, just as a child would display a basketball trophy in his room. Each jar contained the head of a missing policewoman, all in order, all labelled with names and dates. All were tagged, except the first.

I moved the torch to the second corner where I saw a rack with another headless, naked body. The head was sitting on the bench beside it, a hobby in progress.

My guess was that Jake had interrupted him. Where the hell was Jake? As I moved the torch around, I saw a cage. Hayley. I had found her. She was covered in blood and dirt, but she was alive. The cage had a padlock on it. I put my finger to my lips, and Hayley acknowledged my gesture by nodding.

I looked on the bench and only centimetres from the severed head were two silver keys on a small plain ring. I put the gun on the ground beside me, the torch in my mouth, and began to fumble around with the lock on the cage.

The killer was somewhere in the house, or, from the gunshots I'd heard, dead. I had heard no movement at all so I felt relatively safe. I was confident I would hear if anyone started moving around.

Then I heard a sound. It was like a door closing. I reached for my gun but before I could locate its metal handle, I felt the pain in my neck. My vision was going, my mouth was dry. I was slipping away. It took every bit of energy I had to keep my eyes open. I continued to feel around in the dirt for the gun. As I touched the metal butt, everything went black.

Chapter 75

Saturday 15th November 2003 (8.56am)

I awoke to a feeling of sickness, as if I was about to vomit. I went to sit up but my arms were chained.

Where was I?

My vision was still blurry but I could make out a figure in a doctor's outfit wearing a green surgical mask.

Then everything came flooding back. "How are you feeling, Brodie?" the deep voice behind the mask asked.

"Sick," I replied as the bile flowed up into my throat and then out of my mouth.

"I think I'll give you a few more hours to regain your senses. I want to make sure you feel every bit of what I have in store for you."

I vomited again. This time, I could feel it run down my neck.

This was like the nightmare I'd had, except now, it made sense to me. I wasn't in a surgery with a doctor, I was in a cellar with a madman. A man who was about to cut me up and pull out my heart.

"I will leave you to recuperate a little; give the effects of the tranquiliser a chance to wear off. Then I'll be back. I read that you have a heart condition and that you have undergone several operations. I will be back to have a firsthand look at what those doctors did to your heart. I even have a special jar for it."

Mason walked away from me and out of sight. I felt like I was going to vomit again at any moment.

I wanted to live. I had to get out of this somehow.

Chapter 76

Saturday 15th November (9.45am)

"Morning Jake, nice to see you're awake. You were out for quite a while. I can't stay long. I have to take care of your friend and then I have to spend some quality time with your woman. I'm sure you wouldn't want me to rush what I'm going to do to her. My only disappointment is that you won't be there to witness all the fun."

Jake was starting to feel like his normal self again, except that he was in deep trouble.

He was lying in what appeared to be a glass or Perspex box. He presumed the box was in the ground as all he could see out the sides of the box was dirt, the blue sky above, and a nice oak tree providing his feet with a little shade.

His hands were cuffed, not to each other but to either side of the Perspex box. Jake guessed he had only a few centimetres of slack on either side from his wrist to the side of the box. He could almost touch his hands together; his fingers met but he could not clasp them together. His feet were loose, no binding there. He could breathe quite easily, as there were hundreds of small holes in the Perspex top of the box.

Jake had begun to wonder, why had he put him in here. What was planned for him? Was it going to be a slow painful death by way of starvation? That was the only thing Jake could think of. Whatever he had in store had been well planned out, that was certain.

"You can't get out of there," Mason said as he lowered his face down to the top of the box. "You can squirm all you like, but that shit is solid. It won't break. I reinforced all the corners with steel and those handcuffs are police issue. Somehow, a lot of the women I picked up had them around the house."

"You fucker, I'll get you!" Jake screamed as he tried desperately to break the box with his feet, but he knew Mason was right. He couldn't break it.

Mason laughed as he watched Jake try to fight his way out.

"I asked myself, what would be the worst death imaginable. The answer I came up with was starvation. Having your stomach eat itself, chewing off your tongue for food. Lying there for days knowing no one was coming for you, knowing you are going to die and being unable to do anything about it. That would be horrible, wouldn't it, Jake?" Mason's face was almost touching the top of the box. "You've been a good cop so I thought you deserved better—a quick death, shall I say. So I have a choice for you to make. In this bag . . ." Mason placed a large hessian bag on the top of Jake's box, "is a big eastern brown snake listed as one of the world's deadliest. Now, what makes these snakes dangerous is they are very aggressive. If they were trapped in, say, a Perspex box where it's hot, they become more aggressive and might strike out. Actually, I am sure it will strike out. So the choice you have is to provoke it so it will strike you, causing you to die within an hour, or ignore it and prolong your death, in the unlikely hope that someone will stumble upon you before you starve to death."

Mason placed the bag into a small secondary box that adjoined the Perspex box containing Jake. Mason removed the bag and watched the snake slide into the box and down the clear tunnel that joined the two boxes. Once the snake was in the tunnel, Mason pushed down the piece of tin that blocked off the smaller box. The only place the snake could go now was into Jake's box.

"My money is on the snake," Mason said, laughing.

Mason walked back towards the cabin as if he didn't have a care in the world, as if he was a farmer going in for his supper.

Chapter 77

Saturday 15th November 2003 (10am)

"We have Stephen in ICU now," Hanam told Cassie. "His heart has given out, so we have him attached to what we call a mechanical heart. It's used mostly for heart attack victims to provide time for the victim's heart to recover. However, as you know, Stephen's heart will not recover because it's diseased. We're using it until we can find a donor heart. Unfortunately, we don't have long. Maybe two days at the most. The longer he's on the machine, the higher the risk of rejection if we do locate a donor heart." Hanam brushed his comb-over back into place. "All we can do now is pray we find a donor heart before the rest of his body gives up."

Cassie began to cry.

"The nurses will come to collect you when he is settled," Hanam said just before he left.

Cassie put her head in her hands. What was to become of her soul mate? They were young and in love, their lives were supposed to be full of fun, romance and excitement. Now, it was full of sadness and possible death. Even though she had known for months that this day would come, she had never really let herself believe it. Now it hit her hard.

It was a good couple of hours before the nurse came to collect Cassie. By that time, Stephen's mother had arrived. Shelley was in her mid-40s but looked far younger, and some people had mistaken them as sisters when they had been out together. They sat in the waiting room across from each other, waiting to be shown into the ICU. They both knew what the other was going through but had no idea what to say. They sat in silence, each hoping the other would start the conversation.

When Cassie set foot in the ICU, she almost fainted at the sight of Stephen. It looked as though he was hooked up to every machine ever invented.

"Now don't panic about the machines," the nurse said reassuringly, "let me explain. It might help ease your fears. Stephen is hooked up to a normal blood pressure machine. This is the sats machine, which tells us how much oxygen is in his blood. That is the mechanical heart. It's the noisy one." She pointed to the machine in the corner.

"Finally, the tubes are the oxygen: just to help take the pressure off his lungs. We'll be with him here in ICU all the time. We never leave the room. We check on him at 15-minute intervals. Have a seat next to him. Try and relax. He'll probably come around soon. He will be groggy but I am sure he would love to hear your voices."

Cassie sat down, looking from Stephen to Shelley. "He's going to need both of us to get through this."

Shelley looked up with tears in her eyes and nodded.

Chapter 78

Saturday 15th November 2003 (10.05am)

I was lying on the trolley in the cold damp cellar, which smelt of blood and death. My vision had cleared and my vomiting had ceased. I was cuffed to what felt like an old hospital trolley. One hand was cuffed to each side rail and my legs were strapped to the sides, as if I was in a mental hospital. I kept thinking about the nightmare I'd had that night, the one that had made me call Esmeralda to discuss it. I remembered the mask and those piercing eyes. I also remembered the one thing in the dream that I hadn't been able to work out: the silver handcuff key in my pocket. Esmeralda had told me that day to keep a spare and thankfully, I'd remembered to ask Jake for it. Now, I hoped I could reach it.

I moved my body slowly over towards my right hand. I could only reach the tip of my fingers inside the pocket. Searching, I could feel the key but I couldn't get hold of it to grab it. I pulled as hard as I could on the cuff to try and gain those few extra centimetres. The cuff dug into my skin. It felt as if there was blood running down my wrist, but there wasn't enough time to check. He would be back soon.

I pushed hard again, one last go at the key, then I had it, balanced delicately between my pointer finger and index finger. I placed it on the trolley where I could pick it up in a more useful grip by holding the key between my forefinger and thumb. I managed to slide it into the lock of the cuff that was attached to the rail. I could see the blood running from my wrist. Now how to turn it? I knew I had to be careful. If I fumbled and it fell to the floor, my fate was sealed. The fate of the three of us was sealed. If the key didn't turn, it was the same deal.

I moved my thumb and forefinger, stretched out as far as I could, and tried to turn the key, but there was not enough give. I only had one option. I put my hand outside the rail. If I dropped the key now it would hit the floor and be out of reach for good. Unable to see the lock, I moved my hand around, feeling for the keyhole in the cuff. There, it was in. Now to pray for it to turn.

Click! The sweetest sound I had ever heard. My right hand was free, now for the left. I pulled my hand back inside the trolley. The tip of the open cuff clipped the rail of the trolley. Then it happened. It dropped. I had dropped the key with only one hand free.

There I was on the trolley, with my left hand cuffed, my right hand free, with half an open cuff dangling from my wrist and the key to freedom on the floor. There was no way I could reach the key with my left hand still cuffed to the bed.

On my left, my gun sat on the bench close to Samantha's severed head, but several metres away from me. I stood up with my left hand still cuffed to the bed and pulled on the trolley. The brakes were on. I could not reach the brake release pedal at the end of the bed. I had no other choice but to try to move the trolley with the brakes on.

I pulled, using all my weight. The trolley began to move. The wheels didn't turn, they just dragged in the dirt of the cellar floor. I had managed to move the bed a few metres before I began to feel fatigued. I was worried I wouldn't be able to move it much further and there was no way I would be able to move it back. Just a few more metres in order to reach the gun. I took a deep breath, gathered myself and pulled. I could touch the bench but not far enough to reach the gun.

If Mason were to walk in now it would all be over. Suddenly, I heard laughing outside, not far away but not too close either. I had to hurry.

I held onto the bench and pulled with all my strength.

Finally, the cold metal of the revolver touched my fingertips and soon, the gun was safely resting in my palm.

Over the bench, I could finally see inside the cage that held Hayley. I had not called out to her for fear of Mason hearing voices and returning. I could see she was still breathing but her eyes were closed and the pool of blood had increased. My guess was the loss of blood had decreased her blood pressure and she was possibly unconscious. I didn't know how much time she had left.

Still with the fear of getting caught, I gathered all my remaining strength and pushed for as hard and as long as I could. I managed to get the trolley back to its original position. My chest was sore, I could hardly breathe, and I needed to slow my heavy breathing down quickly.

I lay back on the trolley, breathing deeply, trying to return my heart rate to normal.

I hadn't worked out yet how to kill him. Should I shoot him as soon as he walked into the cellar? If I fired at the door from here, it would mean I would need to hit him from 10 metres away. I had only been to the range with Jake twice. That wasn't enough training for me to be sure I would hit him from that distance.

If I missed, I had to hope he wasn't carrying any weapons. I knew I was not likely to win a gun battle, half cuffed to the bed, from where I had no cover. I needed a better plan.

Then I heard footsteps on the loose gravel.

I needed that plan now.

Chapter 79

Saturday 15th November (10.05am)

All that occupied Jake's mind now was how he could kill a two-metre brown snake without getting bitten. The snake had hardly moved. It lay coiled up in the outlet tube just centimetres away from his feet. 'If I'm calm and quiet, it will just sit there, surely,' Jake thought. 'Why would it come up here if I don't move?'

Then he realised it would only be a matter of time before the snake became too hot in the Perspex box. Then what would it do? It would look for shade or water. Jake answered himself, but what shade was there? His pants leg? he answered himself again. Fuck, what then? How long would it be until the snake sought refuge up his trouser leg?

As it turned out, it was only ten more seconds before the snake began searching the air with its tongue and then it began to move. Jake was sure it was looking for escape inside his trouser leg.

Except it didn't.

It crawled along the floor and side of the Perspex box as close to the cool soil as possible. It headed straight for Jake's head. 'What if it senses my breathing, smells my breath? What if it wants to drink the saliva from my mouth?' With these thoughts, Jake closed his mouth and pushed his lips together.

He didn't know a lot about snakes but he knew a few things: if it felt fear or felt it was in danger, it would strike. If you stepped on it, it would bite.

Again, with its tongue leading the way, it made its way further up Jake's body, looking for food, shade or water. Jake wasn't sure which.

In the short time Jake had, he had devised a plan. It wasn't a great plan. Hell, it wasn't even a good plan, but it was the only chance he had. It was simple. Once the snake reached his hand, he would try to grab it around the neck and snap it before the snake had a chance to move into an attack position.

The snake climbed up Jake's left arm and across his face. Jake closed his eyes and held his breath. He could feel the head of the snake on his right shoulder. It began to move down his right arm.

Jake opened his eyes to see the head of the snake cross his elbow. He had trouble seeing its head fully as the body was still moving across the bridge of his nose.

Jake slowly opened his right palm. He was poised ready to strike and he guessed the snake would be too.

He had never touched a snake before this. The skin was different to what he'd expected; it wasn't as slimy as he had imagined, or as scaly.

Jake could feel the sweat drip down his brow. Surely the snake could feel Jake's nerves vibrating through his body.

Jake glanced at the snake again. His moment of truth had arrived. Only one question remained. Was he quicker than a brown snake?

Chapter 80

Saturday 15th November (10.10am)

The gun was hidden and at the ready, with the safety off.

"Good to see you awake. I wanted to tell you how much I respected you, before you meet your demise," Mason said, as he approached the trolley I was chained to.

"You know, I'm surprised that such a smart man got caught by such a novice," I said, trying to provoke Mason, "'cos I mean, this is my first case. Sure, you have the upper hand now but really it must worry you that I managed to catch you." I hoped to provoke him into losing his focus.

"You really shouldn't take credit for other people's work. If I'm not mistaken, it was me who actually sent you the evidence, so you could find me. So I wouldn't flatter yourself if I were you, Brodie."

Mason ripped open my shirt, causing the buttons to fly everywhere.

My plan wasn't working yet so I had to do something soon. Something that would rattle him. Something that would send him over the edge. "Do you know what surprises me, Mason?" Without waiting for the answer, I continued, "With all six girls . . ." I said, purposely reducing the number of his victims.

He snapped. "It was nine I killed, nine of those bitches, and once I'm done here with you, I'll start on her," he looked over at Hayley, "and then I'm going looking for my next one. No one can stop me." He sounded triumphant but his rage was increasing. My plan was beginning to work.

"Ok, nine, I stand corrected. It makes my point worse really. Out of those nine, how come you never got it right? How come it was never the way you wanted it? I didn't think you could fuck it up nine times!"

"Fuck it up? I'll fuck you up in a minute. I think you're forgetting where you are and the predicament you're in, Brodie. I never fucked it up. They were all perfect." Mason was beginning to move around, forgetting his task, which I was glad of because his task was me.

"You say they were all perfect, except we both know that's not true. That's why you had to keep going. They were never perfect. They will never be perfect because the person you really want to kill is already dead."

"You don't know me; don't pretend you do." He was starting to show his anger.

"The one person on this planet who should have protected you, didn't, and yet she's still fine. Why isn't her head in a jar?"

He knew I was talking about his mum.

I was getting to him. His face was becoming redder. The veins in his neck were bulging. Now that I had found the button, it was time to push it.

Chapter 81

Jake took a deep breath and grabbed as fast as he could. The snake reared and struck. Jake only felt a small scratch but he knew immediately that it had got him. He had to keep going. The last thing he needed was to get bitten again and to have an angry live snake in his box with him. Jake managed to pinch the snake's neck between his thumb and forefinger. Then he wrapped the chain attached to his wrist and the side of the Perspex box around the snake's head and jaw. He had the snake trapped. He increased the pressure with his thumb and forefinger and then pulled on the chain. He pulled harder. Snap! Something had broken. Blood began flowing from the snake's neck. Jake was hoping the extended pressure of the chain had done enough.

He'd lost count how many times he'd pulled the chain but when the snake's head finally fell off and landed on his leg, he guessed it was safe to let go of the headless serpent.

He lifted his head and saw what only looked like a scratch on his hand. But he knew it was serious, even though he could not feel anything yet. The effects would take hold of his body soon.

Now that the snake was out of the way, Jake turned his attention to getting out of the box. He tried to keep thoughts of being buried alive away. He knew that as long as Brodie was alive, there was hope that he would get out.

"Think positive thoughts, stay still, think positive thoughts, you're going to be all right, you're going to be all right," Jake kept repeating to himself.

The box had hinges secured by screws, and the handcuff chains were screwed to a metal plate on the box, so Jake was not going to bust them off anytime soon.

Jake looked around the box to try and find a solution to his problem, when he noticed next to his decapitated serpent friend a crack in the Perspex. It had been caused by pulling on the chain to strangle the snake. It was only a small crack, but it gave him the idea that he could perhaps crack the Perspex around the hinge.

However, Jake knew that if he started bashing the hell out of the Perspex, the venom from the brown snake would travel though his bloodstream faster.

He didn't know a lot about it, but he knew that a lot of movement and exertion would increase his heart rate and that would only expedite the effect of the venom.

Chapter 82

"**D**on't tell me your mum didn't know what your dad was doing to you!" I shouted, pushing the boundaries hard. "She knew he'd abused your brothers before you and yet she did nothing about it. She did nothing to protect you either. Don't you think she noticed the man lying beside her kept leaving in the middle of the night? Of course she did! But she left you to deal with the problem. She ignored you, left you all alone in the dark with that monster."

"Don't you ever say my mum was to blame!" Mason said furiously. "She tried her best to protect us. Dad was scum."

His rage was growing but not enough. I needed him to fly off the handle. I wanted him going nuts. I knew I wouldn't be able to distract him when he was focused on cutting me to pieces, so I turned up the anger dial. "Your dad didn't make you into this monster. You're not killing these girls because your dad molested you. You're killing these girls because you're exactly like your dad. Your dad liked seeing you beg, just like you enjoy watching the girls beg. You're just like him except worse."

Then he started to lose it, giving me the distraction I needed.

"I'm nothing like him! Nothing . . ." he began to mutter, clearly losing his focus. Then he picked up the scalpel, still muttering, and jammed it down into my shoulder. The piercing pain was excruciating but I did my best not to show him any weakness. My mind and my mouth were not in sync and I let out a thunderous scream to make him think I was at his mercy.

"I am nothing like my father, you understand?" Mason said, as he twisted the blade embedded in my shoulder.

He stared at me squarely in the eyes. He was truly rattled, and I knew that now was my only chance. I purposely looked behind Mason and then shouted, "Run Hayley! Run!"

She was still in her cage but I knew that Mason would turn and check. He did, and I had only a split second but it was all I needed. By the time Mason swung back to face me, I had already fired the first shot and before I even realised, I had pulled the trigger again. The first hit Mason on the side of his head just above his left cheekbone, while the second hit him just above the right eye, as his head recoiled from the first hit.

By the time he hit the floor, he was dead.

It was time to go and find Jake. By God, I hoped he was alive tied up somewhere waiting for Mason to return. I put the barrel of the Glock to the keyhole of the left handcuff that I couldn't unlock and fired my third shot. Metal flew everywhere and the cuff spun open.

I stepped over Mason's corpse. Blood had pooled around his head and turned the dusty floor into a mess of bloody mud. I went over to Hayley's cage and fired another shot into her lock, then opened her door. Tears were rolling down her face as she crawled out of the cage. I held her up but she couldn't walk. She sat outside the cage, her head facing Samantha's headless body.

"Don't look," I said, helping her up the stairs out of the dark cellar and into the bright sunlight. It took a minute or two before our eyes adjusted. I sat Hayley down on a nearby log, "Are you all right?" I asked, kneeling next to her on a soft patch of grass. "I'm going to look for Jake."

"I'll be fine," Hayley answered.

I looked at her wound and while there was a lot of blood, it wasn't as bad as I'd first thought. I took her socks off her feet and tied them both around the wound. "Keep pressure on it. I'll be back."

She continued to wipe the tears away. "Go and find Jake," she said.

I headed up the front stairs to the door of the cabin, praying I wouldn't find Jake dead on the floor.

Chapter 83

Saturday 15th November (10.32am)

Jake had been pulling on the cuff and then slamming his fist against the cracked Perspex, for what seemed like an eternity. It had hardly made a difference.

He felt sick and had a thumping headache. He didn't think he had much longer. If he was to live, he had to get out of there, and fast!

Vomit was making its way up his throat, and then he could no longer keep it down. By now, he guessed he had performed about 30 hard pulls on the handcuff. Then it suddenly cracked. Jake pulled again and the hinge and surrounding Perspex fell inwards.

Jake vomited again and his vision blurred. He was sure his time was running out.

He began kicking the end of the box but he had no more strength and had to stop. He vomited for a third time but this time his vomit was white and foamy. His eyes began to close. He was losing the fight. He couldn't go on, the venom had taken hold quicker than he'd thought. He had to rest for a moment.

His eyes closed again.

Chapter 84

Saturday 15th November 2003 (10.35am)

I had been through the laundry and the kitchen and had seen no sign of Jake. I entered the lounge and saw a few drops of blood. It looked fresh. I was hoping it didn't belong to Jake.

As I was kneeling there, a tree moving in the wind caught my attention out of the corner of my eye. Then it was as if Esmeralda was speaking to me directly. "An old oak in a forest full of pines." I remembered now that I'd seen it when Jake was about to go into the house. I ran to the kitchen window to get a better look and saw the big old oak tree in the middle of a paddock.

Esmeralda had been right: about the jogger, Mason and the key. She had to be right about this.

The oak was only 300 or 400 metres away but by the time I got there, I was stuffed. My heart felt as if it was going to seize up or explode. I could hardly breathe. I couldn't see anything at the base of the oak. Where the hell was he? Maybe Esmeralda was wrong. What if he was buried? What if he had been buried since yesterday? If so, surely his oxygen supply would have run out by now.

I double-checked around the trunk of the oak. Had I missed it?

Nothing!

Exhausted, I slumped down against the trunk and looked towards the thick forest at the bottom of the gully.

I decided to head for the car and call for backup.

I got to my knees. Then a reflection caught my eye. A refection of glass or steel. Whatever it was, it didn't belong out here. I ran, despite the fact that I thought running was no longer an option.

It was a simple Perspex coffin. Jake lay lifeless inside with vomit all over his shirt and chin. He looked like a ghost. I had never seen him so helpless and vulnerable. I called Jake's name several times and then saw the snake.

Without hesitating, I removed the gun from the holster, fired at the latches on the coffin and lifted the lid. I was ready to unload a few rounds into the snake before I realised it was headless. It was then I realised the vomit was the after-effects of a snake bite. Jake was too heavy for me to move. I had to get the doctors to him, fast, and the only communication for help was located

800 metres away in the police car. I leaned down and felt his pulse. It was very weak.

I knew we were running out of time, but I had no choice. Still puffing from my previous exertions, I began the run across the field towards the car. I wasn't even halfway and I thought I was going to collapse. My heart was pounding, it hurt badly, and my lungs and legs were burning. I had to keep going. It might already be too late but I had to do my best. I continued without even slowing and soon I was amongst the thick bush leading to the rear of the cabin. The bracken brushed my legs and whipped against my ankles. I felt a sharp pain in my left ankle. I had stepped on a stick and half of it had flicked up and stabbed me. It was not enough to slow me down. By the time I got to the car, my heart had gone into palpitations and I was struggling to remain conscious. I knew that the palpitations could cause my blood pressure to drop and make me collapse. I lay across the driver's seat, clasped the handset and radioed in for help.

I was guessing my heart was going about 200 beats per minute. There was no way that I could walk back to Jake in this condition. I had to drive. I didn't care if I wrecked the car, I had to get back and help him.

I decided to drive around the front of the house and head down the side of the cabin to where the big old oak stood.

"We are sending in the helicopter," I heard the voice on dispatch say. "Can you tell us what type of snake it was, Brodie?"

I picked up the radio receiver. "It looked like a brown," I replied.

"They have the anti-venom on board. They'll be there soon, Brodie."

I pulled the car to a halt just in front of the oak.

The car tyres slid in the mud as they struggled to grip the soil. My heart was still palpitating. I held my breath, trying to slow my breathing down.

It was to no avail.

I fell out of the vehicle and moved fast towards Jake. I placed my two fingers on the side of Jake's neck near his jugular. His pulse was present, weaker than before, but still there nonetheless. "Jake!" I called again, but there was still no response.

My palpitations began to thud and thump, thud, thump, thud, thump, hard against my chest. Every beat felt as if it was going to be my heart's last. I was starting to struggle. I headed back to the car to grab some water. I took the water and tipped some over my face. The rest was for Jake.

Hayley was limping her way over, and by the time I had finished wetting Jake's lips and washing his face, she was standing over him. She too checked his pulse. I could tell by her body language that he was still alive.

"The air ambulance is on its way, Hayley, all we can do now is wait," I told her. She took Jake's hand and sat on the dirt with his hand clasped in hers.

"Give him some more water," I said, tapping the bottle on her shoulder. She poured some over his lips and a little over his forehead, trying to cool him down. She took a sip herself and handed the bottle back to me.

"Are you all right? You're very pale."

I explained that I had palpitations but reassured her I was fine. Hayley knew palpitations were not to be taken lightly.

Chapter 85

Saturday 15th November 2003 (10.51am)

It was only 12 minutes before the helicopter appeared overhead and within another minute, it had landed safely.

Both Hayley and I waved the ambulance officers over to Jake. They were no sooner at his side than they had him hooked up to an intravenous drip. As I lay on the grass close to unconsciousness, I could hear the ambo medic tell Hayley the drip was full of saline and anti-venom.

"Hopefully he'll be all right. The next few hours will be crucial. He's lucky to be such a big guy. It really gave him more time."

Unmarked police cars pulled up around Jake's car. One of the ambulance officers approached me about the same time as some of the local cops. Even though I was sprawled out on the ground, I pulled out my badge and instructed the local cops not to go anywhere near the house or the cellar.

The ambulance officer wanted to take me to Melbourne to treat the palpitations. He was a nice enough sort of guy, mid 50s, fit and caring.

"I'm not going anywhere."

"We have to get you to hospital, mate, you can't do anything in this state."

"Give me some verapamil and then I can get in there and sort out the crime scene. I have to make sure everything is done right. So stop stuffing around and give me some verapamil to get rid of these palpitations."

He looked at me. "Ok, lie in the back of the ambulance and I'll give you some verapamil but if they don't stop with that, I can't leave you here like this, ok?"

I nodded. I knew I wouldn't be able to do my job in this condition anyway.

He helped me onto the stretcher and drew the verapamil into a 10-ml syringe. He removed my shirt to connect the ECG. He noticed the stab wound from Mason's scalpel. "We'll get these palpitations under control and then sort that cut out." He started attaching the leads for the heart monitor. My heart rate jumped around, 188, 194, 191. It was all over the shop. Brian injected the first mil through the cannula in my wrist. It was one mil per minute and after 10 mils, they would stop and then take me to hospital for more drastic treatment, including an anaesthetic and then shocking my heart back into a normal rhythm. I was lucky. Up until now, it had never come to that. The verapamil had always worked.

We were up to the fifth mil when I told Brian the palpitations had gone. He looked up at the screen and watched as my heart rate dropped from 192 to 123 to 88 and now 74, which was an unusual rate, but normal for me.

Every time my heart dropped that suddenly, the initial feeling was it had stopped altogether. While the verapamil had done its job, it would take me a while to feel completely right again. But for now, I was right to do my job and finish this mess.

The ambo removed the cannula and again asked if I wanted him to look at my shoulder, but I politely waved him away.

David was being flown in to search and examine the grim finds.

The scene soon became very cluttered. There were patrols arriving from Yea and Seymour, even from as far as Shepparton. From what I knew, the Melbourne taskforce was on the helicopter with David. The chief had rung me and told me very clearly that I was the only one permitted to enter the crime scene until he and David arrived.

I closed off the whole cellar until David and the chief arrived. It wasn't the crime scene that interested me. I needed to know what had made this guy tick. Mason had told me it was revenge against Samantha for killing his father, when he'd wanted to take his own revenge for what his father had done to him when he was younger, but to me that was just his excuse. He killed because it excited him. He liked the control he had over the women and well as the sexual gratification after their deaths.

The cabin was two hours from city headquarters by car but only 20 minutes by helicopter. The chief and his entourage didn't take long to arrive.

My thoughts went back to Jake who was now on his way to Alfred Hospital. More than anything, I wanted to be with him but I also knew that he would want me here to finish this. Anyway, Hayley had gone with him. I would be there soon to see him. He would be all right. Somehow, I just knew it.

"You all right?" the chief asked as he offered his hand to help me up. I nodded in acceptance. I couldn't be bothered with a lot of talking, I was so tired.

"You did a fantastic job, but you should have told us what you were doing."

Again, I nodded. He was right. We should have called for backup. Nothing like hindsight. "Lead the way, Detective," he said, motioning towards the cellar doors. I couldn't believe it. He had called me 'Detective'. Maybe the fact that we had solved the case had made me one of them. Maybe now I would be accepted.

Chapter 86

Saturday 15th November 2003 (11am)

I opened the doors to the cellar, flashed my torch around a few times. It caught Mason slumped in a pool of his own blood at the bottom of the trolley, where he had put me, ready to cut me to pieces.

Slowly, we all entered. The medical officers began taking photos. Flashes kept going off. I saw one of David's team picking up my bullet casings with tweezers. It was like being in a CSI show. It felt surreal.

David left his team to join me. We stood motionless, saying nothing for a while. I think we both had the same thought going through our heads. What type of person would do this? The victims' heads were displayed on a shelf in large round jars. They were all there, all labelled. It was the second time I had seen them.

I knew for sure that the first girl who'd gone missing was one of his victims. With no body, there had been doubts. Obviously, there had been a reason he hadn't dumped her body; not that we'd ever find out.

"Just think the world is a better place because of you. He can no longer kill. You stopped him." David put his arm around me. "Just think how many girls you saved. He would have never stopped."

The crime scene guys had finished taking their photos of Mason and Samantha, and their bodies were bagged. My gun was taken into evidence. I was told I would have to make a full statement to internal affairs, but not to worry. The coroner came in and removed both bodies, placing them into separate vans and taking them to Melbourne for further examination.

The magnitude of what Mason had done finally hit me. It was a torture chamber. I was sure he'd visited the cabin frequently between killings. It was the place he came to remember. Relive his past glories. Relive the murder and the torture and most likely masturbated to the memories of his victims. He would have found it sexually gratifying. I was sure he did a lot of reliving until the memories faded, thus igniting the need to kill again. The wall contained what seemed like all the newspaper articles ever published about him. He obviously enjoyed being the hunted as well as the hunter. The shelf that held the heads of his victims also held plastic lunch boxes that contained the personal effects of each girl. Some had just a few items of jewellery;

others had wallets and keys as well. One had a whole bag of items. I continued to look at the wall while the crime scene guys photographed everything. There were dates listed on the wall and next to each date were names.

What took a lot of my attention was an article about Lance. His photo had been marked with a red circle. As we'd expected, Mason hadn't liked someone else taking his limelight.

I had seen this all before at Quantico. It was nothing new to me. A killer's shrine was common amongst serial killers. I had all the answers I needed.

The sunlight that shone on my face as I walked out of that cellar was the best feeling I had ever had. The sadness was still heavy in my heart for the victims, but the fact that I knew no one else would suffer at his hands made me happy. Now, it was time for me to check on Jake.

I was helped into the back of the ambulance and we asked the driver to radio the hospital to find out how Jake was doing. He agreed and we headed off to the same hospital.

As we started moving away, with the movement of the ambulance swaying me from side to side, I suddenly felt tears roll down my face. Yet I had no idea why they'd come.

Chapter 87

Saturday 15th November (11.30am)

Cassie ran to Stephen's side.

"They've found you a new heart! You're going to get your operation, baby. You're going to get your new heart!"

Hanam strolled through the door with a slight smile, adjusting his comb-over before he spoke. "Well, Stephen, your new heart is on the way. Do you want me to go over the operation again before theatre, or are you comfortable with what I've already told you?"

"I'm fine. I just didn't expect it to happen so soon."

"We never know how long it will take. Some take months; some never happen. The lucky ones have it happen when they need it."

Cassie began to cry.

"You're lucky because you're still healthy enough to cope with the operation. Had it been much longer, you might have been too weak to survive the operation. I'm sure everything will go very well. Don't worry, ok?"

Stephen looked at Cassie and she smiled. "You're going to be fine, baby. I'll be here waiting for you. It'll all be over soon and then we can get on with our lives together." She kissed him on the lips. It was a sweet and lingering kiss, one that made Stephen happy, even if it would be his last.

Cassie tried not to cry any more, but it got the better of her and it was Stephen's turn to comfort her.

"Hey baby, I'll be ok. Don't cry, I'll see you soon. This is a good thing for me. It's a great thing for us. I love you. See you when I wake up."

Stephen looked across from Cassie to his mother. "We'll be here, darling," his mum said, grabbing his hand.

"We have to take him in now," the orderly said. "We'll take good care of him."

Cassie and Shelley both gave Stephen a kiss on the cheek and Cassie finished with one on the lips, surpassing the previous one.

He waved to them as he was pushed through the double doors to the operating theatre.

Cassie and Shelley were now well out of sight and Stephen was on his own. As they wheeled him along the corridor under the flickering fluoro lights, the possibility that there would be no tomorrow filled him with fear.

The surgeon had explained that this heart operation was risky. Stephen knew that but he simply had no other choice. Die now or next week.

Stephen turned his head from the fluoro lights above him to the pale green walls of the corridor.

The orderly's eyes were focused straight ahead. Having done this hundreds of times before, he was calm and collected. He reminded Stephen of a prison warden, walking the prisoners to their death. It made Stephen wonder if what he was feeling was similar to how prisoners felt on their final walk down the green mile. Full of panic and nerves, and helplessness.

"We're here. We're just going to move you onto the table now, Stephen," a voice behind the green mask said. "One, two, three," the voice counted, as they slid Stephen from the bed onto the table, using the sheet to help.

"Stephen, we're just going to put this anaesthetic into your IV now." This was a new voice and a different set of eyes. They were very kind. "I have the anaesthetic here. I'll let you know when we're ready to use it and I'll get you to count back from 10, ok?" he said, as he tapped Stephen on the shoulder.

Stephen nodded, looking into his kind eyes.

"Ok, we're going to put you to sleep now; everything will be fine. We'll see you soon. Stephen, start counting back from 10 now, slow, deep breaths." Stephen began to realise what the prisoners on death row must feel like. Seven . . . six . . . but before he could say another number, a mask was placed over his face and he slipped into darkness.

Chapter 88

Saturday 15th November 2003 (1.45pm)

When I arrived at the hospital a few hours later, my body had recuperated a little and I was feeling a lot better. My emotions, on the other hand, were still all over the place.

They took me in to see Jake. He was sleeping when I went in. His parents were already there at his bedside. He had a drip in his left hand. He looked a lot better than when I'd seen him last.

Jake's mum came over and gave me a hug and an update. He was recovering well, the anti-venom had started to take effect and no major tissue damage had been done. He was a lucky boy. Had he not been so solid, the doctors suggested he wouldn't have survived the bite.

His parents were about to leave. I told them that I would stay with Jake until he woke up.

His mum left after giving her son a kiss on the cheek.

My heart palpitations always brought on an appetite. Maybe it was because my body thought it had run a marathon or driven a Formula 1 GP. Whatever the reason, I was bloody hungry and needed a nice cup of tea as well, so I headed for the cafe while Jake slept. I was hoping he wouldn't wake up while I was downstairs.

I picked up some food for the two of us. I put Jake's food next to him on the dining tray at the end of his bed. Jake was still sound asleep and hadn't even moved. I sat back, grabbed my chicken roll and began to read the paper.

I tried to relax and not think about what had happened to both of us today and how close I had come to being dismembered by Mason. Keeping the thoughts away was almost impossible in the end. I closed the paper, leaned over to Jake and said, "We've got him, mate, you, me and Hayley are all ok. He's dead. I killed him!"

"Good job, Bruce," Jake responded in his half-asleep half-drugged state. He rolled over and went back to sleep. With that said, I knew he was going to be all right.

I pulled the second visitor's chair over for my feet, laid my jacket over my chest and tried to sleep too.

Chapter 89

Wednesday 21st January 2004 (9.00am)

Stephen had recovered well from his transplant. The anti-rejection drugs seemed to be working. He was now only required to visit outpatients for a biopsy every six weeks, providing everything remained stable.

Stephen was enjoying being able to shower independently again and the scar down the front of his chest, the zipper as he called it, was almost fully healed. The scar was still a little raw and he had to be very careful in the sun, but it was free of scabs and he no longer needed to use Betadine.

He couldn't believe that he felt so well. He had never felt this alive. Yet at the back of his mind, he felt different and he had no idea why. Everything about him seemed different since the operation.

He didn't like some of the foods he'd previously liked, he no longer felt the same attraction towards Cassie that he'd had before. He found her a little too chubby for his liking now. He couldn't work out why this was so.

He had even started to have horrible dreams, or were they memories? He couldn't tell, but he had them often.

He kept seeing women he didn't know, dying. He kept seeing places he had never been to.

A cabin was the most frequent image that flashed up in his head.

Stephen shook the dreams from his mind and tried to focus on the positives, how strong and well he felt. His breathing was easy, and his skin had become a normal colour without the blue tinge of before the operation.

Stephen dried himself off and stood in front of the steamed-up mirror. He wiped away enough of the steam so that he could see his face and chest. He leaned forward and stared intently at his reflection.

"Who are you?" he asked. Without thinking or forethought, he wrote one word in the steam, a word he didn't understand, a person he didn't know.

Mason

THE WAITING ROOM

JASPER WOLF

THREE MISSING CHILDREN IS JUST THE BEGINNING.

THE WAITING ROOM

"Every child deserves a hero; some just need one more than others."

~ Jasper Wolf

Dedicated to Clint Anderson
A True Friend and the Real Jake Miller

PART ONE

The Missing

Chapter 1

Shevd had watched the cop run from the tunnel, carrying one of the girls, all hero-like.

Soon he would want to return to the thick of the action. Soon he would want to go back in. Soon he would hear the sound of the gun, and before he could react he would be dead.

Shevd hadn't taken his eye from his scope in minutes. He wanted to see the cop's face when he killed him. All he had to do was wait for him to reappear.

His breathing was steady, his eye focused on the target, his finger relaxed and ready. Even in the heavy rain, he found him. The cop's shoe was sticking out from the base of the tree. He had placed the girl out of danger. Now, Shevd just needed to wait for him to run.

It reminded him of when he was shooting deer as a kid in the Ukraine. "Be quiet and patient," his father would say, "the deer will hear the slightest noise." The deer never knew it was about to be killed. It would be at a stream drinking and then the shot would echo through the forest, but before the deer could react to the sound, it would fall to the ground.

The cop was as helpless as the deer.

I'll get you, Shevd thought.

* * *

The storm had ramped up and it was raining so hard, it felt like hail. I was struggling to see more than a few metres in front of me. The girl bounced in my arms as I ran. We made it to the forest edge and I was hit by the smell of forest freshness and rain. The air was fragrant with the smell of pine trees. Christmas would be here soon, I thought.

The large pine provided Chloe with plenty of cover from the storm. I untied her and covered her with my jacket. "You will be safe here," I said.

She sat silently, curled up into a ball.

In the distance I could hear not only gunfire, but voices, loud voices, yelling. There were more children here somewhere, but how many perpetrators were left? The only thing we knew for sure was that we had found the spider's web I looked at the base of the tree. They were hell-bent on getting out of here. They were not planning on giving up. There was no jail for them. They knew it was death for them if they couldn't escape.

"Mikayla, you need to go back for Mikayla," Chloe said, quivering with the cold.

I knew there were more kids and I had to go back. I couldn't leave Jake. I had to go back. I had to do my job. I had to help. I would never forgive myself if something happened to Mikayla or Jake.

The thought of the tunnels terrified me, the smell of death; it was the cabin all over again, the fear of the unknown and the darkness, the fear of death. I pushed the fear aside and took a deep breath to steady myself. The smell of the pines once again made its presence felt. It was a beautiful smell and I took in as much oxygen as possible ready for the sprint to the tunnels.

I darted out from the tree. I had taken three steps before an ear-piercing crack echoed through the night.

Chapter 2

Two Weeks Earlier

Stevie Bradley was sound asleep and dreaming about Ellie Davis. She had thanked him for picking up the books she had dropped on the way home. He stood close as he handed them to her. Her hair smelt like peaches and her skin smelt of perfume, one he didn't know but that he would recognise again in an instant. Her hand touched his, her skin soft and delicate. She leaned forward into him. His heart skipped a beat, her lips pressed against his and they were soft and a little wet. It was an amazing kiss. Until he was woken by his father. "Get up and get ready for school. You're going to have to walk, your mum has a migraine. I can give you a lift but I'm leaving in 15 minutes." Stevie, who still had Ellie Davis on his mind, didn't really want to be rushed this morning so he decided it would be best if he walked.

The sun was streaming in through his bedroom window so he figured it was a nice day outside. By the time he headed out the door for school it was 8.15. It usually only took him 15 minutes if he cut through the reserve at the end of the cul-de-sac. If he walked around it took an extra 10 minutes.

Stevie was right, it was a beautiful day. The sun was strong and his shadow was long as it walked beside him. He trudged along without a care in the world, hoping his dream would become a reality. His backpack, full of books and his lunch, was slung over his shoulders, and his drink bottle was sitting snug in the side mesh pocket of his bag. He bounced his basketball between his hands, occasionally crossing it over between his legs and then behind his back; he was good at it, he had not missed a step.

Stevie was so busy playing with the ball that he didn't notice the van pass him as he entered the reserve. He continued his dribble on the path up through the park, now doing figure-eights as he walked. He had begun to sweat a little. Walking up the hill dribbling was tougher than he expected. As he reached the top of the park, he placed the ball down and removed his backpack to reach his drink. He placed his bag on the path beside him and the ball rolled to rest against his bag.

Stevie bent down to place his bottle back in his bag when the white van mounted the kerb in front of him. Before Stevie realised what was happening, a man in a joker's mask was upon him. His large arms wrapped around him, pulling him into the van.

Stevie screamed.

His scream was quickly silenced by one of the man's hands smothering his mouth. With one arm free, he felt above for the man's head, trying to locate one of his eyes. All he could find was the loose plastic of the mask. He felt higher. He could hear the van door opening; he was being dragged in. He had little time left before he would be inside it. He pushed his thumb hard on what he thought were his eyes. The man made no noise even though Stevie thought he must be in pain. He heard the man step inside the van. He could see the inside of the van now, only his legs remained on the outside.

Stevie reached for the side of the door with his free hand but it slid straight off. The man was too strong. Less than a second later, he was inside the van and the door was being closed. Before he could say anything, tape went across his mouth and a bag was over his head. Something tightened around his neck.

"If you make a sound I'll fucking kill you, do you understand?"

Stevie nodded. He heard a door at the rear open and close again and then seconds later another door at the front opened.

It had only been a few moments and then they began moving. Stevie sat in the darkness swaying with the movement of the van.

He lost track of how long they had been in traffic but guessed about an hour, he couldn't be sure. The van had stopped many times during his trip, Stevie assumed for sets of traffic lights. The radio was switched off soon after the van started up.

He felt the van make another turn, this one slower, then the van came to a stop. The door at the front opened but he could still hear the motor running. Again the door shut and the van moved forward slowly.

As the van stopped and the motor cut, Stevie could hear loud metal banging, followed by what sounded like locks.

"Out!" the voice called. Stevie felt the bag tighten around his neck and he was pulled to the left.

He felt a hand pinch the back of his neck. He was pushed forward six or seven paces. "Stop," the voice said as the rope pulled him back slightly. "Sit down." Stevie did as he was told. The ground was full of loose stones. "Move forward on your butt until you feel the edge," the voice commanded. Again he did as he was told, moving forward by dragging his butt along the ground. His feet fell into emptiness. "Stop," the voice called.

"Now, you'll need to drop down off the edge, it's not far, you'll be ok."

Stevie sat for a moment. Was he dropping into his own grave? he wondered. Where the hell was he?

Tears began to flow.

Before he could muster the courage to drop, he felt a hard push in the middle of his back.

For a brief moment he was falling, then he stopped suddenly. His ankle rolled and his shoulder hit the ground. He heard a girl scream, then what sounded like someone walking down metal steps.

His hood was removed. His eyes took some time to adjust but when they did he saw the worst thing he had ever seen. Several cells with a path between them leading to a red door. He could see two other children, both of them with their heads down, crouched in the back of their cells.

A hand spun him around. "You scream, you die right here."

Stevie nodded and his tape was ripped off without warning.

Despite the fact that the man was wearing a joker's mask, Stevie could tell he was balding, and big, over six foot. He was podgy. What little Stevie could see of his mouth revealed yellow teeth. The sides of his face and hands were very grubby and it looked as if he hadn't showered recently. It definitely smelt that way.

He was wearing stained tracksuit pants and an old torn flannelette shirt.

The fat, dirty, balding man threw him into a cell on the same side as the girl but there was an empty cell between them. The other boy was on the other side.

The man removed the rope from his neck, and closed the door to the cell behind him.

He stood on the other side of the bars looking him up and down. "They're going to love you," he said as he headed towards the ladder. "Remember, no talking. If you talk, there will be punishments."

He left, climbing the ladder, closing the lid behind him. Stevie's cell went into complete darkness. He could hear movement above and then music. Suddenly the lights went on and he could see again.

Chapter 3

"What's your name?" Stevie asked the girl who was two cells down from him. She looked about a year younger than he was. "Chloe," she answered from her dusty, dark cell.

"Where are we?" Stevie asked. Chloe shrugged her shoulders as if to say, I have no idea.

The boy opposite them put his finger to his lips. "Shhh, he will hear you," he whispered.

Stevie looked around: there had to be a way out. He counted six cells the same as his.

The bars went from the concrete floor to the concrete celling. Each cell had a light attached to a beam that ran above the middle of every cell. In between the two rows of cells was a simple gravel path. It led from the trapdoor to a bright red door that stood like a beacon at the end of the cells.

On the floor of his cell lay a dirty old mattress and a blanket. There was a bowl of water but no food. In the opposite corner was a bucket. He hoped this wasn't his toilet.

The other boy was in the cell at the end of the path on the opposite side.

Stevie could see him but the lack of light made it hard to see all his features. From what he could make out, Stevie was at least a couple of years older than the boy, maybe a little more. The boy had sandy blonde hair and looked fairly athletic for his age. Probably a football player, he thought.

The girl looked young and thin. She was still in her school uniform.

The boy looked familiar; maybe they went to the same school, although he couldn't quite place him. He was in normal clothes but they were worn and dirty.

"What's your name? How long have you been here?" he asked the boy.

"Shhh," he said again. "He will hear you. You don't want him mad." The boy did not answer either of Stevie's questions.

"His name is Scott," Chloe whispered, ignoring the plea for silence.

"Please stop talking, he will come if we make noise," Scott said as quietly as he could.

That was when Stevie recognised him. It wasn't school. It was on the news. He had been missing for over six weeks. Scott Western was sitting opposite him and he was still alive.

Then he looked at Chloe and remembered her too but he couldn't think of her surname. They had both been on the news. Scott had been taken on his way to school.

Chloe had been taken on her way to school. Just like he had.

Before he could tell Chloe and Scott that their families were still looking for them, music blasted from above them and all the lights glowed.

Scott instantly shuffled to the back of his cell and curled up. Stevie turned towards Chloe; she had shuffled back as well.

The trapdoor remained shut.

False alarm, Stevie thought.

Chapter 4

What had the world become?

It was a question that I found harder to answer since the Slayer case. Even though it had been over 10 years since Mason Belic had been placed into the ground, my mind often returned to the events within that dark cabin.

I wondered what reason he would have given for doing what he did. Was there ever a reason or had it just been a sick and twisted fantasy? It was something I would never really know.

Was there more violence in today's world? Maybe crims just received more media exposure these days. Either way, there didn't seem to be any shortage of evil amongst us.

Currently, I had three case files under my review and the days of my private practice were long gone. I was now a fulltime detective. I was given the cases no one could solve.

The first kidnapping was a 10-year-old boy in Sunbury, Scott Western. On his way to school he had vanished and only his bike and bag were found in the gutter. Missing now six weeks. No leads. Nothing to go on.

The second one was a 12-year-old missing girl, Chloe Henderson. She had been walking to school in Boronia and had simply vanished. Missing now two weeks. No leads. Nothing to go on.

Even though these cases were miles apart geographically, they were eerily similar in detail. Both children vanished out of thin air, no witnesses.

Then just two days ago, it happened again. An 11-year-old boy, Stevie Bradley, same MO, was walking to school, never made it. The only item recovered was a basketball lying in the gutter. He had simply vanished.

I was to provide a report on the possibility of the same offender.

Considering it was a different geographical location, two boys, one girl, it was highly unlikely to be the same person. Usually killers prefer a gender, and once they choose one, they stick to it.

Unlikely but not impossible.

My final case I considered cold. It was 16 years old now and bordering on the impossible. Three street workers had disappeared off the streets and all had been found murdered. All three had been posed provocatively, their wrists tied and their legs spread, on the banks of the Maribyrnong River.

All three had worked the streets of St Kilda. I was sure these cases were related, I just wasn't sure why they had stopped. Serial killers usually didn't stop of their own accord. In the late 1990s, the tabloids had been in a frenzy of fear, labelling him the 'Night Stalker'.

Maybe he was dead? Maybe he had moved?

My thoughts wandered back to the children.

Nothing was worse than a missing child. Except three missing children.

After the Mason Belic case, Jake had been physically ok. However, mentally he had been a mess. I suppose being buried alive in box with a snake will do that to you. He had been required to undergo counselling, as had I. Jake wasn't the type of person who would easily open up. He was very reserved at the best of times.

His girlfriend Hayley was given permission by the department to receive counselling from the same psychologist. The joint sessions were of benefit to them both. After six months of therapy, they stopped the sessions and everything seemed normal.

Until a few weeks ago anyway, then Jake started seeing Salma again.

Something was haunting Jake, I just didn't know what.

My sessions always helped me. I had no problem discussing the events from that day. It was the flashbacks and the smells that still haunted me. Usually they came to me in my sleep. Some nights, I would wake up and I could smell the death in that cellar as if I was there again.

Salma George was the psychologist of choice for Victoria Police and all its employees. She was a great psychologist, full of empathy and insightfulness, which only the good ones had. I had known Salma reasonably well before my own sessions began. She and I had taken some of the same classes and had sought each other's counsel on matters from time to time.

Her career had gone from strength to strength and she now also held the position of head of psychiatry at North View treatment centre for the mentally ill. Salma was the type of woman who interested me. Not only on a physical level, as she was very attractive, but also as a woman who surpassed me intellectually. She had seen what evil had done to both sides of the law, the victims and the police. It was a rare perspective and one I admired more every time I saw her. Or was it Salma I was admiring more and more?

Chapter 5

Major General Austin Campbell had been in the SAS Second Commando Unit for over eight years, the last five being spent in high-end intelligence operations in Afghanistan. For the last two years, he had been in charge of the Second Commando regiment. Their creed was 'Foras Admonitio', 'without warning'.

He had done everything in his career, from rooftop sniper, to search and clear scout and finally regiment commander. His tour was over and he was ready to live his life. He had a wife, Sarah, and a daughter, Mikayla, who were at home waiting for him.

He had not seen them in six months and he missed them terribly. Soon, he would be back in Australia and able to hold them both tight. The plane was due to land in Melbourne in just over two hours. The RAAF plane had landed earlier in the Western Australian Army Barracks and the debrief and final sign-off on his latest tour, complete with the Medal of Gallantry, had taken just over four hours. The prime minister had formally presented the medal as part of the Anzac commemorations.

He sat patiently waiting for the plane to reach its destination.

He was in his civilian clothes and his new life had started. He doubted he would ever go back, although his motto had always been 'never say never'. He sat amused by the goings-on of the civilian passengers. In the aisle opposite, a businessman was requesting to be moved from the two children seated next to him. The hostess politely told the gentleman, for at least the second time that Austin had heard, that the plane was full and there were no spare seats.

"Beverage sir?" the hostess asked. The drinks trolley bumped his elbow on the way through. "Just a water, thanks," Austin replied. She passed him a chilled plastic bottle of Mount Franklin water and held out her hand, "That's $4," she said, smiling. Austin would have to get used to this again, paying for food and drinks that were normally provided to him free of charge. He reached in his pocket and clasped a note. It was a fiver, more than enough to cover the charge.

Despite his thirst, Austin sipped his water. It had become a habit not to guzzle it down. After all, he had been trained to survive on very little.

Less than on a 600-ml bottle of water, that was for sure.

The plane bumped and jostled around as it hit a pocket of turbulence and the fasten seatbelt sign flashed on, followed by the accompanying announcement.

Austin tried to relax. He would love nothing more than to close his eyes and have sleep take him. But sleep was hard for him. It had become increasingly harder as his time in Afghanistan had lengthened.

When he did sleep, the nightmares tagged along. They often involved an accident in war, usually resulting in his own death. Then he would startle awake, usually finding himself drenched in sweat. Lately, the dream had involved him clearing a house in the small town of Musa Qala. Every time he entered the third home, he forgot to check the corner. He would turn around just in time to see the AK-47 begin firing at him.

There was nothing he could do.

He died every time.

Well, he assumed he had, but he always awoke before he knew for sure.

With the muttered chatter of the passengers, Austin did sleep and for the first time in a very long time, there were no dreams at all.

He woke when he heard the pilot announce, "We are beginning our descent into Melbourne, local time is 9.25 pm. It's a balmy 22 degrees outside. On behalf of Virgin we would like to thank you for flying with us today."

The plane began its slow descent. The cabin crew checked the overhead compartments and made sure the passengers were buckled in correctly. A few minutes later, the announcement came for the cabin crew to be seated for landing.

The landing was smooth and almost bump free. The plane taxied to the terminal and came to a halt. The seatbelt sign flashed off with a 'ping'. People scrambled for their overhead luggage and almost fought for the door.

Austin had no reason to rush. Sure, he wanted to meet his family who were awaiting his arrival in the airport, but he had waited six months and a few minutes more wouldn't kill him. The aisle cleared and Austin stood up, removing his backpack from the overhead. As he stood, he had to stoop to get his large frame out of the seat.

The air was fresh and the sun was shining brightly, if not strongly, and the Melbourne sky was clear of cloud. Spring was in the air.

* * *

Inside the terminal, Sarah sat with Mikayla on her lap. Mikayla was busy playing on her mum's phone. Subway Surfers was all the rage; nothing kept an 11-year-old occupied like an iPhone. Her pink dress was new and free of food stains; this was a personal best achievement considering she had been wearing it for over four hours. Her blonde hair was tied back in a ponytail with a pink ribbon.

Sarah was not the type to do herself up, but this morning she had taken a little extra care in her presentation. Shaved a few areas that had become unkempt, added a little extra makeup, put on her good jewellery and her special perfume, the one she saved for special occasions.

Chapter 6

Look at you, you're a disgrace. You really disgust me."

Beau Delacroix made no response to his mother's outburst. It was just another episode of her nagging at him. At 33, he was well and truly used to it.

"Is that what you're going to do all day, sit on your fat arse watching TV eating leftovers?" Again, Beau ignored her ranting, but inside he was starting to hurt. He tried to fix his attention on the cartoons on the TV in front of him.

"You've been out for almost eight months and what do you have to show for it? You don't even have a proper job."

"I have two jobs," Beau replied, not looking away from the Tom and Jerry cartoon.

"You can't count them as proper jobs. One is a part-time handyman and the other is a shit-kicker for a signwriting place."

Annabelle stood leaning against the wall waiting for her son to reply. She removed a cigarette from its packet, even though the one in her mouth still had a couple of drags left in it.

"It's hard to get a job when you've been inside, Mum. I-I-I a-a-am d-do-do . . ." His stutter started up as it always did when he was nervous or worried.

"Don't you start that stuttering with me. Maybe you should have thought of that when you were robbing those houses. Maybe if you did something with yourself and made yourself look respectable, you would have a girlfriend. You wouldn't be getting your jollies trying to abduct kids from a playground." She lit the cigarette with the butt of her old one and then discarded the old butt in the fire. Her face was wrinkled, not from age but from smoking. Her fingers were yellow, her teeth discoloured, her hair grey and in need of a colour.

Beau stood up out of the recliner and faced his mother.

"What? You stand up to your mother, do you want to hit me?" Annabelle said as she blew smoke into his face.

Even though Beau was six foot and solid, Annabelle knew she was in control.

"You wouldn't want to have a go at me, I'd knock your block off."

Beau took a step back. "I'm going to the shed," he said.

His mother stepped in front of the doorway that separated the lounge from the kitchen. "What you do you do in there all the time?"

"Fix the vans, practise my painting and play with my trains," he replied, hoping she would let him pass.

She didn't; she had more to say.

"You not doing any drugs in there? Not doing anything you shouldn't be?"

"No, just trying to keep busy."

"Make sure it stays that way, you go back inside you ain't coming back here!" It was the only sentence she spoke without a smoke in her mouth. "When you're done in there, be a good boy and go up and get our Thursday night fish and chips for dinner," she said. "Get me the usual."

Annabelle's usual consisted of two potato cakes, chips, flake, and two steamed dim sims.

Beau nodded in agreement. Annabelle let him pass.

Beau hitched up his tracksuit pants and grabbed the hoodie hanging on the back of a kitchen chair as he passed. He put the hoodie on and raised the hood to cover his head that was now balding. His wispy hair not only knocked his confidence, it made him look way older than he was. Beau's family wasn't rich; in fact, they were downright poor. His dad had died in a car accident when he was young. He had no memories of him at all. His mother had raised him on her own. The only thing his mum owned was an old weatherboard house.

The house stood on an acre of land and had originally been a farmhouse. Now it was on the edge of suburbia. High-voltage powerlines ran across the rear of the property, which was in need of repair.

His mum lived on disability benefits from the back injury sustained in the car accident that had claimed his father's life. Any spare money usually went on ciggies and alcohol and medicine for her back. If money was tight, it was usually the medicine that missed out.

The shed sat directly under the powerlines, and Beau liked it that way. It was away from everyone including his mum. It was big enough to work on six cars, still with room to use the work bench. Even though he had two vans, neither of them were being repaired. It just gave him a reason to get away from his mum. He had other hobbies that he preferred to work on.

The train set was laid out on a two-metre by one-metre piece of chipboard. It was complete with mountains, bridges and stations, trees and little people. The landscape had several settings, one a country town with a coal mine and sawmill. The other end of the set was a more suburban setting that included Walthers Cornerstone Merchant's Row opposite the station. Next was an ice-cream stand. His most prized locomotive was a rare Pennsylvanian Mantua steam engine. It made his coal mine complete.

The train set ran the length of the garage and took up the far right wall. Although it didn't look like it, it could be moved. The vans were on the far left. Against the far back wall sat a long tool bench. On it his computer was especially set up for WOW. It was the only online game he liked.

Under the bench was a set of drawers with the usual workshop tools, spare batteries for his mouse and everyday junk.

Beau loved his trains, but what was underneath them was his real interest.

* * *

Tyler Parsons had only done three break-ins before he had been caught. His stint in the big house was the first, and it was a real eye-opener. He had gone in a petty thief and come out ready for real crime, with the connections and knowledge about how to profit from his ventures.

He had been out exactly four days, and tonight he would put his new skills to the test. No longer was he going to steal TVs and DVD players to sell at Cash Converters.

Tonight was his first big job; well, scouting for it at least.

He was going in to the high end of town. He was after the expensive jewellery, not costume jewellery.

He had been given the name. His instructions were simple. He was to call a number, ask for a Mr Lee, then a private number would call him back with an address. He was to take any jewellery to the address for exchange.

No other instructions were given. The rest he would have to find out for himself.

While in jail, he had also been given what they called 'the word'. It was a simple code that reset all ADS security systems. He was told the code was legit. Unfortunately, there was only one way to find out.

Home owners thought they were enhancing their crime prevention when they stuck the ADS stickers on their windows. In fact, it was the exact opposite. Now that he had the code, the stickers told him which homes he could target.

He knew he had to double-check everything in daylight, before committing himself to the job. On the inside, he had been given an address that was supposedly an easy target. Apparently they were well off and the husband was away overseas. He was an army officer. Only a mum and a daughter were at home. Word in the joint was the safe in the house held valuable jewellery and cash. They even gave him the location of the safe—in the walk-in robe of the master bedroom.

Tyler parked his Mitsubishi Lancer five houses down from the target. His dog sat panting on the back seat. Tyler thought he had bought a Staffy;

however, it turned out he had got something completely different, more likely a boxer. While it wasn't what he had wanted, he loved it anyway.

He had named him Rocky after the movie.

Tyler took Rocky from the back seat and hooked the leash to his choker collar. His plan was to walk him up and down the street a few times. No one ever took notice of a person walking a dog; it was the least suspicious thing someone could do.

He reached his target and even though he was on the opposite side of the street, he could see enough. The home was set back on a large block protected by a brick and wrought-iron fence, and electric gates. The home was large, two-storey, brick, with an upstairs balcony and a tiled roof. It was nice. The right side had a three-car garage, while the left had a gate that led to the back yard and perhaps a pool. The view to the back yard was hidden by two large trees each side of the gate. Rocky was sniffing around the opposite owner's front nature strip, doing his business as he pleased.

Tyler walked on. He would walk up the street for at least 10 houses and then cross the road and come back to have a closer look the second time round.

Rocky was enjoying the walk as usual. To him it was just another fence, just another bush. Just a different scent.

On the second run, Tyler got a better look at the property. He noticed a camera on the gate and one on each corner of the roof, another at the front door. He assumed there were also cameras out the back of the property. He noticed that there was no camera on the balcony.

He had seen enough; he knew his way in. His plan was coming together.

His pay day would soon be here.

Chapter 7

Beau had finished his fish and chips, yet his mother was still nagging at him. Lighting her third cigarette since finishing her meal.

"Louise called for you while you were up the shop, she wanted to know why you hadn't paid her the money this month?"

"Why do you still talk to her? She has nothing to do with us anymore. She divorced me, remember."

"She was too good for you, that was the problem. I knew you would never keep a girl like her." Ignoring his mother, Beau stood up from the table, washed his plate and placed it in the dish rack beside the sink.

"She cheated on me, Mum, and she divorced me. Now I'm stuck somehow, paying for her car."

"I know she cheated on you. Had you done a better job of satisfying her, she wouldn't have gone looking for sausage somewhere else. If you didn't turn into a stuttering mess every time you went out together, she might have been more inclined to stick around."

"I can't help my stutter, it didn't help me that you teased me when I was at school," Beau replied, standing in the doorway ready to end the conversation with his mother simply by heading back to his shed.

"I was only joking around with your friends, trying to make them feel comfortable."

"Is that like walking around the house in next to nothing when I had friends over?"

"Oh, you're being dramatic, Beau. Is it hard for you to believe I was just being friendly and if the occasional friend of yours found me attractive, who was I to argue with a teenage boy?"

Beau simply ignored this comment and headed outside, as he should have done a minute earlier.

He entered the shed and bolted the door behind him. He pulled on the handle to double-check it was locked. All secure, he thought.

Beau removed the red ladder from the wall and leaned it against the bench. He went over to his train set and walked around to the inside corner. He pulled the lever and the train table moved sideways. To the naked eye, moving the train set looked impossible and that was exactly how Beau had wanted it. The set was designed in a box shape, just over a metre high from the floor.

Below the train set was a mat, just a typical indoor thin carpet mat. When the train set was lengthwise, the mat was hidden.

Beau lifted the mat, folding it over itself. He unlocked the four padlocks that held the sunken wooden hatch. The concrete floor had been cut to allow for a door to be installed.

He placed the ladder down the hole and began his descent.

Beau unlocked Chloe's cell and walked in. Chloe was sitting as far away as she possibly could. As the man came towards her, she tried to shuffle back, but there was nowhere to go. He grabbed her by the hair. She began to scream and cry, "Let me go, please, let me go!"

"Q-q-q-q-quiet," he responded.

Chloe tried to keep as quiet as she could. She was aware of Scott's warning. She wasn't the smartest girl in her grade but she was close. She had noticed three things since the man had come down the ladder.

1. The door which he came down was still open.
2. The keys were still in her cell lock.
3. He had a stutter.

The man smelt worse than before. He held her by the throat. His hand felt greasy and his breath stank of onion and garlic.

He grabbed her by the hair with his other hand, leaving the keys in the door and the trapdoor open. He shuffled her towards the red door at the end of the corridor.

He turned the handle. There was no lock on this door. He released her hair momentarily and flicked a switch on the inside wall.

Chloe looked at the room and immediately her heart sank. She could see a bed with cuffs coming from the two rails that ran horizontally between the two end posts. On the concrete wall above the bed was a cross. It wasn't just a plain cross. It was one with 'Jesus' on it.

The balding, mask-wearing man with sweat patches under his arms and stinky breath threw her onto the bed. Chloe thought she knew what was going to happen to her, but at 12 she could not understand the gravity of the situation.

The bald masked man spoke, but not to her. He was speaking to the wall or the Jesus that hung on it.

"Forgive me," he said. He touched his forehead and then his crotch and crossed his chest. Chloe had not seen that before but she knew it was some sort of prayer.

He closed the door, bolting it behind him. He moved towards her. She thought about moving, but where would she go? Before she knew it, her hands were cuffed. He sat on top of her and removed her top and pants. Chloe couldn't move, he was so heavy.

His plump face came closer to hers, the breath was stronger, it was disgusting.

Panic set in. She lay there looking at the Jesus through her tears and wondered where was God now. What sort of God created monsters like this?

Her fears were worse than what she was actually going to endure. Just as he had removed her clothes, he pulled a phone from his pocket. He dialled a number. He waited only a short time before he spoke. "Father, I have what you asked for. Do you want me to send you a pic as per normal?"

He paused as he listened to the person on the other end. "Yes, she is undamaged." Pause again. "It's too soon." Another pause. "Yes, I understand. Ok, I'll see what I can find. Has delivery been arranged for M10?" Beau questioned. "I can't keep him much longer, he's been here too long already." Pause. "Ok, but by next weekend I will need to deliver him," he agreed. "I also found an M11 two days ago. Do you want him?" Pause. "Yes, I can send it tonight." Pause. "Yes, I can find another, why does he want two of them?" he answered the person on the phone. "No, don't tell him I w-w-w-won't. I-I-I-I will get the other one soon, week and a half tops." Pause. "Maybe I could deliver one of the goods on Saturday night and part two next Saturday when I deliver you your outstanding order? That might keep him happy? At least he'll have something to play with for the week." Pause. "Well, I'll deliver part two directly to him on the same night," Beau said, getting frustrated at the sudden extra demands.

He now had four deliveries in two weeks. Two to the 'Priest' and two to the 'Ukrainian Monster'.

Chloe had no idea who he was speaking with, maybe his dad? But before she could continue her thought, his phone flashed. Her photo had been taken; she was just in her undies and nothing else. Who was he sending the photo to? she wondered. Who would want to see her in her undies?

"Why did you take my photo?" she asked.

"For your ransom. Once your parents pay, you will go home."

Chloe didn't know why, but for some reason she didn't entirely believe his answer.

Chapter 8

Father Peter O'Riley had run the Saint Alexius home for children for over 40 years. It was set on 12 acres, just outside the town of Learmonth, 40 minutes north-west of Ballarat. The home consisted of 60 squares of residence. The St Therese wing housed the girls, while the boys stayed in the St Sabinus wing.

There were also an additional two wings that were specially equipped for the Wards of the State. These were troubled children, often abused, raised amongst drugs, prostitution and crime. They were what Father Peter O'Riley referred to as 'damaged'.

Capacity was set at 20 children per wing. There were another 10 per wing for the Wards of the State children.

In the grounds were two grass tennis courts and a separate indoor pool and of course the church itself. Attached to the church was his sacristy and three confessional booths.

As well as running the home for children, Father O'Riley offered Sunday services and confessional for the community. His parish consisted of many of the townspeople and local residents, including a magistrate of the county court, a police senior superintendent, teachers and general members of the community.

He had been preparing for his final rounds for the evening to ensure all the children were in their rooms, ready for lights out, when his mobile rang. It wasn't his normal mobile either, it was what he referred to as his personal phone. It was one that he had bought off the Internet. It had a sim card that was assigned to no one and the phone IMEI could be changed at a whim. In other words, the number could change and in effect, become a ghost phone.

He knew what the call was, even before he answered. His latest order had been fulfilled. He had several clients who had requested specific requirements. These requirements came with a premium price tag of $50,000. Money was cash only, hand delivered at the drop.

"Yes," the Priest answered.

"I'm going to have to send the buyer for the M10 a reminder, a nudge shall we say," the caller said.

The Priest paused.

"Holding him one more week won't kill you. Next weekend, I'll take delivery. I'll have it sorted by then," the Priest said. "Is the product still undamaged?" he asked. "Good, my son," he said when the caller replied.

"Yes, my son," he answered the caller's question. "I never pass up a free M11. Can you send him tonight?" Pause. "Send the conformation pic of F11. And I need you to fill another order. I need another F10-11 white." This was code for female aged 10-11 Caucasian.

"You should never ask why when it comes to the Monster. Do you want me to tell him you can't deliver?" the Priest asked. "Deliver the one you have this weekend. I will tell him the second one will be delivered next weekend. Once you have the second part of the order, text me conformation immediately. I don't want to go getting the Monster angry. He'll be anxious for his delivery." He added, "Meet the Batman at the normal delivery spot." In answer to his question, the Priest said, "No, my son, you will need to deliver both the F11s directly to the Monster himself, you know where to go," he said, and then reminded him, "be there this Saturday night. I'll let M know to expect you."

Moments later, a pic arrived on his phone. It was exactly what the Monster had ordered. However, it was the wrong gender to excite him.

The Priest's ghost phone had only two numbers: one was his supplier's and the other was titled UM.

He selected the picture on the phone and sent it via message to the only other number in his phone.

He then unlocked the glass doors located in the middle of his bookshelf. The bookshelf sat directly behind his desk. He removed a box from the middle of the shelf. To the left of the box was his Bible. To the right was his red stole, folded neatly so the tassels at each end met.

He opened the box. It was a black carrying case made of hardwood with blue velvet interior and black Rexene exterior.

Inside, the communion set included:

The gold cross he wore on Sundays and in the confessional.
The gold chalice he used at Sunday services.
Two candle holders.
Two glass cruets.
One paten.
One pix.
One purificator.

Except for the glass cruets, all the items were gold, and both the cross and the chalice featured ruby stones. The cross had one large stone in the middle, while the chalice had several stones around the lip.

Under the velvet interior was another ghost phone.

He had several more hidden within his office and around his sacristy.

He removed the phone from the box, and sent the photo in a message to the number for 'UM': *F11 x 2 50ea*. He used code to record all his clients, and then also recorded their details in a journal hidden under his mattress. In the subject line he stated, *first part ready for delivery.*

He never named them via text even though he knew them all. Anonymity was best for everyone concerned. Everybody except for himself. He recorded as much detail of the deliveries as he could in his journal. If his empire ever came crashing down, he would bring everyone down with him. The journal was his insurance.

Along with the two letters at the beginning, he sometimes used numbers, e.g. 'J8' meant John 8 to identify the person. In this case, 'UM' stood for the man who was known as the Ukrainian Monster, a man the Priest had never met and never wanted to meet.

The Ukrainian Monster was the only client who made his own rules and while he didn't consider him his boss, he knew he would always do as the Monster asked.

According to the underworld, the Ukrainian Monster was not called by that alias because of what he did to his collectables. It was because of what he did to those who threatened his control, his way of life or his seat at the head of the table.

F11 was the order, yet in this case, it meant two of them. Fifty was the cost: $50,000 each had been agreed to be paid upon delivery.

The phone vibrated. *That's only half of what I ordered. You have 14 days. New price 40 each.*

Agreed, the Priest replied, *delivery direct Saturday night.*

Last chance, was the response from UM.

Beau would have to take a cut in his share. Father O'Riley knew this might cause an issue but he also knew how to best control any such problem.

Anytime Beau wanted to renegotiate or argue with him, he only needed to say, "I will have to ask the Monster and see what he says." That comment always ended the negotiation, always with the same response from Beau. "No, it's ok, I'll let it slide this time," as if trying to convince himself and others that he was in control.

Father O'Riley removed another phone from his bottom drawer. This had several numbers in it, all clients who had placed orders for children. He scrolled down and pressed enter. When he came to C9, he wrote the following message.

Payment overdue. Final date set for next Saturday night. Confirm payment

His phone vibrated.

Can't make payment will need to cancel, the client replied.

Father O'Riley replied, *Unacceptable*

Father O'Riley deleted both messages from both phones and placed them back in their hiding spots.

A threat was necessary. No one backed out of a deal, but that would have to wait for now. It was time to prepare for evening service and then the evening rounds.

It was his favourite time of day. In just a few hours, it would be a great day.

Chapter 9

Sarah Campbell was still sitting in the arrivals terminal waiting for her husband to arrive. Although it had only been six months, it felt like years. Her daughter Mikayla sat next to her, having switched from Subway Surfers to Candy Crush.

Sarah had sat patiently for almost an hour. She was now hoping the time would pass faster than normal. With nothing else to do, she couldn't help but notice the different types of people who visited the airport.

Across from her sat a pretty young businesswoman, dressed in a dark blue pants suit, busy checking her emails on her phone. Probably sent to pick up an interstate business colleague of some sort, Sarah thought.

A few seats down sat an odd looking man, who looked like he was stuck in the 80s. He was dressed in denim, head to toe, his jeans so tight they looked as if they would need to be cut off. His hair was long at the sides and back and spiky on top. He was a cross between Elvis and Mick Jagger. Every time Sarah glanced over, he would smile and give her a wink. She thought, sleaze-ball, and shuddered inside.

She looked away from Denim Elvis and noticed a younger woman sitting to her right. She was naturally beautiful. She looked all of 22 and was done up to the hilt. Sarah thought maybe she was meeting a mystery man from interstate, most likely from one of those Internet dating sites.

Sarah noticed she was missing one of her hoop earrings. She leaned over towards her. "Excuse me, I think you've lost an earring." She pointed to the girl's left ear. The young girl reached for the right ear, and corrected herself when she saw Sarah pointing to the other side.

She reached at her ear with her other hand and felt around for a hoop that wasn't there. She then stood up, looking at her seat and the floor, hoping it had dropped somewhere nearby. There was no luck. It was gone, and she could have lost it anywhere in the airport.

Sarah noticed she spent the next 10 or 15 minutes looking for it, before finally giving up the search.

"You waiting for someone special?" the young woman asked Sarah.

"My husband, he's been away on business," Sarah replied. She had stopped saying he was in the army three tours ago. One time a lady had asked her the same question and when she said he was coming home from Afghanistan, the lady said, "Oh, I see." She might as well have said, "Oh, waiting for a baby killer, are you?"

Now she always replied he was away on business. She was proud of what her husband did and always would be, but answering that way was likely to cause a lot less confrontation.

She looked at her watch: 9.25 pm. Then she looked at her daughter, who was starting to get tired. It was late for her to be up. The arrivals screen to her right flickered and the status of VA116 from Darwin changed to 'landed'. Sarah's view of the screen was interrupted by Denim Elvis. "Excuse me, Mam, I couldn't help but notice you kept looking in my direction. Thought maybe I could buy you a drink, how does that sound?"

A little taken aback by Denim Elvis' forwardness, Sarah responded, "I am sorry, I didn't mean to look at you, I was deep in thought and wasn't really looking at anything."

But Denim Elvis was a persistent one. "Sometimes the eyes see what the mind wants." He winked again. "Now how about that drink?"

"I am sorry, I am waiting for my husband, he is in the Special Forces just coming back from Afghanistan. I see his plane has landed so he should be coming out any minute," Sarah said, looking at the gate and the adjoining bridge.

"I beg your pardon, Mam, I didn't realise." Denim Elvis turned and returned to his seat.

Maybe telling people her husband was in the Special Forces had its benefits after all.

The first two passengers made their way out of the gate. Both were plump older ladies who looked very similar, possibly sisters. They were greeted by a younger woman with three small children. The children were introduced as if they hadn't met the ladies before.

A few businessmen followed the ladies, most busy switching on their phones.

Still no sign of her man.

Then there he was, towering over the other passengers, with a big smile on his face stretching from ear to ear. He looked more muscular than the last time she had seen him. Maybe it was her memory or maybe he had become bigger. Either way, she liked it.

It was an emotional reunion; she cried almost the instant he picked her up and hugged her. His smell was amazing. They kissed lingeringly but not passionately.

Mikayla hugged her dad around the leg. He placed his wife down and picked up his girl, the one he called his princess. She was beautiful. He had noticed she had lost a front tooth, but she was gorgeous nonetheless.

Mikayla fell asleep in the car on the way home.

While she slept, they caught up on what had been happening around the house. What had been happening at Mikayla's school. All the gossip that normal mums have. The one topic they never touched on was the war. She knew he wouldn't tell her and she didn't really want to know.

They arrived home and waited for the electric gate to open and allow them through. The gate shut automatically behind them. They parked in the garage and headed inside.

The one thing Austin loved to do was carry Mikayla to bed. It was one of the best memories he had as a child. Nothing beat being carried to bed by your parents.

He placed her in her bed, switched the lamp on and just sat there staring at her. He wondered if she had done what they had promised each other before he had left for his tour. They had agreed they would both stare at the stars whenever they missed each other.

He had spent many a night looking up at the stars and thinking of his princess. How he loved her!

Tonight, he wouldn't have to look at the stars. She was right here in front of him asleep, with not a worry in the world.

He had been there 15 minutes when Sarah came in. "You ok, babe?" she asked, standing there in her nightgown.

"Fine," he replied.

"You want to come to bed?" she asked as she took his hand.

He could see her nipples through her nightie. He took her hand and followed her to the bedroom. As was often the case, absence had made the heart grow fonder.

Not only had he missed her, he had missed being with her. She took off her clothes and began kissing him. She unbuttoned his shirt as she sat on his lap. There was a new scar; she touched it, and kissed him again. She thought about asking about it, and then thought better of it.

Her hair smelt beautiful; it was a smell he had tried to hold onto while he was in the desert. The memory of her only lasted a week, maybe two, and by the second month, he could no longer visualise her naked.

Her skin was soft and smelt of musk. He wanted this moment to last forever. They reacquainted themselves with each other several times that night. Each time was longer and more enjoyable than the preceding one.

Chapter 10

Since I'd joined the detectives' team, I'd been promoted from a cubicle to an office. Jake sat on the edge of my desk, fresh coffee in one hand, chocolate doughnut in the other.

He had brought me a hot chocolate and a chocolate doughnut. I sipped the hot chocolate. It burnt my tongue and a little of my bottom lip. "Ow," I moaned.

"Careful, Brucey, it might be hot," he said sarcastically.

I smiled.

"So what did you want to discuss?" Jake mumbled with a mouthful of doughnut.

"I have concerns about these cases. Something doesn't seem right, something isn't adding up."

"Run it by me, mate. What are the issues you're having?"

"Ok, Scott Western, aged 10, riding his bike to school, never made it there. Local residents found his bag and bike lying on the footpath. Gone. Vanished."

"Yeah, kidnapping," Jake added, as if to say, what's unusual about that.

"Then a few weeks later, other side of the city nearly 60 kilometres away, 12-year-old Chloe Henderson also never made it to school. No items were left, just never made it, vanished, gone."

"Ok, so another kidnapping," Jake said, "what's your point?"

"We have them listed as two separate cases and most think it's two separate offenders."

"You're not sure?" Jake sipped his coffee.

"The MO is very similar but what bugs me is I've never heard of a paedophile who likes both genders. It's normally one or the other." I continued. "Just two days ago, another boy, Stevie Bradley, 11 years old, totally different location, disappeared going to school. All they found was his basketball lying in the gutter. Something tells me they're all related."

"Maybe one was watching the news report about the boy and adopted the same method because it worked," Jake said. "I think you're reading too much into it. Just relax, not every crime is a serial killer. Quite frankly, the Slayer case was enough to last me a lifetime."

"That makes two of us," I replied. "Maybe you're right, maybe it's just coincidence." Although I said this to Jake, something in my gut told me it wasn't. Problem was, I trusted both.

"Any progress on the "Night Stalker?" Jake asked.

"No, I'm still sorting through potential suspects who have jail sentences that coincide with the cooling-off period. I'm assuming he's alive and in jail, then I'll look into sexual offenders who died after the last killing. Unless we get a new lead, we're going to struggle."

The kidnappings had been grinding in my head all morning. I had to try and settle some of the queries I had.

"Jake, do you think it would be ok if I got involved in these kidnappings?" I asked, unsure of the protocol.

"Aren't you supposed to just review them and make recommendations?" Jake asked me.

"Yeah . . . but I think they're related and I recommend we set up a task force," I answered.

Jake closed his eyes and sighed loudly. "Well, if that's what you think needs to happen, then recommend it, but I doubt the chief will give it to you, you're in Homicide, remember? Not Missing Persons."

I nodded. "I'll make the recommendation that they be considered linked and send it back to the Missing Persons Unit."

Chapter 11

Jake and Hayley hadn't got married, although the idea had been discussed. Hayley had spent the morning in the bathroom vomiting; she had done that every morning for the last week.

She knew she was pregnant. She was late and her boobs were hurting and the morning sickness practically gave it away.

She hadn't told Jake; she didn't really know how to. While she was ecstatic, she knew he was still coming to terms with everything that had happened at the cabin all those years ago.

Maybe it would be a good thing.

Maybe it would help get him out of his slump.

She had been working at the Children's Hospital for over 12 years and had recently been promoted to head of the ICU.

Most of the time she enjoyed her work, but sometimes it was hard. For some reason, the last 14 months had been particularly hard.

She'd had a five-year-old come through the ICU, although this was nothing new. Kids were often in there with leukaemia, heart conditions and injuries.

This incident, however, was desperately sad. Ryan was an everyday child, just started school, fought with his siblings. His mum and dad were hard-working responsible people. The kind every kid would love to have as parents.

* * *

From all reports, Ryan was very friendly, smart and well liked amongst his classmates. He had made lots of friends. As any boy does when they are making their way in school, he had play dates. Friends came over and played on a Saturday or after school. Then he would go to their house; it was the way it worked. Joan, his mother, thought nothing of it when Ryan asked if he could go and stay at his friend Josh's house, after all, she had had Josh in her house.

She dropped him off and arranged with Josh's mother to pick him up at lunchtime on the Saturday. All seemed fine. Little did she know that it would be the last time she would speak to her boy.

At 7 am the next day, she received a frantic phone call from Josh's mother.

"Oh my God, you have to go to the Children's Hospital now. The ambulance is on its way. Ryan needs you!"

"What happened?" Joan asked, now in a panic of her own. "What's going on?" she asked again.

"Please, just go to the Children's, I will meet you there."

Joan got dressed and rang her husband, who was already on his way to work. "Hi, babe, you're up early." But before he could finish, the frantic voice, half-crying and half-speaking, came through the speaker.

"Reece, something has happened to Ryan, he's on his way to the Children's Hospital in an ambulance. Paula hasn't told me what happened, just said it was urgent and to get to the hospital."

"I'm on my way there now," he said after a slight pause.

Reece had pulled his car over. He had no idea what had happened or if Ryan would be ok. One thing he did know was that he had to stay calm. He turned his car around and headed for the hospital.

When he walked through the doors to the emergency ward, he saw Paula sitting in the waiting area crying. "Where is Joan?" he asked.

"She's with Ryan just through there. I am so sorry," she said, but Reece didn't wait for her apology. He raced into the emergency room itself.

The triage nurse escorted him to bed 11. Joan was sitting on the edge of Ryan's bed, holding his hand. At first he looked ok. It looked as if he was asleep.

"What happened?" Reece asked.

"He fell in the pool, no one noticed. He was dead when ambulance officers arrived. They revived him. He had been dead for almost 30 minutes."

* * *

He had remained in a coma ever since, the parents still going in every day to see him. Each and every day they prayed for a change that never came. There was no eye movement, no finger that twitched, no toe that moved.

Nothing; just a lifeless body.

Yet the parents continued to visit. Tomorrow would be his seventh birthday and his first in hospital. There would be no celebration, although Hayley was sure the parents would bring cake and gifts. The parents always held out hope that a new toy might connect with him, somewhere inside, wherever he was trapped.

Hayley and Jake had made a rule not to bring their work home with them. Both of them were concerned that eventually the darkness would consume them both if they lived it 24/7. At home, they tried to put their other worlds aside and concentrate on the more positive aspects of their lives together.

Despite her best intentions, Hayley struggled to set aside the sadness she had over Ryan, but true to her promise, she kept her sadness to herself.

She hoped Jake couldn't sense her sadness although she thought he must. She lay awake, wondering how and why these things happened to the most innocent people of all, children.

Chapter 12

To the wider community, Senior Superintendent Mike McLeod was an outstanding member of the police force. However, the few people who had seen his dark side had a different story to tell.

Mike was not on duty tonight but he was working for a boss no one else knew he had. He sat in the driver's seat of the Black Chrysler 300c that had been provided for him. He was parked on a dirt road just past the gates of the Learmonth cemetery and had been there since 10 pm.

His delivery was due at 10.15. He had been asked to collect and then deliver the goods to his employer tonight. He did as he was asked, without question.

Lights appeared in the distance. This would be his man, Mike thought. He checked to ensure no lights were following him. He was in the clear. As the van headed towards him, the driver toggled the lights in a quick flash. The van moved closer, before slowing to a complete stop.

Mike sat in the car and waited for the van driver to exit before he made his move. The driver exited and stood at the front of the van in between the headlights. It was the Joker.

Mike opened his door and walked towards the fat balding Joker. He looked like something you would normally see at a fancy dress party. Mike was dressed as Batman, well, only from the neck up and minus the cape.

Mike wasn't much taller, maybe just a couple of inches, but he was a lot fitter and well built, plenty of muscle he could use if he needed to. He would probably suit being Batman.

"You got the goods?" Mike asked.

He had met the man several times before but names were never discussed. Everyone that worked in 'the loop' as they called it, stayed anonymous and wore masks.

"You got the envelope?" the fat Joker asked back. Mike pulled a folded yellow envelope out from his inside jacket pocket and handed it over.

Beau thought he had met this man several times before. Surely no two guys were built like this one. He assumed Batman was the Priest's muscle, someone to do his dirty work when required. Beau walked forward and took the envelope from the large Batman.

He had no fear of this man, he had fought plenty bigger than him and had still won. Several times in the joint the gangs had come for him. They thought he was slow and stupid because of his stutter; many thought he was retarded. What they didn't know was that anytime he fought he went to some other place inside himself, somewhere animalistic.

Beau walked to the back of the van and came back dragging a small shape with a rope attached around their neck. The head was covered with a black bag. Beau handed the rope to the big man.

"Is he what was ordered?" the big Batman asked.

Beau nodded, turned back towards his van.

By the time he was in reverse, the boy had been loaded into the back of the black car. Beau wondered if this delivery was for the Priest himself or if he was destined for another buyer.

Was the Priest in the back waiting for his delivery? Beau wondered.

Beau took the envelope and opened it, quickly counting to ensure he hadn't been short-changed. Even though every deal had been correct thus far, it was always best to double-check.

Closing the envelope, he folded it under his seat. Five thousand dollars was his cut. Not bad for a few minutes' work. The Priest had always told him never to pass up on an opportunity, and that he would always have buyers for undamaged goods.

Beau usually picked up the goods as ordered, however, if any other opportunity presented itself, sometimes he just couldn't resist.

The Priest had only three rules.

1. Wait a minimum of two days before transporting to ensure there is no heat.
2. No names.
3. Always wear masks, common ones at that.

Mike loaded the boy gently into the black seat of the Chrysler, ensuring that he didn't hit his head on the way in. This was common police procedure, an everyday habit he was unaware of.

Once inside the car, Mike removed his mask. The inside of the Chrysler had been specially fitted. Separating the front and back seats was a dark glass electric window. The rear seat could lift up if required, providing enough room to hide someone. All the locks were controlled from the front, and there were hidden cameras in the lining of the roof and in the wall that contained the glass separation panel. Alongside the cameras were listening devices.

All products on the way to and from delivery remained hooded and with their feet and hands bound.

Quite often, Mike would hear the hooded children counting the turns, some even counting the time. Others would be a mess from the start to the finish of the trip. If Mike ever heard them counting, he would purposely go around the block a few times or drive a longer, more confusing route. For the smart ones, he would play a loud CD of traffic noise, trains, dump trucks, police sirens, the whole box and dice.

Mike wasn't a paedophile; in fact, he was happily married. Delivering for the Priest was just a job. He simply helped out with the deliveries and the clean-up if required and his reward was money, lots of it.

Chapter 13

Father O'Riley walked the halls with his Bible in his right hand and his gold cross hanging around his neck. Every night, he would start his nightly prayers at 8. He would go from dorm to dorm.

Each dorm had four beds, two on each side of the room. Each bed had a night table beside it. At the end of the room was a communal closet with enough space for all four children. The night table had a top drawer which housed the Holy Bible. Above each bed hung a cross with Jesus on it. On the table was a statue of the Virgin Mary.

Father O'Riley used the same prayer every night in every dorm.

"Children, are you ready for your nightly prayer?" he would ask. Most times the children would already be waiting in silence, kneeling beside their respective beds.

Father O'Riley stood in the middle of the room, Bible open in the palm of his left hand. He began and the children joined in, in chorus:

__Be present, O Lord our God,__

At the end of this day I thank You most heartily for all the graces I have received from You.

I am sorry that I have not made a better use of them. I am sorry for all the sins I have committed against You.

Forgive me, O my God, and graciously protect me this night. Blessed Virgin Mary, my dear heavenly mother, take me under your protection.

St. Joseph, my dear Guardian Angel, and all you saints of God, pray for me

AMEN

At the end of the prayer, the father would perform the sign of the cross. "Bless you, my children." The children would repeat the sign of the cross and climb into their beds. They were allowed to read for a further 15 minutes but then lights had to be out.

When he had finished in the St Therese wing, he headed to the end of the hall, past the night station and west down the St Alexius wing. Then he headed to the two wings that had been allocated to the Wards of the State; and other sources. The St Paul wing held the boys and St Abigail housed the girls.

He would save the boys' ward for last. Both wards had only single rooms; there were no dorms, no groups of four. This was because these were often abusive and violent children, or children who had been abused and needed time to accept the Lord into their lives, before they could be assimilated into the dorms. Some children would only be there for days before being moved on.

Father O'Riley finished in the girls' rooms, leaving them to read their Bibles.

He was expecting a delivery. By now, his new arrival should be safe in his new room in the St Paul wing. There should be five housed there now, four from the State and one from his own delivery service.

He never interfered with the ones from the State or any of the orphans. There was simply too high a risk of getting caught. He had done that once before and it had nearly brought him undone. The boy, 11-year-old Jonathan Lucas, now lay buried at the south-east corner of the cathedral. Father O'Riley told authorities Jonathan had simply run away. He was believed because children often did, although they were usually found. Children running away from a boys' home attracted a state-led police investigation that lasted months. Father O'Riley's only saving grace was that they never found the body, and Jonathan had a previous history of running away which added weight to the father's story.

After the investigation ended, he decided those children who were under his care had to be his biggest asset and they could no longer be used to fulfil his inner demons. Having many children speak highly of you would always help, if he was ever questioned in the future.

He found the best way to satisfy his own requirements was to have his desire shipped in and when he was done with them, they would either be sold or disposed of.

After all, he had plenty of buyers that didn't mind damaged goods, as he called them. They would still fetch between $7,000 and $15,000 each. This one had already been sold and would be delivered in the morning.

He performed his usual nightly prayer for all the ward children, and then went into his new arrival's room.

"Hello, my child," Father O'Riley said as he entered, his face hidden by a hood and a mask.

The boy wondered why the man was dressed as a priest.

"Help me! I've been kidnapped, by a man in the van. Please help me," the boy replied, shaking and in tears.

"No, my son, you haven't been kidnapped. The man works for me;

you have been chosen by God to serve him," Father O'Riley replied as he approached the boy, who was standing in the back corner of the room.

"What is your name, my child?" he asked, now standing within touching distance.

"Stevie," the boy answered, shaking in fear and crying. "I want to go home."

"This is your home now, my child."

The Priest closed the door behind him.

Chapter 14

The next morning, Austin woke early, as he had done every day for the last few years. He lay there watching his wife sleep, holding her tightly, her head resting on his chest.

He stroked her hair and kissed her forehead as she held him tighter in her sleep.

He had slept well, by his standards. Four or five hours, only two bad dreams that he could remember. Maybe the others would show their faces later as the day developed.

The alarm on the bedside table flicked over to 7 am and on cue, the radio came on. Without even a lift of her eyelids, Sarah tapped the button and sent the clock back to sleep.

She snuggled in tighter.

Making the most of her sleep with her man.

By 7.45, they had again made up for lost time and then showered together.

Sarah had decided to give Mikayla the day off school so she could spend the day with her father. After all, the school year was almost finished. Only another week before summer holidays began.

They sat and ate their eggs and bacon breakfast as a family for the first time in over six months. And they enjoyed every second of it.

"So, I was thinking we could go to the movies today or the park? Have some lunch out," Austin said.

Before Sarah could respond, Mikayla piped up, "I want to go to the movies, see *Frozen*!" she said, all excited.

"*Frozen* it is," Austin replied.

Their morning was relatively lazy. The movie wasn't showing until 11.30 and they had nothing that needed to be done before then.

They pulled out of their garage at 10.45, leaving them plenty of time to get to the movies and enough time to queue for the popcorn, ice-cream and drink.

Austin couldn't remember the last time he had had ice-cream. More than six months, at least.

* * *

After spending five hours travelling the country and making his delivery to

Batman, Beau gave himself a treat and slept in. He only had a few odd jobs to do for the local real estate agent, and they weren't booked until the next day, Saturday morning. The last thing he wanted was stay at home and put up with his mother mouthing off all the time. He could hear her now, "Don't you have something useful to do?"

He decided to head out to the movies to see *The Hunger Games* and grab a burger afterwards. He had to try to think about how and where he would find another girl.

Beau had always gone to the movies alone, not because he enjoyed being on his own but simply because he had no friends. He found it relaxing, but it was also a great place to locate suitable targets for the Priest. He had been asked to produce an F7 within the next two weeks, so he was on the look-out more than normal.

He always went during the day. He figured it looked less strange being at the movies by yourself in the middle of the working week than it did on a Saturday night when everyone was out with friends. However, the main reason was parents always took their kids during the day, not at night.

Today was a school day so pickings would be slim.

Beau got a bucket of popcorn, a drink and a choc top. For 11 am, it wasn't the most ideal food in between meals. Beau sat in the lobby nibbling at his popcorn while he waited to be admitted. The lobby was getting busier as more movie sessions neared. That was when he noticed her; she was beautiful, big smile, big brown eyes, hair plaited, cute outfit. He would get a lot for her. Maybe he could bump the price up. The Priest would have to pay more for her. Once he sent her photo, he would be able to ask for more. He glanced away so as not to get caught staring at the young girl. He especially didn't want to get noticed by the rather large and muscle-bound beast who was walking with her. Obviously her dad, he thought. A lady who was obviously the girl's mother accompanied the girl and her dad. The resemblance between mother and daughter was incredible.

They walked past and sat opposite in the foyer, the mother and father talking and holding hands as they sat. The girl was spinning in circles, singing, "I'm going to see *Frozen, Frozen,* for me! How much longer is it?" she interrupted her parents.

"It starts in 20 minutes," her father answered without breaking off the conversation with his wife. The usher came out and asked Beau for his ticket. He held his popcorn with his thumb with the same hand that was holding his drink. He passed the ticket trying to prevent the drink or the popcorn from spilling.

The usher ripped it and returned half to him. Beau knew he had about 110 minutes before *Frozen* finished, taking into account the later start. He figured he wouldn't get through all of *The Hunger Games*, because he had to find out more about this girl. He couldn't let this opportunity pass. There would always be another session of *The Hunger Games*, part two. He set his iPhone to vibrate in exactly 98 minutes.

The film had just started to get exciting when the phone vibrated in his pocket. Beau made his way to the exit. The doors to theatre four where *Frozen* was showing were still closed. Beau took the opportunity and quickly visited the men's room.

For 12 long minutes, Beau sat in the foyer and made out that he was waiting for someone, scrolling through his phone. Pretending he was dealing with important business.

When they left the theatre and walked past him, he inconspicuously took several shots of the girl.

They strode through the foyer, the girl holding tightly onto her father's hand. He looked even bigger than before. Had he grown while watching the movie? The girl was singing. Her voice was soft and angelic. It was a song he had never heard before. He figured it was from the movie they had just watched.

Do you wanna build a snowman?
Come on let's go and play
I never see you anymore
Come out the door
It's like you've gone away
We used to be best buddies
And now we're not
I wish you would tell me why!
Do you wanna build a snowman?
It doesn't have to be a snowman.

Then she started up again. She was so pretty. He had to know where she lived. He was a little concerned that the dad was so protective: hawk-like eyes, looking everywhere. Beau followed them out to the car park. He lit a cigarette as he watched them head towards the car. He thought it was safe now to continue his pursuit. He removed his keys and fumbled through them as if looking for one key in particular, and he saw them hop into a black SUV. Beau made out the numberplate and typed it into his phone.

He copied the number-letter combination into an open message, added two words and pressed send.

Address required

The phone vibrated back.

Why?

Beau typed the second part:

Order for M

He watched as the . . . hovered.
Again Beau's phone vibrated.

Will do

Beau waited in his vehicle for them to leave in their SUV. He followed, but ensured it was at a safe and inconspicuous distance behind.

Chapter 15

"You need to come now. I think I've killed him." The voice on the end of Mike's phone quivered.

"I'll be right there. Don't touch anything."

Mike turned to find his wife Jemma standing directly behind him.

"That sounded urgent. Who killed who?"

"You know I can't discuss work, hun. No one is dead but I do have to go."

He kissed his wife who was still in her morning gown, then quickly headed over to his two sons and pecked them both on the cheek. They were two and they were adorable, born only minutes apart. Identical twins, Brock born first and Clay second.

He rushed out the door as they sat in their matching highchairs. His wife had already begun to wipe up the crumbs from the floor beneath them.

Mike hopped into his car. The story for his wife was that the black Chrysler had been bought with an inheritance. In reality, it had been given for services rendered to the church. Services like this one, services that his wife had no idea about.

Had she known what he had been doing and what his true reason for doing it was, he knew she would leave him and take the twins with her.

He couldn't have that. He'd see them all dead before that happened.

The Priest was waiting outside the Ward of the State wing where Mike had delivered the child not more than 12 hours ago.

"What's happened?" he asked the Priest.

"He was being difficult, trying to fight me off. At first it was fun, you know how I like a bit rough play. But then he got serious and really violent."

Right about the time you tried to butt fuck him, Mike thought.

"Then what happened?" Mike asked.

"I hit his head against the wall. Blood spurted out, and he collapsed," the Priest said.

"Have you checked his pulse?" Mike asked.

"No, I just left. I'll need you to dump him if he's dead."

"Understood," Mike responded. "I'll go check on him first, just to make sure we're not jumping at shadows. Does he still have his hood on?"

"Yes," replied the Priest, "I could see blood soaking through it," he added.

With the boy's hood still on, Mike had no need to cover his face with his standard Batman cowl. He slipped into the room, closing the door behind him.

The boy didn't move.

Didn't even stir.

He was sprawled in the top right-hand corner of the bed, head twisted at an unusual angle.

Upon first appearance it didn't look good. The Priest might be right.

Mike approached the boy, slowly knelt down beside the bed and felt the boy's wrist.

There was a pulse. It was there and it was strong.

Mike was sure he would be ok. He walked over to the basin that was bolted against the stone wall of the room. Cupped his hands and filled them with water. He carried the water back to the boy and splashed it over his face.

The boy moved and groaned, slowly at first.

Then he obviously remembered where he was and what was happening and frantically began kicking out.

"Stop now and be quiet or I will slit your throat where you lie."

Mike's voice was not loud or angry, it was very cold and matter-of-fact.

That scared Stevie very much.

He stopped fighting immediately.

"What are you going to do with me?" he asked, confused.

Stevie could not see the person sitting over him, although he could feel the water and the cool air through the hood. Other than that, he had no idea where he was or who he was with.

"I'll be back for you later," Mike said as he made his way to the door. Stevie could hear a bolt and then the turn of a lock a few seconds later, then the closing of the door.

Where is he going to take me? Stevie wondered, as he sat curled up in the corner of the bed. He could feel cold rough stone against his right arm and palm.

"He's alive," Mike said.

The Priest was leaning against the wall of the corridor, rosary beads in hand.

"Good, I think it's best we ship him off. I'll make the arrangements, can you make the drop? It will either be tonight or tomorrow."

"Just send me the details as per usual and I'll collect him and drop him off."

"Mike, before you go, I have another job for you."

Mike turned and faced the Priest. "What type of job?" he asked.

"A buyer has reneged on a deal; he needs to know he can't do that to us." The Priest spoke calmly.

"Do you want a reminder so he goes ahead with the deal, or am I setting an example?"

"Just a warning he needs to take delivery next weekend, otherwise an example will have to be made of him."

Mike nodded, "Send me his number I'll follow the rest up. The message will be delivered by the end of the weekend."

Chapter 16

I had taken Jake's advice and ignored my feelings about the case, but it continued to haunt me.

Three children, all taken in broad daylight. It wasn't right and I couldn't let it go. Maybe the fact it was kids was what tormented me most.

As a child, I had spent a lot of time in hospital and had seen a lot of other children come and go during my stays. Some would stay only a short time and go back home to normality just days later. They were the ones I was envious of. Then there were the others that came in but didn't leave. They died all of a sudden, their lives over. Extinguished like a new flame before it had a chance to become a fire.

I had survived. I was their envy; they had just wanted to live.

There was the little boy I recalled who suddenly fell over one day, and then the next and the next until soon it was every time he walked. He was just six and he wanted to be a policeman. Within weeks, he couldn't walk and six months later, he was dead. I saw his funeral on the news. The Make a Wish Foundation fulfilled his wish of becoming a police officer and ensured he was buried with full police honours. A year later, I was in hospital for another stint when his brother came in suffering the same fate as his older departed brother. He died too! Life is cruel!

I had driven to the home of Stevie Bradley without even knowing how, my mind on auto pilot while it visited the ghosts of my past. Memories I had hidden deep down.

I knocked loudly and then stood back from the door. The door opened but the security door remained closed. "Can I help you?" the lady asked.

"Mrs Bradley, I'm Detective Brodie Foxx from Homicide. Just wondering if I could ask you a few questions regarding Stevie?"

"Do you think he's dead?" She began to cry. "Have you found him?" I could hear running from the other end of the house. "What's wrong, hun?" the male voice asked. "It's the police, Homicide."

I quickly said, "We haven't found him and we have no reason to think that anything has changed. We're still looking at it as a missing person."

"But you're from Homicide?"

"Please, Mrs Bradley, if I could just have a few minutes of your time, I can explain."

She unlocked the security door. "Of course, excuse me. I don't know what happened to my manners."

Her crying stopped almost as quickly as it had started. It was obvious she was in a state of shock and she had no way of dealing with how drastically her world had changed. Their world as they'd known it had changed forever, and they did not know how to move forward.

I stepped inside their house, which was dark, blinds drawn, TV on. Mrs Bradley was still in her dressing-gown despite it nearing lunchtime. Makeup was no longer a concern. Everything in this lady's life had stopped and tomorrow would never come until there was closure.

"Thanks for your time. I just wanted to ask you some questions. I'm investigating some links between Stevie's abduction and other missing children cases."

"Are the other children dead?" Mr Bradley asked, nervously awaiting my answer.

"No, we haven't found them yet. But they may be connected and if that is the case, we might find a lead into all of them. Did you notice anything unusual leading up to the morning of Stevie's disappearance?" I asked them.

They looked at each other and shook their heads. "Nothing we can think of," his mother said. "It was just like he vanished off the face of the earth. All they found was his ball in the gutter and they only knew it was his because it has his name written on it. He did that to stop other kids from taking it at lunchtime."

"May I look in his room?"

The parents nodded and led the way down the even darker hall. They opened a door. I guessed this door had been shut since Stevie was taken. Except for when the Missing Persons Unit had asked to view it.

Stevie was into basketball for sure. His walls were covered in posters. There was Chris Paul, Kevin Garnett, Lebron James, Kevin Durant. I stood taking it in. His bed was in the corner, desk against the wall with a computer. Photos of friends stuck to the walls next to the posters. Basketball ring attached to his cupboard door. There was a ball sitting on his bed, the one I assumed he had taken to school that day. It sat there waiting for him to return and play with.

"Was he on Facebook?" I asked.

"No, we thought he was too young. He played PlayStation online but that was with his friends."

"Did you ever hear him talking to people he didn't know; names you didn't recognise?"

"No, I knew them all. It was a very select group of friends."

I closed the door and headed back out to the lounge. The Bradleys followed.

"I'm going to walk his route to school and I'll be in touch if I come up with something of interest. Thank you for your time."

I turned and headed for the door, then I stopped. Something registered in my memory from a case I had read about years ago. "I asked you earlier if you noticed anything unusual. Let me rephrase that. Did you notice anything normal but also a little odd, out of place?"

It was like a lightbulb going off. His mother answered immediately, "About a week before, I noticed a van parked down the road. It had a phone logo on the side, but it wasn't for a phone company. Anyway, I remember seeing the same logo, possibly the same van, one other afternoon, except it was parked three streets over. I just happened to pass it on the way home."

"Did you see the driver?"

"No, I didn't pay any attention to who was driving it."

"I'll follow that up but it was probably nothing. If you have any questions please call me any time."

I handed her my card and headed out the front. I needed to re-create Stevie's last movements.

I stood at the bottom of the reserve, ready to cross where he had crossed through the reserve, and looked up. I could see the street at the other end. I set my watch and walked. It took me 53 seconds to walk to the top. It might have taken Stevie less than that. I looked at the houses either side of the reserve. Both were single storey; unlikely they would have seen anything. Across the road were two more single-storey homes and one double storey. The double didn't have great views of the reserve. According to crime scene reports, none of the other residents had seen or heard anything, but I would ask again anyway.

Now, I had to test my theory. I headed back down to my car, started the engine and drove past the reserve at 40 kilometres an hour. I pressed start on my watch and without having to speed, I had reached the top of the reserve with 25 seconds to spare.

I figured that if he had been dribbling the ball, Stevie might have taken a little longer to reach the top. He might have even lost his dribble, which would have extended even more the time available to the suspect. The suspect had 25 seconds minimum to park, lie in wait and then make his move. He knew the area; he knew the connecting streets; he knew Stevie's route. Had someone seen Stevie at the bottom of the reserve they would have had enough time to drive around and cut him off.

Providing one thing.

Our suspect knew how to get there first.

Was our unsub the man with the van?

I knocked on both the single storey front doors, with no luck. There was no one home.

I tried the two storey across the road. A lady answered. I introduced myself and showed her my badge. "The morning the boy was taken. Were you at home?"

"Yes, my children go to the same school. I drop them off." Her voice was soft but matter-of-fact.

"Did you see or hear anything unusual?"

"No, I was busy getting my own two ready for school, and that's a task and a half on some mornings. When we drove out of the driveway, I saw the ball lying in the gutter and I thought nothing of it, to be honest. When the police came by in the afternoon and I found out that the ball belonged to the boy, then I realised all that time he had been missing and my heart sank. I knew he hadn't run away, so did the police. If you run away, you take the ball with you."

She was a lovely lady. Someone you would like as a neighbour.

The phone in her house began to ring in the background. "Is there anything else, Officer?" she asked.

"No. Thanks for your help, I'll get back to you if I need anything else."

I sat in my car thinking things over. Jake was right as usual. The case wasn't a homicide and it wasn't mine. I had to suggest that Missing Persons take this over but first, I had to be sure the cases were similar.

I headed to the street of the second missing child, Chloe Henderson. I had to know if the MO was the same for the boy and the girl. I just had to know.

Again, I made that dreaded knock. I hated it because I knew the parents would automatically fear the worst. "Mrs Henderson, I'm Brodie Foxx from Homicide." I placed my hands forward, palms down, as if to say, calm down. "Firstly, I don't have any news on your daughter, I'm just reviewing the case. May I come in?"

Mrs Henderson let out a big sigh of relief and clasped her hands together, dish towel held tightly between them. She was dressed in around-the-house clothes. Maybe since the abduction of her daughter, appearance had lost the importance it had once held.

"Of course, please, may I get you a drink?"

"No, thank you. I can't stay, I just have a few questions for you if that's ok? Sorry to bring all this up again, but I'll be asking you some questions that you may have been asked several times. I'm trying to stay fresh and look into this as if it just happened."

I removed my pen and unzipped my folder.

"I do it this way to make sure I come to my own conclusions without the influence of other officers or any case file notices. Does that make sense?"

"You're the expert," she replied with a small smile.

"On the morning Chloe disappeared, can you tell me what time she left home?"

"She left at 8.20 as she did each morning. It took her about 20 minutes to walk to the school. It was only five streets away, three this side and two the other side of the highway."

"When did you know that she hadn't made it to school?" I asked calmly.

"Her friend Jasmine rang at around 4 pm. She asked if she was ok. It was then I knew something was wrong." Her eyes were beginning to well up.

"The worst part is Chloe almost made it to the school. She was only 80 metres away from the school. How did she get so close without anyone seeing her? How is that possible?" She looked at me as if I could provide the answer to a question that might never be answered.

"I don't know but we're doing everything we can to find out. Can you show me which way she walked?" I opened Google Maps on my phone. She pointed with her finger, following the streets three prior to the highway, then two after. The last led to the back gate of the school. It was less than 180 metres away from where she was last seen. How she had vanished from this spot was unbelievable.

"Police told me she was seen by the owner of number six. He was out sweeping his path; he swears it was her." Mrs Henderson was mopping up her tears with a tissue she held scrunched up in her left hand.

'No. 6 Elmer Road', I scribbled.

"Would you mind if I look in her room?" I asked nervously, expecting that this would bring on another waterfall of tears.

She didn't answer, only gestured me to follow.

It was at the end of the hall, furthest from what seemed to be the master bedroom.

Her room was typical of any 12-year-old girl's room. There were the latest dolls and plenty of drawing and craft material on a small table in the corner, including a do-it-yourself bead set, lid open with a half-finished project. "I thought it was best I leave it for her to finish when she gets back," said the mother from the doorway behind me.

"That's best," I said, not turning. I could feel a tear in the corner of my eye begin to well.

There were photos on the walls, selfies as the kids called them, of her and her friends pulling faces and making pig noses, tongues out.

"You know that I tidied this room but when I realised she was gone and wasn't coming home, I tried to get it back to just how she had left it. I think it's close but I know it's not how she had it. Is that the craziest thing you've heard? A mum wanting her daughter's room messy again?"

"No." My voice croaked. "It's not crazy, it's what I would want too." The tear dropped this time.

"I even say goodnight to her every night as I pass on my way to bed."

I had no response. I wouldn't know what I would do, so I just smiled gently.

The room was as if time had stopped and hadn't restarted.

It had become the waiting room, waiting for its child to return.

Chapter 17

Mikayla had grown so much in the time Austin had been away. It didn't show a lot in her size, but her maturity and confidence had changed a great deal. Sarah had done a great job with her. Austin couldn't believe she was 11.

They pulled up at the pancake parlour and sat at a table. The place was relativity empty but it was a week day after all. Austin assumed tomorrow would be a different story.

Beau watched them enter the restaurant, waited a few minutes and then entered himself. He sat at a table close enough to eavesdrop, but not close enough to raise suspicion.

Austin didn't usually eat a lot of junk food but he decided to let his strict diet go today. He ordered the steak with potatoes on buckwheat pancakes and salad.

His daughter ordered something called 'Alice in Wonderland', while his wife ordered Hawaiian crepes.

His wife had been talking his ear off, as if she had saved everything she had wanted to tell him. Now she was just opening the vault door and letting it all out.

He liked listening to her sweet soft voice. It was better than the heavy artillery fire he had become used to. She gave him all the family updates. Her sister Debbie was planning on leaving her husband, thought he was cheating on her with a floosy from the office.

Austin nodded and wondered how he had become so distant, so indifferent to problems that other people considered dire. To him this was incidental compared to the bigger troubles of the world.

Maybe it would have more significant if it affected him directly. His line of thought was broken as the phone in his pocket began to vibrate. Very few people knew this number; very few people knew he was in the Special Forces. To most people, he just said he was in the army. If anyone tried to find him, then they would end up receiving one word back: Confidential. Only the general could access his file. They kept the identity of all personnel in the Special Forces secret to avoid terrorist reprisals. You knew the people in your regiment and your superior, but that was it.

He swiped across the green answer button. "Austin, is that you?" the voice at the other end of the phone asked. A smile came across Austin's face, a smile his wife hadn't seen enough of lately.

"Yes mate, it's me, how are you?" Austin replied. "You still working in the Melbourne office?"

"I have a couple of days off next week. Would you like to catch up and go fishing at the lake?" the voice replied.

The 'lake' meant Beechworth, a small Victorian country town and once home to the now empty yet apparently haunted lunatic asylum. It was also famous for having the prison that had once housed the famous bushranger Ned Kelly. Marcus and Austin had done several fishing trips between tours.

"I'd love to but I've just got back from tour and I really want to spend some time with the family. Thanks anyway."

Beau's ears pricked up. Tour. Perhaps a navy or army man, he thought. That would explain his physique.

Austin was about to say his goodbyes when Sarah nudged her husband. "Go," she mouthed.

"Hang on a moment . . . what day were you thinking, Marcus?" Austin asked.

"Leave Monday morning, come back Tuesday night, stay the one night," Austin repeated so that Sarah could hear. She nodded, waving her hand in agreement.

After a slight hesitation, Austin agreed. "Sounds great, but you're driving. What time are you picking me up?"

"Five am."

"Man, it's like being back in the army again!" Austin replied before hanging up.

"Are you sure you're ok with this?" Austin confirmed with Sarah.

"It's fine, you need to relax. About time you enjoyed life a little."

"But I just got back. I think I should be home. Mikayla will get upset."

Sarah grabbed her husband's hand. "She will be fine and so will I, it's only for one night. Go, enjoy, end of discussion."

"Ok thanks," Austin replied, smiling. He knew there was no point continuing a discussion he could not win.

Their meals arrived. Mikayla's Alice in Wonderland was fairy bread on pancakes with ice-cream and chocolate sauce. Way to dress it up, Pancake Parlour, he thought.

He dug into his potatoes that were covered in bacon bits, sour cream, cheese, and chives. They were divine and the steak was amazing. Was the food extra-good, or was it the fact it was one of the few decent meals he'd had in months?

Sure, the food in the army would get you by, but it was nothing like this.

Ahh, so you are an army man, Beau thought. That news aside, he had just learned that the girls would be alone Monday night. That would be his opportunity. He had everything he needed. He left the money on the table along with his half-eaten pancakes and headed out.

* * *

Beau received the one-line message with the address.

It had only taken a matter of minutes. Beau didn't know where or how they got the information and he didn't really care. He assumed the Priest had connections.

He decided to survey the area of his chosen child, but not until Sunday afternoon.

Sunday he would have more time to plan for Monday night. He had to get the planning right. The father was only away for one night.

He didn't want to upset the Ukrainian Monster any more than necessary. It sounded as though waiting a week for part one and then another week for part two was already upsetting him. Beau didn't want that but in this case, it couldn't be avoided.

Tales of the Monster had been rife throughout Port Phillip Prison. The main story told from prisoner to prisoner involved two 'employees' who had thought to turn State's witness and testify against the Monster's extensive operations across Australia.

Despite being under guard and with new identities, they were found one frosty winter's morning only weeks before the trial was due to commence. The four police guards were given Colombian neckties, while the informants were found in a burnt-out vehicle on a remote beach in NSW.

According to police, the fire had been set from the inside. They had been burnt alive. The van and its contents were then set alight from the outside while the cries of the burning men came from within.

The underworld said that the Monster had insisted on lighting the fire himself. He wanted to see their eyes as he struck the match in front of them.

Beau closed his phone and headed home. He needed some sleep before he was to make his delivery after work tomorrow and as he was visiting the Monster tomorrow night, he had to make sure he had his wits about him.

Chapter 18

Jake sat down in his usual spot for his Friday afternoon therapy session.

"So Jake, how have you been this week?" was the first question Salma asked.

"Same as always," Jake replied.

"You still having the dreams?" Salma asked.

"Yes," Jake replied.

"How many times did you have the dreams this week," she probed.

"Three out of seven."

"Jake, it's time I was frank with you. You've been coming here on and off for over 10 years and you increased your number of sessions a few months ago, but I can't help you if you don't tell me what the main concern is. Each week, you answer the questions, say you're ok and then give me nothing. If you want to start to heal, Jake, then you need to talk to me." Salma paused and waited for Jake to respond. She would wait until the end of the session if need be.

It took over three minutes before Jake finally spoke.

"The issue I keep coming back to is life. How do I plan for the future with Hayley when I know there are people out there who lie awake planning evil acts? Acts that I don't know about. Acts that I can't control . . ."

Salma interrupted, "I'm sure that in your line of work that is not a new feeling?"

"No, it's not, not at all, but before that, I assumed I might get hurt by doing my job, not that others would. Since the cabin I don't feel like I can protect them any more."

"Them?" Salma questioned.

"Hayley is having a baby. I guess she's about 10 or 12 weeks."

"You mean she hasn't told you?" Salma frowned.

"No, she hasn't, but she forgets that I'm a detective. She's afraid of how I'll take the news."

"And how will you take it?" Salma asked immediately.

"I'll be rapt," Jake said, "but how would I be able to protect them from all the evil? What if there's another Mason Belic? Brodie thinks there are hundreds of them roaming out there."

"Jake, you need to see the good in the world too. There are people out there like you making it safer for the rest of us. You'll never be able to control all the bad ones and you'll never be able to predict crimes. All you can do is your best, and you have to make your peace with that."

Jake sat deep in thought for a moment.

"I used to think fate was good or bad luck that just happened to people, but the whole Mason case made me realise that there are people who interfere with fate and send it in a whole new direction."

"But don't you see the flaw in your argument? You could say that about things that are not evil in the least. Let me give you an example. A driver of a truck leaves for work on a cold Wednesday morning. It's been raining with heavy thunderstorms most of the night before. The truck driver's power goes out. As a consequence, his alarm doesn't go off on time and while he isn't late by much, he leaves for work five minutes later than he would have if his alarm had gone off. Before you ask what this story has got to do with the price of fish, let me finish.

"Due to being late out the door, the driver decides to skip breakfast and go to McDonald's drive-through on his way to the first job. By the time he receives his meal, he's further behind schedule by two minutes."

She sipped her honey and lemon tea on her desk.

"As he's eating his McDonald's in the truck, his concentration is slightly distracted. He doesn't see the light change and goes through a red light. His truck hits a car crossing the intersection. He kills a mum and two children. Every day he blames himself. But the purpose of the story is that fate sometimes consists of several little things. If it hadn't stormed the night before, he would have left on time, he wouldn't have needed to stop. If the queue at the drive-through had been one car longer or one car shorter he would have either made the light or most likely not been the first at the lights. Sometimes there is no one to blame, some things just are, you understand?"

Salma paused, taking another sip. "Now, I agree there are those who plan evil acts, but that is why we need people like you. Without an army of good the world will fall into despair."

Jake nodded.

"Before you go home I want you to write a list of all the good qualities you have and all the reasons you became a police officer. Then I want you to go home and tell your beautiful wife Hayley why you are glad to be having a baby."

Jake nodded again.

This time, Salma thought she saw a glimmer of acceptance in his eyes.

Chapter 19

ike received two texts from the Priest, each from different numbers. Both were received in the hour after he had left the Priest.

The first was a time to deliver the boy and collect the sum of $50,000. The delivery was set for tonight. Midnight. Usual place.

The second text was a number followed by: *Give warning. Confirm delivery next Saturday.*

It only took him 20 minutes of looking through the LEAP Victoria Police database to match up the number to a person. The photo that appeared on the screen was an individual called Neil Figal.

Figal had spent eight years in prison for three separate incidents. Two were for indecent assault of a minor and one was attempted kidnapping.

Good information for Mike to have.

He had to work today and tomorrow, but he had Sunday off. A good time to pay him a visit. A good time to deliver a warning.

Mike had managed to spend the evening meal at home with his wife and kids. It was a time he really enjoyed. His wife again questioned him about the morning phone call and what she thought she had heard.

"So who was killed?"

Mike knew the best way to lie was to mix it with a little truth. "The call this morning was from Father O'Riley. He was concerned that a young ward of the state who was sent back to his family had been killed. It was a rumour he had heard through the congregation. We looked into it. The young fella is doing fine and it was obviously some unfounded rumour. Jemma, remember you can't say anything. I could lose my job if you do."

Jemma nodded. "Well it's good to hear all is ok. That's the problem with a town this size. Too many rumours from bored housewives." She placed her hand on his and smiled.

"I need to head out tonight," Mike said. "I've had complaints from the council about people dumping rubbish at the cemetery. I told them I'd check it out myself."

"Can't someone working tonight do it?" Jemma asked, disappointment ringing with every word.

"It will only take an hour. I promise I'll be back by 1 at the latest."

Mike finished his dinner, bathed his twins, read them a story each, and managed to relax a little and watch some TV with his wife, although neither of them watched. It just provided background noise while Jemma discussed the latest events. The most important was Christmas, which was only three weeks away. What were they going to get the twins?

Chapter 20

Beau knew he would be on the road for the next 24 hours. He might have a sleep on the way back but until the drop was made, he would be wide awake.

He locked the shed from the inside and slid the train set from vertical to horizontal. He opened the trapdoor. He removed the red ladder and placed the two hook ends into the specially crafted holes to hold it.

The ladder reached all the way down except for the last 50 centimetres. Beau put on his standard joker mask and then headed down the ladder with a hessian sack tucked into the waistband of his grey tracksuit pants.

He approached Chloe's cell for the second time in days. "Looks like someone loves you. Your ransom has been paid. Put this on," he said, handing the sack through the bars. Chloe did as she was told. Soon she would be home: she just had to play it cool for a little while longer.

She pulled the hood over her head and darkness fell.

She heard the lock undo and the cell door open and an instant later a hand grasped her elbow.

She felt the rope tighten around her neck.

"Need to go up the ladder. Now I will guide you," he said to her. He placed her right foot on the first rung. "Now you move your other foot."

Chloe lifted her left leg but missed on her first two attempts, then clunk, the toe caught the metal rung. She managed to hold it there, preventing herself from slipping off.

She only missed two rungs for the rest of her trip up the ladder. The second and last miss hurt her the most. She had become over-confident and her knee clipped the rung above. She grimaced, not that Beau could tell; her hood hid her anguish.

Beau already had the rear doors of his van open. He ushered her into the back, sat her on the same side as the sliding door, on the floor, then looped and tied the rope to the welded metal hoop.

He folded the rope in two and threaded the loop through the metal hoop. Then he removed the rope from Chloe's neck and pulled the loop through, creating a slip knot before replacing the original loop back around Chloe's neck.

He locked both doors from the outside using the key. The windows in the back of the van had been highly tinted. He placed the ladder back and returned the train set to the original position. Down below was one boy, the one the media had called Scott.

Beau hit the road for the Monster at five minutes after 11 o'clock on Saturday morning.

Chapter 21

Tyler had cased the house several times over the past few weeks but he had decided that Monday would be his day. He had thought it best that he break in while the mum was out collecting the girl from school.

In the 15-minute window he had while she was out, he would have enough time to find and crack the safe, bag the loot, sneak out to the back door, jump the back fence, and sprint across the neighbour's back yard and down their drive. Their front fence was not only lower, but it was brick and easier to scale. Simple job.

If he got caught, what would be the worst that would happen to him? Another six-to 12-month stint in Port Phillip. He had decided to take a small weapon, not a gun but a butterfly knife. That way he would be protected if the big guy he had seen with the lady was more than a friendly visitor. He would at least be protected.

It couldn't be the husband, who according to Jack his cellmate was away at war. But he wanted to be prepared.

If he got this score he would be set for the next two years, according to his informant. The hardest part was getting rid of the goods but now that Jack had set that up with Mr Lee, he was good to go.

The way it worked was 60% went to Tyler and 40% went to Lee. Out of his 60%, he offered to put 10% in a safety deposit box for Jack until he was released.

Tyler put Rocky in the back of the car and cranked the window. He watched.

The man was still there. What the hell was going on? Who was this guy? Maybe he was on weekend leave, that could be a possibility, Tyler thought.

Tyler started his car. He had no choice; guy or no guy he was all set to do the job and come Monday he would ensure it was done.

Chapter 22

Beau arrived at two wrought-iron gates with one word written across them in big bold letters. 'PALANOK'.

To the right side of the gate was a long brick wall with built-in camera, buzzer and speaker. Sitting to the side of each gate was another camera. This was no ordinary house, it was something a king would live in, Beau thought. He only saw four other houses in the street. This was a very exclusive house in a very exclusive street. Beau guessed that each house was on acreage, most likely five-acre lots.

Beau had put on his Joker mask on arrival at the gates. Now he wound down the driver's side window and pressed the button. "Yes," the voice replied in a strong accent, which Beau assumed was Russian. He wouldn't have known the difference between a Russian and a Ukrainian. "I have a delivery for Mr Pavlychko." Beau was very glad the word 'Monster' didn't slip out of his mouth.

"Take off the mask," the voice replied.

"Can't do that, sorry. Does he want the delivery or not?"

* * *

In normal houses, the rumpus room was for the family to enjoy activities such as billiards, darts and table tennis. Igor Pavlychko's rumpus room was more often used for business and drinking.

Igor was known by the outside world, incorrectly, as a Russian crime boss with a quick temper prone and to violent rages. Usually resulting in someone's death. He was in fact a Ukrainian crime boss and there was a big difference: Ukrainians were more violent and less tolerant.

His three business associates, as he called them when introducing them to someone new, were the only three people on this earth he trusted. Too many other people wanted him dead, either to take over his business or to remove his business.

Alexi, the Monster's most senior guard and trusted ally at six foot eight, sat on the right side of the sofa. On the left sat Shevd. He was not as big as Alexi but still a big guy, at just under six foot four.

Shevd was a more skilled killer than a brute fighter like Alexi was. Alexi would kill you up close and personal while Shevd would kill you without your even realising he was near.

The man standing at the intercom was the Monster's third trusted ally, known only as Andrei. He had unknowingly saved the Monster from an assassination attempt by a rival drug cartel while they were in the Ukraine.

It was after this that the Monster had organised their lives in Sydney and set up the lifestyle they all wanted.

It was believed that prior to his chance meeting with the Monster, Andrei had been fighting the Russian invasion in his home province of Crimea. During the war with Russia, he killed over 65 Russian soldiers, leading fellow officers to name him Andrei after Ukraine's worst serial killer, Andrei Chikatilo.

When they had first arrived in Sydney, drugs were 90% of the business, with local prostitution filling the other 10%. The business was now more than drugs. Igor found he had a liking for prepubescent girls. He also discovered they were a hot item on the domestic and international markets, and they sold well, extremely well.

Over the past five years the trafficking part of the business had become half his business. He now employed several local suppliers; the priest of a church in Ballarat was just one. Not only was the Priest a paedophile, he was a paedophile hungry for cash, and as a middle man you could make a lot of money. Igor also liked the fact that it removed him from the dirty work. For doing the dirty work, Igor paid the Priest well and sent through the occasional toy-boy to keep him happy. Igor knew the Priest had his own supply chain and he was sure that this Joker was at the top of it.

Igor made sure he never met the delivery people. He left that to his men to handle. Anyway, it was unnecessary for him to be there, and the fewer people who knew of his existence, the better. The last thing he wanted was to be fingered by some two-bit paedophile delivery man trying to downgrade his sentence.

* * *

"The Joker won't remove his mask. Do you want me to go take care of it?" Andrei asked.

"It's ok, send him in," said Shevd.

"We will teach him some manners; the boss wants his delivery," Alexi replied. Then he communicated back through the intercom, "Let him in."

The gates buzzed and began to open. Beau drove the van up the long, tarsealed driveway, lined with pine trees and gums. The brick fence, measuring a metre and a half with 50-centimetre wrought-iron spikes atop it, ran from the gates along the property boundary. Every four metres there was a brick pillar two metres high.

By the time Beau reached the homestead, he had driven over 500 metres. In front of the house, the drive opened up into a circular turnaround area, in the middle of which sat a large concrete fountain.

Two men in suits stood at the door at the top of the terracotta steps. They looked like secret service agents.

Beau slowed the van and shut off the engine. He unloaded the cargo, holding the rope and leading Chloe up the front stairs.

"Here to see . . ." he addressed the suits but before he could finish his sentence, the smaller of the two said, "Follow me." Then he opened the door and led the two of them inside the expansive home. The other suit stayed outside at the doorway.

The front door opened into a large tiled foyer. Off to the left was an expansive lounge with an open stone fireplace. To the right was what looked like a second lounge but there were only two chairs, both high-back Chesterfields, one opposite the other. To the right of each chair was a side table with an ashtray and a wooden box. In the middle of the two chairs was a chess table with some pieces lying face down on each side of the table, while others were placed across the board in various positions.

Beau did not understand the game or why anyone would waste their time playing. He found the combat missions on *Call of Duty* more fascinating and a lot more fun.

Beau followed the suit through a hallway past an in-house gym and into some type of games room.

Alexi stood. "Remove the mask," he said in a thick accent.

"I've been told to keep it on when dealing with clients," Beau replied calmly.

"Do you think we are clients? We pay the Priest, who I assume pays you. We are your bosses," Alexi said.

Beau paused, unsure what to do. This guy was huge, at least 6 foot 5, built like the Hulk. A real-life monster. Was he about to disrespect the Monster? He thought better of it. If push came to shove, he wouldn't be able to match him for brute force. He was sure this must be the notorious Monster. Made sense, he thought. The other two were too small.

Behind the Monster, two men were sitting on the sofa. One was about six foot while the second man was a little taller, maybe 6 foot 2.

One on three would be suicide.

His thoughts were interrupted by more talking; another voice, a stronger accented voice.

It was the six-footer who spoke.

"He told you to take off the mask. You don't want him to ask you again."

Beau had summed up the situation and thought it best to do as asked.

He removed the mask, revealing his bald head. The wisps of hair on the sides had fluffed up with sweat.

"Now show us your licence," Alexi demanded.

Beau frowned, but did as he asked.

"You have family?" Alexi asked.

"Just live with my mom, my deadbeat dad is dead, well, as far as I know he is."

"You work for the Priest, yes?" Alexi said, confirming his own statement.

Beau nodded.

"You realise two girls were required?" the other seated man asked.

Beau nodded again. "He just told me yesterday. I have a second one almost ready."

"This is not acceptable to us. You understand?" the seated man continued.

He stood for the first time, and put his hand around Beau's throat and began to squeeze. "I don't think you understand that we run this show."

Beau didn't reach for the gun tucked into the back of his pants. Pulling it out now would surely end his life.

"You come in here with your mask, and then you bring half the deal. Who the fuck do you think you're dealing with? We're not some drug-fucked paedophiles who don't care about their stock or its quality."

His grip stayed firm around Beau's neck. He was finding breathing increasingly difficult.

"I think it's time to send a message to the Priest. Maybe we could mail you to him. Would that send a message?"

Beau thought the guy was going for his gun, but instead he pulled a knife and pressed it against his eye.

"Wait," he said. "What I have is very special. One more week and she will be yours. I have a photo of her on my phone."

The guy withdrew his knife and took Beau's phone from him.

Shevd released his grip from Beau's throat and handed the phone to Alexi, who was towering over him. The man took the phone and disappeared down the rear of the home and returned a few minutes later. He replied with one word, but it wasn't a word Beau recognised.

It sounded like 'fin eel'; maybe it meant fine or finally. Beau couldn't be sure.

Who had he shown the photo to?

The big guy turned back to face Beau. He placed the phone back in his jacket pocket.

"You tell the Priest we pay $40,000 total. That girl must be here by Saturday night," Alexi said in his thick accent.

"Now, you don't deliver, I will see you personally and I will take your eyes and the eyes of anyone else close to you," Shevd butted in. "Do you understand?"

Beau nodded.

The man Beau took for the Monster had returned to his seat on the couch.

Shevd took two steps back and folded his knife and replaced it in his pocket.

Beau turned to head for the door.

"Where do you think you're going?" the man leaning next to the intercom asked.

"Show us the merchandise, we need to make sure she is what we ordered."

"I can't have her see my face."

"Don't worry about it, you will never see her again."

Beau removed the rope and then the hood and bowed his head. No matter what they said, the less the girl knew about him, the better.

The girl stood there barely clothed, mouth taped, face red and fringe wet with sweat.

She looked at the men sitting on the couch and immediately began to fret.

"You satisfied?" Beau asked without looking up.

The Monster nodded. Beau turned towards the front door; he had been here way too long already.

His delivery moved to follow him, arms outstretched, crying as Beau left.

Better the devil you know, hey girl, Beau thought to himself.

She would be desperate at the idea of being left with three guys who looked ready to have their way with her. Especially when one was the size of two.

After all, Beau had not touched her.

By the time Beau reached the door, they must have removed her tape because he heard her scream. The scream was followed by an almighty slap. Hand across her face, Beau thought.

Twenty minutes later, in his van heading for Melbourne, he was still fuming. "Fucking Russians," he muttered to himself. "Who do they think they are? Speaking to me like that." The guy with the knife hadn't fazed him. He had seen his type before. All threats, most likely a lousy fighter. He could probably beat him and the guy standing by the intercom at the same time, if it came down to a fight for life or death. But the big guy, presumably the Monster, there was no way. He was bigger than anything he had ever seen in jail.

Beau began to think about the following week. That delivery might be his last. They might decide to terminate him once they had the goods. He had to ensure he made the delivery but more importantly, his best chance of survival was to get the girl- at any cost.

Chapter 23

Mike collected the boy just after 11 pm. The delivery had been arranged for midnight at the cemetery, a secluded and private spot for such a transaction.

He had been waiting for 13 minutes, according to the clock on the dash. It was now 11.53 pm and soon the man who was due to collect would be here.

Mike could see the boy in his mirror. The glass privacy panel was down and the boy sat shaking, nervous. The Priest had left him in a pretty bad state. His eye-socket might be fractured, not to mention the abuse his body had taken. Mike doubted the Priest had restrained himself after knocking the boy out. He'd probably put him in that state during the rape and kept going until he was finished.

Lights in the distance shone through the front windscreen, breaking into Mike's thoughts. The car turned at the crossroad, disappeared for a few seconds and then the lights reappeared.

The driver stopped about 10 metres away from where Mike was parked. Mike exited his vehicle and stood next to the front right tyre. The boy remained in the back of the car.

The driver of the other vehicle turned off his engine and shut off his lights. He was wearing no mask; he was in a suit and tie, looking very professional. It was if he was here to buy a new car.

He looked like a typical paedophile, sleazy and slimy. The suit didn't fool Mike for a second. It just made him look like a crim ready to face the judge.

He was tall with thick black hair, narrow eyes, almost Asian in appearance. His nose was small and pointy, his frame thin and wiry. He was probably stronger than he looked, but there was nothing about him that concerned Mike.

"Evening," the gentleman said. "Are you wearing a Batman mask?"

"What I am wearing is none of your concern," Mike answered. "What *is* your concern and what should be your only concern is, do you have the cash for the purchase?"

"Yeah sure." The man in the suit reached into the passenger side of his vehicle and removed a large bag. He walked forward and handed it to Mike.

"Your licence?" Mike held out his hand.

The gentleman seemed stunned. "What do you need that for?"

Mike stared at him and repeated, "Your licence."

"I think I will just take my money back and leave," the gentleman said, ignoring Mike's second request for the licence. He reached for the envelope, his fingertips clasping the corners, before they were wrenched downwards towards his own wrist.

"I suggest you show me your licence, now," Mike said.

The gentleman laughed. "Is this hand thing you're doing supposed to hurt me?" he said, half-jokingly.

"No, it doesn't hurt, not until I do this." Mike pushed the elbow of the arm he was holding against his stomach and pushed his hand down, hard.

Excruciating pain travelled up the gentleman's arm.

"Now, are we getting that licence?"

The man nodded. "Ok, ok, please stop."

Mike released his grip a little, but not enough that he couldn't reapply it in an instant if he had to.

The gentleman handed his wallet to Mike, who removed the licence and took a photo of it with his phone, then handed it back.

"Now, Mr Ian Welling. I know where you live. If the money is not all there I will come for you. If at any time in the future you allow the boy to escape from whatever dungeon you and your rock spider mates plan to keep him in, call me immediately and we will find him."

Welling nodded.

"Don't wait. Call immediately," Mike emphasised.

"You won't have to worry. We have a room all set up for him. He will be secure," Welling replied.

Mike nodded. "Now I will get the boy and you will put him in your car. Under no circumstances do you remove the hood until I am gone. After that, it's up to you. Then you will go back to doing what you do and you will never see me again."

"Agreed," Welling said. He was all smiles now. Such a sleazy smile.

Mike removed the boy from the back of the Chrysler and led him out by the rope around his neck.

He handed the rope to Welling. "All yours."

He didn't like Welling much and given the opportunity, he would enjoy ending his life.

Chapter 24

After dealing with Welling, Mike was looking forward to issuing his warning to Neil Figal the next day.

Figal, French heritage, Mike guessed.

The drive to Preston was a good hour and a half.

He arrived in the middle of Sunday afternoon, unannounced.

At his doorstep.

He knocked, his four usual quick raps.

A small man arrived at the door dressed only in a pair of shorts and a dirty (once white, now grey) singlet.

"Yes?" the small man said with a slight touch of a French accent.

Mike considered Welling a sleaze, but he had nothing on this guy.

This guy was a lot smaller, a lot thinner, definitely on some sort of drug. Ice, most likely. His left arm was full of holes and his skin was scratched to pieces; his eyes were dark and recessed, half sunken into his skull; his teeth were yellow. He was dirty.

"You Mr Figal?" Mike asked.

"Maybe, who the fuck are you?" the short man asked.

His right shoulder was leaning against the door frame and his right arm was out of view. Mike knew he had a weapon concealed on the other side of the door. His first thought was a baseball bat, but he immediately dismissed that from his mind. He was too heavily involved in the drug scene for a bat to provide adequate protection. Mike's next thought was a gun, most likely a shotgun.

"I take it you're Figal. That shotgun you have beside the door won't help you. If you keep fucking around . . ."

Figal had no sooner raised the shotgun from the floor than he felt pressure on his ribs. "I'd show your other hand right now," Mike said. Figal released the gun and placed his right hand against the door jamb.

"The Priest has asked me to ensure you're ready to take delivery of the goods on Saturday night. He doesn't like to have orders cancelled. Now, I can see that you probably don't have the money to pay for the order, so here is what I will do for you. You will pay a cancellation fee of $5,000 within seven days. You will deliver it to me where and when I ask."

"I ain't giving you fucking 5k man, no way, tell the Priest to go fuck himself."

Mike didn't wait to see if he had finished speaking. He whipped the shotgun up from the man's ribs to his chin, clipping him on the jaw with the barrel.

Figal jolted backwards with the hit and probably would have fallen had Mike not had him by the belt with his left hand.

"You don't understand, Figal. I was told to come here and make sure you follow through with the order. Now, I'm giving you a break, I'm letting you off. If I go back and say you said 'get fucked', he will send me back. If I come back, there will be no more warnings, it will be the end you. So I am giving you an out and the out is $5,000."

"What, you think I'm stupid? You think I won't just move once you leave? You would never find me again."

With the gun firmly pressed against Figal's ribs, Mike reached into his back pocket and flashed his badge. "I bet you're on parole and I bet if you run I'll find you."

Figal couldn't believe that a crooked cop was shaking him down. What the fuck.

"Now how much of that can you pay today?"

"I don't have any money, I swear, I just bought a hit," Figal answered.

Mike knew this was a lie. If he had just bought a hit, it would be running through his veins, right now. He figured he was coming off a three-day bender and was almost ready to buy again. He would be cashed up.

"I will be in contact with you in seven days. You better have the money when I ask for it or there is nothing I can do for you."

Mike removed the shotgun from his ribs and pivoted as if he was about to turn away, then without warning, his pistol came down. It was fast and ferocious. This time Mike wasn't holding him to protect the fall. Figal stumbled backwards and fell into the hallway. Mike stepped through, took him by the throat and whipped him again. He was out.

Mike rifled through his pocket and found his buyer's roll: $1,700 in total, all in hundreds. He took the shotgun and left the residence, closing the door behind him.

It was a quick call to the Priest on the drive home, only a matter of a few sentences. Most of his calls to him were like this.

"He has no money. He's agreed to 5k, I have $1700 with me."

"What do we do with the goods?" the Priest asked quietly.

"We could always get $3,000 for a weekend with the Judge. Holidays are coming up and the Judge is always looking for some play toy to take up to the lake house."

"But then what do we do with it?" Still quiet, almost whispering.

"Maybe we give it to the Monster, to try and smooth over the relationship. He could always use it on the plantation," Mike suggested.

"Sounds like a lot of trouble for us, Mike. Might be time to just cancel the order."

Cancel the order was code for killing the child. The Priest very rarely resorted to this. However, occasionally things went wrong and loose ends needed to be tidied up. Mike had cleaned up a lot of the Priest's loose ends in the past, but he had planted enough evidence over time to ensure he wouldn't be the only one going down if anything ever went wrong. As his dad had always told him, don't paint yourself into a corner. His other saying was, don't burn your bridge while you're standing on it.

"I think we can avoid cancelling the order. Five thou isn't a bad return, plus we need to gain some bonus points with Monster."

"All right, but if M doesn't want it, you'll need to cancel the order."

With that, the call went dead, and Mike continued on his drive back home to his wife and twin boys.

Chapter 25

As always, Marcus was punctual and reliable. He arrived at exactly 3 am so that they would get to Beechworth at 6, be out on the water by 6.30, and be talking about Afghanistan and the boys by 6.45.

Fishing had never been the purpose. When he and Austin had first started going on trips to Beechworth, it was to relax between tours, to try and forget all that they had witnessed, as well as spend time with their mates away from the war zone.

If war had taught them one thing it was mateship. It was part of their creed to 'never leave a man behind'. They had respect for one another and they had their backs. That was what made the SAS so strong.

Today though, it was just the two of them. Marcus had been injured in the last tour and sent home and Austin had now retired. They had been best mates in the battalion. They had gone through their induction training together and been on all their tours together. The only tour they had not gone on together was Austin's last.

During the three-hour trip to Beechworth, they discussed everything from politics to music, anything except the war. Their conversation centred on Marcus' new line of work with ASIO, Australia's secret service.

"So, what is it you do exactly?" Austin asked.

"Because I know you understand the meaning of 'classified', I can tell you," Marcus answered. "I'm a glorified computer hacker for the government. My technical title is 'security analyst'. I follow suspected terrorists, networks, Facebook accounts, bank accounts, religious leaders, money trails, weapon purchasers. All online. I also do phone taps, but they're getting smarter, using handwritten notes to pass messages now, and I can't hack a note. But that's just the terrorist side of things. I also work on government security. Making sure government sites are secure. The last thing we want is some nutter hacking into the prime minister's travel itinerary."

"So you can look into anyone's personal files?" Austin asked.

"If you give me a name, I can give you everything on them. Same with an address or a licence plate." Marcus continued, "It's different from the war. Not only are we trying to fight them over there, we're now trying to quell the uprisings over here as well."

Austin nodded. He didn't want to go into a discussion about Marcus' injury. The topic was still raw. He could see that Marcus had a severe limp and thought it would remain that way for the rest of his life.

Marcus had arranged a boat, rods and equipment to be ready at the cabin upon their arrival and in accordance with his plans, they were out fishing at 6.45 am. The sun was rising, the wind was cool without being cold, and the temperature was pleasant.

The water was calm and their boat hardly broke the surface as it floated on the lake. Rays of sunlight bounced off the water. The lines dangled, free of nibbles. Not that capturing anything made any difference; they would put it back, regardless. The wee craw fishing lures were not working today.

Marcus sat at the bow while Austin was at the stern, one arm resting on the throttle handle. Marcus passed him an egg and bacon roll and a cup of coffee. The coffee was hot and the egg and bacon roll still warm. Both went down with delight.

It took longer than the usual 15 minutes, but the war conversation raised its head eventually. It was Marcus who said, "In case I haven't said it enough, thank you," he began.

"You don't need to thank me; you would have done the same," Austin replied.

"I know, but if you hadn't come back for me, they would have killed me," he reiterated. "Do you have dreams about that day?" he asked Austin.

"Sometimes," Austin replied, staring out at the lake. "Sometimes I dream that by the time I kill them and get to the Humvee, it's on fire and I can't get you out."

Marcus sipped his coffee, "Sometimes I dream you don't come back and I'm stuck there and I burn to death. Luckily, neither of those things happened. You came back."

"Sorry I was so long. I had to kill six Afghani soldiers to get to you. It wasn't easy, you know. But you never had to worry, you knew I was coming back, we were both coming home or we were both dying there, I was never leaving," Austin answered.

"Excuses, excuses," Marcus joked.

"How is the leg coming along?" Austin asked.

"I'll have the limp forever, but as the doctors say, a limp is better than no leg. I was lucky. Had we driven over the antipersonnel mine directly, I would have lost both my legs. So in a way, I'm lucky we just clipped it," Marcus replied.

"You seen much of the others?" Marcus asked.

"No. All of them except Leeroy were going back. Like us, Leeroy retired. I think he lives up north Queensland, so I doubt we'll get to see him much. The others should be back by June, so we'll need to plan another trip after that. By then, it'll have been 18 months since we were all together," Austin replied.

The line on Marcus' rod began to buzz as it was taken by something. Marcus quickly placed his coffee and roll down to attend to his possible catch.

They spent until lunchtime fishing, then went for a round of golf. It was a relaxing day and it was not until the third hole that Austin realised how much he had needed this. Sarah had obviously seen that.

Their lunch was just a quick bite at the clubhouse between the front nine and the back nine.

Their real meal was tonight. It was a prime Angus T-bone weighing in at one-and-a-half kilos. Dubbed 'the Texan', it was named after the US State of Texas. It came with baked potato and a side salad. If you ate it all, the rest of your table ate at half price. Both Marcus and Austin had never finished the meal. However, tonight could be the night.

First, they had to finish their lunch and work up their appetite before they tackled the Texan.

Chapter 26

Tyler had planned to wait until the lady of the home went to pick up her daughter at 3 pm from school. This trip usually took 15 minutes, but half an hour if they went to the shops after. He had not seen the man at all today. He must have gone back on tour, just a weekend stopover perhaps.

He would need all of the 15 minutes to cut the cameras and disable the alarm, locate the safe, and get the jewels.

The gates opened. The lady's Mercedes drove out, turned down the street and drove out of view.

Countdown.

Tyler drove around to the back of the home to the neighbouring street. He parked two houses down from the target's rear neighbour. He knew they would be at work and there was no gate to scale to enter the property. They had an open drive that led directly to the back yard. The drive was empty, just as it was supposed to be. Tyler pulled down his balaclava, scaled the back fence and sprinted across the back lawn. He was at the back wall of the house within seconds. He cut the two lower cameras with ease. It was the higher ones that would prove the challenge. He had to do them from the inside. He went to the rear laundry door, placed the bump key inside, a simple trick he had learned on the inside. He had bump keys for four and five tumbler locks. He tried the four-tumbler lock key, placed it in the lock and hit and turned. Nothing. Hit and turn, nothing. Hit and turn, nothing.

He tried the five-tumbler key. Placed it in the lock, hit and turned, nothing. He did it again with the same result. What was he doing wrong?

This was eating into his tight schedule.

"Come on Tyler," he muttered to himself.

Still nothing.

Then he remembered the O-ring. It stopped the key from bobbing in and out. He fumbled through his pocket. How could he have forgotten it? His fingers clasped it and he quickly removed it and slid it down over the key.

He stayed with the five-tumbler key already in his hand, placed it in the lock and followed the same steps as before. Bang. He hit the key with the end of the screwdriver and turned the lock. The door opened.

Now the race was on. He had to turn off the alarm. He had 30 seconds. It had already started beeping the second the door opened. Beep, beep, slow and regular at first. Tyler closed and locked the back door behind him. He sprinted towards the internal access door to the garage.

There it was, right on the wall where it was supposed to be. Now to enter the code. The master code, 1739, the four corners, starting top left, finishing bottom right.

Beep, beep, beep, the alarm continued, now beeping a little faster. "Fuck!" Tyler hissed.

He knew the prisoners had been fucking with him. Lies mixed in with half-truths. Some type of initiation, he thought.

He was going to go down for this if he didn't get out and soon. The alarm was about to sound any second. He headed back towards the laundry door, then stopped. Lies with half-truths. Was the safe a half-truth? Tyler changed direction quickly and headed for the stairs. Beep, beep, beep, very fast now. Soon the siren would scream out. He headed for the master bedroom, removed the screwdriver from his pocket, ran into the back of the robe. There it was. The box that sent the signal from the alarm to the security firm. Tyler stood on a suitcase and reached above the shelf. He cracked the case in one quick motion.

Once while studying videos on bump keys, he had come across how to deactivate and reset an alarm. Tyler removed the case and pulled the red wire. The alarm sounded for an instant before being silenced. He looked for the safe in the bottom of the robe. Nothing, another fucking lie. Then something shiny grabbed his attention. It was a bolt. The safe had been bolted here to the floor once upon a time but must have been moved. But to where?

He checked his phone; 3.11 pm. Only four minutes before her return. He was way behind and time seemed to be running extra fast.

Tyler raced down the stairs, nearly tripping on the step third from the top, regaining his balance by grabbing the railing. A vision of him lying in a pool of blood at the bottom of the staircase when the wife came home flashed through his mind. He headed straight to the study. He looked behind a painting of a colonial style picture of early settlers. No good, just wall.

Where would it be? Why would they have moved it?

Tyler's phone beeped, telling him 3.13 pm. Two minutes until her return.

The bolt flashed into his mind again. What had the safe been bolted to? Chipboard. Why move it? Too easy to pick up and take away. Needed to be bolted to something stronger. Concrete. It had to be here somewhere, but where?

The floor was all smooth, nothing bolted to it.

Tyler looked under the desk. Nothing, just a filing cabinet to the right-hand side.

Then he looked at the desk and cabinet again. The desk was deeper than the cabinet. Something was behind it.

Tyler moved the cabinet, just sightly, so he could see behind it.

Jackpot! There it was, bolted onto the concrete slab through the carpet. Wouldn't be able to pick this one up. Good thing he knew how to crack it, but that would take time, time he didn't have now. On cue, his alarm sounded at 3.15 pm. He could hear the gate moving. She was back, right on schedule. *She* was on schedule but he was behind.

He was out of time and empty-handed.

What was he going do now?

Leave with nothing?

He had an idea, but he had to act fast.

He needed to reconnect the alarm and then get up into the manhole. Tyler slid the cabinet back to its original position and sprinted up the stairs. He reconnected the wire, tapped the cover back on with the handle of the screwdriver. He could hear the alarm beeping as if it had just been set. It was counting itself down 30 seconds and then it would be rearmed.

He made sure everything looked undisturbed, as best he could in the limited time he had.

The garage door had opened and the engine was switched off and they were coming inside.

"Wait honey, we need to check the mail," Tyler heard as he lifted the lid of the manhole. He stood on a shelf with bath towels and pulled himself up into the roof cavity. As he dropped the lid back into place, the alarm sounded its final beep.

He let out a huge sigh of relief.

The stroll to the letterbox gained him only 30 seconds but he needed every one of them.

Now all he had to do now was wait. Wait until they were asleep, then he would have all the time he needed to crack the safe.

Then an awful realisation came to him.

He had left his screwdriver in the master bedroom. He couldn't leave here without it. Even though he was wearing gloves, he had used the screwdriver without them. His prints would be all over it.

* * *

Beau sat inside his van waiting for an hour to pass since the last light, in the top right corner of the home, went out at 11.30 pm. No doubt the master bedroom. It had only been out for half an hour. He had to be patient a little longer. He had not seen the man from the movies, so this confirmed he had gone away, and that was a good thing.

His plan would go to perfection and the girl would be his. He had to get her, otherwise the Monster would end him, he was sure of it. Now that the Monster had seen a photo of her, he could not substitute her for another if this went wrong.

Beau had done his research on her house. The back way was the easiest but there were cameras. He would have to put his paintball skills to the test.

His plan was simple: first, cut the power. Most cameras stopped recording once the power was cut. Very few had an uninterruptable power supply attached. But he had to get to the house itself in order to cut the power. Next, he would need to hit all four back cameras with orange paint from his paintball rifle. It was state-of-the art, had cost him almost $1,500, the infrared telescopic sight a large chunk of the cost.

Beau snuck past the car parked in the drive directly behind the girl's house. It was hard to use the scope while he was wearing his joker mask, but he managed it.

He stood on the fence, aimed up at the bottom camera but noticed the cable was hanging. It had been cut. He scanned across to the other lower camera. Same deal, cable cut. He scanned up to the top camera. The top one was intact, as was the one on the other side. Possibly they'd had an attempted break-in and hadn't yet had them fixed. Didn't matter, wasn't his problem, just made his job easier. Only two shots needed. He doubted the rifle would be powerful enough to break the camera. He only needed the paint to cover the lens.

He scanned again, his finger resting against the metal trigger. He slowed his breathing and squeezed. The paint ball flew, hit its target and splattered paint over the camera. There was no crack. Nothing broke. Everything was going to plan. He scanned the telescope across the home and repeated the process. Fifteen seconds later, he was over the fence and heading for the back door.

With his rifle slung over his left shoulder, Beau used his screwdriver to apply pressure on the lock, while with his right shoulder he pressed against the door. He was having trouble seeing. The mask kept slipping. With all the cameras disabled, he removed the mask and placed it in his back pocket.

Soon enough, the lock popped and the metal lock and screws fell to the floor, clunking on the tiles of the laundry floor as they landed.

Chapter 27

Sarah always took a couple of nights to get used to sleeping by herself again.

Every time Austin left for duty, the week after was always the toughest.

The clunk downstairs immediately startled her from whatever light sleep she had managed to find. She sat upright, frozen, listening for the slightest sound.

Nothing.

A stair creaked ever so slightly and she knew someone was in her house. Someone was coming up the stairs.

Her thought immediately turned to Mikayla. Her bedroom door was shut, she was hopefully asleep. Sarah grabbed her phone and called the police. She hopped out of bed and hid in her wardrobe, hoping she could tell the police what was happening without being heard.

"Police Emergency," the voice on the line answered.

"Someone is in my house."

"Address ma'am?"

Sarah replied as quietly as she could.

"A patrol car has been dispatched, ma'am. It's on its way. Do you know where the person is, ma'am?"

She listened. Nothing. "No, I'm not sure."

She stood in her wardrobe shaking, listening for any sound, any clue as to the intruder's whereabouts. Then there was another creak, not a step this time. This time it was a door opening. The door to her daughter's room.

She could hide no longer, she had to act. Phone still in hand, she turned to leave when a silver object on the shelf caught her eye. Before she had assessed what it was, or even thought about who it belonged to, the screwdriver was in her hand and she was heading out of the bedroom.

Her daughter's scream filled the whole house. It was only one but by god, it was a good one. A scream to be proud of!

By the time Sarah was on her landing, she could see a man descending the stairs carrying Mikayla in a bear hug with one big paw over her mouth.

"Put her down and get out of my house!" she yelled and ran towards the intruder.

She threw herself at the man as he reached the last step, grabbing at his jacket. Her phone flew from her hand, coming to rest at the bottom of the stairs. Now she had dropped her phone and lost her grip on the intruder. The intruder was heading towards the back door. This was no robbery. This was a kidnapping.

Mikayla tried desperately to free herself from her captor's grip.

After a failed first attempt, Sarah jumped on her daughter's attacker as he neared the back door.

The attacker held the girl in his left hand and reached over his left shoulder with his other hand. He grabbed the woman by her hair and rammed her face and forehead into the back of his head, like a reverse head butt. After three quick reverse butts, he felt the woman slide off his back.

Beau turned to see her slumped on the floor, screwdriver still in hand. She had seen him so he had no choice.

"Don't hurt my mummy!" Mikayla screamed as he raised Sarah's limp unconscious body up off the tiled floor. Beau answered the child's screams with a back-hander that sent her sprawling across the room. The sound of the leather glove against her skin ricocheted throughout the room.

Mikayla heard her mum scream and then thud to the floor, the screwdriver she was holding now embedded in her throat. The man was still holding her mum. What had he just done, had he killed her?

"Mum!" she screamed, before his big paw covered her mouth again. "Scream again and I will kill you. Do you understand?" he said carefully, as he moved his hand down from her mouth and placed it firmly around her throat. "I will snap your neck just like a chicken."

Her tears turned to anger. Her mum was dead and this man was taking her. But why? Was this a dream, a nightmare? She would wake soon.

Wake up, she begged herself, but the nightmare continued. The big guy flung the back door open and rushed out into the night air. It was cold. The wind was blowing and it was icy. For a big guy he was really moving. She could see her house getting further away. As he ran faster, she bobbed around in his bear-like grip.

They reached the back fence and before she knew what was happening, she was airborne and free-falling. The fence came and went under her as she flew through the air. She let out a small scream that was cut off when she thudded to the earth. Before she had even regained her breath, she was back inside the bear grip.

Now he was sprinting down the street and they approached a white van. He removed his hand from her mouth and threw her inside. Sliding along the metal floor, she crashed to a stop when she slid into a wire mesh frame. The door slammed behind her.

Seconds later, they were moving, fast at first, sharp corners. She rolled from one corner of the van to the other as the van skidded sideways.

This was no dream, she had just been kidnapped and her mum had been killed. Where was he taking her?

She couldn't see anything. Everything was blacked out including the view to the front driver's cabin. She tried to count the streets. She started out well until she took a tumble and then missed a few after that.

Twenty minutes later they were still driving, at normal speed now. She could hear the bells of a train crossing. A few seconds later she could hear the train pass, then the bells stopped and they continued driving. Soon after, they came to a complete stop and the engine was cut.

The driver's door opened and closed. Soon he would come for her, or so she thought. She heard a loud dragging sound followed by slamming, as if metal had hit metal.

She moved towards the back doors of the van, slowly, so her movement wouldn't be noticed, if he was still around. The steel mesh was also on the inside of the van doors. There were two large metal plates where the handles should have been. She assumed they were there so no one could open the back doors. But she would still try. She had to.

She placed two fingers in through the metal mesh and wiggled them down behind the metal cover. She could feel what she thought was the plastic door handle but she couldn't get her fingers to the edge to pull.

She was trapped.

* * *

The girl's scream startled Tyler, who had drifted off to sleep in the roof cavity. His watch was set to vibrate at 1 am, but the scream beat him to it.

The cries of "Put her down and get out of my house!" brought him back to reality.

Who else was in the house?

Maybe the man had returned, a custody dispute perhaps. He reached for his butterfly knife, which was in his back pocket. It was hard to grip with the gloves so he took his right glove off and threw it into the crawl space of the roof.

Maybe the husband or ex-husband had come back for the girl.

Whatever it was, the commotion had stopped and he had to get out of there as fast as he could.

Tyler raised the lid of the manhole and peeped out. No one was there, no one he could see anyhow. He waited a few seconds and peeped again and again. Still no one. He lifted the lid enough to slip out. There were no sounds. From the top of the staircase he could see a mobile phone on one of the lower stairs glowing. It was still on, still calling someone. As quietly as possible, Tyler stepped down slowly, taking care not to use the rail so as not to leave fingerprints with his right hand. Was there still someone in the house? As he came to the phone, he saw the number on the display. Triple zero. The police would be on their way. He had to get out of here now!

From the bottom of the stairs he could see the tiled hall that led from the front entrance, and the back dining and kitchen where he had entered. Slumped in the middle of the tiles directly in his path was a body, the mum's body.

Tyson's ears pricked up at the sound of distant wailing sirens. He could study the scene no more, he had to leave and leave now. Tyler darted around the body and out through the open rear door. He sprinted across the back yard as if he was in the trials for the Olympics. He had never run so fast. His heart felt as if it was going to explode. He was anxious, sweaty and dismayed at what had unfolded. What the fuck had just happened?

It wasn't until 20 minutes later when he finally felt comfortable with the distance he had put between himself and the property that a shocking thought hit him for the second time that night. Like a baseball bat to the nuts. He had left the screwdriver at the property. He then reflected on the scene: a screwdriver had been protruding from the mum's neck. Couldn't have been, could it?

"Fuck!" he screamed, bashing the dash of his car and rocking back and forth in his seat. "Fuck, fuck, fuck!" he continued screaming.

Chapter 28

Nothing worse than being woken by a ringing phone at 3 am. "Hello?" I answered.

"Sorry to wake you, buddy, but we have a homicide." Jake's familiar voice.

"What do you mean 'we'?" I asked. "I'm on cold cases, not homicides."

Jake took no notice. "They believe it's a child abduction gone wrong."

I sat bolt upright. "What do you mean an abduction gone wrong?" I asked.

"It's not clear yet but early reports are a girl may have been taken from her room. I thought you would want to get involved early. It may be related to the others," Jake replied. "I'll text you the address. Get there as soon as you can."

"I'm leaving now," I answered, already half dressed.

Jake had hung up.

Being in Kew, Jake would have got there first, but not by much. When I arrived, several officers showed me through to the rear of the property where the crime scene had been established.

I pulled out my torch and my notepad. It hadn't taken me long to establish my own system when examining a crime scene. Although it sometimes went against standard protocol, I liked to walk myself through the scene before getting all the information from the officers. That way my first impression was mine, not someone else's.

Gloves, torch and notepad, my tools of trade. The torch was slimline and lightweight, so I could hold it under my arm if I had to. The first thing I noticed when escorted to the rear of the property by the uniforms was the surveillance system. There were four front cameras, one side camera and four rear. The rear ones had been painted with orange paint, and on the ground was a skin of paint. I asked the uniforms to pick it up and bag it, have it ready for examination. There were other skins near the other cameras as well.

When I examined the cameras, I could see that the cables to the two lower ones had been cut at the connection point. When I got to the door, it was already being dusted for prints. They had collected the broken pieces of the lock for individual testing at the lab.

Inside a lady lay in her nightgown, lifeless on the cold tiles. The positioning of her feet was of particular interest to me. It looked like 'dead man fall', which meant she was dead before she hit the ground. Her legs had crossed on the way down. This could have been because she'd died suddenly. I was guessing she had been beaten, lifted up, stabbed in the throat, and then dropped.

I made my way to the bottom of the stairs. Jake was questioning a neighbour, with a uniformed officer taking the statement. We exchanged nods and continued with our tasks. There was an evidence marker, number six, sitting next to a phone on the second bottom step. I'd noticed evidence markers up to 27 as I passed the rear doors and was sure there were more yet to be found and marked.

I walked wide of the phone and headed up the stairs.

At the top, three doors were ajar, the closest a girl's room. At the landing end of the staircase was the master bedroom.

I started there. I wanted to leave the girl's room until last, because that was where I would need to focus most of my attention. The master bedroom looked like any other. While the bed sheets were messed up, there didn't appear to be any evidence of a scuffle in this room.

I walked through to the en suite. All was neat and tidy; again, no signs of a struggle. I looked into the wardrobe on my way past. It looked normal enough. I noticed the alarm box was on the wall above the robe shelf. I had almost walked past when I noticed a scratch and a dent.

Better to be safe than sorry. I'd hate to miss a vital clue. I waved my torch over it. Definitely scratched on the lip. It could have been done on installation, I supposed. There was also an indent under the scratch, which made me wonder if the lid had been tampered with. I called down to a uniformed officer to send the fingerprints unit up once they had finished with the door, and then headed to the girl's room. The night light was still in the on position although with no power, there was no glow. The doona still covered most of the bed. I touched the bed. Hell, it was still warm.

I sat on the corner of the bed. Who would do this? I wondered. Was it the same person responsible for the other three kidnappings? If so, this was a big concern. He had become desperate. While the others had been taken from the streets in broad daylight, this one was worse because it showed me the criminal had evolved from opportunistic to targeting his prey. Tonight he had shown he was willing to do whatever it took to acquire his prey.

If he was targeting them, I needed to know how. Maybe he was a neighbour. As soon as I thought of that possibility, I discounted it. It was unlikely that an unemployed man who took kids from the street in a van would be able to afford to live in such an affluent area.

Which led me to wonder, how had he targeted this one? Maybe this was different from the others. Maybe this was a kidnapping or a ransom ploy gone wrong. Whatever it was, it was too soon to try connecting them. I had to find some stronger evidence before I could consider them related.

I sat looking at the room. It was now another waiting room, a room waiting for the return of the person who brought everything here to life. Nothing upset me more than seeing a child's room full of possessions lying idle. Barbies sat in their house and their cars, soft toys on a shelf above the foot of her bed, clothes were laid out on a seat, obviously ready for the day ahead. The lamp that would normally bring the cut-out characters' shadows to life, dancing on the walls as the shade slowly spun around the globe, stood still.

I sat there staring into emptiness. I was praying not to a god but to a higher being. My prayer wasn't for me, it was for time and more of it. It suddenly registered that I had better speak to Jake and get a full briefing.

Halfway up from the bed, I saw it. How had I missed it? How had they all missed it?

Maybe, like me, they hadn't thought of it. I walked out of the girl's room, half stooped over, not taking my eyes off it.

In the linen press there were towels strewn over the floor.

"Officer, bring me a chair." I switched my flashlight on and examined the messy linen closet. I worked the torch up. The lid of the manhole was three-quarters of the way off. The section not obscured by the cavity looked as if it had dirty marks, maybe prints. I shone the torch across the cupboard from celling to floor. The two bottom shelves had dirty marks on them, maybe from a shoe. An officer arrived with a chair. I didn't want to disturb anything that had been left behind. I stood on the chair and looked inside the cavity. It was dusty but empty. No girl, but someone had been up here recently.

I asked Forensics to make sure they searched the roof space immediately, just in case she was there. It was standard procedure to check the whole scene for a missing child, yet there was no harm in stating the obvious.

Forensics had finished at the rear door. The lock had been torn right off. Springs and metal lay across the tiles, every piece marked with a numbered cone detailing its evidence number.

I stepped through the doorway and headed to the back of the home. It was dark. I could see the cameras but only just. I shone my flashlight on the back wall of the house. The cameras were covered in orange paint.

I walked across the yard to the back fence. Luckily, the rungs were on this side. I stood on the bottom rung and looked into the neighbour's yard and saw what looked like orange casings. I shone my torch across the top of the fence. There was some orange paint on one of the palings, and what appeared to be a strand of green hair.

I called an officer over, and asked him to wake up the neighbour and ensure the back yard was secure until the forensic technicians had a chance to completely check the scene.

* * *

Jake had seen all he needed to have a fair understanding of what had happened here tonight. Someone had broken in to rob the place and had been confronted. That confrontation had ended in Sarah Campbell's death. Her daughter either witnessed the attack and had been taken to be disposed of later, or was taken in order to extort money from the family.

It seemed to Jake that the intent of the home invasion was more likely that of robbery than of kidnapping. Robberies had been rife in the area over the last few months.

Jake had finished speaking with the neighbours on both sides. Neither had seen or heard anything out of the ordinary and both described the victim as a very nice and easy-going neighbour.

Only one of the neighbours had met the husband. Apparently, he was away a lot with work. Apparently, he had been back all weekend but no one had seen him since Sunday night.

Jake decided it was best to try and contact him, find out where he was and what his movements had been over the last day or so.

The neighbour told him the husband's name was Austin.

Jake cycled through Sarah's recent calls and found a call from 7.30 Monday night only five minutes long, an outgoing call to Austin.

Jake's thumb hovered over the number before pressing on it. It rang three times before it was answered. "Babe, is everything all right?" the half-panicked, tired voice asked.

"Is this Austin Campbell?" Jake asked.

"Yes, what are you doing with my wife's phone?"

Jake paused. "My name is Detective Jake Miller. I'm with Homicide. We were called to the property by your wife. Upon our arrival we have found her deceased. I am sorry."

There was a stunned silence on the other end.

"I am ringing to ask, is your daughter with you? She's not here at the house and we're desperately trying to ascertain her whereabouts," Jake said.

Austin was clearly upset. "No, she's not with me, I'm away on a fishing trip with a mate. We're up in Beechworth and it'll take me over three hours to get back. I'll be there as soon as I can."

"We'll still be here when you get back. I can organise a police car to drive you back. Save you driving at this time if that helps you out at all?"

"It's ok, my mate will drive, we'll leave now."

Jake hung up the phone.

"Listen up people: we have a missing child believed kidnapped. Please put out an APB for her." He moved over towards me. "Well, if what he's telling us is true, he didn't do it. He's away on a fishing trip up state. They're checking the phone towers to confirm he is where he says he is and we're having both calls examined; the call I just made and the one his wife made at 7.30. He would have had time to get here and kill her but not enough time to get back."

"How did he sound?" I asked.

"Genuinely distraught," Jake replied. "What type of person does this, Brodie, what type of person steals a child from the safety of their bedroom?"

"Clearly whoever did this was desperate. But we may be looking at a different offender to that of the other kidnappings. The others were more opportunistic, don't you think?" I asked.

"It appears that way," Jake replied. "Forensics have a lot of work to do here. Feel like a coffee? I have something important I need to tell you."

Concerned and quizzical, I accepted.

Chapter 29

When Marcus woke to thumping on his bedroom door, he instinctively knew something was wrong. He opened the door to a man who looked void of all life, whereas hours earlier, he had seemed full of life.

Austin had been crying. "Mate! What's wrong?" Marcus asked.

"Sarah's been killed and Mikayla's missing."

"What? How?" Marcus asked, trying to register what he was being told. "Oh my god," were the next words out of his mouth. "What happened?"

"I don't know, I just had a call from Homicide. They were called to my home and found Sarah dead and Mikayla missing. I really need to head back home now, if that's ok."

"Of course, no problem," Marcus answered, already throwing things into his duffel bag. "Meet at the car in two mins," he said.

Austin nodded and headed back to his room.

It took Marcus a little longer than two minutes. By the time he got to the car, Austin was already waiting.

"Mate, it's raining; why didn't you just wait on the porch?"

Austin shrugged. "Let's just go."

They drove in silence. Every time Marcus looked over to speak, he noticed Austin blankly staring out the window into the darkness.

An hour in, Austin finally spoke. "I'm going to find who did this and kill them and anyone else who had anything to do with it."

"Buddy, don't go doing anything stupid, they might find Mikayla, she will need you, now more than ever," Marcus replied.

"Can you get me my kit?" Austin asked, ignoring Marcus' warning.

"Don't go down that path, now is not the time to be making these decisions, let the police do their job," Marcus said, almost pleading.

"Can you get me my kit?" Austin repeated.

Marcus nodded.

"I can organise for it to be sent to Melbourne for reassignment and just not reassign it."

"Good, get it done. The sooner the better, I don't have much time. They better not hurt Mikayla." Austin returned his focus to the dark emptiness outside the window.

Marcus knew if Austin had been at home, Sarah would be alive and Mikayla would be asleep in her bed. Marcus knew it was just cruel fate, but he couldn't help feeling responsible. He was the one who had pressed Austin to go on the fishing trip.

Marcus turned slightly towards him. "I am sorry man. It's my fault, you should have been there. I took you away on this dumb fishing trip."

Without turning, Austin answered, "Don't blame yourself, the only people who are responsible are those who did it and they're the ones who'll pay."

"Whatever you need," Marcus said.

"What will the police learn about us when they do our background checks?" Austin asked.

"Police will get 'army employed, honourable discharge' in your case. The ASIO and SAS part will remain confidential. The only people who will ever know about the status of ASIO employees like us are the general and the prime minister and the defence minister. We're covered by the highest classification in the country, that's how we stay safe from terrorist reprisals," Marcus said.

Austin didn't speak again for the rest of the trip, but Marcus knew that he was thinking about poor Sarah.

Chapter 30

Jake and I sat down at the local McDonald's, the only place open at 5 am. I was eating a McMuffin and Jake was drinking his coffee.

"So what did you want to tell me?" I asked, full of curiosity.

"After this homicide I'm going to retire from the force."

"What? Why?" I asked.

"I don't think I'm making a difference anymore, maybe I never was, maybe I've just woken to the realisation that justice no longer exists."

"You're one of the best cops that has ever been."

"Maybe. You know Karl and Amanda from when we were kids?"

"Yeah, I remember it well," I replied.

James Mitchell had been sentenced to 20 years for the murder of Karl and Amanda when they were children. He stole the car they were passengers in. He'd convinced the jury that he didn't mean to kill the children, that he couldn't even remember doing it because he was drug affected.

"Mitchell is likely to get out of Northview at Bendigo. He'll probably be declared no longer a threat to himself or society. I can't believe he was found not guilty by reason of insanity. What's the point, seriously?"

"How do you know he's getting out?" I asked.

"Salma told me, she's on the advisory board. She's one of the psychiatrists who makes the decisions and she said they're having trouble finding fault and they can't just keep him in there. He's been out on visits to his mother's for months."

"Maybe he has got better, maybe he was insane?" I proposed.

"Let me tell you, he was acting, he was full of shit. What many don't know is that at the time he was arrested he was living with his cousin. Police found an eight-year-old boy strapped to a bed in the spare room. He had been raped dozens of times and he'd been there five days and was close to death. Luckily, the boy survived. Spent two months in the hospital and was mentally scarred for life but he survived. Kidnapping was added to the sentence for Mitchell. He didn't care, he was too busy acting the loon trying to avoid life sentence for the murders. The kidnapping charge was the least of his issues. His cousin, what was his name?" Jake tapped the table, trying to remember. "Anyway, he was just as big a scumbag, he had raped the boy too, but the police were so keen to send Mitchell away when Ian . . ." Jake turned his head to the left and looked up as if searching his brain for the last piece of the puzzle, "that's it, Ian Welling. When Ian offered to testify, his charge of rape was pleaded down to a short sentence for accessory after the fact for the kidnapping, but he was just as bad. Two scumbags, both hooked on drugs, both child molesters, both under 25." Jake shook his head and sipped his coffee.

"Is that what this is all about, a light sentence, a plea deal?" I asked.

"No . . . possibly . . . to some extent, I'm not really sure," Jake answered. "Our work gets undone. We catch whoever is doing these kidnappings and he'll run around like a loon and he'll get off, or be sent to a farm, or plead it out for a deal.

"After Ian did his two years, he raped a boy in a park, he got seven, was out in five with good behaviour. Good behaviour! He raped two kids before he was 30! Good behaviour shouldn't be an option. But it is."

Jake took a deep breath.

"Plus Hayley is having a baby, she hasn't told me, but I think she's afraid that I won't want it."

"Do you want it?" I asked straight out.

"Of course I want it, I was just hoping the world would be better, but it only seems worse. I don't understand the world anymore. Look at all the kidnappings and murders we have piling up."

His coffee was almost finished.

"We work our asses off and the courts send them back out to us a few years later," Jake continued. "Now we have terrorists on the streets, the world's gone mad. I don't feel I'm making a difference anymore," he repeated, swishing his remaining coffee around in his mug. "Maybe it's that I don't want Hayley to get that phone call. I never used to care about what happened to me but since I found out I'm going to be a father, I'm shit scared of getting killed doing this job."

"What will you do if you don't do this?" I asked.

"I've been offered a job at Professional Investigations. It's $100,000 a year and fewer hours."

"Are you going to find taking photos of guys cheating on their wives exciting enough for you?" I asked Jake. I had finished my McMuffin in four bites. They didn't seem as big as they used to be. My hash browns were cold. I should have eaten them in the reverse order.

"Probably not, but I won't be disappointed with the outcome all the time. I think they would be happy to take you on too, if you wanted to come," Jake responded.

"Thanks mate, but it's not my cup of tea, I love working the cold cases. It's where I'm best suited. So when are you leaving?" I asked.

"Not sure yet, I think I need to give four weeks' notice." Jake paused.

"What do you think of the murder?" he asked.

"I'm not sure Jake, I don't know if it was a kidnapping gone wrong or a burglary that turned into a kidnapping, in an attempt to get some ransom. It could be either."

Jake's phone buzzed. The caller ID came up as 'Pete IT'.

"Hey, Pete, what you got? Ok, good to know, we'll be back in five." He hung up. "They've accessed the computer and the crowd that stores the security footage. Let's go have a look." Jake slid out from behind the table.

"Maybe it'll explain the orange shit on the cameras," I suggested.

"It might even provide us with a killer," Jake said.

Even though the ride back to the Kew crime scene was short, it gave me a bit more time to ask Jake about the one positive piece of information our chat had provided.

"So do you want a boy or a girl?" I asked.

"Not fussed," he said. "The name I have will suit both."

"What's that?" I asked.

"Indiana," he replied.

"Like Indiana Jones?" I questioned.

"Yep."

"That's awesome, what does Hayley think of it?"

"She doesn't even know I know she's having a baby."

"If she didn't tell you she's having a baby then how do you know she is even having one?" I questioned.

"I'm a detective, it's what I do."

"Ok, do me a favour. Before you say anything else to anyone else, talk to her, please."

"It's ok Brucey, we're going out for dinner tonight. I'll tell her I know and it'll be all good," Jake said.

* * *

By the time we arrived back at the crime scene, Jake had switched back into detective mode.

In the study, Pete sat at the desktop playing feedback from the various cameras.

"Come and look at this," Pete called out as he noticed us enter the property.

"What have you got?" Jake asked.

"I was going back through the cameras and at 12.30 the top left back goes black. I think that's the paint. If at the same time we look at camera two, we can see a small reflection from what appears to be a scope just over the back fence."

It was hard to make out and identifying someone from this footage would be impossible. But it at least gave us the time the suspect entered the property.

"What time did the victim first call dispatch?" Jake asked the Forensics team.

"Twelve forty-three," one of them answered almost immediately.

"Ok, cameras out just after 12.30, phone call 12.43, all seems to fit. What time did the officers first arrive?"

"Twelve fifty-two," the same man answered. Obviously it had been his job to detail the calls made to establish a window.

"So we have nine minutes from call to arrival, during which a lady was killed and a girl taken. Let's get filling in those nine minutes, people," Jake ordered.

Chapter 31

It was after 7 am and Austin Campbell was sitting in front of us.

He was clearly devastated, as any loving husband and father would be, and both Jake and I ruled him out as a suspect immediately.

"We are sorry for your loss," Jake began. "Our biggest concern right now is to establish where your daughter is. So any information you can provide us could be vital. If you need to stop at any time, please just let us know."

Austin nodded.

"We are aware that you have just returned from duty in Afghanistan and that you have now retired after four tours."

Again Austin nodded.

"In the last few months had Sarah raised any concerns about home security?"

"About six months ago she installed a security system, a monitored one. She had some jewellery in an upstairs safe and there had been some break-ins in our neighbourhood so I suggested she get an alarm system installed. Anyway, she told me that when the guy came he suggested moving the safe from the robe to the study so it was more secure and at the same time further away from her. That way if someone ever did break in, they wouldn't be confronted and they would just take what they'd come for and leave. We took his advice and had it shifted. As far as I know, no one has ever attempted to break in. Sarah was only concerned because of what had been happening in the area," Austin said.

"Austin, we're of the opinion that this may have been a break-in and your wife disturbed him. Rather than leave empty-handed, we think he took Mikayla for a ransom. It means he's less likely to do her harm if he thinks she's his pay cheque," Jake suggested.

Austin nodded.

"The good news is we've collected a lot of evidence, we have a weapon and several prints as well as two possible shoe prints. They've been sent to Forensics for analysis."

"Well, that's a good start," Austin said. "What do you want me to do?" he asked.

"We might need you to appear in an interview, it may help keep Mikayla alive. When you do, just remember that every time you mention your daughter, mention her by name, invite a ransom, because that way if we're wrong we might at least give him the idea that he could score big. If he isn't planning on keeping her around, he might see the benefit." Then Jake asked him, "If we organise the interview, would you be happy to do it? We really need it done as soon as possible."

"Please. Whatever will help get her back," Austin said.

It was only 45 minutes later when Austin found himself sitting in front of dozens of cameras at the St Kilda Road police station.

"Thank you all for attending the press conference," Jake said to the media. "Overnight, Victoria has suffered one of its most heinous crimes. A young mother was murdered and her daughter has been taken from inside the family home."

He stood aside for Austin, who was visibly upset. The recent events had begun to take their toll.

He began, "I would like to say to the person or persons responsible that what's done is done. However, you have the opportunity to prevent the situation from getting a lot worse. Mikayla is only 11 years old. It's important that Mikayla is brought back to me. If you have Mikayla, please just drop her at a street, don't hurt her. Mikayla is all I have left. I am open to paying a reward for any information leading to her whereabouts and her safe return."

Jake held up a photo of Mikayla. "Any information on Mikayla's location will be handled in the strictest confidence. Let me just add this: if you have information on this crime but had no direct involvement in it, you will be offered immunity. Please call Crime Stoppers with any information, no matter how small or insignificant you may think it is. Thank you," Jake finished, before stepping away from the media desk.

Austin left the interview and sat down in an office cubicle at the heart of the Homicide division. He sat there, head in hands, trying to keep the worst thoughts away. He knew he had to stay strong but he didn't know if he would be able to.

He remembered something Marcus had said. "She needs you."

He decided to keep saying that to himself until he had her back.

Whatever it took, he was getting her back.

Chapter 32

Beau had been disciplined as usual. He had kept his mask on, but on entering the girl's home, he had taken it off and placed it in his pocket. Usually he would have kept it on, however, he was scared the big guy from the movies, her father, might be there and if he was, he didn't want his vision limited.

He had seen him leave but he couldn't be sure he hadn't returned and he couldn't afford a surprise attack.

* * *

He had never killed before, well not on the outside anyway. Once, on the inside, he had been forced to show his mettle and set an example of what happened to those who thought he could be used as a sex toy.

As with most new inmates, the weak ones were targeted, eyed by the gangs and then when the opportunity presented itself, attacked. Attacks usually happened in isolated areas of the prison so the attackers were not interrupted by prison officers. On occasion, officers were paid to walk in the opposite direction.

Beau had been on the inside for only two weeks when he first noticed he was being watched. He had drawn the attention of the gang known by all other inmates as the 'Husbands', because those they targeted would become their 'wives'.

Beau suffered a close encounter where he was nearly raped by the Husbands in the toilet block, only to have the assault broken up by an uncorrupted guard. The fact that Beau had been incarcerated for child molestation only made the target on his back bigger.

Beau understood the prison world and knew that he would never be free from attacks. He also knew if he put up a fight, people might think twice before attacking him again.

Beau remembered it as if it was yesterday. He was finishing a job in the laundry room where he had been stacking the shelves of the laundry cupboard. The shelves were six feet high and four feet wide and they were enclosed within a steel cage so that the goods would not be stolen.

He was on his last shelf when he noticed the guard at the far end of the hall nod and walk away from his post. The guard at the entrance at the other end of the hall also left his post. Beau instantly knew something was up and prayed it wasn't going to be about him. But then he knew. Three men, all members of the Husbands' gang, approached him. The three of them all working together would get what they wanted, and what they wanted was a turn. Luck was with Beau on that day. He would normally have said God was with him, but Beau knew there was no god, especially in a place like that.

The first one entered the cage, with the second man about three metres behind him. The man was bigger than Beau and so Beau did the only smart play he had available. He went on full attack. His first move was not a punch or a kick, but a head butt. The top of Beau's forehead matched perfectly with his attacker's nose, and the force of Beau's strike was ferocious. The man went flying backwards, his body slamming against the door of the cage, forcing the door closed and his Husband mates trapped outside. It was difficult to open a door with a dead weight behind it. Even though Beau's attacker was bigger, he was in no state to offer assistance to his gang members trying to enter the cage. His nose was spread across his face from the head butt and his vision was blurred. Before he knew what was happening, Beau had him up against the gate. Beau had fed a piece of packing wire through the cage door and he now pulled it tight around the man's throat.

Beau pulled the packing wire tight so it cut into his attacker's throat. His two gang members could only stand and watch.

The blood trickled at first and then as the wire really began to cut deep, it flowed. The two remaining gang members remained circling outside the cage like a pack of half-scared, half-hungry wolves, trying to work out if there was going to be a meal or not.

The standoff continued for another three minutes before being broken by a new shift of laundry workers walking in. Both the men on the outside fled the laundry, as did Beau as soon as the Husbands were out of sight.

One thing was certain: no one would talk about who had killed the gang member. Everyone's privileges were restricted for two weeks, but still no one spoke. A message was sent to Beau through his cellmate. It was clear and simple.

'You're dead.'

Just as his murder of one of the Husbands had angered them and moved him to the top of their hit list, it had not gone unnoticed by other gangs, especially those who wanted to keep their prison virginity intact. The death in the laundry room sent his whole cell block into lockdown, all privileges were withdrawn and everyone was confined to their cells 24 hours a day. No one was going anywhere until answers were found. Of course, no one would talk, no one would snitch. You snitched, you died. Eventually, life in the prison would just move on.

During the lockdown, his only visitor was an elderly priest. "I hear the Husbands have you high on their wanted list," the priest muttered.

"In prison, everyone wants something from you," Beau replied.

"I could have you moved away from the Husbands into a special rehabilitation program for the remainder of your sentence. A nice prison far away from here. Do you believe in God, my son?"

All Beau heard was 'away from the Husbands'.

"Yes, I believe in God," he answered. He would believe in aliens if it kept him alive.

"Good. I will take care of the details," the priest said, leaving Beau alone once more.

After he left, Beau wondered what the priest might want in exchange.

* * *

This time, however, it was an innocent woman who hadn't deserved to die. But getting caught would have meant death for him. There would be no way he would be able to avoid the Husbands for another jail term, or satisfactorily explain to the Monster he was empty-handed and without the girl he had promised.

He drove the van back to his home, opened the shed and moved the train set. Then he opened the hatch and took the red ladder down from the wall.

It was a routine he knew well.

He placed his mask on, not for her, she had already seen him, but for the boy who was still below.

He had taken a sack from under the driver's seat. Before he removed her from the van, he needed to cover her face. The less she saw of the surroundings, the better. Beau walked to the back of the van, opened the rear doors and placed it quickly over her head. She went to scream at the sight of his mask but thought better of it when Beau raised his massive hand ready to slap her again.

He took the piece of rope, placed it over the hood and guided her down to the cell. He placed her in the same cell that held the Monster's last delivery. He didn't speak to either of his current captives.

He removed her hood, closed the gate behind him and disappeared up the red ladder.

Chapter 33

Austin booked himself into a hotel, hoping he might be able to get some sleep.

Forensics were still at his place and according to detectives, would be there for quite some time. The idea of sleeping in the same house where his wife had been slain didn't appeal, although he knew he would have to go back eventually.

Sleep was well overdue, but the events of the worst night of his life prevented it. He had lost his wife and his daughter. Although he didn't yet know the fate of his daughter, the unknown was killing him more, yet at the same time the possibility of her being alive was the only thing keeping him going. He needed to take matters into his own hands, find his daughter and those responsible.

But where would he start?

He decided the only lead he had might be at his fingertips. What did the surveillance cameras show? Nothing, maybe something? The police had been interested in looking at them. The good thing about storing information on the Cloud was it couldn't be stolen or confiscated, even though he guessed his house computer may have been taken as evidence. Best of all, information on the Cloud could be accessed by any computer, tablet or iPhone anywhere in the world, as long as he knew the site and the password, which as the owner, he did.

There was a computer bank in the lobby of his hotel for $2 per hour. It would do.

He got up and made his way downstairs, then began reviewing the film from the 2 am mark on the camera, working his way backwards. As he wound back in the evening, the cameras went from black to light, from nothing to vison. Suddenly there was a picture and he could see something through one camera. As he rewound, a splatter disappeared and then the same thing happened with the second rooftop camera. Then he could see a man on the fence, a man with a gun. There was no other disturbance. However, there was a fault; the two lower cameras remained blank. Austin checked the time: 8.41 pm. They were still out. He rewound the day further to 6.12 pm; they were still blank.

The front cameras showed nothing of interest and the two working back cameras remained free of clues.

He rewound further and decided to continue rewinding until he saw something, anything. Then he saw the most beautiful sight in the world. It was his wife and daughter, checking the mail, just after 3.15 pm. They had just arrived home from school. The back camera remained out.

He rewound further. They hopped back in the car and disappeared down the road backwards. The gate closed. Then he saw it.

The back camera came to life and a hand moved away from it. Then the other camera came to life. It too had a hand move away from it.

Then he saw a second unknown man. Austin watched this at normal speed. He could rewind more later if he needed to.

Just after 3 pm, he saw the man jump over his rear fence. He was of average height, neither particularly tall nor particularly short. He was reasonably bulky, although compared to Austin nearly everyone was puny. The cameras did not show a close-up, not that a close-up of a balaclava would be of any help.

Austin didn't know what happened to the man after the second camera went out. He seemed to vanish. He switched to the side camera. He was hoping the man in the tape wasn't aware of its presence. It was positioned high up near the eave, semi-obscured by a conifer, and it would be almost impossible to cut.

Austin clicked on the live view. The camera was still actively recording! He could see Forensics looking at the door. He selected the recorded file from 2 am, just as he had done with the others.

He began to wind it back. It started off with no one in sight, just his side path at night with a couple of shrubs blowing in the wind. Just after 12.30 am, the same time as the other cameras had been shot at with a paintball, a second man appeared at the side door. He was bigger and fatter than the first man who had cut the cameras at 3 pm. And he was wearing a joker mask.

Were they working together? Austin wondered. Maybe one was doing some casing work for the other. Then the man removed the mask. Austin zoomed in. He couldn't see his face because his head was down while he concentrated on the lock. It didn't take the man long to break into the house. Austin played the tape at normal speed; three seconds it took him to bust the door down.

Three seconds didn't provide much by way of identification, apart from his size. Five seconds later all the cameras went blank. Power been cut, Austin thought.

So the man with the joker mask jumps the fence at 12.30 am after shooting at the cameras with paint.

Then the guy busts in the door.

Cuts the power, so there's no footage of him leaving.

Austin wound the camera back again to 3.13 pm. The other man appeared at the side of the home. He took longer to get into the house and he was still wearing his balaclava.

There was footage of him entering but not leaving. Austin double-checked the footage, then triple-checked. Definitely no footage of him leaving.

Austin wondered if they had left together. Were they in on it together? He had better call the detectives.

But first he had one more call to make, to his security company.

Austin provided his security details to the receptionist and was transferred to the security department.

"Security," a man answered.

"Hi, I need to check my security from yesterday. I'm wondering if anyone tampered with the system."

"Let me have a look for you, Mr Campbell." There was a short pause as the man checked. "The system was activated at 8.30 am and then deactivated via pin code at 10.47." Makes sense, Austin thought. Sarah probably dropped Mikayla at school, did some shopping and then came home.

He paused. Austin could hear him typing at the other end of the phone.

"It was then reactivated via pin at 2.57 pm. Then there was a four-minute period when no signal was being received, between 3.11 and 3.15 pm."

"What does it mean?" Austin asked.

"Could be a couple of things. Most likely cause is that your home lost power," the technician replied. "The alarm was rearmed without a code just after 3.15 pm, which tells me the power must have come back on. It was then deactivated via pin code some 30 seconds later."

"What else could it be?" Austin probed. "Could it be a faulty wire in the box?"

"Someone who knew what they were doing could have removed the wire inside the main control box and reconnected it to bypass they system," the tech answered. "But it's highly unlikely. To do so they'd have to have an understanding of how these alarm systems work. They'd have get to the wire inside 30 seconds. Not likely," the tech said. "I'd say you had a power outage," he confirmed. "Is there anything else I can help you with?"

"No thanks, that should do. If I have any other questions I'll get back to you."

Austin hung up and leaned back in his chair. What had the first guy been doing, and why had he hidden in the house for so long? Surely they must have been working together. It must have been planned.

What were the odds of two different criminals working the same target on the same day? Two million to one?

Now it was time to contact the detectives.

Chapter 34

Jake wasn't surprised to receive a call from Mr Campbell. He assumed it would be to check on the progress of the investigation. When, however, he offered new information, Jake was taken aback.

What information could it be that he didn't know already? Was Mr Campbell involved in the murder of his wife? Had the guilt got to him? Was he going to confess?

Jake doubted it, but he had to know what the man knew.

Jake came over to my desk and hovered over me. "Mr Campbell wants to see me, says he has information, might be worth you tagging along."

"Sure thing, I need time to think anyway," I replied, closing the file of Scott Western. "Did he say what information he has?" I asked as we headed to the elevator and down to the underground secure parking.

"No. He just says he has information," Jake answered.

"Interesting."

We met Mr Campbell in the foyer of the Hilton and then followed him to the lobby to a row of computers. He clicked on the screen. There were eight squares all showing different aspects of his yard.

"This is the footage from the cameras at my house last night," he said.

"Mr Campbell," Jake interrupted, "we have already gone through the footage from last night."

Austin clicked on a small link that said '2'.

A new page loaded showing one more square, the side of his house.

"Then why has there been no footage of this man?" Mr Campbell pointed to a man at the door wearing a joker's mask.

Jake looked at me and I looked at him.

"What camera is that?" Jake asked.

"It's the side camera, most people don't think I have one because it's partially hidden by the pencil conifer we have growing next to the gate. If you're looking for it on the web, it's also hard to find because the page holds the first eight cameras only," Mr Campbell explained.

We bent in to get a better view. Mr Campbell went through the footage again. He was correct; it looked like a fat man wearing a joker's mask. He then wound the footage to earlier in the day. Another man appeared in the camera's view.

This was a skinnier, smaller man than the one we had just seen wearing the joker mask. This one was in a balaclava.

"What time is this?" Jake asked.

"Just after 3 pm," Mr Campbell replied. "I don't have any footage of either of them leaving, which leads me to suspect they both left after . . . after they killed Sarah."

"Can you go over them again please, Mr Campbell."

We took several more looks at them. I now knew where the green hair that I had found on the fence came from. It was from the joker's mask.

However, with his mask removed, we could see nothing of use.

"You're the psychologist, what do you think?" Jake asked me.

"I agree with Mr Campbell. It seems unlikely they were operating separately, but one thing doesn't add up. Why did the second guy break in if he already had someone else on the inside?" I asked.

Both Jake and Mr Campbell could offer no explanation.

"Also," said Mr Campbell, "I rang our security company. They told me there was a four-minute outage between 3.11 pm and 3.15 pm. Their interpretation was that it was likely due to a loss of power."

"I doubt that, but we can check with the power company," Jake said without hesitation. "I think the first man removed the cable and then reset the alarm. It's a trick many burglars use. Usually they enter the premises, disconnect the alarm, take what they're after, and then reconnect the alarm just as they're leaving. Not only does this stop the alarm from going off, more importantly, when the owner comes home the alarm is still armed and there's no sign of a break-in. In some cases, it's days before people realise things are missing. Crims often do this when stealing credit cards. They take the credit card and go spending," Jake explained. Then he continued, "Thank you for this valuable information, Mr Campbell. We'll keep you updated on any developments. If you have anything else you find or think of, please let us know. Once Forensics have finished, I'll call you so you can move back home. Should only be another day, or so."

Mr Campbell stood up and shook Jake's hand and then turned to me with his hand held out. I accepted and shook it. Mr Campbell didn't let go, instead he asked, "The other kids that went missing, has any ransom been demanded?"

"No," I answered, "no one has sent in a ransom note."

"Then why do you think this guy is going to demand one?" Mr Campbell asked.

"Because this abduction is different from the others. This abduction was done from the home. The others were carried out on the street. We feel that maybe they broke in, were disturbed, didn't have time to get whatever they were after, so instead took your daughter," I replied.

"But it's just a theory," Jake added.

"Yes, it's just a theory we're going off," I confirmed.

Mr Campbell finally let go of my hand. "Ok then, well, we will soon see," he said.

We turned to go back to the station when he spoke again.

"Just so you know, there is no way in hell I am going to sit here while my daughter is out there somewhere. I will do whatever I can to bring her home."

Jake turned, "It's best not to get involved in a police investigation. The best thing you can do is stay home in case they call with the ransom demands. Getting involved could only hinder our investigations," Jake said.

"I can't do that, Detective. Getting in your way is my least concern. I will do whatever it takes to bring her home."

Not only had we been made to look inept by the Forensics team because they had missed an entire camera, we now had a dad challenging our work.

Jake didn't bother to reply. He understood Mr Campbell was upset and there was no point trying to tell him otherwise. After all, if he wanted to walk the streets, how could we stop him?

"Ok," Jake said to me, "so we have two men we need to identify, and that's where we start. Once Forensics run the prints through the database and we get the results, we'll will be able to compare them to the footage."

Chapter 35

Beau hadn't slept past 11 am in years, however, the sleep debt owed from the weekend and Monday night had caught up with him. Even when he woke he was still tired. If it hadn't been for the fear of the police knocking on his door and the evidence still sitting on the passenger seat of his van, he would have stayed in bed for a few more hours.

Instead, he got dressed and was headed out to his shed when his mum stopped him in the kitchen. "Where did you get to last night?" she screeched.

"Went to the movies," he responded automatically. "What's it to you anyhow?"

"While you were out, another girl was taken, this one from her home, and I know how much you like young girls," she replied.

Annabelle leaned into the corner of her kitchen bench, one cigarette in her mouth and another at the ready in her fingers. "You better not be up to no good, ya hear me, because you'll be out on your ass quicker than you can say jack rabbit."

Beau reached into his pants, removed the ticket stub. "I was at the movies. See? The 11 pm session of *The Hunger Games* part two." Beau had bought the ticket not to convince his mother, but to provide an alibi just in case the police ever asked. He brushed his mother aside and headed out to his shed.

"Aren't you going to have breakfast?" Annabelle asked him with her head poking out the door, ciggy still in her mouth.

"I'll get something later," he called back without even turning to face her.

Beau unlocked the shed, and locked it again from the inside. He flicked on the TV, removed from his bar fridge a bottle of milk, smelt it—not off, but on the edge—took two paper bowls, two plastic spoons, and two mini packets of cereal from a cupboard built into his work bench.

He removed the red ladder from its hanging spot on the wall and leaned it against the work bench. He turned his train set, revealing the trapdoor, unlocked it, placed the ladder into its usual position. He put on his joker mask and put the bowls, cereal and spoons in one hand and the bottle of milk in the other. He held the ladder, the milk handle hooked around his thumb.

When he arrived at the bottom, the girl screamed, while Scott remained silent, lying curled up in a corner of his cell. "Don't know why you're wearing the mask. I've seen your fat ugly face!" Mikayla screamed at him.

Without speaking, Beau placed the bowl and milk on the gravel path, opened the cell, stepped inside, and grabbed Mikayla by the throat. "Unless you want to end up like your mother, I suggest you keep your mouth closed."

Mikayla grabbed at his hand. It was firm and strong. Even using both hands she couldn't pry his fingers away. She was struggling to breathe. This was it. She would die like her mum. Tears rolled down her face. She began smacking his leathery hand. Suddenly he released her and air flew into her lungs, causing her to cough. She dropped to the floor, trying to regulate her breathing.

Slumped in the corner, Mikayla watched as the Joker bent down to pick up the bowls, cereal and milk. This was her chance. Something inside her called 'run!' She didn't hesitate, she didn't think, she just ran. Like a professional runner, Mikayla was off. She pushed on the big man's hip as she passed him on the path. Being stooped over, he lost his balance and fell. Mikayla didn't look to see if he had gone over or not. Her attention was squarely on escaping. Her hands clasped the old red metal ladder. At first her legs couldn't agree on which one was moving first, so for an instant, she stood there motionless, then her right leg decided to take charge and step up.

At any moment she expected the Joker to grasp her foot or to feel a hand on her shoulder, but there was nothing. Surprisingly, she was free. She reached the last rung; still nothing. She gathered herself out of the hole and searched for the door. She saw what appeared to be a door off to the side. Sprinting, she reached for the handle, arm outstretched. The tips of her fingers withdrew at the touch of cold metal. She pulled down on the handle and pulled again. The handle turned all the way but the door resisted and remained shut. Mikayla pulled again, nothing. She looked up. There was a bolt with a padlock through it, "Nooo!" she cried.

"You thinking of going somewhere?" the Joker asked, half muffled by his mask.

"Please, let me go. My dad will be looking for me." Tears began to well but the fear of being beaten dried them up before they began falling.

"You shouldn't have run; you've made me mad now."

Mikayla looked for a way out. She could only see one other door, a big sliding metal door big enough for cars to go through. It had big bolts top and bottom and was also padlocked.

She could see no way out of the garage. There was no way out of this mess. The Joker was upon her now. The mask didn't scare her; it was the gaze from the dead-looking eyes that lay behind it. She tried to prepare herself for the beating she was about to get. He grabbed her face, squeezed her cheeks with his fingers and squeezed hard. Her cheeks touched each other and her mouth was deformed like a fish. She was ready for the rest, but nothing came.

Instead, he eased his pressure and took her by the hair. "If you try to escape again, I will kill you," he said slowly and deliberately, "regardless of how much they're paying for you."

Who is paying for me, she wondered, who was he talking about?

Chapter 36

When James Mitchell killed the two children, pleading he couldn't remember doing it, the truth was that being drug affected had made the killing so much more intense. He remembered every second of it. Some days he lay in his bed reliving it.

James knew if he ever got caught he would do his best not to go back to jail. Being declared clinically insane was both good and bad. The bad was he had to deal with all the 'nutters', as he called them, walking the hallways. The good was it was like a free motel, just with padded rooms for the naughty ones.

It had been hard playing the part and selling his version, but he had done so from the moment he was arrested and he'd laid it on thick. His main defence was that the 'shadow people' had made him do it. He could hear them and sometimes see them, usually when he was going to sleep. During his questioning, he asked the detective to protect him from the shadow people, that they would be coming for him.

His hardest task was still to come. Now he had to prove that he was no longer insane. How long that would take was anyone's guess, but it didn't matter to him. Anything would be better than being constantly raped and beaten in jail. Most prison inmates didn't take kindly to child molesters, let alone ones that killed as well.

He had spent 20 years in Northview at Bendigo, the high security home for those found by a court to be 'not guilty by reason of insanity', held there by the Commonwealth until it was deemed suitable for him to return to society.

Everyone at Northview had been good to him, no one had tried to rape him. It was better than prison. He had decided to wait several years before even showing a sign of improvement, then he would phase in and out. Sometimes the shadow people were there, sometimes they were gone, sometimes he could comprehend what the doctors were saying, other times he would accuse them of being involved and trying to plot his death.

For the past five years, he had exhibited stable behaviour; no mood swings, no imaginary shadow people, no voices, all calm. He had become a model patient. He could be good when he had to be, and now he had to be. He needed out. Inside, his monster was back and growing stronger, day by day, week by week, his hunger for children stronger than ever. The constant news reports of the missing children over the last few months had fed his monster's hunger.

Chapter 37

Hayley had decided tonight was the night to tell Jake. She stood beside Ryan's bed, distraught at the sight of the motionless boy.

She was holding a stuffed Garfield in her hand and she leaned over and tucked it under Ryan's arm, patted his sweaty head, leaned in and kissed his cheek. "Here is Garfield. He needs your cuddles," she whispered. Of course, there was no response.

She had asked Jake if he would be able to make dinner tonight, if she booked somewhere. He'd said that after seven would be best.

Hayley cleared her mind of her personal issues and went about taking the morning obs. By the time she returned to Ryan, his family had arrived for the day, hoping their bedside vigil would bring him around.

"Excuse me, do you know how my son got this toy?" his mother Joan asked.

"I bought it for him," Hayley responded. "I hope you don't mind, I just thought something new to cuddle might help."

"Don't be silly, Hayley, of course we don't mind. Thank you so much, you're such a sweetie," Joan responded.

She leaned down and placed the Garfield back in the bed with Ryan. Then she walked over to Hayley who was standing at the end of the bed, chart in hand, and threw her arms around her, saying a simple, heartfelt "Thank you."

Hayley had got to know Ryan's parents over the time he had been in hospital. They didn't deserve this; no family did. They were good people and had they been there, Ryan wouldn't have drowned.

It always seemed that fate only visited the innocent, not the guilty.

"The doctors will be around shortly. After they've been, I'll give him his sponge bath and freshen him up a little. Maybe then we could even put on some of his favourite music and have that playing for him," Hayley said, smiling.

Joan nodded, "That would be great. Thank you." There was no smile to accompany the nod.

Hayley had never seen her smile. Who could blame her? It wasn't as if the current situation called for it. Maybe she would never smile again. If Ryan died, she doubted it.

Chapter 38

After our meeting with Austin Campbell, Jake rang ahead to Forensics asking to meet with Grace, the head. She had taken over from David in the spring of 2009, when David had passed away. She was great at her job and even though she was easy going, she was tough on her crime scene investigation team to ensure its integrity.

Grace met with Monique (our chief of Homicide), Jake and me in the conference room. She had already gone over the crime scene report supplied by her team. "Hi guys . . ." she began.

Jake interrupted her, "Your technicians made us look like idiots."

"Jake, I've spoken to them about thoroughness and how they need to be on their game every scene. They understood they made a mistake, Jake, they can't do anything about it now," she continued.

Jake calmed himself.

"Ok, let's move forward," Grace said. "I have good news. We have the match from the fingerprints on the screwdriver and on the manhole. I've reviewed the footage from the side camera. Based on the arrest records and the fingerprints we found at the scene, we have a match." Jake was about to say something. She held up her hand. "There's more. We also found a glove in the roof cavity. The fingerprints found on the manhole and the screwdriver are the same. There's also a match to a partial print on the back door."

She slid a file across the desk to us.

"Tyler Parsons was convicted and sentenced for B&E. Looks like he's back to his old tricks, except this time he's added murder and kidnapping to his repertoire."

Jake finished flicking through the file and passed it to me. Grace was right; the prints matched the screwdriver and the manhole, and the video footage showed an extremely close resemblance to the photo of Tyler when considering body size.

Jake thanked Grace for her report. He then turned to Monique. "We need to organise SWAT to clear Tyler's house. Then we'll need Forensics to look for any sign of Mikayla in his car or house," he said.

"We already have a sample of Mikayla's hair from the brush in her room, so if we find any, we'll have a comparison back quickly," Grace answered.

It was 35 minutes before SWAT was ready to clear Tyler's home. We had been waiting outside his house for 15 minutes before Sal from SWAT came across the radio to let us know they were two streets away.

"Looks like he's home," Jake told him. "There's a car in the drive and it's registered to him, but we haven't seen anyone yet."

"Satellite shows three exit points, one at the front, one at the rear and one on the left, so we'll send four in from the back, two on the left-hand side and four at the front. Once we have him I'll give you the all-clear so you can enter," Sal said.

"Hey Sal! We need this one alive. He has an 11-year-old girl somewhere and he's our only lead."

"Will do our best, Detective, but can't guarantee anything. If he opens fire, we'll have to take him down."

Less than a minute later, the all-clear came through from Sal.

We entered the property. This time there were seven Forensic's technicians following us in, led by Grace herself.

When SWAT had entered the house, Tyler was sitting on the couch, eating a bowl of spaghetti.

We walked through the door to find he was cuffed, spaghetti stains all over his shirt and the rest spread over the lounge room floor. They removed him, placing him in the back of Jake's squad car.

Jake and I immediately began searching the house for signs of Mikayla. We came up empty-handed. I decided I had to talk to Tyler now. If we waited until we were in the interview room at the station, it could be too late.

I opened the rear car door and knelt in the doorway. "Tyler, you need to tell us where the girl is. Whatever happened at the house we can sort out later. Where is she?"

He didn't answer, just sat there silently staring out the window.

"Tyler, do you want to go inside for the rest of your life? They'll throw the book at you if you don't help us."

Tyler said, "I don't know about the girl or the dead lady. I had nothing to do with it."

"Tyler, if you had nothing to do with it, then I will help you, but you need to help us first. Where is the girl?"

He gave no response.

"Tyler, who was the other guy you were working with? Tell us who the big guy was."

Still nothing. This wasn't working. He wasn't giving me anything, so I had to change tactics.

"Obviously you want to protect him, but so far it's your prints on the screwdriver. Right now, you're going down for the lady's murder and now you want to go down for the girl too? If we can't find her, we'll charge you for both their deaths. We don't need a body to charge you. Do you understand? Tell us who he is, don't go down for something you didn't do."

Tyler looked up. "I don't know who he was, I was hiding in the roof waiting for the mum to go to sleep so I could have a crack at the safe. Then I heard screaming. I panicked and ran. She was dead when I left. I never saw the guy or the girl." Tyler was shaking.

"You expect me to believe you don't know the guy you were working with? If what you say is true, that she was dead when you left, then how come the screwdriver has your fingerprints on it? How could it have been used to kill her, Tyler?"

Tyler shook his head, "I must have dropped it, and the other guy picked it up and killed her," Tyler said, still shaking his head.

"Tyler, the only prints on the screwdriver are yours and the victim's. Quite a coincidence, wouldn't you say? How does he pick it up and kill her and not leave any prints?"

Tyler looked up, "He must have had gloves on."

"So you're telling us that you dropped your screwdriver and the other person picked it up and killed her, and it was this other person, who you don't know, who took the girl as well?"

Tyler nodded. "That's the truth."

"You must be the unluckiest burglar of all time."

Tyler mumbled, "I am."

"Tyler, if what you're saying is the truth, why didn't you come in and see us? Why did you flee the scene that night?"

Tyler rocked back and forth in his seat, "I didn't think you'd believe me."

"This is your last chance to tell me the truth. Come clean. Who are you protecting? Where is the girl? You'll be looked on favourably by the courts if you help us find the girl."

I waited for Tyler to speak. If I spoke now I'd lose for sure.

He replied, "I've told you what happened. It's the truth. I'm only telling you the truth. I can't tell you what I don't know."

"I can't help you if you don't help me. We know you're not telling us the truth. You're going back to the police station where you will be formally charged for murder and kidnapping as well as breaking and entering."

I shut the door.

Tyler began to cry.

"Read him his rights, then take him to St Kilda Road," I instructed the officer accompanying him. "We'll be back there to question him again soon."

Jake was still searching the house. "Did he tell you where he put the girl?"

"No," I responded.

"Arseholes never do; they rarely tell you where their victims are. Even years later when the trial is all done and dusted, they still don't."

"Some psychologists believe they enjoy the control," I replied.

"What did he say?" Jake asked as he walked the back yard looking for any freshly dug ground.

"He said that the other guy killed the mum and must have taken the child. He said he was in the manhole, heard a scream, went to leave the house, and saw the lady dead on the floor." I stopped walking. "Normally, I'd say it's crap, but on that video the two entered at different times. Maybe they weren't working together."

Jake turned and eyeballed me, "They were working together. Don't doubt yourself."

"If they were, then why would he go down for something he didn't do? Why wouldn't he just give him up?" I asked Jake.

"Jail is better than death. If you rat out your boss, maybe he'll kill you and your family," Jake said.

"We could protect him," I fired back.

Jake laughed.

"You have to understand, Brodie, some of these people are connected, sometimes giving up someone just isn't worth it!"

I looked at Tyler's dog in the yard. It was a gorgeous boxer, practically still a puppy. He had the best of everything, best bowls, best bed; the lead hanging in the doorway was leather. Hanging next to it was a winter jacket Tyler obviously put on him on his walks. Most likely the dog slept inside with Tyler, same bed, would be my guess.

Maybe that was my way in.

Chapter 39

Austin had seen the two men in the video footage and he knew his daughter's time was running out. He couldn't decide if they were working together, and if he was honest with himself, he didn't care. He would chase them both down and he wouldn't stop until he found them.

The man who had killed his wife had his daughter. He had little doubt that Sarah had died trying to prevent Mikayla's abduction.

Still sitting in the hotel lobby at a computer terminal, Austin scrolled through his phone contacts and pressed the green call button to Marcus.

"Hey buddy, how you coping?" Marcus answered sombrely.

"I need my kit," Austin said.

"It's on its way to you, everything you need."

"I also need information on the following missing children." He reeled off one by one the three names he knew of. "I also want some tracking devices as well as bugs. I need to find this guy and I'm running out of time."

"I'll send it to you today. I take it you're staying there tonight?" Marcus asked, confirming what he already knew.

"I'll be here until I get my kit and then I'm gone until I find her," Austin replied as if it was going to be a sure thing.

The ability of Marcus to provide him with what he needed in such a short time shocked even Austin. Two packages arrived at his room within two hours. The first bag was his kit. It contained all his weapons. Marcus had done the smart thing and removed the uniform, replacing it with some casual clothes in a suitcase with two false bottoms. Austin unzipped it and removed the jacket and jeans, a pair of black shoes and a belt.

He flipped the bag over, unzipped the other side. It contained a laptop bag, a phone and a set of keys. He removed the items, placing them all on the bed. He opened the laptop bag. In one slip was a MacBook Air, in the other were three folders, each with a name printed on the lip. It was a dossier on each kidnapping. Austin could have got all the information from the internet himself but it would have taken him a while. In the front of the bag was the laptop cable.

He turned the phone on. A text message came up.

It was from Marcus.

Laptop has email address only we can view. If u need anything checked email/text me

In bag four trackers to place under a car & follow on GPS. I've set them into yr phone. Numbered 1 to 4. Most I could organise in limited time. Also a jammer—blocks central locking to get into car to plant device

Keys for government car. Been checked out 4 weeks for repairs.

After that will be reported stolen

Will help you as much as I can. If u get caught doing something illegal you're on yr own. I'll say u went rogue and all our communications will be deleted

Austin typed a reply.

Do whatever you have to do, I understand

Five seconds later he had deleted both messages.

Austin then removed the false bottom of the case. There were two identical handguns, both SIG p228 9mm, holding 12 rounds each. It was a light handgun, better for going house to house and in hostage situations.

Then there was a Walther P99 semi-automatic pistol holding 16 rounds in the magazine, a machine gun H&K G36 with five 30-round clips, and finally an L96A1 sniper rifle fitted with the Schmidt & Bender telescopic sight and with one 12-round clip.

There were three titanium suppressors, two for the handguns, one for the sniper rifle.

Finally, were his knives, both kukri. He had used them in Afghanistan. They were designed to kill. Unlike a standard kitchen knife that struggled to cut tomatoes, these would cut through flesh as if it was paper.

Marcus had done a good job. Good thing he wasn't a terrorist; he could start a one-man war with weapons like these. If all went to plan, Austin wouldn't need to fire a single shot.

The phone rang, startling him at first, then he realised it could only be Marcus.

"Hey," Austin answered.

"Turn on the news," Marcus said.

Austin fumbled with the remote that was sitting on the bedside table in the shade of the lamp. He clicked the remote several times and found the Sky news channel. 'Man in custody for Campbell murder', read the caption.

"I'll call you back," Austin said.

He picked up his own phone and dialled Jake's number.

"Have you found my daughter?" he asked, without waiting for the normal exchange of pleasantries.

"No," Jake said. "We're still looking. The man we have in for questioning said he never saw your daughter. We're trying to validate his version of events."

Another caption scrolled across the screen.

'Man identified as Tyler Parsons of Victoria.'

"Is the man you have Tyler Parsons?" Austin asked.

"Austin, I'm trying to find your daughter. Let me get back to you as soon as I have solid information I can share."

Austin replied sheepishly and somewhat apologetically, "Ok, sorry," and ended the call.

He picked up the other phone and called Marcus back.

"The police won't confirm who it is," Austin said, "but if the news sources have named the person of interest, it must have been confirmed. Otherwise they could face a massive legal bill."

"I've emailed you Parsons' criminal history, it's all thefts. No rape convictions or child abuse of any kind. So murder and kidnapping would be new for him," Marcus said. "If you want my suggestion, I'd start looking for links between the other kidnapping cases and Mikayla's," Marcus added. "It'd be foolish to dismiss the possibility Mikayla's isn't linked to the other three. Maybe he had a reason to break in and take her."

"Maybe you're right, perhaps there is a reason we don't know of yet," Austin said. "Maybe I need to go back to the beginning."

Marcus spoke again. "So we agree? We both think it's possible that Mikayla's kidnapping is related to the others?"

"Forget the fact that they were different circumstances for a second because really when you think about it, all the kidnappings were slightly different. Maybe they were all targeted? Maybe he planned to strike when he did?" Austin said.

"Maybe he planned to break in because he knew you wouldn't be home or he saw you leaving?" Marcus suggested. "Can you remember anyone watching you over the last few days?"

Austin thought about that. Had he noticed anyone out of the ordinary?

Was it out of the ordinary to be at the movies alone, like the fat guy he saw on Friday?

Was it out of the ordinary for the fat guy to go to the Pancake Parlour for lunch, just like they did?

Was it out of the ordinary to park near the movies?

Did he park?

Or just fumble for his keys?

What car did he get into? Did he see him get into a car or just stand in the lot?

What car did he get into?

Austin couldn't remember. Maybe because he didn't see him get into a car.

Was the big guy the same guy as on the tape? Possibly; maybe.

"Austin, hello?"

"Sorry," Austin replied. "Someone may have been watching us at the movies. It may have been the bigger guy in the surveillance footage," Austin replied.

"The bloke with the joker mask?" Marcus asked.

"Yeah . . . maybe . . . not sure," Austin answered.

"Well it's a start," Marcus replied.

Maybe the best place to start looking for Mikayla was with the other lost children, Austin thought. Time was ticking and as each hour passed, the chances of finding her alive were diminishing. It had been 12 hours already.

After the first 24 hours, the chance of finding her alive was 50%, and each day after that was 2% less.

Chapter 40

By 2 pm, we had searched Tyler's house thoroughly twice through. We had uniformed officers going over the property a third time, just in case anything had been missed.

Tyler sat in interview room four. He remained cuffed. Looking at him through the mirror, we saw he was sitting still, head down and emotionless.

"So, what do you think?" Jake asked me.

"I know I've said it before, but I don't know why he would be protecting someone. Why wouldn't he just give him up?"

"Thick as thieves," Jake replied.

"Maybe he doesn't know the guy. Maybe he's telling the truth?" I posed to Jake.

"You saying two different guys hit the same place on the same night? I doubt it. We already calculated the odds of one in a million," Jake said.

"One in two million," I corrected him. "I keep thinking about the back door. If your guy's inside, why do you need to break in again? It's not logical."

"Maybe we give him a polygraph? Let me see how I go. Fresh person, fresh approach, and then we'll offer the lie detector test."

"Sounds good," I replied, ready to go in. Jake grabbed me by the shoulder and held me back.

"Did you write notes on what he said in the car?" he asked.

"No," I answered. Jake rolled his eyes, ever so slightly. "I recorded it on my phone though, does that help?" I asked, pushing Jake towards room four.

We sat down opposite Tyler. Jake introduced himself. Before asking him any questions, he asked if he was thirsty, if he needed to go to the bathroom or if he wanted something to eat. Tyler asked for a can of Coke.

"So, Tyler. Just before we start, please be aware you do not have to answer any questions without your lawyer present. You have been charged with breaking and entering at this time. This interview is being recorded. Do you want your lawyer to attend this interview?"

He shook his head.

"Please answer yes or no for the recording."

"No!" he replied firmly.

"Can you tell me what happened on Monday 10th December and Tuesday the 11th?"

"Well, I broke into the house at about 3 pm. I switched off the alarm using my screwdriver to pop the case in the master bedroom. And then I went looking for the safe."

"Ok, then what happened?" Jake's tactic was never to ask another question until they were finished with their story. He believed this gave them enough rope to hang themselves with.

Tyler continued. "It wasn't where it was supposed to be, so I did a quick search and I found it in the study. Except while I was there, the lady came home. I heard the automated gate."

"Ok, then what?" Jake asked.

"So I had to rush to reset the alarm so it would still be good when she walked in. Otherwise she would know something was up and I'd get caught. The alarm was rearmed and I was up in the roof before she entered the house. My plan was to wait till 1 am when they were asleep and then go for the safe. Then at 12.30, maybe a little after, I heard screaming, the girl screamed. It startled me. Woke me up. I think I'd been dozing and then the lady said 'Put her down!' or somethin' and 'get out!'. But I don't know to who she was talkin' with."

"So what did you do?" Jake asked calmly.

"When I heard no more screaming, I got out my knife. I had one in my pocket. I remember throwing my glove away, so my knife didn't slip. I climbed down from the roof and went downstairs. Her phone was still on the step and I walked past it, it was glowing because the rest of the house was dark. I saw the lady on the tiles. I didn't stop 'cause you guys were on your way. Then I ran out the back and jumped the fence and then I was in my car, gone."

"Do you know who this other person was?" Jake asked, still very calm and unemotional.

"Man, I never saw the dude and I never worked with him. I work alone."

"You would agree it would be rare to have two people rob the same house at exactly the same time who were not working together, would you not Mr Parsons?"

"I don't think he was robbing the joint. He had no reason to go upstairs. He could have got to the safe from downstairs," Tyler replied.

"You said earlier that you went to the master bedroom for the alarm and the safe wasn't there. Why did you expect it to be there?" Jake asked.

"That was the word in prison. It was supposed to be in the robe," Tyler replied.

"But it was in the study, wasn't it?"

"Yes," Tyler answered.

"Maybe the other guy got the same info you got, that's why he went upstairs?"

"I suppose, but I didn't hear him come past me," Tyler added.

"But you were asleep, maybe you missed him?"

"Nah, I would have woken up, I wasn't sleepin' that heavy," Tyler answered.

"Ok, can you clear something up for me?" Jake asked, going through the photos of the crime scene.

"Is this your screwdriver?" In the photo Jake showed, the screwdriver was embedded in the lady's throat. Jake had done the right thing by the family and concealed her face with a Post-It note.

"Might be, I can't be sure," Tyler answered.

"How did it get in the lady's neck?" Jake asked.

"I don't know, I was up in the roof," Tyler replied.

"Where I have an issue is that the screwdriver only has two sets of prints on it: yours and Mrs Campbell's."

"Maybe I dropped it. I can't be sure," Tyler answered. He had almost finished his Coke and maybe it was the caffeine or the questions but he was starting to fidget.

"You know what I think?" Jake began. "I think you went in to rob the house, as you say, while your partner waited outside. When you didn't come out, he waited in the car until it was dark, then he went in to see what the fuck had happened to you. But in doing so he woke them up and when you had to leave empty-handed, you went for the girl as ransom. But on your way out, the mum tried to stop you, and one of you killed her!"

"No, no, not at all. No, that's not what happened!" Tyler rebutted.

"Tyler, I have been doing this for a long time and the evidence doesn't lie," Jake replied. "Now, I can help you. Tell us who the other guy is and where the girl is. If you help us find the girl and if you didn't kill Mrs Campbell, then we will help you. You don't want to go down for two murders you didn't commit, do you?"

"Two? Who else is dead?" Tyler asked.

"What do you think will happen to the girl if we don't find her?" Jake asked.

"I don't know who he is, I swear." He thumped his hands on the table. "Fuck, how many times do I need to tell you the same shit?" he said, frustrated.

"Will you do a lie detector test?" Jake asked.

"Hell yeah, cause I'm tellin' the truth, no problem," Tyler replied.

"Ok, we will organise that. Sit tight. Is there anything else you need, another Coke?" Jake asked.

"Yes please, and somethin' to eat. You guys messed up my leftover spaghetti this morning." Tyler pulled up his shirt to show the stain from the spaghetti sauce.

Jake got up to leave.

It was the only time I spoke in the interview but I wanted to leave him with something to think about.

"Maybe you should think about what's going to happen to your dog if you go away. We'd have to send it to the pound, and they never find another home for them so within two months he gets the green needle. Just think about that and if you remember anything let us know."

I didn't wait for the response.

We left the room. Jake turned to me, "Did you just threaten to have his dog killed if he didn't give up information?" Jake asked, almost laughing.

"Possibly, it's been a long night."

Chapter 41

Austin could wait no longer. He had to start looking. He had spent the last hour reading the files on the three missing kids while he was waiting to hear back from the cops. No call had come. He could be waiting a while yet.

He would head out and do some investigating of his own. He arrived at the residence of the Bradley family just after 1 pm. At first, he sat in the car and looked around. This could be any street in any suburb. He knocked quietly on the door, not loudly like a police officer.

A dishevelled woman in a dressing-gown appeared at the door. She was wearing no makeup, had not done her hair and didn't look like she cared. Her face was drawn, and her eyes had heavy dark rings underneath. Sleep had obviously evaded her.

"Hi, my name is Austin Campbell, my daughter was kidnapped and my wife was killed." Austin got straight to the point. "I was wondering if I could ask you some questions to see if there is any connection between our children's abductions?"

"Oh my God. I saw you on the news. Please come in, you poor thing," she said, giving Austin a hug as he passed through the doorway.

"Your son Stevie was on his way to school when he was taken?" Austin asked.

She nodded, "His basketball was found at the top of the park so we assume that he was taken from the court that meets the other side of the park."

"Did he normally walk to school?" Austin asked as they both took a seat at the table.

"Tea?" Mrs Bradley asked.

"White, no sugar please," Austin replied.

She flicked the kettle and removed the cups from the shelf above the stove.

"I was supposed to drive him, but I had a migraine that day," she replied. "He had walked two days that week and most of the week before."

"Do you think someone had been following him?" Austin asked.

"The police asked me if I had noticed anything out of the ordinary, but I hadn't, except I had seen the same van a few times over the last week."

"How did you know it was the same one? They're a common vehicle," Austin said, sipping his tea. It was good and strong.

"I don't for sure but it had the same yellow logo on the side. It was some type of phone company."

"Do you know which one?" Austin asked.

"No, I'd never seen it before. I've looked for it everywhere since."

Austin pulled out a pen and a piece of paper. "Could you draw it?"

She took the pen and paper. Austin took another sip of his tea.

A few seconds later, she slid the paper back. The logo wasn't so much a phone as an old-style phone receiver. Austin folded the piece of paper and put it safely in his shirt pocket.

He then turned his questions from those of an investigator to those of another concerned parent. "How are you coping?" he asked.

Mrs Bradley suppressed a cry. Then she looked herself up and down. "You can probably tell, not very well, I hate myself, it's my fault. If I had been ok that day, he would be here with me now."

Austin, who had almost finished his tea, gently touched her hand. "I need you to listen to me. It's not your fault. The person who did this is responsible and I tell you one thing; I will find him, I will not stop until I know who took them! But you need to do me a favour."

Mrs Bradley frowned, hesitated, "Ok, what do you need?"

"You need to stay strong, because if I bring your boy home, then I don't want him to see you like this, ok?" She nodded, and began crying.

"How can you stay so strong?" she asked.

"I need to be strong for her, I need to be strong for all of them. Whoever did this has unknowingly made it my mission and I won't stop until I find them."

"I hope you find the bastard that took them. If you do, what will you do?" she asked.

"End him," Austin said without hesitation and with total conviction.

It was the first smile that Austin had seen from her.

"I will stay in touch with you. I wouldn't advise telling the police I was here; they aren't too happy about that. I'm poking around," Austin said as he stood ready to leave.

"I found them of little assistance anyhow. I'm glad that you're out there looking. Thank you."

Austin kissed her on the cheek, and headed back to his car.

Time was ticking.

Chapter 42

Monique Keller was my third police chief in 10 years and she was by far the most driven. The last two had been men who were past their prime, where Monique was still hungry to kick ass. While she took cases very personally, she was strong enough to handle the burden.

Monique sat on the driver's side of her desk while Jake and I sat on the side that usually meant we were in trouble. As usual, she was dressed immaculately today, in a dark blue pant suit, her gun holstered to her right hip. Her red hair was tied up in a complicated looking ponytail.

"So gentlemen, tell me, where are we at with the Campbell murder? Has the suspect provided any further information?"

"We've interviewed him three times. His story is the same, nothing's changed."

"Do you think he's telling the truth?" she asked.

Jake and I exchanged glances.

"Well, Detectives, you must have some thoughts."

Jake answered, "We both think that he may be telling the truth. The reason we say that is Forensics found no evidence of the girl in his house or his car. Only evidence we have is the fingerprints on the screwdriver and the back door. The two main questions we can't yet answer, but that give weight to Tyler's version, are, why would someone who was working with someone else lock them out, and why would one person enter so many hours after the first if they were working together? He's just finished doing the polygraph with Dr Swan, so those results might lead us somewhere. Either way, we need to find the other offender to find the girl."

Monique picked up her phone, pressed four digits and spoke. "Have you finalised the results of Tyler Parson's polygraph? Great, bring them by my office." She hung up. "Raymond will be here in a few minutes. Let's talk about this other suspect. What are we doing to find this guy?" Monique asked.

Jake sat forward. "We've put out the footage of him in the mask, asked for anyone who may know this person to call Crime Stoppers. We've mentioned the paintball aspect. I wouldn't imagine many people would have that combination. We're also still going door to door but until we have more to go on, we are where we are." Jake sat back in his chair.

"Do you think this is related to the other kidnappings?" Monique asked.

"I'm not sure at this point. It's something I'm considering. This seemed well planned, while the others appeared to be more opportunistic. Although having said that, the perpetrator may have planned the others. Maybe their best time was on the way to school?"

I added, "Maybe he changed his MO in this case because Mrs Campbell drove Mikayla to and from school. So there was never any opportunity to strike. That's my best guess anyway."

"I think we start working these. If they are connected and we get a ransom note, then we reassess. Whatever, don't mention to the media that they're connected, or the whole city will go into a panic," Monique said. "You studied at the behavioural science unit in Quantico," she said to me. "How many serial kidnappings did you study?"

"In most of the cases I studied, the children were murdered soon after the abduction. Ransom is very rare," I replied. "That's why I think they're connected."

"Do you think they could still be alive?" Monique asked.

"We haven't found a body in any of the cases. So I would think they are still alive, especially if they're being taken for the purpose of sexual gratification. Either that, or we just haven't found them yet," I replied.

"Maybe they're being sold?" Jake chimed in.

"It's possible. However, I'd say if they were younger that would be more of a possibility. A two-year-old for example won't remember they were abducted. Someone desperate for a child will pay for a two-year-old. They can be raised by someone else and will never know what happened. But an 11-year-old, they will remember being taken," I said. "It's possible that we could have a paedophile who's not fussed on gender and it could be possible that he's keeping them somewhere. But I think we need to be prepared for the worst."

"Don't they usually go for one gender or another?" Monique asked.

"There was a case I remember studying in Quantico. The man was Lewis Lent. He kidnapped a girl from near her house then a month later, a boy from a movie theatre where he worked as a janitor. So a single offender can have desires for both," I said.

"Come in, Doctor." Monique waved in Dr Raymond Swan.

He stood at the side of her desk where he could better see us all.

"What was the outcome?" Monique asked, her chair squeaking as she twisted around to face him.

"Technically, he passed. But when we discussed the fingerprints on the screwdriver, there were inconsistencies. He passed when I asked him if he was working with anyone, if he killed Mrs Campbell and if he knew who had killed Mrs Campbell.

"The only question that he didn't pass on was 'do you know why your screwdriver was found in the victim?' He answered no but the graph suggested this wasn't truthful. So he didn't fail but it wasn't a pass either. He knows more than what he's telling us, but if I were to go to court, I'd have to say it's a pass."

Raymond placed the results on the desk, and Monique immediately handed them to Jake.

"Well, Detectives, I suggest you go look under rocks. Do whatever you have to do to find this guy and the kids.

Chapter 43

It was just after 3 by the time Austin arrived at the home of Chloe Henderson. He knocked in the same quiet way. Mrs Henderson answered the door and asked, "Can I help you?"

At first glance, Austin knew this lady was holding it together a lot better than Stevie's mother. She was wearing makeup and was reasonably well dressed. Hell, she was dressed.

"Mrs Henderson, my name is Austin Campbell and as you may have heard, my daughter was taken last night. I think the kidnappings may be related. Do you mind if I ask you a few questions?" Austin asked.

"I recognise you from the conference, how are you holding up?" she asked as she opened the door.

"I'm trying to stay busy so I don't dwell on it," Austin replied.

She offered Austin a tea or coffee but he declined. He explained he had just come from the Bradley's home. She had heard of the other cases but had never sought to communicate with them. She hadn't thought she would be able to handle it and so she was suffering alone. Being a single mum, she relied on her parents and the police to provide support.

Austin listened intently and when Mrs Henderson said something of interest, he made the occasional note in his notebook. It wasn't until she showed Austin into Chloe's room that he realised his daughter's room was sitting at home waiting for her to return. It hit him. Tears began to well up in his eyes but as the emotions began to flow, his mind ticked into military gear. Stay focused on the mission, the mission, bring them home, he reminded himself. He took a deep breath and moved away from the door.

"Can you tell me about the last person to see Chloe?" Austin asked.

"I don't know much more than what the police told me," she answered, suggesting that what she knew was insignificant.

"What was that, if you don't mind sharing?" Austin replied.

"They said that the man at number six, Mr Lubic I think his name is, was apparently out sweeping his path when he saw her walk by. When he looked again, she was gone. A hundred and eighty metres more and she was at the school gate."

"Did they ever mention a van or any vehicles?" Austin asked.

"No, the police are at a loss, a total loss." Mrs Henderson shrugged.

"What was the name of the street where she was last seen?" Austin asked.

"Elmer," she answered almost instantaneously. Another note for his book. "Do you think they are related, Mr Campbell?" she asked.

"Yes I do, until something shows me otherwise. I will search until I find them."

"If you find the prick that took my daughter, hurt him for me, make him suffer before you hand him in," she said.

"I don't want to upset you any more than you are already, but if I find him I won't be handing him in, that's for sure," Austin replied.

"That suits me even better." She led him to the door.

"Good luck!" she called as he headed down the path.

He was back in the security of his own car. It was almost 4 pm. Time was ticking. He thought it was best to follow up the lead on the last person to see Chloe alive. The Lubic man at number six Elmer.

Then he would visit the home of the missing Scott Western.

Chapter 44

Mikayla sat back in her cell. She was still surprised she hadn't been beaten or hurt for trying to escape. The music continued to play some type of slow rock, she couldn't make out the song, it was just all noise.

"How long have you been here?" Mikayla asked the boy who sat back in the far corner of his cell.

"Shhh, he will hear you."

Mikayla pointed her index finger to the celling. "He can't hear us, he has the radio on too loud."

Scott listened intently for a few seconds. The girl was right, the music was loud, he would never hear them talking if they were quiet.

"I don't know how long it's been," but then he looked at his wall and began counting, "I've had 24 breakfasts, but I don't think I've been given breakfast every day, so it might be longer."

"Do you know what's behind the red door?" Mikayla asked.

"It's a bedroom. He takes you there and takes photos of you and he sends the photos to people. When I first arrived, there was a girl he took in there, I think he did things to her, there was a lot of screaming."

"What happens to them after that?" Mikayla asked.

"I dunno, I guess he sends the photos to your family so they pay." Scott shrugged.

"Why are you still here if everyone else has paid? Why haven't you been sent home yet?" Mikayla asked.

"My parents don't have the money, they wouldn't be able to pay . . . I just want to go home," Scott said, starting to cry.

"When my dad buys me back, I'll make sure we pay for you as well so you can go home," Mikayla said, trying to stop his crying.

* * *

Stevie had been chained to the bed for three days now. He'd had very little to eat or drink.

The room was plain, nothing out of the ordinary, nothing different from a standard bedroom in a normal house. There were curtains over the window and a door. In the corner opposite the bed, there was a TV. It was on the cartoons, as it had been for the last three days. He thought he had seen the same *Scooby Doo* cartoon every day, sometimes twice.

He thought he was going home when the man with the mask put him in the van, but when he met the Batman he knew it wasn't true. Then he met the Priest with the strange opera mask. He had seen it once before on a poster of the *Phantom of the Opera* billboard in the city.

Even though he couldn't remember it in detail, he knew the Priest had hurt him. If it was anything like he had been through in the last three days, he was glad he couldn't remember it fully.

The last three days had been hell. At first they just took photos, then they crawled into bed with him. Every time they did, he went somewhere else, usually into the cartoons on at the time. He would imagine himself solving a mystery in *Scooby Doo* or killing Yo Sammity Sam with Bugs Bunny. He visited a lot of cartoons in three days.

He had only been in the room for three days but he knew it like the back of his hand. He knew all its little secrets, all its little intricacies. Like the curtains. They must have been bought specially for this room and likely for this purpose. Even though they were new, they were thin enough that any light behind them would make them transparent, except the light never changed, so Stevie was pretty sure the window must be boarded up.

He knew it took his kidnappers exactly five steps from the door to the bed.

He knew there was a daddy long-legs spider in the far corner above the bed. It must have been comfortable because it hadn't moved in two days.

In three days, he had worked out that there were hidden cameras in the room, one in the smoke detector and one behind the mirrored door, opposite the bed. Even though he couldn't see it in the middle of the night, he could hear it, even above the TV.

His wrists were burning; the skin had been broken by the handcuff. He could see a red tinge from the bleeding around the edge of them.

He lay on a bare mattress, in just his briefs, shivering. Yesterday had been hot, but today was cold, and he felt it. He had no blanket, not even a sheet. Goosebumps had formed all over his body. His lips were dried and cracked and his throat hurt. He was desperate for a drink. When was the last time he'd had one? He couldn't remember.

As he lay there breathing what he thought would be his last breaths, one thought entered his head. Ellie Davis and her beautiful smelling hair, and that wonderful exotic perfume, and those lips that one day he wanted to kiss for real, to see if they would be as soft and beautiful as he imagined.

That smell, her smell, it was all that kept him going.

As if on cue, the man that he had only seen in a suit or naked walked through the door. He was holding a glass of water in his right hand and a plate of sandwiches in his left.

Stevie began to salivate just at the thought of eating and he licked his lips. They stung as his tongue ran over the cracks. The man placed the plate and glass on the table at his right-hand side. He didn't speak, he simply sat on the bed and undid Stevie's right cuff. He then stood and headed out, but before he got to the door, Stevie spoke. "Thanks for the food and drink, sir." The man paused for a few seconds, as if contemplating a response.

Stevie knew what would happen when they tired of him or wanted something else to video. He had seen on the crime shows what usually happened to the missing kids. Often they would be found dead and were soon forgotten when the next one went missing. He knew if he was to stay alive he had to try and befriend them; get them talking. Maybe get them to drop their guard.

The man in the suit was the nice one, if there was such a thing. It was like choosing between two monsters. His name was Ian.

The second man was called Bill. He was home all the time and had a drug issue. He was a few inches shorter than the man in the suit, scruffier, not quite bald but with thinning hair. He was always in tracksuit pants and a singlet, which looked to be the same ones every day. But the worst thing about him was that he was dead-set mean. The meanest, angriest man Stevie had ever seen. It seemed that he didn't just want to rape but he wanted to watch him suffer. He'd noticed the needle marks on Bill's left arm, which looked like a swarm of mosquitos had attacked him.

Ian left and locked the door and as soon as the bolt sounded, Stevie got stuck into the food. He sipped the water. He needed to savour it.

Stevie sat on the bed eating peanut butter and jam sandwiches, watching cartoons, and for the briefest of instances he felt like a kid again.

Chapter 45

Mr Lubic answered the door. He was a tiny man, dwarf-like in stature. "Hello," he said in his thick accent.

"Mr Lubic, I was hoping you could help me. I'm Austin Campbell. My daughter was kidnapped and it may be related to the kidnapping of the girl who was taken while walking to school near here. Can you show me where you last saw her?"

"Yes, yes, terrible it is, come I show." He took Austin out the front of his house and stood on the footpath, "I was standing here, I sweep, I look in that direction," he said, pointing to the start of the street, "girl was walking, I see her coming closer and closer, as I sweep. As she walks past she is very close to me, so that's why when police ask me I am sure it's her. We were only few feet apart. She is not paying attention as she passes by, she is on the phone, moving thumb up and down, doing whatever they are doing. The wires are in her ears, I could hear the music as she passed."

"Did you see her go all the way to the school gate?" Austin asked.

"No, my phone rang and I hurried to answer it. When I came back out she was gone, I thought she was in school grounds. Didn't think any more about it."

"How long were you on the phone?" Austin asked.

"About thirty seconds. It was hospital, confirming my appointment next week. I said yes and hung up and then I was back out. I even remember looking up road to school, before I began sweeping again. The street was empty."

"Would you mind helping me for a few minutes? I want to walk from the point she reached when you went inside."

"Yeah, sure no problem," he answered.

Austin began walking towards Lubic. "You're going too fast. She was walking slow, because she was playing with her phone."

Austin slowed down his pace. "Is this better?" Austin asked.

"Better," Lubic answered.

The two men re-enacted the scenario as before.

When Lubic returned from inside, Austin was five metres from entering the school gate.

"Ok. Let's do that again. This time I want you to take an extra 15 seconds inside." They ran the test again. This time when Lubic returned to his sweeping, he looked up as he had done that day, and instead of seeing nothing he saw Austin on the path inside the gate heading for the oval.

Austin made his way back to Lubic. "You could still see me, and even if you were inside another 15 seconds, I still wouldn't have been out of sight."

"No, I could easily see you, I have a lot of carrots, grow them fresh out the back. Good for eyes."

"Are you sure we have the timing right? Could it have taken you longer? Could it have taken you longer than you recall?"

"No, no, it was very quick call. I think the first time was even a little too long. I went inside, pick up phone, say 'hello', they say 'Mr Lubic,' I say 'yes,' they say 'it's Helen here from Monash Medical Centre just confirming your appointment at 10.30 Thursday.' I say 'yes, no problem,' she say 'I see you then.' I say 'thank you' and I hang up."

"You came straight back out. You didn't go to the toilet or get a drink?" Austin asked, trying to eliminate any potential complications to Mr Lubic's story.

"No, I came straight back out," he said emphatically.

"Ok, ok, just confirming," Austin said. "You know that means someone took her from the street?" he said, gazing down the street where she had vanished.

It was an unusual street, he thought. The left-hand side was all standard residential development, while on Mr Lubic's side, it was one-acre blocks. Five hundred metres beyond the back fence ran the high-tension powerlines.

"There are a lot of criminals around these parts. They let out the sexual offenders and for some reason they let them live close to a school," Lubic said. "You know, in the village where I grew up, you touch kids, they cut your balls off. They need to have that here."

"Had you noticed any cars or anyone acting strangely that morning or even the days prior?" Austin asked.

"No, everything was the same. The only cars I saw that morning were dropping kids off."

"Thank you," Austin said before he leaned in to shake his hand.

Mr Lubic held his hand. "I hope you get her back; I hope you find them both." He let go of Austin's hand and headed down his driveway to his front door.

Austin sat in his car trying to imagine what had eventuated. He asked himself was it likely that someone drove up while Lubic was inside on the phone? It was such a small window of opportunity that Austin doubted the chances.

He picked up his ghost phone and dialled the only number stored in it. "I hope you're not ringing me to clean up a mess?" Marcus answered.

"You know that I don't leave a mess," Austin said. "Looking for some information. What do you have on registered sex offenders living in the Elmer Road area of Bayswater?" he asked.

"It will take me a few minutes to access that database. I'll call you back," Marcus replied.

The phone call ended.

Austin sat in his car wondering if it had been a lucky or a planned abduction.

He must have dozed off because he saw his wife smiling at him at the airport, and he kissed her. Had the ringing phone not butted in, he might have had one more kiss.

"You're not going to believe this," Marcus began, "there are 15 registered sex offenders within a two-kilometre radius! And there's one in the very same street. It's the second-to-last house according to the satellite map. His name is Beau Delacroix. He lives with his mother. He did a two-year sentence for attempted abduction of two girls in a park. He was released only four weeks before the first child disappeared."

"You're right, I don't believe it, but I did expect something similar," Austin responded.

"He was interviewed as a witness in regard to Chloe's disappearance. He said he had left before that and arrived at his first job at 9.15. His alibi checked out, although it's impossible to know if he left when he said he did or if he was two minutes later. His house and garage were searched. There was no evidence of her anywhere. But he remains a suspect. As do five other sex offenders in the area."

"I might go pay him a visit," Austin said. Before hanging up, he remembered to thank Marcus for his assistance.

* * *

Austin had briefly thought about pretending he was a detective for this next visit, yet he suspected they would recognise him from his TV interview. Everyone else had, so he dismissed the idea.

He walked up the driveway of the house at number 18 Elmer Road. It was built of older style clinker brick, which suggested it was an original house and had been there for decades. Austin wondered if, in fact, it might have been the original farmhouse before the land was subdivided. The driveway went down the side of the house and led to a large freestanding garage, a big one, possibly for six or eight cars.

Austin approached the security door with the mesh falling away in the corner. He rapped his knuckles on it three times. Instead of sounding like knocking, it sounded like he was trying to bust the door down. Maybe he'd rapped a bit hard.

The door opened and the cigarette smoke made him cough. It was disgusting. He carried on regardless. "Sorry to bother you. My daughter was kidnapped and I was just looking into Chloe's kidnapping to see if there might be any links. Do you mind if I ask you some questions?"

The woman at the other end of the cigarette was old, wrinkly and had skin the colour of a potato sack. The smoking had aged her, that was certain. She was a masculine looking woman, the kind you expect to see in hillbilly horror movies.

She drew on her cigarette again, "Yeah, I saw ya on the news the other mornin'. Not good losing a kid, but I don't know how I can help ya."

"I just wondered if you had seen anything on the morning the other girl vanished, that's all."

"I'd love to help but as I said to the coppers, I wasn't even home, dole money had come in and I was doing me shopping," she said.

Austin immediately imagined her gambling.

"Was anyone else at home, your husband perhaps?"

"Don't have no husband, I fucked him off long ago. Useless fat heap of shit he was."

"No kids?" Austin asked.

"No, live here all by my lonesome. I have to go now, I have something on the stove. I hope you find your girl," she said.

Austin knew there was no husband but wanted to see if she was protecting her son. According to her, she had no son.

As she began to close the door between them, a white van pulled into the driveway and drove past them down to the back shed.

"Who's that?" Austin asked, followed quickly by, "I thought no one else lived here?"

"He's never home, so it's like I'm by myself. That's want I meant." She closed the door before Austin had a chance to ask any more questions.

He walked down the step and back onto the driveway, his eyes remaining firmly on the man in the shed.

He headed directly for the big sliding door.

As he reached the entrance he could hear loud music playing. It sounded like INXS.

"Excuse me," he said. The man had his back to him and continued to unload something from the top of his van.

Austin tried again, "Excuse me!" This time he said it a lot louder. This time the man turned.

"Whatever you're selling, we don't want any," he said, continuing to unload.

"I'm not selling anything. I want to ask you some questions about a missing girl."

The man stopped his unloading and came to the entrance of the garage.

"Who you looking for?" Beau asked.

"I just wanted to ask you some questions about the morning the girl disappeared. Do you remember that morning?" Austin asked.

"I've told you guys everything I know," Beau answered. He had recognised Mikayla's dad the moment he drove past him in the drive. He was praying the father wouldn't recognise him from the movies.

"No, I'm not with the police. My daughter was kidnapped yesterday and I'm trying to see if there was maybe a connection between her kidnapping and Chloe's, the girl who was kidnapped on her way to school," Austin replied.

Austin tried to compare the man standing in front of him with the man in the mask. Could it be the same guy? Definitely the same build. Could be the same person, could be a hundred other fat guys. Austin knew one thing; he had met this man before, somewhere.

"As I told the police, I left probably five minutes before the time she would have passed my house. I saw her on the other corner of the highway. Apparently some guy saw her in this street. I don't know who, but he was the last to see her."

Austin got the feeling something wasn't right.

"The cops think I had something to do with it, but I said how could I have if someone else had seen her after me? They checked out the job I attended and the time I arrived and left," he added without prompting.

"I never suggested it was you; just wondering if you had seen her at all," Austin said smiling, "and you did, so that helps greatly. Sorry, how rude of me, I'm Austin." He offered his hand for shaking. "Beau," the man replied, as he took Austin's hand and shook it.

"What do you do for work?" Austin asked.

"I'm a handyman. Work everywhere really. I have a big day ahead tomorrow. Really need to get this van unloaded," Beau replied.

"Yeah, sure, sorry," Austin replied. He scoured the garage for anything that might have belonged to his daughter, but there was nothing. He was about to turn and leave when Beau stepped behind his van, leaving the side in clear view.

It read 'One Call Handyman'. Underneath was a picture of the handle of an old phone receiver. He had no doubt this was the logo Stevie's mum had seen.

And he still couldn't shake the feeling he had seen this guy before.

Chapter 46

Hayley and Jake had not been out to dinner in months, but it felt like years to Hayley. They had never been more distant from each other than they were right now. Hayley hated herself for keeping secrets, and tonight she was going to tell Jake she was expecting their baby.

Jake came directly from work and they met at the Crown Casino. It had an abundance of restaurants to choose from. They decided on Chinese. It was expensive but worth it. They chose the seven-course banquet. The courses were small but by the time they hit the fried ice-cream for dessert, they were struggling to finish it. Even Jake had trouble fitting it in, but he would always find a way.

"Jake, there's something I've been meaning to tell you."

Jake put his hand on hers. "It's ok, I know." He paused. "I know about the baby and I'm ecstatic."

Hayley looked utterly shocked. "How did you know?" she asked.

"I'm a cop, remember?" Jake replied. "You might be thinking I've been a bit distant lately, but it wasn't intentional. In fact, I was distant because I was trying to get some things straight in my own head." Jake took a deep breath. "I've decided that I'm going to leave the force and do private detective work."

Hayley sat there, even more shocked. "But you . . ." She paused, trying to understand. "You love that job," she continued, "why would you quit?"

"I do love it, but I love you and Indiana more."

"Indiana?" Hayley questioned.

"Yeah, Indiana, our boy, or girl, that's going to be the name," Jake said, smiling.

"Ok, let's discuss the name later," Hayley began. "Why are you quitting the force?" she asked again.

"It's because I love you and I don't want you getting that call, the one that says I'm not coming home. Call me selfish but I don't want to miss any of our future because some drug-fucked crim got lucky and shot me. Plus, I can't do my job properly if I'm worrying about it every day."

Their first course of spring rolls arrived but neither of them even looked at them.

"I'll give my notice soon. I just want to help Brodie clear some cases first. Also, they need time to replace me."

"You're irreplaceable, honey." Hayley laughed. "Whatever you want, that's ok with me." She smiled, and it seemed to say 'thank you'. Maybe deep down she had wanted him off the force too. Maybe Jake knew her better than she knew herself.

They spent the rest of the dinner talking baby. What they needed, what colour the baby's room should be and of course the name came up again, several times. Jake was sure she was accepting it as a boy's name. If they had a girl she would need a bit of convincing.

They decided not to find out the sex of the baby. They were happy with the surprise. He had almost eight months in which to convince her, if that's what it took.

Chapter 47

The air was crisp and salty. A gentle breeze broke the heat. The warmth from the sun on his back filled his soul. Water flowed over his feet and retreated with each wave. He walked along the beach like a man at peace with the world. "I love you," a voice next to him said. He turned. Sarah stood there, shining. The wind caught her hair, her hand touched his. She smiled and pulled him in. He had never seen her look so beautiful. She nestled her head under his chin. As he hugged her, he looked up the beach and could see Mikayla in the distance. She was drawing a heart in the sand with a stick. Above the heart was the letter 'I', below was the letter 'U'.

He turned his gaze back out to sea, smelling the ocean with every breath.

"You need to save her before it's too late," Sarah said to him.

"She is just there," Austin replied. He was still enjoying the hug.

"Look again," she whispered.

He turned back towards the beach where his daughter had been drawing in the sand.

She was gone and there was no heart. Instead was the word 'HELP!'

Austin felt his wife disappear in his arms.

Save her, before it's too late. The words rang in the air.

Austin awoke crying. He was sitting in his car. 'Save her, before it's too late,' still rang loudly in his head. Had he been asleep or was it a vision? He couldn't be sure. Whatever it was it was vivid. Was it a snapshot of heaven? While he didn't believe in heaven, he was sure he had already been to hell, or as close to it as he wanted to get.

Could it have been his wife's spirit? Could she be caught in the in-between? Many cultures believed the spirit would be trapped between earth and heaven if business remained unfinished.

Austin pondered the possibilities for a moment and then concluded that with the sleep deprivation and the tragic circumstances of the last 24 hours, it was most likely to have been a dream. The message was clear, however; he had to find her before it was too late, and time was running out.

He had parked the car at the end of Beau's street. While he had strong suspicions about Beau, he couldn't focus all his effort on one suspect. He had to make sure he looked at every possibility.

His cell rang, and Marcus flashed up in the caller ID.

"Hey," Austin answered, sluggish and tired.

"I'm just ringing to let you know the police have arrested Tyler Parsons. It's only for B&E, but more charges are expected. I managed to find the name and address of his last cellmate. His name is Jack Taylor. It might be worth making a house call. I'll send you an email with the details."

"Yeah, ok. It'll be my next stop. Any news on Mikayla?" Austin asked.

"Nothing. Sorry," Marcus replied.

"I'm getting more and more convinced her kidnapping is related to these other disappearances. Something big is going on here," said.

"Whatever you need, I'll get it for you. Keep me updated."

"Thanks buddy. I'll let you know how I go at Jack's."

Austin hung up. During the whole time he had waited outside Beau's house, while he had been awake, his eyes had been focused on the driveway. Staring at it for over four hours. No movement.

Before he moved on to Jack, he needed to be able to track Beau. That way he would always know where he was.

The idea of breaking in to his shed to plant the tracker had crossed his mind. He also wouldn't mind another look inside that shed.

Chapter 48

I had to follow up the two remaining leads. One was the first kidnapping, Scott Western's. I wanted to go and speak with the parents. The other was the last witness to have seen Chloe Henderson, Mr Lubic.

As I neared the Western's house, one thing struck me; the similarity between the areas. Not a geographical similarity, a suburban one. All the abduction sites were the same: quiet neighbourhoods, normal suburbs, normal kids. This person was a master at blending in.

I knocked and this time, a man answered. He was tall, but not quite as tall as me, about six foot two. He had a barrel chest, broad shoulders, toned arms, and he looked as if he dedicated a fair amount of his time to the gym.

I introduced myself. "I'll get my wife," he answered, without even introducing himself.

Moments later, a blonde lady appeared at the door. "How may I help you?" she asked in a bright cheerful way that I hadn't expected. I was taken aback.

I explained how we now believed the cases were connected and I was going over each case to see if we could find a common thread that might give us a new lead.

Mrs Western showed me through to the dining/kitchen area. I stood in amazement; the feeling I had interpreted as cheerful was in fact determination. This woman had thrown herself into searching for Scott and I had just entered ground zero. They had made posters and maps. The maps had a red pin with the words 'Last Seen' in the colour ledger at the bottom.

From the look of it, they had been doing an investigation of their own. She sat at the table and offered me a seat opposite. As I moved the chair to take my seat, a white cat darted from under the table into another room.

"So, Mrs Western, could you tell me what happened?"

"Audrey, please," she replied.

"Audrey," I repeated.

"It was like any other school morning. Scott got up, had brekkie, packed his lunch and headed off to school on his bike."

"Now, the school is Sunbury State Primary, just six streets over, correct?" I asked.

"Yes, that's the one. He always rode his bike to school. He loved riding his bike, he was always on it, even after school he would be out the front riding it until dark."

"So on that morning, there was nothing unusual. Scott went to school as normal?" I asked.

"Yep, I went on with my day, thinking he was in class. All that time he needed me and I didn't know . . . It wasn't until lunchtime when I went up to the shops for some groceries and I saw his bike on the footpath. At first I thought I must have been mistaken so I went and checked the bike. It looked like his. I rang the school, and they told me he wasn't there, that they thought he was off sick. They had no reason to think otherwise.

"I stood there on the side of the road staring at his bike while I waited for the police. I had no idea what to do. It was like I was in a haze, but at some point in that haze I knew falling apart would be of no benefit to Scott and I had to stay strong," she explained.

She leaned in across the table.

"Neville, my husband, on the other hand, it's torn him apart. They were really close. He just mopes around. I was hoping he would be influenced by my positivity, but it's like he's resigned himself to the worst," she said, sounding sad.

"Could you make us a cuppa, darl?" she called out to him.

Without a word, Neville heaved himself out of his recliner and turned his eyes away from the TV. His walk was slow and it seemed to take him a huge effort. By the time he had placed the cups on the bench, he had sighed several times, as if to protest his chore to his wife.

"How would you like your coffee?" she asked.

"I'd prefer a tea, if it's not too much trouble," I replied.

"Of course not, how would you like your tea?"

"Just white, thank you."

Neville begrudgingly walked over, placing the cups on the table. He even made a second trip, this time placing a plate of biscuits on the table.

"Audrey, did you notice any strange cars or vans hanging around the neighbourhood before Scott's disappearance?"

"No, everything appeared normal."

"Scott didn't mention strange cars or a van following him in the days leading up to the abduction?"

"No, and he would have said if he'd noticed someone. I always told him to be aware of stranger danger," she said.

She had several more sips from her cup, chewing a biscuit between sips.

My tea was hot and strong, just the way I liked it. The biscuits were only store bought but they were chocolate chip and moreish. It was a good thing Jake wasn't here or they would be demolished.

"Audrey, do you mind if I look in Scott's room?"

"Not at all, I'm sure he would love you to see it," Audrey said.

She stood up from the table, cup of coffee still in hand, and headed back past the front door through a lounge where Neville had retaken his seat in front of the TV.

Scott's room was bright and clean and based on the rest of the house, this was probably how he had left it the morning he'd left for school.

His shelves displayed several statues, which looked like figurines from various video games. There were also sports trophies on the shelf and several posters on his wall. One was labelled 'Black Ops 3', whatever that was, and the other 'The Last of Us'. I assumed these were other video games.

It was another waiting room, waiting for its child to come back and return it to life.

"Does Scott have a Facebook account?" I asked.

"No, he isn't old enough. A few years off for that yet," she said.

She finished her coffee.

"What do you think about a private detective, Mr Foxx?" she asked.

"Some are good, some are bad, some just in it for the dollars. I know we haven't found anything yet but rest assured, we're throwing everything we have at this case. We want to solve these crimes," I replied.

"Thank you, but it's been six weeks now and with every new missing child, Scott gets forgotten about just a little bit more," she said.

"No one will forget, and all of us at the station are working hard. If anything, the new cases are providing leads. We are hopeful they will lead to a connection between all of the abductions. Keep up with your posters and promotion of Scott, it's always good to get his face out there as much as possible," I said.

I handed her my card, "If you think of anything, please, let me know, no matter how small."

It was almost dark when I reached the solitude of my car.

Mr Lubic was next.

But he would have to wait until tomorrow.

Chapter 49

The man at number 18 obviously wasn't going out tonight, Austin realised, which meant one thing. He had no choice but to break in. He decided the best way was around the back. Going down the drive and past the house was just too risky. He would have to enter through the reserve at the rear with the high-tension lines running through it.

Austin drove to the end of the street and turned left. He parked his government SUV at the kerb. He opened his bag and removed his knife and pistol. He also took his case of lock picks. He had noticed the padlocks on the side door; they were good quality, yet nothing he couldn't bypass.

The grass in the reserve was knee high. The lines overhead buzzed. His head hurt. How they were ruled safe was beyond him. He had no doubt that in five or 10 years, there would be a class action proving they were responsible for tumours and brain cancer. An Erin Brockovitch-type case.

He passed Mr Lubic's back yard, and could see him seated at his dining room table eating spaghetti for one. He must be lonely, Austin thought.

He made his way down the row of houses. The large shed at the rear of number 18 stood out like a lighthouse.

The lights in the shed were off, but the ones in the house were still ablaze.

Normally, he would wait. But time was one thing he didn't have a lot of. He was hoping that any noise he made would be drowned out by the TV in the house.

Austin climbed the fence and waited. No one stirred. He moved slowly to the side door and again waited; again, nothing stirred. He began on the bottom lock. This was a risk, as he couldn't watch the door at the same time as he was crouched. So he had to be quick, and quick he was. It took him all of 15 seconds before it was open. With the top lock, he could keep one eye on the house while he fiddled. After opening the bottom lock, he had found the secret, and the second one was open in less than 10 seconds.

Austin inched open the door, listening for any creaks. It was quiet for the first few centimetres and then the tin door gave its first cry of angst. Austin waited. Still all quiet in the house. He pulled the door faster, hiding behind it, and waited. Still all quiet.

Austin pinned the door against the shed wall so it wouldn't bang shut with the wind. That would certainly send the fat guy running.

The darkness of the shed would normally require a torch, but Austin had his night-vision goggles with him. His first task was to plant the tracker on the van. Then he would look for clues. He made his way to the van and removed the tracker from his pocket. He slid it under the van and placed it between the axles.

He slid back out, checked the door. All clear. There were drawers and cupboards under the work bench. He rifled through them looking for anything; children's backpacks, clothes, anything that might disclose if he had taken them and where he had put them.

There was nothing. To the far right there was a train set with locomotives, mountains, stations, and people. He had his own little world on the train board. Yet there was nothing that suggested he was a kidnapper. Above the bench were tools and a red ladder. Again, nothing screamed kidnapper.

He had expected more. Then a thought came to him. He hadn't checked the van itself. It was reversed in so the rear doors were at the work bench end. He carefully pulled on the handle of the rear door. The van was unlocked. He looked inside. The back was clear except for two large 'U' bolts bolted to the floor, halfway between the back door and the cab. Then he noticed the doors were caged, as was the cab.

The back of the van was like one big cage. Could this be how he was doing it? Once the children were in here they would be trapped.

He quietly closed the back door and went to check out the cab itself. He opened the passenger door. It was full of junk food, packages, notes, an invoice pad; nothing incriminating. Austin flipped open the glove compartment. One empty eye stared back at him.

A mask.

A joker's mask.

Rage filled every vein of his body. His hand went to his gun. He was ready to kill. Then a thought interrupted his rage. If you kill him, how will you find her? A gun to his head might make him talk? But if it didn't work, the kidnapper might never go to her again, he might just leave her where she was to die. The risk was too great. He had to follow him from afar. There was no guarantee the Parsons guy hadn't taken Mikayla. After all, Austin hadn't yet been able to find anything that led to any of the missing children.

If this guy had taken the kids, then where the hell was he keeping them?

Without warning, he was blinded. Someone had switched the shed lights on.

"Who's in here?" a loud, deep voice called out.

Austin slid down the van and scurried noiselessly to the front. He removed his knife. He heard the fat guy move to the back of the van. Austin stayed low and circled him.

Beau had come to check on his cargo before he turned in for the night and he'd noticed that the side door was open. He also noticed the locks hadn't been cut, but picked. What were they looking for? Were they just looking for gear to hock, or were they poking around in his other business? Either way, he was going to find out and give them a hiding they wouldn't soon forget.

The back of his van was wide open. He poked his head around the corner of the door expecting to see someone sitting in there waiting for him, but it was empty. He clasped the door ready to pull it shut when he was struck. Something or someone struck him on the back of the head and everything went black.

His thumping head was the first thing he noticed when he regained consciousness. He touched the back of his head. There was a big lump and the skin had broken, although there was only a little blood.

Beau got to his feet, looked around, couldn't notice anything missing. When he had ensured he was alone, he locked himself in as he always did before checking on his prized possessions.

Chapter 50

For the first time since Stevie had been kept there, he'd finally had a night where he wasn't abused. Maybe it was the fact that the captors were too high or too tired. Either way he was glad.

The only downside was he had not been given any food or water since yesterday lunchtime. He had lost track of the days. Today could have been any day, but he thought possibly Tuesday. He had counted two mornings since Bill had requested the Sunday night special. Even though Stevie had never seen the sun, the cartoons were an indication of how much time had passed.

Stevie had purposely saved his water. He would only have a sip every hour or so but no matter how hard he tried to ration it, it simply wasn't enough. Ten minutes after he had sipped it, he was craving another sip. Despite the water he'd had, his lips were still cracked and dry because he was so dehydrated.

Then the pains came, pains in his stomach, a craving for any form of nourishment.

The captors had been hitting the drugs pretty hard. The last time he saw them they were still high and they had been that way for at least a day.

Stevie heard the lock turn and then the door opened. "I'm ready for some morning fun, how about you?" Bill stood there in the doorway, naked. Stevie begin to shake at the thought of what was about to happen. "I need to go to the toilet," he said softly, "please, I'm busting."

"You better hurry the fuck up." He took a set of keys that hung on a nail on the outside of the door.

Bill walked over, one hand playing with the keys, the other playing with his cock. He unlocked the cuffs. "There you go, hurry back." Stevie stood up, his legs turning to jelly. He hadn't walked in hours. He swung his legs over, planted his feet on the carpet and was about to stand when he was restrained. Bill put his arm across his chest from behind. "Remember: try to escape and I will kill your family." He licked his ear. Stevie stood, headed to the bathroom. It was filthy. There was vomit to one side of the bowl where someone had obviously thrown up but missed. He did his business, trying not to vomit himself. He rinsed his hands, ducked his wrists under the cold water. They stung, badly, but only at first. After a few seconds the water calmed them. He quickly put his face under the dirty tap. He drank like there was no tomorrow, guzzling as much as he could. A trip to the toilet was a rarity for him. Who knew when or if he would get another.

When he arrived back at the bedroom, Bill had fallen asleep. "What the fuck took you so long?" Bill asked, one eye now wide open.

"I was just freshening up," Stevie replied.

Bill patted the empty space next to him. Gesturing him to come.

The morning hell with Bill, luckily, didn't last long. Maybe it was the drugs, whatever the case, he was glad.

Stevie lay in bed watching the morning cartoon as usual. Scooby Doo had made his standard appearance.

He could hear Ian and Bill eating. He guessed it was eggs and bacon by the smell. God, he would give anything for a slice of bacon.

He tried to listen to their conversation. Often, the jingles and theme songs of the cartoons prevented him from hearing what they were saying. However, this morning their conversation was louder, the men were almost arguing. Something was going on.

"We just can't let him go," Ian said.

Stevie's ears pricked up.

"I'm not saying we fucking let him go, I'm saying we can't keep him much longer, plus he's starting to get boring, he doesn't even fight back anymore," Bill said.

"So, what you're saying is we kill him?" Ian asked.

Stevie heard that loud and clear.

"Yeah, just strangle him and dump him up the bush. No one will ever find him. If we bury him," Bill answered.

"That's how my cousin James got caught, got high, went for a drive and went crazy," Ian replied.

"We will bury him," Bill repeated.

"A dingo will dig up his fucking bones, scatter them all over the fucking bush and then some girl guide on a field trip will stumble across a leg bone. Next thing there's a search party, they find the body and a piece of fucking hair or DNA that links him to us. I watch *NCIS*, you know. That's how they get caught," Ian added.

"Don't panic, before we cover him over, we pour bleach all over him and then we burn him. Once the fire does its work, we fill in the hole," Bill said.

"Ok, so when are we doing it?" Ian asked.

"Kill him Friday, bury him Friday night," Bill suggested.

"What do we do until Friday?" Ian asked.

"We party. Take a couple of days off. We go on a bender, enjoy ourselves and on Friday our heads will be clear. Then we get rid of him," Bill said.

"Ok, we start the bender tonight, but come Friday, you better not fuck it up," Ian said.

Stevie had just heard his fate decided over eggs, bacon and morning coffee. In about three days' time, he would be dead. He had to get out of here and maybe the bender would give him a chance. He only needed one . . . even half a chance would do.

Chapter 51

Chloe had spent the last two days coming to grips with knowing that she was no longer going home. She had been sold to a monster and she was living with a man she only knew as Igor. He was a small man with cold eyes, and she had feared him instantly. She had been raped more times than she could count and it wasn't just the raping, it was the beatings that went with it, either from him or from his goons.

She was told she was free to roam the house but that if she tried to leave, she would be killed and so would her family. Igor told her she would end up like the other girls.

Igor's guards watched over every part of the house 24 hours a day.

On the second day, she was moved to his country house. Until then, she did not know he had another house. Soon after arriving there, Igor raped her again. This time, she fought. Igor bashed her, then he had his goons take her to the cellar. It was no ordinary cellar. This one was more like a dungeon, accessed via a secret door in the library. Chloe couldn't see a lot, with her face bruised and her right eye closed over, but she could make out being carried through a series of underground tunnels that led to a big brick room. In the room was a single chair.

The big man that they called Alexei or Alex plonked her in the chair. She was semi-naked, blood had dripped down from her face and onto her chest, her vision was blurry, her cheek stung, in fact her whole face was in pain. She had been hit hard.

As she landed on the chair, it rocked and almost tipped over.

Alex chained or cuffed her hands, she couldn't tell which, but she could feel the cold metal against her wrists. She moved her fingers around, and then she felt the links in the chains. The chains were tight and her wrists hurt.

Alex took her by the hair to raise her slumped head.

"Keep your head up," he demanded in a strong accent.

She did as she was asked.

She could see Igor standing in front of her.

He was holding a small blade in his hand.

What was he doing? Was this it? Was she about to die? Her tears flowed and panic set in. Without warning, Igor slashed her already aching face. This was it; this was how she was going to die. He was going to cut her to pieces.

"Turn your head and look at me," Igor commanded.

Chloe turned to face him.

"Now if you fight again, I won't stop cutting you," Igor said.

"Hang her in the next room."

Alexi dragged the chair under the archway and down a tunnel into a second room.

Igor ordered Alexi to unchain her hands. Then he placed the chain around her feet instead. He smiled and dragged her off the table by the chain. Her head clipped the edge of the table as she swung downwards. He put the chain over a spare hook that hung from the beam.

Something bumped into her or she bumped into it.

She turned her head to see what she had hit. She screamed.

It looked like a body. It was hanging by the feet and it was covered in blood. It spun as it hung, and when it stopped spinning, Chloe saw that it was a girl, just like herself, except her hair was matted with dry blood. She was obviously dead. Her face was frozen as if she had died in fear, her eyes wide open.

Chloe's body filled with fear; she wanted to run, but she couldn't move. She didn't want to look, but she couldn't look away. Even when she closed her eyes, she could still see the hanging girl.

She couldn't breathe. Something was wrong. What was happening to her? Why couldn't she breathe? Panic had set in.

"Relax," Igor said. "This is what we call an example. If you want to stay alive, then I suggest you don't fight me," he said.

Chloe nodded in understanding.

"This one fought. The choice is yours, I will leave you here to think about it."

"No, don't leave me here," Chloe cried out.

But she was left hanging next to the dead girl.

Their eyes met as they swung.

Chapter 52

I'd been hoping for a good night's sleep, yet I had a feeling I wouldn't get one for a while. So many questions kept entering my head.

In the dark, surrounded by silence, I let my subconscious answer the questions with the first thought that came to me.

Why haven't we received a ransom?

Because it was a kidnapping, just like the others.

Are they all related?

MO suggests it's likely.

Is the van linked?

Yes.

Is Tyler telling the truth?

You know he is.

I believed in my natural instincts and the first response of my subconscious was usually reliable and correct.

If my subconscious was correct, then I needed to find evidence that either supported my thoughts or led me to someone else. Either way, until we found who was responsible, we had little chance of finding the kids.

* * *

It was just after 9 am when I arrived outside Mr Lubic's home.

He was already out the front tending his garden. He was busy planting some shrubs just outside his front window as I walked down the drive.

"Mr Lubic?" I called.

His head turned and he looked up. "Yes?" he answered.

I flashed my badge. "Do you have a few minutes to answer some questions?"

"This about the girl again?"

"Yes, it is."

Mr Lubic stood. "I am going to have a cup of coffee, would you like one?"

"Tea, if you have it?" I replied.

He nodded and headed inside.

I followed.

"What can I help you with, Detective?" Mr Lubic asked.

"I've just taken over the investigation and I wanted to speak with you myself. See if any detail was missed or if you remembered something new?"

"Like I told the guy yesterday, I saw her walking and when she was approaching, my phone rang. I went inside for 30 seconds and when I came outside she was gone," Mr Lubic explained.

"Did you say the man yesterday?" I queried.

"Yes," Lubic replied.

"Was he a policeman?" I asked, confused.

"No, he was the father of the other girl. He called in to find out what I saw, exactly. He was a hell of a nice guy. I hope he finds his daughter," Mr Lubic answered.

"He came to see you?"

"Yes. Said he was following up some leads. We even did a test of how far she would have walked while I was inside on the phone. Funny thing, the police never asked me to do that . . . do you want to know the result?" he asked me, but didn't wait for me to answer. "She wouldn't have made it to the school, not even if we added an extra 15 seconds to the call. So I should have seen her when I came out of the house."

"We know she disappeared between here and the school, is that what you're saying?" I asked.

"No, after running the test, he believes she disappeared between here and number 20 and never even made it to the school gate," Lubic said.

He placed the tea in front of me at the kitchen bench.

As I added the milk, I pondered my next question.

"What did he do after he left here?" I asked calmly.

"He went door knocking as far as I know. Sat in his car for a while. Some people were not home I guess, then he left. You don't think he is involved, do you?" Mr Lubic asked.

"No, he is not involved. He's just trying to find his daughter," I answered.

"I think he is trying to find them all. I think he has made it his mission," Mr Lubic replied.

I didn't respond.

"Let's move on to why I'm here. I have read your statement." I passed him a copy and he began to read it.

"Does that still ring true, nothing that you think needs adjusting?" I asked.

"No, that's what happened. It's still fresh. I may be old but I'm still dealing with a full deck, if you know what I mean," Mr Lubic said, tapping his head.

"I don't know if you were ever asked this or not, but did you notice anything unusual that day?" I asked.

"Man yesterday asked me that but not the police," Mr Lubic replied.

"What was your answer?"

"No, just a normal school day."

"What about a van? Did you see any vans around, white ones?"

"Every day the man at number 18 drives one. He's a handyman," Mr Lubic replied.

'No. 18 has a van,' I scribbled.

A girl vanished in a 30 to 45-second window when this elderly man was inside and no one saw anything.

My only new piece of information was that number 18 had a white van.

My next stop, number 18.

Chapter 53

Austin was certain he had found the person who had taken Mikayla. Only problem was he doubted he still had her and from the brief search of his garage, if he did, it was somewhere else.

Austin was going to play his meeting with Jack one way, and one way only. He was going to hope that the unwritten rule of crime applied. Children were off limits.

Austin pressed the doorbell and waited. According to Marcus, Jack had just been released and was living at this address with his sister. Austin was assuming he hadn't found work yet.

His wait seemed like an eternity, but finally the door was answered, but not by Jack. A woman stood in the doorway. Her long, dark, curly hair was flowing in the wind. She was wearing jeans shorts and a white blouse. Her perfume hit him immediately. She was smiling from ear to ear, happy and pleasant. "How can I help you?" she asked.

"Is Jack here?" Austin asked.

"He's asleep as per usual," she replied, still smiling. "Are you the police?" she asked as if expecting them.

"No, my daughter is missing and he shared a cell with someone who may know her whereabouts. I really would like to talk to him."

"I'll go wake him," she replied.

She left Austin standing in the doorway.

"Jack, get your butt up. Someone is here to see you!" she shouted. She pounded on his door with her fist. "Jack, get up. Someone is here."

She returned to the front door after few minutes of yelling and banging.

"He's coming. Did you want to come in?" she asked hesitantly.

Austin could sense her concern and declined the offer. "I will wait here. I'm sure you have things to do."

The lady smiled but didn't insist.

Austin knew he had made the right decision. She was probably put out enough, having her brother just out of jail living with her. Last thing she would want was his mates calling over or worse still, unannounced strangers.

If the man who arrived at the door was Jack, he was shorter than his sister and that was rare. Maybe they had different fathers, Austin thought.

"Do you know Tyler Parsons?" Austin asked immediately.

"Yeah, what about him?"

"He broke into my house. Cops say he killed my wife and took my daughter," Austin said.

"Why you asking me? Cops have him. Go ask him," Jack said.

"You did time with him. I want to know about him," Austin replied.

"Look man, I dunno, you'll just have to ask him," Jack repeated.

Austin took a breath, "Can you help me, please. The police seem determined to say he did it, but I just want to find my daughter," Austin said.

"All right, I'll tell you what I know," Jack said.

He drew a cigarette from the packet, held it in his sleeve and lit it. He leaned against the brick pillar of his sister's porch.

"I shared a cell with him in the last 12 months of his sentence. The 11 months prior, he shared a cell with a guy named Neil Figal. He was French, I think. Anyway, he was in for the rape of a 12-year-old boy in a shopping mall. Figal was doing the last year of a four-year sentence. Let me just say that other prisoners don't do you any favours when you share a cell with a paedophile. One of the gangs had a particular problem with peds, and most of them assumed that Tyler was one of them. I don't know if you've seen the guy, but his looks don't do him any favours in dispelling the rumours. He's 25 and can hardly even grow a beard. Just looks like a person who would, how would you say, venture down that path."

He squashed the butt of the cigarette against the post between his thumb and forefinger before flicking it into the garden bed.

Before he began his next sentence, he had lit up and begun to suck on the end of another cigarette.

"Anyway, there's a motorcycle gang called Death Angels. They have a reasonably big contingent on the inside as well as the outside. The Death Angels have a huge problem with peds on the inside and they pride themselves on making their lives hell."

Jack stopped to let out a cough that sounded like his lung was about to be ejected. He thumped his chest a few times with his fist and then continued.

"One winter's morning last year several members of the Death Angels heard of Figal's mall escapade and offered Tyler a way to prove he wasn't one of them. It was simple: he had to send Figal a message from the Death Angels and if he did, they would lay off him. I don't know exactly what happened in the cell that night, but it resulted in Figal being sent to the infirmary and Tyler to solitary. Figal never came back into the main population. He had to be placed in lockdown. When Tyler reappeared, I was his new cellmate. We hit it off straightaway. He was in there for B&E. He'd never hurt anyone, he just wanted to get rich. The beating he gave Figal was not in his nature, it was foreign to him.

"Having been around, I taught him a few tricks of the trade and gave him some names that could get him set up on the outside. So I believe when he robbed your house, he was just after some cash or jewellery. He would never take your daughter or harm your wife, that's not him. If he was caught in the act, he'd just make a run for it."

Jack sucked the last of his second smoke and sent it away into the garden bed, which was obviously his own little dumping ground.

"That's what I suspected," Austin said. Having received that information, he was ready to leave. Now, he could focus on the man with the van.

Austin held out his hand to thank Jack but before he could, Jack spoke. "Before you leave, I have something else you might like to know."

Austin removed his hand, "Such as?"

"Tyler told me that Figal mentioned to him they now had a supplier of kids. They sent in their order via text and then the order was completed and delivery arranged. It made him sick. Figal didn't say who the guy was, only that a priest held the kids until delivery was organised. He said kids were sold anywhere from $10,000 to $50,000. It might be worth you seeing this guy. Whoever took your daughter may have sent her to this priest."

Austin had always imagined that his daughter had been kidnapped by a paedophile and was being held in a hotel room, or a house somewhere. It had never crossed his mind that she had been kidnapped and on-sold.

"If you want good news, I think she's alive somewhere. If I hear any more, I could give you a call."

"Do you know where this Figal guy lives?" Austin asked.

"Wouldn't have a clue, but you seem like a resourceful guy, after all, you found me," Jack replied.

Austin handed over his private mobile number. "Thank you again," he said.

He extended his hand for a second time. This time, Jack took it and shook it firmly.

As Austin headed back down the driveway towards the gate, Jack called out, "Good luck!"

Austin waved to acknowledge his well-wishes.

He called Marcus. Apparently, finding Figal might be a little harder than Austin had first hoped. He didn't even have time to put the key into the ignition when his private phone rang and the caller ID came up as private.

Chapter 54

Less than a minute after leaving Mr Lubic to enjoy the rest of his morning tea, I knocked on the door of number 18.

A burly man who could have once been well built but had let himself go was in the driveway working on a van.

"Excuse me, sir," I said, flashing my badge as I approached.

"Yeah?" he said.

"I'm Detective Brodie Foxx. I'm investigating the disappearance of a girl who went missing . . . well, we believe she may have even gone missing from this street," I said.

He wiped his hands on his overalls as he approached. "I won't shake your hand. Mine are dirty. I'm Beau," he introduced himself. "What do you guys want now? I've already spoken to you guys several times. Do you wanna take me in for another lie detector test I suppose? Don't you guys fucken speak to each other?"

"Yes we do, I have the file here. I'd like to go over a few things if I may. It's been plonked on my desk. Just want to ensure everything's been done properly," I said.

He looked uneasy and in my book, that moved him up on my suspect list.

"Well, can we get on with it? I need to fix me truck and if I don't, I got no job, you understand?"

"I understand, I'll be quick. On the morning she went missing, you were home until 8.45, is that correct?"

"If that's what it says, then, yeah. I can't remember. But it sounds about right."

"Did you see the girl as you left?"

"I didn't notice her in particular. There were a lot of kids walking to school. You guys rang my job. They said I was there, you even checked my house, my van. I had nothing to do with it," Beau said.

"About the van. How do you explain the traces of bleach found all over the floor?"

"As I said, at the time, I was doing painting. On the trip home from the job, some of the bleach spilt and it took me a good hour to clean it up. Stunk to high heaven for a week."

It was plausible. But I had my doubts.

"What about the steel mesh you have in the back, why do you have that?"

"Just to hook stuff onto, tie wood to when I'm taking it to jobs. Sometimes I even have to take my Bond saw to jobs and it's heavy and if I don't chain it in, the fucker slides everywhere." Then he added, "You should be following up on the dirty old man that supposedly saw her walking this way, maybe he was the last to see her for a reason."

"We're following up all leads, Beau, we're just trying to eliminate you as a person of interest. Well, I think that's all. Thanks for your time," I said.

I put the photos of the van back in the file and turned to leave. Before I did, I had a revelation, maybe it was a voice, maybe it was the investigator in me nagging at me.

Check out the van for yourself, my internal voice said.

I turned back, "Is that your van?" I asked, pointing down the drive.

"Yep."

"Do you mind if I have a quick look?" I asked.

"You guys have done that already, but go ahead," he replied.

As I walked down the side of the van, a cold shiver went down my spine. I knew instantly this guy had just become number one on our list, not just for the disappearance of Chloe Henderson but for all of them.

I couldn't let him know I thought there was any connection.

What made me shiver was the logo on the side of the van. It was a big phone with the words 'One Call Handyman' and below that, a picture and a phone number.

I took a photo of the logo. I needed to show this to some people. Thoughts were racing through my head. Definitely needed to organise another search warrant.

I walked further down the driveway, stuck my head in the shed. I was looking for Mikayla, not that I was telling him that.

"If you want to look through the property again, you'll need a search warrant," his voice came from over my shoulder.

"No need for that," I replied.

"I'd like to make a formal complaint," Beau said.

"What about?" I asked, thinking police harassment.

"The dad of the latest girl to disappear was here yesterday, asking me all sorts of questions and then last night, he broke into my shed and hit me on the back of the head," Beau said.

Classic deflection procedure. First Mr Lubic and now Mr Campbell, I thought.

"How do you know it was him, did you see him?" I asked.

"Well no, but who else would it be?" Beau asked.

"Unless you saw him, I can't really do much, but I will have a word to him about his visit."

"Typical fucking cops," Beau replied.

"Thanks for your time," I said.

The logo was exactly what was described to me by Stevie's mum, coincidence maybe, but unlikely.

I rang Jake but had to deal with his voicemail. While I waited for his return call, I rang Mr Campbell.

"Hello?" Austin answered.

"Austin, this is Detective Brodie Foxx, can you talk for a few minutes?"

"Sure," Austin replied.

He sounded as if he was expecting horrible news so I said hastily, "I have nothing new to report, so don't panic. I'd like you to come into the station. Around 3? There are a few issues we need to discuss."

"Yeah sure, I'll be there," Austin replied.

As soon as I hung up, Jake rang back and I filled him in on the van's logo.

"While you're on your way back to the station, I'll organise a warrant," Jake said.

Chapter 55

By the time I got back to the office, it was nearing 2.30 and Jake had just received word that the warrant had been partially approved. We had requested permission to plant listening devices as well as for a physical search of the two vans, the house and the shed.

However, the judge only approved the physical search, his reasoning being that having a van that was seen at one kidnapping and that resided near another was not enough evidence to suggest that they were responsible for the crime. He could thus not approve a listening device.

We had organised for Forensics to come with us on the search, with both Beau's vans to be impounded for 24 hours and analysed in the crime lab. I had just put the finishing touches to the paperwork and sent it to the captain for execution when my phone rang. Mr Campbell was in reception. He was early. "Jake, he's here," I said.

Jake was on the phone, so he pointed to interview room one.

I met Mr Campbell in reception. "Come through, would you like a coffee?" I asked.

"No thanks," he said.

I ushered him into interview room one. It was small, with a desk, three chairs and the standard two-way mirror.

"Am I in trouble?" he asked.

"No, we're just short of space around here," I replied.

I sat down on the side with two chairs, and he sat on the one opposite me. The chair next to me remained empty.

"Jake will be joining us in a second, he's just finishing up a phone call."

Jake entered, offering his apologies.

"Mr Campbell, we've asked you here today to give you an update on the investigation," Jake said. "We've arrested Tyler Parsons for breaking and entering. While he admits to being in your house, he told us that he was in the roof so he could rob the place in the early hours of the morning."

Austin wasn't completely sure that Beau was responsible, but he knew one thing: the more pressure the police put on him, the less chance he would have of being led to Mikayla. His biggest risk right now was Beau going underground, and leaving Mikayla to die of starvation.

"He claims he never got a chance to rob the safe and he never saw the man that he claims killed your wife and took your daughter," Jake continued. "He says that your daughter's screams startled him. He waited in the roof until the commotion was over before leaving and on the way out, he found your wife dead."

"Do you believe him?" Austin asked.

"We can't be sure. The lie detector test was inconclusive," I replied. "We're only 68 hours into the investigation of Mikayla's disappearance and your wife's murder. We have hundreds of leads that we're continuing to follow up. During the investigation we've also been looking into the possibility of Mikayla's abduction being linked to the other missing children."

"I thought you felt it was a ransom and it wasn't related? Isn't that what you told me?" he asked.

His temper had begun to rise. The whole situation was getting to him and I could see it.

"Stay calm, Mr Campbell, we're doing everything we can to find Mikayla."

He sat back and relaxed a little.

"During the investigation it came to my attention that you have been conducting something of an investigation of your own," I said.

He was about to speak when I raised my hand and then Jake butted in.

"Now we can't stop you looking for your daughter and we can't stop you interviewing people, but just be sure you don't go breaking any laws when you're doing it."

Campbell knew what Jake was referring to but just in case he hadn't got the hint, I knew Jake was about to explain it to him plain and simple.

"Mr Delacroix claims his shed was broken into the night you visited him. Do you know anything about that?" Jake asked.

"I know it's a bad area. I went and asked him some questions. He said he was at work; him mum was there and she verified it. I will do anything to find Mikayla. The other missing girls are the only lead I have. What else am I going to do? I can't put up posters forever."

"We know you're not going to stop looking but if you find anything, you need to tell us. Our suggestion to you is not to go breaking into places looking for your daughter. If you have any suspicions you want followed up, call us. No point getting yourself put in jail. You can't look from there," Jake added.

"Will do. I don't have anything that will help your investigation," Austin answered.

"Before you go, we're about to conduct another search of the residence, the shed and the two vans Beau Delacroix has on his property, so I don't want you to be surprised when you hear it on the news," I said.

Austin was halfway to the door but decided to sit back down.

"If he has her and he is holding her somewhere else, if you search there and he goes underground, Mikayla could starve to death, all of them could."

"We know it's a risk, but he has no other property we know of. If he has them, they're probably there. If we don't find them, then we can probably eliminate him as a suspect."

"Eliminate him? Why?" Austin replied. The anger had returned.

"We won't have any reason to think he's involved," Jake said.

"He's been sighted at two kidnappings!" Austin replied.

"Both of which were indirect. We've searched his property and van previously and they were all clean. He has undergone a lie detector test in the past and it was inconclusive. We simply have nothing to tie him to any of the abductions. We've struggled to get a warrant this time around, and in the eyes of the law, coincidence doesn't equal evidence," Jake replied.

We stood up, telling Mr Campbell we would stay in touch.

Austin stood again, ready to leave. He had a million thoughts going through his head. Should he tell the police about the mask? Surely they would find it. What if the fat guy found himself under constant surveillance and went underground with Mikayla left starving somewhere? Austin knew if he mentioned the mask, he would be admitting to breaking and entering and he would be held overnight at least. Tomorrow was Thursday and he could afford no time in jail. He still had a few leads to follow up.

He kept quiet.

"Thank you," he said as he left.

Chapter 56

Three unmarked cars and a van all arrived just after 4 pm. Jake and I were in one car; the other two were occupied by members of the Missing Persons Unit and uniformed officers. The van held Grace and three members of her Forensics team. Jake was first onto the property, warrant in hand. As he knocked, three members from the Missing Persons Unit split up. One followed Jake, the other two headed straight for the shed.

I followed Forensics into the garage. We were prepared to cut the locks but Beau was happy to let us in.

"Detective Miller is giving your mother a copy of the search warrant if you want to see it?" I said.

"It's fine, Detective. I have nothing to hide, please look around," Beau replied.

"We need to impound your vans. Should only be for 24 hours," I said.

"I have work on Friday. Jobs to do, so I better have them back by then," Beau said.

"We will do our best," I said.

Forensics took the keys and drove the vans out to the street where the tray trucks were waiting.

"Do you mind if I keep working on my locomotives while you look around?" Beau asked.

I looked over his shoulder. He had a big board set up with mountains, a town and several stations. He had the works. There were locomotive parts spread out in one corner of the board, obviously the one he was repairing.

"Sure, no problem. Just don't interfere with the search." I began to look through the cupboards. They were full of things that a kidnapper, or a handyman, would use: duct tape, rope, cable ties. Our biggest problem was we didn't have anything to compare to. As none of the kids had been recovered, it was impossible to know what these items had been used for.

We confiscated everything.

My hopes were resting on finding some of Mikayla's hair or DNA in one of the vans.

Jake received a rude response from Beau's mother. "This is police harassment. My boy hasn't done anything. He's been a good boy."

Jake didn't even respond. He handed her the warrant, headed past her and went straight for Beau's room. If he had any souvenirs from his victims, Jake doubted that he would keep them out in the open in front of his mother. He would do what a teenager would do with a packet of smokes. Hide them at all cost, or cop a belting.

Jake opened the first drawer of the three-drawer side table. There was a pile of dirty magazines, pens and a few odds and ends. Nothing of interest. The next drawer held socks and undies. Jake removed it, emptying the contents onto the floor. Again, nothing of interest. The bottom drawer held football cards, dozens of them, just dumped there. Again Jake upended the drawer and the cards fluttered to the floor.

Jake left the drawers all askew and the contents where they lay. He lifted the mattress off the bed. Nothing. Under the bed was another stack of magazines and a video tape, marked XXX. Jake tossed it aside. He picked up the pile of magazines and flicked through them, hoping something incriminating would fall out.

Nothing did.

Jake moved over to the robe. It consisted of one shelf with hanging space below. On the shelf were some DVDs, not porn, and a stack of CDs. The shelf itself was relatively empty. An old shoe box sat in the other corner. Jake's hopes rose, only to be disappointed by a pair of worn Blundstones.

Nothing, he thought, there's nothing fucking here.

"I hope you're going to clean all this up?" Mrs Delacroix yelled. She was standing in the doorway and smoke was drifting into the room as she spoke.

"I am sorry, Mam, we are not a maid's service," Jake replied.

"You fucking pigs are all the same," Annabel replied.

Jake left Beau's room alone and headed for his mother's, taking extra time in upsetting her room. After the pig comment, anything goes, he thought. By the time he had finished, it looked as if a three-year-old had chucked a tantrum in there.

Jake checked kitchen cupboards, cereal packets, Milo tins, anything and everything. He checked the sofas, both in the cushions and down the back.

Jake had not been looking for the girl. He doubted she would be here; all he was after was a sign that Beau had once had her. But there was nothing.

By the time the whole crew had finished, they had searched the home top to bottom including the roof cavity. It was clean.

Jake was hoping they'd had better luck in the shed.

"You got anything?" he asked me.

"No." I shook my head.

I looked over at Beau. He didn't even look worried. Too calm for my liking. Even an innocent person gets upset when the cops are searching your home. It didn't faze him in the slightest and that made me think he knew we wouldn't find anything. Not because there was nothing to find, but because he had removed it or hidden it. Clearly, something was wrong with this picture.

PART TWO

The Priest, the Cop and the Judge

Chapter 57

ather O'Riley had received a text. It was only one word but he knew exactly what it meant.

HEAT

He picked up the phone and called the man he always called when things got a bit sticky and requested a meeting with Mike. He didn't want to do this one over the phone.

Mike came over as soon as he could and sat across the desk from the Priest.

"I need you to fix a problem," Father O'Riley said.

"Don't you always," Mike said. "Who hasn't paid us this time?"

"It's more serious than that, I'm afraid. Our supplier is under pressure from the police."

"What do you expect me to do? I can't go putting myself into the investigation. That'll only compromise our position," Mike replied.

"I want you to send them on a different path. Give the dogs a new car to chase, so to speak," the Priest said.

"So you mean stage an abduction. Using the same sort of car. Take the attention away from our supplier?"

"That's exactly what I mean," the Priest said.

"What car does he drive?" Mike asked.

"It's a white van," the Priest replied.

"What do you want me to do with my catch?" Mike asked.

"I have no orders to fill at the moment and therefore no use for any goods. So what you do with it will be up to you," the Priest said.

"I don't kill children," Mike replied.

"You may not have a choice," the Priest responded.

"I always have a choice," Mike replied.

"Do you? When the goods are not delivered to the Monster, what choice will you have then? What choice will your family have and those beautiful twin boys? Will they have a choice?" the Priest said.

"The Monster doesn't scare me," Mike replied.

"I believe in God, and the Monster is the closest thing to the devil I have seen here on earth. Maybe you should be afraid," the Priest countered.

"I will sort it out. Don't you worry. Maybe after Beau makes this delivery to the Monster, we get ourselves a new supplier."

"I think that is a certainty," the Priest agreed.

"Leave it with me. I'll make sure a kid is taken care of and I might even have a way of putting our mate Figal in the frame."

Chapter 58

James Mitchell had spent more than enough time in this nuthouse. He needed to get out. The desire to kill was growing stronger every second. He only had one more review to pass, and that was with the board that oversaw the hospital.

He wanted to be back where he could satisfy the urge that was growing inside. Even without the drugs to feed it, the monster had continued to live inside, and now it wanted out. He had managed to keep it quiet in the corner of his mind while he had visitations with his mother. Soon, his monster would refuse.

* * *

Salma looked through her notes several times. She had to make her decision by 5 pm. Other members of the board were doing the same. Reviewing a criminal who had been found not guilty of a crime by reason of insanity was not about now finding him sane, it was more about eliminating any reasons he would still be considered insane or a threat to himself or society.

The facts were clear to her. James had been out on visitations with his mother at weekends and even for weeks at a time. He had been off his antipsychotic medication, his voices and delusions had disappeared years before, and any reference to the 'shadow people' had vanished close to a decade before. If his case was before the court today, she would not be able to find him insane. Had he still shown the signs he had displayed when he was arrested, there would be no doubt at all.

After deciding her own stance, she read through all her colleagues' reports and was pleased to find they agreed with the diagnosis and thus the conclusion to release Mr Mitchell.

Salma began to type her report.

She concluded that Mitchell should remain on the Sexual Offenders List but that in her professional opinion, he no longer posed a threat to the community.

Chapter 59

Finding a white van was easy enough. Taking a kid off the street would be a more difficult proposition. It wasn't something you did on a whim. Mike knew that he had no real choice, despite what he had said to the Priest. If the choice involved angering the Monster or not, you chose not to, every time. At five foot five, the Monster hadn't achieved his reputation because of his size. He was a vicious killer who had been rumoured to kill an enemy's entire family, including their children and the grandparents.

Mike didn't want to kill a child, but what else could he do? Take him to the country and let him go? What if he came back and was able to identify him? That wouldn't work. What was he to do? How was he going to kill a kid?

He left his car in the parking lot several rows down from where he had taken the van. Now all he had to do was find a kid, boy or girl, it didn't matter. He drove the streets of the local neighbourhood; the surroundings were all unfamiliar. He was hours and hundreds of kilometres away from his home town. He was now in the Joker's territory. The streets were all the same, houses crammed next to each other, rarely a difference between them, cars in the drives. Kids were in school, well the good ones were. It was the ones who decided not to attend that he was looking for.

He put some distance between himself and the shopping complex where he had found the van. He had passed through dozens of suburbs, the names of which he could no longer remember. It was late morning and at this rate, lunchtime would come and go and he would be no closer to fixing the Priest's problem. The longer he drove the van, the more chance he had of getting caught.

A sign caught Mike's attention. Northland Shopping Centre. Surely an opportunity would arise. He drove around to where the cinemas were located, hoping to find some kid heading in alone. Every kid he saw either had a mate or a girlfriend with them. Taking two was out of the question. Double the problem, double the risk and double the guilt. No one ever took two at once; no one except the Beaumont killer. He'd taken three off a busy beach. How had he done that? Confidence, nothing more, Mike answered himself.

He decided to park in the lot outside the cinema and wait. It was a safer option than to keep driving around. He sat watching, cap on, head down. Mother after mother passed the van and occasionally a group of children, but never a single child. He had his clipboard up. Whenever an adult walked past, he held it in front of his face as if he was working.

He emptied the contents of his wallet into his jacket pocket. Preparing for the ambush.

He was about to try another location when he saw a boy. He guessed he was about 12. He was walking towards the van, about 15 car spaces down from where Mike was parked. His hair was dark brown and it was spiked so he looked taller. Mike guessed he might have wagged school for a girl, a date maybe, maybe his first ever. He was dressed nicely in jeans, shirt and a red jacket.

This was his chance, and he might not get another.

Mike got out, opened the side door, dropped his wallet and kicked it under the van, just enough so it was out of sight.

Now he waited.

The boy got closer. Seven cars.

Three cars.

"Excuse me?" Mike said.

The boy stopped, turned, unsure if he was being spoken to.

Mike took a quick glimpse around for witnesses. None.

"Yes?" the boy answered politely.

"Can you help me?" Mike asked.

"What with?" The boy was hesitant.

"I dropped my wallet and it slid under the van. I'm so clumsy. I've just had an operation and I can't get it, I really need to get my daughter's birthday present."

The boy stood in front of the van, being careful to keep his distance. He crouched. He could see the wallet; the man was telling the truth.

"Yeah, sure mister. I'll get it for you," he said, moving around to the side of the van. He bent down and collected the wallet.

"Here you go." He handed it to Mike.

"Thank you," Mike said. He took the wallet with his left hand and pushed hard with his right. The boy flew back, through the open door of the van. Mike had punched the boy hard in the face, twice. The back of the boy's head hit the floor of the van and bounced back with the next punch, which was even more vicious.

The boy lay on the floor of the van with blood flowing liberally from his nose and mouth. Pain was shooting up his face. His eyes were watering.

His vision was going blurry. What had happened? He couldn't be sure. He heard the door shut. Now he could feel the van moving, he wanted to run, he needed to get out, but he couldn't even see the door, let alone move.

He was dizzy, he could taste blood flowing down his throat.

They were travelling faster now, but his vision was still hazy.

Where was he going? Had he been taken? His eyes flickered between light and dark, until darkness came.

Chapter 60

Grace went over both vans with her team, there every step of the way, more hands-on than she would normally have been. She knew her team would be thorough, but she wanted to ensure every box was ticked.

But after going through the vans, they had nothing; not a hair, not a fibre, no bloodstains, not a single fucking thing. She could tell the van had been cleaned regularly and with bleach. Bleach was a killer's best defence against any trace evidence and this guy knew it. She had heard the story of the spill, but this was no spill, this had been used methodically and carefully to remove anything left behind. She thought he must have hosed the back, scrubbed it, then bleached it and hosed it again. She was hoping for some trace evidence that had caught on his clothes and been transferred to the front cabin, but there was no such luck.

* * *

It was early afternoon when Grace came into my office. Jake was standing by her side like an eavesdropping schoolgirl, trying to get the latest gossip. I could see it in his eyes; he was hoping they'd found something.

"What did you find?" I asked.

"Nothing. They were both clean. He's used bleach all over the place. He was covering up something," she replied.

"Unfortunately, using bleach is not a crime," I replied, although we all knew I was just stating the obvious.

"What about the house? Did they find anything there?" I asked.

"No, it was clean, no trace of any children in the house or garage," she replied. "If he has them, he must have taken them somewhere else."

"Why don't we ask him to do another polygraph test?" Jake interjected. He'd done one for us when Chloe Henderson had disappeared.

"Why would he agree? He passed the first one, I don't think he'd volunteer for a second," I said.

"It was inconclusive," Jake corrected me immediately, "I think it's worth a try. How about we bring him in for questioning, put some pressure on him and see where that leads?"

"Nothing to lose," I agreed.

"Let's keep the vans here while we question him," Jake said. "It'll make him think that we found something."

"Let's go get him," I said.

I picked up my folder and car keys and we headed for the elevator down to the car park.

We drove to Beau's. At first we sat in silence, which was unusual for us. Then Jake spoke. "We have our ultrasound in six weeks and we'll find out what we're having."

"How are you getting Hayley to accept the baby's name?" I asked.

"It will be Indiana. She'll agree, she's warming to it," Jake replied.

I wound down my window even though Jake had the air-con on. I had been feeling sick of late. I wasn't sure what it was, but something wasn't right. I had made an appointment to see my specialist and until I knew more, I would keep it to myself.

"You ok there, Brucey?" Jake asked.

"Yeah mate, I'm fine, just feeling a bit sick in the guts," I replied, trying to wave it off.

"You're probably hungry and it's way past lunch. Do you wanna grab a quick bite before we pick up Beau? It's not like he can go anywhere." Jake laughed.

"No, it's all good, I'll be ok," I answered.

Truth of the matter was that eating was the last thing I wanted to do.

"What do you really think is this guy's involvement? What does your gut tell you?" Jake asked.

"I don't know, my gut says he's involved, but my head asks for the evidence. There isn't any, so my brain tells my gut that it's wrong and to look elsewhere," I replied.

"Ok, so your gut says it's him. Now why would there be no evidence?" Jake asked.

"Because it's not him?" I answered.

"Ehhh! Wrong," Jake replied, making a buzzer sound like a wrong answer in a quiz show. "Think. How did you find Mason?"

"Esmeralda found him," I responded, referring to the psychic who had confirmed the identity of the serial killer.

"No. Think. You were led to him because he made a mistake and killed someone he knew. Correct?"

"Correct," I replied, "but what's this got to do with Beau?" I wasn't sure where Jake was heading.

"Maybe Beau knew the girl who walked past his door every morning? We didn't find any evidence of Mason at his home. He had a secret place. Maybe Beau has a secret place too?" Jake suggested.

"You think he's keeping them somewhere else?"

"Possibly."

"I'm sure they don't have any other property. Where would he take them?"

"Maybe he has a house elsewhere that's not in his name. Maybe he has a sick and twisted friend. Hell, that Cleveland guy had three girls in a room for 16 years, one even had a child and the neighbours knew nothing of it," Jake replied.

"I don't know about Beau being able to keep four kids in a house undetected, especially when he's elsewhere. But we agree on one thing: they are alive somewhere," I answered.

"Let's bring him in for questioning and we'll see what he has to say for himself," Jake said.

Chapter 61

James Mitchell didn't have many visitors and the few who came were usually family. But when his cousin was sitting opposite him in the visitors' room, he was the last person James had expected to see.

"What the hell are you doing here? Do you know I'm about to get out?" James asked.

"Yes, that's why I came," Ian Welling replied. "We've set up a surprise for your homecoming, one specially delivered by the Priest," Ian continued.

James knew that it was possible their meeting was being recorded. "I'd love to see the Priest again if I get out, but it's unlikely I'll be able to spend time with you, Ian, due to our past. I hope you understand."

Ian knew exactly what he meant by saying 'see the Priest again'. He wanted an order.

"How are things on the farm?" James asked.

"Still having trouble with the wild pigs up there. They're becoming a big nuisance. Need exterminating," Ian said.

James knew all too well that wild pigs meant cops.

"I'll be able to give Dad a hand on the farm if need be," James replied.

"That'd be great, I'm sure he'd appreciate the help. I hope I'll see you up at the farm at some stage," Ian replied.

He stood and left.

James sat in the visitors' room alone. Thinking.

The pigs were still causing problems.

Had they ever stopped?

In the whole time he had been here, he had learned one thing. The pigs had put him here.

Finally, he would make them pay, one by one.

Chapter 62

Austin knew Beau was out of action for the day, so chasing other leads was his next best option. He was waiting for Marcus to come up with Figal's address. He had given Marcus the details the previous night. Jack had told him he had a supplier. Austin knew if he found the supplier, he would be one step closer to finding his daughter and hopefully, the others.

Marcus had told Austin he couldn't risk going back into the office late at night. He had taken a lot of risks already and if he got caught searching things he wasn't supposed to be searching, the whole operation would be in jeopardy. Austin knew without Marcus' intel he would have to rely on the police and that was simply not an option.

The clock on the bedside table clicked over to 11.30 am. Austin sat on the bed, which remained made. He hadn't slept in it lately; he just lay on top of it when the urge to sleep became too great. He had dreamt of Sarah every time. The same dream over and over. Every time, Mikayla was walking ahead of them on the beach and every time, he and Sarah were happy. Then Mikayla was gone and Sarah began to fade. She cried out for him to find her before it was too late. Not only did he dream the same dream, he woke up exactly the same way, staring at an empty beach, listening to the screams of his dead wife. Every time he woke, he was in a cold sweat.

He sat taking in the view of the city and the world below carrying on around him. He had not gone home since the police first called him. He couldn't bear the thought of stepping inside that house again. He had been in contact with Sarah's parents; they understood. Her father made him promise that when he found who had killed Sarah, to make it painful. No doubt about it, was Austin's response.

Usually he was a patient man, but the wait for Marcus' call was driving him insane. He wanted to be on the move, finding out what Figal knew about the so-called delivery man.

Another 15 minutes passed before his cell phone began to jump off the bed.

"Sorry I took so long, but I had to ensure my system hadn't been breached," Marcus began. "The only Figal I've found is a Neil Figal. He was Tyler's cellmate only for two months. In for kidnapping and molestation. He has an address in Prahran listed as his permanent place of residence. You got a pen?" Marcus asked.

"Sure," Austin replied.

He scribbled the address and collected his already packed bag from the floor.

He was getting close; he could feel it in his bones.

Chapter 63

Stevie had noticed a drastic change in the way he was treated, especially by Bill. He no longer tried to hide his drug problem. He had been injecting on the bed and throwing the needles into the corner of the room. Last night, Stevie had been forced to lie still as Bill sprinkled and sniffed white powder off his stomach.

Stevie couldn't remember the last time he had eaten. It might have been the morning he overheard their plans to kill him and bury him in the woods. Since then, he had spent every waking moment trying to figure out a plan to get out of there. He knew if he was still there Friday, he would be dead.

He sat on his bed, cold and shaking, busting to go to the toilet and desperate for a drink. He had considered drinking his own urine but the thought of it made him feel sick. They were always willing to let him go to the toilet. He guessed it was only so they didn't have to clean up the mess. Every time he went, he guzzled as much water from the tap as he could handle.

The frequency of the attacks increased, and the brutality also increased. Not only were they high and drunk at the same time, they seemed to be continually feeding themselves with more white powder, needles and vodka. Stevie hadn't slept since they'd discussed their Friday plans, but neither had the men. Whatever it was they were taking, it was fuelling them. He had worked that out.

"We're almost out of C, and we used the last of the H last night. I want to speedball tonight. Can you get me some more H?" Bill asked.

"You better slow down, you'll overdose if you keep going," Ian replied.

"I know my body, just one speedball for our last night with the boy. Then we'll get rid of him," Bill replied.

"Where am I supposed to get the money for the H? I'm down to my last grand and that was meant for rent."

"Just give me 500 for the H and I'll get you some cash next week," Bill replied.

"How are you going to get me some cash next week? You're unemployed," Ian said.

"I have my ways, don't you worry," Bill replied.

"I don't want you hurting anyone to get the money," Ian said.

"Ok, I promise no one will get hurt," Bill said.

Ian handed over the 500 and Bill was immediately on the phone to his dealer.

Chapter 64

It took Austin just over half an hour to reach Figal's. From the kerb it looked like a house belonging to a low-life. The lawns were unkempt weeds, as high as a man's knees. The windows were filthy and the blinds were closed. The driveway had an old Toyota sitting under the small free-standing carport. Austin thought it must be at least 20 years old, with faded paint and bald tyres. It would be lucky to get a road-worthy.

He crossed the front lawn, the weeds whipping his ankles as he walked. The man who answered the door was a small, dishevelled, unwashed scum-bag. Looked like he was high. "What you want?" he asked. The door was cracked open just enough to see through the door. The security chain hung above the man's chest.

"I'm looking for Neil," Austin said.

"I'm Neil. Did the copper send you to rough me up for reneging on the deal?" Neil asked.

"No one sent me. I have a business offer for you," Austin replied, confused.

"You a cop?" Neil asked.

"No, far from it, I'm hoping you can help me," Austin said. "Tyler told me to look you up," he added.

"How do you know Tyler?" Neil asked.

"Friend from inside," Austin answered.

"Hold on," Neil replied.

Figal closed the door so he could unlatch the security chain.

Austin noticed that inside was like outside, only dirtier and darker. The TV was buzzing with some porn movie and the table consisted of an ashtray, a lighter, some cigarettes, a spoon, and some needles.

Neil lay down on the couch and went back to watching porn. The couch was old and dirty. It looked like something that he had picked up off the street.

"Watch this chick, she's amazing," Neil said.

Austin didn't even glance at it; he was here for one reason only.

"Do you want to sit down?" Neil asked.

"No, I don't plan on staying long. I was just after some help."

Neil reached under the couch cushion he was lying on and removed a black pistol.

Looking down the eye of the barrel, Austin remained as calm as ever. It wasn't the first time an enemy had pointed a gun at him.

"Now, tell me who sent you, was it the cop?"

Austin raised his hands, "I told you, I don't know anything about a cop, Tyler sent me," Austin replied.

"You see, that's where your story hits a snag. Tyler beat the shit out of me on the inside and we aren't exactly friends. So I will ask again: who sent you?"

"It was one of Tyler's previous cellmates while you were in protective custody. He told me about you," Austin replied.

Neil just lay there staring at Austin, finger on the trigger ready for action.

"I'm looking for people who might have bought a girl recently. My friend said you told Tyler you had a contact? I'm looking for my daughter."

"Empty your pockets, put everything on the table," Neil demanded.

Austin followed Neil's orders, placed his keys, some loose change, a knife, and his wallet on the table.

"Big blade, not wise to bring a knife to a gunfight," Neil said. "Take your clothes off," he instructed.

"What? Why?" Austin questioned.

"I wanna make sure you're not wearing a wire," Neil replied.

"How many times do I need to tell you I'm not a cop?" Austin asked.

"Till I believe you," Neil scoffed.

Neil began to flick through Austin's wallet, then he paused. Austin knew exactly what he was looking at. It was a photo of Mikayla.

"You're her dad, you were on the news," Neil said. "Did you come here to kill me?" he asked. "Because you're barking up the wrong tree there, I didn't take her."

"I just told you I'm looking for my daughter," Austin repeated. "Anyway, I know you prefer boys. I'm not here for you, but I just want your contact, and I'll pay you for it," Austin answered. He threw $500 on the table. "All I want is your contact."

Neil lay on the couch, shocked at the cash and at the stranger's brutal honesty.

"The cop I was asking you about, he was sent from higher up the chain, if you get my drift, he was sent to punish me because I reneged on my order," Figal said.

He placed his gun on the table and handed the photo back to Austin.

"Why did you renege on the order?" Austin asked him.

"Can't afford it at the moment," Neil said, counting the cash.

Austin knew why. He was spending all his cash on drugs. "How do you place an order?" he asked.

"Well it isn't like McDonald's, that's for sure. I was given a name and number on the inside and once they check out your credentials, they contact you. I would say they have the copper do the check first, then once satisfied, they get in touch."

"This copper, you know what station he's from?" Austin asked.

"It wasn't like he left me his card, he flashed his badge, told me I owed five large, had a week to pay it, then he near broke my nose and took my roll, took my enforcer too," Neil replied.

"What about you ring your contact. Say you want to place another order for a friend. Then I help you out with the cop?" Austin said.

"Once you're done with them they wipe you. I have no doubt when the cop comes back for the money, he'll be here to rub me out. They don't like loose ends," Neil answered.

"So, what are you going to do when he comes back?" Austin asked.

"I have this." He indicated the black pistol. "Self-defence, I guess you'd call it. I tell you what, I'll give you my contact's name for $500 and his phone number for another $500. The rest is up to you," Neil offered.

Austin agreed, dropping another bundle of cash on the table in front of Neil.

"But let me warn you. They recognise you, they kill you," he added.

Austin thought about what other options he had. He could kill him, he thought, but where would that get him?

"What do they do with the kids they take?" Austin asked.

"They sell them to people like me," Neil said.

"Who's your guy?" Austin asked.

"His name is Ian Williams or Welling or something like that. I can't remember exactly," Neil said.

Neil was busy going through his phone, looking for the number, Austin assumed.

"Put this number into your phone." He read out the 10-digit mobile number.

"He did a stint in Barwon two years back. If he's changed his number, it's because he had heat on him," Neil said.

Neil then removed a small bag of white powder, placed a little of it in a cut-out plastic bottle, added water, and watched the powder dissolve. Then he poured out a spoonful. His thumb scraped the lighter to life. Neil's eyes widened as the concoction boiled on the spoon. He drew the boiled substance into the syringe. He repeated the boiling process two more times.

He had all three needles lined up ready to go.

"If you want to have a shot, it'll cost you $50. That's on top of the $1,000. If not, get your shit and fuck off out of here, let me enjoy my afternoon."

Austin had what he came for. He took his belongings and left Neil to ruin his life even more. Good riddance, he thought.

Chapter 65

Mike could see in the rear-vision mirror that the boy was out cold. He drove the van at normal speed through the traffic, trying to think of a place where he could dump him. He knew he had crossed the line when he took the child, and once that line was crossed there was no going back.

In his mind there had always been a difference between them and him. He was the cleaner, the man who fixed problems and cleaned up after the Priest. For that, he was paid well. He had always been able to separate himself from them. Now he was the same as them. He had joined their depraved world and he would surely pay.

Mike shook the thought from his head. He needed to concentrate on the task at hand. He pulled over in an isolated side street, Googled 'Northland' in his phone and then clicked on 'maps'. He pinched the map to get a broader view. Then he saw it, 'Billabong Sanctuary'.

It was connected to the Yarra River, a secluded place only about 20 minutes away, located just behind a golf course. In the early afternoon with kids at school, it was likely to be deserted.

Worth a shot, he thought.

He drove slowly out of the side street and towards the reserve.

His only worry was the boy waking up. He didn't want to be stopped at the lights with a kid screaming in the back. He had ensured all the doors were key locked so escaping was not an issue, but noise might be. He had thought if he woke he would turn the music up as loudly as it would go.

By the time Mike reached the first golf course, the boy had begun to stir. Luckily he was only a minute from the reserve entrance. The road turned to gravel, and the ride became bumpy. Mike swayed from side to side, with the occasional jerking forward when the van hit a pothole. The equipment in the back rattled around as tools shifted from side to side.

Mike drove the van a long way down the road, near the water. The van beeped as he reversed to the water's edge. He stopped and got out and scanned the area. No one around. The section of the second golf course that adjoined the reserve was tree lined, with large pines providing a screen. The only real concern were people walking around the reserve.

Mike looked in all directions as he made his way to the rear of the van. There was no one about.

It was as clear as it was going to get. He opened the rear van door, just one, and grabbed the boy by the feet. He pushed his feet together and slid the black cable tie around his ankles and then pulled hard. The boy screamed in fear. Mike leaned in and took him by the jacket. The boy did everything in his power to fight back and Mike was impressed. He even wished there was another way.

Mike rolled him over, pushed his knee into the boy's back. He clasped both the boy's hands together behind his back and held them tight in his left hand, and cabled them with his right. He pulled it tight. He grabbed an old oily rag from the shelf and used it to gag his mouth. He knotted it tight, catching some of his hair in the knot. He tied the hands the same way as the feet, and then tied the hands to the feet and to each other using a long piece of rope that had been used to tie down a wheelbarrow in the back. Now he needed something heavy.

There it was, a crowbar. He attached the crowbar to the rope with more cable ties. He rolled the boy back over. His expression was one of immense fear, his eyes wide and terrified.

"I'm sorry mate, you were just in the wrong place at the wrong time."

The boy tried to speak but Mike had no idea what he was saying. Maybe that was a good thing. It was hard enough as it was.

Mike took the boy by the ears and lifted his head, ramming it into the metal crowbar tied behind him.

The boy's lights were out almost instantly.

* * *

The freezing cold water brought him around. He was shocked to find himself sinking. Had he been thrown in? He couldn't remember it if he had. Even underwater, Samuel could still taste the oil from the rag in his mouth. Now it was being flooded with dirty dam water. Samuel bit down hard on the rag, quickly cutting off the water. He held his breath. He tried to kick. If he could kick, he would be able to get to the surface. He pushed hard with his legs. The rope between his legs and his hands held tight. Samuel could feel the steel rod that went from head to toe. If he could just free himself from it. He clasped the cold wet metal pole and pushed down hard, trying to feed it through. It moved. It was moving. Adrenaline pumped through his veins, he was going to get out of this. Suddenly there was hope. It had to happen quickly, he couldn't hold his breath much longer. Soon his body would force him to breathe. Samuel kept feeding the pole through. Suddenly, it would go no further, it was stuck.

His fate was sealed.

He opened his eyes. He could see the light filtering through the murky water. It was a beautiful view, a fitting one considering it would be his last, he thought.

I wish I had gone to school, Samuel thought, as the water began its final journey into his lungs.

Chapter 66

Mike tried to forget what he had just done, but he thought no amount of time would let him forget. He stood watching the boy sink to the bottom of the dam. After four minutes, he knew it was done.

He didn't need to look up Google on his phone, he knew where he was going. He had been there before. Best part of it, his destination was just minutes away. If all went well, he would be home just after dinner and no one the wiser.

Fifteen minutes later, Mike parked the van in the driveway behind a faded old Toyota. He took the cloth that was sitting on the passenger seat and began to wipe the dash, steering wheel, gear stick, and door handle. He wiped the outside of the door handle and the back doors before heading through the carport and towards the back door.

Mike was prepared to break the door down, but before he kicked it in, he turned the knob just to check. Lady luck was on his side. He moved quietly through the laundry. The TV was on, as was the stereo, which was pumping music. Mike looked through the kitchen and saw Figal lying on the couch. There was an open bag of coke on the table and two empty needles, one still full of mixture.

He had obviously used one shot of coke, perhaps done a line and then soon after, injected the other shot. Now they had worn off and he was on a downer, and sleep was his body's way of coming down. Mike removed a separate injection from his inside jacket pocket and put his knee on Figal's chest, instantly waking him.

"What the fuck are you doing, you bastard!" Neil yelled. "I don't have any cash. It's not due yet!" he continued.

Mike didn't reply; he didn't speak or even acknowledge his presence. He could feel Figal try and lift him off, but he knew he wouldn't have the strength from underneath. With one knee into his chest and the other knee pinning Figal's right arm to the couch, Mike was free to inject his hot shot, a lethal drug combination, into Figal.

He stayed on top of Figal until his eyes rolled back into his eye sockets. It looked like he was turning into a zombie. He started to foam at the mouth and his body began to convulse. Mike got off him and stood by the couch and waited for the convulsions to stop and for his lungs to close and his heart to stop. The hot shot was a guaranteed overdose.

It took only three minutes for Neil's body to stop shaking. Mike leaned over and felt for a pulse. There wasn't one.

He wiped the syringe he'd used and then placed it in Neil's left hand. Then he let it drop to his side.

Mike then spent the next five minutes planting evidence: hairs, carpet fibres. He even found an old sleeping bag in the hallway closet that he threw into the van. He took Figal's shoes and banged them together inside the van front cabin. Finally, he took the tissues from the coffee table and threw them on the passenger side floor.

* * *

By dinnertime, Mike was sitting across from his wife and twins. What he had done today would haunt him in this world and the next but if he wanted the money to keep flowing in, he had to keep the Priest safe. Fifteen thousand a month was a retainer he had become accustomed to and he could no longer live without.

His wife smiled at him the same way she always had. How horrified she would be if she knew the truth. What would she think if she knew what he had done? He could keep the lies to himself; no one would have to know. He would take the boy's murder to his grave.

He had to.

Chapter 67

"Do you know why you've been called to this meeting?" Salma asked.

"No, not really," James Mitchell said.

"The Board of Northview can no longer find reasonable grounds to hold you here for ongoing treatment. We believe you do not need any further treatment. This is a meeting to discuss the specific conditions of your release back into society."

"Ok," James nodded.

"I will list the conditions and then we will go through them one by one. Ok with you?" Salma added.

"That's fine," James answered.

"Your release is subject to the following. You undergo weekly drug and alcohol testing. You provide us with a permanent residential address. You no longer associate with known sex offenders or people with a criminal background. You maintain an ongoing therapy plan with an approved therapist. You provide an undertaking to return to Northview should you notice any change in your condition.

"Do you have any questions?" Salma asked.

"I have a couple," James said. "How do I not associate with my family? Some of my family are convicted felons."

"We have excluded your family. However, with family like Ian who came to see you the other day, even though they are family I would suggest you associate with people that are more appropriate. Is there anything else?"

"No, I understand. You want me to live out there like I have been in here, clean," James replied.

"I'm glad you understand the effect that drugs and alcohol could have on your mental wellbeing," Salma said.

"I don't want to go back to what I was. I've come such a long way and I want to stay like this," James lied.

"That's what I expected. You've done very well in turning your life around. You should be really proud of yourself," she said.

"Who do I have to see for therapy?" James asked.

"Any doctor you choose. As it is a condition of your release, it is paid for by the government."

"Can I choose you?" James asked.

"No, sorry, I only see patients at the hospital. I don't have a private practice. But if you tell me who you're seeing, then I can call them occasionally to keep updated on your progress. Would that be all right?" Salma asked.

"You would do that for me?" James said. He couldn't believe she hadn't realised he was playing her.

"Sure, I want to see you succeed in life," Salma replied. "Do you understand all the conditions as I have put them to you?"

"Yes," James answered.

"Do you understand that they form part of your release?"

"Yes," he answered again.

"If you will just sign here and initial here," Salma pointed to the places on the contract where he needed to sign.

James signed without hesitation.

Chapter 68

Beau had been in the interview room for more than three hours. His constant responses of 'no comment' were becoming trying.

"Beau, we know you're involved, tell us what you know," I said. "No comment."

"It's not just coincidence that you were near to both of the abduction sites," Jake said. "We're searching your house now, so why don't you just tell us? We're going to find the evidence."

Beau sat in silence.

This wasn't working; he was staying quiet and I needed to try a new tack.

"You know, the only thing I really want to know is, how you took Chloe on her way to school without anyone seeing? How did you do that?"

Beau looked up and smiled and for a second, I thought I was going to get the answer. Just for that second. I thought he was going to crack. Then he repeated the words, "No comment."

I knew then that we wouldn't get anything. Even if the children were alive, he would let them die even if he was in jail. We would never get anything out of him.

I knew from his smile he had done it and he would love to brag about it, but previous experience had taught him to stay quiet.

"If you tell us where the children are, it will help you at sentencing," Jake said.

"We're taking a break. Can I get you anything, a Coke or a coffee?" I asked.

"No thanks," Beau replied.

We left the recording running, hoping we would catch a slip, but unfortunately for us, Beau sat there staring into space with that insolent smile across his face.

"What do you think?" Jake asked.

"He's dying to tell us but he just doesn't want to get caught. We didn't find any evidence in the searches. I don't think we can hold him much longer," I said, stating what we both knew.

"I agree. I think he had something to do with it. Maybe we could ask Monique for a surveillance budget?" Jake said.

Monique had the phone glued to her ear but she motioned us into her office as we stood in the office doorway.

After about five minutes, Monique hung up her call. "So where are we at?" she asked.

"We have diddly-squat, no confession, no evidence, but our guts tell us he's involved somehow. Every question we ask he says 'no comment'," Jake said.

"Has he asked for a lawyer?" she asked.

"No, he's just playing the silent game. We were hoping we could get a surveillance budget?"

"Firstly, what sort of surveillance order do you think the judge will give me with no evidence? I don't have just cause to get approval for wire taps or recording devices, especially after the searches turned up nothing. Secondly, my boss won't approve the man hours required for 24-hour surveillance, not on what we have. I suggest you go find more evidence. I'll rephrase that: go find some evidence."

Jake sighed, looked at me and nodded towards the door.

"Detectives," Monique called out.

Both of us stopped and turned.

"Don't get fixated on that suspect. If the evidence isn't there, it may be because he isn't involved."

Jake nodded.

"You have until Friday, that's all I can authorise. If you don't find anything in that time, I want you to investigate other leads."

"That's just over 24 hours," I said.

"I'm stretching it at that, Detective. I can't have all my resources following a guy for weeks, when it may not be him. If we're seen to be focusing on the wrong guy, the media would have a field day and I would get the sack."

I opened my mouth ready for a response when I was cut off.

"Time is ticking, Detective."

Jake grabbed me by the shoulder and we headed back to the interview room.

"Wait," I held Jake back. "Both of us think this is our guy, that he has them and is keeping them somewhere, which is why we haven't found any evidence or any bodies, right?"

"Correct," Jake replied.

"So we need him to drop his guard. At the moment, he's feeling he's the number one suspect, so he'll stay well away from wherever he's keeping them."

Jake nodded, more out of politeness than understanding.

"If we tell him we've crossed him off our list, he might just lead us to them."

Jake nodded.

"You organise his van from the compound and I'll go and give him the good news," I said.

I sat opposite Beau Delacroix. We needed evidence and we needed him to give it to us.

"Sorry to take so long, Beau. I know this has been a stressful time for you, but I'm pleased to tell you we've be able to eliminate you from our suspect list."

I watched Beau's body language and everything about it was wrong. Normally, people are relieved, but Beau came across as confused, unsure how this could be. This only increased my suspicions.

After he had calculated a response, he replied civilly with, "Well, about time."

"Your van is being brought around from our depot and will be out front in a few minutes. You can wait in the foyer."

Chapter 69

Chloe had swung next to the dead body for several hours. The smell was so bad she had vomited twice. Since being admitted back into the house a day and a half before, she had complied with everything she'd been asked to do without complaint. She never wanted to go back down there again.

She knew that the cellar was where they all ended up once the captor was done with them. The girl she had seen swinging from her feet had obviously bored him.

Igor wasn't at the house the whole time. Sometimes she would see him and the other three baddies, as she thought of them, leave by helicopter from a back paddock. In the front paddock was a large shed full of dogs. On the days she was locked in her room, Chloe would look at the woods at the back of the property. Depending on the time of day, she would see an older man with grey hair and black boots open the dog-house and let them run around for a few minutes. He would blow his whistle and all the dogs would exit the building like a wild pack. There were all different types of dogs. She recognised a few. There was a Rottweiler, a German Shepherd and a Doberman. The old man would then enter the building with a wheelbarrow and broom. Chloe guessed he was cleaning up their mess and feeding them. Usually he attended to them morning and afternoon. The man seemed to be working quickly today. The dogs had only been out for a short while when the man reappeared. Normally he took longer to do the job.

There was no helicopter yet. Maybe it would come later, she thought. It had left with the four men the day before but as far as she knew, they had not returned. The security men still stood guard. She could see one of them standing to the left of her window under the verandah. He too was watching the dog-man work. The bottom of the paddock abutted the woods. From the house to the wood was only four paddocks away but it seemed like miles. Chloe guessed it would only take two minutes to run from the house to the woods and out of sight of the house security. Was running into the woods her way out?

That might be the easy part. Getting out of her room and out of the house was a whole other complication.

Sometimes, when Igor had his way with her, she would stay in his bed.

Early one morning, she had got up to use the toilet and quietly peeked out the door. No one seemed to be on guard and the door was open. She thought about running then, but was too terrified. She would take the chance if it ever arose again. Maybe when Igor returned, he would want her to share his bed. Maybe she could pretend to fall asleep and hope that he would let her lie there. Then she would have to wait for him to fall asleep.

If she was caught, she knew she would also be made an example of for the next girl and be left hanging in the cellar. But if she didn't escape, she would more than likely die in the cellar, one way or the other.

Chapter 71

Jake had been keeping an eye on Beau since his release from custody. We had 24 hours to find some answers and I was out chasing some answers of my own. I was used to specialists keeping me waiting for hours on end. But my GP had always been good and he definitely broke the mould.

"So, what can I help you with today?" he asked. He was a polite doctor, in his late 50s with grey hair. English background but only a slight accent. He wore bifocals and looked at me over the top of them.

"I'm feeling nauseated all the time," I said.

He put the blood pressure cuff on my arm.

"Are you still eating normally or have you lost your appetite?" he asked.

The cuff went tight for a few seconds before it slowly released the air and the pressure.

"I get hungry, but I just feel sick. Do you think it's something bad?" I asked.

"You always fear the worst, don't you. It could be any number of things. I wouldn't worry just yet," he replied.

I was a worrier, but I had bloody good reason to worry. I had been sick from the moment I was born. Hell, my parents had been told I wouldn't make it past three weeks, but I'd always been a fighter.

"Let's take some bloods. That will rule out a few things and hopefully narrow it down. Have you been feeling lethargic at all?" he asked.

"Yeah, a little during the day. Sometimes after lunch I just want to sleep, but I've been working long hours at the moment."

"You may need to consider slowing down. You're not fit and healthy like the other officers. You keep going like this, something will have to give and that something will be your health," he replied.

"I can't stop. I have to solve this one. Too many kids are being hurt, if it costs me my life so be it, I won't stop," I replied.

"I'm not suggesting you stop. I'm just saying slow down a bit, get some more sleep. Remember, you can't save anyone if you're dead."

I took the slip he handed me and headed out to a second waiting room, where I took a number from the wall and sat down to wait to be called.

Being number four, I assumed there would be three people ahead of me but when the nurse came out and called "number three" I was pleasantly surprised.

I hated having blood taken and the one thing I could never do was watch as the needle went into my arm. The nurses at these centres were usually first-go masters, and this time was no exception.

I'd experienced many a time when four tries had still not been enough and thought that some of the nurses seemed to feel that if they wiggled the needle around under the skin, they might hit the vein. I often wondered during these episodes if they thought they were digging for oil?

There was no digging required this time.

Chapter 72

Jake had been watching Beau's house just on two hours before a call he least expected came in. It was Monique. "You won't believe this, Jake," were her first words.

"What happened?" Jake asked.

"Another boy was taken today from Northland. We need you to get on it now," she said.

"What about Beau, do I stay on him?" he asked.

"Forget him, this happened while he was in custody. It's obviously not him. I need you to come back to the office. We have some leads I need you to follow up."

When Jake got back to the station, the place was buzzing. He walked through the auto double doors to see Monique in her office madly waving to him, her phone attached to her ear as usual.

"Hold on," Monique said to the person on the phone, and then pressed a button and placed it on her desk.

"We've found a child's body. Could be the boy that was taken today. Here's the address." She waved a piece of paper at Jake.

Jake opened the folded sheet of paper which read Billabong Sanctuary Northland.

* * *

Jake rang me on his way to Northland. I met him at the top of the road at the scene. The latest development surprised me. I was sure we had our man, I was sure Beau was him. Even though we had nothing to prove my theory, I didn't like to go against my gut instinct. I thought it through some more. Could I be right and wrong at the same time? Could Beau be involved but be working with someone else? Maybe there were two of them.

I didn't dismiss the idea totally, but the possibility of two kidnappers working together didn't feel right.

I followed Jake's car down the dirt track. It was getting on dusk and Jake had his headlights on.

When we pulled up, Forensics were already on the scene. Instead of Grace in attendance, it was Philip, one of her more senior forensic analysts.

I will never forget the first time I saw the dead boy. It was an image that will stay with me for the rest of my life. He had already been removed from the water. He was lying on his back, and his legs and hands were bound, crumpled beneath him. His eyes were wide open as if bewildered at what he was seeing. It didn't seem to be a look of fear, but more one of amazement. Had he seen what was on the other side?

I often wondered where the spirit went when you died. One day I would find out.

The boy's hair was filled with dirt and sand. There was a twig stuck behind his ear, like a spare pencil. His skin was wrinkly and bloated, with blotchy patterns all over his face, neck and hands.

"Was he dead before he was dumped?" I asked Philip.

"Unfortunately not, he was alive when he was put into the water. He suffered an excruciating death. Drowning is a horrible way to go. Once your lungs fill with water, the body goes into convulsions before the victim becomes unconscious and eventually dies."

"A golfer spotted him floating in the dam early this evening," Jake said. "He'd been weighed down with a crowbar. Police divers recovered it after they dragged the body from the river."

Philip continued, "From what I can establish so far, during the boy's convulsions, the cable tie holding the crowbar broke. But by that stage it was too late for him to swim to safety."

They gently moved the waterlogged body into the plastic bag.

"Did you find his shoes?" I asked.

"They weren't on him when we took him out. Police divers have looked in the dam for them, but haven't found them. They could still be down there somewhere," Philip answered. "We need to get him back to the lab to undergo further tests. The longer he's out here in the elements, the less chance we have of collecting anything of substance. Water is our worst nightmare," Philip said.

"We'll meet you back there. You taking him to St Kilda Road I take it?" I asked.

Philip nodded.

They loaded the boy into the van and headed away from the scene. Jake was already walking back to his car.

I stayed to survey the area and saw that tyre moulds and shoe casts had already been taken. What a horrible crime, a boy with his whole life ahead of him, taken and thrown while alive into a dam, how inexplicably disgusting, I thought.

I knelt down, hands resting on my knees. I looked at the water and then up to the fading sky. Wherever the boy was, I was hoping he was at peace.

"You all right, Brucey?" Jake asked as he realised I wasn't following him.
"No, not really, who would do this to a child?" I asked.
"That's what we have to find out, mate," Jake replied.
"God help him when we find him," I said.

Chapter 73

Stevie had watched Ian and Bill go from acting like 'normal' people to completely crazy. They switched from being abusive and evil, to caring and jovial, and then back again. He didn't know what mood they would be in or what was in store for him each time they entered the room.

He knew they had done with their drugs and now they were finished, he noticed they were getting sleepy and continually trying to wake each other up.

It had been a few hours since he had last been raped and from what he could tell, both the kidnappers had fallen asleep. His door was shut but they had not locked it the last time they had left. He remained cuffed to the bed with his right hand, his left hand free. Although he could still only reach from one side of the bed, now he had a free hand, he would be able to rummage through the drawers that had previously been out of reach.

He started with the right-hand side, hoping he would find a screwdriver or a paperclip. He had two options: pick the lock of the cuff, or unscrew the bar that ran through the cuff.

He rummaged through the first drawer. There was a coin. He thought about using it on the screw that held the iron bar to the bed but realised it was too wide to fit the screw. There was nothing of use. He quietly slid the drawer shut again and moved on.

The next drawer was empty.

Stevie rolled over to the other side of the bed. This side was a lot harder to search, as he had to reach across his body.

This time he started with the bottom drawer first. Inside were a couple of old magazines and a notepad. Again he slid it closed quietly.

There had to be something. This last drawer was his last hope. Surely there would be something in here he could use.

He slid the drawer open but it only opened a few centimetres before it got stuck. He pulled harder but the angle didn't help and the drawer didn't budge. He reached his hand in and slid it across the bottom of the drawer. A sharp pain hit his pinkie finger. He wondered if he had been stabbed by a used needle.

He pulled his hand out and inspected his finger. It was bleeding but it seemed more a cut than a prick.

He sucked the finger and dived his hand back in again, a little more carefully this time, padding the bottom of the drawer. This time there was no sharp pain, only the cold touch of metal, something thin and sharp. It was only a couple of centimetres long but it could be of use. He slid his fingers over it again, trying to lift it out, but he couldn't grasp it. Stevie slid the object towards the front of the drawer, using the front panel of the drawer to lever it up. He clasped it between his fingers.

He slowly withdrew his hand and the object shone. It was a blade of some sort. He immediately knew that even if it wouldn't help with the cuff, it might help with the bed screw.

He knelt on the bed and threaded the blade into the head of the screw. His only luck of the day was that the screws were not the Phillips head type. Stevie applied some pressure, praying that the blade didn't break before the screw moved.

The screw stayed put and the blade remained intact. He applied a little more force. It moved slowly at first, then turning it became smooth and easy. Stevie removed the blade from the head of the screw and used his fingers to unwind the remainder.

He then put the blade into the second screw head. It was all that remained between him and being free from the bed. He turned with what he thought was the same amount of pressure as before, but this time the blade snapped, flew up into the air and fell down onto the back of the bed. Stevie realised he had just enough blade left to grip onto. If he lost any more of it, he wouldn't be able to apply the pressure required. He threaded the broken blade into the screw head and turned it again slowly. Then he increased the pressure, paused before adding a little more, then another pause and more pressure, pause, pressure. This method went on for several tries, until finally the screw gave up its fight.

Seconds later, the screw was in his fingertips and he had slid his cuff down and over the free end of the metal rod.

He quickly screwed the rod loosely back in place so that there was no risk of it slipping and making a noise. Dressed in just his jocks and a white t-shirt, Stevie crept towards the window and drew the blinds. The window that had once been there was now boarded up, as he had suspected, and only a few thin bars of light filtered through. There was no way he would be able to get out that way without making a racket. Even though it was filthy, the carpet felt soft between his toes. He made his way over to the door, hoping the floor wouldn't creak as he walked around the room.

The door was shut; he had no way of seeing where Bill and Ian were. If he opened it, would they see him? Would the door squeak if he opened it? Had it squeaked before? he asked himself but he couldn't remember. It was something he had never noticed or thought about until now. How had he not noticed? Maybe he had been too pre-occupied about what was coming to notice any noises. He had no choice but to try it. He held the small broken blade in his hand, poised ready to unleash whatever damage it would inflict. He had wrapped the spare cuff around his right wrist as well, so it wouldn't dangle or hit on something as he tried to escape.

He turned the knob and pulled on the door just enough to create a crack. He had only a limited view through the crack, but he couldn't see anything. The house was in darkness.

He opened the door a little further. This time, the door let out a groan as the crack widened.

Stevie expected to hear one of the men come running down the hall towards him, but no one came. The house remained quiet and dark.

His feet moved briskly and quietly as he tiptoed across the carpet.

He paused at the end of the hall, staying as still as possible. He even tried to calm his breathing. He wanted to have no noise to impair his hearing. With everything within him as calm and as quiet as possible, he stood and listened.

He could hear the muffled noise of the TV coming from his own room, and the sounds of another TV coming from the left. Once his eyes adjusted to the darkness, he poked his head around the corner of the hall wall and studied his surroundings. The first thing he noticed sent his head recoiling around the corner. He had made out a pair of bare feet hanging over the edge of the couch. He didn't know which one of his captors they belonged to. He calmed himself once again, put his head around and listened. He was hoping for some snoring. At first he didn't pick it up but within a second the noise was unmistakable. It was low, but it was there. Whoever the feet belonged to was asleep.

He had two choices: head for the back door past the sleeping man with the bare feet, or head towards the front door, towards the unknown. He was hoping the feet belonged to Bill, and that Ian was somewhere else entirely.

He decided to head to the front. The last thing he wanted was to risk waking the devil while it slept.

He tiptoed across the kitchen tiles. The floor was sticky and the bench was a mess, with most cupboard doors ajar. He caught a glimpse of the knife holder sitting next to the stove and thought about taking one of them for protection, but the thought of staying in the home longer than he needed to prevented him from taking it. He heard talking coming from the other side of the kitchen. He was hopeful it was a radio or a TV, and not people. He poked his head through the door. The lounge was on the right, and another bedroom door was on the left. It was ajar but he could not see inside. The TV in the lounge was on and it looked to be the source of the talking; some sports show. There was no sign of the other man. Had he gone out? Was he in the room, just feet away? Was he sitting on the lounge couch?

The longer he waited, the more chance he had of getting caught. He had to go for it, now. There was no benefit in waiting. He took a breath and prepared himself.

He moved quicker than he ever had before, or so he thought. The lounge room came and went and before he knew it, the cold metal door handle sat firmly in his hand. He turned it and pulled; there was no resistance at all. It flew open in his hand and had he not had his wits about him, it would have flown wide open into the wall behind.

Beyond the door was a mesh door, a security door. He pulled on the handle. It didn't move.

"Hey Bill! The boy, he's trying to escape, quickly, the front door, Bill!" someone hollered. At the sound, Stevie could see a man approaching from the bedroom. He flicked the snib and tried the handle again. It flung open and the cold night air rushed in. He stepped out onto the porch before a hand grabbed him tight, the fingers digging into his neck.

"Quick Bill, he's getting away!" Ian called again.

Stevie spun to try and break the hold. As he turned, he saw and then felt the impact of Bill's elbow being thrust into his face. The pain was sharp at first, then he felt nothing.

When he woke up, Stevie knew where he was he before his vision returned. His hands were both cuffed above his head, and the bar that he had just removed was back.

"Where did you think you were going?" Ian asked.

"Home," Stevie replied.

Bill climbed on the bed and sat on Stevie's torso. "Let's just kill him here," he said.

"No, not here," Ian replied.

Bill didn't listen. He grabbed Stevie by the throat, and began to squeeze.

"Bill, not here!" Ian yelled.

"Bill, stop!"

Bill didn't stop. If anything, he squeezed harder.

Ian could see he was killing the boy.

"William, if you kill him here, we get caught."

Bill released a little at first and then totally eased his grip. He felt the boy beneath him gasp for air. By the time he climbed off the boy, he was breathing again. Even though he was unconscious, he was alive, for now at least.

A loud noise rang through Ian's head and it took him a few seconds to come back to reality and realise it was their own doorbell.

Bill turned towards him and they stood staring at each other.

Chapter 74

Within two hours of watching the boy's lifeless body being loaded into the coroner's van, we knew who he was and had a fairly good idea of how he had ended up in the bottom of the dam.

He was Samuel Sadiq, who was born in Australia and had grown up in his large family with five sisters. His parents owned the local café and life had been good to them all. Samuel enjoyed school and had been doing well, but today was a special Thursday, it was the day that the new James Bond movie was due to be released and he couldn't wait to see it. Two of his friends had also skipped school to see it with him. Their plan was to meet at the cinema for the 1 o'clock session. When Sam didn't show, both Ben and Nick thought he had chickened out and they went ahead without him.

When Ben found out that it was Sam who had been found dead, he thought he had better come forward. Although he knew he would cop a hiding from his father, he decided to tell Sam's parents about their movie plan.

Jake and I had gone to the Sadiqs' and we were sitting in their living room. "Hi Ben, I believe you have some information for us?" I asked him calmly. He looked nervously towards his parents who were sitting with him.

"I am sure your parents will go easier on you if you tell us what happened," I said.

"We all agreed to skip school so we could see the new Bond movie. It came out today. We were meant to meet at the movies at 1 pm, that way we would all be back home at 4."

"Did you see Sam at all today?" I asked.

"No, he didn't show up. We thought he was sick or he'd chickened out. We didn't think much of it. I tried texting him, but he didn't reply."

"So you watched the movie and what did you do when you got home?"

"I rang Sam to tell him about it, but his sister told me he hadn't arrived home from school and they'd rung the school and he hadn't been there all day. So I told her we were meant to meet at the movies and he didn't show up," Ben said. "Now he's dead and it's my fault, all because I wanted to see the stupid movie." Ben was crying now, filled with guilt and sadness.

"Ben, you can't blame yourself, you've been a great help. We will find who did this," I replied.

I took a piece of paper from my notepad and wrote 'CCTV, mall', and passed it to Jake.

Jake took the note and headed outside while I finished up with the family.

The Sadiq family were distraught, as any family would be when they lose a child. In situations like that, the only thing you can do is find the person responsible and make them pay. Anything you say seems insignificant.

I joined Jake outside a few minutes later.

"How did you go?" I asked.

"The mall management will have some techs there within 30 minutes to go through the footage. Do you think we need to search all of it?" Jake asked.

"Possibly, did they say how many techs they were sending?" I asked.

"Four," Jake replied.

"That should be enough, though it still might take a while," I said.

"Did you get a photo we can use for comparison?" Jake asked.

I nodded. "It's in the file. We better get going if we want to meet them there."

Chapter 75

Austin stood on the porch in the dark. He had just rung the doorbell. He knew they were home; he could hear the TV. He pressed it again. He was counting on these guys being as willing to sell information as Neil had been.

Seconds later, he made out movement inside the home. Moments after that, the door opened. "Can I help you?" a middle-aged man asked.

"I was looking for Ian, Neil sent me. He said you would be able to help me," Austin said.

"Don't know any Neil, sorry you're mistaken," Ian replied.

"Neil Figal," Austin repeated. "You were friends down in Barwon."

"Oh yeah, you mean Figal, yeah, what about him?" Ian replied.

"He said you have a contact who can get me a very exclusive product," Austin replied.

"How do you know, Figal?" Ian asked.

"I did a stint with him myself. Let's just say we all have similar interests. I'm after the contact, the one you use they call the Priest," Austin replied.

Ian looked directly at Austin, then behind him, and even down the street a little, as if to check he was alone. "Come in," he said as he unlocked the security door.

Austin stepped inside. He knew one thing instantly. Crims didn't make good housekeepers. The place smelt, and there was drug paraphernalia everywhere. They were not hiding their addictions.

"Bill, we have a visitor," he said to a man who appeared from a back room wearing track pants and a singlet that had once been white. His pants were low and almost falling off his arse.

"This is . . . sorry, I didn't get your name?" Ian said.

"Wayne, but most people call me Al."

"How do they get Al out of Wayne?" Bill asked.

"My last name is Alfred. So I guess Al just stuck," Austin said.

Bill chuckled to himself. "It's better than mine. I got called Worm by all the girls."

"Girls can be cruel," Austin answered.

"They're fucking dumb sluts, is what they are," Bill said.

Austin saw the sudden change in Bill's personality and they had only been talking 90 seconds.

"So, why you here?" Bill asked, unaware of the conversation Ian had already had in the doorway.

"He's after the Priest's number, says he knows Figal from down the Bay," Ian answered on Austin's behalf.

"Why didn't Figal give you the Priest's number?" Bill asked.

"He said he'd had some recent trouble with the Priest because he cancelled an order, and now some cop was after him," Austin replied. He even raised his hands as if to say, I don't really understand.

"Apparently you'd be able to hook me up for a price?"

Ian and Bill looked at each other.

"$5,000 large and maybe we can point you in the right direction," Bill replied.

Austin removed a wad of cash and counted out $2,500 dollars, placing it on the coffee table in front of them, just as he had done at Figal's.

Then he returned the remaining funds to his pocket. "I'll give you the balance when I get the details."

"How do we know you're not a cop?" Bill asked.

"You don't, I can't prove it. I can only tell you I'm not a cop," Austin replied.

"Ring Figal," Bill said, pulling a revolver from the back of his pants. "You look like a cop," he said.

Bill pointed the gun at Austin's head.

Austin remained calm.

"Ask him if he knows of Wayne here," Bill continued.

Austin panicked a little on the inside. He had made up his name on the way over. He hoped Figal would catch on. He would, wouldn't he? If he didn't, Austin was a dead man.

Ian selected a number in his mobile and held it out, speaker on. It rang, and rang. Then click, 'You've called Figs, leave a message.' Then it beeped.

"He was pretty high when I left. Suggested I fuck off and let him enjoy his afternoon," Austin said quickly.

"Oh fuck, he could be out of it for days," Ian said.

"Still doesn't prove he's not a cop," Bill said.

Austin removed his shirt and handed the gun sitting in his belt to Ian. "You have my weapon. I'm not wearing a wire. I'm only asking for a phone number. Even if I was a cop, which I'm not, you can't go to jail for giving me a phone number," Austin said. "Think about it," he added.

With both their guns pointing at Austin, Ian and Bill looked at each other. "It's just a number," Ian said.

Bill nodded.

"I told Figal if I got the number, I'd help him with the cop if I could find out who he is. Do you guys know him?" Austin asked.

Ian shook his head, "No, but I reckon the Batman is the cop," he said.

"The Batman?" Austin questioned.

"The Batman does the delivery. It's a guy in a Batman mask," Ian replied.

"So why do you think this Batman is a cop?" Austin asked.

"When I got my last delivery he asked for my licence," Ian said.

"That doesn't prove he's a cop," Bill said.

"No, but it was also the way he held my wrist. I've had a cop do that before. Last time I was arrested, actually," Ian said.

"Fuckin' pigs," Bill added.

"Friends have told me some got their deliveries direct from a guy in a Joker mask," Ian said.

Austin knew about the Joker.

Soon the Joker would know about him.

Chapter 76

Jake and I met the mall staff at 6.30 on the Thursday evening. They had called in two of their senior CCTV specialists to help look for evidence of Sam.

They colour copied the pic I had given them from the file and pinned it next to each screen with Blu-tack, then began their search.

Our guess was that Sam had spent the morning at the shops until the boys' 1 o'clock movie began.

"What would you have done before a movie when you were 12?" I asked Jake.

"You know that answer, Brucey," Jake replied.

I did know that answer, which was 'eat'. It reminded me of the time Jake had consumed a full family meal, including four burgers, four fries and four drinks before a movie and was still hungry enough to order popcorn.

"Can we check the food court from 11 to 1 first?" I asked the CCTV specialists.

"We normally start with the toilet areas. That's usually where kidnappings happen," the security guard replied.

"I think you'll find most rapes happen in the toilets but most abductions happen from the car park. I think what my partner is trying to establish is if he even made it into the mall," Jake replied.

The security officer accepted the request and forwarded the instructions to his colleagues to search the cameras from the food court.

Only a few minutes in, one of the officers said, "I think I've found him, here, ordering at KFC at 11.47 am."

I stood up to compare the footage to the photo. Jake was leaning over the other side of the security officer when his phone buzzed.

Jake stepped aside and I heard him answer, "Miller," in the background.

The image in front of me looked like Samuel.

"Brodie, we have to go," Jake called out.

I turned away from the screen, wondering why we needed to leave.

"They may have found Sam's offender," Jake explained.

I turned back to the security guy, pointed to the screen. "This is him. I want you to find out where he goes every step. Then I want you to copy it, so it flows like a movie. Can you do that?" I asked.

"Yes sure," the officer said, "now that we've found him, he'll be easy to follow."

"Make sure you don't erase any of the footage by accident," Jake added.

"Don't worry, Detective, it's all backed up in the Cloud."

"Thank you," Jake said.

"We'll send an officer down to collect it," I said as we left.

"You seemed extra nice today?" I said to Jake.

"They had to come back into work when they'd only just finished for the day. They were doing us a favour," Jake replied.

"So what do you mean we might have him?"

"They found a stolen van in a guy's driveway. Apparently he's a known sex offender and there's evidence all over the place."

"Let's go question him. Find out what the fucker has to say for himself," I said.

"We can't, he's dead, overdose," Jake replied.

"You're fucking kidding me, right?" I asked, even though I knew he would never joke about a case.

Then it hit me: why would a man steal a van to kidnap a child, only to drive it home and overdose? Something smelled and it smelled bad

Chapter 77

Austin was standing in Ian and Bill's lounge, still half-naked and still with two guns pointed at him, one of them his own. "Isn't it entrapment if I say I'm not a cop, but I am?" Austin asked Bill and Ian, who again exchanged dumbfounded looks of uncertainty.

"Can I put my shirt back on now?" Austin asked.

Ian picked it up off the floor and handed it to him.

"If you don't mind, I'll feel safer if I hold on to the piece until you leave," Ian said.

"Sure, no problem, I trust you," Austin replied.

"Here's the number. You need to text your order in a specific format and he'll text you back with a price. If you don't use the format he won't even respond."

"How will I know the format?" Austin asked.

"I'm going to tell you, fuck-head," Ian said, laughing. "You need to put M or F and then the age of the goods. That's it; nothing else, no other information. Then you'll get a price and a date. Just before the date sometime, even on that day, you'll get your delivery instructions. Do you understand what to do?"

"Yeah, sounds easy enough," Austin replied.

"Now, this next piece of info is for your own benefit. I heard of a buyer who turned up to the drop and tried to negotiate. I heard he was cut up, fed to some guy's dogs in New South Wales, someone they call the Monster."

"I don't plan on negotiating," Austin replied.

"I don't know how true this, but I don't plan on testing it," Ian said.

Austin followed through with his end of the bargain, placing the balance of the money on the coffee table. He was about to ask to use the bathroom so he could plan his next move, when Bill interrupted him. It couldn't have worked out better.

"Do you want to see the quality of the product? We have one here now if you want to take a look," Bill said.

Ian's eyes widened; he was furious, and Austin had noticed.

"Are you fucking insane? What if he's a cop?" Ian asked.

"I'm not a cop, I already told you that," Austin said before Bill had a chance.

"Then we fucking kill him," Bill answered.

Bill pointed towards the hallway, motioning with the revolver.

"Follow me," he said.

All Austin could think was, please let it be Mikayla and please let her be alive.

He followed Bill past the kitchen.

The smell and the mess were disgusting. He could see the homemade drug kit lying on the table in front of the second TV.

Bill entered the hall.

Austin could see the shiny lock, high on the outside of the middle door. He knew right then that they were keeping someone.

Possibly Mikayla.

What if it was Mikayla?

Then Austin wondered what would happen if they opened the door and his daughter was on the other side. Sure, he would be able to stay in character, but there was no way she would. The first word out of her mouth would be 'Daddy'.

He knew what the consequences would be for them both if that happened.

He couldn't risk it, he had to act now.

Chapter 78

The suspect's home was only a few minutes from the mall and several blocks from the victim's residence.

Jake parked on the opposite side of the street. We both got out and as was custom, we surveyed the scene before we went any further. I noted there was an old Toyota in the drive under the carport and a van sitting in the driveway behind it.

Police tape had been put up across the whole front of the property, from one neighbour's fence to the other.

Jake lifted the tape and stepped under it, then held it up for me. The back doors of the van were open and Forensics were going through it. Grace looked up. "You might want to start inside the house, there's more in there. We're almost done. I'll come and get you shortly when we're finished."

Jake led the way and I followed. We crossed the lawn, which was well overdue for a mow, and went in through the front door. Jake flashed his badge at the officer standing in the open doorway, and then we stepped inside.

Two steps inside into the lounge, we stopped. A short balding man lay dead and naked on the couch. He had foamed at the mouth. One of the Forensics guys was looking him over.

"OD?" Jake asked.

"Looks that way," the Forensics officer replied.

I looked at the syringes all lined up on the table, all used. I noticed a syringe down the left-hand side of the couch, as if it had fallen out of his left hand. I looked at his left arm; it was full of holes. Then I looked at the right; there was only one.

I asked the doctor to pick up the syringe from down the side of the deceased and place it on the coffee table, and then I compared the syringes. Three were the same type and brand, but the one on the couch was different.

"Why do you think he changed arms?" I asked the doctor.

"I was wondering that myself. Normally, they only change when they're having trouble with a vein, but the veins in his left arm seem reasonably good considering the high use. So I don't know. Maybe he had a bit of trouble with his last shot?" he theorised.

I wandered through the house. There were more syringes in the top drawer of the bedside table, together with spoons and several lighters. These were to provide for the late night or early morning fix. Why was his last hit in a different syringe? I asked myself again.

Grace came in.

"I have some things that I need to show you," she said.

I followed her outside to the van.

"What have you got?" I asked.

"I found a pair of child's shoes and from the description the parents gave, I think they belong to Sam. I have a jumper on the passenger floor which belongs to the deceased in the house."

"How do you know it's his?" I asked.

"It's the matching jacket from the pants on the floor in the lounge. There are also muddy shoe prints on the driver side floor and the back laundry floor. They both match the shoes at the back door. Finally, I have hairs. I have no doubt that they will belong to the deceased."

"Sounds like an open and shut case," Jake replied. He had followed me outside.

"It does, doesn't it? But among all this incriminating evidence, I've found very little from the boy, and no prints from anyone. None belonging to Sam and none belonging to the deceased," Grace said.

"I'm not sure what you're getting at?" Jake replied.

"I have enough incriminating evidence for a conviction 10 times over. But why would you wipe down all the prints, yet leave hairs and jumpers and shoes all in the van?" Grace questioned.

"Maybe he came home, was halfway through cleaning, and needed a fix. Got carried away and OD'd. Who the hell knows, but this is a person who has kidnapped kids in the past."

"Possibly, just seems unusual," Grace replied.

"Everything about this case is fucked-up, Grace, starting with a boy thrown into a dam alive," Jake said.

Jake left us at the van headed back into the house.

"Don't worry about it, Grace, he's not upset with you. All these missing kids are starting to get to him," I said. "I have a few questions about this case too, something doesn't feel right," I said.

"Like what?" Grace asked.

"Well, who steals a car to commit an abduction and then parks it in their own drive? Who uses a different syringe and arm for the fatal dose? Why is this kid found within hours of the kidnapping and the others are still missing? Like you, I think it seems odd," I said.

Grace looked at me. I could see she was pondering the questions I had posed.

"But also I think we need to consider the fact that the drugs may have affected the suspect and the scene is odd because we're not dealing with a rational human being," I added.

"Let's just keep an open mind for now and see what the investigation and the science tell us. After all, I have a lot more left to analyse," Grace said.

"Agreed," I answered, "although it's going to be difficult getting answers from a dead suspect."

Chapter 79

Austin was now standing less than a couple of metres from the bedroom door, between the two paedophiles. He towered over both. They each had a gun, yet he knew he was in control, he had the advantage, he just had to be precise. The SAS had taught him precision, and in a few seconds he would put it to the test.

A trained soldier notices everything. Austin had already noticed that Ian, who was in front of him, was beginning to handle his gun in a manner that would render it useless when he needed it most. He was holding it by the butt, his trigger finger no longer in the trigger guard. Also, Austin had flicked the safety off when he'd handed it over.

Bill, who was in front of him, held his gun well but he was in the wrong position to keep himself safe. Ian needed to be armed and ready should an attack from behind occur. He was the one in position to prevent what was to occur, but he was not ready.

Austin's only dilemma was psychological: did he kill them both or leave them alive? Killing them would be justified, simply for what they had done to the child behind the door. If that was Mikayla, death would be a certainty. If he left them alive, he would be identified and then questioned by the police, at length he assumed. That would certainly prevent him from tracking Mikayla and that couldn't be allowed. If he let them live, he wondered how long it would be before they were out of jail and doing this to someone else's child.

Poised to strike, Austin waited for Bill to reach for the bedroom door handle. Then he struck. He grabbed Bill around the neck with his left arm, and spun his body to face Ian. Bill was now his shield. Bill tried to ram Austin into the wall to break his hold, but he only succeeded in breaking the plaster.

Ian was fumbling with his weapon, trying to place his finger back on the trigger.

Austin had Bill's arm well under control. He wasn't trying to wrestle the gun from him, he only wanted Bill to fire it. After all, Bill shooting Ian was better than Austin doing it.

Ian pulled the trigger, only to be answered by a click rather than a loud bang. Austin watched as Ian fumbled for the safety. By the time he had located it, it was too late. Bill's gun had exploded, and Ian was flying backwards through the air, his gun leaving his hand as he thudded against the wall. Blood flowed from the right side of his chest.

Bill was nearly unconscious in Austin's hold. Austin crouched down, Bill's neck still firmly held by his elbow. He removed his blade from his boot and without further thought, slit Bill's throat, from ear to ear.

Sending blood spraying, like a garden sprinkler.

Ian screamed like a girl.

Austin walked over, picked up his piece.

"Wait here, I'll be back to deal with you," Austin said.

Not trusting that Ian would obey his order, he lifted Ian's foot with one hand and kicked down on his knee with the other, hard and forcefully, shattering his kneecap instantly and sending another girly shriek from him through the house.

Austin opened the bedroom door, hoping to finally see Mikayla again. When he saw the boy, he was disappointed and happy at the same time. He recognised Stevie immediately. His mother would be ecstatic at his return.

"Stevie, it's ok. I'm here to help. I'm looking for my daughter, Mikayla, she was taken just like you, have you seen her?"

The boy sat there shaking.

"Stevie, I need you to help me otherwise I can't find her. Please, she needs your help," Austin begged.

"I never met a Mikayla, I met a Chloe and a Scott. The Joker took them, like he took me." He paused.

"The Joker?" Austin asked.

"Yes, he had us hidden in cells. He used to come down on a red ladder, then take us to the room with the red door and take photos of us and send them to someone."

"Did the Joker bring you here?" Austin asked.

"I don't know. I was in a car for hours and then in another car for even longer," Stevie replied.

Groans came from the outside the door.

"Don't worry about him, I'll take care of him. Have you ever seen someone dressed like Batman?" Austin asked.

"No, only like the Joker," Stevie replied.

"Now, I'm going to get you out of here, but I need you to promise me you didn't see me because I need to keep looking for my daughter. If the police question me, I can't be out looking for her," Austin said. "Can you do that for me?"

"I promise," Stevie replied.

Austin walked back to the bedroom doorway, took Bill's keys, bank roll and mobile. He threw the keys to Stevie so he could unlock the cuffs.

"I'm going to close the door so you don't have to see this," Austin said.

"No, don't go, please don't!" Stevie cried.

"Stevie, it will be ok, you're safe now," Austin replied, still standing in the doorway.

Stevie stopped crying and began undoing the cuffs.

Austin knelt down beside Ian. His breathing was shallow. He hadn't been hit in the heart, but it looked as though his right lung had been punctured and it would be filling with blood.

"I will give you a choice, a quick death or a slow death, your choice. Either way, you die here today."

"Please don't, please, I will stop," Ian began.

"Save your begging for God for when he judges you," Austin replied. "What do you know about the Joker?" he asked.

Ian frowned, confused. "I don't know anything about a Joker, I only met the Batman, I swear," Ian spluttered.

Austin knew he was telling the truth.

"Does the Batman work for the Priest?" Austin asked.

"I think so," Ian replied.

"Who does the Priest work for?" Austin asked.

"I don't know; I don't think he has a boss," Ian replied.

His breathing was becoming shallower, his time for answers was running out.

"Everyone has a boss, tell me who it is and I'll make it quick," Austin said.

He placed the knife that had slit Bill's throat against Ian's.

"I don't know, I swear. Wait, the Batman mentioned to me a person called the Monster. He told me he would protect me if the boy escaped," Ian replied.

"Thank you," Austin said.

He slit Ian's throat, left to right. He stood out of the way, so as not to be covered in spray, and then he opened Stevie's door.

"Come here," Austin said.

Stevie walked towards him. Bill was slumped in the doorway.

"Step over him," Austin said.

Austin led Stevie along the hallway and they headed for the front door. He wiped Bill's phone and handed it to Stevie.

"I want you to stay here until you count to 100 then you step outside and walk across the road to the neighbour's and call the police. If they're not home, use this cell phone. You don't need to worry about these two anymore. They're dead. Just look ahead and count, do you understand?" Austin said.

"Please don't leave," Stevie begged.

"I promise I won't leave until you're safe, I will be watching you until the police come. Ok?"

Stevie nodded.

"Now count," Austin said.

"One, two, three, four," Stevie began. He did as he was asked and did not look back and went outside as soon as he hit 100 and stepped out into the street.

Austin waited in the safety of his vehicle and when he saw a lady in an apron take him inside, he knew Stevie would be safe, but true to his word, he stayed until the police arrived.

Chapter 80

When another double murder call came in, I looked up to the sky to see if it was a full moon tonight. This one spiked my interest a lot. Initial reports were that one of the kidnapped boys had been recovered.

There was a full moon and it looked as though I would still be awake when it disappeared and the sun took its place.

"What the hell is going on today? Why are we finding these guys now?" Jake asked.

"I don't know if we're finding them, or if their organisation's imploding, but I agree something's going on," I replied.

The call gave us an address in Brunswick, another suburb that was renowned for low-life scum, like many others it seemed.

Jake placed the address in the sat nav and we headed straight from the Neil Figal crime scene to the Welling one.

When we walked in, we saw it looked like any other drug house in any other suburb. There were empty bags, needles and powder on the table, and the kitchen was a mess, full of the evidence of drug use.

Another overdose, I thought.

Then I saw the mess in the hallway, the blood sprayed wall to wall. The first victim had been identified as the owner, Ian Welling. According to police reports, he'd had several convictions for kidnapping and child molestation as well as some minor drug-related convictions.

The other man slumped in the doorway was still being formally identified, but it was believed to be Ian's lover, Bill Halstead. Jake and I were both scribbling down notes. We believed it was good to collect our initial thoughts prior to Forensics delivering the scientific evidence.

Jake stepped over the slumped body in the doorway and entered the room. I followed. The empty cuffs on the bed were the first thing I noticed, and I am sure that struck Jake too.

It took a while for me to register the noise in the background and it wasn't until I heard the laugh of Woody Woodpecker that I looked up and saw a TV set on the Boomerang 24/7 cartoon channel. Something you might do if you were keeping a child.

I pointed at the TV with my pen and Jake nodded. He was studying the bedside table as well as the bed and the cuffs. Then he moved over to the bodies and looked at them. "Forensics are here," I said.

He looked up.

"Ok, let's go interview the boy," Jake answered.

"He's across the road, with Child Services," I replied.

We walked to the neighbour's house where three women were sitting in the lounge room. Stevie was sitting in an armchair by himself, wrapped in a blanket and sipping a hot chocolate. Ambulance officers were assessing him and hooking him up to what looked like an IV. He was probably dehydrated.

Jake walked over and sat on the floor in front of him. He wanted to be lower to seem less threatening. I took a chair from the dining room table and placed it on the carpet next to the ambos. I knew if I sat on the floor I would look like a turtle on its back trying to get up again.

Jake opened his notebook.

"Hi Stevie, I'm Detective Miller but you can call me Jake. And this is Detective Foxx, you can call him Brodie."

"Stevie, can you tell us what happened?"

"Do you want me to start at the start?" he asked, sipping his hot chocolate.

"If that's what you feel comfortable with, Stevie," Jake replied.

"I was walking to school when someone dragged me into a van. I was locked in the back and I couldn't get out. We drove for a while, I have no idea where we were going, I couldn't see out."

He stopped and had another sip of his chocolate.

"I guess it was about an hour, but when we arrived, I had a bag put over my head. I couldn't see anything, I was pushed down a hole, I landed on gravel and there were cells, like a jail either side of the path."

Stevie was using his free hand to show how the cages were on both sides.

"At the end of the path was a red door. He would take us there to take our photo and then he would send the photo to someone. When he took my photo he rang someone about me. I could hear him say I was a good-looking lad."

"Did you ever see the person who took you?" I asked.

"No, he always had a Joker's mask on, or I had a hood on," Stevie replied.

I could see he had finished his hot drink. "Would you like another? I asked.

"Yes, please," Stevie replied, jumping at the offer. "I didn't stay in the cages for long, a few days maybe, then I was taken to meet another man. I remember leaving the van and sitting in another car. It smelt nice. The man who drove the car took me to a place. I don't know where or what it was but it was like an old castle on the inside with wooden doors that had old handles on them. I was sitting on the bed when a priest with a mask on walked in. He tried to rape me but I fought him off."

"What sort of mask was he wearing?" I asked.

"I don't know. It only covered his eyes and half of his face," Stevie said. "I can tell you, he was old. His hands were wrinkly and his hair was grey," Stevie added.

"Was the mask like the one in *Phantom of the Opera*?" I asked. Without waiting for his response, I Googled it on my phone and showed him the picture.

"Like this?" I asked.

"Yes, sort of," Stevie replied. "Then the man who took me there picked me up and took me to someone else."

"So the man who took you to the priest and then picked you up again, did you see him at all?" I asked.

"No," Stevie replied.

"What about the car?" Jake asked.

"No, I always had my hood on," Stevie replied.

"And you have no idea where you were taken, just that it was an old building?" Jake asked.

"Yes," Stevie confirmed.

"Did you see the man who held you in his car?" Jake asked.

"No, I had a hood on. The next time I could see, I was here. The man that took my hood off was Ian. They locked me in the room, put handcuffs on the bed and they did bad things to me. They were going to kill me tomorrow, and bury me in the woods."

Stevie had handled the whole experience really well, up until this point anyway.

"How do you know that?" Jake asked.

"I heard them say they were getting sick of me. They said the best way not to get caught was to dig a hole and burn me in it, before burying me."

"So, how did you escape?" Jake asked.

Stevie had been waiting for this question.

This was where he had to keep his promise, and keep it he would.

"I was trying to escape, using a blade I found in the drawer. They used it to cut the drugs. Anyway, I took the blade and I was unscrewing the screw in the bed that held the bar to the bed when I heard the doorbell ring. Then there was arguing, it was hard to hear what it was about with the cartoons on. I heard someone say, I think it was Bill, he was always an angry man, something like, that's the last time you screw us.

"Then I heard what sounded like fighting, people throwing each other around into walls, then after it stopped, the bedroom door opened and a man I had never seen before threw me the keys. I could see Bill lying on the floor, I didn't see Ian till I left the room."

"Did the man who threw you the keys say anything to you?" Jake asked.

"He said, 'you're free', and told me to count to 100 before leaving. Which I did."

"What did this guy look like?" I asked.

Truth mixed with lies, Stevie reminded himself.

"He was tall." True. "He had red hair and a beard here." He pointed to his chin. False. "He was really pale." False. "That's all I really remember of him," Stevie said.

"What about when he spoke. Did you notice any accent?" Jake asked.

"No, he sounded normal," Stevie replied.

"We have some photos of people we need to show you. Can you tell us if you have seen them before?" I asked.

I showed him the photos of Beau and Tyler.

"Do you recognise any of these men?" I asked.

"No, I don't, but I had a hood on or they had a mask on. The big one could have been the Joker but I can't be sure," Stevie said.

"These people," Jake nodded in the direction of the Child Services staff, "are going to take you to the hospital now, and then take you back to your family. We'll come back to ask you more questions tomorrow. Make sure you get plenty of rest."

"Have you found any of the others?" Stevie asked.

"Others?" Jake questioned.

"The others in the cells," Stevie answered.

"You never told us you saw others in the cells," Jake said.

"Both Scott and Chloe were there when I was there, but I got moved first," Stevie explained.

"So they were still there when you left?" I asked.

"Yes, I was last in, first out, Scott had been there the longest."

Jake took a pen and a spare notepad from his inside pocket. He handed them to Stevie. "Between now and tomorrow I want you to write down anything you remember, no matter how small. Ok?"

Stevie nodded.

As we left the house, Jake turned to me. "Looks like we're in the middle of a big spider-web."

"Agreed. Let's go see what Forensics have come up with."

Chapter 81

"So, is this how you repay your mother?" Annabelle asked, cigarette in mouth.

"I have no idea what you're talking about," Beau replied.

"Maybe this will help?" His mother threw the object at him. "Good thing the coppers were searching you and not me!" she said. "Just as well the police didn't find it," she added.

She put up your hand to prevent Beau from speaking.

"I know you're involved in those kids somehow, so don't fucking lie to me anymore. Whatever you're doing, get out of it, now."

"Mum, I have nothing to do with it, I swear," Beau answered, still fiddling with one of his engines.

"Don't treat me like an idiot, I know where you keep them, I know where the money comes from. Get rid of them now. If you don't, they'll catch you. We have enough to tide us over for a while," Annabelle replied.

Beau realised he had been treating her like an idiot. She knew exactly where the money had been coming from and exactly what he was doing.

"Ok, I'll get out of it," he replied.

Annabelle flicked the cigarette into the dirt and headed back into the house.

He wanted to get out but there was no way out. The Monster wanted him dead. The army man would too if he knew his girl was still down below, and he knew the Batman despised him. Tomorrow, he had to make two deliveries, one to the Batman and the other to the Monster.

If he made the delivery to the Monster, he would certainly wind up dead. He'd never leave. Maybe he would be fed to the dogs, which was what he heard had happened to a dealer who tried to screw with the Monster.

He had spent two weeks trying to come up with a way out, but no ideas had come. Maybe this would be the end of the line for him. Death was what he deserved for what he had done, and he knew it.

Maybe, just maybe, if he provided the army man with the delivery address, he could deliver the girl to the Monster and let him deal with the Monster. All he had to do was stay out of the way.

It was a chance, but a chance all the same.

Chapter 82

Austin only heard about the child murder and the suspect's overdose when he arrived back at his hotel room. He had still not dared to venture back home, not until he had Mikayla.

They were saying that Figal had kidnapped and killed the boy and then died of a drug overdose. One thing Austin knew for sure; he hadn't kidnapped any boy that day, because he had been there with him. Figal couldn't have been where they said he was. His death sounded like a hit. Austin didn't know who had ordered it, although he suspected the Priest and the Batman were involved.

Tomorrow was Sarah's funeral. He assumed that the police would be there although with all the recent deaths including the missing child's, he doubted the presence would be as large as it might have been.

Austin called Marcus. He wanted to know what he could find out about the man they called the Monster.

The phone rang a few times before Marcus answered.

"Hey mate," Marcus answered, always trying to stay upbeat for the sake of his friend.

"I need to know if you've ever heard of a guy called the Monster."

"We had tracking on a guy in New South Wales two years ago nicknamed the Ukrainian Monster. We thought he was bringing in illegal weapons, but they found nothing. I know local police had been investigating drug rumours, but ASIO pulled out when there was a lack of evidence," Marcus replied.

"I heard through a source he was buying and selling kids. Find out what you can. I know who the Joker is. He has Mikayla somewhere. I should go and confront him," Austin said.

"Mate, I don't know. He was questioned by police for eight hours and he gave them nothing, so why would he tell you?" Marcus asked.

"I have better negotiating techniques," Austin said.

"Torture is not a technique, is it?" Marcus said.

"It's often the most persuasive," Austin replied.

"So when are you going to persuade him?"

"I have a few other leads to follow before I get to that point. But it's tough knowing he's involved."

"You sound undecided," Marcus said.

"I am. Because if I show up again, he might close up altogether and then I'll never find her," Austin replied.

"What time do you want me to pick you up tomorrow for the funeral?" Marcus asked.

"The service is at 1 pm."

"Ok, I'll be at your hotel at 12. It'll give us time to talk on the way."

"Thanks, mate," Austin said.

The suit he had sent to the hotel cleaning service had been returned immaculately pressed and ready for what tomorrow held.

He ordered himself a steak and vegetables from room service. It had been a long time since he had eaten a full meal and his stomach was craving a decent feed. It was good.

While he ate, he watched the news. The media couldn't get enough of Stevie's 'miracle survival', as they put it. Reporters were interviewing neighbours asking stupid questions like "how did you not know they were holding the boy?" "Didn't you see anything suspicious?"

The head of the Missing Persons Unit praised Stevie, and said this would hopefully lead them to the other missing children.

"We will not stop until this investigation has uncovered the whereabouts of all the missing children, and the people responsible will be held accountable."

Austin didn't have much faith in the Missing Persons Unit or in their spokesperson, based on the results. So far he had one; they had zero.

After hearing the same news repeatedly, he switched channels. He needed to rest his mind, although he doubted whatever he watched would do that. Sport was usually the best. Since being stationed in Afghanistan with troops from the USA, he had discovered an enthusiasm for NFL and baseball.

Austin flicked to ESPN. The NBA game of the day was on, Golden State v OKC. Steph Curry was doing his thing and Russell Westbrook was trying not to be outdone. Amazingly, he had OKC in touch with the rampaging Warriors.

Sleep came quickly to Austin as it had on several occasions over the last few days. He found himself on the beach again, yet his family was nowhere to be seen. He headed up the beach, the waves rippling against his feet as he walked along the shoreline. A light breeze blew and he breathed in the salty tang. He heard birds squawking in the distance. Seagulls, probably. He felt the warmth of the sun on his face.

In the distance he could see a figure; it was kneeling. He couldn't make out who it was from this distance but as he drew closer, he could see it was Stevie, in his stained white t-shirt and underwear.

"Stevie, is that you?" Austin asked as he approached.

"Yes, thank you for saving me," Stevie said. "I am sorry you couldn't save your wife." Stevie was looking at the gravestone that was erected on the beach in front of him.

"It's not your fault. I will find the person who did it and they will have a gravestone of their own."

Austin bent down to tend to the weeds that had sprouted in front of the stone.

"Why are you here, Stevie? You should be at home with your family," Austin said.

"I need to tell you, time is running out, people will start to panic after today."

The earth groaned, and a second grave began to build itself from the earth, like a jigsaw puzzle putting itself together. Within seconds, it was standing next to Sarah's.

It read 'Mikayla Campbell'. He stopped reading; he couldn't bear the pain.

"Not much longer now," Stevie repeated.

Austin tore his eyes away from the grave and looked back to where Stevie had been, but his body was fading. Then it disappeared.

Austin woke in his usual cold sweat. The basketball was still on, and Curry had just sent it into overtime from a deep corner three. He turned the TV off and slept, his mind emptied of all the horrors of the past week.

Chapter 83

We were standing outside the home where Stevie had been kept waiting for Forensics to finish.

"What do you think went on here?" Jake asked me.

"Based on what the boy said, it was a turf war over drugs or a drug deal gone wrong. There was arguing. Maybe they were buying more drugs and felt they got ripped off, maybe they were going to kill him with the boy and he fought back, killed them both," I replied.

"Why would he let the boy go, considering the kid had seen him?" Jake asked.

"You know, code of honour with some crims, won't hurt kids. Until we find him, we won't know why he let the boy live."

"Hmm, I don't know. It seems wrong to me," Jake replied.

"How so?" I asked.

"I don't understand how it ended in the hall. I don't believe the boy's story for some reason. It seemed too detailed, too specific."

"I'm not sure why you're having trouble with this, Jake. To me it adds up. Ian and Bill were on a three-day bender and ordered some more of whatever. They accused the redheaded man of short-changing them on the deal. There was a scuffle and they lost. He opened the door, saw the boy and threw him the keys. Told him to count to 100 before leaving. Which he did. I think it rings true. But if you think something is wrong, then I trust you," I replied.

Grace had left the Figal scene to come and join us at the Welling one. Today her department was being pushed to the limits. She approached us and said, "I've reviewed the scene here and just wanted to discuss the initial findings with you guys. The evidence suggests that the two men had a scuffle with an unidentified third man, at which point Bill fired his .38-calibre weapon, hitting Ian in the right upper chest. We're waiting on Ballistics to come back, but we believe it's the same gun. Then during this scuffle, both Bill and Ian had their throats cut. From their wounds, it appears it was the same knife. That's why we think there was only one man. Ian was left to bleed out for a few minutes prior to having his throat cut. We also noted his kneecap was smashed, most likely during the scuffle."

"How do you know the Welling victim was left to bleed out?" I asked.

"There was an excessive amount of blood around the gunshot wound. Had his throat been cut soon after being shot, we wouldn't have found that," Grace replied.

"What do you think the man was doing, while Welling was bleeding out?" I asked.

"Ransacking the joint, would be my guess," Grace replied.

Chapter 84

The rain had kept Chloe awake. She had always been scared of thunderstorms but up here in the mountains they seemed worse, ferocious, alive even.

She heard the helicopter arrive and the three men returning to the house. She was terrified; he would be coming for her. She wasn't sure what she was more afraid of, the storm or Igor.

The only benefit Chloe noticed was that once the rains came, the security guards withdrew, to where she wasn't sure, but they were no longer standing watch where they had been. Had they moved inside? Maybe they were in the gatehouse?

They were answers she needed to know.

The sooner the better.

She crept out of her bed and turned the door handle. Igor had never kept her locked in. He trusted her fear and he trusted his men to keep her in the house.

The door creaked a little. She waited, but no one came. She stepped into the hallway and swiftly made her way up to the entrance of the large family room, where she could hear men talking, laughing, but not in English. It was a language she had heard in the house before, but she didn't understand it.

The man who usually stood guard outside the family room door was not there. She needed to check if the guard who usually stood outside the master bedroom was there, and so she turned and headed back past her own room and towards Igor's suite.

The only way she would be able to tell if he was there was to go in. If she went in and woke him, who would know what might happen.

She opened the door. He was asleep, she could hear his breathing. It was slow and steady. She walked past the bed, and made her way through the large open hexagonal space. It was a room that belonged in a castle. She slowly opened the door that led to a patio where she had once had breakfast. His guard was not there. No one was out there. Maybe this was her chance, maybe she was looking for an opportunity that was now right in front of her.

She placed her right leg out the door while she contemplated her opportunity. Her nightie was getting wet from the rain. She slid her back through the small gap in the door and was ready to follow with her right leg when a large crack of lightning hit a tree just beyond the dogs, and it burst into flames.

She jumped back and almost screamed with fright from the lightning crack and before she realised, she was back inside the room with one wet leg.

"Are you going somewhere?" a voice said from the bedroom.

"I was coming to see you. I hate thunderstorms. Will you keep me company please?" Chloe asked.

"Sure, come in here," Igor said.

He pulled back the sheets for her to climb in.

Chloe took a step, then realised her leg was wet. "I just need to . . ." She pointed to the en suite bathroom.

He nodded and said, "Hurry up."

She realised her nightie was wet and her only option was to dump it on the en suite floor, or have him discover that she had been out. How would she explain?

She reappeared in his room, without her nightgown.

"Can you keep me warm?" she asked. "I hate the rain, especially bad storms with lots of thunder and lightning."

"You know, my grandfather used to believe that there was a single god called Perun and it was Perun who would throw down lightning and thunder when he was angry at the world," Igor said.

"Why would God be angry?" Chloe asked.

"Some people believed he got angry if you had done wrong, or not prayed enough. So when the thunderstorms came, people saw them as a warning. If your village was hit by lightning, people would think that you had angered Perun," Igor explained.

"Did you believe it?" Chloe asked.

"I believed what my dad told me when I was young. I learned as I grew older that this world has no god."

He began to touch her, as he always did.

She closed her eyes and realised she too was learning that this world had no god or if it did, it hadn't shown itself.

PART THREE

The Monster and The Spider's Nest

Chapter 85

It was raining. Austin thought it was God setting the tone for the day ahead. As he stepped out of the hotel lobby and into Marcus' black SUV, which was identical to his, the rain hit the windscreen like a million tears falling from heaven.

Since Afghanistan, Austin had found it difficult to reconcile his life and his religion. He believed in God and that one day he would stand before Him and be judged. However, he didn't believe in the Ten Commandments. He simply believed that as long as he lived an honest life, he would be ok when he stood before God.

Then when he first killed in Afghanistan, he asked the USA soldiers how they thought God considered their killing in war. One soldier told him that it was for the greater good. Killing evil was allowed, and the killing of terrorists was protecting the good of the Afghan people. The theory of the greater good made sense.

Maybe he was right, maybe he was wrong. The Bible could be interpreted a million different ways and when his time came, Austin was ready to meet his maker.

He was sure that Sarah was one of the good ones.

"Did you find out anything about the Monster?" Austin asked Marcus.

"Hi, how are you Marcus? Thanks for the lift," Marcus replied sarcastically.

"I'm sorry, mate. I haven't been normal lately, I just can't even think straight with Mikayla still missing. I don't want to go today, I know that sounds crazy but Sarah would want me to be out there looking for Mikayla, not at her funeral," Austin said.

Then he turned his attention to the rain hitting his window.

"I will know more today hopefully," said Marcus. "As I said last night, New South Wales police are still investigating him. I rang a friend in the New South Wales organised crime unit. He's going to get back to me as soon as he can establish where the investigation stands. I wish I'd never invited you to go fishing. I wish I could go back in time and change it all. I just don't know how I can best help you, other than getting Mikayla back for you." Marcus was clearly distressed.

"We've been through this," Austin said. "It's not your fault. It's no one fault, except the Joker and whoever he works for. You know that, we both do, and I'll set it right soon."

The church was already filling an hour before the service. Aunts and uncles, army friends, Sarah's work colleagues, Mikayla's school friends. By the time Austin and Marcus arrived 30 minutes before the service, the church was full. Any latecomers would be restricted to the steps of St Michael's.

The reverend was an older gentleman who had known Sarah and her family for years. He was a close family friend and had conducted baptisms for both Sarah and Mikayla.

"How you holding up? Any word on Mikayla?" Father Doyle asked Austin as soon as he arrived at the altar.

"I'm holding myself together. I need to be strong for Mikayla although there's been no word on her yet, Father," Austin replied.

"Stay strong. The Lord is with you in these trying times."

Brian, Sarah's father, and Helen her mother, both hugged him. "How are you coping, dear?" Helen asked. "You haven't been back to the house yet," she added.

"I'm ok, I just want to find Mikayla and I won't go back home without her, I may never go back. I am so sorry I wasn't there to protect her," Austin said as the tears welled up.

"Oh darling, don't blame yourself," Helen said, hugging him again.

Father Doyle called for everyone to be seated.

The whispered conversations ceased and people who had been standing in the aisle sat down. Austin sat in the front row with Helen on one side and Marcus on the other.

Sarah's nieces and nephews moved down the aisle, quietly handing out the order of service booklets to any who had missed them.

'In loving memory of Sarah Jane Campbell, 1977–2014.'

Below the date, a large photo of her, in happier times.

Father Doyle led a hymn and then said, "Before we begin the service, the church and Sarah's family ask us all to remember Sarah as she was and not to dwell on the evil act that took Sarah from us. We are here today to celebrate the life of Sarah Jane Campbell who has now returned home to our Lord and Saviour the Father."

Sarah's father Brian went up to the lectern to read the eulogy.

He stood proudly in a black suit with a red tie, his hair neatly brushed across his forehead.

"Sarah, you were and will always be our angel.

"From the day you were born, you were full of laughter and love. Nothing was ever too much trouble for you, you showed more kindness to strangers than some struggle to show their own family.

"You and your sister Heather both shared a love for living and a kindness for your fellow man that is rarely seen.

"You were a beloved wife, a fantastic mother and most of all, a wonderful daughter who I was lucky to call my own.

"While you were taken from us all way too soon, I pray you're at peace, and although I shall never see that cheeky smile again, I will hold you in my heart forever.

"Love you, Scare Bear."

By the time he left the lectern, he was inconsolable.

Father Doyle returned.

"I had the pleasure of performing Sarah's baptism when she was a girl. She attended mass in this very church. She could sing like the angels. I was lucky enough to conduct her marriage ceremony when she wed her husband Austin. I was then delighted to perform Mikayla's baptism. While to many, myself included, Sarah's loss seems like a tragedy that we cannot comprehend, we must have faith that the Lord our Father has a bigger plan for all of us.

"Whilst we will weep, we should take comfort in knowing that Sarah is with our Lord. I would like to take this opportunity to say a prayer for the safe return of Sarah and Austin's daughter, Mikayla."

After the service, only immediate family and Father Doyle went to the grave site.

"Ashes to ashes, dust to dust," he began.

Austin faded away from the words and became fixated on the coffin. He remembered their wedding day, the birth of Mikayla, the love they shared, all the loving glances that had passed between them that had meant so much more than words could ever say.

He would miss his wife, every day. Finally, he realised the life he had known was gone forever.

Chapter 86

Beau had spent Friday at home in his shed preparing for the night ahead. He knew the probability was that he would not return home, even if he managed to escape the Monster's clutches.

He had decided not to run. What good would it do him? He couldn't outrun the Monster, and even if there was a chance, running wasn't his style. He had also decided not to give the army man the Monster's location. After all, what was in it for him? There was a small chance he would be allowed to leave the Monster's place unharmed and with the payment he'd receive for the girl, he'd have a shitload of cash. He had no intention of passing it over to the Priest this time. He was going to start a new life for himself.

He took his mother out for lunch. Nothing flash, just the local pub, extra cheap meals. It was a good feed and he needed it, with the long weekend in front of him.

They arrived back from the pub around 1 pm, which gave him a good hour to prepare before he had to leave for Ballarat. Beau had an 8.30 pm appointment with the Batman and he had to have completed his delivery to the Monster's by Saturday night, although he was considering dropping her off early, on Saturday morning. That way, the Monster might be less inclined to kill him.

With the news in overdrive about the discovery of the boy, he had called the Priest, asking to drop off Scott earlier and head for NSW. The Priest agreed that he would be better off in NSW than staying home. Beau reassured him there was no way Scott knew him or where he lived, and he had nothing to worry about.

Beau doubted the Priest believed what he was saying.

Beau turned on his train set and drove all of his locomotives into their rail yard, possibly for the very last time. When they were all in and secured, he pulled the lever to move the train table sideways.

Moving aside the mat, he unlocked the four padlocks, lifted the trapdoor, placed the ladder down the hole, and put on his Joker's mask.

He descended the ladder with two ropes and hoods in his right hand and the keys to the cells in his left.

"Good news. You're both going home. Both ransoms have been paid," he said to the children.

Mikayla and Scott were curled up in their respective cells, terrified. As the Joker descended the ladder, their fears increased.

He passed the hood and the rope through the cells.

"Once they're on, I'll unlock you."

Since her escape attempt, Mikayla had been wary of the man in the mask. He had threatened her with death, and every day she was worried that he would see his threat through.

She had never believed they were going home, and even when they put on the hoods ready to be moved, she believed in her heart she was heading for her death.

They were led up the ladder and into the van. The two children sat together against the side and for the first time in a week, Mikayla touched someone other than the Joker. They held onto each other tightly. He had been trapped there longer than she had and was desperate for someone to cuddle. She could feel her hands being cuffed and then heard him cuff Scott's hands too.

They listened as the Joker got into the front seat and started the van.

The radio came to life.

"No matter what, we stick together," Mikayla whispered.

"Always," Scott replied.

The music was turned up, suddenly the truck slowed, she thought she heard muffled talking, and then the music was back up.

The van was moving. Everything was dark because of the hoods.

"Mikayla?" the voice from the front of the van called.

"Yes?" Mikayla replied.

"Could you take your hood off, if I asked you to?"

"I think so."

"Take it off but if I hear any commotion back there, I will stop the van and it will be the end of you, do you understand?" the Joker said.

"Yes," Mikayla replied.

"I have food in the back. You will be able to reach it. Take your hood off, untie Scott's hood but leave it on. He will be able to eat with it on."

She could smell the hamburgers through her hood.

"It's a long drive," the Joker explained.

"I thought you were taking us home?" Mikayla queried.

"I am, but the drop-off point is different. No more talking, just eat and then the hood goes back on. Got it?"

"Got it," Mikayla replied.

"Can't wait to get the Monster's money and go fishing," Beau muttered to himself.

Chapter 87

Jake and I arrived at Stevie's home. He showed us where he had been walking when the driver from the van took him, which was from the top of the path. We walked back to his house with him. He seemed a lot calmer than he had been the day before.

Mrs Bradley, who had been totally detached, had come back to life. Having her boy back was a much needed early Christmas gift. She was busy in the kitchen, making tea and coffee, slicing cake and putting biscuits out. His nanas and aunts were kissing and hugging Stevie and asking him how he was. He didn't give them much. He always answered with a "fine" or an "ok".

It was a defensive answer to prevent further prying questions. I had done the same after one of my horrific hospital stays. Family would ask, "how are you, how are you feeling, glad to have you home", when all I wanted was to push the memory of it all as far back in my mind as possible. I thought Stevie would want his experience boxed and filed as far back inside his head as it would go.

His mum kept him within sight. If her gaze left him for a second when she poured a cuppa or cut a slice of cake, it returned immediately after to check on him. If he moved or went to the toilet without her knowledge, the fear came flooding back.

We sat in another room, in privacy, to question Stevie again. We had asked his mum to join us while we questioned him but he wanted to talk to us alone, and she accepted that.

"Thanks for talking to us again, Stevie," Jake began.

"That's ok," he replied.

"You said yesterday that you saw both Chloe and Scott who were being held in the cells near you. Can you draw a sketch of what the cells were like?" Jake asked.

"I did, in the notepad you gave me yesterday," Stevie replied.

Stevie opened the pad and showed us the drawing. There was a pathway down the middle and cells on each side. He had put a 'C' in Chloe's cell, an 'S' for Scott's and an X for his own.

Under the drawing were two other words:

Red ladder.
Blue train.

"What does red ladder and blue train mean?" I asked.

"Every time he came down to feed us or take photos, the red ladder would drop down first. We all used to freak every time the ladder dropped. Sometimes he would say we were making too much noise, so he would hit us or make an example of one of us. One day when we were talking, I thought we were whispering but we must have been too loud. He came down and gave Chloe a hiding like I have never seen. I thought she was going to die that night. It was horrible, and we couldn't even help her," Stevie said.

Jake looked at me. We both knew to tread carefully. Stevie was at breaking point.

"Do you think you were underground?"

"I think so, but I couldn't see dirt because the walls were plastered. It was like a room."

"And you mentioned a blue train. What can you tell us about that?" Jake asked.

"I remember one day he came down with his Joker's mask on and he was dancing around showing us his shiny new train. It was bright blue. I asked him did he like trains and he said, 'This isn't a train, it's a locomotive'," Stevie said.

I looked at Jake but could see he hadn't realised the connection I had made.

"That's all we need, Stevie," I said.

Jake stayed seated and couldn't work out why I was suggesting we leave already.

"Let's leave Stevie to enjoy his day, hey Jake?" I gave him a significant look and then said to Stevie, "If we need anything else, we'll be back in touch, ok Stevie?"

Before I was seated in the car, Jake started, "Why the fuck are we leaving? I have heaps more questions!"

I put my finger up. "Wait a minute, mate." I was flicking through the files, then I reached for the yellow envelope and tipped the contents into my lap. They were photos of the search of Beau's house.

One of the rooms.
Several of the van. Where was it?
One of the yard.
One of his mum's room.
There! The one I was looking for, the shed. I handed it to Jake.
I kept looking through the photos for the other one I wanted to show him.
"What! A shed? This helps me a lot," he said sarcastically.

"Look on the wall," I replied.

He looked in the background and squinted.

I handed him another.

"On the table, at the station," I added.

It was like looking at a cryptic picture. You don't see anything until someone asks you to look hard.

Once he saw the ladder, he knew what I knew.

Beau was involved.

Chapter 88

Chloe now knew the best time to escape was during a storm. The guards retreated indoors. Her only issue was conquering her fears and heading out into the storm.

She had managed to endure the night with Igor with only one horrible episode. Usually, there were multiple episodes, but he had fallen asleep straight after. She was left awake, sobbing, to listen to the rain and ponder her escape.

She did not get out of the bed, although she contemplated running for it several times. She thought about running into the storm, down past the dogs and over the fence into the woods. She thought about the lightning hitting the tree on the edge of the woods, earlier in the night. Would that happen to her? Would she attract the lightning? She knew people got hit by lightning and most died, but she wasn't sure what attracted the lightning to people. Was it just bad luck? She wasn't sure and she wasn't going to find out tonight, anyway.

She finally managed to fall asleep and the next morning, when the sun peeked through the blinds, she awoke. Igor, on the other hand, was still asleep. She snuck off back into her room before she was made to endure another horrible episode.

Her own bed was cold, at first, but it warmed quickly and soon she was fast asleep.

The sound of someone screaming at her brought her back to stark reality hours later. He was small but he had a loud and intimidating voice and when he was angry, it was even louder.

It took her a few seconds to understand what he was going on about, not because of his accent, she had become used to that, but because she was half-asleep. It wasn't until she saw her nightie in his hand that she caught on.

"It's wet. You were trying to escape! Have you forgotten what I do to those who want to leave?" Then he said to Alexi who was standing behind him, "Send her to the cellar!"

Chloe put her hands out. "Nooo! Wait, please. I wasn't trying to escape."

Alexi had manoeuvred around Igor and grasped her by the hand.

"Make sure you beat her a little for the lie," Igor added.

"No! Please, I'm not lying," Chloe insisted. She dug her feet into the carpet, but against the brute strength of Alexi her resistance was futile.

"You lie! The nightgown is wet. When you were in my room you were standing by the door, except you were not just standing there, you were ready to run, weren't you?" Igor approached, slapping her face without warning. He slapped her so hard, it made a cracking sound and left a large red mark across her cheek.

Tears streamed down her face, but she didn't let out her normal blubbering cry. She held it in. Tried to remain strong.

"My gown was wet because when I went to the toilet I wiped my hands on it after I washed them. Nothing else."

Igor stood looking at the gown as she was talking. He was trying to remember if in fact she had gone to the toilet, as she said. Maybe she had, he thought. He was still half-asleep, and thought a little more. He did remember her saying something when he had found her staring outside.

"Take her to the cellar!" He couldn't afford to show her any kindness. Kindness was often taken as weakness.

Chapter 89

We arrived at Beau's home without a warrant, hoping they wouldn't make a fuss about another search.

Jake did his usual police knock on their front door and I stood a metre behind him, staring down the drive at the shed I was so desperate to search.

Mrs Delacroix answered. "You again! What do you think, that I'm running an illegal brothel this time?" she asked sarcastically.

"We would like your permission to search the shed again," Jake replied.

"Ok, sure, as soon as I see your warrant I'll open it up for you," she replied, blowing smoke into Jake's face on purpose as if to say, fuck you.

"Sorry to shock you, but we don't need a warrant, we believe your son is in the process of committing an indictable offence and as such, we have grounds to search the premises," Jake replied, smiling.

"Oh bullshit. You need a warrant if you want to search. I know my rights. This is police harassment! I'm ringing your boss!" she shouted, running back inside to get her phone.

"I take it you are refusing to cooperate with a police investigation?" Jake called after her.

"Bet your fucking ass I'm refusing. This isn't an investigation; this is a witch hunt. If you have your way, you'll soon have him hanging from the gallows," she replied.

Annabelle's thumbs and fingers were busy on the phone. Within seconds, it was at her ear.

Jake removed himself from the stoop and headed for his car boot. He returned with bolt cutters in his hand.

"Mrs Delacroix, this is your last opportunity to let us in."

She replied by holding up her middle finger. "I would like to speak with Mr Roosevelt," she said to whoever answered the phone. "Well it can't wait till Monday. Can I have his mobile number?"

She disappeared inside the house again and when she reappeared, her fingers were busily punching digits into her mobile. "Mr Roosevelt, it's Annabelle Delacroix. I have police officers here wanting to search the premises again and this time they don't have a warrant. They said they don't need one because they believe a crime is being committed." She paused. "Hold on, I'll ask," she said.

"Detective, what offence is my son supposedly committing?" she called out to me.

"Kidnapping," I replied, as I followed Jake to the shed.

"Kidnapping," she repeated into her phone. "What do you mean they can search without a warrant!" she argued.

Jake had made light work of the bolts on the side door and before I reached him, he was inside the shed.

When I walked through the door, even though I had flicked on the light switch, the light was still flickering as it warmed up.

Jake had removed the ladder off the wall and was inspecting the dirt that remained on the bottom stoppers.

Annabelle had made her way down to the shed. She was off the phone and screaming at us, "Get out of here, immediately!"

"Mrs Delacroix, you have to step out of the way or you will be arrested for interfering in a police investigation," Jake said calmly.

"Well, you better arrest me then, because I'm not going to stop interfering!" she retorted.

I didn't need anything else. I took her by the arm, placed a cuff on her wrist and took the other wrist behind her back to meet it, locking them in place.

I took the chair from inside the shed and placed it outside, then sat Annabelle on the chair and told her not to move. She was no danger to us. We just wanted her out of the way.

I stepped back inside the shed, where Jake was now inspecting the blue train that Beau had been holding in the photo I had shown him.

"Ok, so Scott said he saw these items when the Joker went down to them. We've checked the back yard; there's nothing there. How do we know he doesn't have them somewhere else and he just takes the ladder with him?" Jake asked.

"It's possible I suppose, but how would that account for the train he showed them?"

"Maybe he bought it when he was out visiting them and he just happened to have it with him," Jake replied.

"Maybe," I said, unconvinced. "Wherever he's holding them, one thing we do know is that he was always going down to them, correct?"

"Correct," Jake replied.

"So it must be underground somewhere. We couldn't see anything in the back yard, what about in here under the old van?"

The van was rusted, with bald tyres, no hood and no motor. What he was using it for was anyone's guess. Jake opened the door, moved the gear stick to neutral and pushed. I stood at the back and also pushed, but Jake was doing most of the work. It rolled to a stop just outside the shed. Jake put it back in park position.

I stood there looking at the solid floor. There was nothing under the van. Jake looked at the empty space with a look of pure perplexity. I was sure he was trying to comprehend how it wasn't there. Beau's mother only smiled, the cigarette hanging in the crooked corner of her mouth.

She smiled only briefly but Jake saw the look in her eyes, a look that said, 'I have beaten you.' He had seen the same look many times from guilty people who thought they'd got away with murder.

It was Jake's turn to smile. "You know," he said to her, "I should have guessed you were involved in this. Your son's not smart enough to be doing this on his own."

"I have nothing to do with nothing, don't try pinning it on me because you can't find anything on him. I won't put up with that shit," she replied.

"Brodie, get a divvy van here to take her back to the station. We'll question her later."

I walked to the car to make the call while Jake stayed in the shed and surveyed the empty space. However, before I walked up the drive, I gestured to Jake to walk with me, out of earshot of the prying old woman.

"There's nothing there. It's a concrete floor. There's only an empty space and a train set. He must have them hidden somewhere else," I said.

"The train set. The forest for the trees, Brucey!" Jake replied, his eyes lighting up.

He turned and ran back to the shed.

I followed him back inside the shed and he was already down on his knees, head under the wooden table.

"Help me look," he said.

"What are we looking for?" I asked.

"An unlocking device," Jake replied as he continued to feel around.

"What are you thinking? That it'll unlock a secret passage?"

"Just look," Jake replied.

"This isn't *Scooby Doo*," I said.

Jake just looked at me.

I grabbed what I thought was a handle to lift the table, except when I pulled up, it moved towards me, not up. The whole train town moved. I pulled more. The table fitted perfectly, sideways as well as lengthwise. When it was sideways, it revealed a mat.

Jake flung the mat across the garage. He looked up at me, all smiles.

"We have him now!" he said.

He ran across the shed to the door where he had left his bolt cutters and 20 seconds later, the wooden hatch had been ripped from its hinges and thrown across the other side of the shed to join the mat.

I turned to grab the ladder but before I could pass it to Jake, he had jumped down.

"Fuck!" was the cry that rose from below.

For fear of snapping my fragile ankles, I used the red ladder and headed down after Jake. I landed on a soft bed of gravel. Goosebumps rose up on my arms and all the hairs stood up at the back of my neck. It seemed as if shadow men were lurking in the corners. The path was like the yellow brick road, except it didn't lead to Oz. It led to a red door, the red door of hell, I thought.

On each side of the path were concreted cells only separated by bars. There were food trays, old mattresses, old ratty blankets. There was everything to suggest kidnapped kids, except the kidnapped kids themselves.

The lighting down here was flickering. Before I could refocus, Jake had gone from two feet in front of me to the other end of the path where he was now kicking in the red door.

He let out another cry of profanity. This time it had 'mother' in front of it.

I didn't know I could have goosebumps on goosebumps until I walked into the room with the red door. The endless, horrific possibilities of what Beau had done to these kids flooded through my mind and my rage grew.

Jake was pounding his fist into the wall. He had already flipped the mattress and accompanying spring mattress. He was a giant ape, going crazy.

I began rifling through the drawers opposite the now overturned bed. It wasn't until I opened the second drawer that I found the phone. It was taped to the top of the first drawer. This was something Jake had taught me to look for when searching a house.

"Got a phone!" I called out to him.

Jake had stopped hitting the wall and his head was now buried in his elbow. He was leaning against the wall.

"Awesome," was his muttered response.

Surprisingly, the phone was unlocked, no pin required. I scrolled through the contact numbers. There was only one.

Priest.

Chapter 90

The dead girl who had hung in the cell with Chloe a few days before had now become a rotting corpse. The odour was horrific and the skin was falling from her bones. Chloe no longer had to fear the stare of the dead girl, as her eyes had fallen out.

There was nothing she could do to prevent the pungent smell from wafting up her nose. It made her feel sick. She hoped she could hold in the nausea, but doubted she would be able to.

"Enjoying the smell?" Alexi taunted.

"No, and I didn't try to escape," Chloe replied, as she swung slowly alongside the dead girl.

"This is your last chance. He likes you, yet you keep trying his patience. No more chances for you. Next time this will be you. No threats, it will be you for real."

Alexi paused. "You understand?" he asked.

"Yes, I understand," Chloe said.

Chloe was wearing her pink singlet and pyjama pants. Her left slipper had fallen off in the scuffle or soon after. It now lay on the ground just behind her head.

"We are having another guest joining us tomorrow night. She is your age. I want you to make the room next to yours for her. You will find more clothes in your room. Some for you, some for her. For now, Igor said you have to think about what you have done for a while longer. Then I will come back for you," Alexi said.

"No, no, please, don't leave me here with her and that smell!"

Her cries went unanswered. Alexi left and she was left in darkness. She could hear the flies buzzing around her, and on occasion she would bump against the swinging corpse and the sticky, decomposing flesh.

The smell was even stronger and this time, there was no keeping the contents in her stomach and she vomited.

She guessed most of it was matted in her hair.

Chapter 91

Austin had been sitting at the gravesite for a good half hour, his back resting against the trunk of a large oak near Sarah's grave. She would have loved this spot for sure; she'd loved nature.

When they first started dating, they would often go on picnics, find a large shady tree, set out their blanket and just talk the afternoon away. They would sometimes even spend it doing the crossword from the daily paper. Occasionally they would fool around, if the mood was right, but most of all, they just loved being together.

He distractedly picked apart an acorn that he had found on the ground and talked to himself. The sun was full on his face, but he didn't try to shade his face or block the sun. He just sat there enjoying the warmth, with his head rested against the trunk, basking in the most brilliant sun he had seen in weeks. Even today, the sun had been missing all day until now. He rested his eyes for only a few seconds, or so he thought. It was time enough for him to find himself on the beach again. The wind, the sun, the smell of the sea air were all strongly present. He could see Sarah. She was waiting further up the foreshore, her curly hair blowing in the soft breeze. There was no Mikayla, and no headstones, no boys standing further up the beach, only Sarah and him.

She smiled at him, kissed him on the lips, a lingering kiss. He could feel her love and feel her breathing as he held her in his arms.

"I love you," Austin said.

"I know, I will always love you too," Sarah replied. He nestled her head under his chin.

"Mikayla's gone now. You were too late, you were too late for her. You were too late for us both."

Austin held her by the shoulders and stepped back to answer her, but before he could reply, she turned to dust in front of him. He awoke with a start. The cemetery caretaker was poking at his shoe with the end of his shovel.

"Didn't mean to startle ya, the rains are coming back, ya might want to take some cover."

"I have to go now," Austin replied.

"Didn't mean to bother ya," the older man said.

"You were no bother. Thank you for waking me."

All the other mourners had moved on to the wake, Marcus included. Austin had promised to meet him later so Marcus had loaned him his car.

He walked back through the cemetery and out the front gate to the car park. He had left his phone in the console of Marcus' vehicle.

The words "too late for Mikayla" rang through his head. Austin tapped on the tracking device app.

The last thing he had expected was to see its location register as Hume Highway, Northern Victoria. He held his finger over the triangle that represented Beau's van. The icon showed Beau had been stationary for three minutes.

Beau was stationary but he was at least an hour and a half away.

Where they hell was he going?

Chapter 92

"Put out an APB on Beau's van. We need to find this guy now and get him to tell us what he's done with the kids," Jake said to me.

"Will do," I replied.

I moved out of the room and back up the ladder, passing the officer who was now standing on guard duty at the shed door. I headed towards the divisional van and opened the back door, directing myself to Beau's mother.

"We found the underground cells, Annabelle. Your boy's in big trouble now. If you have an ounce of decency in your body, tell us where the kids are. Tell us where he is."

"Fuck you!" she replied angrily.

I shut the door, leaving her in the darkness of the van.

The day was drawing to a close and we'd had several brief afternoon showers. The officer in the divisional van processed the APB for Beau's van through to head office. All units state-wide would now be looking at every van and for those plates. If Beau was driving around, we had a good chance of finding him. If he had gone underground, then we had little.

"I'll call Forensics," I called down to Jake, who was still in the cellar, "get them out here as soon as possible."

"Get put through to Communications. After that give them the Priest's number listed in that phone. We need to find out who and where that person is," Jake replied.

"Will do," I replied.

The sergeant in Communications asked me for the sim followed by the 10-digit number. I gave him both.

"I'm afraid it's untraceable. It was bought off the internet. The only way I can trace it is if you keep him on the line for two minutes, or if he answers I can triangulate the nearest cell tower to the receiver," the sergeant said. "Give me a minute to set everything up and then make the call," he added.

I selected the only contact in the phone and prepared myself to make the call.

"All set," came the sergeant's voice over the phone.

I called the Priest.

"Beau, is the delivery ready?"

"Yes, where do I need to drop them?" I replied.

He hung up without saying anything.

When I redialled, it no longer rang.

I tried four times with the same result.

"I rang the number in the phone, the Priest," I said to Jake, "and he was expecting Beau and a delivery."

"You think Beau's delivering them somewhere?" Jake asked.

"Yes, Communications are trying to triangulate the signal for us."

"Couldn't they trace the call or the other number?" Jake asked.

"No, apparently they're untraceable and they can only trace the call," I replied.

"The call you made, how long did it last?"

"Only seconds," I replied.

My phone buzzed. It was Communications.

"It was answered in Learmonth," I relayed to Jake. "The closest cell tower to the phone is the one near the Saint Alexius home for children."

"Learmonth, home for children?" I confirmed with Communications.

"Yes, that's correct Detective, it's north of Ballarat. I can send you the location of the tower it was sent to."

Before I had time to thank the sergeant, he had sent the message to my phone.

"Thank you!"

I ended the call and asked Jake, "Did you get all that?"

He nodded. "Yes, and we need to go!"

"I think Beau's kidnapping the kids and somehow they're moving or selling the children through this home," I said.

Jake stood, trying to take in all the information.

"When I called the number, whoever answered asked if the delivery was ready. Then when I asked where I needed to take them, the person hung up. I assume it was the Priest, seeing as it was the only contact in the phone."

"Let's go and find out who and what's in Learmonth." Jake said.

Chapter 93

Hayley was standing beside Ryan's bed.

"We're going to have to turn off his life support, his vitals are not improving," Professor Wise said. "The readings on the Glasgow coma scale have stayed at four, but his brain waves haven't changed."

"What are you going to tell his parents?" Hayley asked.

"I think it's time they understand that turning off life support may be the best option. He will only continue to deteriorate for some time until his eventual death," Professor Wise replied. "It's the hardest part of the job, especially when it involves a child."

"I imagine it would be." Hayley smiled, but she was quietly disgruntled at the lack of understanding that she too had similar problems in her job.

"When are the parents in next?" the professor asked.

"Usually, they come and stay for dinner until the end of visiting hours," Hayley replied.

"Could you page me when they come in tonight?" Professor Wise asked.

"Of course, no problem."

After the professor left, Hayley read through Ryan's chart, as she did every morning. She listened as the professor's heels clicked slowly down the hall.

Hayley touched Ryan's hand, "I know I tell you this every day, but honey, you need to come back to your family before it's too late. If you wait much longer you won't be able to come back."

She rubbed his arm on her way to check the IV, and then ran her fingers through his hair as she left him.

Visitors came to all the other patients, but none came for Ryan. Other kids who were well enough played cards or did colouring, drew pictures, but Ryan just lay there with no sign of life. Hayley did her rounds, noticing with one child after another the parents there talking, waiting, helping their children recover. Every time she checked on Ryan, she thought how sad it was that there was no one there for him.

Her shift was one hour off finishing when the parents walked in. She did as she was asked and paged Professor Wise, who arrived soon after.

Ryan's sister sat next to him eating a bucket of chips from the canteen. Her headphones were on, her head was bopping, and her mouth was chewing. Hayley walked over to her. She touched her hand to get her attention. The girl removed her headphones, but continued to eat. "Maybe you could tell your brother what's been happening at school. He would like that," Hayley said.

"Can he hear me? Mum says he can't hear."

"He might be able to hear you. It's like magic. Some people have it but we never know until they wake up," Hayley explained.

The girl sat there for a few seconds contemplating what Hayley had said. Then she leaned forward and began talking to her brother as if he had been away on camp and they had a lot of catching up to do.

That's it, just talk to him, Hayley thought.

Meanwhile, Professor Wise was saying to their parents, "Mr and Mrs Davey, we are concerned that there has been no improvement in Ryan's condition over the past few months. If anything, all the treatment we are giving him is only keeping him alive, but it's not improving him. I am afraid we have to consider the possibility that Ryan won't come out of the coma. In fact, I would suggest that there is a 99% chance that he will die within the next 12 months. As hard as that is to hear and for me to say, I have no medical reason to keep the machines going."

Mr and Mrs Davey didn't burst into tears, didn't fall screaming to the floor, in fact, they were completely calm and accepting of the information.

"We suspected this day was coming. We haven't been preparing for his funeral or anything, but we have been preparing ourselves for this day," Mrs Davey replied.

"Let me be clear," Professor Wise continued, "we are not saying you have to turn the machines off or that you have to do it soon, but over the next little while, if nothing changes, we will need to start making some formal decisions around Ryan's future."

The couple sadly agreed.

Chapter 94

"Mike, we have a problem," the Priest said into his phone.

"Another one. What now?" Mike asked.

"I just had a call from Beau's phone, but it wasn't Beau. The man asked me when to deliver the goods."

There was a silence followed by tapping on a keyboard. "He has an APB out on Beau," Mike replied.

"Beau is due to deliver the boy within two hours," the Priest told Mike.

"Then what? He's on to the Monster's?" Mike asked.

"If the cops don't get him first," the Priest replied. "The fat fuck will take us both down with him. Maybe we should cancel him while we can?" he suggested.

No response.

"Mike, do we cancel him?" the Priest repeated.

"I was thinking," Mike replied. "Here's what we'll do. If he turns up in two hours, we take the delivery and if all looks clear of cops, I'll give him some new plates and send him on his way to the Monster. That way, the Monster gets his cargo and we know he won't be leaving the Monster's place."

"And if it goes bad?" the Priest asked.

"I will take him down myself," Mike replied.

"We can't have him exposing us," the Priest said.

"He won't get to talk, don't worry. Either way, he won't be a problem for us any longer. By the way, when the cops come, you better have a good reason made up as to who accepted that call from Beau's phone," Mike said.

"But it's a ghost phone, it can't be traced!" the Priest said, panicking.

"You answered a call, old man, the phone can't be traced but the call can be," Mike replied. "Be ready." He hung up.

Chapter 95

I hated flying, but especially by helicopter. They looked as if they didn't belong in the sky and then once they were airborne, I always wondered what would happen if the engine blew.

Jake had organised for the helicopter to take us direct to Ballarat. It was the closest big town to Learmonth. The Ballarat sergeant said he would meet us at the helipad and take us to the tower in Learmonth.

As we stepped off the chopper, the promised cruiser was waiting and set to go.

"I thought we were meeting Superintendent McLeod?" Jake asked.

"I'm Constable Evans. Mike had a domestic violence issue he had to take care of, a repeat offender he had to see to. He sends his apologies; he directed me to take you wherever you need to go."

Evans began to tell us about the town, acting more like a tour guide than a police officer.

"Constable?" I asked, interrupting his guided tour.

"You can call me Dale," he said.

"I wouldn't think you would get many domestic violence issues out here?" I chirped from the back seat of the cruiser.

Dale took his eyes off the road so that he could look at me. I would have felt much better had he just used the rear-vision mirror.

"You would be surprised. A lot of men out this way still think it's the way of life. Dinner not on the table when you come in off the farm, beat the wife."

Cars passed us regularly, at high speed. Maybe it just seemed fast because Dale was also speeding.

"We also get a lot of people from the Ararat Prison. Being the closest biggest town, a lot of people relocate up here once their sentence is finished," Dale explained.

The car pulled up outside the children's home in Learmonth and I was amazed by its size. It was a large bluestone property, vast in width and length. I couldn't see the end of it. We walked towards reception, passing offices on both sides of the long hallway. The building had very high ceilings. Rows of leadlight windows depicted religious scenes. The lights were replica heritage candle fittings. Our shoes clicked along the stone floor. I felt like a school kid again on his way to the principal's office.

This time, however, it could be the principal who might be in trouble, I thought.

Dale approached the desk and told reception we were there to see Father O'Riley. There was no objection.

The door to his office was large and wooden, the carpet was red and the office had a warm welcoming feeling. His desk was a dark wood, mahogany or blackbutt, I wasn't sure.

The man on the other side of the desk stood as we entered. He was older than I had expected. For some reason, I had expected a young priest, but he was probably 20 years older than Jake or me. He was dressed in a long black gown with some sort of red jacket over his shoulders, pinned at the front.

"Nice to meet you," he said in a softly spoken voice. He offered us his hand.

We shook his hand and then he gestured us to some chairs. We sat down, not at his desk, but at a small table to the side of the room with matching club chairs.

"What brings you here, gentlemen?" he asked softly.

"We want to know if you know a Beau Delacroix."

"I can't say I do. It's not a name that I am familiar with. I'm sorry, should I?"

"He's a convicted felon," Jake replied.

"Not all of God's children are perfect, some stray too far from the flock unfortunately," the father replied.

"Could you explain why the cell phone tower you have on the roof here received a call I made from Beau's phone?"

Father O'Riley gave me a confused look. "No, I can't. I'm very confused by these questions," he said.

"We found a number with the name 'Priest' in this phone." Jake produced the phone from his jacket pocket. "We want to know why your name is in this phone?"

"There are a lot of priests in this world," Father O'Riley replied.

"Yes, there are, but they don't all work here. Whoever answered the phone answered it here, and you're the only priest here, correct?"

"Correct," Father O'Riley answered.

"So again, we are back to you."

"I can't offer an explanation, I'm afraid. I have had very few calls today. Please check for yourselves."

"May I look at your phone?" I asked, holding out my hand.

"Of course, I have nothing to hide," he said. Immediately, my ears pricked up. It was usually one of the first things guilty people said.

He handed over his phone. I scrolled through it.

"What is this outgoing call just before six? Who did you call?" I asked.

He placed his glasses on and looked at the phone. "That was to Mike, the superintendent."

"The police superintendent? The one who was supposed to pick us up?"

"Yes, the same one."

"Why did you call him?" Jake asked.

"To confirm his wife was handling the supper for the Sunday service."

Jake looked at me in a way I had seen before. It said, something's not right.

"Father, don't you find it strange that only a few minutes after this mysterious person answered the phone, you called the superintendent?" I asked.

"Detective." His voice was stronger now. "I don't know who answered your phone call, but I can assure you, it wasn't me. Feel free to ask my staff and check their phones, for I am as concerned about this as you are."

"Apart from staff, do you have other people here during the day who would be making calls within the building?"

"We are a church as well as a youth home. We have staff and other people coming and going. Many people come to the church to pray, others to confess. I really am sorry I can't be of more help."

"Thank you for your time. We will be in touch if we have any further questions," Jake said.

"I hope you have luck in solving your case. Paedophiles belong behind bars," Father O'Riley said.

Both Jake and I picked up the stumble the Priest had made, but now was not the time to call him on it.

Chapter 96

Austin had caught up to Beau. He had stopped for dinner, not the standard drive-through but a dine-in restaurant. He needed to refresh and recharge. By the time he was on the move again, Austin was only 20 minutes behind him.

Over the next hour, Austin caught up to him. He wasn't close enough to see him but he was only about 30 seconds behind. He could see Beau was turning into the main entrance of a local cemetery, according to the map. Austin took the street that ran alongside the cemetery. According to the tracking device app, Beau had parked close to the top of the cemetery. Austin needed to be a little higher. He drove up the hill a little and took Marcus' car off-road into the undergrowth. It wasn't entirely hidden but it was out of sight, enough. Along the ridge of the cemetery ran a windbreak of trees. They provided Austin with perfect cover.

By the time Austin actually gained a visual on Beau's van, Beau was out of it. He was wearing a mask, standing opposite another man who was also wearing a mask.

Daylight was fading and the shadows were at their longest, so Austin could barely make out the other mask. His best guess was that it was a Batman's mask. The man wearing it stood in front of a black Chrysler as if it was his Batmobile.

Austin was too far away to see with any great detail. But he couldn't risk trying to get any closer, not until he could be sure where Mikayla was.

* * *

The Batman had been waiting for 15 minutes and was about to call the Joker but before he could remove the phone from his pocket, a van turned into the entrance. This was his man. Deal time. Mike was always nervous around deal time. Mike's crime scenes were usually full of deals that had gone south, mainly because he had caused them.

"You're late," the Batman said.

"Sorry, got held up," the Joker replied.

"You realise the police have an APB out on you?"

"No," the Joker said.

"Well, you better not have led anyone here. You won't leave the cemetery if you have," the Batman said, pulling out his Glock.

"Don't threaten me. No one is here. No one has followed me. I have the goods. Let's just do the deal and we can both be on our way."

"The Priest wanted me to check that you're on your way to the Monster's?"

"Yep, and you can tell him it will be my last delivery."

"Get the cargo. I'm already late for the Judge," the Batman replied.

* * *

The light was fading fast as Austin watched the shadowy figures. He could pick out some words, Judge, Priest, Monster, but what did they mean? It sounded like some bizarre comic book. He could just make out the Joker go to the back of the van and return to the Batman with a hooded captive. It could be Mikayla. In this light, it could be anyone.

Austin was ready to pounce, end them then and there, both of them, but one thing worried him; what if it wasn't Mikayla? What if she was somewhere else? He could kill one of them, and torture the other. But what if he killed the wrong one, the one who knew where Mikayla was? In a gun battle, two against one, he might not have the opportunity to let one live. The risks were too high.

He watched. The Batman handed over a package and in return, the Joker handed him the captive's lead.

The Batman placed the child in the back of the Chrysler and the Joker returned to his van. The deal was done.

The question now was, which one should Austin follow?

Chapter 97

Justice James Aaron had served on the bench at the local magistrate's court for the last seven and a half years. He was a well-respected member of the community, yet he had a secret, and it was a secret only two people new. The police superintendent and the Priest.

He liked boys, and from time to time he would rent them, just for the night, then they would be shipped off again.

Shipped off to whoever had bought them.

The superintendent delivered them and he assumed the Priest organised them. The Judge paid well for this service and extra well for his privacy.

He had lit the fire at his lake house in preparation for his young companion. The room was warming up, there was a soft drink in the fridge chilling and pizza was in the oven.

A fox sat atop the mantelpiece and a bearskin lay on the floor in front of the fire. The lights were low.

All he could do was wait. He would be here soon, he kept telling himself.

The Judge never needed a mask, after all, the kids would never see him again.

Headlights flickered through the window as a car approached.

My guest, the Judge thought.

He walked out to the porch to meet his guest. It was the man he was expecting, the superintendent, the man who always brought his guests. He watched from the porch as Mike opened the rear of the car and removed the guest.

The boy was taller than the others he'd had previously. Mike led the boy past the Judge and into the home. The judge handed him an envelope containing $8,000.

"I'll pick him up at 6," Mike said, and then left the two of them standing inside the entrance.

Mike headed out the door and back into the Chrysler. The Judge watched the taillights disappear as the car left the property.

Once he could no longer see them, he removed the boy's hood.

Scott took a deep breath.

* * *

Austin had watched the exchange from the side of the drive, hidden behind the trees lining the drive. He could finally make out the plate and had committed it to memory.

He had now seen the delivery man without his mask. He would find him in good time. His only concern now was the child. It wasn't Mikayla. He regretted not following the van but now that he was here, he had to save the boy.

The windows were open and he could see the man hand the boy a towel and point him into a room, presumably the bathroom. The Judge sat by the fire waiting for his guest to shower.

It was Austin's opportunity to strike. He sneaked further up the drive, past the living room, around the back of the house. The door off the kitchen was open. He stepped inside onto a slate floor. His boots echoed upon it. He had only moved two steps before he noticed a shotgun hanging on the wall above the table. It was probably for the snakes. They would be rife in the fields up here, Austin thought.

He removed the gun from the wall, and stepped out into the living room.

"I take it you're the Judge?" Austin said. Gun sighted.

The Judge, startled, spilled his wine over his crotch. "Get the hell out of my house!" he demanded.

"Give me the boy," Austin said.

"Who are you?" the Judge replied.

Austin ignored his question. "Do you know who the Monster is or where I can find him?"

"Never heard of him," the Judge replied.

Austin moved closer, towering over the Judge, the barrel of the gun only inches from his face.

"Who is the Monster?" Austin asked again.

"I don't know," replied the Judge.

Austin cracked the gun across the Judge's nose.

"Last chance: who is the Monster?" Austin asked, barrel pressed against his cheek.

"I don't know," the Judge replied.

"Then you can't help me." He lowered the barrel and pressed it against his chest, pulling back the trigger.

"I would normally offer you a chance of redemption but you crossed that line long ago, I'm afraid," Austin said.

Seconds later, the gun exploded and the Judge was sent flying backwards, landing askew in the chair in which he had been sitting moments earlier.

Austin rummaged through the dead man's jacket and found his phone. If he did know the Monster, the number would be here.

Austin entered the bathroom and found the boy cowering in the corner.

"Don't panic, don't be afraid, I'm here to help you. The man is dead, let's get out of here. When we leave, just concentrate on the front door. Don't look at him no matter how much you want to."

They left the bathroom hand in hand, Austin leading the way. The boy looked at the man, he couldn't help it. He had a huge hole in him. The room was covered in blood and it looked as if he had pissed his pants.

The crisp night air hit them after the warmth of the fire in the house. Scott had to run to keep up with Austin. They made their way through the bushes, to the side of the drive where an SUV waited.

"Get in," Austin said, opening the door. Scott got in the driver's side and climbed over to the passenger seat.

Austin got in, throwing the gun over into the back seat. There were no neighbours to worry about. No one would have heard the shot out here. He figured he had until 6 am before anyone would find the Judge's body.

Austin headed back towards the cemetery. He needed a little distance between himself and the house before he worked out what to do next. Everything depended on where Beau was now.

He pulled the car to a halt.

"What's your name?" he asked.

"Scott," the boy replied.

"Ok, Scott, when you were in the van, was there a girl with you?"

He nodded.

"Was her name Mikayla?" Austin asked, holding his breath.

"Yes, she looked after me," Scott replied.

"I'm her dad," Austin said, choking out the words. "I need to find her."

He looked at his phone. The tracking icon still showed the van was in the cemetery.

Waiting for the Monster, are you? Austin thought. Maybe I'll show up instead.

Chapter 98

Beau had waited at the cemetery for the Batman to leave. He had never liked him and he felt better after he was gone.

He decided he had better take note of the Batman's warning about the APB and make some changes to his van.

He removed two large magnets from the rear of his van. One for each side. They were for a non-existent dog grooming business. They covered his handyman logo well.

He removed the set of spare plates he kept in the back, along with a screwdriver, and began to unscrew the old plates and screw on the spare ones. He was finishing off the rear plate when the screwdriver slipped from his hand and rolled under the van.

He knelt down on all fours and ducked his head under. Then he saw it. The flashing green light.

It was a tracking device.

He was being tracked, but by whom?

Those two detectives?

Most likely.

The nosey dad?

Possibly.

Either way, the trace ended here.

He removed the magnetised tracking device and gathered his screwdriver. He finished fastening the plate, then took his screwdriver to the device. He scratched two letters into each side of the tracking box.

FU.

Chapter 99

Austin drove back to where the GPS indicated, except there was no van. Nothing. Was this a setup? Was someone in the tree line waiting for him to exit his car, before picking him off with a rifle? Not likely, but a possibility. He scanned the trees but saw no one.

His phone said 30 metres away but there was no van. He decided to track it on foot. He needed to know what was going on. Where was the van and where was his daughter?

The boy sat in the front, peering over the dashboard, like a puppy watching his owner. Austin's shadow lurked large across the road. A gust of wind blew and his eyes scanned the tree line. His eyes darted between locations he would have chosen if he was up there himself lying in wait. All the possible sniper nests looked empty. He hoped that was the case.

He moved forward slowly, always scanning, always listening. Nothing moved; there was no sound. He continued towards the flashing triangle on his phone.

There it was. On the ground. His tracker had been removed and left in the dirt. He picked it up. It had a message for its owner. FU.

Austin returned to the warmth of his vehicle. "Scott, do you know anything about a man named the Monster?" Austin asked.

"No, I never heard of him," Scott replied.

"Did you hear where he was taking Mikayla?"

"No. He bought us burgers, told us to eat up because it was going to be a long trip. Then a few hours later, we stopped for a while. I don't know how long it was but it was a long time. We ate another burger he brought back for us."

"There was nothing said to Mikayla?" Austin asked.

"No," Scott replied, "I was just told to get out, and you know the rest."

"What about when you were in the other car, did he say anything to you?"

"Not a word," Scott replied.

Austin got out the phone Marcus had given him and held it to his ear. No point scaring Scott with any gruesome details he might hear on speaker phone.

Without exchanging pleasantries, he reeled off the number plate of the Chrysler. "Can you get me address? This is the only lead I have," Austin said.

"I have it. It's registered to the church," Marcus replied.

"Send me the address," Austin said. "Thanks," he added, but before he could hang up, Marcus spoke.

"Wait, six months ago there was an insurance claim. The insurance company had a Mike McLeod listed as the driver."

"A lot of companies have multiple drivers," Austin replied.

"He's the police superintendent," Marcus said.

Austin was speechless while his brain processed this information.

"Send me his photo and his address."

The person who had delivered Scott to the Judge was none other than the police superintendent. This was big. It involved a judge, a high-ranking police officer and a priest. Austin wondered how high this went. He would do whatever it took. He had already killed a judge and he was prepared to burn the world if that was what it took to get Mikayla back. He would deal with the consequences. Consequences didn't matter as long as she was safe.

Nothing outweighed her safety.

He needed to find out where Mikayla had been taken and there were only two people who might have that information. Time was running out but he was closing in.

"I'm going to give you this phone," he said to Scott, "and you are going to call this number and ask to be put through to Detective Jake Miller. If they won't put you through, tell them your name. They will protect you."

"Where will you be?" Scott asked.

"I have to find Mikayla," Austin replied. "I will leave you somewhere safe until Detective Miller can get to you. When he asks you about the Judge, just tell the truth. That you were in the bathroom and you heard a gunshot. That's all you need to say. I will tell them everything later. Are you ok doing that?" he asked.

"I am ok. You need to find her," Scott replied.

Austin stopped outside the 24-hour McDonald's in Ballarat.

"Ready?" Austin asked.

Scott nodded and Austin pressed dial on the mobile.

"Is Detective Miller there, please?" Scott asked.

He paused, and covered the phone. "They're putting me through."

Austin heard the voice on the other end. It was him all right.

Scott said to him, "My name is Scott Western, I was kidnapped. I escaped. I'm in the McDonald's at Ballarat. Can you please come and get me? I don't want to speak to anyone else, just you," Scott said.

He pressed the speaker button so Austin could hear the reply.

"We're in Ballarat. We will be there soon. Don't go anywhere," Jake replied.

"I'll be waiting for you," Scott said. Then he said to Austin, "They're coming here, you'd better get going."

"Go inside and wait," Austin replied.

"Good luck finding her," Scott said.

He exited and headed into McDonald's.

Chapter 100

Jake and I were finishing dinner, which consisted of a cold hamburger and a can of drink in the cold night air at the back of the children's home. We didn't have time to have a proper break but we had to eat. Constable Evans was kind enough to have some food brought to us.

We knew the Priest was lying; we just couldn't prove it yet. We suspected he was a key figure in the kidnappings and needed to find out how he fitted in. We had come to a standstill. The only contact from Beau's dungeon phone could no longer be tracked.

There was nothing else to follow, until Jake's phone rang.

The phone call was brief and although I was standing near him, I was too busy finishing my food to pay much attention to what he was saying.

"You're not going to believe this!" Jake said when he hung up.

"Believe what?" I asked.

"That was Scott Western. He wants us to pick him up. Come on, let's go!"

"The missing boy?" I asked.

"Yes, come on, he's waiting for us at McDonald's in town."

I automatically thought he meant Melbourne and that we were in for another chopper ride, and started to head for the car.

"No Brucey, he's just over there," Jake said, pointing across the road to the golden arches.

"If you weren't so vague all the time . . ." I mumbled.

We both ran. All I could think of was, was he ok, how had he escaped, where were the others. By the time I reached McDonald's, my lungs, thighs and calves were burning. "You all right, Brucey?" Jake asked. He had only jogged and wasn't even breathing heavily.

"I'm fine," I gasped.

We spotted Scott instantly, sitting by himself staring out the window. As we approached him, Jake said, "Scott, I'm Detective Miller, and this is Detective Foxx. Are you ok? Are you hurt in any way?"

"No, I'm fine," Scott replied bravely.

"Are you hungry?" I asked him.

"A little, I didn't get fed much," Scott replied.

Even though he had already had two hamburgers today, he had a long way to go to make up for all the meals he had missed.

"I'll get you a burger," I said.

As Scott ate his cheeseburger meal, we both questioned him about his capture. His story was very similar to Stevie's. He had no idea who had taken him, or why. He had stayed underground somewhere, which we now knew was Beau's shed, and then he was transferred several times, until he ended up in an old man's home. An old man whose first request had been to take a shower. "He said he wanted me clean!"

Then he continued, "When I was in the bathroom, I heard what sounded like a big crash, but the water was running so I couldn't hear it properly. When I opened the bathroom door, the old man was dead, flipped over in his chair with a big hole in his chest. I saw his phone on the table, picked it up and left. I just ran."

"Ok, first thing we do is find out who he is. Can I have the phone you picked up?" Jake asked.

Scott handed the phone over. It had specks of dried blood covering the silver case.

Jake searched the menu, while ringing the office on his own phone. "Need a record check on 0418 . . . He rattled off the rest of the digits and then waited. "Can you text them through to me, please?" Jake asked.

Then he stood up. "Give us a sec, ok, Scott?"

Scott nodded, a mouthful of cheeseburger making it impossible for him to reply.

We stood three booths back, "This is big. The phone belongs to the magistrate."

I frowned. "Are you saying we have a paedophile magistrate?" I asked.

"A dead one, possibly," Jake responded.

"Where did the magistrate live?" I asked.

Jake looked at the addresses sent via the text. "One address was here in Ballarat, the other just outside of Learmonth."

"How did the boy get here?" I asked.

"Walked?" Jake surmised.

"If he was held here in Ballarat, maybe, but if you're a paedophile judge then you wouldn't have a child at your house. Especially when you have a secluded home out in Learmonth. And he couldn't have walked from there, that's about 50 ks."

"Are you saying the boy is lying?" Jake asked.

"Lying is harsh, omitting most likely," I replied.

Jake strolled back over to Scott's booth.

"Hey Scott, how did you get from there to here?" he asked.

"Hitched. When I found the road, I ran along it until someone passed. A farmer picked me up. He was on his way to pick up his daughter from the train," Scott replied.

Every day he had sat in that cell, Scott had believed he was going to die. There was no way he was going to hinder the man who had saved him from saving his own daughter, Mikayla.

We walked away. "That's a lie," I said to Jake. "There's no way a kid who's been abducted and probably abused is going to jump in a car with a stranger. I just can't imagine it. Look at him, he's still shaking."

"The kids in Ohio ran to the neighbour's house and grabbed the first person they saw. People react differently in hostile situations," Jake replied.

"I still don't buy it, but let's go and look at the crime scene."

"We'll call in the superintendent and ask him to put the boy under guard in hospital. He'll need to be checked out anyway," Jake said.

I grabbed his arm. "Wait! We don't know who's involved, we don't know how deep or high this paedophile ring goes. This is a small town; we need to be really careful."

"You might be right," Jake replied, "but we don't have a choice. We need to admit him and place him under guard."

By the time we did the paperwork and had Scott under guard in the hospital, it was past 12 and we hadn't reached the second home of the judge yet. The judge's residence in Ballarat township was undisturbed.

Dale was back as our driver. "Seems like you guys came to town on the right day. Lot of action today," he said, smiling.

Both of us ignored his comments and Dale mumbled something under his breath and returned to driving.

Chapter 101

Austin was surprised when Mike left his house at 11.52 pm. He had been hunkered down in his car waiting for Mike to leave. There must be a problem, maybe Scott's call to Miller.

His old drill sergeant used to say, if the enemy makes a mistake, then make him pay for it.

Austin's opportunity had now come early.

He crossed the street and jumped the side fence and in less than 15 seconds, he had gone from the passenger seat of his car to being a balaclava-clad man inside the superintendent's home. His military training had once more served him well. He crept down the hall. The household appeared to be asleep. There were twin boys in their cots in one room and his wife asleep in the main bedroom.

Austin placed his hand over her mouth. She woke with a start. "I want you to call your husband and tell him to come home. If you do as I say, I won't hurt you or your children. Do you understand? If you promise not to scream, I will remove my hand. Will you be quiet?" he asked.

She nodded. Austin passed her the phone from her bedside table.

"Hi babe," he answered, "it's early, is everything ok?" he heard Mike ask her.

Austin ripped the phone away from her ear.

"Depends on what you do next, Chief," Austin said.

"Who is this!" Mike screamed.

"Who I am is not important, what I want is," Austin replied.

"What do you want?" Mike asked.

"In return for your family's lives, I want you to come home. We need to have a private discussion. You will come around the back, take your clothes off and enter through the back door. Once you're clean, we will talk in private. Let me warn you: plan anything or call any of your staff, it won't be pretty."

"You have my word."

"Do as I ask and I will leave your family safe."

"Ok, I'm almost back home." He hadn't wasted any time. As he was speaking, Austin heard him running and then the sound of his car starting up. "I'll do as you ask. Just don't hurt anyone," Mike begged.

"That's up to you," Austin replied.

Austin heard the Chrysler pull into the garage as he finished tying the last knot to secure Mike's wife. Then he sat on the inside of the rear door, shotgun pointed at Mike. "Gun belt first." Mike threw the belt, complete with the cuffs and the Smith & Wesson M&P .40 Calibre. It was fastened in the newly designed thigh holster.

Austin removed the mag as well as the spare cartridge. He tucked the gun into the back of his waistband and pocketed the ammo. Next came the vest, then the clothes.

Mike stood there in the freezing midnight air in nothing but his boxers. "Turn around," Austin demanded. He wasn't hiding anything; there was nowhere to hide it.

Austin threw Mike the grey robe he had taken from his bathroom. Then he flung his cuffs back at him. "Put these on," he demanded. "Behind your back. Now back up to the door."

Austin grabbed Mike by the cuffs and tightened them further. Then he pulled him back inside the home and sat him down on a dining room chair.

"I'll show you your family before we leave, so you know they're safe."

Austin led Mike to the rooms, showed him his twins and then his wife. She made a muffled cry as Austin closed the door and led Mike back into the dining room.

"I know you've been dealing children to paedophiles all over the state. All I want is the Monster's address. I won't lie to you, you can't save yourself, but give it to me and it will save your family," Austin said, calmly and matter-of-factly.

"This is the way it will work. I will ask you once for the address. If you don't give it to me, I will kill your wife. Then I will ask you again. If you refuse, I will kill one of your boys. Then I will ask you one more time. If you don't tell me what I need to know, then I will kill your other son. Do you understand?" Austin said.

Mike began to talk.

"Don't say anything unless it's the address," Austin interrupted him.

"I don't have it," Mike said. Austin rose from the table. Then he begged, "Wait, please wait. I can get it. I'm the only one who knows who has it."

Austin stopped a few metres away from the table.

"Please, I'll get it for you now. Just grab my phone and I'll get it."

Austin picked the phone up from the floor.

"Is the number saved under Priest or Father?" Austin asked.

"Father," Mike replied.

"How long does it take to get to the church from here?"

"About 20 minutes," Mike answered reluctantly.

"When you talk to him, tell him you need to pick him up in 25 minutes," Austin said.

He placed the phone on the table, engaged the speaker and levelled the gun at Mike's head.

"Don't do anything stupid."

The phone rang out, and there was no message bank.

"Dial it again," Mike suggested.

Austin pressed the button again followed by the speaker button.

It almost rang out the second time, before a tired, sleepy voice answered. "Everything ok with the Judge?" the Priest asked.

"I need to come and see you, it's important," Mike said.

"What is it?"

"It's best we don't discuss it over the phone," Mike said.

"Whatever you think is best."

Austin hung up the call.

"I told you the consequences of not getting the address," Austin said.

"He won't give it over the phone. You'll have to persuade him. You can kill me and my family but you still won't have the address," Mike replied.

"All right, but if I don't get it, God won't save anyone. It's time I had a chat with the father anyhow," Austin replied. "Where's the Chrysler?"

"In the garage," Mike replied.

"We'll take that. I'll drive." Austin pulled Mike up from the table, collecting the phone on the way.

"Remember: you want your family to stay safe, you get me that address. I don't want to come back here."

Mike had achieved his aim. He had led the man out of his home and away from his family. Now he had to work out how to take him down.

He would make him pay for threatening his family. Who the fuck did this guy think he was?

Chapter 102

Deputy Doofus, as I had come to think of Dale, kept his mouth shut. He hadn't said a word to either Jake or me since we had ignored his last comment.

When we arrived at the Judge's lake house, the light from the living area was shining through the open front door like a lighthouse beacon leading the way.

Apart from the open door, there were no signs of a disturbance from the outside.

It was a beautiful home, built largely from stone and slate. It had large, expansive rooms, and floor-to-ceiling windows to take in the views.

We stepped inside, where the scene was exactly as Scott had described; a man tossed into his armchair with a huge hole in his chest. The blood splatter was significant. The shooting had been performed at close range.

"Constable, call your office. We're going to need Forensics and officers here to help secure the scene," Jake said.

Deputy Doofus was turning green at the sight of blood. He seemed glad of a reason to get out of the house.

"Check the bathroom for me, Brucey," Jake said.

I knew that Jake was trying to verify Scott's version of events and from the evidence, it was looking good. The towel was wet and on the floor, there was still water in the bottom of the shower; it added up.

When I returned to the living room, I noticed Deputy Doofus outside hurling his guts up in the garden bed. Jake was down on his knees looking at the coffee table. I assumed he was checking for blood splatter.

"Doesn't look like there's any trace evidence there?" I said to Jake.

"No, the kid said he took the phone from the coffee table, correct?"

"That's what he said. He's a kid, maybe he picked it up off the floor. He'd have been shit scared and wouldn't have had a clue what he was doing," I replied.

We began our search of the home. The kitchen door wasn't open but it was unlocked. There was a gun rack, but no gun. Based on the half-empty box of shells I found in the bureau next to the rack, it was a shotgun. We also found a spent shotgun casing on the floor near the fire. Our jigsaw pieces were fitting together. The intruder had entered via the kitchen, taken the gun off the wall, loaded it, and killed the Judge. Probably never knew the boy was there.

Maybe this is about the boy, I thought, but how? It didn't seem to be connected to the other murders, or maybe there was a link? In the double murder case, one of them was shot with the other's gun. Maybe that was just a coincidence.

"Who would come in to kill someone without a weapon?" I asked.

"Maybe they knew the Judge had a gun," Jake replied.

"I was just wondering if it could have been someone known to him."

I went into the bedroom. This room didn't look disturbed at all, but I wanted to try and find out what sort of man this judge had been. What sort of man becomes a magistrate and keeps such a dark secret? Jake came into the room and began rummaging through the walk-in robe while I went through the bedside table.

"Looks like he was into something big," Jake said from the closet.

"What have you found?" I asked.

He dumped a black leather shoulder bag on the floor. It was full of bundled cash. Hundreds of thousands by the look of the overflowing bag.

The bottom drawer of the side table contained mainly cufflinks and tie-pins, but I came across a jewellery box. Why would a jewellery box be in a man's drawer? I opened it. It was a jewellery box all right but it was full of cocaine.

"Jake, there's a box full of coke."

I received no response.

"Jake?" I called out again.

Still no response and so I turned towards him and saw him standing there, holding something.

"Jake, what have you got?" I asked.

"Get the constable."

I called Deputy Doofus, who meandered in like he was circulating at a dinner party with cocktail in hand.

Jake showed us both a newspaper clipping. The article was about how pillars of the community were helping the prisoners of Ararat rehabilitate. In the attached photo were four men: Justice Aaron, Father O'Riley, the prisoner Ian Welling, and the fourth man was a uniformed officer.

"It says Palanok Pty donated a million dollars to get the inmates' rehabilitation program 'Restart' off the ground. I bet they'd be pissed if they found out they'd donated to paedophiles," Jake said.

"We know four of these men. Who's the policeman in the picture with the Judge and the Priest?" Jake asked Constable Evans.

"That's Superintendent Mike McLeod."

"Where is he now? Considering his magistrate has been killed in his own home, I thought he would be here," Jake said to the constable.

"We can't get hold of him. He isn't answering the radio and we rang his home and it just rings out. The station sergeant has sent a cruiser to his house."

"Let me know the outcome," Jake instructed.

Once Evans was out of the room, Jake turned to me. "Well, at least now we know they all knew one another."

"What do you think was going on here?" I asked him.

"I think they were organising drugs, weapons and kids and they were sending them wherever they needed to go. This might just be the tip of the iceberg."

"Maybe we're getting too close and someone is erasing any leads before we uncover them," I said.

"I agree, but with syndicates like this, there's usually a head, a rich drug lord. Someone has to be bringing the drugs into the country," Jake said.

"Maybe our Judge here was the boss? Look at all the cash," I said.

"He's rich but he's not in the drug lord. There's someone else."

"Maybe the Priest," I said.

"Maybe he's putting the cash into the church," Jake suggested. "I think we need to pay him another visit when we're done here."

"Detectives!" Evans called, running down the hall towards us. "The unit arrived at the superintendent's house. When they knocked, they heard a cry for help so they broke in to find his wife tied up and the superintendent missing."

"Did she see who took him?" I asked.

"No, she said he was wearing a balaclava, apparently he was a big guy."

"Maybe we should go see the Priest now?" Jake said.

"Constable, can you contact the Priest?" I asked.

"I can ring the children's home, he lives in the monastery at the rear of the chapel," Evans replied.

"Take us there now. He may be in danger."

Chapter 103

Austin drove the Chrysler while Mike directed from the passenger seat next to him.

"When we get to the church, you call him, tell him to get into the back of the car."

As they turned into the church, Austin pressed redial on Mike's phone.

"Yes, I'm ready," the Priest replied.

Mike said, "I'll be there in a minute. When I do, get in the back, we need to talk in private."

Austin stopped the Chrysler and seconds later, the Priest in his black robe with red trim came out from around the back.

He got in as Mike had asked him to. The partition between driver and the back seat was up.

"Mike, what did you want?"

No answer.

"What did you need to talk to me about?"

Still no answer.

The Priest tried the door handles. The childproof lock was on. He couldn't get out.

He banged on the Perspex. No response.

Was there someone in the passenger seat? He thought he could see a silhouette, but it was very hard to tell as the partition was tinted.

Mike's voice came through the speaker. "Not long now, Father."

Austin didn't drive to the cemetery where Beau and Mike had met earlier or where he had parked Marcus' car. He drove past the entrance to the end of the road.

"Get in the back," Austin ordered Mike.

It was now or never for Mike; he had to strike. He got out and instead of heading to the passenger side back seat, he headed around to the driver's side back door.

"I can't open the door," he said, holding up his cuffs behind his back.

Austin reached for the handle and Mike attacked.

He head-butted Austin. It wasn't his first option but it was probably the best of his remaining options.

The head-butt collected Austin on the side of the nose rather than flush on the bridge. It dazed him and sent him staggering backwards and with blurry vision, but Mike still didn't have the advantage.

He charged Austin with his shoulder down, hoping to send him flying, but Austin quickly recovered. He regained his balance and although his vision was still affected, he could see Mike rushing him and knew what his intention was.

Austin stepped aside like a matador at a bullfight. Because Mike had built up such a huge head of steam, and he had his hands cuffed behind his back, he missed his target and crashed face first into the ground.

Austin turned him over with his boot.

"As I said at the house, I won't kill your family if I get the address. As for you, you can't save yourself. Do you have any last words for your family?"

"You said you wouldn't kill me or my family if I got you the address."

"I said I wouldn't kill your family, they're innocent. You're not innocent, you're a money-grabbing child killer. You might not have killed them your-self but you knew what the outcome would be. There's no way out of this for you.

"Now, the lives of your family are in the Priest's hands. Let's hope he gives me the address."

He pulled out his pistol.

Fearing his own imminent death, and the loss of all hope, Mike did the only thing he could do. He rolled over, gathered himself and ran past the car towards the graveyard entrance. He was fast, considering he was in a night robe with his hands cuffed behind his back. But the bullets were faster and with Austin at the other end of the gun, they were accurate.

Austin fired twice and the second bullet hit within an inch of the first just under Mike's shoulder blade.

Mike fell and became still.

Austin opened the rear door of the Chrysler.

"What in God's name is going on here?" the Priest asked.

"Mike is dead," Austin replied. "Now I want my daughter, and apparently a man called the Monster has ordered her? I want his address and I want it now."

"If I refuse . . ." the Priest began.

"Then two things will happen. I will kill Mike's wife and twin boys, and their deaths will be on you. Secondly, your death will be excruciating. I have tortured many people when I was in the army and I was very good at it," Austin replied.

"Why kill Mike's family?" the Priest asked.

"He promised me the address in exchange for their lives. You're the only person alive who has it. I live up to my promises. You give it to me, they live; you don't, they die. Simple."

"What happens to me?" the Priest asked.

"It's too late for you, you're no better than the Judge or Mike," Austin replied. "You're even worse."

"You killed the Judge too?" the Priest asked. "Not much incentive for me to give you the address."

"Mike's twins are the best incentive of all. I'm sure you don't want two more children's deaths on your soul as you make your way to answer to Jesus?" Austin said.

"If I give it to you, he won't let you in, he won't see you. You're out of your league, you don't know what you're dealing with. He isn't called the Monster for no reason, you know," the Priest replied.

"Then I will get what's coming to me, won't I. Why don't you let God decide?" Austin replied.

The Priest bowed his head.

"So what's your decision?" Austin asked.

"If you're going to kill me, I'd like to pray on God's soil and with his gracious air flowing through my lungs, if you don't mind."

Austin slid out of the car and waited for the Priest to move.

Then he shut the door.

"I don't fear death, sir, so kill me if it is your will. I have made my peace with God, I have admitted my sins to God and he has forgiven me, as he will do for you." The Priest's voice was shaking.

He was on his knees, head bowed, rosary beads and cross clasped tightly between his fingers. He looked up and gave a smile, a smile he had given at most Sunday services.

"Tell me, Father, how many kids were there? How many years?"

"Hundreds, over decades," he replied.

"Why did you do it, Father?" Austin asked.

"The Monster pays well, too well."

"Give me the address."

The Priest hesitated.

"Don't make me go back to see Mike's twins."

Austin repeated the address into his phone. He was going to check it with Marcus.

Marcus confirmed that the property was registered to Igor Pavlychko. His police record listed his alias variously as the Ukrainian Monster or just the Monster, and showed he had been raided by police in January last year for suspicion of human trafficking. Officers thought he must have been moving the cargo around, because they'd searched both houses and his boat and had come up empty. He hadn't even been there; he must have been tipped off.

"This guy is bad," Marcus said. "We had two of his ex-employees who said they'd testify about what they'd seen in return for protection. But while they were in witness protection, they were killed. Even the officers protecting them were executed. If you're going there, be careful," Marcus warned. "Call me if you need help."

Austin hung up the call.

"Well, Father, have you made your peace?" Austin asked.

"I know where I'm going. Really, you're giving me a gift," the Priest replied.

"You're mistaken, Father, you're under what many call the security illusion," Austin said.

The Priest frowned, confused.

"You believe in your faith so much and think that because you've been a leader in the church, you cannot be lost and you'll be granted immunity from the consequences of your evil deeds." Austin pressed the barrel of Mike's gun against the Priest's head.

"But you've overlooked something very important. 'But if a righteous person turns from their righteousness and commits sin and does the same detestable things the wicked person does, will they live? None of the righteous things that person has done will be remembered,'" Austin said, quoting from Ezekiel.

"You know your scriptures," the Priest said.

"Then you know what comes next," Austin said.

"As you must," the Priest said, and began in his loud sermon voice, "'Because of the unfaithfulness they are guilty of and because of the sins they have committed, they will die.'"

Austin fired a single shot, ending the sermon and the Priest. His body slumped back. Austin dragged him and placed him onto the back seat of the Chrysler. He would need him later.

Jumping into the driver's side, he headed for the address the Priest had given him.

Chapter 104

It was like *déjà vu* walking on the echoing floor of the children's home. We had been there only hours earlier. I felt as if I was in a loop.

The lady at the reception desk was considerably older than the one who had been on duty earlier. She did as Jake asked, and tried calling the Priest at his home. "He's not answering, I'm afraid. He was in earlier when Mike called. Maybe he went out."

"How long ago did the superintendent call?" I asked.

"About an hour, maybe an hour and a half," she replied. "Feel free to knock on his door. His residence is at the back of the chapel. Just go around the side," she said, pointing to show us the way.

The door to his residence was closed but not locked. His bed was unmade as if he had been in it not long ago. There was no sign of him or of a struggle. He had just vanished.

"Let's think about this. We have a dead paedophile judge, a police superintendent who was taken at gunpoint, and now a priest who knows them both. A priest who received a call from Beau. What are we missing, Jake?"

"A second phone," Jake replied.

Jake began pacing. All he needed was a hat and a pipe and he would look like Sherlock Holmes. "The call was traced here. The Priest handed us his phone but he said his phone wasn't the number that Beau called. But what if he has more than one phone?"

"A ghost phone, just like Beau had," I replied. "What do you think is going on?"

"Could be someone is trying to take over the Priest's territory?"

"Either that or the Priest might be afraid we're getting too close and he's now trying to keep his contacts quiet, if you know what I mean."

"You search his office, I'll search here." Jake began rummaging through drawers while I headed to the office.

His office was open, so I helped myself. I searched his desk. There were some keys, pens, pencils. Normal stuff, nothing out of the ordinary. Maybe we were barking up the wrong tree. Maybe he was innocent. Maybe he wasn't like the Judge.

I moved to the glass cabinet behind the desk. It was locked, so I took the keys from a drawer and tried each of them in turn. Finally, one turned. I opened the box sitting in the middle. It was a black carry case made of hard-wood with blue velvet lining and black Rexene exterior.

Inside the communion set were:

The gold cross he wore on Sundays and in confessional.
The gold chalice he used at Sunday services.
Two candle holders.
Two glass cruets.
One paten.
One pix.
One purificator.

"Should you be in here?" a deep male voice called from behind me. Half stunned, I spun towards the voice and in doing so, my grip slipped and the box fell to the floor. The contents bounced and flew in different directions.

"We have concerns for the father's welfare. Do you know where he might be?" I asked, showing him my badge.

"At this time of night, he would be asleep, I would suggest," the male security guard replied.

"We've checked there; he's missing," I replied.

"That's terrible," the guard said.

"Why does a children's home have a security guard?" I asked.

"It's for the security of the staff. Some of the kids don't want to be here, and they can get quite violent."

"I suppose," I replied.

We stared at each other briefly and then the security guard said, "I better get back to work."

I looked down at the damage I had done to the box. The contents were all over the floor, and the box itself was broken. The lid was twisted and one of its hinges had snapped.

Among the contents on the carpet was a silver iPhone. I switched it on. There were only two numbers in the contacts list; one 'UM', and the other was digits only, no name or initials beside it. The only messages in the inbox were from UM. In the sent box were dozens of coded messages, the last one 'F11-x2-50ea'.

I thought about calling UM's number, then stopped myself. Maybe if we sent a message, we could get a trace on the phone.

I began looking for more evidence, in books, under shelves, under the desk, but it wasn't until I picked up the Old Testament and flicked through it that I found a second phone. It had one stored number, which coincided with the unnamed number on the silver iPhone.

Why send messages from one phone to another; what was the point? I wondered.

Jake appeared in the office doorway. "I found a journal, it's more like an inventory, actually," he said, placing it on the desk. There were hundreds of entries. The last few matched exactly those in the silver iPhone.

I told Jake about the phone and he took it from me and checked the messages. "I think this guy is ordering kids! Look. 'F11' must be female aged 11, then here 'M12' would be male 12 years old. The figure next to them is the amount he's prepared to pay," he suggested.

"Why do they buy so many kids? What can they do with that many?" I asked.

"Most of them would be sold overseas. The boys probably work in the fields, picking opium usually. They pay $50,000 to $100,000 for a kid and get 10 to 15 years' worth of work out of him. The girls they put into the overseas prostitution market. They get a mint for overseas girls, especially under-age ones," Jake replied, grimacing. Then he added, "This guy, UM, I'd say he's our kingpin. Our rich drug lord."

"Why did the Judge and the other two paedophiles that were holding Stevie have kids if they were meant to be sent overseas to this UM guy?" I asked.

"Maybe the Priest is renting them out before delivering them, like a double dip at profits. He'd get paid twice for the same kid!"

"Maybe they found out these kids were being defiled before being sent. Maybe they weren't getting what they were paying for," I said.

"It's possible this UM person found out and he's sending a message."

Chapter 105

Mikayla had sat in silence since Scott was removed from the van. She knew she was being taken to her death, or something worse. Her father had always told her to believe in herself and that she could do anything, so she had decided wherever she was being taken, she would take her first opportunity to escape. She would get out or die trying.

Beau had been driving the van very fast, taking corners sharply, and she had been tossed from side to side for what felt like hours.

"You lied about us going home, didn't you?" Mikayla said.

"Yes, but you knew I was lying, you're a smart girl," Beau replied.

"Yes, I did. So where am I going?"

"You'll be at your new home in a little while. You should be happy. There's another girl there," Beau said.

"What other girl?" Mikayla asked.

"Hard to remember; all you kids, so many deliveries."

There have been so many he doesn't even remember us, Mikayla thought.

"The people who bought me, what do they want with me?" Mikayla asked.

Beau went to look at her in the mirror, but the view was blocked by the plastic he had installed years ago. He saw only his own reflection. His eyes threw back a look of disgust at himself.

"I don't know," he replied. He did know; he just couldn't tell her.

It was easier when they didn't speak to him, he thought. He lowered his window. He had started to feel sick. He needed some fresh air.

"Are they going to rape me?" she asked.

Beau ignored the question and turned the music up, loud. He would hear no more questions.

Beau hadn't come up with any better plan to get out of the Monster's house alive than by simply delivering the girl early, hoping to get into his good books. Then he would vanish. The Priest would come looking for him when he didn't return with his cut of the money. The Priest had a bad reputation when it came to clients who reneged on deals or cheated him. The result was usually death.

While the Priest was a concern, he was the lesser of two evils right now. He knew the Monster would kill him if given the order.

He doubted the Priest could physically do it himself.

He would find out soon enough.

Chapter 106

By the time Jake and I had rummaged through the Priest's private residence as well as his office and chapel, we had found 13 phones and dozens of buyers. All had had young children placed with them. We had managed to reconcile one of the phone numbers to Ian Welling and now knew that the Priest had supplied Stevie to him.

However, all the other orders paled into insignificance when we compared them to the number of orders to 'UM'.

Jake had requested tech support to trace the phone, however they hadn't yet got back to him.

"I think it's safe to say the Priest is the middle man. He organises the orders and I would imagine the delivery of them too," Jake said.

"I agree," I said.

Apart from Jake rummaging through the rooms at the chapel, the church was eerily quiet. How did a person who devoted his life to love not see the evil living inside himself? A place of hope, love and faith should not know such evil.

When Jake was quiet and all was still, I could hear rain falling on the church roof. It was the most peaceful sound I had heard all day.

Unfortunately, it was broken by the stomping feet of Deputy Doofus.

"I've just received a call from the groundskeeper at the cemetery. We've found the superintendent."

His sombre expression told us what we'd expect to find. "Take us there," Jake said.

"Organise some tarps and tents. We'll need to secure what evidence hasn't been washed away with this rain," I added.

"Already done, Detective," Evans replied.

"Good job," I said.

As much as I thought he was a doofus, good work deserved praise and he had made a smart decision and deserved to know he had done the right thing.

The drive out was quiet and sombre. The heavy rain combined with the darkness reduced visibility and made the country road feel even more isolated. Constable Evans was very shaken at the discovery of a colleague's body. Jake and I had been lucky enough not to experience that with anyone we had directly worked with.

We had been driving for about 15 minutes before we saw blue and red flashing lights off in the distance.

When we arrived on the scene, most of Ballarat's available officers were there, as well as a few from neighbouring areas. Jake had already contacted Monique and requested control. Like him, she believed the recent deaths we were investigating were all related and so she gave her approval.

We produced our badges and strolled through the police line without any issues.

As usual, Jake and I worked from the outside in. As always, we started by getting information from any witnesses, the first respondents, forensics, or pathologists. Then we would move onto the body itself.

The groundskeeper was an elderly guy who had lived on the property since 1999. He received cheap rent and a weekly cheque in return for taking care of the grounds. When he had first started, he had 187 gravestones to take care of and four bare acres of lawn to mow, while now, there were 369 gravestones and two and a quarter bare acres.

"Can you tell us what you heard?" Jake asked.

"I was woken by a loud bang, followed closely by another. I was asleep and I mean, man! I sat straight up in bed; scared the crap out of me. Loudest bang I ever heard. I grabbed my gun and went out onto the porch. By the time I got to the end, I heard one more loud bang. I still couldn't see anything, so I got in my truck to drive to the entrance of the cemetery but before I could, a car passed me. It looked like a black car. It was really travelling. Then when I drove to the entrance and was about to turn in, I saw a lump on the ground about 10 metres away. I got out, realised it was a person and called you guys."

"I take it you didn't get a plate on the vehicle, or the make and model?" I asked.

"It was really dark. I'm pretty sure it was black, and it was a bulky, square shape," he replied, clearly annoyed at himself that he couldn't offer more.

"It's ok, the officer here will take your formal statement and we'll be back in touch with you shortly. Thanks for your help," Jake said.

"Could you do it?" I asked Jake.

"Do what?" he quizzed.

"Live on a cemetery," I replied.

"Fuck, hell no, that's scary shit. I have nightmares about dead people as it is, you?"

"No way, if I wanted ghosts I'd go to Picton Town," I said, referring to one of Australia's most haunted towns.

The first units had done a great job securing the scene and protecting the evidence against the elements.

The ambulance officers reported on initial examination that the deceased had died from two bullets to the heart. However, they wouldn't be able to confirm it until the autopsy had been completed and the toxicology report came back.

Because we'd arrived so soon after the murder, the body hadn't begun to decompose. The superintendent only smelt of stale urine.

Jake went to the left-hand side of the body while I went to the right. The victim's face was planted in the mud. He was only wearing a bathrobe. His black hair was knotted and covered in mud. His hands were cuffed behind his back and his feet were bare. Whatever he had done, it must have been something pretty bad to be left like this, at a place like this.

I noted the two bullet wounds.

"Have you found a third wound?" I asked Jake, referring to the fact the groundskeeper had mentioned three gunshots.

"No, maybe the third bullet missed him," he replied.

"Maybe, but these two are grouped pretty close together. Within about two and a half centimetres, would you say?" I asked.

"Yeah," Jake replied. "Maybe he fired a warning shot, who knows. Let's save the questions for when we have all the evidence, otherwise we'll be out in this shit for the whole night."

"I'm going to see if I can find the casings," I said. "Based on how he's lying, the shots came from up there." I pointed with my torch into the darkness beyond the entrance.

I had walked about 15 metres before I found a partial tyre print, then what appeared to be a shoe print, then a casing, then a second casing, and a few metres over, a third.

I looked at one of the spent casings. It looked like a .40-calibre; standard police issue, I thought. Second person killed tonight most likely with his own weapon.

By the time Jake strode up the track, I was almost soaked through.

"What you got?" he asked.

"Three spent .40-calibre casings, tyre tracks, and one big fucking question," I replied.

"What's the question?" Jake asked.

"Who does this belong to?" I pointed my torch to the ground.

There was a pool of blood next to the tyre cast. It had begun to wash away with the rain, but it was clear that it was recent.

"There's no trail of blood, just a pool, so I doubt it belongs to the victim," I suggested to Jake.

"Interesting," Jake replied.

"Another victim, perhaps?" I probed.

Jake's phone buzzed.

"Miller," he answered, "what you got? Palanok?" he repeated into his phone. "Text me the addresses."

He hung up and shone his torch away from the pool of blood and then bent down and picked something up.

"What is it?" I asked.

"Looks like it's from rosary beads. There are heaps of them, look." Jake shone his torch over them.

"Do you think that the Priest killed the superintendent?" I asked.

"We need to see Scott. I have more questions for him," Jake said urgently.

Chapter 107

The rain had turned into hail and visibility went from limited to near impossible in the car. Yet Constable Evans drove us without hesitation. When we finally arrived at the hospital to visit Scott, Jake directed Evans to wait in the Cruiser.

Jake hadn't spoken on the way over. I could tell he was working on a theory, I just had no idea what it was.

Scott had been placed on a drip to replace lost fluids. He was all skin and bone.

Jake sat on the edge of the bed at Scott's feet. I stood, notepad open, pen poised.

"Scott, the man who saved you is in danger. We need to help him."

"What man?" Scott replied.

Yeah, what man? What the hell are you talking about? I thought.

"The man who saved you from the Judge. Was it Mikayla's dad, was Mikayla in the van? Do you know where they were taking her? We need to find them, Scott, they could be in danger!"

"The Joker said our ransom had been paid and he was dropping us off at different places. We knew he was lying. He always lied."

"We? Is that you and Mikayla?" Jake asked.

"Yes," Scott replied.

"Did he say where he was taking her?" Jake asked.

"No," Scott replied. "Only that this was his last delivery," he remembered.

"Jake, you got a sec?" I asked.

We stepped into the hallway outside Scott's room. "Where are we going with this? Do you think Austin is involved?"

"The phone the Priest used to place his orders was registered to a company called Palanok. Palanok donated the money to get the prisoner 'Restart' program going. But they weren't donating money; they were funding their own paedophile ring. It was their plan from the start. They had the Judge, the police chief and the Priest running the program. They must have all been in Palanok's pocket in some form or another."

"That's like a pub funding AA programs," I replied.

"Yep," Jake said.

"But I don't understand what that has to do with Austin."

"Austin saved Scott, and Stevie said he killed them with their own gun. Why, you ask?" Jake said. "Less evidence. When I saw the Judge had been killed with his own gun, that made two in one day. Big coincidence. Then the policeman; he was killed with his service pistol. That's three. Someone's hunting them. May I suggest a person straight out of the army with a classified army file might be behind this?" Jake said.

"You were right," Jake continued, "a kidnapped kid wouldn't have hitched a ride, but I couldn't work out why he was lying. Now I know; Scott is not trying to protect Austin, he's trying to save Mikayla."

I was dumbfounded.

"What else do we need from Scott?" I asked.

"I want to know if he ever heard the name Igor or Monster. If he heard Beau say it, then it probably confirms where Beau is heading."

Scott had almost dozed off when we entered his room again.

"One more quick question," Jake said as he woke him. "Did the Joker say what he would do once he had made the delivery?"

Half-asleep, Scott answered, "He said he would take the Monster's money and go fishing."

"Go to sleep now, Scott. Your parents will be here soon. We'll see you again in a few days.

Chapter 108

Chloe wasn't sure when she had blacked out, but she had dreamt the eyeless girl hanging next to her was talking to her. "Get out," she said, "this will be you." With every word spoken, a sliver of skin fell from her face onto the blood-soaked, dusty floor. When Chloe woke, she could hear the sound of flies buzzing around her head. She was worried they would go up her nose or mouth. She could feel one crawling across her eyelid.

"Ooww!" she screamed, as Alexi removed her from the chains and carried her over his shoulder. He weaved his way through a labyrinth of connecting tunnels, knowing when to turn right, when to turn left and when to stay the course. At one point, Chloe saw a flash of daylight and swore she heard the sound of barking. She could see the flicker of lights as she bounced around. He then hit the stairs, taking two at a time, and she could see all the upside-down books placed neatly on the shelves in the library, although she could make none of them out.

He sat her down on the bed. "Get cleaned up. We have a visitor arriving tonight, you need to look your best."

Despite the fact that she was now away from the dead girl, she could still smell her. The smell of death at its worst was a thick fatty smell, and it stuck with her. She could smell death even deep in her hair.

Even after her shower, she could still smell it, in waves.

She put on fresh clothes and felt much better about herself, but it was all a façade. She was beginning to think if she remained here, she would be the next girl hanging in the tunnels, or maybe, that was just the dream talking.

It would have only been 8, maybe 8.30 in the morning, as she studied her reflection in the mirror, and she couldn't help but notice how gaunt and sickly she was looking. Her cheekbones were drawn, her eyes were sunken and she looked neglected, she thought.

Then she realised that was her now.

Plain and simple, she was abused and neglected.

Chloe heard the slightly muffled sound of the intercom buzz in the other room.

"The Joker's here," the voice over the intercom said.

"He's early, let me check," Alexi replied.

Chloe then heard his heavy footsteps walk away down the hall and while she could still hear voices, she couldn't decipher what was being said. She heard the footsteps return.

"Let him in but we won't be letting him out," Alexi said. "The boss wants to feed him to the dogs."

"Show him in!" Igor himself ordered.

* * *

After passing the guard at the gate with relative ease, Beau was feeling positive about his chances of coming out the other side. The drive along the winding road up to the country house seemed longer today.

By the time Beau set foot inside the property, he had his excitement in check and was able to give the impression of a calm, disinterested delivery man. He had Mikayla behind him, with a hood over her head.

"I apologise for being early. I didn't want you to have to wait any longer, because you have waited long enough already," Beau said.

"It's fine," Alexi said, dismissing Beau's apology with a careless wave of his hand. "Show us the goods," he demanded.

"Sure . . . Monster . . . I mean . . . Mr Pavlychko," Beau replied.

Alexi stood there laughing.

"I am not the Monster, and I would be very careful using that word around here."

"I wouldn't use that word at all unless you were interested in finding out its origin," a small man at the back of the room said.

Beau knew he had made a mistake, one he was hoping he would escape from.

"Sorry," Beau apologised immediately.

"So, you're the Priest's bagman," the small man said. He stood and walked over in front of Alexi. "Show me what I have bought."

It was only then that Beau realised the small man in front of him was in fact the Monster. It also provided a lesson between myth and reality. Beau thought he would be able to grab him by the neck with one hand and hammer him to the ground with the other. The only thing that scared him about the Monster was the big guy standing next to him, and for that reason he was cautious and apologetic.

He removed the hood, revealing Mikayla as he had promised. "Same as in the photo," he said.

"You have a fantastic eye for quality," the Monster replied, as if he was looking at a painting or an antique.

"Always aim to please," Beau replied. He hoped he appeared genuine and not some slimy scum-bag who couldn't wait to get the fuck out of there. "The Priest said you would have the payment?"

Igor nodded, and clicked his fingers. Andrei, who had been standing in the corner of the room, observing, waiting and ready to act if his boss called, stepped forward and handed a yellow envelope to Beau.

"You will find it's 10,000 short. I took the 10,000 as compensation for the inconvenience, Igor said.

"I shall let the Priest know. If he has an issue he can speak with you," Beau said. He had no intention of speaking to the Priest. Any money collected he intended to keep and use to start his new life. He waited anxiously, wanting to leave but not wanting them to smell the deception.

"Get the new girl cleaned up," Igor said.

Alexi took Mikayla by the arm and led her away.

Beau watched the girl being escorted to the rear of the home and out of sight.

"Is there anything else you need?" Igor asked.

"No, I'll get going now. It's been a long drive and I have a long drive ahead of me," Beau replied.

Igor nodded to the security guard standing behind Beau, giving him the approval to open the door and send him on his way.

Back in his van, Beau was driving down the drive towards the gate, just shy of half a million dollars in his bag and with a new life on the horizon. He hadn't lied to Igor, he did have a long drive except he was heading north, not south. The Gold Coast would be his new destination.

Igor turned to Shevd. "Take out his tyres. Andrei, hunt him down, and make sure you hide the van."

Andrei was about to head off when Igor spoke. "Don't kill him. He needs to see what a true Monster is."

"Yes, boss," Andrei replied.

Shevd took up his position in the attic. He saw the van turn right off the tar-sealed drive and out of the gate, headed down the dirt road and away from the house. He aimed at the rear tyre of the van, calmed his breathing, paused and fired. The shot cracked loud throughout the house and across the land. The van swerved and swayed.

Shevd could see the fat man disembark the cabin and inspect the rear tyre. Shevd fired again; this time, the bullet hit the front tyre. Beau's immediate reaction was to head back to the cabin but the third bullet to the driver's door put that thought out of his mind. He was darting around looking like a trapped animal.

With no idea where the shots were coming from, Beau didn't know where he could go for cover. His immediate thought was to run for the woods. The trees would provide some cover.

He sprinted down the dirt road, going left across the front of his van, when a shot rang out and a bullet landed in the dirt just centimetres from his left foot.

The bullet made him turn right, which kept him closer to the house than he would have liked. Beau decided it would be best to enter the woods at the closest point and then weave away from this place. Otherwise they would be firing pot shots at him all day long.

He ran in a zigzag pattern as fast as he could towards the edge of the woods. The woods began 500 metres from Beau's current position. Then something sent him sprawling onto his belly in the dirt. In the split second it took him to gather himself, he heard a shot ring out.

A sharp pain pierced his calf.

Shevd watched through his scope as the fat man gathered himself and hobbled into the woods at the end of the street beyond Palanok. He could have killed him if he wanted to but the boss had ordered he be brought back alive.

Shevd scanned the area. One of the guards was already on his way to remove the van, and as he scanned back to where Beau had entered the woods, he could see Andrei about 150 metres behind him.

Chapter 109

We were in the hospital café, and Jake was confident that Austin had killed both the Judge and Mike. While I thought it was a possibility, I couldn't rule out that the hits on them both had been performed by a rival cartel, or even the Priest himself.

"So, if it is Austin, we need to arrest him," I said.

"Do we have a case?" Jake asked.

"You said he killed five people. Three paedophiles, the Judge and Mike."

"I'm not sure about one of the paedophiles. The two that died where Stevie was found yes, Judge yes, and Mike yes, but Brodie, what evidence do we have?"

I sat back and thought about it. What evidence did we have? Ballistics? Killed with their own weapons, so there was no murder weapon to speak of. Fingerprints on the guns? Forensics hadn't come back yet so it was possible. Trace evidence? Nil. Witnesses? Neither Stevie nor Scott had seen the murders committed.

Hell, we didn't have a lot. Our only hope was prints.

"You're right, we don't have a lot," I replied. "Where do you think Austin has taken the Priest?"

"I'd say he took the Priest to find out where they shipped his daughter," Jake said.

"Igor," I said.

"Based on the orders, it's a likely destination."

"Let's go then," I said.

"Hold your horses, Brucey. We can't just go into New South Wales and storm the home of some suspected crime boss. Monique would have a fit. I'll call her to organise a raid, but she'll want her New South Wales counterparts in on it."

Jake paced the hospital café as he talked on the phone. Each time he passed, I caught a snippet of his conversation with Monique. As the call grew longer, I became increasingly concerned with what appeared to be our boss's reluctance.

Jake hung up the call and sat down, staring at his half-drunk cup of coffee, which had now gone cold.

"What's the verdict?" I asked.

"She said New South Wales police have been investigating Palanok Investments for years now. They suspect he's involved in trafficking drugs and prostitution. They had some witnesses, ex-employees that had turned State witness, but they were murdered before the trial so the State had to drop the case."

"What the hell are we dealing with here?" I asked.

"It's big. Everyone who's tried to bring him down is dead!" Jake exclaimed. "Monique's trying to get approval for us to search the residences and question him about the phone and the orders. She advised against a raid. She seems to think he has someone in his pocket, high up in the New South Wales Police Force. She believes he would get tipped off over any potential raid by them."

"Well he obviously has more than one informant, not just Mike," I said. "Will they get tipped off if we go?"

"For our sake, let's hope not," Jake replied.

I kept the possibility of the Priest being our shooter to myself. The more I thought about it the less probable it seemed.

When Jake's phone did finally ring, it was Hayley, not Monique. She was checking in to make sure Jake was all right. He had been slack in reporting to her. She always worried about him when he was away.

"Honey, I have to go, I promise I'll call you soon," Jake said, taking the phone away from his ear and looking at the screen. "Babe, I have another call I need to take." He hung up and accepted the new call. This time, it was Monique.

"What's the plan?" he asked.

When the conversation ended and he had he hung up, he was all smiles.

"Ok! She's got us a permit to search the residence and suggests that we interview him about the phone. New South Wales police are picking us up at Jenolan and taking us there."

"Tactical?" I asked. After the last time I'd gone into a property looking for a hostage, I really wanted Tactical on the scene.

"No, just detectives. It'll go smoothly, don't panic," Jake said.

I must have looked worried. Jake hugged me, which he hadn't done in a long while.

I was dreading the answer before I asked the question. "How are we getting there?"

Jake smiled, "You're not going to like the answer. Helicopter."

The helicopter looked in good condition, not as if it was going to fall apart mid-flight.

At least that's something, I thought. "How long is this flight?" I asked.

"About four and a half hours. We have to stop in Albury to refuel, then we land at Jenolan," Jake replied. "Igor's place is about 20 minutes' drive from there."

The flight was a lot smoother than I'd expected and before I knew it, we were refuelling.

"Forensics have cleared both scenes, so now we wait to see if they come up with any evidence that will help us link Austin or anyone else to these crimes," Jake said.

He had obviously received an update from one of Grace's crew.

"Let's hope they find something," I replied.

We were only on the ground 15 or 20 minutes before we were back in the air heading towards the Blue Mountains.

As the helicopter flew inland over forests and old farming homesteads, my heart started to flutter a little. My memories, smells and fears about the cabin from 10 years previously came flooding back, despite the effort I put into keeping them under control. Anxiety combined with a heart condition was not a good combination. It only lasted for a few seconds, but it reminded me of how vulnerable I really was.

Chapter 110

Austin drove north to NSW with the dead Priest slumped and bleeding in the back seat.

He had set the navigation system for the Palanok residence in the Blue Mountains, the address where the Priest had organised Beau to make the delivery. His daughter.

It was nearing 9 am and Austin had been driving for over eight hours. He had hardly slept. His eyes were heavy and despite his sleep deprivation training, there were only so many days he could go without sleep. He needed a quick nap, just half an hour.

He pulled off the main highway and drove about 500 metres up a side road. It was a secluded spot, remote enough for a nap. Austin stared into the brush at the side of the road, seeing only his daughter's face. Then he fell asleep.

The beach came to him, as it always seemed to lately. Sarah was there, as beautiful as ever, hair blowing in the light wind; the smell of the ocean, the waves crashing, the water gently flowing over his bare feet, seeping between his toes. Sarah was staring out to sea. Austin placed his hand on her shoulder, where her skin was soft and smooth.

She turned and smiled as soon as he touched her. Her smile was wide and comforting. "You need to go and get our daughter, before it's too late."

Austin looked up the beach. Mikayla was playing in the sand. Drawing a heart shape with a stick.

"She needs to be with you, not here with me," Sarah said.

"I don't want to leave, why can't we all stay here together?"

"It's not your time," Sarah replied.

Austin woke in his usual cold sweat. The image of Sarah had been so vivid again; he could smell her, feel her.

He felt he had been asleep for hours. When he looked at the clock he realised he had been asleep for two hours! He was angry with himself. His daughter had been sold to some crime lord and here he was sleeping. He pounded his hands on the dash and yanked the steering wheel back and forth out of sheer frustration.

He had to forget his mistake and move on, before it was too late.

Chapter 111

Igor liked what he saw when he looked at the new girl. She was much prettier than Chloe. He wasn't completely sure what would become of Chloe. At this stage, he thought he would ship her out to the Ukraine. One of his pimps had been requesting a younger girl for the crew he was running. The one thing Igor was confident about was that he would keep the new girl for a long time. Unless she decided to fight him. If she did that, well she would end up in the tunnels with the other bitch, the one who had taken a piece of his ear one night.

Once Alexi had taken her off to clean her up and give her some fresh clothes, he was on his way to 'introduce' himself when he was interrupted by a call on his cell phone. The caller ID read 'Hutch'. The cop's nickname was taken from the 70's TV show *Starsky & Hutch*.

"Yes," Igor answered. He never used his name when he answered his phone.

"You have visitors coming. They'll be there soon and they'll be looking through both properties," the voice said.

"What the hell am I paying you for?" Igor replied.

"They're from Victoria so I have no control. Apparently someone's taken out a few of the Priest's crew," the voice explained.

"How long we got?"

"Half an hour, maybe less. I only found out when they landed. We were kept totally out of the loop on this one."

Igor angrily hung up without another word and turned to Alexi and Shevd. "We need to clean up. Cops are coming. Everything into the tunnels and get Andrei back with the Joker to hide him down there. Make sure he covers the exit so they can't see it from the outside."

"Yes, boss," they replied and immediately got moving to do as they were asked.

"Alexi, put the girls down there too. Make sure everyone down there is tied and gagged. I don't want some scream giving us away.

One moment Mikayla was getting changed into fresh clothes and the next she was being yanked by the arm and thrown over the big guy's shoulders. The other girl, who Mikayla didn't yet know by name, was grabbed by the neck in a lot more vicious and hostile way.

Mikayla couldn't understand what was happening. Chloe began screaming the moment they started to descend the stairs and Mikayla realised why when they came to the room with the table and the hanging corpse. Then Mikayla let out a scream that would have woken the corpse had it not been stifled by Alexi's big hand, squeezing her cheeks together and her mouth shut.

The men hung both girls upside down. Mikayla had never felt terror like this. Her heart was racing and the tears flowed uncontrollably down her cheeks. The thing hanging beside her barely resembled a human being, let alone a girl.

The other girl was hanging on the other side of the corpse. If Mikayla hadn't had a gag in her mouth, she was certain she would have vomited. The smell was disgusting, the worst smell she had ever experienced, and the flies were in their hundreds. Maybe thousands, swarms of them.

* * *

The blood trail led deep into the woods, further than Andrei thought the Joker would have reached with his injury. As he went deeper, the blood was fresher, brighter. Andrei was getting close.

Then it stopped altogether.

Andrei had killed many people in many different wars. But this was the first person he had lost track of. It was also the first time an injured man had climbed a tree to ambush him.

He felt like an idiot. He was standing there looking at a pool of blood on a log trying to locate the next trace, when out of nowhere the fat man landed on him.

Andrei was sent flying and his gun soared out of his hand into the foliage.

Beau hammered both hands down on the Monster's henchman who had been tracking him and then took the man's head and rammed it into the tree trunk, repeatedly. The man stumbled backwards, dazed.

Beau took advantage of his opponent's momentary daze, and unleashed a flurry of body and facial punches.

There was far more fight in the fat Joker than Andrei had anticipated. He clearly wasn't a trained fighter; he just fought with brute force.

It took Andrei a few seconds to gather his arms in a position that would adequately protect his head. Then he could begin to feel the punches two from the left, then one big punch from the right. This series continued several times. Two and one. Two and one.

Andrei timed his strike.

Two and one, and as the one recoiled, he struck hard and fast, palm out, hitting him flush in the nose. Beau wasn't just dazed, he was nearly out of it. His vision came and went and when he could see, his eyes were teared up.

Blood streamed down his face and down the back of his throat. He had lost sight of his attacker. He resorted to swinging haymakers, hoping one would connect. All they did was use up what little energy Beau had left.

Andrei calmly headed over to search for his gun in the scrub where it had fallen. He climbed over a downed trunk and landed on a pile of sticks and twigs, which cracked under his weight.

Beau heard the sound and turned and without thinking, rushed in the general direction. With his vision still severely affected, he could not see the fallen tree and hit it at full speed, sending him semi-cartwheeling over the fallen log and on to the other side, crashing into another tree.

Andrei immediately heard the crack of the fat Joker's neck as his body wrapped itself around the tree but the head stayed in position. It was the first time Andrei had seen a man kill himself by running into a tree.

Igor would not be happy with him, he thought. He'd wanted him alive.

Chapter 112

Jake and I were picked up by two NSW vice detectives. One was called Deakins and the other Hutchinson. "You can call me Deak and we call him Hutch, you know, that TV cop show from back in the 70s? Never thought I'd be working with a star," Deak joked.

Deak was the senior of the two by about 10 years, I guessed. He was a lot less fit than Hutchinson, and going bald, but to his credit he was going graciously, making no attempt to cover his bare head with a comb-over.

Hutchinson had a bit of swag about him; nice new suit, perfect blonde hair, every bit of him resembling a successful businessman rather than a seasoned detective.

"Is this it? Is this all the help we get when we go to sweep a crime lord's property?" I asked, exasperated.

"We've been down this path ourselves and we came up dry; there was nothing there," Hutchinson answered.

"What my partner is trying to say," said Deak, "is that finding the evidence is really tough. We did a search ourselves. We even had witnesses who said he was trafficking drugs and weapons, but the place was clean."

"We have information he might be trafficking children. Ever had information on that?" I asked.

"That's a new one, it's always been drugs or weapons," Hutchinson replied quickly.

"How far is it to the homestead?" Jake asked.

"About 15 minutes," Deak replied.

The road was bumpy and it wound around the mountain. Maybe it was the ride, or maybe it was the fact that I was six foot four and stuffed into the back of a midsize, either way, it was not the best car ride after a five-hour helicopter flight. My stomach was feeling the effects. For a second, I thought I was going to bring up my last meal.

"We'll need a vehicle," Jake said.

"What for? I thought you were just asking a few questions and searching the two houses. That's what we were told. Right, Deak?" Hutchinson said.

"That's what we were told," Deak confirmed.

"You seem a little defensive there, Detective." Jake deliberately didn't use the nickname we'd been given. "We're not stepping on your toes, are we?"

"Hell no, I was just worried I hadn't done something I should have," Hutchinson replied. "Believe me, we want this scumbag as bad as the next guy. Just not sure why you'll need a car, that's all," he added.

"We might need to stay in town a couple of days. Can you organise one for us or not?" Jake replied bluntly.

"Yeah, we have another detective meeting us there. He can come back with us after the search and you can have his vehicle."

"Perfect," Jake said.

I had always imagined a crime lord's home as being one of sheer opulence. While this one was massive, it was not opulent from the outside. It was a graceful heritage home. The security guard waved us through and the gates opened to admit us. The driveway wound up to the homestead, which sat high on the crest.

What looked like two private security guards met us at the door.

"Can we please see the warrant?" one of the guards asked.

"We would just like to ask Mr Pavlychko a few questions," Jake said.

"Mr Pavlychko is a very busy man. Any questions for him can be sent to his legal counsel." The man handed him a card.

"I'll raise you," Jake replied.

He handed across a copy of the warrant Monique had organised before we boarded the helicopter. Then he reached for the front door handle, but the guard stepped across, blocking Jake's access. "I suggest you move, before I move you," Jake said. He stood a good 10 centimetres taller and when he was eye to eye with someone, Jake was a menacing figure.

The guard thought about standing his ground, but then reconsidered.

Jake walked in as if he owned the place, and I followed.

When we stepped inside the house, it was as if they were all waiting for us. There was a room full of businessmen, yet little to no business was taking place.

"My name is Igor, why do you wish to search my home?" he asked.

"It's in the warrant, but the highlights are: kidnapping, human trafficking, drug trafficking, and the sale of prohibited firearms," Jake answered.

"It's absurd, my business is legitimate," Igor replied.

"What exactly is your business?" Jake questioned.

"We import and export products all around the world but they are legitimate businesses. Mainly computer equipment," Igor detailed.

"How many employees do you have?" Jake asked.

"A hundred and seventy-two, why?" Igor asked.

"Do they all get company phones?" Jake returned.

"Some do, but not all, it depends on how long they've been working for us. Is this leading somewhere, Detective?" Igor asked.

"Do you know a priest by the name of Peter O'Riley in Ballarat?"

"Yes, we supported his outreach program for reforming offenders. Is he ok?" Igor pretended to be concerned.

"Can you provide me a list of your company mobile phone numbers?" Jake asked.

"I don't have any of them on me but I could get them to you. I really don't know why you're asking me these questions," Igor said.

"We have reason to believe one of your company phones has been used to place orders for children, from the Priest in Ballarat."

"That's disturbing. I have never really trusted priests. They always seem to be up to no good. We will provide you with any support you need," Igor replied, knowing as long as they didn't find the girls, the phone would lead nowhere. It was the other evidence that would seal their conviction. "Where would you like to start your search?" he asked.

"We will go room by room," Jake said. "You're welcome to watch, but get in the way or prevent us from going somewhere, and you will be detained," Jake warned them all.

Igor allocated one of his security guys to show us around, not that we needed him to guide us. We were going to look anywhere and everywhere. Any piece of the puzzle would do.

We searched the house room by room, all 570 square metres of it, and all of it was clean. Not even a joint, let alone kids in chains.

We searched the grounds, wire fence to wire fence, all 25 acres. There were hay bales and a tractor, and one huge compound that housed what seemed like hundreds of dogs and one large machinery shed. After Beau's house, we were looking for secret rooms everywhere, but there were none to be found.

After finding the hidden treasures at the Priest's, we even searched inside books, looking for photos or the like. We took their computers to be analysed.

The roof cavity only had spiders and more spiders.

There seemed to be nothing of use.

We were about to go inside and talk to Igor and tell him we had found nothing, when Jake pulled me aside.

"What do you think?" he asked me.

"They seemed to be expecting us, don't you think?" I asked.

"Yes, my thought exactly, as if they were tipped off." Jake pulled out his mobile and dialled the number that we had found at the Priest's. The phone from which all the orders were placed. Jake dialled. I heard the recorded message, 'the number you have called could not be reached at this time'.

"You realise we could be looking at the next victim? Whoever killed the Judge and the superintendent, this is his likely next stop," Jake said.

"Unless we're at the killer's," I replied.

"Unlikely, he wouldn't have made it back in time," Jake said.

"He could have sent someone."

"Let's rattle his cage. You keep an eye on his body language," Jake said.

We stepped back inside and met Igor in the library. He was sitting there pretending to work.

"You're all clear. If you could please follow up those phone numbers for us, it would be of great assistance," Jake said.

"My pleasure, I will assure it's done as soon as possible," Igor replied.

"Oh, and one other thing," Jake said, as if it was an afterthought, "we think it's important that you are made aware that your safety could be compromised."

Igor frowned, unsure how that could be.

"Why would I be in danger?" he asked.

"Well, someone has killed the Ballarat superintendent as well as the chief magistrate. Both were involved in the outreach program you sponsor."

"Why do you think that affects me?" Igor asked.

"We haven't been able to locate Father O'Riley either. As you were all involved in the outreach program, we believe you may be next."

"Any ideas who it is?" Igor asked.

"Not yet, but if you have any concerns you should call us immediately," Jake replied.

"Will do," Igor said.

"You have a lot of dogs, what do you use them for?" I asked.

"Hunting wild pigs," Igor replied in a cold and threatening manner.

We left the residence. Hutchinson and Deak looked pleased, as if to say, told you so.

"You still want to stay?" Deak asked.

"Yes, at least for 24 hours," Jake replied.

After Deak and Hutchinson's colleague arrived and the car was handed over to us, Jake and I sat waiting in the car opposite the front gate. I wasn't sure what Jake was expecting to happen or why we were still there.

"What are we doing here, buddy? There's nothing here."

"Something isn't right. Everything was too neat, like they were expecting guests. You thought the same."

"Yeah, but there was nothing there. If they had any kids hidden, they must have moved them off-site. They're not going to go there now, with us out the front, they're not that stupid."

"Call Deak. Tell him we're leaving, that we're going for dinner and then back to the airfield. They can pick the car up from there in the morning. Say we'll leave the car key with the duty manager."

I made the call and passed on the information, just as Jake had asked.

He waved at the gate security, thanking them for their assistance, started the vehicle and headed off.

I was thinking about what I would have for dinner, desperate for a nice steak, when Jake turned the vehicle in a totally different direction from what I expected.

"Where are we going?" I asked.

"It's called foxing. We both think they were tipped off and I'm hoping they'll get the call that we've left," Jake replied.

"How does this help us?" I asked.

"If they do have the girls, I'm hoping they'll move them. If they don't, I'll show up again at 6 am unannounced and have another look."

We had driven around to the west side of the property. We could see the side of the home sitting up on the crest. There were four square paddocks between us and the house. The two paddocks closest to the homestead sloped down from the peak of the home and then levelled out to two horse paddocks. Sitting in the far left paddock was their own helicopter. We could have landed here, I thought to myself.

Everything looked the same as when Jake and I had inspected the property, everything except the tractor. It had been moved back into the shed. Probably because of the thunderstorm that was on its way.

Even though dusk was still a few hours off, the sky was darkening with gathering storm clouds.

* * *

Igor had been pacing the library waiting for the phone to ring to give him the all-clear, but no call had come. The library had been swept for bugs; it was all clear. His staff continued to sweep the rest of the house, but it was a slow process and Igor didn't want to be confined to his library for much longer.

He had a new toy downstairs and he wasn't allowed to play with it. It reminded him of when he was a boy; they would celebrate Christmas on Christmas Eve, yet he would never get to play with his presents until the next day.

Alexi and Shevd were sitting in the library opposite Igor's desk.

"What are we going to do with the phone?" Alexi asked.

"Do you know who ordered the phone and put it in the company name?" Igor asked.

Alexi stood up, all six foot eight of him. "It's my fault, boss. I asked Rostov to pick up a ghost phone. I don't know what he did, I thought it was a clean phone."

"You gave the order; it wasn't followed. That was his choice. Tomorrow we will meet with Rostov and fix the situation," Igor replied.

"I will ensure that the phone doesn't lead to you in any way. Perhaps it would be best if Rostov wasn't around to give his version of events," Alexi said.

"Make sure he's found with evidence other than the phone, in fact, use Chloe. I'm sick of her anyway. Kill her, and leave no evidence," Igor ordered.

"I will fix it, boss," Alexi said.

"What happened to Andrei? Did he bring the Joker back?" Igor asked.

"Andrei is in the tunnels. The Joker tried to kill him. During the scuffle, the Joker tripped over, hit a tree trunk and broke his neck."

"What is done is done. Make sure he is buried deep. Send Andrei to clean it up, after all, it is his mess."

"Yes boss," Alexi replied.

Igor's phone vibrated on his desk. It was a message from Hutch.

All clear, the trouble from the south have left with their tails between their legs

"They're gone, Shevd. When the sweep is complete bring the girls back up and check the motion sensor is still active on the south tunnel exit."

Shevd nodded. "When will they be finished with the bug sweeping?" he asked.

"Go ask them, 'quietly'," Igor emphasised.

Shevd slid the study door open and slipped through, closing it behind him.

"Who do you think killed the Judge and Mike?" Alexi asked Igor.

"My bet is on the Priest. He was probably getting heat and he cashed in his own insurance policy. He wouldn't let them turn him in. I'd say he's disappeared because he doesn't want to be found. You know what they do to paedophile priests on the inside," Igor said.

"We will need a new supplier," Alexi said.

"Don't panic, business will continue. There will be plenty of rock spiders to supply us and there will be plenty of cops who won't be able to refuse the money."

Alexi laughed. "I'm sure you're right."

"Until we find the replacements, we will just have to use our connections in other states a little more," Igor said. "Now I want you to do me a favour. Find the Priest. Ensure he can't do our company any harm. We need to silence him."

"I will ensure it is done. I will put the feelers out for him."

Shevd opened the door. "We are all clear, they didn't bug us."

"I will go tell Andrei to bury the Joker and get the girls while I'm down there," Alexi said.

"Good," Igor replied.

Chapter 113

Austin pulled the car over onto another remote road near the village of Edith. He was waiting for nightfall. Marcus had rung to tell him the police had found the superintendent and the Judge. He also informed him that a warrant had been executed on Igor's properties by Victorian Police. Significantly, the police had found nothing.

"Maybe she's not there?" Marcus said.

"She's there somewhere, surely, and if she isn't, they'll tell me where she is whether they want to or not," Austin replied.

"I can't keep feeding you this information. Someone will find out eventually and there's only so much I can erase," Marcus said.

"I understand. Jump out when you need to," Austin replied.

"Let's see where Igor leads and then we'll reassess," Marcus said. "But don't go storming the place now! There's police still floating about."

"Don't worry, I was waiting until tonight. If they do have the children and they want to move them, they'll probably do it then." My guess is they'll head straight for the helicopter."

Austin suspected the police would be following his trail. He had left too many dead people behind for them not to start putting some of the pieces together.

He had Googled Igor's address and noted on street view that the house was big, and surrounded by several acres. The only way he'd be able to get in undetected was through the forest at the rear. It would provide him with the cover to gain entry into the home. He had already saved two of the missing kids and he was confident Mikayla would be in there, somewhere. If not, the predators would tell him where she was.

Austin was approaching the night knowing there was a very real possibility that he could be arrested or killed without discovering Mikayla's wellbeing or location. But he had no choice; he would do whatever it took. His personal safety was of little consequence. Mikayla's safety was his only thought.

He set his watch alarm for 10 pm, released the boot lock and removed his duffel bag. He laid his weapons out. He had decided he would only take the two pistols and the sniper rifle. Even though they were all silenced, they would still make a slight noise.

The rifle had a night-vision scope, top of the line. He attached it, loaded the rifle and placed it back in the boot. Better to be safe than sorry, he thought, as he slipped the bulletproof vest over his head and slid his first pistol into the holster. He placed the second pistol into his belt holster. Finally, he removed his night-vision goggles and fitted them on his head. When he needed them, he would just flick them down.

For now, he could do nothing but wait and soon enough, he dozed off.

Everything was the same; the smell, the wind, the sea, the water over his feet, his wife's bright smile, and of course the warning, except this time it was more urgent. "Hurry or you will lose her for good. This is it, wake up and go."

Austin woke. He was in more than just a cold sweat; he was soaked. His watch alarm was screaming at him, over and over. He looked out into the darkness and then drove the seven kilometres to the area where the property met the forest on the west side. There were four large paddocks between the forest and the homestead.

He managed to manoeuvre the car about 50 metres into the forest. Weaving through the trees was harder than he imagined, especially with the headlights off and only the moonlight to guide him. But now, the car was well camouflaged amongst the trees.

He removed the Priest from the back seat and laid him on the ground next to the tyre. He was now more than 10 hours dead and smelling, but it was nothing new to Austin.

He opened the boot, removed his rifle and slung it over his right shoulder. Then he removed the jerry can he had filled at his last petrol stop and tied it over his shoulder with one of the Priest's shoelaces.

He was set to go.

Chapter 114

Chloe had almost become used to the smell of rotting flesh, but she would never get used to the swarms of buzzing flies crawling all over her face.

When the big guy finally came for them, Chloe was forced to walk while he carried Mikayla over his shoulder. She struggled to keep up. When he took the steps to the library two at a time, she stumbled and was dragged up the last few steps, scraping her knees.

Arriving back in the main house there were two things she noticed; one, it was dark outside, two, it was raining. Most importantly, it was heavy rain and it sounded like it was going to storm.

Chloe had realised the second Mikayla entered the room that Igor's use for her was over and soon she too would be the rotting corpse in the tunnels. They had to escape. The impending storm could be their only chance.

Alexi threw them in the room, saying, "Get cleaned up."

"We need to get out of here. We need to escape, before we end up like that girl in the tunnels," Chloe whispered as soon as they were alone. "Let's just make a run for it."

"They have guards everywhere," Mikayla replied.

"During the storms, they come inside and stand by the fire, it's our best chance. They can't know we're gone or they'll set the dogs onto us, and they have a lot of them."

"How long have you been here?" Mikayla asked.

"About two weeks," Chloe said.

"Did you ever meet the girl in the tunnels?" Mikayla asked.

"Not while she was alive," Chloe said.

"If either of us gets a chance, we'll make a run for it then. We can't die here," Mikayla said.

"Ok, but let's try to escape together," Chloe said. "If he tries to do stuff to you, let him. If you fight him, he'll get the big guy to take you to the tunnels and he'll beat you bad."

Mikayla didn't need to ask her if she had been raped; she knew that Chloe was speaking from experience.

Thunder cracked overhead.

* * *

The heavy rain was going to affect his plan; nonetheless, Austin had to proceed.

He carried the Priest's body through the woods. It was only about 500 metres but the terrain was tough going, even with his night-vision goggles. He rested the body next to a tree while he took a look at the house though his scope. He noticed there were people on the balcony. They looked like personal security guards. He shifted the scope and saw a dull glow appear between the spaces in the stacks of hay. He could just make out a gate behind the hay. Where did it lead? he wondered.

By the time he had finished sweeping the property through the scope, he had seen six men outside and at least four more inside. He was going to be outnumbered ten to one.

Austin negotiated the electrified fence surrounding the paddock and dragged the Priest through after him. He had sighted the dog house through the scope, and while he didn't have time to kill them all, he needed to delay the guards' access to them. He placed simple cable ties in between all the doors. That would slow them down a great deal.

When he reached the bottom of the paddock, he sprinted to the hay, took a large armful and returned to where he had left the Priest. He rolled the Priest onto the hay, removed his silver cross and began to pour petrol all over the body.

Then he hung the cross around a stick and dug it into the ground. He poured a trail of petrol away from the body towards the gate.

He lit the petrol.

The flames instantly lit up the night sky, even in the rain. Then they took hold and the Priest's body began to burn.

Austin couldn't just stay there; he needed them to come looking for him so he could search the house. He sprinted from the fire past the helicopter back to the hay.

He lay patiently camouflaged within the hay.

Now he had to wait.

* * *

Igor was about to take Mikayla to his room when he saw a large bonfire burning in his back paddock. Was this the Priest coming for them as the police had warned him? he wondered. He would deal with whoever it was.

His men came rushing in from the balcony.

"Alexi! Take three of the security team and go see who is there. Bring them to me dead or alive. Shevd, go to your nest in the attic. If you see anything running around in the woods, kill it," he ordered.

"Alexi, lock the girls in their room, find who is out there and kill them."

As Alexi left, four more members of his private security came rushing inside.

"Stay with the boss!" Alexi ordered.

Another three guards came running in. "You three, one at each door, stay inside, stay low, turn off the lights," Alexei said as he left.

Igor sat on his bed surrounded by his three guards. The house was in darkness. He waited, listening for any sound of conflict. He would have felt better if he had heard some gunfire. Then at least he would have known they had located someone. A rattlesnake loose on the property was very unnerving.

It seemed like an eternity, but in reality it was only a couple of minutes before Alexi returned. When he came through the door, Igor's heart skipped a beat. His mind had told him that the next person through that door would be the Priest, and when the door opened for a split second, that was who he saw. It was Alexi holding a silver cross out in front of him.

"I found the Priest," Alexi said.

"Did you take him to the tunnels?" Igor asked.

"He's burning in the back paddock. Someone set him on fire and left this for us." He handed Igor the cross.

"A message," Igor said.

A large bang cracked overhead. Gunfire? Igor asked himself. No, it was thunder. Normally Igor was fearless, yet tonight he was unusually skittish. He reminded himself that he had killed rivals before and he would again.

When you throw down the gauntlet, be prepared for the fight, Igor thought.

* * *

When the grass burst into flames, Jake and I were taken by surprise. We suspected whoever was killing the Priest's crew had arrived, or that or it was the Priest himself.

"Did you see anyone?" Jake asked.

"No, just flames," I replied.

Jake jumped out of the car and took cover behind the passenger rear guard. I went behind the passenger front wheel.

"Tell me if you see anyone," Jake said.

All the lights in the house went off, and we were in total darkness.

"They've gone into lockdown. There are two sides here now and we'll be in the middle, so be careful," Jake said.

"Why? Are we going in?" I asked.

"We're police. It's what we do," Jake said. "Why don't I go to the back door and you go to the front, that way . . ." Jake was interrupted by four men who appeared in the paddock seemingly out of nowhere.

"Where the hell did they come from?" Jake whispered.

"I think they came from behind the haystack," I said. "There were no downstairs rooms, were there?" I asked.

"No, maybe they have a secret room somewhere just like Beau," Jake replied.

"I'm so sick of hidden passages and this Scooby Doo shit," I replied.

"Let's go," Jake replied, laughing at my Scooby Doo comment. "Stay close to me," he added.

We were a good 500 metres away from the fire. We couldn't see who the individuals were, but we could see that they were armed, guns pointing in all different directions.

They studied the fire for about 30 seconds before making their way back to the house. The big man was in the lead.

Jake passed me a vest from the boot.

"Where's yours?" I asked.

"The car only has one," Jake replied.

I handed it back. "Jake, you take it."

He refused, as I knew he would.

"Jake, it's not for me, it's not for you, it's not even for Hayley. It's for Indiana." My arm was still extended holding the vest out to him. After a slight pause, he reluctantly took it.

"You stay behind me and do everything I say," Jake said as he put the vest on.

"Of course," I replied. "Just remember, Jake, watch out for snakes." I smiled.

"Don't go there," he growled.

"Still too soon?" I asked.

"Yep."

"After 10 years, if not now, when?" I asked.

"Give it another 10 years," Jake replied, still traumatised at the thought.

* * *

Austin waited for the four men to pass. Not one of them had even looked in the hay. He stepped into the tunnel, drew his pistol and moved forward. He hadn't been inside a tunnel since Afghanistan and it wasn't something that he wanted to be exploring again. He needed to be quick and clinical about this. When he reached a T-intersection, he wasn't sure whether to go forward, left or right. He stepped left and waited in the shadows. He could hear the men coming back. He had to start picking them off one by one, to even up the numbers.

Three men came running past, all in quick succession. The fourth, who had the duty of closing the gate, came lagging behind. Austin waited for the feet to pass before stepping out and taking him. He put his arm around his throat and before he even had the chance to react, the knife slid straight into his back. Austin quickly withdrew his knife from the man's back and slid it across his throat, holding his hand over the man's mouth to prevent any gurgling cry from escaping. He then dragged him into the depths of the tunnel out of sight.

He saw the other three men continue straight ahead and thought it best to follow. He reached three stone arches. Behind each arch was a large room, big enough to park a bus. It was the middle arch that attracted Austin's immediate attention. He had smelt this smell many times before; it was death, the smell of lingering death.

He looked at the hanging corpse in the middle of the arch, like a decomposing wind chime swinging in the draught that blew up the tunnel from the entrance.

Austin walked up to the hanging girl to check that it wasn't Mikayla. He knew immediately that she had been there for some weeks, if not months. He stepped past her to what appeared to be a torture area. There was a large wooden table laden with knives, meat cleavers, steel rods, pliers, and chains.

Many had died here, probably all children, Austin thought. He moved to the end arch and stepped in. Almost empty, except for a few yellow plastic waste barrels in the corner, with the words 'dog food' painted on them. Austin unclipped the bracket holding the lid on, and lifted it. The smell hit him. It was beyond disgusting; it was so bad he vomited instantly. When he regained his composure, he took another look because he simply couldn't believe his eyes. Dismembered body parts apparently for the dogs to eat.

Austin heard voices, yet with the echoes in the tunnels, he had trouble distinguishing where they were coming from. He ducked down behind the barrels. The men were in the arch where the dead girl was, too close for comfort.

He strained to hear them. It was the police, Foxx and Miller. They were half-smart; after all, they had followed him here.

Austin knew what he was about to do would definitely mean jail but it also meant he had triple the chances of getting Mikayla back. That was his only objective.

He stood up and went to the arch. "Officers, I need your help."

Jake spun away from the hanging girl, his gun pointed directly at Austin.

"Don't shoot me," Austin said.

"Put your gun down," Jake demanded.

"Shhh," Austin gestured, "Remember where we are. It's nine against three."

"It's ten against three," Jake corrected him.

"Not any more," Austin replied.

"Drop your gun," Jake again demanded.

"I just want my daughter. Then you can take me in, but I'm not giving up until she's safe," Austin said.

Jake stood firm.

I stepped between them. Austin could have killed me if he'd wanted to, but I knew he wouldn't. He just wanted his daughter. I imagined if I had kids I'd be in the same desperate position.

"You agree to turn yourself in once it's over?" I asked him.

"Agreed," Austin replied without hesitation.

"He's ok, Jake. He wants what we want. Lower the gun, Jake."

Jake obliged.

"Do you know where they went?" Jake asked.

"No, only that they ran that way," Austin said, pointing down past the third arch.

We took two steps towards the third tunnel. Both Jake and I looked at the barrels in the corner. "Do you know what's in the barrels?" Jake asked.

"Body parts," Austin replied. Then he said, "Let me go first. I'll distract them. Buy you some time to search the residence. In about five minutes you follow, just find Mikayla and anyone else who may be up there."

Jake and I looked at each other and Jake said, "Sounds like a plan. Yell out if you need help."

Chapter 115

Igor was shocked. Who would be waging war on his business if it wasn't the Priest? Maybe a rival, but he couldn't think of anyone who would be so bold and direct.

"Make sure the house is secure," he ordered.

Shevd buzzed Alexi on the intercom. "The police are here. Only the two from Victoria from what I can see. They just crossed the back paddock and headed into the tunnel."

Alexi looked at Igor for a reaction.

"Kill them," Igor said. "Maybe they're in on it with Mike. Maybe the police want to take over the operation." It wouldn't be the first time the police have run a crime syndicate, Igor thought.

Alexi buzzed back. "Igor said shoot them all!"

"Yes, boss," came the reply through the intercom.

Igor asked Alexi, "Where's Andrei? Is he back from burying the fat Joker yet?"

"No, boss," Alexi answered.

"Get him back here now!" Igor demanded.

Alexi nodded. "Will do, boss."

He went to leave but Igor stopped him. "Alexi, wait." Alexei turned to face Igor. "Bring the new girl to me," Igor said.

"Yes, boss."

When Alexi returned, he had Mikayla by the hair. Igor could still hear Chloe screaming in the other room.

He was about to tell Alexi to go and shut her up, but then he thought better of it.

"Why don't you use that noisy bitch as bait?" he suggested. "When the cops come to get her, they'll come face to face with you."

"Good idea," Alexi replied, "I'll tie her to the bed and wait in the bathroom for them."

Alexi left Igor with Mikayla sitting in his room. As he left, he said, "I'll be back when it's over."

He headed in the darkness towards Chloe's room.

Chloe and Mikayla had been sitting together in the room, trying to understand what the commotion was down the hall, but with the thunderstorm raging, they could only catch bits and pieces. When Alexi barged in and took Mikayla, it was totally unexpected. Chloe had seized her opportunity and sprinted for the door, only to get yanked back into the room by her ankles. Alexi then grabbed her by the foot so she was hanging by one leg and then flung her across the bed where she landed in the far corner of the room, collecting the lamp and cutting her leg on the bedside table as she hit the floor.

She watched as Alexi took Mikayla from the room. She was being sent to Igor; there was no doubt about it.

She was still sprawled in the corner when Alexi returned a few minutes later. He had a length of rope in one hand. With the other, he dragged her out of the corner by the hair and slammed her down onto the floor. He quickly tied her hands and feet together using the rope. He left Chloe's mouth untaped.

Send them to me, he thought as he left the room. He entered the bathroom from the adjoining room, Mikayla's, and waited.

Send them to me, he repeated.

Chapter 116

Austin followed their flashlights to the arches and after leaving the detectives, he came to a second T-intersection where one tunnel veered off to the left and one to the right. Or he could go straight ahead.

This was a labyrinth, he thought, and he felt like a little mouse being tested.

He decided to go straight ahead but eventually, after passing a tunnel to his right, he came to a dead end. He turned around and returned to the tunnel leading right. Within 20 metres, he came to a flight of steps heading up to a door.

He stood at the bottom of the steps, thinking. They would be waiting on the other side of the door. He inspected it. The door swung left to right, so he expected whoever was waiting for him would most likely be waiting in the corner. He thought about trying to draw them out, but didn't think they would be stupid enough to make the same mistake twice.

He had wasted enough time. He had stormed many houses. This was no different. He removed his SIG p228s, one in each hand, and fired four shots in quick succession. The door shattered and the hinges flew off and landed somewhere on the stairs above him.

No one returned his fire, so he slowly ascended the steps. About half-way up, he knelt down. Now he would see if they were lying in wait. Austin re-holstered his handguns and removed the rifle from his shoulder. He aimed the sight of the rifle to the bullet hole in the door, hoping to get a glimpse of the other side, using every centimetre of voyeuristic vision available into the library. He caught sight of a man down on one knee, gun pointed at the door. The man looked prepared and calm. Waiting.

He was about to pull the trigger when the man caught a glint of light on the scope and hit the floor. Austin guessed he had moved to the other corner.

He moved up the stairs, drew both his guns again and kicked hard at the door. As soon as his boot left the door, he opened fire.

Vonkov was a loyal member of Igor's private security team. He had been sitting in the library waiting for whoever was on the other side of the door to show themselves. Then he would quickly erase the problem. He almost shat his pants when four shots were fired through the door, the last missing his neck by centimetres. He had expected someone to walk through the door, not shoot through it. He was the one who was supposed to be doing the shooting.

After the shots, he steadied himself; now they would step through. But they didn't. He looked at the hole in the bottom of the door. He couldn't see anyone, but thought he caught a glimmer of reflecting light, from a rifle scope he thought. Dropping down, he crawled to the other side of the library.

And waited.

No one came.

He waited a bit longer.

Where the fuck is this guy? Vonkov wondered.

Without warning, the library door was blasted open and it crashed to the floor. In the darkness, he didn't realise that the hinges had gone.

Vonkov fired several shots from his nine-mil Beretta.

Austin fired twice and dived against the stone wall at the top of the stairs. A bullet skimmed his leg; another flew over his head and ricocheted down into the dark labyrinth of tunnels.

He took a breath, his back as far up against the wall as possible. In the library, he could see parts of the shattered door on the floor, but no waiting gunman. He stuck his head out a little further; no fire came.

He peeked even further and saw a man dragging himself across the floor, leaving a trail of blood behind him. The shooter. Austin had hit him twice. He stepped into the library, approached the crawling gunman and fired once more. It was direct hit at close range and it shattered the man's skull.

Austin stepped over the body in the library doorway and headed down the hall. He had only taken a few steps towards the back of the house when the front door opened and another security guy charged in, firing as he entered.

* * *

We'd only been waiting three minutes when we heard the exchange of gunfire. Jake reacted instantly. By the light of his torch, he located the steps at the end of the right tunnel. I stayed a few metres behind him.

Jake crept forward up the steps, pistol drawn standard style, in a thumbs over thumbs, fingers over fingers grip. As he entered the library, he swept the room with his arms out, finger on the trigger ready to shoot. There was a body on the floor in the doorway.

Jake saw a man run through the front door and fire at someone he couldn't see. Before he could pull the trigger, the man flew backwards through the door. Jake continued to creep forwards towards the entrance hall, poking his head to see beyond the library doorway to look down the hall. Austin was crouched in the alcove under the stairs reloading his gun.

"Seven to go," Austin said.

Jake nodded.

"You go upstairs; I'll clear down here," Austin said.

Jake nodded again and waved me over to him. I had planted myself at the top of the cellar stairs into the library.

"We're going upstairs. If we find any kids, I want you to take them to the forest. Then just lay low, you got that?"

"Yes," I replied.

As we headed upstairs, more gunfire rang out as Austin made his way through the home. I kept checking behind us. None of Austin's combatants came running up the stairs after us.

We came upon three doors, two on the left, the other at the far end of the hall. The first door on the left was about three metres before the second door and four and a bit metres to the door at the end of the hall.

Jake opened the door. A girl was lying on the floor with her hands and feet bound and tied together. Jake picked her up and passed her to me. "What's you name?" he asked gently.

"Chloe," she said.

"Go," Jake said to me.

I took her and ran. Past the body at the library entrance, back down the stairs to the tunnel, my torch bobbing around. A cold wind swept up the tunnels. The girl clung to me tightly. Even though it was dark outside, as we neared the end of the pitch-black tunnels, the entrance became visible under the night sky.

* * *

Jake didn't realise he was in danger when he handed the child to Brodie. Out of nowhere, a wire came from behind him and pulled tight on his throat. He managed to slip his free hand under the wire to prevent it from choking him. Not many people were as solid as Jake, and very few were bigger, but without even seeing his attacker, he knew he was in trouble when he was lifted off the ground.

The only advantage Jake had was his attacker was using both hands. Jake still had his gun in his right. He reached around and fired the gun under his left armpit, hoping to hit him in the body.

His assailant only choked him tighter. Jake threw himself backwards against him, hoping to get some relief from the strangulation, but this only angered his attacker.

Jake fired again. This time, the big guy cried out in anguish. I hit him! Jake thought.

He fired again, and again, and the big guy groaned in pain and dropped the wire to the floor. Jake stepped away, turned, and aimed at the big guy who was several centimetres taller than he was. Even with three bullet holes in his left side, the big guy made a run at him. Jake only managed to fire one more shot before he was picked up off the floor and slammed into the wall next to the open door. His gun went flying as his hand clipped the door on the way through, the plaster from the wall crumbling around him. He felt blood trickle down the side of his head.

How's this guy still going? Jake thought. I've shot him four times! The man slammed him into the wall again and he couldn't help but think he reminded him of the Hulk.

The big guy's hands were around Jake's throat again, lifting him off the ground. Jake kicked, but because both his feet were off the ground, he couldn't get any traction.

Using what he had with the odds against him, he fought dirty, reaching out and plunging his thumbs into his eyes. The big guy released his hold and as soon as Jake's feet hit the floor, he ran at him with his shoulder and sent him crashing to the floor. He was down for the count, Jake thought. He turned to retrieve his gun from the doorway floor when Austin came into view. Jake smiled at him but Austin yelled, "Down!" Jake hit the floor and Austin fired his own pistol three times before Austin himself was hurled backwards onto the hall floor.

Jake turned. All three shots had hit their mark and the big guy was finally silenced.

Jake checked on Austin. There was no blood; the bullets had hit his vest.

"Fuck, that hurt," Austin said.

"Stay down for a few seconds, regain your breath," Jake advised.

"I think I might have a couple of broken ribs," Austin replied.

"You killed the big guy, if it's any consolation," Jake replied. "We found a girl. Chloe. Brodie's taken her to safety."

"Fantastic. Now let's go find Mikayla and the fucker behind all this," Austin said.

Chapter 117

Shevd had watched the cop run from the tunnel, carrying one of the girls, all hero-like.

Soon he would want to return to the thick of the action. Soon he would want to go back in. Soon he would hear the sound of the gun, and before he could react he would be dead.

Shevd hadn't taken his eye from his scope in minutes. He wanted to see the cop's face when he killed him. All he had to do was wait for him to reappear.

His breathing was steady, his eye focused on the target, his finger relaxed and ready. Even in the heavy rain, he found him. The cop's shoe was sticking out from the base of the tree. He had placed the girl out of danger. Now, Shevd just needed to wait for him to run.

It reminded him of when he was shooting deer as a kid in the Ukraine. "Be quiet and patient," his father would say, "the deer will hear the slightest noise." The deer never knew it was about to be killed. It would be at a stream drinking and then the shot would echo through the forest, but before the deer could react to the sound, it would fall to the ground.

The cop was as helpless as the deer.

I'll get you, Shevd thought.

* * *

The storm had ramped up and it was raining so hard, it felt like hail. I was struggling to see more than a few metres in front of me. The girl bounced in my arms as I ran. We made it to the forest edge and I was hit by the smell of forest freshness and rain. The air was fragrant with the smell of pine trees. Christmas would be here soon, I thought.

The large pine provided Chloe with plenty of cover from the storm. I untied her and covered her with my jacket. "You will be safe here," I said.

She sat silently, curled up into a ball.

In the distance I could hear not only gunfire, but voices, loud voices, yelling. There were more children here somewhere, but how many perpetrators were left? The only thing we knew for sure was that we had found the spider's nest. I looked at the base of the tree. They were hell-bent on getting out of here. They were not planning on giving up. There was no jail for them. They knew it was death for them if they couldn't escape.

"Mikayla, you need to go back for Mikayla," Chloe said, quivering with the cold.

I knew there were more kids and I had to go back. I couldn't leave Jake. I had to go back. I had to do my job. I had to help. I would never forgive myself if something happened to Mikayla or Jake.

The thought of the tunnels terrified me, the smell of death; it was the cabin all over again, the fear of the unknown and the darkness, the fear of death. I pushed the fear aside and took a deep breath to steady myself. The smell of the pines once again made its presence felt. It was a beautiful smell and I took in as much oxygen as possible ready for the sprint to the tunnels.

I darted out from the tree. I had taken three steps before an ear-piercing crack echoed through the night.

Chapter 118

As Austin and Jake stood in the hall staring at the door at the end, an ear-piercing crack echoed above them.

"That was a sniper rifle," Austin said immediately. "There's a shooter in the attic."

Jake's thoughts immediately turned to Brodie and a chill ran down his spine. He had to push the thought out of his head and focus on what he had to do now.

"How can I get up into the roof?" he asked Austin.

"There might be alternative access from the laundry room downstairs," Austin suggested, "rather than the stairs the shooter will have taken to get up there."

"You read my mind," Jake replied.

He rushed downstairs towards the laundry room, seeing two bodies sprawled one on top of each other. By his calculation, there were four criminals left.

As he entered the laundry, he revised his count to three. There was another body, gun still in hand, his torch on. A single gunshot wound to the head had ended his resistance. Jake reached up, pulled the cord for the ladder and brought it down as quietly as possible. Whoever's up there will be expecting me, he thought.

He climbed the ladder slowly and quietly and peeked through the opening. Seeing no one, he shone his torch into the darkness. A blanket and a rifle lay in front of the lever window. The room seemed empty and there was no sign of the shooter.

Jake moved further into the roof cavity to get a better look. He had his gun just in front of his face ready to discharge at the slightest movement. Before he had moved another step, the shooter rushed out of the darkness. The silver glint of the gun caught Jake's immediate attention. His reflexes lightning fast, faster than he or his attacker could possibly imagine, Jake managed to knock the attacker's arm down and when the gun discharged, the bullet only grazed his already injured thigh. Before his attacker could get a second shot off, Jake slammed the attacker's arm hard against the timber beam, sending the weapon flying into the darkness. His attacker quickly resorted to equalling the odds by kicking Jake's hand hard and sending the pistol flying into a corner.

Jake was yanked up by his throat. "I just killed your mate. You're next." The man was big, although not as big as the brute who had almost killed him in the girl's room. He was about Jake's size. Jake didn't know if he had the fitness to go toe to toe again. It didn't seem he had much choice.

The man was punching him hard in the kidneys.

"Your partner didn't even know what was coming. The look of surprise on his face, it was so exciting, but so short. He died quickly." He sounded disappointed that Brodie hadn't suffered more.

* * *

Andrei had just finished burying the fat Joker when he heard gunfire coming from the homestead. He headed back immediately, stumbling across a black Chrysler dumped in the woods and noticing a bonfire in one of the paddocks. Unwelcome guests.

He saw Shevd nail one of them as he was running for the homestead.

Andrei had survived four wars and had killed a great many people, but one thing he never did was put himself in a position where he might get caught in the crossfire. He wasn't about to start now.

He waited patiently in the dark forest. He was going to see how this played out before he went in guns blazing. Shevd was a nutcase with an itchy trigger finger. He wasn't going to test his loyalty by running across the open paddock too.

* * *

Austin was standing outside the door at the end of the hall.

He knew his daughter was on the other side. He didn't know how he knew, he just did. Parental instinct. He approached the door handle, taking it lightly in his fingertips. His arm was outstretched to protect his body from attack through the door.

He turned the handle and swung the door inwards. His daughter was standing there, in nothing but a t-shirt and undies. She was crying.

Igor was sitting on the bed behind her with a knife to her throat.

"Daddy," Mikayla sniffled.

"Well, didn't I pick the right hostage! Looks like I have the advantage," Igor said.

"Alexi! I have him!" Igor called.

"If you're looking for the big guy, he's busy trying to put his brains back inside his skull," Austin said calmly.

"How about you drop your weapon, or I'll cut her open from ear to ear," Igor said menacingly.

The knife was pressing against her soft delicate skin. The slightest movement from the little man behind her would cut her throat. Austin couldn't risk shooting him. He knew he would hit him, but the chance he might slit her throat as he fell backwards was too great.

"Why don't you be a man and face me without using a child as a shield," Austin said quietly.

"I don't think that would be very good strategically for me right now," Igor replied.

"Should have expected it, all you Russians are cowards," Austin said.

"I am Ukrainian," Igor replied proudly.

"Even worse. At least the Russians have pride. You guys don't know the meaning of the word." Austin was trying to get him riled up.

"No, we are just not stupid. I do not need to fight you. I have your daughter. Why waste my energy? Why give up my advantage? I think it's time you put the gun down or I kill her, now," Igor growled. "I was just leaving."

He stood up. He was only about five foot five and of slight build.

"I'm not going to let you leave with my daughter," Austin said calmly.

"I don't think you really have a choice," Igor said.

"You know, if you flee, I will find you."

"Maybe, but will she still be alive when you do?" Igor taunted.

He manoeuvred Mikayla towards the door, the knife still pressed tight against her throat. Then he exited the room and backed up the hall.

The fight upstairs continued and then a loud bang was followed by a crash and Jake and Shevd came crashing through the celling and bouncing off the kitchen bench to land on the tiles below. Austin spun around and saw that neither man seemed to be winning.

"Looks like your cop friend is in trouble," Igor said, "what are you going to do, help him, or save your daughter?" he mocked.

Austin owed Jake no favours, but he had done the math; if Jake died, the man he was fighting would set his sights on him, and then it would be two against one. He could kill the guy easily but then it would provide the little man with the opportunity to slip away. Where would he go? To the helicopter? The woods? The tunnels? Probably the helicopter, with his daughter as insurance.

Whichever option he chose, Igor would still have Mikayla. He would still have the advantage.

He had to decide quickly.

"It'll be ok, sweetie, I'll see you again soon," he called to the retreating figure of his daughter.

He turned his back on her then, the hardest thing he had ever had to do, and jumped the railing, landing just outside the kitchen. Out of the corner of his eye, he saw Igor lead his daughter through the library and into the tunnel.

What Austin had decided to do was the only way to get her out alive, he persuaded himself. He would save Jake and then he would save his daughter.

He heard Mikayla scream, "No Daddy! Don't leave, don't let him take me!"

The words hurt more than any wound he had ever suffered, but it was the only way out.

He entered the kitchen to see Jake backed up against the oven, his attacker about to run him through with a knife.

He rushed up behind him. No hesitation, no time to waste. He took the hand holding the knife and twisted it back on itself, at the same time grabbing the attacker's head with his other hand and ramming it into the glass range hood. Shards of glass pierced the man's forehead and smashed to the floor. Jake grasped a large fragment and rammed it into his opponent's inner thigh. Blood sprayed from the gash.

The man didn't stand a chance.

Austin rammed his elbow down hard on his extended arm, breaking it. The man screamed in pain.

Jake took advantage of his freedom and scrambled towards his service pistol, which was lying several metres away on the floor. He was about to issue his standard call, "Freeze!" But he was too late. Austin had taken the kitchen knife from the man's hand and slammed it into his neck. The shooter fell to the floor. Blood flowed onto the floor as if from a leaking tap.

"I'm going after Mikayla!" Austin panted. "Take my rifle and go up to the attic. If you get a clear shot, take it. He'll be focusing on me, not you. Whatever happens, don't let him board that helicopter!" He moved quickly through the library and into the tunnels.

Jake moved a lot slower, having sustained two beatings, a cracked rib and damage to his leg. He collected the rifle, headed to the laundry and climbed the ladder back into the attic. There was a huge hole where he and the shooter had fallen through. He had to make sure that when he jumped, he landed on a beam so that he didn't fall through the celling again.

He jumped and for a split second, thought he had overshot it. But he landed on the beam like an Olympic gymnast.

He removed the gun from his shoulder holster and laid it on the window ledge. He looked through the scope of Austin's rifle and saw Igor running towards the woods away from the homestead. The helicopter was in Jake's line of sight and because he couldn't tell which option of escape Igor had chosen, he decided to eliminate one for him.

He fired several shots into the windscreen of the helicopter and then three more into the motor. It was a good choice. Igor veered away from the helicopter and the incoming bullets and headed into the forest instead, dragging Mikayla closer to him to prevent any chance of being picked off.

Jake aligned the sight, hoping for a clear shot. But he couldn't risk it. Mikayla was too close; he might hit her.

He watched as Igor continued running with Mikayla.

Then he saw Austin appear from the tunnel and run after them.

Unable to get a clear shot, he knew his best course of action was to go and help Austin. He gathered Austin's rifle and by the time he had exited the tunnels, the three of them had disappeared into the woods.

Jake was struggling to run. He reached the spot where Brodie was lying, then paused and checked his pulse. It was weak but it was still present.

He raced over to the helicopter as fast as his gimpy leg would carry him and called for backup and an ambulance. He chanced another look over at Brodie but he had to hurry. He had to catch up with Igor and Mikayla.

Scrambling through the fence, he headed into the woods in pursuit. The terrain was tough going on his injured leg but he pushed on regardless. He couldn't see them. It was too dark. Then he saw what looked like the outline of a rocky ridge away on the horizon. Maybe they were headed there?

He sat on a nearby log to gather himself, placing Austin's rifle at his side. How could he have forgotten the scope? He picked it up again and placed the scope against his eye, scanning the ridge. Austin was manoeuvring between the trees. Jake scanned ahead of Austin. There they were! Igor was holding a gun in his right hand—he must have collected it on his escape—and with his left, he was still holding tightly onto Mikayla.

It looked like Igor was running out of ground to retreat to. Soon, the woods hit the water catchment. Surely he wasn't planning on swimming across it? A stand-off was imminent.

Jake lay down on the ground, checked his mag; two rounds left. Good, he thought, I only need one shot. He rested his check against the butt and kept his eye focused against the scope.

He was waiting for the prime shot. He couldn't risk Mikayla getting injured.

* * *

Austin was within striking distance.

"There's nowhere else to run, little man. It's over," Austin said.

Igor spun around and faced Austin, his gun against Mikayla's temple.

"I guess you're right. Neither of us wins," Igor said.

"You win this time, boss," said a strange voice out of the darkness.

Austin twisted to his right.

A tall man stood in the shadows, his gun pointed at Austin's head.

"Andrei, kill him."

Where had this guy come from? Austin wondered. He thought he had killed them all.

No time for debate.

Austin reacted by aiming his gun at Andrei rather than at Igor.

Andrei hesitated.

"Just shoot him!" Igor ordered.

"Shoot!"

* * *

Jake didn't see the other man until Austin spun around and pointed his gun at him.

Without missing a beat, Jake squeezed the trigger.

A loud crack broke through the night air. He watched through the scope as Igor's head whiplashed backwards. Then he adjusted the scope over to the other man. Before Jake could set his sight on the mystery man, three more shots rang out.

Jake lost sight of Austin.

When he finally saw the mystery man, he was coming straight towards him and he had to duck for cover. The man was firing continually.

Jake had only one shot left.

He took cover behind a tree. Three more shots rang out. One passed his nose. One just missed his back. He stole a look around the tree. The man was now about seven metres away and gaining.

The mystery man continued his movement towards Jake, continually firing.

Bullets kept thudding into the tree at Jake's back. Others flew near his face.

Jake was pinned down.

Between shots, Jake stole another look. The man was closer; too close to use the scope now.

Then he heard footsteps.

He risked another glance.

The man was out in the open. He had to act now.

He could hear the man pause in his advance, planning his next move.

Jake aimed quickly with his naked eye and fired.

His aim was true and the bullet pierced the man's chest just left of centre. He dropped to the forest floor instantly.

Jake looked through the scope again. He could see both Austin and Mikayla on the ground. Austin was still but Mikayla looked as if she was moving.

He headed up the hill. He didn't know how much longer he could stand up.

Reaching them, he saw that Mikayla was pinned under her father. He knelt down beside them.

"He shot my dad," Mikayla cried.

Jake rolled him off his daughter and felt for a pulse. There was a strong one.

"Austin!" Jake called.

Jake rolled him back over and lifted up his shirt. Three bullets were buried in the back of his bulletproof vest. He had dived in front of his daughter to prevent her from getting hit.

Without his vest he'd be dead.

Austin came to with a deep breath and a sigh of anguish.

"You better get out of here," Jake said.

"I thought you were going to arrest me," Austin replied.

"I never saw you take the car. Dump it. Find a hotel. I'll look after Mikayla until tomorrow. I have your number. I'll call you to come and collect her. You were never here."

"Thank you," Austin said.

"Are the guns registered?" Jake asked.

"No, they're ghosts."

"Then leave them," Jake said.

Austin whispered into Mikayla's ear, gave her a hug and a kiss and then disappeared into the dense brush.

Jake took Mikayla by the hand and headed back towards Brodie. Chloe was still under the tree where Brodie had left her and as Mikayla approached her, she ran to Chloe and they hugged and cried. Then they all sat next to Brodie and waited for help to arrive.

Chapter 119

They say you can smell your death before it happens. It's true. From the moment I stepped out from behind that tree, the smell of the pine forest and Christmas had disappeared, replaced by an impending sense of doom. I ignored the fear and just kept on going towards the tunnels. But the fear came on stronger than before, like a warning.

When I took my next step, I heard an earth-shattering crack.

I felt the burning sensation in my chest immediately, and even though my heart hadn't stopped, I could feel my slow demise and my body beginning to go cold.

I died there that Sunday morning in the pouring rain, staring face-up at the thunderous sky. For the last few minutes of my life, the feeling of doom was replaced by an overwhelming sense of calm.

Once your body dies, your soul disconnects and for the first few minutes, you watch over your body and see the events around you. I saw the gun battle play out in the woods between the four men. I saw Austin dive in front of three bullets to protect Mikayla. I saw Jake come perilously close to joining me in the heavens.

Then I saw something unexpected.

Jake letting Austin go.

Maybe Jake realised Austin would have done the same thing for him.

I watched Jake return to my side and kneel down, crying. He was angry, sad and guilt-ridden all at the same time. I just wanted to tell him I was ok, and not to worry.

But I would never be able to tell him anything ever again.

By the time the paramedics arrived, I could see their efforts were futile, yet they didn't give up.

Jake rode with me to the hospital.

The paramedics continued working on me all the way to the Sydney Royal Prince Alfred Hospital.

They revived me once in emergency before sending me to the operating theatre, where they put me on by-pass while they tried to work their magic. It didn't seem to help. I died again in ICU. Again, they revived me. I doubted it would last.

Then a voice called to me from . . . well, I don't know exactly where from, but wherever they were calling from it was all white. It wasn't heaven, it was the in-between. A place you go when you're stuck. Although I didn't think I was stuck; I thought it was pretty clear that I was dead but for some reason, I had to stay in the white.

"They need you," a voice called out to me.

It was the voice of a young boy. I did not recognise it.

* * *

Jake sat in the waiting room, waiting to speak with the doctors. He had seen gunshot victims before. He knew the likely outcome. Brodie was cold when he finally got back to him and he had no pulse.

"Detective Miller, we've managed to repair the damage done by the bullet," the surgeon told him. "Your friend was lucky. Had the bullet been a couple of centimetres lower, we wouldn't have been able to repair the injury. I won't lie to you; his chances are slim and his heart has undergone incredible trauma. Since the operation, he's flat-lined and we've revived him. His brain was without oxygen for a long time, so even if he does survive I doubt he'll ever be the same." He paused and looked at Jake. "Right now, he's under heavy sedation and the next 48 hours are critical."

Hayley arrived at Sydney airport. Jake had checked them into the Hilton Hotel, knowing they would be there for several days, possibly weeks. Monique needed Jake to go over the crime scene with her. He was the only adult survivor.

The only one who had made it out.

Monique had asked him some questions over the phone. "Internal Affairs are going to want to know why you were still there. Why were you staking out the house, when the search turned up nothing? What made you go in and who started the shooting? How did the Priest end up there?"

All tough questions, when he was trying not to involve Austin in any of the answers.

Given the circumstances, Monique was agreeable to him writing out his statements of events over the next 24 hours and going through it with her initially, and then later with Internal Affairs when they did their review.

When Monique arrived at the hospital the next day, and once she had read Jake's statement, they commenced the official interview. Internal Affairs would come after Homicide had completed their enquiries. Monique had other officers with her although she was the only one who asked the questions. Jake thought it was out of consideration for him. He was sure she was cutting him a little slack.

"I have a few concerns over some inconsistencies," Monique began. "You say while you were staking out the home, the first you knew of any unusual activity was when the Priest was set alight?"

"Correct," Jake replied.

"I take it you assumed he was delivered by one of Igor's men. Do you have any way of confirming this assumption?"

"No," Jake replied.

"You say you believe this employee of Igor's killed the Judge and the superintendent. That's another assumption, I take it?" Monique asked.

"Yes," Jake said. "It was one of them."

"And now they're all dead," Monique stated.

Jake was answering her questions in a semi-comatose state with only one real concern: Brodie.

"We also found a man in the tunnels with his throat cut. Do you know anything about this?"

For the first time, Jake didn't know, and that was the best answer he could give. "I never knew about him. Maybe they thought he had tipped us off?"

"There was a SIG p228 used, which is a really unusual gun, used only in the military. Any idea where this came from?" Monique asked.

"I don't know, there were a lot of weapons lying around. I think I picked it up off the floor after I was thrown through the ceiling. Monique, I know it's a mess, but we just busted the biggest crime gang in Australia! They kidnapped children, lending them out to paedophiles and then selling them overseas. And you're asking me about a pistol?"

He stood up and took a deep breath. "I was going to leave this until everything had settled down, but I'm leaving the force. I already told Brodie. He asked me to stay on until we'd solved the kidnappings. I gave him until the end of the year."

"Jake, don't overreact, we're just finalising the statement." She frowned. "We've done this many times before."

Jake placed his badge and his pistol on the table. "It's not about the questions. I've made my decision. You have my statement; I can't offer you any answers other than what I've already told you. I did what I had to do to save those girls. So did Brodie."

"I can't get you to change your mind?" Monique asked.

"No." He began to walk away when Monique called after him.

"I thought you might like to know that we found Igor's number in Hutchinson's phone. That crooked detective contacted him twice that day, a phone call before you arrived and a text just minutes after you called him to say you were going home. So for the record, you were right." Monique was smiling.

Jake paused. It mattered little now.

"Internal Affairs will want to question you as part of their investigation so expect to answer more questions when you return to Melbourne," she reminded him.

He left the interview room and headed back to Brodie's bedside in ICU. Hayley was there waiting for him with a fresh coffee.

Jake told her he had quit the force. She knew it had been coming, but they'd only had one discussion about it. Now was not the time to discuss it further.

Jake just sat there staring at Brodie. One thought ran through his mind.

I should have given him the vest.

Chapter 120

I was still in the in-between. The boy who had called me stood before me fully clothed but soaking wet. I looked at him and he smiled at me.

"I was told I had to wait for you," he said.

"Why?"

"The girl asked me to tell you they need your help."

"What girl?" I asked.

"The dead one. The one from Picton Town. He's still out there, you know."

"Who's still out there?" I asked.

"The Hat Man," he said.

"How can I do anything about it? I'm dead."

"You need to wake up. You need to go to her" he repeated. He pointed to the white door behind me. "She is waiting for you in there."

"Why are you here?"

"I drowned." He pointed to a hospital bed below mine. The floor had disappeared and it was like looking through glass.

"They think I fell in but I was pushed. Josh pushed me."

I looked through the floor again and could see the accident happen, as if someone was showing me a live replay. The boy was trapped under the pool cover and he couldn't get out.

I watched as he was rushed to hospital. I could see his parents' bedside vigil. I could see the doctors and nurses. I could hear the conversations. I could see Hayley. I had heard about this boy; this was Ryan. Jake had told me all about him.

"You need to go back. Your parents are waiting; your room is waiting for you back home."

He looked at me. "Help the girl, she is waiting," he repeated.

"I will, if you go back."

He hugged me. Then he vanished.

Chapter 121

2 Weeks Later

I had been transferred from Sydney to The Alfred Hospital in Melbourne. I was still trapped in the in-between. I watched Jake from above. He was having trouble coping with everything that had happened but he had done the one thing I least expected, covered for Austin.

I watched as Austin took Mikayla to visit her mother's grave for the first time since they were reunited. They walked hand in hand, down the stone path towards the large oak that overhung her plot.

Mikayla started to cry as soon as she read her mother's name on the headstone.

She drew closer to her father.

"It's ok honey, this is a good place full of Mummy's love. Why don't you go and replace the flowers, she would like that," Austin said.

"Will you come with me?" Mikayla asked, still a little scared.

"Yes of course, we will do it together," Austin replied

Mikayla removed the old flowers and handed them to her dad. They weren't dead but they were starting to wilt.

"Do you think Mummy knows we're here?" Mikayla asked.

"Yes, I think she watches us from above and if you talk to her she can hear you," Austin replied.

"Can she answer us back?" Mikayla asked, looking up at Austin.

"Not by talking, but sometimes if you look carefully she will send you a sign to say she has heard you." Austin rubbed her back and put his arm around her shoulder.

Austin looked back up the path to see a face he didn't expect to see, not here anyway. Jake stood atop the hill waiting.

"Honey, I need to go talk to Jake. You remember Jake, from the house?"

"Of course Daddy. He helped save me."

"Why don't you stay here and talk to Mummy for a minute. Would you be ok to do that?"

Mikayla nodded.

Austin walked towards Jake.

"I didn't mean to interrupt," Jake apologised.

"It's ok, what can I do for you?" Austin replied.

"Just wanted to let you know, Homicide have come to the conclusion that the Judge and Mike were killed as part of a turf war between the Priest and the Monster and Beau, all ending at the Monster's residence.

"Homicide believe Beau may have been the mystery man that set the Priest alight and began a one-man war against the Monster. They have located his van dumped in nearby bushland but are yet to locate him," Jake finished.

"Why didn't you arrest me? You don't owe me anything. I wouldn't have resisted once Mikayla was safe," Austin said.

"She needs you. She's been through so much; she can't lose you as well as her mum. Sometimes the good guys need to win." Jake smiled.

"Thank you," Austin replied. "So they won't be looking for me anymore?"

"They never were. Homicide has closed the case," Jake replied. "Even Internal Affairs have closed their case on me," he added.

"I heard that you quit the force? What you going to do with yourself now?" Austin asked.

"Private detective, no politics, better pay. There's plenty of work if you want to join me. You'll need to pay the bills somehow," Jake replied.

"Thanks for the offer but I need to be with Mikayla right now. She's very traumatised," Austin said.

"I understand. You have my number if you ever need anything," Jake replied. He turned to leave.

"Jake, how are the other kids?" Austin asked.

Jake turned back, "They're doing ok, going through counselling, but the main thing is they are home with their parents and they're alive because of you." Then he turned and left.

Austin stood and watched Mikayla who was still deep in conversation with her mother. She had taken up a seat on the lawn next to her mother's resting place. Austin had no idea what she would be talking about, but he was glad she was talking to her. It must be doing her good, he thought.

"I'm sorry Mummy, I wish I could have stopped him. I hope you can hear me. I want you to know how much I love you and how much I will miss you. I will get Daddy to bring me here as much as possible, so I can talk to you."

* * *

From the in-between, I watched Mikayla continue her conversation with her mother.

It was a heart-warming one-way conversation. Then out of the darkness, a beautiful lady appeared at my side. A lady I had only met once before, when I'd inspected her dead body in her house.

"Sarah?" I asked.

"Yes, Detective."

"But you're dead?"

"Yes, but you can always come back to the in-between to watch over people. It's once you cross over you can't go back to the land of the living."

"So am I dead?" I asked.

"No, you haven't crossed yet," Sarah replied. "You have more people to help. You need to go back, but first you need to talk to the girl you promised you would help. Remember?" She pointed to the white door behind me.

It looked ominous.

"I will," I replied.

"Thank you for saving Mikayla," she said.

"Anytime," I replied.

Sarah clasped her thumbs together to form her hands into wings. I watched as a red, blue and green Rosella appeared next to Mikalya. It landed right at her feet. It wasn't frightened, it didn't fly off, it hopped up onto her leg and just sat there.

It didn't chirp or flutter around, it was very still and quiet, perched on Mikayla's leg staring at her as if it didn't have a care in the world.

"How did you do that?" I asked.

"You can do a lot of things from the in-between," Sarah replied.

"You need to save some others," Sarah repeated, "you need to go back."

Then as quickly as she appeared, she was gone.

* * *

For the first time since Sarah's death, Austin stepped foot inside his home.

Sarah's parents had made sure the property no longer had any traces of the tragedy that had occurred there.

"We don't have to live here anymore if you don't want to," Austin said, as they opened the front door together.

"I don't know if I will be able to, Daddy," Mikayla replied.

"How about you go to your room, pack your favourite things and we'll go to Grandma and Pops?"

Mikayla agreed and headed to her room.

She sat on her bed and looked at her photos, her posters, some of bands, some of friends, some of her mum and dad. She thought of Chloe and hoped she was ok. She opened the curtains to let some afternoon sun into her room. Sitting on the brick windowsill was the Rosella from the cemetery. Instantly, Mikalya ran to the doorway and called her dad.

Fearing she was in shock of some kind, he bounded the stairs two at a time.

"Honey, what's wrong?"

"It's the Rosella from the cemetery, it's here. Do you think Mummy sent it?"

It did look remarkably similar to the one they'd seen at the cemetery. "How do you know it's the same one?" Austin asked.

"Its eye has yellow around it, see?" She pointed to the left eye.

"So it does," Austin said. "Maybe Mummy sent it to tell you she is ok."

"I think I will be ok to stay here, Daddy. Mummy is here with us."

"Ok, let me know if you change your mind." Austin left her to settle in.

* * *

I turned away from the room below me and focused on the mystery door. The door itself was solid white, but the glow from underneath was a bright red and it filled me with an immense fear.

Epilogue

James Mitchell had only been released for two days. He couldn't believe his cousin Ian had died. He'd been shot, apparently in a bad drug deal along with his lover Bill. But James didn't believe it. He believed the cops had killed them both.

Ian had warned him that if anything happened to him, the police would be involved. It looked as if he was right.

James sat on the couch at home alone, watching the idiot box, flicking from channel to channel. He paused on the special report of the Pavlychko crime operation. It had all come crashing down due to the investigative skills of Detectives Brodie Foxx and Jake Miller. The scroll across the bottom read that Detective Foxx was in a critical condition in hospital after Australia's largest paedophile ring had been busted. Ten had died in the police shootout. The scroll continued. The Restart program funded by Palanok and overseen by Justice Aaron had been a front for the Pavlychko crime operation.

As the news report continued, it became apparent to James that it was biased in favour of the police.

Arrogant bastards.

The news detailed how suburban paedophiles had been buying children from the ring run by the Pavlychko company. Photos of the three dead paedophiles were shown, including his recently deceased cousin Ian.

James shook his head in disgust. He hadn't had any kids with him, he was being used to make the police look better. James decided the police needed to be taken down a peg or two, they needed to be held accountable for the error of their ways. They were a deceitful organisation, and he would bring them to their knees.

Starting with Miller. Miller would find out what it was like to lose his family.

He would soon feel his pain.

He watched the next news item.

A young boy who had drowned in a friend's pool had miraculously awakened from his coma.

SOME TOWNS HAVE EVIL, SOME TOWNS ARE EVIL
PICTON
JASPER WOLF

PICTON

"Horror is like a serpent; always shedding its skin, always changing. And it will always come back. It can't be hidden away like the guilty secrets we try to keep in our subconscious."

~ Dario Argento

Foreword

Dear Reader,

Before you go any further I must warn you that *Picton* is the third book in the Jake Miller series and to fully appreciate this book, you need to have read *Hunted* and *The Waiting Room*.

Picton has been by far my scariest, and most enjoyable adventure; I'll not say why here as it may spoil the story before you. However, I spent many late nights writing and looking over my shoulder at the slightest sound.

I'll say this is my first and hopefully not my last adventure into the crime/ horror genre, and I hope you enjoy reading it as much as I did writing it.

On a personal note, as I write the foreword I am a week away from being placed on the heart transplant list, so this could very well be my last book. I would like to leave my readers one piece of advice I unfortunately learnt way too late. Do what you love; life is too short, so follow your dreams no matter how far away or unattainable they may seem.

I'll be posting updates on my health when my operation occurs.

If you want to follow everything Jasper Wolf, follow my Facebook page or Twitter and if you want to join my mailing list please sign up at www. jasperwolfauthor.com

Chapter 1

Picton Town NSW December 1916

Two nights before, Anne had played with black magic—powers beyond her control. Ruth and Stanley had told her it would be fun to talk to the spirits, summon the dead. How wrong they were.

They all sat in a circle on Stanley's lounge room floor. In the middle of them all was his handmade wooden Ouija board. On it were all the letters of the alphabet. 'Yes' was carved on the right and 'No' on the left. Stanley had crafted a pointed cursor, a simple triangle with a hole cut into the middle to allow the letter to be seen.

All three of them placed their hands over the cursor, and all three of them let the cursor take control. At first there was nothing, no movement, only stillness, and the candle flame remained steady.

Then Anne felt a cold breeze blow past her, as if someone had opened a window. The candle almost lost its battle to stay alight. After a flicker, it kept aglow.

Anne could smell sulphur. It was strong.

"What's that smell?" she asked.

"Shh, something's here," Stanley said.

"Stop trying to scare us." Ruth sounded cranky.

Before Stanley could reply, their hands flew across the board. Everyone screamed, including Stanley.

"Are you dead?" Stanley asked the air around him.

Their hands once again flew across the board and landed on 'Yes'.

Stanley asked a second question. "What's your name?"

The cursor moved to the letter S.

"You're doing that!" Anne yelled at Stanley.

"I am not."

Anne withdrew her hand from the cursor.

Ruth followed her example.

"Take your hand off it then, Stanley," Ruth requested.

"If I do, it will stop working," he replied.

"Yes, because you're doing it," Anne said.

He removed his hand and shuffled his bum backwards away from the board.

The cursor stayed resting on the S.

"See, it was you," Anne said.

The cursor sat like the chiselled lifeless piece of wood it was.

Ruth joined in bagging Stanley. "You're a mean prankster, Stanley Roberts."

"But, it wasn't me. Seriously, I didn't do it."

As Stanley began his second round of pleading, the cursor flew to its second letter. C.

All three gasped and screamed. Anne almost jumped into Stanley's lap and Ruth wasn't far behind her.

The cursor paused and then moved again to its third letter, A, and then the fourth, T. The cursor kept moving.

With each movement the girls screamed, and sometimes Stanley screamed too.

Ruth held Stanley's hand so tightly her knuckles were turning white.

The cursor came to a stop.

"Scat. What does that mean?" Ruth asked the others.

"I don't know," Stanley replied, his voice shaking.

The cursor answered. It flew to the letter D, paused, and then moved on to the letter E and then A, followed by T and finally H.

The three of them slid themselves further away from the board. Death had been spelt out to them.

They were terrified.

Stanley reached in to collect the board and end the game. It had gone too far. As he reached for the board, he was violently thrown back by an invisible force that he could not resist. Within an instant, Stanley found himself on the other side of the room. The board itself levitated and began to spin in a clockwise direction. The cursor hovered just above it, eerily still.

Without warning, the board and cursor flew in opposite directions, as if someone had aimed the cursor at Ruth, and the board at Anne.

Anne managed to duck the fast-flying board. Ruth struggled to see the smaller cursor in the dimmed room, and it clocked her on the temple as it flew at her.

The cut wasn't severe, but it was no graze either. Anne raced to Ruth as she hit the floor, tearing up her yellow and white polka-dot summer dress to provide gauze for Ruth's head. Her mum would be furious if she knew she'd ripped her new summer dress on purpose. Her mother had bought it for her at the start of the school term. It was light and perfect for her to teach in, especially in the December heat. At twenty-one, she was still her mum's little girl.

She padded the torn fabric on Ruth's temple.

"Apply pressure," Ruth instructed. She would know; she was a nurse after all.

"You'll be okay," Anne said.

The board and the cursor had both come to rest in different areas of the room as if a spoilt child having a temper tantrum had thrown them. Seconds later, in a final act of defiance, the spirit blew the candle out.

The girls screamed as the room descended into complete darkness.

* * *

Anne shook the memories of the séance and continued her walk to Stanley's home, just under four kilometres from the school, on the outskirts of the township. Anne had left the school and headed down the dirt track out of town. She would need to walk about a kilometre before cutting through the Redbank Range Tunnel. The last train wasn't expected until 5.20 and she should make the tunnel with plenty of time to cut through it before the train arrived.

The town was expanding rapidly. A second railway line was being added and was due for completion within six months. No more having to time crossings through the tunnel. Trains would be re-routed, and the tunnel would become obsolete.

Stanley should be on his way home from working on the line. His job was to lay the sleepers. Twenty-five men from Picton had gained jobs on the railway with years of work, soon to come to an end.

The summer dust swept up against the bottom of her dress as she headed south out of town. While the séance had given her a fright, it was nothing compared to the horrifying encounter of the night before.

Chapter 2

Melbourne 2016

Jake had spent the last eleven months beside Brodie's bed and had seen no improvement. Brodie was in a coma. Lying in the paddock as long as he had without a pulse had starved his brain of oxygen for too long.

Early on, the doctors had suggested his parents shut off the life support, but after everything their son had fought through in his life, neither of them could do it. They just believed he would come back to them.

Jake, true to his word, had left the police force; after all, it had almost destroyed him. Monique had suspicions about Austin's involvement in what had happened at the house of the 'Ukrainian Monster', but Jake knew there was little evidence to pursue it further. Monique was the chief inspector within the homicide department where Jake had worked.

Jake had received the all-clear from Monique only weeks after the shootout at the Ukrainian Monster's house. The internal investigation was now closed. While the Police Integrity Commission investigation had had suspicions that others could have been involved in the shootout at the Monster's, they hadn't been able to prove anything. Thus, they had found that Jake and Brodie had acted reasonably while conducting their investigation.

Over the past eleven months, Monique had made several attempts to get Jake back on the force. Jake had declined every time.

With Hayley pregnant, Jake was finding it harder and harder to visit Brodie, but as he always had, he made sure he found the time. Even after their daughter Indiana was born, Jake still visited.

Being a new dad didn't stop him.

When Jake visited he made sure he was as normal as possible. He would always remain upbeat, treat Brodie the same as if he was sitting in his lounge room. Jake would simply have a one-way conversation. He would update Brodie on all the happenings of the NBA, the trades, how poorly the Knicks were still going (despite signing Rose), and how the young Wolves were still on the rise. Jake knew Brodie loved his Wolves.

Sometimes Jake would read the paper or do the crossword. On some occasions he would even ask Brodie for the answer to the trivia question; of course, no answers were ever supplied. As the months went on, this became more difficult as Brodie's body had clearly deteriorated.

As the days, weeks and months passed, Jake's mood remained upbeat in front of Brodie. Jake didn't dare let his demeanour slip once while he was in his presence.

After Ryan returned from the abyss that he described only as the in-between (a place between heaven and earth), it provided Jake with hope. Hope that Brodie would also find his way back. According to Ryan, he had been able see and hear everything, but he was trapped and couldn't find his way back into his body.

Jake had begun his new job. It was a lot more boring than the police force, but that suited him just fine. Most cases he was investigating were wives asking for their husbands to be followed, as they suspected them of cheating. Most of the time they were right. It was a girl at the office, someone at the gym, a neighbour, or a mum at the school. Occasionally it wasn't an affair but a gambling addiction. On the rarest of occasions, a man would request his wife be followed, and yes, sometimes they cheated too.

The most excitement Jake had encountered was when he had been confronted by a husband he was trailing. Somehow, Jake had become lazy and been spotted, the first time in over fifteen years. The husband had assumed Jake was the other man. Jake had learnt one thing quickly since starting in the private detective business; those who cheat assume everyone else is cheating too. It's their justification.

Conscious of not wanting to put the wife in any danger, Jake had to think quickly. He was lucky he knew his subject well.

"You fucking my wife?" the large, fat, sweaty man yelled as he ran out his front door towards Jake's car. "Why are you following me?"

As the man bashed on Jake's window, his sweaty, hairy belly rubbed against the glass.

Jake pulled his gun and tapped it on the window. "Step back, sir," Jake replied.

The slob saw the gun and backed away immediately. Jake got out of his car and towered over the sweaty unkempt man who was only five foot three, or five-five at a stretch.

"Sir, I am following you. I am hired by the department of Human Services to ensure you're not claiming your welfare benefits illegally," Jake answered.

The man stood there, mouth gaping, unsure what to answer.

Jake didn't wait. "I have found nothing to report, I am pleased to say." He paused. "I'll make sure you won't need to worry about this again." Jake was about to get back into his car, as if he was in the clear.

"Not so fast, fella," the slob replied, grabbing hold of the door before Jake had a chance to close it. "What benefits you got me down as claiming?" the man asked, belly hanging over one side of his grey trackpants, his butt cheeks poking out the top.

Jake knew he was being tested. "Your disability benefits, Tony. It's clear you're suffering severe injuries from your work accident. When you came out the front door, you could barely muster a jog, even though you were full of adrenaline. In the three days I've been following you I haven't seen anything that raises any suspicion. I really am sorry for the invasion of your privacy, but unfortunately some people cheat the system and then the good people like yourself end up missing out."

Tony looked at Jake. Jake returned a polite smile and tugged on the door for a second time. This time Tony let Jake close it.

Jake had no concern about taking Tony down. It would have taken little effort, but he couldn't blow his cover. If Tony had found out his wife had hired him, or worse still, thought Jake was having an affair with her, who knew what Tony might have done to his own wife. This way at least he would think it was unrelated.

Chapter 3

Picton December 1916

Anne couldn't get the thoughts of last night's visitor out of her head. She had to tell Stanley. At first, she thought it was just a dream, well, a nightmare. Now she didn't know what it was.

It was the night after the séance. Anne had almost put Stanley's stupid games behind her. She was tired and with classes to teach again the next day, she needed an early night. She had decided to read only a couple of chapters of her latest book on loan from the school library. *The Rainbow Trail* was a western. She loved to read, and she loved to teach. English was her favourite subject.

She had been sound asleep. It was the smell that woke her; the same smell as that night at Stanley's.

Then, when her eyes adjusted, a dark shape, a creature of some kind, was there standing at the foot of her bed watching her. It resembled a man, with head bowed, a wide-brimmed hat covering its face, and it was wearing a long black trench coat. Without obvious movement, it slipped to her side, its head raised, its face with eyes blazing fiery red, shaped like a cat's. The rest of its face had no discernible features. She couldn't even tell where its mouth began or ended or how it spoke; yet words came out. There was no real nose. She could see no nostrils, only snake-like holes.

Anne went to move but couldn't. She was paralysed. The only part of her body she could control were her eyes. She looked at the mantel clock that sat ticking on her night stand. The small hand was on the 3 and the large hand was just past the 6. It was slightly after 3.30 in the morning. This thing in the hat hovered next to her. Was it a man, or was it a creature? She wasn't sure.

Anne tried to move her hand to pinch herself. She must have been dreaming, she thought. She couldn't move. A dream, she told herself. *Wake up!* Anne screamed to herself. The scream echoed through her head, as if it confirmed her nightmare.

The thing reached into her bed, taking Anne's arm. The smell intensified. Its hands appeared out from under the sleeves of the long jacket. The fingers were long and bony with long grimy nails.

Anne remained paralysed in her bed watching the creature out of the corner of her eye run its disgusting fingers down the side of her stomach.

"Soon," rasped out of his invisible mouth. "Soon." It sounded again before he simply vanished into the shadows.

Anne sat bolt upright, her paralysis gone. Her heart was pounding. It was about to explode through her chest. What had just happened, where had it gone? The door had remained closed. It hadn't exited via the door. The creature had simply vanished. Anne began to wonder if it was a figment of her imagination. Must have been, she thought. It must have been a strange dream where she was dreaming while she was awake.

Only one way to tell, Anne thought, and quickly looked to her right. Her clock showed just past 3.30. The hands continued to tick away. It wasn't a dream. The creature in the hat was real, and he had been here for her.

Anne didn't sleep much the rest of the night. In fact, she didn't sleep at all until the first glimpse of daylight broke through her window at 6.10 am. It was only then she managed to gain an extra forty-five minutes before the sunlight woke her.

With the dream still reverberating through her mind, Anne headed to the bathroom, collecting her clothes that were laid out across her dresser-chair, ready for the day ahead. She placed them in a pile neatly next to her at the bathroom basin. Anne placed the plug in the basin and began to fill it with cool water. There was no time to heat the water on the stove this morning. She took a fresh hand towel from the rack on the wall and dipped it into the cool water. It was cool against her skin without being cold. Anne unbuttoned her nightgown. It softly dropped to the floor leaving her standing in only her white underwear. She washed her face and neck. Anne dunked the washcloth in the water and began on her arms. Before she pulled the cloth from the water for the third time, her eyes caught their refection in the mirror. They were showing signs of tiredness and stress. The dream last night certainly hadn't helped.

She washed her face again to try and freshen up some more.

She put her fresh singlet on and as she pulled it down over her breasts, she noticed marks on her side; three of them to be exact. They looked like burn marks and they were where that man had touched her stomach in her dream. Had he been real after all? She inspected the marks closely. They looked as though she had touched a hot oven. It was as if Hat Man's three nails had burnt her as he stroked her.

The man in her room had been real after all. What had he said to her? "Soon?" What did that mean?

Anne finished getting dressed. She was panicked now. She needed to speak to Stanley. After work would be her earliest opportunity. She knew the thoughts of Hat Man would consume her mind for the day.

Was this the man they had summoned? Surely not. Who else could it be?

Chapter 4

Picton 1916

Ruth had begun the first stint of her double shift at the tuberculosis hospital at 7 am. She would work until 3 and then return at 11 for her first night shift until 7. She was on night duty for the next three days, followed by four days off. Nights were always the worst shifts, but they were always followed by the days off. The nights dragged, and the days off flew past.

Ruth wore her required striped nurses' uniform, with accompanying hat, her watch pinned to her left breast. Her first job of the morning was to take the morning obs.

There was nothing she could do for her patients. There was no cure. They were all dying, some sooner than others. They had all contracted the 'white plague', TB as it was commonly known. Her patients came to the hospital not to get better but to die peacefully without spreading the disease to the wider population. Ruth made sure she always wore a protective mask to cover her mouth. The most common way the disease was spread was by spittle from person to person.

This was a horrible disease; it infected the lungs of the patients and caused them to eventually cough up their lungs piece by piece.

Her first patient was a lady in her mid to late fifties, June. She had contracted TB while returning from England on a ship. The disease was in the late stages, she was coughing up blood with nearly every cough.

"Morning," Ruth said through her mask.

"Morning," June coughed back to her, spluttering into her handkerchief.

"How did you sleep?" Ruth asked.

"Not very well, a lot of coughing," June replied. This sentence came out cough-free which was a real rarity.

Ruth smiled sympathetically. "I'll get you some breakfast shortly."

"I had a visitor last night," June replied.

"Oh, lucky you. Your family came to visit?" Ruth asked as she checked her chart for the previous night's baseline readings.

"No. I had never seen this man before, strange looking fellow, came in after midnight, seemed to come out of the shadows." Her talking was interrupted by a fit of coughing and her handkerchief was again smeared in blood. She took a sip of water from her night stand leaving a trace of blood on the lip of the cup. "He was a tall lanky man, long bony fingers, no real face, no real mouth. He wore a long coat and a wide-brimmed hat, which was quite strange for this time of year, don't you think?" she asked.

Ruth frowned. "Visiting hours finished at 7. I'll check the logs to see who visited. Maybe it was a dream?"

"He was here, my dear, I can assure you of that."

Not wanting to upset an already dying patient further, Ruth just agreed and added, "It was probably another patient's visitor looking for the way out. Now, what do you feel like for breakfast?"

Ruth waited for June's latest coughing attack to subside, before being told, "Toast and tea."

"Once you have had a shower and breakfast, I'll bring you your first glass of milk for the day, then we will pop outside for exercises before it becomes hot."

"I think the milk and the exercise is really helping at keeping the TB at bay; maybe soon I'll be well enough to go back home?" June asked.

"Possibly, if you keep improving," Ruth answered noncommittally.

June got up and headed to the bathroom down the hall, nightgown almost touching the floor. As June entered the cubicle, she immediately noticed her reflection. She had become even more pale and gaunt than the weeks before. Death was closer now. Her hair had turned another two shades of grey, or so it seemed, although her hair colour was the least of her worries. June wiped some dried blood from the corners of her mouth.

On the underside of her forearm she noticed three burn marks. How had they got there? She didn't know. She hadn't cooked anything in a very long time.

She rinsed the burns under some water. They stung a little, and she quickly tried to dab them dry. The skin around the red marks began to fall away.

Who was the man in the wide-brimmed hat and trench coat, and what was he doing in the hospital?

Chapter 5

Picton 1916

Anne felt the entire day at school was a waste. Her mind had been elsewhere. She was sure the children hadn't learnt anything. She had not told a soul about her 'Hat Man' visitor from the night before; not even her mother. After all, who would believe such an absurd tale?

She had to speak with Stanley as soon as possible. It was that simple. She left the schoolhouse as soon as the bell rang and began the one and a quarter mile walk to Stanley's house. She had plenty of time between the 4.30 train and the 5.20 train, neither of which carried passengers. She would need to cut through the Redbank Range Tunnel to save more walking.

The wind flared up as the afternoon went on. The dust swirled, and Anne dipped her hat to try and avoid the dust. She arrived at the entrance to the Redbank Range Tunnel.

She heard the steam train, but with so much going through her head she just assumed the train had passed through the tunnel. After all, it was 4.39. Anne wasted no time and headed into the tunnel.

She walked into the darkness, and the small arch of light at the other end guided her way.

As she walked she tried to rehearse what she would tell Stanley of last night's events, but it didn't even sound believable to her. She hoped he would understand.

She was almost a quarter of the way into the tunnel when a whistle of the train startled her. It was close, but it hadn't gone through the tunnel yet; it was still behind her. The end of the tunnel was still at least a hundred yards away. Anne turned to see the train approaching. There was no way she could make the end of the tunnel in time. Anne panicked. She hitched up her dress and sprinted onwards. After a few good strides Anne caught a glimpse of the halfway alcove. How had she forgotten it? This was the very purpose of the alcove, to provide refuge in case someone got trapped inside the tunnel with the train bearing down on them. It was only twenty yards. She would make it. She would stand in the alcove, wait for the train to pass and continue on her way. She would be safe.

She darted into the alcove, breathing heavily as she caught her breath and waited for the train to pass. A waft of sulphur arose from behind her. It was a smell that immediately brought back the horrors of her nightmare. She turned to see what was emitting the foul odour. The darkness of the alcove met her with blazing red eyes and a wide-brimmed hat. "I told you I'd see you soon," the creature with no discernible mouth said, grabbing her by the arms.

He towered over her small frame.

"You were just a dream," she faltered.

"No, I am very real; I have come for your soul."

Anne wondered why she hadn't felt the train pass. It wasn't that far behind, was it?

Was the train even real, or was it another trick by this thing, this Hat Man? A trick to lure her into the alcove. Anne shook her head. How could he invent a train? This man was real; he was standing right in front of her, holding her. But he wasn't a physical form, he was more like a shadow of a man at best with no discernible features apart from the hat and the red eyes and the long yellow fingernails.

"Soon I'll taste your fear," Hat Man said through a hole in his face that he used for a mouth.

Before Anne had understood what Hat Man had muttered, she was hurled into the air from the alcove and onto the front of the locomotive, hitting the attached cattle catcher. She died almost instantly.

The engineer had no idea where she had come from. One second the tracks were all clear, the next a girl had dived in front of the train. He had no time to react.

It would have to wait until they arrived at the next station. He would need help from the local constable.

Why would a young girl with her whole life ahead of her jump in front of a train?

Did she jump or was she pushed?

Had someone been in the alcove with her? The engineer thought he had seen the shadow of someone, but he couldn't be sure.

Chapter 6

Picton 1916

Ruth had returned for her second shift in less than twenty-four hours. It was just after 11.30 when word came to her that Anne had been hit and killed by a train and her body was now in the hospital morgue beneath the wards in the south wing.

Ruth was shocked when Beth, the night supervisor, broke the terrible news about Anne. Beth had offered her the opportunity to go home but Ruth thought it was best to keep busy and had decided to stay at work.

She couldn't understand why Anne would kill herself. She had been so happy only days ago.

Had she now thrown herself in front of a train?

Beth had given Ruth some time to compose herself and freshen up. Even after the tears had gone, revisited and gone again, Ruth still couldn't believe her friend was dead.

Maybe it was a mistake. That was it. The authorities were wrong. It was someone else. After all, a train would cause a lot of damage to a human. Maybe mistaken identity? It was likely.

She needed to see for herself. She needed to be sure it was Anne lying in the morgue.

She headed down to the south wing. The buildings between the tuberculosis hospital and the southern wing of the hospital were connected by a covered breezeway. Even though it was summer, the cool night air hit Ruth as soon as she stepped outside.

She walked along the cobblestone path lit by a few smaller street lamps. She reached a sign:

Southern Wing
< Pathology
Morgue >

The south wing was almost deserted. As she passed the corridor that led to pathology, she could see a pathologist walking between rooms, holding some samples. Probably another case of TB, she thought.

As she descended the hall that led to the morgue, the drop in temperature hit her. Goosebumps covered her arms and shoulders. She should have brought her cardigan, she thought, as she drew closer to the morgue and the temperature continued its decline.

She had only visited the morgue once before but couldn't remember the hallway being this cold. As she approached the entrance she could see the icy air of the morgue escaping into the hall; someone had left the door open. That would explain why the hallway was so cold. The morgue itself was in complete darkness.

"Hello? Anyone here?" Ruth called out as she stood in the doorway.

There was no response; only silence.

The gas lamps along the wall were out. She only had her kerosene lamp to see by.

Ruth held out the lamp and moved it in a circular direction to survey the room. For a second, she thought she glimpsed a man in a hat standing in the corner to her right.

She quickly swung her lamp back. It first glowed on a pair of feet that hung out from beneath a sheet on a nearby table. She continued around to the right side of the room. Had she seen a man? As the lamp brought light to the room, Ruth saw that the thing she had thought was a man in a hat was in fact a simple coat stand holding what it should, a long coat and a hat.

Normally the morgue smelt of death, but today it smelt like bad eggs.

Ruth entered the room, the lamp glow guiding her way. She was hoping the body she was looking for was on the left side of the table, close to the door. She didn't fancy walking across to the far side of the room. Ruth was convinced her friend wouldn't be here. There had to be a mistake. Anne wouldn't jump in front of a train. It just couldn't be true.

She read toe tag after toe tag until she had checked all the bodies on the left side of the room.

She crossed to the darker side of the room and began at the first table. Her dusty lamp glow shone the way. She stood at the foot of the furthest table from the door. She lifted the sheet and inspected the toe tag.

'Anne Cornwell', it read.

It couldn't be. Ruth thought this simply couldn't be happening. It must be a mistake. She felt hot and flushed. Her emotions were about to take hold once more; soon the tears would be flowing. She had to keep it together; after all, it still might be a mistake. She had to confirm it was in fact Anne lying on the table; she would have to identify her for herself from other than a toe tag.

Ruth took the cloth sheet between her fingers and steeled herself for what she might see. She took a deep breath and drew the sheet back.

The body hadn't been cleaned yet, and the mangled mess that lay in front of her was more horrific than she could ever have imagined. The body barely resembled Anne; it was a mess of flesh and bone. One eye was missing, and the right arm was gone from the shoulder. Her hair was matted and torn away from her scalp, and the right side of her face was almost missing. It had taken the full impact of the train.

Ruth moved the sheet down a little farther. The damage was just as bad. A couple of ribs poked out of her side just below her missing arm. Both her legs were intact, although the right was severely broken in several places; her right foot was at right angles.

Ruth had confirmed her worst fear. This torn and crumpled mess lying before her was Anne and she was dead.

Her shock at the sight of Anne's mangled body finally found its voice and Ruth wailed.

After several minutes of standing in the darkness crying over her lost friend, Ruth tried to compose herself.

Seconds later, the questions came.

Did she really kill herself?

Why?

Ruth drew the covers over Anne. She had seen enough. The vision of her shattered remains would live in her memory forever.

As she pulled the sheet over her deceased friend's head, she noticed burn lines running horizontally, wrapping around the left arm.

Intrigued, Ruth lifted Anne just enough to see the back of her arm and shoulder. The lines continued.

What could have burnt her in such a fashion?

The train wouldn't have been hot?

It was the most puzzling thing she had ever seen.

She would have to ask the medical examiner, once he was done with the autopsy.

She finished covering Anne and began to leave the morgue.

Suddenly, the coldness she felt in the hall was back.

Her spine tingled.

Her arms suddenly exploded in a forest of goosebumps. She felt someone watching from the darkness.

A being.

She flung the lamp around, and each wave of the lamp arrested her fears. Nothing but the empty room showed itself in the light.

Ruth calmed her nerves, and headed for the door, all her fear gone. There were no ghosts. It was just her imagination running wild.

By the time she reached the door, her sadness had returned as had the questions about Anne's final moments.

She dragged the door closed behind her but before the door shut completely, the dark room spoke one word. Ruth heard it loud and clear.

"Soon."

Ruth freaked out, and fear now encompassed her whole body. She screamed, almost dropping her lamp.

She ran all the way back to the breezeway.

Something had spoken to her.

A ghost was the most likely answer, as ridiculous as that seemed.

Did she even believe in ghosts? She slowed to a brisk walk in the breezeway.

Beth welcomed her back to the ward with, "Oh my God! You look horrible. Are you all right?"

"Just a bit shaken," Ruth replied.

"I shouldn't have let you go down there. Why don't you just go home?" Beth suggested, for the second time that night.

"No, it's all right. I'll finish my shift," Ruth replied.

"Then go make yourself look a little better and get back to your rounds," Beth instructed.

Ruth gathered herself and made her way to the bathroom. She wiped away the running make-up and applied a fresh coat. She undid her bobby pins, redid her hair and pinned it back into place. She looked at herself in the mirror and was pleased with the improvement. She smiled a fake smile and the mirror smiled back.

The hurt behind her eyes remained.

The question her eyes held remained.

Why? Ruth went from patient to patient checking their blood pressure and pulse. Her lamp provided enough light to do her duties without waking the patients.

She arrived at June's bedside. There was no doubt she had begun to love this patient, a lady in the last days of her life and all alone, yet she always provided her with nothing but kindness.

Ruth could see June wasn't in a deep sleep and she would probably wake when she started taking her obs. Ruth quietly and softly rolled her nightgown sleeve and began to apply the blood pressure cuff, while at the same time listening for her pulse through the stethoscope. One-thirty over seventy. All good, she thought.

She placed the lamp on the table next to June, so she could remove the stethoscope from her ears. Then her eyes caught sight of the marks in the dim light, marks that seemed burnt into June's skin.

The resemblance to the marks on Anne's arm was incredible, if not identical.

Ruth quietly shook June. "June, wake up."

"What is it darling? What the matter?"

"How did you get these marks?" Ruth asked.

June looked at her arm, still half asleep. "Sometimes when he touches me he burns me a little."

"When who touches you?"

"The man in the hat and long coat that comes to visit me. Don't worry, they don't hurt," June replied. Her cough had woken with her.

"How many times has he visited you?" Ruth asked.

"About five times. You know what's strange? While he's here I don't cough at all. I feel twenty again," June replied.

June reached for her hanky, ready to deposit the blood she had just coughed up.

"Is he coming to visit again?" Ruth asked.

"He said he would come back, soon."

'Soon.' That was the word she had heard in the morgue. Had she seen Hat Man? Had he been there?

She needed to find this man.

Chapter 7

Melbourne 2016

Jake sat in his new office situated in Port Melbourne. It was a lot more lavishly furnished than the one he was used to at homicide. He had just finished his report on Tony Aldrich. He was cheating with a lady who frequented the local watering hole. He had suggested his client, Samantha Aldrich, get a divorce and an AVO. Jake was worried her husband would become violent, considering the way he'd approached Jake outside his home earlier.

Jake had even offered to be there while she packed.

While she appreciated his caring, she shrugged off his concern saying that Tony was too weak to become a wife-beater.

Samantha said that next time he left for the pub, she would pack her car and go. He would never see her again.

Jake placed his report into a large yellow envelope along with the photos of the women to whom Tony had taken a liking. Samantha was going to come in, pay her bill and pick up her file.

Jake wanted to see her, but unfortunately, he had an appointment with a new client so on the way he delivered the envelope to the reception area, leaving it in the 'to be collected' tray.

His appointment wasn't far away; only a few minutes' drive.

Jake pulled up at the kerb. The home was one that only the affluent could afford. It was a big home, behind black wrought-iron gates, with a circular driveway and a buzzer at the front path.

Jake pressed the buzzer.

"Yes?" an unfamiliar voice replied.

"It's Jake Miller from Elite Detectives. I am here for an appointment with Mrs Bassil," Jake said into the metal box.

The gate popped open and Jake stepped through onto the brick pathway and headed for the door.

Jake was met at the door by a tall thin woman, attractive, yet she came across to him as very cold and indifferent.

"I am Mrs Bassil, but you can call me Karen. Please come in."

Jake followed her down a tiled hall to a hexagonal dining room. Everything in the home was immaculate. Not a single thing was out of place. The house reminded him of a display home.

Jake sat where Karen directed. She sat opposite.

The table was a dark mahogany with a high sheen; recently polished, Jake thought. In the middle of the table sat a large jug of iced water with slices of lemon and lime floating amongst the ice.

"I asked you here because I need you to find out who killed my daughter," Karen said. She was calm and matter-of-fact.

"Mrs Bassil, we don't usually do that sort of work. We generally focus on missing persons, insurance and adultery investigations."

"It's Karen."

"The police are the best ones to handle homicide investigations," Jake added before she could continue.

"The police have investigated. In fact, the coroner has even handed down his finding."

Jake was a little puzzled. "Why don't you start from the beginning, and I'll see what I can do to help you."

Karen poured herself a glass of water. "Would you like some?"

"No, thank you."

"In July 2014," Karen began, "my twenty-one-year-old daughter Gemma went to a small town in NSW called Picton Town. It was the weekend starting Friday the 4th."

Jake had heard of this town, but he couldn't remember from where or how.

"Gemma was there with a friend on a girls' weekend, as many college kids do. While she was there, she had a terrible car accident. Her friend Paige, who was the driver, was killed. While Gemma survived, she was never the same. She blamed herself. She was already going to counselling due to the death of her father but despite all the help, a month later she returned to Picton Town, rented the same room as she had the month before, and according to police, killed herself."

"You say Gemma was already in counselling because of her father? What happened?" Jake asked.

"In late October 2013, my husband of twenty-two years suddenly died in his sleep. He was fit and healthy. It was totally out of the blue. Gemma was nineteen going on twenty. It hit us all very hard. To help her cope the doctor offered free counselling," Karen replied blankly.

Karen took a drink to clear her throat and prevent the tears. It was still a raw subject, all these years later.

"Sorry for your losses, I really am," Jake said.

Karen could feel the sincerity in his tone.

"Have you spoken to the counsellor about her state of mind? Had she been concerned about her depression?" Jake asked.

"According to the psychologist, Gemma blamed herself for what happened, but never showed any signs of self-harm. She wasn't on any antidepressant medication," Karen answered.

"Were you told how Gemma died?"

"I was told Gemma was found in the bathtub with a radio," Karen replied. "The radio was found at the bottom of the bath next to her feet, and a wash cloth was covering her face."

"I can see why you're puzzled. It's a hard position to get yourself into, that's for sure," Jake replied. "Did you know why Gemma went back to Picton weeks later?"

"No, I don't even know why they chose to go there the first time."

"Were you given Gemma's belongings after she died?" Jake asked.

"Yes. They sent me a bag of her personal belongings; jewellery, phone, wallet, keys. But I sold the car. Easier than having it trucked down here. I didn't have anyone to help me collect it, so I sold it; got a fair price for it," Karen answered.

"Do you know if the police investigated the phone and her social media accounts?"

"Yes, they did, but she hadn't made any posts or sent any texts or even called anyone since the day she left," Karen replied.

Jake was taking notes.

"Do you still have the phone? Do you know if her Facebook page is still active?"

"I have the phone. It was one of those new iPhones. We closed the Facebook page just after she died."

"Can I look in her room?"

Karen sat shocked, looking at him.

"Have I said something to upset you, Karen?"

"No, but how did you know her room was still, well, the same?" Karen asked.

"I just assumed. Generally, parents leave the room exactly as their child leaves it, until they have closure. It's normally more consistent with missing children, but I can see you haven't reached closure yet," Jake explained.

Karen stood up and headed down a side passage that adjoined her living area. The door to the room was shut. Jake had expected it to be a shrine, and he was correct.

"Excuse the clothes on the floor. I just couldn't bring myself to tidy up," Karen said.

Jake stood in the doorway and observed the room. The walls were covered with photos and twenty-first birthday cards, and there was a double bed, covered in heart-shaped throw pillows of assorted colours. A beanbag sat in one corner, and a desk with a mirror in the other. On the desk sat a silver Mac laptop, and a jewellery box. Next to the desk was a large matching bookcase, full of books and magazines.

Karen stepped into the room. "This was Paige," she said, plucking a photo from Gemma's wall. "They'd been best friends since year seven, inseparable they were."

Jake took the photo. They were both attractive girls, with big smiles and their whole lives in front of them. Paige had long, flowing, brown hair while Gemma wore her reddish-blonde hair in a shorter, punkier cut.

"May I have a look around? I don't mean to pry, but it's important that I try to find out as much about Gemma as I can," Jake said.

"Sure thing. However, please excuse me." Karen left without another look into her daughter's room. Jake wondered about her quick exit. Maybe she doesn't like being in here, he thought, but almost instantly dismissed that idea. No, that couldn't be it. The room was immaculate, everything in its place. She was obviously in here often. Maybe she didn't like watching a stranger in her daughter's room, a room that had now become sacred to her.

Jake stood in the middle of the room and tried to absorb all that was Gemma; everything she had been and everything that had made her tick. His attention was drawn to the desk and the bookcase. What a person liked to read often provided a good insight.

Jake began to look through the books. A lot of Stephen King, Dean Koontz, Joe Hill, and others. Jake removed one book he hadn't seen before, something that interested him. It was an older book according to the cover; published in 1959. *The Haunting of Hill House* by Shirley Jackson.

Jake read the blurb. It was a horror story, a story about a poltergeist living in a haunted house. It sounded very similar to Stephen King's *The Shining*.

She liked horror stories, Jake thought. So did a billion other people. Nothing unusual there. He was about to put the book back when something caught his eye. It was a second row of books hidden behind the front row of novels. The hidden volumes were not published books, but handwritten journals with a gold spine. They were A5 size, lined up in year and month order. Jake removed the first one and turned to the first page.

1st Jan 2014.

It's New Year's Day. I can't believe I'll be twenty-one this year. I can't believe you have been gone 4 months already. Time has gone so quickly, since you passed. I swear the funeral was only yesterday. Mum has struggled, but I suppose you can see that from 'up there'. If there is an 'up there'. I used to have such faith. Now I don't know what to believe. The last 6 months has left me asking so many questions about faith. How does a man as healthy as a bull die in his sleep? Where was God to protect you?

Anyway, enough about God, last night was the first New Year's since I was 16 I didn't go to a party. Paige and I just stayed home and watched movies. It was a good night. Paige suggested we go to Picton in NSW. Apparently, it is a well-known Australian ghost town. (I had never heard of it.) She thought having evidence of the afterlife might help me renew my faith in God. I am not sure I am ready for such an adventure, yet. Maybe in July when I get to the mid-year break? If I make it, that is, even though this is supposed to be my second-last year at uni, it might be my last. I am really not enjoying it. I love the law, but the theory is so boring. I don't know if I can grind it out for another two years.

As always . . . until tomorrow. Thanks for listening, love you with all my heart.

Love Gemma xxx

Jake took one last look around her room. He now had an idea of who she was and why she had gone to Picton Town. He doubted Karen knew about the diaries and was probably too upset to be in the room to search for them. She had stood back from the doorway the whole time he was in the room.

"Would you like that water now?" Karen asked him as he returned to the dining area.

"That would be great, thank you," Jake replied, approaching the table where he had sat only minutes earlier.

"Karen, obviously I would have to do further investigations, but from what you have told me and what I have seen in her room, Gemma didn't appear suicidal. However, that doesn't mean she wasn't suffering depression. Suicide often occurs after the person suffers a depression that is so dark most of their family is totally unaware they were suffering, until the body is discovered."

Karen gave him a look of contempt, as if she had been told this before.

Jake knew exactly what the look meant.

"Now, I am not saying she was depressed or suicidal, but you asked me to investigate and find the truth about Gemma's death. If the truth is that she killed herself, are you going to be prepared to accept it?"

Karen looked at him. It was a gaze that Jake thought would burn through his flesh. "Yes, I'll accept whatever the investigation finds," she answered.

Jake could tell it was hard to say, but he believed her. She would accept his findings.

"Here is what I think we need to do," Jake began. "We need to go back to when she began therapy after her father's death, all the way through to the car accident and Paige's death, and then look at the reason she went back to Picton Town. Do you have any idea why she went back?" Jake asked straight out.

"No, she didn't talk to me about it at all. On August 15th, it was a Friday morning if I remember correctly, she got up early and left. I thought she was just going shopping. She never came back."

"Didn't she have a bag with her?"

"She did take one, apparently, full of clothes. The police returned it to me, but I never saw her put it in the car. Maybe that's why I just assumed she was going shopping," Karen replied.

Again, Jake believed her.

"Whatever the reason she went back to Picton Town, we need to know," Jake said.

One thought ran through his head; not many people pack a bag of clothes when they plan on killing themselves. Usually, they take nothing.

"I don't know why she was there. All I know is, Saturday lunchtime I got a knock on the door by two uniformed police officers. They passed on the details about Gemma's death. I was told to contact Inspector Connolly for further information. Right there, my world stopped," Karen replied.

Jake let her compose herself before he continued. "I'd like to involve a friend of mine, Lucas Taylor, who worked in homicide in NSW. He made detective and more importantly, he is a good guy. He specialised in missing persons and homicides, including the infamous backpacker murders, and like many ex-cops he now does private sector work. I'm sure he would be willing to help with the Picton side of the investigation. It would definitely speed things up. He would have connections," Jake offered.

"Is this friend of yours going to cost me a lot extra?" Karen asked.

"By the time you deduct all the travel I would save from my end, it will probably work out even, and you have the bonus of two of us working on Gemma's case for you."

Jake didn't think Karen was concerned about the cost. He thought she was just ensuring she wasn't being ripped off.

She thought about it, as she sipped what was remaining in her glass.

"Very well then, that will do fine," she replied formally.

"I'll organise a contract for you and I'll also need you to sign a release form authorising me to speak to Gemma's psychologist," Jake said, only pausing to finish his own glass of water. "The contract will have our fees and the estimate for the first fourteen days' work and then we'll review. How does that sound?"

"Fine. How long will it take to get started?"

"I'll have the forms to you tomorrow, so the day after. I'll also give you a list of things I'll need for the investigation."

"Such as?" Karen asked.

"All Gemma's journals, all the items from that night, the jewellery, and a photo of her and Paige."

"I don't understand. Why do you want the journals? They are private between her and her father. I haven't even read them." Karen wasn't angry, but she was getting irritated.

"I understand how emotional and personal all this is for you, I really do. This is the worst thing a parent can experience, but if you want the truth, you need to let me in so I can do my job. You need to think of me as a lawyer, a priest and a doctor. What you tell me, stays with me and will die with me."

Jake stopped speaking, sat back in his chair and waited. She needed to decide what she wanted; the truth, or the fantasy of her daughter that currently existed in her mind.

"Okay—I'll organise what you need. You can pick it up tomorrow when you drop off the contract," Karen agreed.

Jake thanked her and headed for the door.

All night, he expected to get a call from Karen cancelling the investigation. Jake could tell her memories of Gemma were clearly beautiful and untainted, and he thought she would probably choose to preserve those over finding the truth.

It was a rare occasion for Jake. He was wrong. No such call came.

Chapter 8

Picton December 1916

T he day of Anne's funeral was a humid overcast summer's day. It was a day that Ruth knew was coming, yet one she dreaded more than any other day she could remember.

She hadn't been asked to speak at the funeral. Those privileges were left to the parents, aunts and uncles and the school headmaster for whom she had worked. However, Ruth felt compelled to say a few words about her best friend, whom she had known for many years.

She needed to say goodbye.

She approached the iron gates of the St Mark's cemetery. High on the hill within the grounds were the chapel and adjoining graveyard. Tombstones were set amongst weeping willows and several large oak trees. A small stream flowed beyond the graveyard but within the grounds.

The chapel was filling fast. While Ruth didn't know some of the mourners by name, she recognised them from the school where Anne had worked. Even from the gate she could make out Anne's mum, whose head was covered with a black veil, leaning against the shoulder of her taller, thinner husband. The local hardware owners, the O'Brians, entered. He tipped his hat. They shook hands. The wives hugged. Next to offer their sympathies were the Woodstocks, the town's stock and feed owners. Even the local publican Mr Doyle had closed the pub and was in attendance. He dipped his hat.

"Condolences, Miss Ruth," he said, as he passed her on the path and headed towards Anne's parents at the chapel.

Ruth had taken only two steps when a voice called her name, stopping her in her tracks. Ruth spun back towards the gates. Stanley stood there, tall, strong and strapping, dressed in his black slacks, shoes and hat. Even his shirt was black. Maroon braces held his slacks up.

"Sorry. I didn't mean to startle you," he offered.

"It's all right, it's just such an awful day. I think I'm on edge. I haven't been getting much sleep this last week," Ruth replied, watching the wind blow the loose leaves around the graveyard.

When Ruth's eyes finally met Stanley's, she could see he too was sleep deprived.

"How are you coping?" she asked.

"I can't believe she's gone," Stanley replied quietly.

"I know. Such a tragedy."

"I was going to ask her to marry me, on New Year's Eve. Well, that was the plan. Now it's all gone. Why would she have done this? She was happy, wasn't she?" Stanley asked.

Ruth sighed. "As far as I knew she was. I don't understand it either."

Silence filled the air between them.

"How have you been sleeping?" Ruth asked after a short pause.

"I haven't been getting much at all," was Stanley's quick response.

"Same here."

They continued walking up the hill towards the chapel. Ruth stopped and took a breath. "This may sound weird, but have you seen a strange man in a hat around town?"

Stanley froze. "I had what I thought was a drifter break into my house two nights ago. He said he would be back soon."

"Was he wearing a long black coat?"

"Yes."

"What did you do?" Ruth asked.

"I couldn't do anything. I was paralysed. I think he drugged me or something, because I couldn't move. I'll be ready for him next time, though, I bought myself a Colt six-shooter. If he shows up again he'll get all six, for trespassing," Stanley said.

"Don't go doing anything silly."

Stanley frowned down at her. "Silly! Why are you asking about this guy? Has he been bothering you too?"

"I haven't seen him, but he's been visiting one of the patients at the hospital, and no one knows who he is," Ruth replied.

"Maybe that's where he got the drugs he used on me." Stanley sounded as if he had just put two and two together. He added, "You know, the strange thing was, the next morning, when I woke up, I had these marks on my stomach." He untucked his shirt, revealing three horizontal burn marks about two inches long that began just above his hip bone.

Ruth's jaw dropped.

For a split second she thought she was in the morgue again, looking at Anne's body.

The marks on Stanley were identical to those on both Anne and June.

"I have seen those marks on other people. Those exact burns, same length, same direction," Ruth replied, dumbstruck. "Do you think this mystery man may have had something to do with Anne's death?"

"I don't think she jumped in front of the train, that's for sure," Stanley said.

The church bell sounded. The service was about to start. Stanley straightened his tie and they hurried up the gravel path to the church.

After the funeral, the mourners were invited to join the family at the pub for the wake.

Ruth couldn't handle any more sadness that day, and instead gave her apologies to Anne's parents and made an early exit.

She needed to find out about this man in the broad-brimmed hat and the long coat who had been visiting her patient.

Chapter 9

Picton December 1916

By the time the wake was over, Stanley was slightly drunk and totally exhausted.

He had to be at work in just over twelve hours. He couldn't afford to give up another day's pay.

Once home, Stanley prepared an egg on toast and a cup of tea to settle his stomach and took two aspirin to clear his head. After dinner, he headed straight to bed. As he had done since he bought the pistol, he checked and double-checked that it was loaded with the safety off, and then slid it under his pillow. He hopped into bed and turned out his kerosene lamp. The glow of the glass dissipated after a minute or two but by then, Stanley had already fallen asleep.

During the early hours of Tuesday morning, Stanley was woken by a rancid smell. Whatever it was stank to high heaven. Stanley initially thought something was burning. He sat up and sniffed repeatedly, trying to identify the smell.

After a few second his eyes adjusted to the darkness. At the foot of his bed he could see a man in the wide-brimmed hat and long coat. It was as if he'd appeared out of the shadows, as if he had drifted in through the wall.

Hat Man's eyes were red and fiery, his face pale with no discernible features apart from those piercing red eyes. What man had red eyes? Was it a man or some sort of creature? He wasn't sure.

Stanley slid his right hand under the pillow. He could move. Tonight, he had not been drugged.

Tonight, this stranger, this 'Hat Man', would experience the power of his Colt first hand.

"What do you want? I have no money if that's what you're looking for." Stanley's hand wrapped and then tightened around the mahogany butt of his hidden pistol.

"I want your soul," Hat Man replied in a voice that was deeper and more evil than anything Stanley had ever heard.

"My soul?" This man standing before him had either been smoking the mushrooms near the tunnel or had escaped from an asylum. Either way, he wasn't right in the head.

"Get out of my house, you bum, before I kill you where you stand!" Stanley demanded.

He tried to sound strong and authoritative, yet his voice quavered a little upon the delivery of the message.

"Stanley, do you really think that Colt under your pillow is going to stop me?" Hat Man asked softly.

At first, Stanley wondered how he knew his name, then something else struck him. How did he know that he had a gun or what make it was?"

"How—?" Stanley began before he was cut off by Hat Man.

"How do I know all these details? It's like I am reading your mind, isn't it Stanley?" Hat Man questioned, giving a sinister grin.

For the first time, Stanley saw the semblance of a mouth and what appeared to be teeth. They weren't pearly white either. From his quick glimpse, they looked yellow and jagged.

Stanley removed his hand from beneath his pillow, clutching the Colt, and pointed it straight at the Hat Man or whatever the thing standing in front of him was.

Stanley expected Hat Man to run or duck, at least dive away from the pistol's barrel. Hat Man however, didn't even flinch. He stood his ground at the end of Stanley's bed.

With the gun pointed directly at the stranger, Stanley was surprised at how steady his hand was. Stanley aimed the sight at the man's chest and without thinking any further, he pulled the trigger.

A loud crack filled the quiet night air. A quick flash of light momentarily brightened the bedroom and the smell of burnt gunpowder briefly replaced the sulphur stench that had permeated the room.

A split second after the flash, Stanley expected to see the intruder fly backwards and then fall lifelessly to the hardwood bedroom floor.

Yet no fall came, no blood, no injury. Instead, there was a second smaller yellow flash where the bullet should have hit its target. It was as if the bullet had simply vanished.

Instead of letting out a cry of anguish as Hat Man should have done when the bullet struck, he simply smiled, this time giving Stanley a full view of his jagged yellow teeth.

It must have been a misfire or a dud bullet, Stanley thought.

Stanley wasted no more time trying to determine what had happened to the first shot and squeezed the trigger for a second time. As soon as the shot rang out, he fired again and again. Each time, the end of his barrel blazed, the smell of burnt gunpowder filled his nostrils, and the bullets flashed yellow and disappeared. There was no impact on the target whatsoever.

Hat Man stood firm as the shots burst into small balls of yellow light in front of him, just before they were destined to hit him.

Hat Man snarled hideously and gave another sinister smile.

Stanley sat in his bed, frozen with fear and disbelief. Surely, they all couldn't have been duds? Maybe the mystery man was wearing a metal plate over his chest like that Bushranger Ned Kelly had done back in 1880. Maybe that would explain the yellow flashes. Maybe they were the bullets hitting the metal.

As soon as that thought had entered his brain, he dismissed it. There was no sound of bullets hitting metal, no ting, or ricochet.

Stanley adjusted the aim of his Colt just in case there was a metal plate protecting his chest. Stanley aimed right between the intruder's eyes, dead centre of his forehead, just south of his brimmed hat.

Again, his arm was steady, again he squeezed the trigger. There was another crack and again, a split second later, another burst of light at the end of the barrel, just as it had done on the previous four occasions.

This time there was no smile, no sinister laugh. Hat Man stood his ground, unshaken.

They must be duds, Stanley reaffirmed to himself as his fifth shot failed.

"Now, you will be mine." Hat Man spoke in a deep horrifying voice.

Stanley had his finger firmly on the trigger, and he was ready to fire his sixth and final shot. Stanley pressed down hard, squeezing as he had done five times before, but the trigger didn't move. It was as if the safety had been engaged.

Stanley squeezed harder, but the trigger didn't budge. Stanley panicked, quickly looking at the side of the revolver to check the safety.

It was off.

Stanley looked up, fearing Hat Man had advanced on him. Instead he was standing patiently with his right hand up like a stop sign. Stanley froze, although he didn't know why.

Hat Man pointed his finger and thumb into the shape of an imaginary gun and placed the tip of his finger against his forehead.

He gave a beaming smile, revealing those horrible teeth once again.

Stanley's hand mimicked the Hat Man's gun finger and he placed the barrel of his Colt against his own temple. The warm metal barrel nestled firmly against his skin.

Stanley quickly grabbed his gun hand with his left hand and tried to lever the gun away from his own temple. It was immovable, like a rock. He tried a second time. pulling his arm down with all his weight, yet he could not stop himself.

Still smiling, Hat Man created an imaginary trigger finger with his third finger, which he began to squeeze.

Stanley could feel his own trigger finger beginning to constrict. He was now applying pressure to the trigger, with the barrel resting against his temple.

Stanley knew he didn't have the strength to pull the gun away from his head; the power Hat Man was using was too strong. Stanley thought if he couldn't move the gun away from his head then maybe he could move his head away from the gun.

He shifted his head backwards, but the gun remained pressed against his head.

As Stanley moved his head forward trying to get it away from the barrel, he noticed Hat Man compressing his trigger finger even further. He felt his own finger apply more pressure to the trigger. No matter how much he tried to prevent it moving, it did as Hat Man instructed it.

Stanley knew he didn't have much more time before the gun would fire. He quickly shoved his left thumb behind the trigger, in an attempt to prevent it depressing any further. He cried in pain as the trigger depressed further, in the process cutting into Stanley's left thumb. This thing was no man, Stanley thought.

The house began to tremble, and the windows rattled as if an earthquake was coming.

"Please stop this, please don't!" Stanley cried.

"I'm sorry, but you summoned me, so I have come for you. Soon you will be part of me," Hat Man replied.

"Part of you?"

"That's what happens when I collect your soul," Hat Man said, smiling.

Before Stanley could mumble a response, Hat Man pulled his trigger finger and touched his palm.

The trigger on Stanley's Colt depressed further, and the back of the trigger began to cut into his thumb again. The pain was excruciating but it ended quickly for Stanley.

The last of the bullets in the Colt fired, spraying Stanley's brains and skull fragments across his bed and his room.

After everything went black, Stanley found himself staring at Hat Man. What had happened? Did the gun misfire again? Then he gazed back at the bed. He could see himself there, dead. He was now a translucent representation of his body.

He stood over his bloody body trying to reconcile what had just occurred.

A cold breath that tickled the back of his neck interrupted his thoughts.

Stanley turned to see the thing, the Hat Man, standing toe-to-toe with him. His bony fingers unfolded from his hands into ten tiny spears and before he knew it they were inserted into his translucent stomach. Hat Man's mouth opened up.

Everything Stanley had inside him was being drawn out, all the love, all his memories were being taken. He was being taken with them; Hat Man was digesting him head first. The last thing he saw, before being swallowed by the darkness, was a bright, incredibly warm light that seemed to be calling for him; a light he would never reach.

Chapter 10

Picton December 1916

Five hours after Stanley had been killed, Ruth sat down next to June as she ate her breakfast.

"How did you sleep?" Ruth asked.

"Wonderfully well." June sat up in her bed, her tray table in front of her. She began with her toast and poured her tea. June liked her tea strong, so she only added a smidgen of milk.

"Have you had any visitors recently?" Ruth asked, wanting to get straight to the point.

"As a matter of a fact I saw Scat last night, before he had to go to work," June replied.

"Scat?" Ruth recognised the name from the séance.

"Yes, that's what he calls himself," June replied placidly.

Maybe it was a coincidence, Ruth thought. Unusual name to be a coincidence . . .

"Do you know what Scat does for work?" she questioned.

"Oh, um he did tell me . . . let me think." June paused. Her eyes went to the right and up as if she was searching her brain for the answer. She took a gulp of her tea. As she placed the cup back on the tray table, a bit spilt over the lip, staining the crisp white sheet.

A few seconds later, her eyes returned to centre. She had found the answer. "He is a collector," June stated.

"Do you know what he collects?" Ruth probed.

"I don't think he has ever said . . . but it must be something rare. He always seems to be working long hours."

June could feel her cough building. It was about to erupt the way it did each morning, once she became active. June retrieved her handkerchief from the bedside table and placed it next to her tray.

"Did he say anything else to you last night when he came to visit?" Ruth asked.

"Yes, quite a lot. In fact, most of it was about you and your friend."

"What about me, what friend?" Ruth asked quickly, desperate for June to spill the beans.

"Your friend Stanley." June's first cough came; it was coarse and full of phlegm.

Ruth waited eagerly for June's cough to subside.

"What about Stanley? How does he know Stanley?" Ruth asked impatiently.

"He said he needed to collect something from Stanley. Something very rare, then he said, he was coming to see you." June coughed again.

Ruth sat in the chair beside the bed, trying to comprehend what she was being told. What could Stanley have that a collector would want? She knew for certain he didn't own anything rare or of great value.

"Do you know where this Scat was going after he left you last night?" Ruth asked, still trying to get a handle on what Stanley might have.

June thought, trying to recall. Her eyes went back to their search mode. When her eyes returned to their normal position she said, "Now that you mention it, I think that's when he mentioned Stanley; I think he said he was going to collect something from Stanley."

Ruth was becoming frustrated now. "June, this is really important. Can you tell me what he said, word for word?"

"Sorry dear, but I don't remember everything like I used to."

"Please try?"

June sipped the remaining tea. "To the best of my recollection, as Scat was leaving I asked him where he was off to this late. It must have been 2 am. He replied by saying, 'I'm off to collect some goods from a man named Stanley. He is a friend of Ruth, your nurse. Matter of fact I need to collect something special from Nurse Ruth soon too.' That was it. I'm sorry; that's all I remember."

Ruth decided she had to speak to Stanley, but it would have to wait until after work. She had no way of contacting him out there on the railroad.

"Thank you. It's a big help," Ruth said to June.

"What does he need to collect, dear?" June asked.

Ruth ignored her question. "Before I take your morning obs, is there anything else you would like to eat or drink? How about a glass of milk?"

"No thank you," June replied as she pushed her tray table away.

Ruth spent the rest of the day wondering what on earth this man could want with Stanley and herself.

Nothing came to mind.

At the end of her shift, she passed Nurse Mary Crankshaw in the lunch room where she was making herself a cup of coffee before her shift began.

"You worked graveyard shift last night, didn't you?" Ruth asked Mary.

Mary turned from her coffee and biscuits. "Yes, I certainly did. I'm back to do the afternoon shift already."

"June told me she had a visitor at 2 am, but there was no one listed in the visitor's log, and to be honest I can't imagine you allowing visitors in at that time of night . . ."

Mary frowned. "She didn't have any visitors. Hasn't had any for weeks, not since her son came up from Melbourne. And you're right; I wouldn't allow anyone in at that time of night. I need this job. It keeps food on the table. If I did that, management would surely send me packing."

"I didn't think so," Ruth said.

"You know, she may be beginning to lose her marbles. She's been telling me all sorts of stories. She even said her friend was looking forward to meeting me," Mary said.

"Did she mention a name for this friend?" Ruth asked.

"She did. It was a peculiar name. Um . . . what was it?" Mary pondered. "Scar I think. No, that's not right, I can't recall, sorry."

"Scat?" Ruth questioned.

"Scat, yes that's it. She comes up with some whoppers all right. The other day she told me Scat was going to take her out of here. Free her from this prison, she told me, or something absurd like that."

"Maybe she's already lost her marbles?"

"Looks that way. Let's hope we never get like that, hey?" Mary replied.

Ruth felt much better after speaking with Mary, yet how would June know about Stanley? She had to speak to Stanley as soon as possible, and decided she would head over to Stanley's straight after work. She only had handover to do and then her shift would be finished.

Handover seemed to take a month of Sundays. Those last fifteen minutes seemed like an eternity.

The walk to Stanley's house was forty minutes, if she used the Redbank Range Tunnel. She doubted she would be able to go through that tunnel anytime soon. She knew she would have to go the long way, which would add an extra twenty minutes, but she thought it would be better than facing that dark tunnel where Anne had met her fate.

Chapter 11

Melbourne 2016

As soon as Jake arrived at the office the next morning, he began on the investigation contract for Karen. He also placed a second call to Lucas. Jake assumed he was swamped in cases and that was the reason he hadn't returned his call yesterday afternoon.

Jake had his list in front of him, tabulating the most important things he wanted Lucas to follow up first, although he assumed Lucas would know exactly where to start.

Jake removed his brown leather jacket, hung it over the back of his chair and settled into his seat. He was enjoying wearing a leather jacket, shirt and jeans; far more comfortable than the suit and tie required during his years in homicide.

He dialled the Sydney number with the (02) prefix. He had to get in touch with Lucas to prepare the contract. In a worst-case scenario, if Lucas was too snowed under, Jake would make the trip to Picton Town himself.

The phone rang four times and just when Jake thought it was going to revert to message bank again, a muffled voice answered.

"This is Lucas," the voice groaned.

"Is that Lucas?" Jake questioned, thinking he may have dialled incorrectly.

"That's what I said," was the blunt response.

"It's Jake Miller from Vic Homicide. We worked on the Satan's Son's bikie cartel a few years back."

"Hey Jake, my phone didn't recognise the number. How ya doing?" Lucas asked.

"Good, I'm doing private work now. I hear you're doing the same up there." Lucas's northern slang drove Jake crazy. The shortening of words like 'you' to 'ya', Jake could tolerate, but what really irritated him was the mispronunciation of words like 'something' and 'nothing'. Lucas always pronounced them 'somethink' and 'nothink'.

Despite Lucas's Central Coast slang, Jake knew that his detective skills were second to none. Sometimes Jake wondered if Lucas was an even better detective than he was. He didn't think that of many people.

"Yeah, going on two years next January. It beats putting guys away and seeing them out on bail a few weeks later, plus I don't need to wear the suit and tie anymore," Lucas replied. His voice was still a little quiet and muffled.

"Have you got a few minutes or is this a bad time? You sound as if you're in the middle of something."

"Yeah. I'm okay, for the moment. I'm on a stakeout, so if I have to fly, I'll call ya later today," Lucas said.

"Understand. I have a case I need your help on."

"An interstate affair?"

"Suicide."

"Suicide? Why ya investigating a suicide?" Lucas asked.

"Victim's mum has hired me. She thinks her daughter was murdered."

"Guessing the coroner ruled suicide?" Lucas questioned.

"He sure did, and very quickly too."

"What was the cause of death?"

"Electrocuted in a bathtub."

"Sounds like suicide to me," Lucas said.

"That's what I thought at first and it probably is. Problem is, the radio was found in the tub at her feet."

"Hmm, that raises questions. You have sparked my interest here, Jake. So, what do ya need from me?"

"She died in a hotel room in a small town called Picton, not far from you. Her mum doesn't know why she was there. Police believe she went there to commit suicide. I want to know if you would be interested in doing a few days of investigation. Find out what she was doing there. You have a good nose for finding the truth. While you're investigating what she was doing up there I'll start looking into her background from down here," Jake explained. "What muddies the waters even further is this: just six weeks prior to her death on the weekend of the 4th of July, the victim and her friend were involved in a car accident where her friend was killed."

"Victim's name?" Lucas asked.

"Gemma Bassil."

"Gemma driving?"

"No, her friend Paige was. Police reports indicate they were both highly intoxicated."

"So, it ain't her fault. Not like she is going to have the guilts," Lucas mused.

"Wait, there's more. After being pulled from the wreckage, Gemma told police that a drifter in a hat had been tampering with their car, while they were ghost-hunting at the Redbank Range Tunnel."

"What the hell is that?" Lucas asked.

"I don't know; might be worth researching before you leave though."

"Who said I'm going anywhere?"

"When I tell you the fee you will . . ."

"Why, what's the fee?"

"$15,000 for the first fourteen days, split it 50-50. Then we reassess where the investigation is."

"Sounds reasonable. Do ya have a pen? I'll give you my email." Lucas sounded interested.

"Go ahead," Jake said.

Lucas reeled off his address and Jake promised he would send all the information he had, as well as a copy of the contract by the next day. Jake said goodbye and was about to hang up the phone when he heard a voice say something on the other end. Quickly, he raised the receiver back to his ear.

"Yo, Jake, ya still there?" Lucas was saying.

"Yes . . . sorry," Jake replied.

"What hotel did she die in?"

"It was the Intercontinental."

"You know that hotel is supposed to be haunted, don't ya?"

"Don't tell me you believe in ghosts, Lucas?"

"N-n-no, not at all, but ya start wondering about all those stories."

"You'll probably only have to stay a few days, just sleep with the light on," Jake advised.

Lucas chuckled. "I'll take my Beretta, just in case."

"I don't think you can shoot something that's already dead," Jake answered, laughing.

"If I see anythink, then I'll find out." Lucas became more serious and asked, "What dates did she stay there?"

"There are two dates I need you to investigate in 2014. The first is when the accident happened, the 4th of July weekend, and the second is six weeks later, on the weekend of the 16 and 17th of August. I believe she was found dead on the morning of the 17th, by hotel staff. Got that?"

"Sure."

"Okay. Thanks." Jake hung up the phone and flicked his track pad. His computer came to life. It sat idle on the Google search page.

Jake typed three words.

'Picton Town Ghosts.'

Chapter 12

Picton December 1916

The December afternoon heat had died down about halfway through Ruth's walk to Stanley's house. It made the longer trip more bearable. Sometimes, she even felt a touch of a cool breeze as she walked down the path that detoured the tunnel where Anne had met her demise.

By the time Ruth passed the tunnel, the cool change had clearly come, and the clouds were rolling in. It made climbing the hill that the tunnel cut through a little easier. There would be a thunderstorm tonight. She hoped she would make it back home before the heavens opened.

Arriving at Stanley's farm, she headed through the gate, which had been left ajar. Luckily, his animals were kept in the back paddocks adjacent to the shed.

The cloth sheets that Stanley used as makeshift curtains were closed, covering the dirty, dusty windows. A couple of flies landed on the inside of the window before disappearing out of sight.

Ruth tried to peer through the gap in the sheets, but the lounge, the same lounge where they had performed that séance, appeared empty. Since then the world had changed.

Ruth stepped off the porch and headed around to the right side of the home where a dirt path had been cut into the brush. The horizontal cedar panels were fading in the summer sun.

Ruth walked around but could see nothing through any window, except when she peered into the bathroom. While the room was empty, apart from a towel crumpled on the floor, Ruth noticed more flies, or probably the same ones, she thought, flying around the inside of the house.

At the back porch, resting against the wall was Stanley's bicycle. He must be home.

"Stanley!" Ruth called.

There was no response.

Ruth moved towards the back door. She knocked loudly and waited.

"Stanley, you home?" Ruth called again.

Still no response.

The sun was getting lower, but it was still an hour or so before dusk.

She knocked a second time, this time, louder, almost thumping on the door. As her hand hit the door, she noticed her arm was covered with flies. She tried to shoo them off, but they clung to her. They were normally bad in the summer heat, especially before a thunderstorm, but this was the worst she had seen them.

Ruth looked at the bike again. It was usually with Stanley. Suddenly she got a bad feeling in the pit of her stomach. She turned the handle on the back door. It was locked.

Ruth turned towards the back paddock. About fifty yards away from the back door was the outhouse, and beyond that, two large paddocks with a tin hay shed in the middle. Ruth stepped off the back porch and walked down the roughly cut path towards the outhouse.

She made it halfway down the path before stopping. The long grass was not an ideal place to be walking on a hot summer's day, especially in her nursing shoes and not her riding boots. She squinted. She could see the horses and cattle in their respective paddocks, but when she turned her focus to the shed, she saw no movement. If he was feeding the animals he would be going to and fro from the shed to the paddocks.

"Stanley!" she yelled as loudly as she could. Again, there was no response, and no one appeared from the shed.

"Stanley!"

She waited. Still there was no movement from the shed.

Ruth headed back to the house. She turned to face the road, thinking maybe he had walked to a neighbour's place; his closest was a hundred yards up the hill and across the road.

Ruth's gaze returned to the gate. It was open when she arrived. What if that drifter had paid Stanley another visit?

She needed to get in and check if Stanley was in there. Check if he was all right.

She returned to the first window she had looked through at the front of the house.

Ruth dug her nails in under the bottom of the window, pulled and managed to prise it open enough to climb through. The floorboards inside groaned under her feet.

The house was dark and smelly. A large mat lay in the middle of the lounge room floor and two high-back armchairs faced the window. In the corner sat a guitar and next to the window was a small table holding a radio and a clock, which showed it was just before 6 pm.

"Stanley, you home?" Ruth called out.

She listened for a response as well as any movement.

There was none.

Ruth moved through the kitchen. A frying pan lay in the sink, unwashed, and flies flew from room to room. She could hear them buzzing about the place. A plate sat in the drying rack, ready to be put away. An unlit kerosene lamp sat on the table.

She headed towards the bedroom. The door was shut, and she knocked. More flies lingered around the bottom of the door.

There was no answer and she couldn't hear any movement.

Ruth wrapped her hand around the doorknob. It whined as she turned it gingerly. A great sense of dread came over her.

Flies landed on her face.

Nothing could have prepared her for the sight that awaited her on the other side of the door. Stanley lay dead in bed, his eyes wide open and filled with fear. Blood was splattered across his bed clothes and the floor. Some had even reached the other side of the room.

Flies were not only crawling over Stanley's face, but they had followed the trail of blood across the room.

Ruth approached the bed slowly. She went to the right-hand side of the bed to avoid all the blood. As she reached it, something silver on the floor glistened up at her. She knew instantly it was his revolver.

She passed it by without touching it. She knelt on the bed, careful to avoid his right hand which hung slumped over the edge, and reached across to feel his neck for a pulse. But as she suspected, there was none.

Going by Stanley's expression, someone or something had terrified him.

Shaking with grief and fear, Ruth realised she must get the police and ambulance.

She looked up at the back of the bedroom door. Just to the left of it she noticed there were five holes in the wall. She wondered why he had fired the gun before he'd turned it upon himself.

Had he fired at an intruder perhaps? Maybe the drifter?

She leaned over Stanley's body. The left side of his head was missing, splattered on the floor and wall beside him.

Ruth screamed and instantly felt sick.

She frantically ran to the front door, released the lock and flung open the screen door. She made it down three steps of the front porch before she vomited violently.

Ruth tried to collect her thoughts. She needed to call for help. The nearest phone was located at the general store ten minutes away. As she ran, she wondered if Stanley had turned the gun on himself. Had he been suicidal? Sure, he'd been upset at the funeral, but who hadn't been?

Yes, Stanley was worried about the drifter, the 'Hat Man' that had been around town.

Something was terribly wrong.

Ruth still looked awfully unwell when she arrived at the store because the storekeeper asked her, "Are you feeling all right, Miss Martin?"

"Not at all, Mr Wade. There's been a terrible accident at Stanley's farm and we need to contact the police and an ambulance." Ruth's voice had begun calmly but ended up in a full-on sob.

Mr Wade, who was in his early fifties, placed the cloth he was cleaning the counter with on the till, and called for his wife.

Elsa came running from the back of the shop.

"Elsa, please get her water and a chair, while I call the authorities." Mr Wade headed out the back to the phone.

Elsa nodded and filled a glass from the tap and sat Ruth down behind the counter.

Mr Wade returned.

"They're on their way. What on earth has happened?"

"Stanley is dead; looks like he shot himself," Ruth sobbed.

"Oh, my goodness!" Elsa squealed in horror at the news.

After about ten minutes, the police arrived and a few minutes later the ambulance. Both arrived by carriage. Cars were not available in Picton yet although according to the mayor, they weren't far away.

Ruth tearfully explained to the sergeant how she had found Stanley. The only thing she omitted was why she had come to see him. She thought if she told the police she had wanted to talk to him about a mysterious Hat Man, they would have her on the first bus to the insane asylum.

Instead, Ruth just stated that she wanted to see how he was coping after Anne's funeral. After all, Stanley and Anne had been dating for nearly two years.

The sergeant asked if he had been drinking heavily at the wake. Ruth explained she had left after the service and hadn't attended the wake, so she couldn't say what condition he was in. The sergeant took down everything she said.

"Miss Martin, the ambulance is going to take Stanley's body to the morgue in Picton."

Poor Ruth doubted she would ever be able to forget the image of Stanley in that bed. She feared it was burnt deep into her brain.

"Would you be able to drop me at St Mark's, please? I really think I need to talk to Pastor Dwyer," Ruth said to the policeman.

"No problem. It's on my way back to the station, so hop aboard."

He offered his hand to help her, and she lifted the hem of her uniform and stepped into the carriage.

As they headed back towards town, all Ruth could think of was that maybe, the mysterious Hat Man was somehow involved in her friends' deaths.

Chapter 13

Melbourne 2016

With the contract signed and the initial fee paid, Jake sat in the waiting room of Gemma's psychologist.

From the furniture and the décor, Jake immediately concluded that Mrs Jermaine was running an extremely successful business. The magazines were new, the tables were all dust-free, the counter was shiny, and the silver lettering glistened under the lights.

A photo on the cover of one of the gossip magazines caught his attention. It was a photo of two parents, the Walters, who had been investigated for murder. Jake had been a part of the investigation. Early on, everyone thought the mother had murdered her children in their sleep; suffocated all three.

All the investigators wondered how anyone could do such a thing, especially to their own children. Jake always waited before reaching a conclusion until all the facts were in. He felt it affected his ability to stay open-minded. His biggest fear was that his emotions would push him in one direction and he would end up missing vital evidence that would solve the case.

He was especially proud of himself that he had managed to stay focused in the Walters' case. While many in the force had condemned the couple, Jake had just done his job.

When the toxicology reports came back, there were many red faces along the halls of justice. It turned out that the culprit was in fact a faulty space heater. Apparently, it hadn't been serviced and was leaking carbon dioxide. The deadly gas had killed the children in their sleep.

While there was no crime, the Walters' lives were changed forever.

It was another ten minutes of patiently waiting before Mrs Jermaine called Jake into his office. She wasn't what he expected at all. She was dressed very casually and looked every bit the caring mum. She wore a long black skirt below her knees, long black boots and a white shirt and cardigan. Her hair was brown, short and tucked behind her ears.

The office had the usual armchair, located opposite an urbane-looking black and silver couch. Her desk was opposite, with two chairs in front of it. She took her seat behind it and offered Jake one of the chairs.

"Apparently you're investigating the death of Gemma Bassil?"

"Yes, that's correct."

I have told everything I know to the police. I don't see how I can help you any further, Mr Miller."

"Please, call me Jake."

He noticed she didn't offer her first name in response. She wanted to keep this formal. He doubted she would be anything like this with her clients.

"I'm not conducting a police investigation, just trying to ensure the police investigation was accurate and provides closure to the family."

"Was it accurate, Mr Miller?"

"I haven't completed my investigation yet, but on the surface, it appears so. Mrs Jermaine, may I ask you a few questions about Gemma's treatment?"

"I'll answer what I can, but some topics may be privileged. I am sure you understand physician–patient privilege."

Jake couldn't understand why she was being so evasive. It was more than patient privilege. He wondered if she was hiding something.

"Firstly, privilege dies with the patient and if I have to get a court order to release your file on Gemma then I will, but I would prefer not to. This is not a witch hunt, Mrs Jermaine. I am not here to cause trouble, or to cast doubt on your expert opinion. I just want your help to put this case to rest," Jake said firmly.

She leant back in her chair and thought for a second, before unclipping a set of keys from her office key chain. She huffed, stood up, retrieved a file from her cabinet, and returned to her desk.

She slid the file across the desk.

"I'm not trying to be difficult, Jake, and while I know I did everything I could to help Gemma, it doesn't stop me from feeling responsible. I always wonder if I missed something."

"I wouldn't beat yourself up about it. One thing I have seen in my time on the force is people are very good at burying dark secrets deep inside themselves. I'm not here to lay blame for her suicide. I am here just to confirm that it was suicide, that's all, Mrs Jermaine."

"Please, call me Kelly."

He nodded.

"You think she died some other way?" Kelly asked.

Jake shuffled in his seat and opened the folder she had slid to him. "It's possible it was an accident, or even foul play."

"You think someone killed Gemma?"

"I don't, but I don't rule anything out until the evidence suggests otherwise."

He had flicked through three pages of notes, scanning them as he went. Nothing abnormal caught his eye. To him it was a typical psychologist's patient who was suffering depression from the recent loss of her father followed by the tragic loss of her best friend.

"Do you mind if I ask you a few quick questions?"

"Of course, although all the notes are in my file there."

"Some of this may not be in the notes. Did you know that Gemma was writing a daily journal?"

"Yes, I was the one who suggested she begin a diary. It was done as a coping mechanism for the loss of her father. I suggested she talk to her dad by writing the journal."

"Have you read any of the entries?" Jake asked.

"No, it was her personal diary. She didn't offer to show me, and I didn't ask to see it. Have you read them yourself?"

"Some entries, but not all of them," Jake replied. "How emotionally stable did Gemma seem to you, when you last saw her?"

"The last time I saw her was two weeks after the car accident that killed Paige. Gemma came in to see me. She was on the mend physically, but she was still a mess mentally. Even though she was extremely upset by Paige's death, I never saw the symptoms of self-harm. Depression yes, self-harm, no."

"That would have been late July 2014?"

"Correct." Kelly flicked through her file. "It was Monday the 28th to be exact. From my notes here, Gemma said she planned to go back to Picton. She told me it was no accident."

"The crash?"

"That's right. Apparently, before they had the car accident they were being followed by a man who had scared them."

"What would going back achieve?" Jake asked.

"Apparently, he was a local. Gemma had told the police after the accident that they were being followed. Somehow, I don't think the police took her information too seriously. "

"Did she say how the accident happened?"

"No. Just that they were being followed."

Jake finished writing notes and laid the pen and his notepad on his lap.

"Maybe she wrote about it in her diary," Kelly suggested.

"I could find no diary for July 2014. It's like that month never existed for Gemma," Jake replied.

"Maybe it's because she had the accident that month," Kelly offered.

"But I don't even have the July diary. You would think there would be entries up until the time of the accident. The August diary is also missing."

Jake continued, "So, Gemma saw you on the 28th of July 2014 and then a few weeks later on the 17th of August she was found electrocuted in a hotel bathtub?" Jake confirmed.

"Sadly, that's what happened. Yet none of us knows why." Kelly sighed.

"I wonder what changed between those two dates?"

Kelly shrugged. "We all ask that question."

Jake put his pen in the inside pocket of his leather jacket and closed his notepad. "Thanks for your help." He extended his hand and shook Kelly's firmly but gently.

"Jake, let me know what you find, please."

Jake, who was halfway out the door, turned and answered in the affirmative as he left her office.

Chapter 14

Picton December 1916

Two gas lanterns at the entrance to St Mark's Anglican Church lit Ruth's path.

Pastor Joseph Dwyer was only twenty-one. He was a baby-faced pastor with pleasant facial features, of small stature and slight frame. He always appeared happy and at peace with himself, as if he didn't have a worry in the world.

Stationed at St Mark's, he worked under Pastor Philip Fletcher who was due to retire in the next few years, and who provided sound guidance in Joseph's spiritual development.

On the night Ruth came bursting through the doors of St Mark's, Joseph was about to prepare for a date; his second with young Laura Hayfield who was three years his junior.

Ruth had tears streaming down her cheeks, her eyes red and bloodshot.

"Are you all right my dear?" Pastor Dwyer asked.

"No, I've had a terrible week," Ruth replied.

Joseph knew exactly what she was talking about. He had performed the service at Anne's funeral after all. He could tell, yesterday at the service, she wasn't coping well.

"Sit please." He motioned her towards the front row pew.

She sat, as he took up a seat beside her.

"Did you want to talk about Anne?" Pastor Dwyer questioned.

"Anne and Stanley." Ruth dabbed a tissue to her eyes, trying to dry up the flow of tears.

"Stanley? Is he having problems dealing with Anne's death too?"

"He's dead!" Ruth blurted. "The police say he may have killed himself sometime last night. I just found his body in his bedroom." Ruth burst into another flood of tears.

Pastor Dwyer sat on the pew, stunned by the news of Stanley's death.

"How did he die?"

"Suicide apparently; shot himself." Ruth sobbed.

"I spoke to him yesterday at the wake, and he didn't appear suicidal. In fact, considering the occasion, he was quite calm," Pastor Dwyer said.

"He appeared fine at the funeral, when I saw him. I should have stayed for the wake, but I just needed to go home and have a good cry."

"We all need a good cry sometimes. There is nothing wrong with that. Nothing to be ashamed of," Pastor Dwyer soothed. "I'm sure they are in a better place. They are with the Lord now."

"I came here because I don't think Stanley or Anne killed themselves. Something strange is going on in this town," Ruth said.

Pastor Dwyer looked at her with an expression of confusion. "I don't understand what you mean, Ruth. Anne stepped in front of a train. Maybe it was a tragic accident, but it's clear that's what happened. As for Stanley, I understand that his death is raw but if the police say he killed himself then they are usually right, my dear." He placed his hand on hers. "Death is a very hard thing to understand. It is what tests our faith the most."

Ruth looked up at him. Kindness shone in his eyes. "Yesterday, Stanley told me he was having trouble with a drifter in town."

"A drifter?"

"Apparently the drifter has been visiting a lady I care for in the hospital as well."

"What sort of problems was he having with this drifter?" Pastor Dwyer asked.

"Stanley told me he had broken into his house. That's why he had bought the gun; for protection."

"Have you informed the police of this person?"

"No." Ruth hesitated.

"What is it, my dear? Is there something else you want to tell me?" he probed.

"I'm afraid you'll think I'm crazy. In fact, I think I'm crazy," Ruth replied.

"I'm sorry. I don't follow. Why do you're think you're crazy? I promise I won't judge."

"When Anne died I saw her body in the morgue. She had an expression of fear that was so intense, it was like she had seen the devil himself. She looked horrified. While I was there I noticed that she had these strange horizontal lines on her stomach. There were three of them. They were like burn marks. Anyway, while I thought it was strange I didn't think any more of it until . . ."

Pastor Dwyer sat on the edge of the wooden pew, listening intently. "Until?" he prompted.

"Promise you won't think I'm crazy?"

"I promise."

"Until I did my rounds and found that the patient who has also been seeing this man, 'Scat', or whatever she calls him, also had the marks. Then to add to my concern . . ." Ruth looked up.

Pastor Dwyer's mouth was agape, his hands trembling.

"Pastor, are you all right?" Ruth asked.

He sat glued to his pew edge, unemotional, frozen.

"Pastor?" Ruth asked. She touched his shoulder. "Pastor?" she called again.

"What was the name you said?" he asked quietly.

"Scat."

"The church speaks of the seven deadly sins. Well, each sin has a demon. A demon is often referred to as Satan or Scat."

"Why would a demon be here on earth, and what would he want with us?" Ruth asked.

"If it is a demon, then he would be on earth to collect souls. That's what they do," Pastor Dwyer said quietly.

"How and why would one be after them?" Ruth asked.

"Usually demons only come to earth if they are called upon, summoned, if you will." Pastor Dwyer sounded grave.

Ruth tried to place her hands over her mouth before the gasp came out, but she was too late.

"What have you done, Ruth?"

"Stanley, Anne and I did a séance last week. We thought it was harmless. We were just fooling around," Ruth explained.

"Messing around with the dark powers is never a good idea," Pastor Dwyer chided.

"I see that—now. How do we kill this demon?"

"I don't know if we can, as he is not human. Only something of pure good can destroy something of pure evil."

"You're pure and good, Pastor."

"Thank you, my dear, but I think it may take more than me to rid the town of his presence. I'll need to write to the church and seek counsel from my superiors. A demon is beyond my experience," Pastor Dwyer admitted. "Until I get a response from the archbishop, I suggest you wear this. It will give you some protection, help keep you safe."

Pastor Dwyer rose and walked to his dais. He took a silver cross and necklace from a box and placed it around Ruth's neck. "It was what I wore before I was ordained," he said, offering a half smile.

Ruth thanked him and relaxed a little.

"How many marks did you say were left on Anne?" Pastor Dwyer asked.

"Three . . . why?"

"It could be his mark. Most people think of this as the 666, but during my studies I learnt that each sin has a specific demon.

"The demon for Pride is Lucifer. That's why everyone refers to Lucifer as the devil: really, he is just the first demon on the list.

"Envy is Beelzebub. Wrath is Sathanus or Scat, and so on: every sin has a demon. I think it is this demon we are dealing with and he is leaving three lines because he is third in line, so to speak."

"In line for what?" Ruth asked, confused.

"To rule hell, I suspect. If he is a demon of some kind, as we suspect, I would think you would be safe within these walls, as we are on sacred ground. If you ever feel he is after you, get here, or to any church. I'll telegram my superiors, and in the meantime it's probably best you don't discuss this with the townspeople. We don't want to unnecessarily scare anyone, and we don't want you taken away to the loony bin." Pastor Dwyer gave a grim smile.

Ruth nodded but didn't answer. What would the townspeople think of her story?

"Do you know what this being looks like? I assume he has taken on a human form of some kind?" Pastor Dwyer asked.

"According to Stanley and the lady I look after, he wears a long coat and a wide-brimmed hat. Shouldn't be too hard to spot, in this heat."

"He might look out of place, but he won't feel the temperature. The only thing he is after is souls."

"What does he do with the souls he claims?" Ruth asked nervously.

"He feeds on them: they become a part of him."

"Thank you, Pastor, please let me know when you hear back from the church. I'll keep you updated if I see anything," Ruth said.

The pastor again put his hand on Ruth's. "Stay strong. The cross should keep you safe," he encouraged.

Ruth stood, preparing to leave the security of the church. She made her way down the aisle and headed towards the wooden arched doors.

"Would you like me to walk you home?" the pastor offered.

"No, thank you. I have troubled you enough already. It's only a few minutes away. After all, I have this to protect me." Ruth rubbed the cross between her fingers and them tucked it in under the top of her dress, so it rested against her skin.

Her emotions were running wild as she stepped out of the church. She was full of sadness and disbelief over Stanley, thankful for Pastor Dwyer's cross and fearful of the unknown demon. Of all the emotions, fear was the most prominent one running through her.

She walked the whole way, continually checking that the cross was still nestled between her breasts.

Chapter 15

Picton January 1917

Ruth had spent the two weeks since seeing Pastor Dwyer on holiday. She had taken a week off for Stanley's funeral and another week for the Christmas break.

Today was her first night back at work. As usual, her first point of call when beginning work was to do handover at the nurses' station followed by patient observations.

"Good to have you back," Beth said, giving her a hug. This was something Ruth had not experienced from her matron previously.

"Before you start, I have something to tell you," Beth said.

Ruth could tell Beth was unsettled but did not know why. Maybe she was about to fire her . . . no, she'd just said it was good to have her back.

"June passed on last night. I was going to contact you, but I thought no point disturbing you when you would be in today," Beth said.

Ruth stood there, a little shocked. Sure, June had TB but compared to some other patients, she was in reasonable health.

Ruth didn't feel much of an emotional reaction. She thought there would be sadness, yet no tears came. Maybe she had exhausted so much sadness over the past three weeks, she simply had none left.

"How did she die?" Ruth asked.

"In her sleep, peacefully," Beth replied.

"Has her family been contacted?"

"The hospital called them first thing this morning. They are organising the funeral."

Ruth hadn't noticed that Beth still had hold of her shoulders.

"One other thing. You will need to take June to pathology," Beth continued.

"Why can't the orderly take her?" Ruth asked fretfully.

"Ray is not back until tomorrow and as you know, the pathologists need to do the blood tests within twenty-four hours of death. Because Ray is not here you will have to take her," Beth replied.

Ruth sighed, but agreed.

Beth gave her another quick hug and then picked up the patient charts and began discussing them one by one.

Over the last few weeks since seeing Pastor Dwyer, she had thought very little about Hat Man, or the absurd possibility of a demon strolling her town. Yet walking down the hallway that led to the morgue, the thoughts flooded back, and the possibility of a demon Hat Man again seemed very real. All the fear she had felt that night at Stanley's came rushing back. It was as if fear had replaced blood in her veins. The closer to the morgue Ruth came the more uneasy she felt.

Without any conscious effort, Ruth's hand clasped her necklace. It wasn't until her fingertips touched the coldness of the cross that she realised she was playing with it.

Where had the fear come from?

She walked closer to the morgue door. She passed the corridor on her right that led to the pathology centre. A breeze from the empty hall hit her. Fear built with each step she took. She took a deep breath, trying to calm down, trying to reassure herself that everything would be all right.

The morgue was dark, cold and quiet. The lamps were again out. Ruth's only light was her hand-held lamp.

Goosebumps instantly rose all over her skin as soon as she entered.

She was hoping June's body would be located on the entrance side of the morgue yet somehow, she felt it wouldn't be. The bodies were always lined up in order; the newest ones awaiting autopsy, or if the cause of death was under investigation, were together, while the ones ready for burial were normally in the fridges nearest the door. As Picton was a small town, it only had three fridges. With the TB outbreak, this was far short of what was required. As a result, many of the deceased were lined up on trollies throughout the morgue. Ruth looked to her right where she thought she had seen the shadow of Hat Man last time. She moved her lamp in that direction. This time she could clearly see the coat rack was empty, which helped ease her tension.

She guessed June was the most recent death in the hospital, so she went to the furthest trolley on the far side of the room, the darker side, the same place where Anne's remains had lain just weeks ago. The lamp glow led the way through the trollies of the deceased. She came to what she thought would be June's body, only to find it was an elderly man; in his eighties, by the look of him. DOA was written on the toe tag. Ruth recognised him as a local but couldn't remember him by name. She moved along to the next trolley in the queue. She removed the sheet and June was staring back at her. Beth had said she had died peacefully in her sleep, yet the look on her face resembled horror or fear, rather than uninterrupted peace. Her expression seemed odd.

She drew the sheet further down and inspected her arms and stomach with the torch. Ruth could see the three burn marks she had witnessed earlier. They had faded somewhat. Maybe it was due to no blood being pumped around her body, she thought. Ruth brought the covers back up. As they reached June's chest, she had once last look at her face. It certainly was a fearful expression rather than one of peace.

Ruth swung the lantern around the room just to double check she was still alone, make sure there was no Hat Man, make sure none of the deceased had woken.

Everything was as it should be. Nothing had moved, nothing had changed.

Ruth hung the lantern on the end of the trolley and went to flick the trolley's brake off with the top of her foot, only to find air. There was no brake. This was a new scissor-lift trolley, which had the brakes on the other wheel. She again used her foot and disconnected the brake. The trolley glided as she pushed it past the lines of deceased patients and headed out into the hall, towards the pathology corridor. There were no dodgy wheels on this trolley—not yet anyway. Ruth pushed the bed back the way she had come, turning left at the corridor. The goose bumps had left her, at least for the moment.

She manoeuvred the trolley through the twin doors into pathology.

"Hello?" she called.

"Right with you," came the reply from behind the reception counter.

Ruth waited. She had stood away from the trolley and away from June. She had been as close as she needed to be and closer than she wanted. She would be so glad when this job was done. She had seen enough death to last a lifetime. Lately, she had begun to feel like a mortician rather than a nurse.

"So, what we got here?" the abnormally tall man asked as he emerged from behind the desk.

Ruth went through June's details with him while the pathologist checked the wrist and ankle bands in order to confirm the details were correct. Ruth stuttered nervously a couple of times, trying to sound more professional than she felt.

"Where is the orderly? Normally he brings the bodies," the man said. He must be over seven feet tall, Ruth thought, as he spoke.

"Holidays," Ruth replied.

"Ahh, the luck of it, off on holiday while we're stuck here, hey?" he asked rhetorically.

"Oh no, we're the lucky ones. I'd rather be here than at some resort," Ruth joked.

The tall man laughed a snort of a laugh, followed by a little giggle that didn't belong to a body of his size. "You got the chart?"

Ruth took it from the end of the bed and handed it up to the tall man.

"Thank you."

As she headed for the door, a loud voice from above called her back. For a second, she thought it was God speaking to her. "You need to stay here with me. It's against protocol to leave me with the body."

Ruth turned and stood in the doorway, unsure what she was supposed to do.

He moved June into the room, pulling a second trolley by her side.

"This will only take a minute."

The tall man placed the large needle into June's wrist and it filled with bright red. In all he took seven vials of blood.

Ruth watched.

"You can take her back now. The blood results will be back from the lab late tomorrow."

According to the tall man's signature, his first name was William, but she couldn't make out his last name.

Ruth had started wheeling June back through the double doors when she realised she was holding her necklace again.

She had the crumpled chain pressed tightly between her hand and the silver handle of the scissor trolley.

Since Pastor Dwyer had given it to her, she had hardly thought about the Hat Man and she still hadn't seen him. Whatever had happened was over now.

She entered the dark morgue, wheeling June back to her original position, with one hand on the trolley and the other already clasping her necklace. Her lamp swung as it dangled from the end of the trolley. As she crossed to the darker side of the room, the hairs on her neck stood up as if they were all screaming at her. She instantly stopped, turning to looking over her right shoulder.

She clearly saw a man in a long coat and a wide-brimmed hat. The eyes burnt at her.

She screamed.

She was still holding the necklace and screaming when the chain broke as she reeled around in fright, and the cross fell from her hand to the floor. Seconds later, she felt it make contact with her foot. Where it was now she had no idea.

Ruth stood, feet pinned to the floor as if they had been nailed to the spot. She turned her body from the waist, removing the lamp from the trolley and holding it out towards where she thought she had seen the man.

Nothing!

No one was there. Except for the dead, she thought.

Jumping at shadows, she thought again.

Her thoughts returned to her necklace. Where had it gone? She hung the lamp back on the trolley. The lamp provided just enough light under the trolley for Ruth to see her necklace. She bent down to collect it. As the tips of her fingers gathered the chain off the floor, she remembered the chain was missing the most important part. The cross. It had fallen from the chain.

Down on hands and knees, beneath June's cold lifeless body, she searched the floor trying to locate it. The lamp flickered, and Ruth looked up. It was as if a strong wind was trying blow it out.

Maybe it was running out of kerosene.

A cold breeze blew up from behind, causing her goosebumps to return. Her lamp flickered again. Just a few more minutes, she begged. Her prayer went unanswered as her lamp flickered again. Seconds later, a loud bang came from behind her. She jumped up and spun around at the same time.

Her fear had returned, as she could see the door had closed. Just a breeze, she thought, but without her lamp she couldn't see anything.

All she wanted was to get her cross and get back to her ward. She'd had enough frights for one night.

Ruth turned her lamp down to try and save fuel, but she was nearly in pitch black and she could barely see the floor.

She knelt and resumed her search. Almost instantly she located the cross on the other side of the trolley. She tried to move the trolley, but it wouldn't budge. She clicked the brake with her toe, but it was already released. She pushed harder the second time but still it wouldn't move. Something was wrong.

Before she could bend down to see what the problem was, the corpse at the end of the line sat straight up, opened his eyes and screamed.

Ruth screamed back.

Then the female corpse opposite sat up and screamed.

Ruth screamed again.

They were alive.

She needed her cross to protect her. Pastor Dwyer had said she would be safe with it on. She fumbled on the floor beneath June. She climbed halfway through the scissor lift; her fingers touched the edge of the cross trying to bring it closer to her.

The screaming continued. Ruth finally clasped the cross between her thumb and forefinger.

"He's here for you," June said, leaning over the bed.

Ruth screamed again and scrambled backwards, dropping her cross once more.

June's eyelids were wide open but the eyeballs themselves were rolled back.

Ruth could feel feet behind her, but she was too scared to look. She wanted to remove herself from under the scissor lift but couldn't take her eyes off June who although dead, was leaning over the bed speaking to her.

"He is here. Scat is here for you."

The other dead bodies that had been screaming moments ago were now chanting, "Scat, scat, scat."

She knew exactly who Scat was.

Still crouched under the scissor-lift bed, Ruth looked over her shoulder. She could barely make out a pair of legs and what appeared to be the bottom of a trench coat.

Her whole body began to shake. Terror ran through every vein. Her heart was racing. She could feel a pulse throbbing in her neck. Frantically she again looked for the cross, but she couldn't locate it.

She turned back to where June had been hanging over the side of the trolley. She was still there, smiling now.

"Time's up!" June screamed

"Time's up!" The other voices joined in this new chant.

A pair of claw-like hands with long yellow nails grabbed Ruth's ankles and pulled.

Ruth was dragged along the floor. Whoever was here for her, wanted her out from under the bed. She grabbed onto the base of the trolley bed, trying to prevent herself from being dragged out.

Her legs were high off the floor. She could feel someone's fingers burning through her stockings. Soon the fingers would burn her legs.

Her shirt had become untucked. Ruth was losing her grip. Whoever had her legs was yanking hard.

Her hold on the trolley gave way.

There was nothing to hold onto.

Her nails dragged along the concrete as he pulled her out.

Ruth flipped over, kicked hard and screamed as loudly as she could. "Help!"

How could the pathologist not hear her screaming?

Couldn't hear with the morgue door closed, her brain answered immediately.

She screamed louder.

"Help, hellllp!"

"Time's up," the chorus of the dead replied from above.

She could see the man pulling her, the drifter or demon in the hat. What-or-whoever it was, really wanted her. She had no doubt it was the one that had killed Stanley and now it wanted to kill her.

Still sliding, Ruth grabbed another of the bed's arms and held on for dear life.

Her attacker yanked once more. Ruth's grip held firm.

The trolley wobbled and groaned as the tug-of-war continued with Ruth underneath.

Suddenly the scissor lock gave way, sending the bed crashing to the floor.

The scissor arms acted exactly as they were designed and folded onto themselves, crushing Ruth's throat.

The pressure on Ruth's throat was enough to crush her windpipe. For the next few frantic seconds, Ruth desperately struggled to free herself from under the fallen trolley, but she failed.

Ruth thought she had just passed out. It wasn't until she saw her lifeless body lying tangled with her head trapped under the scissor-lift stretcher that she realised she was dead.

She stood motionless, staring at her corpse. A loud snarling noise bellowed from the shadows behind her. She spun, still disorientated, unsure as to who or what she had become. She turned, only to find herself face to face with the creature that had been chasing her. The Hat Man.

Hat Man moved so quickly Ruth didn't even see it happen. It wasn't until she looked down that she saw Hat Man had stabbed her with his fingers. Hat Man's fingers were woven around her invisible insides and back out like shoelaces.

A bright light appeared near the door, strong enough to illuminate the whole morgue. It was warm and inviting. Ruth tried to move towards it, but Hat Man's grip was strong. He ran his face up and down her neck. When he brought his face level with hers, he opened his mouth. The first thing that hit her was the rancid smell, a smell of decomposing flesh. The second was his teeth, which were yellow and oddly shaped.

Without any warning the jaw unlocked, its teeth protruded from its face, and a whirlwind of air began to pull at her, dragging her into Hat Man's mouth.

Into a dark abyss of screaming souls.

Chapter 16

Picton December 2016

Lucas passed the sign that read 'Welcome to Picton, the Stone Quarry Town'. In front of the brick and stone sign was a flowerbed full of annuals, mostly yellow. The Mazda 3 he drove was a lot smaller than the police Commodores he was used to as a detective, yet it was more economical and a much nicer drive. Lucas hadn't quite made the jump from a suit to casual wear. He still wore the slacks and the business shirt, but no tie, and on hot days he rolled up his sleeves.

He slowed to fifty ks as he entered the town. It was the first time he had been in Picton. There was so much of Australia he still hadn't seen.

As he passed the sign from the north, the road slowly descended around a long sweeping bend. In a few kilometres, he would be in the heart of Picton. His first impressions of the town were nothing like he'd thought they would be. Before he'd left, he had done his online research of the town and the Picton Intercontinental Hotel where Gemma had died, and he'd been expecting something far different. The town was represented as one of Australia's most haunted towns, with numerous ghost sightings including in that hotel. In the early 1900s, the hotel had been used as a tuberculosis hospital. According to the internet, a ghost still roamed the halls. Other reports and sightings included a woman who had been hit by a train on the way to visit her boyfriend, now haunting a local disused railway tunnel, and two young teenagers who were seen from time to time roaming the graveyard of St Mark's cemetery, hand in hand.

Lucas didn't believe in ghosts and he wasn't about to start now. After all his years in New South Wales Homicide, he was more concerned about the crimes committed by the living. Even in the weird cases that involved ritual killings and black magic, the investigation always revealed a human was responsible. Sure, he had a few criminals who claimed they were possessed and couldn't control their actions, but he had never arrested a ghost.

The closer he got to the town centre the more normal it appeared. It was a bright, vibrant, quaint little town that seemed to be a hive of activity. He pulled up at a set of lights at Menangle Street. One way was the Picton Intercontinental Hotel, the other St Mark's cemetery. Lucas had booked the same hotel room where Gemma had stayed, hoping to start investigating from where she had been found and work backwards.

The hotel was on the high side of the road. It was an old two-storey Victorian building painted white, with a beautiful wrought-iron balcony. He guessed from the outside it had thirty or forty rooms maximum.

Lucas parked his car in the nearby vacant parking lot, retrieved his bag from the boot and headed inside the hotel.

The old-world charm of the building remained despite the recent renovations, with new carpet and drapes as well as a fresh lick of paint.

Behind the mahogany reception desk stood the receptionist, a short elderly lady with frizzy white hair. She was wearing a bright floral blouse with tan slacks and according to her work tag, 'Isabella Elliot', she was the owner.

"May I help you?" she asked with a smile.

For the proprietor of a hotel that was apparently haunted, she did seem surprisingly chirpy, Lucas thought.

"I have a reservation under Lucas Taylor." Lucas removed his wallet to produce his ID and pay the $100 deposit to cover the mini bar. He had been through this process countless times before.

"You're the private detective that rang a few days ago. You requested the same room that . . ." She didn't quite know how to say it.

Lucas butted in. "Yep, the same one that Gemma stayed in."

"We don't normally let out that room. In fact, I really would prefer if you took another. I would be happy to show it to you during the day. It's the same as all the others on that floor."

"No, that one will be fine, thanks."

Isabella nodded in agreement and grinned widely before continuing with the checking-in process. Her demeanour didn't seem sincere.

Lucas clearly saw her gulp. He had spent many years reading people. "Is there something wrong with the room?" he asked.

"No, not at all. I just don't like going in there ever since I found her," Isabella replied.

"You found her?" Lucas questioned.

"Unfortunately. Such a horrible sight to see someone take their life like that."

"I can imagine. Don't panic, I won't require housekeeping. I'm a bit of a neat freak." Lucas tried to lighten the mood.

"I will be fine. I have to face my fears sooner or later."

Despite the honesty of her answer, Lucas couldn't help feeling there was another reason. She didn't want him in the room either.

"Here you go." Isabella handed Lucas his credit card and ID and a small envelope containing two magnetic cards. "Up the stairs and last room on the right."

There was no offer of help with his bag, not that he needed it, but it reinforced that this was a small hotel in country NSW.

The staircase was carpeted except for the first two steps. The grand and spiral staircase with its highly polished wooden handrail and handcrafted timber supports was quite impressive. The staircase didn't resemble one from a cheap country hotel, that was for sure.

Lucas swiped his card and entered his room. The wall on the left was brick. Immediately on the right was the bathroom, with a vanity opposite the shower and a claw-foot bath along the far wall with a toilet between the shower and the bath. He would take a closer look later.

Beyond the bathroom was the double bed complemented by two side dresser tables. Over the bed hung a large chandelier. Opposite the double bed a TV hung on the wall, under which sat a set of drawers. To the left was a freestanding cupboard. Out of curiosity, he opened the cupboard. It was empty but for some coat-hangers swinging on the rail.

Jake had mentioned to him that there were two of Gemma's journals missing; July and August. If the room had been sealed since her body was removed, then maybe the diaries were still here. He would look for them later. First, there was something he needed to see.

He stood beside the vanity. There was a gap of about eighteen centimetres between the vanity and the edge of the claw-foot bath. Lucas searched through the cupboards under the vanity, looking for the radio that had fallen into the bath. He wasn't surprised it wasn't there; probably taken away by the police for evidence.

He wondered if a radio that toppled from the vanity edge would fall into the bath. From what he could see, it would have fallen through the gap between the bath and the vanity. The gap seemed too big for the radio to reach the bath.

He needed to test his theory.

Chapter 17

Picton January 1917

The sergeant had seen many deaths in his time as a police officer, yet the suicides of Anne and Stanley had been two of the most gruesome sights he had ever witnessed.

That was until he walked into the morgue late on a hot Thursday afternoon in January. He had been called in by the hospital director, Mr Richard Lumley, to investigate a fatal work accident.

Mr Lumley met the sergeant at the door. "Thank you for coming so quickly, Sergeant."

Richard had known Sergeant Lee Amly for many years, but he thought under the circumstances he'd best use protocol.

"It's all right Richard, you can call me Lee," Lee replied, trying to ease the situation. "Tell me what happened."

"Well, William from pathology saw the morgue door wide open. He went to close it and he found, well, um . . ." Richard stopped.

"It's okay, take it slowly."

"He found her crushed on the floor."

"Is William still here?" Lee asked.

"Yes, he's in the tea room."

"I'll need to take his statement. I'll look at the scene first, then have one of my men take his statement so he can go home. Sounds like he's been through a lot," Lee said. "Has anyone apart from William been in there?"

"Just me, but I made sure no one touched anything. We didn't even go near the body. What we saw from three paces was enough." Richard swallowed.

Lee took a step towards the morgue. Richard put a hand on Lee's chest. "It's bad, really bad," he muttered, as if to say, don't go in there. They locked eyes for a second or two before Lee brushed him off and headed inside. It was his job.

The morgue was bright and clinical; all the gas lamps were on and in full glow. The light bounced off the white walls and the concrete floor. Corpses were laid out on the trolleys; four rows of four. The last row, the one furthest from the door, was a little askew. It had three bodies in the row and one trolley sitting in the aisle.

Lee took three steps inside the morgue before stopping. Richard was correct; the sight was horrendous.

A nurse was lying half under a bed, her fear-filled eyes staring at the underneath of the trolley. Blood had pooled on the floor from a cut in her head and dried in her hair. Upon closer inspection, he saw her throat had severe bruising consistent with strangulation.

He knelt, but he couldn't quite see under the bed without lying down on his stomach, and that was out of the question unless he wanted to drag himself through the crime scene.

He rose and stepped back so he was level with the third row of corpses, and then lay flat on his stomach. Under the trolley that the nurse was propped up against, he noticed a small pool of blood.

Behind her he could see a shiny silver necklace. Half the chain was clasped in her hand while the other half was curled up on the concrete floor. A cross lay not far from the end of the chain. He noticed dry blood around the nurse's nose and mouth. Her face was aghast, eyes and mouth wide open, shock and horror written all over it.

Had she seen her impending death?

It looked like a fight.

An attack.

Had the chain fallen off before she died? Was that the reason her head was under the scissor function of the bed? Or had someone killed her?

Had it come off in a struggle?

It looked as if she had collected the chain before the struggle. Maybe she was under the bed when William came across her?

Maybe the pathologist William had had other ideas for the nurse. Maybe that was why there was a struggle, Lee thought. Possibly.

He looked at her legs. Her stockings had runs in them, as if someone's long nails had caused them. He would check the skin for scratches.

It was time to see William.

Lee walked in and sat on the chair opposite him. William looked tired and scared. In the middle of the table sat a barrel of biscuits and around the edge were strewn a few cups.

Sergeant Lee introduced himself.

"You found Ruth, William?" Lee asked.

"Yes sir."

Lee noticed that even when seated William towered over him.

"How tall are you?" Lee asked.

"Six-ten," William replied.

"Wow, big boy! Can you show me your hands? Just put them out for me." Lee demonstrated, holding his hands out, palms facing upwards.

William complied, and Lee noted he had long fingernails for a man. His hands were clean; no cuts, no abrasions.

"Can you tell me what happened?"

William spoke slowly and quietly. "I went to put some bloods in the lab fridge—that's where the lab collects them from. Ruth was going to take the deceased back to the morgue. When I was coming back from the lab I felt a cold draught up the morgue corridor. I went to check it out and saw that the door was wide open. People forget to close it sometimes. When I arrived at the door, I saw her there on the floor. It scared me. I thought she was dead. I didn't intend to go near her but . . . I thought I better check her pulse."

"Go on."

"When I checked her, she was already gone," William said, his complexion becoming paler.

"Did you touch her anywhere apart from her neck?" Lee asked.

"No, I don't think so, maybe I might have placed my other hand on her leg while I was taking her pulse. I can't remember."

"Did you attack Ruth, William?" Lee asked.

"What! No sir, definitely not. I just said I found her like this. I didn't kill her. I only checked her pulse. I don't know how she died. I didn't hurt her, I swear."

Lee wasn't sure he believed him.

"William, we are going to run some tests on your hands, so you won't be able to leave until we have the results back. One of our officers will take you to the courthouse for the night," Lee said.

William nodded and put his head in his hands.

Lee called Richard into the lunchroom. "How long has William worked here?"

"Only a few months. He just moved over from South Australia," Richard replied. "He had impeccable references."

"Did you check them?"

"As best I could, yes."

"I'll have the coroner look over the body, but my initial thought is, this was no accident. To me there was a struggle. The victim grabbed onto the trolley to try and get away from her attacker when the scissor mechanism malfunctioned."

"You think William was the attacker?" Richard asked.

"It appears that way, I'm afraid. We're running some tests, but let me finish the investigation before we make a firm finding. We're going to have to close off the morgue for the next few hours, while we finish our investigation."

"Sure, no problem. Let me know if you need anything," Richard replied.

"Thank you for your cooperation."

"Would you like us to inform Ruth's family?" Richard asked.

"It's best if we do it. If you could just provide me with Ruth's details, I'll send my men to inform her family in person."

Chapter 18

Picton December 2016

Lucas had done a quick search of the room, but had come up short on locating any diary. He headed back down the spiral staircase towards the reception area.

Isabella was at the desk attending to a young couple who appeared to be checking in for a dirty weekend away. The guy had his hand down the back of his blonde girlfriend's jeans, playing with her pink thong, while she was nibbling on his ear between each conversation with Isabella.

Lucas remembered when he was that young and in love. It seemed a lifetime ago . . . or was it just a different life? A life where he had been truly happy, a life before the cancer hit and took his love from him.

Isabella handed them the key envelope as she had done with Lucas. "Don't let the ghosts scare you," Isabella said.

The ghost rumours of this town were obviously good for her business. Encouraging them made her a bit of a charlatan, Lucas thought.

The couple were so excited they almost snatched the keys out of Isabella's hands.

Lucas thought the excitement had more to do with the pink thong than the possibility of seeing a ghost.

The guy hoisted his girlfriend over his right shoulder and picked up his wheelie case in his left hand. He took the steps two at a time. The girl squealed, and slapped his back, giggling all the way up the stairs.

"I hope they're not in the room next to me," Lucas joked.

"Right next door," Isabella replied. "I could move you, if you like?"

Lucas knew it was her ploy to have him switch rooms.

"No, thanks. I'm sure I'll get used to their rumbustious frolicking," he said, smiling.

"Something else I can get for you?" she asked.

"I have a couple of questions for ya, if you have time."

"Sure, fire away."

"The first time Gemma and Paige stayed here, did they say they were having any problems?"

"When they weren't in the bar they stuck to themselves pretty much. On the first night they were here, I think it was the Friday night, they were asking about ghost tours. They were keen to try and see a ghost. Mind you, most of our tourists are here for the ghost tours," Isabella replied.

"Which are?"

"I suggested the three most common places tourists go to see ghosts."

"Where are they?"

"Well here, obviously. This place used to be the old tuberculosis hospital. Rumour has it, there is a nurse that still haunts the halls. Although I haven't seen her, some have. My staff claim to have had her visit.

"Second is the Redbank Range Tunnel, or the Mushroom Tunnel as locals refer to it now. Some believe a girl on the way to visit her boyfriend tried to cut through the tunnel, only she misread the train timetable and was hit by the train. Her mangled body was carried on the cow-catcher all the way to the next station.

"Thirdly is the cemetery at St Mark's. It used to be the town church. Now it's a private residence, owned by the church, occupied by the former pastor, Elijah Dwyer. His father was also a pastor of the church. He lives there with his granddaughter, Olivia. They are very rarely seen outside of the church grounds. People have claimed to see ghosts of children running through the graveyard. One of them is supposedly Elijah's brother, who died when he was twelve, playing with a friend on a pile of sleepers."

"How does a twelve-year-old die playing on a pile of sleepers?" Lucas asked.

"Apparently the pile collapsed on him and his friend, crushing them both."

"Do ya know if the girls actually went out ghost-hunting?"

"I assume so, but they were in the bar when I last saw them."

"What about the Saturday? Did ya see them that day at all?"

"No, but they were in the bar again Saturday night. Garry had to stop serving them. They got a bit narky. He's working tonight if you want to ask him the details. He starts at 7. I'd hate to give you information that was wrong or misleading," Isabella replied.

"I'll catch up with him later then. Oh, do ya have a radio that was the same as the one that ended up in Gemma's bathtub? I want to run some tests."

"The police have done all those tests, hun. You'd be wasting your time."

"Yeah, well. I'm employed to run my own investigation, not just concur with the police findings." He could see she was put out by his comments, but he stood firm.

"I could borrow one from another room for you," Isabella offered.

"I'm pretty sure I'll end up with the same results as the police, but at least I'll be able to tell Gemma's mother I tested every theory." He tried to soften the blow. He realised he might need more information and there was no point getting her offside unnecessarily.

"What theory is that?" Isabella asked.

"She had the radio on too loud and it vibrated off the edge into the bath."

"That's what the police think happened too."

"Speaking of police, who is it best to speak to about the deaths?"

"They were both handled by Inspector Mike Connolly, except he's stationed in Thirlmere, which is just south of Picton. I used to have his card, but I think I chucked it out about a year ago. I didn't think I would need it again."

"That's okay, I'll track him down."

It was too late in the day to speak with Connolly. He'd save that task for first thing in the morning.

It was probably best to get his bearings around town, then come back and grab some grub and speak with Garry in the pub, before going ghost-hunting.

He stepped out into the December heat. He could almost see the heat smouldering off the tarmac of the carpark. He noticed a black Mercedes packed two spaces over from his Mazda.

No wonder the girl checking in had been excited; her man had money and looks.

Chapter 19

Picton January 1916

Pastor Joseph Dwyer, upon returning to the church after grocery shopping, found Sergeant Lee waiting.

"Sergeant, what do I owe the pleasure on this fine morning?" he asked.

"Unfortunately, it's not pleasure. It's business, Pastor," Lee replied.

Dwyer's smile faded. "Please come in."

The St Mark's Protestant Church was unlocked, as always; people in this town were good, honest folk.

Pastor Dwyer held the heavy wooden arched door open for the sergeant and then followed him inside.

It was only a small church. It would seat about seventy-five people, with standing room at the back for another twenty-five.

"What is this about then, Sergeant?" Pastor Dwyer asked.

He had taken a seat on the altar step, so he was facing Sergeant Lee who was sitting in the first pew.

"I was hoping to speak with Pastor Philip."

"Unfortunately, he has gone to Sydney for some tests."

"Oh, I knew he had been unwell, but I didn't realise he was that sick; please pass on our prayers."

"I'll pass them on, thank you. Is there something I can help you with?"

"Do you recognise this?" The sergeant extended his hand, showing the pastor a silver cross in his palm.

The pastor took it and rubbed his thumb down it from top to bottom, before flipping it over to look for the church's inscription.

'ST. MARKS' was engraved on the back.

"Yes, that's one of the church crosses," Pastor Dwyer replied, handing him back the cross. "Do you mind if I ask where you found it?"

"At a murder scene, I am afraid."

"Not Ruth Martin?" Pastor Dwyer cringed.

"I am afraid so . . . How did you know?" Sergeant Lee asked.

"A few weeks ago, after Stanley's death, one of your men brought her here. She was scared someone was after her, so I gave her the cross."

"Did she say who that might be?" Lee questioned.

"She told me he was a drifter who had been following both her and Stanley. She said he wore a wide-brimmed hat and a long coat and that he called himself 'Scat,'" Pastor Dwyer replied.

"What type of name is Scat?" Sergeant Lee joked, beginning to chuckle.

"It means devil," Pastor Dwyer replied, instantly silencing the sergeant's chuckles.

"Why would someone call themselves that?"

"Maybe he is a man with mental issues, maybe he is a devil-worshipper, who knows?" Pastor Dwyer replied.

"Well, we caught him," Sergeant Lee said.

"What do you mean, you caught him? I thought Stanley killed himself . . ."

"Stanley did kill himself, but maybe the drifter followed Stanley to find out more about Ruth. I mean, we found Ruth's killer. He worked at the same hospital where she worked."

"Are you sure it was him?"

"Evidence suggests it was. Ultimately, it will be for a jury to decide. Thanks for your help, Pastor. I needed to confirm this cross was Ruth's before the trial. Her parents couldn't identify the necklace as hers, but if you say you gave it to her, your word is good enough for me."

Chapter 20

December 2016

The temperature was in the mid-30s and despite the strong northerly wind, the heat was becoming unbearable. Lucas's shirt was damp down the centre of his back and under his armpits. He was standing out the front of the church grounds. The church had been fenced off from the cemetery and a 'Trespassers will be Prosecuted' sign hung on the church side. Lucas ignored the sign and headed into the church.

A gust swept across the graveyard, taking the loose leaves and twigs with it. Lucas made his way on to the slate stepping-stones leading to the church doors. The wooden arched doors were closed. He turned the old black wrought-iron handle to the right and pushed. The door was unlocked, but heavy. It opened inwards, revealing a small standing area at the back of the church. Straight in front of him, about twelve rows deep, was the altar.

The altar was on two levels. On the first lower step were candles and candelabras. The second held the podium.

The church was empty; not a soul around.

"Can't you read? This is a private residence. It's no longer a church," a voice uttered from the rear of the stage.

"I just wanted to ask the father a few questions," Lucas replied.

"The father, as you call him, is long gone, I'm afraid," the old man replied, coming into view. Lucas guessed him to be in his early to mid-eighties.

"I want to ask him about some ghost sightings. Do ya know anythink about that?"

"I am not a tourist guide, so please leave."

Lucas thought about pushing the issue further, but he had other leads to follow before he began causing trouble around town. "Sorry." Lucas raised his hand, as if to say, 'my fault', and headed for the heavy timber door.

By the time he had made his way out of the church gate he could see there were people in the graveyard. Normally he wouldn't have noticed mourners, but these weren't normal mourners. They were tourists looking for ghosts.

It would have only been just after 5 pm but they were out getting their photos before dark. Lucas assumed they would be taking more during their night ghost tour, but these were the before shots so to speak, before the town became scary, or spooky or whatever it became at night.

Lucas assumed it would be like every other town at night and just become dark.

He approached the three chattering women taking photos of the old gravestones.

"Excuse me?"

"Hi," the youngest of the three women replied.

"Do you mind If I ask why you're taking photos of a graveyard?"

"We're hoping to capture the ghosts of the children playing," she said, smiling. "I'm Ellie."

Lucas hadn't intended to chat up Ellie, but she seemed to find any conversation flirty.

"Lucas," he replied, offering his hand. "I hadn't heard of the ghost children in the graveyard. I have heard of the nurse at the Intercontinental and the lady in the Redbank Range Tunnel, but nothink about any children."

"Oh, you're staying at the Intercontinental?" Ellie said, smiling.

Lucas didn't reply. He just smiled back.

"Legend has it that three children were killed when a pile of sleepers collapsed, crushing them. Apparently, two of them, a boy and a girl, have been photographed running through the graveyard, hand in hand," Ellie offered.

Her friends had moved deeper into the graveyard without her. "I'd better go; are you going on the tour tonight?" she asked, stepping away from him slowly.

"No. No tour for me, although I'll probably see ya at some of the sights," Lucas replied.

"Well, maybe I'll catch you in the bar at the hotel later tonight. I'm sure that's where we'll end up," Ellie replied, smiling again.

"Sure."

He stood and watched her run a little to catch up to her friends. She turned once to see if he was still there, and grinned when she saw he was. He supposed that meant something. At least it had when he was last dating.

He guessed Ellie was in her early thirties. That's how old Tara, his wife, was when the cancer finally took her life. He hadn't even thought of dating anyone else since. As far as he was concerned, his love life had died along with the love of his life.

As much as Lucas enjoyed a little flirting, he would never have considered anything physical. He still considered it as cheating.

He may not have been the best husband in the world, worked too much, maybe neglected his wife too often, but one thing he had been in his marriage was faithful.

Every time he thought of Tara, the image that came to his head was her at her absolute worst. It was just hours before she'd lost her painful year-long battle with the big C. Her face was pale and drawn, her eyes dark and hollow, her breath shallow. She looked as if she was at death's door. She was. Yet it was this memory that stuck with him the most. Maybe because it was the last time she told him she loved him. While he could clearly see her ruined cancer-riddled body, he could just as clearly remember her sweet soft voice, and the last words she spoke. 'I love you.'

These words replayed many times in his head as he walked out of the graveyard.

He didn't have time to go to the Redbank Range Tunnel before dinner. He would just have to see it at its scariest in the dark. He needed to test his radio theory before he went out tonight. He needed to know if this had been just an accident or someone wanting to make it look like one.

Lucas was extra hungry. Maybe skipping lunch had something to do with it.

He headed back to the hotel for an early dinner.

As he pulled away from the kerb, he could see the three ladies of Ellie's party taking a selfie in front of the St Mark's sign.

Everyone was taking selfies these days.

Chapter 21

Picton December 2016

When Lucas arrived back at the hotel, Isabella was still at the desk. Lucas wondered if she ever left.

"I have that radio for you," she said as he came through the door. She held it out in her hand for him.

"Do you mind holding it for me? I'm going to grab some dinner first," Lucas said.

"Sure, no problem," she replied. "I'll be here. Just collect it when you're ready."

He turned and headed to the bistro on the right.

At just before 6, the place was almost empty. The only other people there were two elderly couples, one at each end of the bistro. Here for the 'early bird specials', he thought. I must be getting old, eating dinner at this time of day.

Lucas did not go out much since his wife's death, as he hated sitting at a table by himself, being judged by all the other couples, not to mention the restaurant staff themselves. They were the worst. They treated him as if he had the plague.

He preferred just to eat at home and while he couldn't cook, he could heat a frozen meal in the microwave. Macaroni and cheese was his favourite and for the times he required something a little more substantial, he could always dial a pizza.

He sat down at the bistro, flicked through the three-page menu and while there wasn't a lot of choice there were some classic dishes: roast of the day, bangers and mash, steak. Lucas ordered a steak, chips and salad. He hadn't eaten a steak in months.

While he waited for his meal to arrive, he headed up to the bar for a drink.

"You Garry?" he asked, ordering his Coke.

"No, I'm Ben. Garry comes in after 7. Does the rush hour with me, then takes over the evening shift," Ben replied.

Lucas turned looked again at the two old couples in the restaurant and wondered about the rush hour.

"Rush hour?"

"It gets crazy busy in here between 7 and 8. We're booked solid every weekend," Ben replied.

"I'll come back after 8 then. Thanks for ya help," Lucas said.

Lucas tried to eat the steak slowly to savour the taste, but he was so hungry, he ended up scoffing it down, every last skerrick of it. He only took a break mid-meal to grab a second Coke from the bar. The food was good. Maybe the place would get busy.

Lucas wiped his mouth and waved at Ben as he left the bistro. Ben waved back, holding a white towel in his hand.

"I'll take that radio now, if it's okay?" he asked Isabella.

She reached down under her desk without replying and lifted it onto the counter.

"Where's the radio's normal home?" Lucas asked.

"Usually they're on one of the bedside tables."

"When you found Gemma, was the bed made or unmade?"

"Ohh . . ." Isabella stood for a while, rapping her fingers on the desk. "You know, I honestly can't remember."

"It's okay. I'll ask the detective tomorrow."

He collected the radio from the desk and headed upstairs.

From the moment he stepped into his room he could hear his neighbours and clearly, they were enjoying themselves. Lucas suspected they had been in bed all afternoon.

He plugged the radio in and switched it on and sat it as close to the edge of the bathroom vanity as possible, without it toppling over.

He removed the towels from the rail and placed them in the bath to ensure the bath was dry. He knew water and electricity didn't mix. He folded the towel to provide a cushion for the radio. He didn't want to damage the bath or the radio itself if it happened to fall into the bath. He doubted it would happen.

Lucas turned up the music, drowning out the screams and moans of next door. The radio blared. It was set on some local pop station that played a variety of music; some new, some old.

By the third song, the radio was vibrating on the counter, but not enough to send it off the bench and into the tub.

He hung the cord over the edge, switched off the radio and hopped into the bath. He lifted one leg out of the bath and dangled it over the edge. He then swung his leg to see if accidentally, it would catch the cord. It did. He pulled, the radio fell, but not into the tub. It fell between the vanity and the tub.

Lucas set it up again, with the same result. He tried the leg experiment a further twenty-seven times, before the radio hit the side of the tub and bounced in. So, it was possible; unlikely, but possible.

The more likely option was someone had purposely pushed the radio into the tub and then left.

He would find out more once he had spoken with Inspector Connolly. The crime scene photos would reveal a lot. He doubted they had investigated it in any detail. If it looked like suicide and there were no other suspicious lines of enquiry, that was usually the conclusion.

Lucas lifted himself from the tub and turned down the radio. He was surprised when he couldn't hear his neighbours.

Lucas decided to give Jake a quick call with his preliminary findings.

The number rang only three times before Jake answered.

"How is it going up there?" Jake asked.

"It's a pretty quiet town. Not a lot going on, that's for sure. I just wanted to tell ya I tested the electrocution theory. It's pretty unlikely," Lucas replied.

Lucas described to Jake how he had tested the radio, volume up, leg out, twenty-seven times. He went through how he had to hook his leg in the cord.

"So, it's possible," Jake said.

"But not likely," Lucas said. "I'll know more once I've seen the actual crime scene photos, tomorrow."

"Let me know your thoughts once you have," came the reply.

"Oh, before I go, I thought of somethink today," Lucas said.

"What's that?" Jake asked.

"I thought, how come we don't have any photos of before the girls' car accident from their first visit?"

"I don't follow. It was all on Facebook," Jake replied.

"Exactly. We got what was posted on Facebook from Paige's phone, but there was zip posted from Gemma's phone. It's as if she didn't take any pics. I just find it strange, that's all, but maybe it's nothink," Lucas said.

"I'll have a look into it," Jake said.

Jake knew Lucas was right. There were photos missing. How had he not thought of it sooner?

"No problem. I'll call ya when I know more. Probably tomorrow arvo sometime," Lucas said.

"Thanks; speak to you then," Jake said robotically, still thinking about the photos.

Lucas knew it would be a long night. A quick catnap now before he caught up with Garry would be a great idea. At first, he thought he'd have trouble falling asleep by 7 pm but after a long day, waking up was the hard part. He ended up sleeping until 8.30 after hitting the snooze button three times. Finally, the noise of his neighbours woke him.

He swapped his suit jacket for his suede one and headed out to see Garry.

* * *

Melbourne December 2016

When Jake hung up the phone, Hayley was sitting at the table feeding Indiana some goo from a jar.

"Nmmmm."

"Nmmmm," Hayley repeated as she tried to feed her.

Indiana just babbled. So far, her only words were 'mum-mum' and 'da-da'.

"Everything okay?" Hayley asked Jake.

"Yeah, yeah. It's fine. Just thinking about a case is all. Do you mind if I go do some work for a few minutes?"

"Sure, that's fine. We're finished here anyway. I'll put her down, then our stew should be ready."

"Meet you back here in half an hour then?" Jake joked.

"It's a date," she replied, giggling.

Jake made his way down the hall to the study.

After the slayings case, Jake and Hayley had decided it was best to start again somewhere fresh, together. Hayley didn't really care about the location as long as they were together.

Jake had thought a little more practically, including about their travel time to work. In the end they'd settled on a two-storey townhouse in the Docklands. It was quiet, charming, overlooking the dock, and just a short distance from Etihad Stadium and the city itself.

Jake's study was smaller than he was used to, but it was still practical and functional. Jake took Gemma's phone out of the plastic bag of things Karen had given him. He pulled out the phone. It was an iPhone 5c, the newest model when it had been purchased back in 2014.

Jake clicked on the photos icon. Several folders appeared, with different titles. One was favourites, one titled 'selfies', one 'places' and one, 'my photos'.

He looked through the photos, then began to search backwards. The first photo he found was dated 11 July 2014, a week after the accident that killed Paige.

Jake checked the phone settings. He wanted to see if Lucas's missing photo theory was correct.

He thumbed through the settings.

He then hit the mobile setting, and pressed on the arrow. He looked at the current period; thirty-eight days.

It only had photos from the 11th of July. Gemma had been released from hospital after the accident on the 9th, so Lucas was correct. There was a gap between Gemma's last Facebook post and the new phone. Two young girls would definitely take photos when they went on a ghost tour.

He would have to wait until tomorrow to find out for sure, but he was certain there was an earlier phone of Gemma's still missing.

* * *

Picton December 2016

Lucas couldn't believe the change in the bistro. It had gone from almost deserted to full within the space of a couple of hours. It was the good food, Lucas thought, but it was not exceptional. Maybe everywhere else was just poor by comparison.

He could see Garry behind the bar from the entrance. He stood out like a sore thumb standing next to Ben.

Garry was in his late fifties, short and fat with grey hair. His arms hardly reached past his belly, and Lucas wondered how he reached the bottles on the high shelves.

Nevertheless, Lucas could see why the hotel employed him. He moved quickly, was always smiling and seemed to be able to joke with the customers easily.

Lucas bustled his way through the queue to the order line. The noise was incredible. It seemed to bounce off the walls and reverberate around the room.

"What can I get you?" Garry asked him, just before he had taken his seat at the bar. Lucas had snared one that had just been vacated.

"Coke please," Lucas replied.

"Sure, no problem," Garry said without hesitation.

"I wanted to ask ya a few questions. Isabella suggested you would be the best person to speak to," Lucas said.

"Sure, what can I help you with?"

Lucas removed the photo of Gemma and Paige from his pocket. "The girl on the right died in a car accident, and the girl on the—"

"I know what happened. I told the police everything I know," Garry interrupted.

"It's been a few years. I wasn't sure you'd remember."

"I'll never forget. I volunteer for the State Emergency Service, and I got the call to come cut her out of her mangled car," Garry replied.

Lucas couldn't imagine him being able to do any physical work.

"I'm sorry. Do you mind if I ask you a few questions about the accident?"

"Shoot, but make it quick."

"Had they been drinking?"

"They'd both been in here on the Saturday night, and neither was fit to drive," Garry replied.

"How did they appear to ya, were they happy, having a good time?"

"The one that died in the car accident seemed a lot happier than the other girl. She was drinking and dancing a lot more than the other girl, seemed keener to go on the ghost tour. The taller redhead just seemed like she didn't want to be here."

"So, they said they were going on a ghost tour?" Lucas asked.

"The shorter girl was really excited, wanted to know the best places to go to see a ghost. I thought they were going on one of those guided buses. Had I known they were planning on driving, I would have called the cops," Garry said.

"So where did you suggest they go to see a ghost?"

"I didn't. I've lived here for fifty-three years and I've never seen anything. Hocus pocus if you ask me, so I suggested they speak to the Brown brothers, Dave and Anthony. They claim to have seen several. Between you and me, I think they use it as a pick-up tactic." Garry shrugged.

"Where would I find these brothers?" Lucas asked.

"You might be in luck," Garry said as he stepped back and looked into the dining area. "There they are, far table. They usually come to the bar after dinner, so if you want to wait here I'll introduce you when one of them comes up next. The big one is Dave. He's a little slow, but the older, smaller brother, Anthony, he's switched on."

"One more quick question. Gemma, the one who survived the accident, claimed to police that a man had tampered with their car while they were in the Redbank Range Tunnel. When you arrived at the scene, did you notice if the car had been tampered with?"

"Mate, I could hardly tell it was a car. It was wrapped around a telephone pole. It looked like an old crushed can. How that Gemma girl lived was a miracle in itself," Garry replied.

"Oh, I see. Thanks for your time." Lucas spun on the bar stool and looked over the sea of people.

It took him only seconds to spot the Brown brothers. They were both big; the shorter one would have been six-five and the other six-seven. Both were dressed in shirt and jeans. The taller one, who had lighter brown hair, was wearing a striped shirt and the shorter one's was checked. They both looked like farmers, big and muscular, with tough leathery skin from many hours spent in the sun. Their hands were rough from all the manual labour.

That was just Lucas's assessment from afar. He always liked to test himself as to how close he could profile someone from their looks.

The brothers were still eating.

He ordered another Coke and again turned to watch the hordes of people scoffing their food. He saw the table with the laughing ladies; the one to the far right was Ellie. She looked up at him with a mouthful of salad, smiled, and blushed a little too.

Lucas returned a smile and then looked away. He didn't want to come across as some creepy stalker. He thought of buying their table drinks, but he wasn't sure, so he didn't. He didn't want to start something he wasn't ready for.

He turned back towards the bar, taking another sip of his drink.

Garry was at the other end of the bar serving the young couple from the room next door. They still appeared to be all over each other.

It's going to be a night of little sleep, he thought.

After about twenty minutes, the shorter brother approached the bar to buy a jug of beer. Lucas could see him talking to Garry, and Garry pointing in his direction.

The brother approached Lucas.

"I hear you're asking about the girls who died here a couple of years ago?" he said.

"Yeah, I'm Lucas."

"Anthony," the man replied.

"Garry told me you and your brother were with the girls that night?"

"We were drinking with them here. Paige, the one that died that night, was asking us about the best place to see a ghost. Where is the scariest place? That's what she wanted to know. We told them about the Redbank Range Tunnel, the cemetery and of course this place."

"Had they had a lot to drink?" Lucas asked.

"They were drunk. I was shocked when I heard that she had driven that night. Especially on P plates." Anthony shook his head.

"You didn't go with them?"

"No, my brother likes to drink too much."

"After the accident, Gemma claimed someone had been tampering with the car and thought it could have caused the accident. Do you know anything about that?" Lucas asked.

"Are you accusing me of tampering with their car?"

"No, no, don't misunderstand me, I meant to ask ya if you had heard of that happening around town." Lucas hastened to calm the situation.

Anthony looked at him without expression, and then seemed to make up his mind. "What I'm about to tell you is off the record, doesn't get repeated, understand?"

Lucas nodded, more than a little curious at what he was about to say.

"This town has a lot of secrets, a lot of ghosts and a lot of demons. Maybe it was Hat Man. He's been killing people in Picton for the last hundred years," Anthony said.

Lucas hadn't read anything on the internet about anyone called 'Hat Man'.

"What do you mean . . . a hundred years? How's that possible?"

"Some think Hat Man is a creature, a monster, some sort of demon summoned to earth from hell itself. According to town legend, a group of young people did a séance to speak to one of their mothers who had passed. It opened the door. All three died in unusual circumstances. Many other townspeople have died in unusual circumstances over the years, and some think that the Hat Man was responsible. Apparently, he lives in the shadows, or he is the shadows. The town doesn't publicise it because if it gets out, the tourists won't come and our town dies. They promote the ghost sightings . . . just not the cause of the ghosts." Anthony sounded serious.

"Do ya think Paige was a victim of this Hat Man?" Lucas asked.

"No, she was just drunk, and they shouldn't have been driving. Maybe she was a little freaked out from the Redbank Range Tunnel and, well, when you're panicked and half drunk, accidents happen." Anthony shrugged.

"What about Gemma when she returned in August? Did the Hat Man have anything to do with her death?" Lucas asked.

"I can't say for sure it wasn't, but I don't think so. The last time I saw her she was depressed about her dad. I don't even know why Paige brought her here. It's not like this is the place to bring someone to cheer them up. I would have thought the Gold Coast would have been a better choice."

"So, you didn't see her when she returned in August."

"I didn't even know she was in town."

Lucas had never heard such a bizarre story in all his life. A summoned demon, killing people? It went against everything he believed. There was always a logical conclusion to every death. Demons had never been one of them. He was sure Anthony was having a lend of him.

"Before you go, Anthony, what do you and your brother do?" Lucas asked.

"We run our dad's farm. He retired five years ago, so we've taken it over."

"Cattle?"

"Mostly cattle and sheep, and a few crops."

"Thanks for ya time, much appreciated."

"No problem, if you need anything else, just ask."

Anthony took his jug of beer and headed back to the table to his brother. He was more muscular up close than Lucas expected; not only was he tall but he was very solid.

Chapter 22

Picton December 2016

Lucas sat in his car outside St Mark's cemetery, window down, cool night breeze on his face. It was nearing 11 pm and a busload of tourists had just arrived. Surprisingly, they were mostly women of all ages; girls with small bottles of bubbly, and older women with their Stephen King books in hand, their glasses hanging around their necks, all chattering away.

A middle-aged, curly-haired, plumpish woman stepped off the bus and clapped her hands.

"Hi everyone. I'm Megan Lupia, your spirit guide for tonight. To have the best chance of an interaction with a spirit, it's important to remain quiet and move slowly through the cemetery and stay together, so I can tell you about significant historical events."

She led them in. The chatter continued but at a much lower level.

Everyone joined the group, except for one girl in her late twenties, petite, wearing glasses and kind of cute, in a dorky sort of way. She stayed behind them, busy taking notes, scribbling fast in something that could only be short-hand. A writer, Lucas suspected immediately.

Lucas followed them in, even though he wasn't part of the group.

"Who do ya work for?" Lucas asked quietly, coming up beside her.

"*The Australian*," the lady replied.

"What's your piece about?"

"All the unusual deaths that have occurred in this town over the last fifteen years."

"What do ya mean?"

"There have been nine women who have died in unusual circumstances in that time. All of them were from out of town. All of them came here for ghost tours." She swapped her notepad for her camera as she spoke.

"I'm here investigating the death of Gemma Bassil," Lucas told her.

"She's just one of the nine," was the response.

"What do ya mean—died in unusual circumstances?" Lucas continued.

"Well, three either fell or hung themselves from the Redbank Range Tunnel bridge, and one hung herself from the hotel roof. Police claim they were all suicides." She used her fingers to indicate quotation marks around the word 'suicides'. "Then there was Gemma's 'suicide'. There were even two girls who drowned in Stonequarry Creek that runs at the bottom of the railway bridge, and both deaths were ruled accidental. One apparently tried to save the other and drowned trying."

Lucas wondered if she had heard the rumour about Hat Man. He was close to telling her what he had heard but thought it best to wait until he had a better understanding of what was going on here.

"You know, on top of those nine," she added, "are four women who just disappeared. Came here on ghost tours. Vanished off the face of the earth."

How had he not known this? Lucas wondered. How had it not come up? Had he been too focused on his case and not seen the bigger picture?

"Have you got a card?" Lucas requested.

She took a card from the plastic sleeve at the back of her pocket book. She flipped it over and wrote a number on the back. "This is my room number. For some reason, cell phone service is really patchy in this town. If you get any information you think might help me solve some of these riddles, it would be great."

"I'll call you if I come up with anythink," Lucas replied, handing her his card.

"Nice to meet you, Lucas," she said, looking at the name on the card.

Lucas just replied with, "The pleasure is mine." He hadn't yet looked at her card.

"Are you two going to join us?" said someone at the front in a quiet but firm voice. Lucas and the journalist hurried to join the group.

"Now, on the path just beyond those two large headstones is where people have seen the ghosts of two young teenagers who were killed playing on the railway sleepers. They were crushed to death when the sleepers fell on them. Some wonder why they haunt the graveyard when they were killed on the train line. Well, it's believed this is because one of the boys killed that day was Thomas Dwyer, brother of Pastor Elijah Dwyer and son of Pastor Joseph Dwyer.

"Elijah Dwyer still lives in the church today, with his granddaughter," Megan said, pointing to the church behind the neighbouring fence.

"Now, if you don't see anything, don't get disappointed because many people will take photos and then later on when they look at them you may see the kids in the background," she said, as she moved through the tombstones.

Members of the tour group were all taking photos, not only of the graveyard but of the church next door.

Lucas walked back to the car.

His head was racing. How had he not picked up on the four missing girls, the nine unusual deaths? He couldn't understand. Once a death was ruled an accident or a suicide, it was case closed. But the missing girls . . . how had they not shown up when he'd Googled Picton?

Maybe they weren't known to be missing here.

Maybe they weren't known to be missing at all. Maybe they were back-packers, and they had been reported missing but just not from here. Possible, he thought.

He needed to talk to the reporter more. He flipped her card over, 'Talia Baxter Investigative Reporter', it read.

She was following something, and it had led her here.

The tour bus took off, leaving a cloud of smoke behind it, heading south through town. The streets were all but deserted.

Lucas watched, ready to follow. He placed the card inside his wallet before starting his car. It was facing north, and he needed to double back. As he turned the car around, his lights flooded the graveyard. He flicked the gears into reverse and looked up out of habit, and there they were, where she said they would be: playing, running, chasing each other, like kids do, except they were dead. He wound down his window, his car idled, but the wind carried their voices above the sound of his car.

They were both dressed in olden-day clothes, the girl in a dress and the boy in shorts and a shirt.

He could hear them laughing, as if they didn't have a care in the world, as if they were at peace.

They ran behind a large tombstone, one first, then the other and just like that, they were gone.

Vanished.

He looked to the right of the graveyard, and a face peered back at him. It was the pastor.

Had he been watching his brother play?

Lucas couldn't be sure.

That was his first encounter with a ghost. He feared it wouldn't be his last, before his time in Picton was up.

He headed south in pursuit of the tour bus. It shouldn't be too far ahead.

He came to the intersection of Menangle and Argyle Street. He looked south and saw the taillights of the bus disappearing around the bend. He punched the Mazda and caught up with it.

He followed the bus for a few minutes before it slowed and pulled off to the right, coming to a stop just inside a side street.

The street that had no name.

Where the street met Argyle Street, a sign read, 'Closed to the Public. Trespassers will be Prosecuted'.

Lucas pulled up behind the bus and watched the women disembark.

The tour guide would get upset when she realised he was piggy-backing on her tour.

"Megan?" he called from his car.

"Yes?" she replied, looking for the voice that had called her.

Lucas approached her and took her aside. "Sorry, I'm investigating a young lady's suicide and I asked my office to book in one of your tours while I was in town. Anyway, long story short, they didn't. Do ya mind if I tag along?" Lucas asked.

He gave her a hundred-dollar note. "For the inconvenience," Lucas offered.

"That's fine," Megan said, smiling, and took the note. "Just follow along." She turned towards the crowd of people huddling at the bus steps. "Okay, local council prohibits vehicles up this road, so we have to go on foot from here. Some people ignore it and drive, but I don't want to be shut down."

Lucas followed the tour group up the private road for about four minutes, until they arrived at a green gate set about a hundred metres in front of the tunnel.

It read 'No Pedestrian Access Permitted Through the Tunnel.'

The gate was only a metre high and did nothing to prevent people from entering the tunnel.

Why did they want to stop people from entering the tunnel? Lucas wanted to know. What was the big deal? Wasn't as if trains still used it.

Megan addressed the group in front of the sign. "This is the most evil place in Picton. The ghosts that haunt the tunnel have a dark, malevolent energy. Bad things have happened in there over the last one hundred years.

"Many people have gone through the tunnel and have experienced nothing. Others have gone through and seen a lady in a dress, running through a tunnel. Some have heard a train or felt a cold chill, or something brush past them." Megan paused and took a breath. "Yet others have seen the dark entity that they refer to as 'Hat Man'. I have not seen this entity myself, but I have had people on my tour come screaming out of that tunnel, who claim he was in there. So, pair up and we will do it one pair at a time. If we all go through at once you won't get anything out of the experience."

Talia Baxter approached Lucas, "Do you mind being my partner?" she asked, peering at him through her glasses.

"Not at all, but if you're hoping for a big strong man to protect you from evil spirits, then I think you're barking up the wrong tree. I might run out of there screaming before you," Lucas teased.

Talia laughed. "I'll keep ya safe," she replied, still giggling a little.

"I'd like that."

They waited their turn to head into the tunnel.

Other members of the group were coming out saying they could feel a presence. Some claimed to have felt something touch their legs or their arms. But no one claimed to have seen a ghost, let alone the legendary Hat Man.

Lucas and Talia stepped over the gate and headed into the tunnel. They passed two elderly ladies who had just emerged from the tunnel. Both shook their shoulders several times as if trying to shake off a chill. They passed Lucas and Talia fifteen metres from the entrance.

"How was it?" Talia asked.

"Really creepy," one replied, but kept walking.

"Sounds like we're in for a treat," Talia said.

This time Lucas was the one laughing.

When they arrived at the entrance they both stopped and looked. They couldn't see to the other end. It was just an abyss of darkness. Lucas and Talia switched their torches on and stepped into the tunnel. To the crowd watching it was if the tunnel had swallowed them, just like the couple before them, and the ones before that.

Lucas found the tunnel cold and eerie when he first entered, but the deeper they walked into it, the more the nature of the tunnel changed. It went from cold and eerie, to a heavy dark feeling, more of a presence.

Anthony's words came flooding back. 'Apparently, he lives in the shadows, or he is the shadow.' This tunnel is one big shadow, Lucas thought.

They continued to walk, the gravel crunching beneath their shoes.

At the midway point of the tunnel was an alcove. It was ten metres ahead, just on the perimeter of the torch glow. Lucas assumed the alcove had been built into the tunnel for pedestrians to duck into and avoid an oncoming train, but he couldn't be sure. It didn't seem like a very practical idea.

Without warning and for no reason, the temperature dropped significantly. It went from being a mild and pleasant summer's night to bitterly cold within a few steps.

"Are you cold all of a sudden?" Talia asked.

"Freezing," Lucas replied. He shone his torch on Talia's face. "Do ya want to keep going?"

"Yes," she replied in a low but excited whisper.

They continued into the tunnel, into the cold, into the shadows.

They arrived at the alcove. It was about a metre and a half deep and a metre and a half wide, enough for two people to step into when a train passed.

Lucas shone the torch ahead. Nothing, only more tunnel and darkness. He turned back towards Talia. She had her back to him, looking back the way they had come. He stood next to her.

"Do ya want to keep going?" Lucas asked again.

There was no response, so he lifted the torch beam to her face. It was frozen in a stare.

"Talia?" he asked.

"Do you see that?" she replied, hardly moving her mouth.

Lucas lifted his torch to shine down the direction they'd come.

She was walking towards them. She was young and dressed in olden-day clothes.

"Is that a ghost?" Lucas asked.

"It's the ghost of Anne Cornwell. She died in here," Talia whispered.

Lucas remembered reading about it, when he'd researched Picton.

"She was hit by the train," Talia said, her voice trembling.

A loud whistle blew, then the sound of an oncoming train filled the tunnel.

Anne appeared to be running, although she had no feet.

She was floating.

She came straight towards them.

Within a second, she went straight through them.

Lucas felt a shiver, as if his soul had just been stolen. Every hair on his body was standing up.

Anne disappeared into the tunnel.

Talia and Lucas both whipped around and looked into the alcove, but she was gone.

"Wow!" Talia said. "We saw her." She was excited.

Lucas's chest felt heavy pressure. The air had grown thick. He felt he was struggling to breathe.

His torch dimmed.

Something was wrong.

All his senses were screaming at him. Every instinct in his body was telling him to run, leave, get out. The messages to his brain were all the same and they were relentless.

But his feet wouldn't move.

Before he could get his feet moving, a tall dark shape appeared from the corner of the alcove.

Out of the shadows, Lucas thought.

Suddenly, it took the shape of a tall man, about six-seven, way bigger than Lucas, and his eyes were ablaze.

Lucas stumbled back, tripping over his own feet and falling to the gravel.

He heard Talia scream as he was on his way down.

He couldn't take his eyes off this thing, whatever it was. It came towards them. Talia turned and ran, stepping over Lucas on her way. As the shadow stepped out of the corner, Lucas could make out it was wearing a hat.

Hat Man, Lucas registered.

He gathered himself. Once he was on his feet, he sprinted to try to catch up to Talia.

"Keep running!" he called out to Talia.

Lucas glanced over his shoulder. The thing, the man, was still behind him and was closing in.

Lucas pushed himself faster, head forward, back straight, knees high, arms pumping. He was going as quickly as he could.

A black mass flew past and stopped in front of him, floating in mid-air.

Talia was ahead of it. She was almost out.

The thing hung there, floating, now more a dark cloud than a man. Suddenly the cloud formed again.

It was another man. Not the one with the hat. This one looked like how he imagined the devil himself would look. It had horns, eyes of fire, wisps of blue steam coming out of its nostrils, claws for hands, and it was skinny. Evil personified.

"Soon!" it screamed at him.

Its mouth opened up, releasing a swam of flies.

The swarm flew straight at him.

They were thick and black, noisy. It seemed there were millions of them.

Lucas closed his eyes, covered his face and crouched down.

The sound stopped.

Then nothing but darkness. Lucas looked behind him and saw only his torch lying in the dirt.

For the second time in as many minutes, Lucas got up from the dusty gravel floor of the disused train tracks and headed towards the exit.

He would leave his torch where it lay. There was no way he was going back for it now.

He was never going into that tunnel again!

Chapter 23

Picton December 2016

Lucas emerged from the tunnel to find a pale and panicked Talia on her knees, trying to gather her breath. Megan was there beside her also trying to comfort her, as well as asking what had occurred. After all, it could mean big things for her business. If someone had sighted the mythical Hat Man, ghost-hunters from around the world would come to try and capture a glimpse.

"Are you all right?" Megan asked Lucas, not wanting to leave Talia.

"Yeah fine," he replied, although he was far from fine. He continued walking over to Talia who was trying to recover on a log. She seemed to be in shock. Lucas had seen it many times on the job, usually after a violent crime. The whole bus appeared to have gathered around her to get their fill.

"You got a blanket and water?" Lucas asked Megan.

Someone in the crowd came forward with them.

Lucas wrapped the old checked picnic blanket over Talia's shoulders and sat down next to her. He held the water bottle while she sipped it. Talia was still shaking but gradually settling down.

"So, what happened in there? She came out all frantic. I don't understand what happened," Megan said.

Lucas recounted the events of the tunnel, including Hat Man and his several transformations.

"So, you're a medium, what do you think?" Lucas asked Megan.

"To me it sounds like you met a demonic entity. Generally, they don't want to be disturbed and will do anything to protect their space," Megan replied. "I've only read about them," she added.

"I take it no one else is going into the tunnel?" Lucas asked.

"I think it's best if we cancel it for tonight," Megan agreed. "Would you two mind if we caught up tomorrow just so we can go through what happened? So I can document your experience?"

Lucas shrugged. "That's fine by me."

Talia just nodded in agreement. She was still in her own little world.

"How about we meet for a morning coffee?" Megan suggested.

"I can't do it till lunchtime. I have a meeting in the morning," Talia replied, without making eye contact.

"Lunch is fine. There's a nice coffee shop opposite the church. How about we meet there?"

Lucas agreed, and Talia nodded.

"Are you right to walk back to the bus?" Lucas asked.

Talia nodded again and stood up, holding the blanket tightly.

"Do you want to go back in the bus or would you like me to drop you at your hotel?" Lucas asked.

"Would you mind?" she muttered.

"Of course not."

They headed over the green gate and began the walk back to the car. Megan and her busload of ghost-hunters walked just ahead.

Lucas could hear the crowd chattering. Some of it was downright mean.

"Can't believe we didn't get to go in the tunnel," one of them said.

"Just because a pair of idiots get a bit scared," someone responded.

"Such a rip-off!" a third one added.

By the time they reached the car, they had heard several comments. Talia hadn't said anything, and Lucas wondered if she'd even heard them. He wedged the brochure that Megan had just given him between the passenger seat and the console.

"Where ya staying?" Lucas asked.

"Picton Inn. It's on Argyle, just after the creek." The firmness had returned to her voice. The shock was passing, Lucas thought.

He drove off and a short time later, they pulled into the circular driveway for hotel guest pick-ups and drop-offs.

"Thanks for your help," Talia offered.

"No problem. Are you going to be okay for your appointment tomorrow? Do you want me to take ya?"

"Thanks anyway, but I'll be fine. I just got a little shook up tonight is all." Talia gave him a small smile.

"Where ya going tomorrow anyway?" Lucas asked.

"They don't know I'm coming yet, but I know they'll be home and I want to ask them about some of the missing girls."

"Who is they?" Lucas asked, puzzled.

"Just a couple of locals. I don't want to say too much until I know more."

"Be careful, don't go walking into something."

"I've done this for years. I can handle myself."

Talia sounded confident but after what he'd seen tonight, Lucas wasn't so sure.

"I'll see you at the café, tomorrow," Talia said. "Thanks again," she called on her way into the hotel reception.

Lucas headed off north to his hotel. Finally, he could think over what he had seen tonight. It wasn't the most horrific sight he had seen. The Ling family murders still held that trophy, but it was only one of a few times he had feared for his life.

Generally, he was good at putting bad experiences to one side and moving forward, yet he feared this one would haunt him for some considerable time.

When Lucas walked into his hotel just after 1 am, reception was closed, while the bistro was finishing up. He could see the Brown brothers, standing at the bar talking to a couple of girls.

He gazed around the room looking for Ellie, although he didn't know why. Maybe he just wanted someone to talk to; maybe he wanted more. He decided it was a situation best left alone.

His room was dark and quiet. The neighbours were obviously asleep.

Lucas threw his keys on the bedside table and sat on the bed, attempting to gather his thoughts. Something was going on in this town, something evil, and he had no idea what to do. He looked in every dark corner of his room, expecting some creature to jump out and attack him. Nothing did. He flicked on the TV, something to break the quiet. He needed something funny, something that would take his mind off things, just until he could sleep.

The Exorcist was on the first channel he flicked to. He watched just a split second, but it was enough. The next channel was showing a comedy, an old one but a goodie, more for teenagers than for someone in his early forties, but still it was light, and it was fun.

He watched about ten minutes before he could feel himself drifting off to sleep. Suddenly he was woken by the sound of running water. He sat bolt upright in bed. The sound was clear; unmistakable. It was someone running a bath. He rolled off the bed and dived for his bag. Within seconds the Beretta butt was safely in his palm and his fear dropped a little. His clock read 4.11 and the TV was showing snow.

He approached the bathroom doorway, as he would enter a suspect's home, cautiously protecting his body, gun low, double-gripped and at the ready. He glanced inside the bathroom. No one was there . . . unless they were hiding in the shower. He entered the bathroom and looked into the bath. It was dry. Had he dreamt about someone filling a bath? Was it his subconscious acting out? Both were possible, but he doubted it. He had clearly heard running water.

Instantly the room went cold, just as he had experienced in the tunnel. Pressure began to build in his chest again. A shiver ran through his body. Lucas could have sworn that something passed behind him, but when he turned there was nothing there. He stepped one foot into the entrance. He could see both rooms without moving. He could see both rooms were empty. This was crazy!

Returning to the bathroom, he placed his Beretta on the vanity and ran some water. He needed to wake up and make and sure he wasn't dreaming this whole thing.

Cupping his hands, he scooped the water and splashed his face. The cool water felt delightful, refreshing. He felt better already. He caught sight of his refection in the vanity mirror.

His reflection sent him stumbling backwards, almost onto the toilet seat. His skin had gone all pale, ashen in fact, and his eyes had huge black rings around them, but worst of all what Lucas thought was fresh water running down his cheeks was in fact blood. It trickled from both his eyes.

He quickly rinsed his face again, splashing his eyes and cheeks several times. He watched the blood drip into the basin. He reached for the towel hanging on the nearby rack. He dried his face. He looked at the white towel expecting to see it soaked in blood. It was clean, like new.

Lucas took another look in the mirror. He was fine. He must be imagining these visions. The shock of the tunnel must have had more effect on him than he realised.

He needed to settle himself down and go back to sleep. His face was fine. He was fine. He just needed to get some sleep.

He went back to his bed, continually trying to tell himself that it was all in his mind; he had been through a traumatic experience. He switched the TV channel, wanting something to calm him. *The Exorcist* was still on, showing the same scene as before as if it had been paused all this time. How could that be?

He flicked again. *Anchor Man* was on, so he settled for that.

After an hour of TV, no sleep and no further visions or noises, Lucas decided to get up and do some research into those missing girls.

He switched every light in his room on and fired up his laptop. He searched for 'Missing Girls Picton'. Nothing came up.

He typed 'Thirlmere Missing Girls' into the Google search bar. Two girls' photos came up. Bree and Natalie had been backpacking from Melbourne to Queensland. They had reached Thirlmere before vanishing. He typed in 'Maldon Missing Girls'. Nothing came up. He tried 'Razorback Missing Girls'. One girl was reported missing. Eighteen-year-old Peta Reid had been driving north in her red Ford Laser (REX 780 was the plate). He would remember that plate. He'd had a dog called Rex once, a beautiful German Shepherd. She had been driving south along the Old Hume Highway just four days before Gemma and Paige's accident. Lucas knew the road well. It was, after all, the same road he used to get into town. He Googled other neighbouring towns but couldn't find any more missing girls.

By the time he had completed his Google searches, it was just after 6 am.

Thinking he might try and get a couple of hours' sleep before breakfast, he flicked the TV over to the news and closed his eyes.

Chapter 24

Melbourne December 2016

Jake waited until after 8 before he rang her. He'd had very little sleep and needed some answers.

The phone rang four times before a drowsy Mrs Bassil answered. "Hello?"

"Mrs Bassil, it's Jake Miller here. Do you have a few minutes to talk?"

"Yes, sure Jake, what can I do for you?" Her voice was instantly more attentive.

"I need to know what you're not telling me," Jake said.

"I—I don't understand. Sorry," Mrs Bassil said.

"Mrs Bassil, if you want the truth about your daughter then I need to know everything."

"Jake, I seriously don't know what you're talking about. I have told you everything."

"No, you haven't. Let me start you off. Why did Gemma buy a new phone when she was released from hospital?"

"She lost her last one in the car accident and the police never returned it." Mrs Bassil sounded puzzled.

"Why didn't you tell me that?"

"I didn't think it was important." He could hear the shrug in her voice.

"Every detail, no matter how small, is important to me," Jake said firmly.

"Okay, sorry," Mrs Bassil offered.

"Now, tell me why the girls went there the first time. And don't tell me you don't know, Mrs Bassil!" he added before she had a chance to reply.

"They were going there to speak to her father." Mrs Bassil sounded reluctant.

"But he's dead," Jake said bluntly.

"Apparently there's a place in Picton where you can speak to the dead."

"What do you mean . . . a place?" Jake asked.

"Paige didn't say. Just that there was a place where you can communicate with the dead. She and Gemma went there so Gemma could say goodbye to her father. I don't know what this has to do with Gemma's death, honestly."

"It may have nothing, or it may have everything," Jake said. "After the accident did she say if they actually went to this place?"

"Yes, they had been there, and she had spoken to her father. She claimed they saw someone tampering with Paige's car, and then the accident happened."

"Did she tell you about the conversation with her father?"

"No. I didn't ask. I don't believe in that stuff, but I know she needed closure, so I didn't say anything to dissuade her," Mrs Bassil said.

"Mrs Bassil, whatever the reason Gemma went back to Picton may be related to why she died. At the moment, we're trying to figure out how Gemma died, and knowing why she was there in the first place is a big piece of that puzzle."

"I'm sorry, but I don't know anything else. I don't know why she went back."

"If you think of anything can you please let me know? No matter how small, okay?"

She agreed, and Jake hung up.

The phone rang instantly.

* * *

Picton December 2016

Jake answered the phone as if he had been sitting on it.

"Jake, it's Lucas."

"I have some news for you," Jake said.

"Me first," Lucas insisted. "I met a woman named Talia, an investigative reporter for *The Australian*. She said she was looking into the nine recent deaths in Picton that had either been ruled accidental or suicide, and also the four missing girls."

"What girls?" Jake asked.

"That's what I wondered, so I did some research into it. They all disappeared in nearby towns."

"Do you think that the nine deaths and the four missing girls are related?"

"I don't know. It's hard to make a murder look like suicide but it's possible. I don't know how jumping off a roof can be anything but suicide, for example," Lucas responded.

"Maybe they were pushed?"

"Possibly. I do think it's likely that the four missing girls are all related to the same case. It's too coincidental otherwise," Lucas said.

"Serial?" Jake asked.

"I'd say so. I should also tell you that there was an incident last night."

"What sort of incident?"

"Last night I swear I saw the devil."

It wasn't the bar fight incident that Jake had been expecting to hear about. "Go on."

"I went on a ghost tour to the Picton Redbank Range Tunnel and while I was in there with Talia, we saw the ghost of the girl who was hit by the train a hundred years ago, Anne Cornwell. Anyway, just after she vanished, this thing—black, tall, wearing a wide-brimmed hat, appeared from nowhere. Its eyes were red like fire. It reached for us, trying to grab us, and I tripped. Talia just ran for it. Meanwhile, this thing got in front of me, changed from a man to a devil creature, horns and all. Then without warning, it became a swarm of flies. Then it just vanished. Locals call him the Hat Man. Some say he's responsible for all the deaths around here."

"Yeah good one," Jake retorted, expecting Lucas to burst out laughing any second.

"Jake, I'm serious. That wasn't the end of it. When I got back to my room I was woken by someone running water in my bath. When I got up to look, there was nothink. I splashed my face with water trying to wake myself up a little. When I looked up, there was blood coming out my eyes, I looked like a dead man. This place, this town, it's haunted. In fact, I think it's evil," Lucas said.

Jake didn't know what to say. He had never heard such a bizarre story. "It's probably just your mind playing tricks on you. Maybe go stay somewhere else?" Jake suggested.

"I'll be okay," Lucas said. "So, what's your big news?"

After everything Jake had just heard, his news didn't seem so exciting any more.

"Oh, it's nothing really. I just wanted to tell you I spoke with Gemma's mum and found out why Gemma and Paige went up there. They were going, would you believe, to . . . well . . . speak to the dead."

"What?"

"Paige had heard of a place that made communication between the living and the dead possible. Don't ask me how, or where it is, but they went to communicate with Gemma's father. According to her mother they had been to this place just before they had the accident."

"But they crashed on leaving the tunnel."

"Maybe that's the place then."

"I'm not going back there. That place is pure fucking evil."

"She also said she met some boys there," Jake continued.

"I have spoken to the boys . . . men, rather, if you mean the Brown brothers. I met them in the pub. I don't think they went to the tunnel with them, but I'll look into it further."

"Also, Gemma is missing a phone. It's an iPhone 4. She lost it during the accident. The police never returned it and as far as I know it hasn't been recovered," Jake said.

"Okay . . . tunnel, Browns, phone."

"Are you sure you'll be okay up there?"

"Yeah, I'll be fine." Lucas replied. "Can you ring your cop friend about the missing girls? I've sent you an email with the details of the three I found."

"Sure."

"I'm having lunch with Talia, so I'll ring you when I'm done and let you know what I've found out."

"I'll try and have some answers for you by then," Jake replied.

"Thanks champ."

"Hey Lucas, with what you know, all the deaths, missing girls, haunted hotel, what does your gut tell you?" Jake asked.

"I think there's a killer in town. Who or what that is, I don't know yet, but I'll find out. One thing is for sure; I don't think it's the ghost I saw tonight."

* * *

It was only a few minutes' drive from his hotel to the town of Thirlmere, just under eight kilometres south of Picton.

Lucas hadn't made an appointment to see Inspector Connolly. That was the way he liked it. He got to see them answering on the fly and was more likely to get a more truthful result. He knew all cops weren't honest ones; he had seen that first hand.

He also knew from experience that a lot of country stations were grossly understaffed. Meaning, they didn't have the manpower to invest in a case where there appeared to be an obvious answer. So often the obvious answer was the answer they settled on. However, it was not always the correct one.

Lucas parked just across the road from the station, which was neither large nor modern, but more substantial than Lucas had expected.

Lucas made his way into police reception. The constable at the desk seemed put out by his request to see the inspector.

"Is he expecting you?" she asked.

"No."

"What's it regarding?" she asked in a huff.

"Gemma Bassil case," he said, showing his PI badge.

She buzzed through to a back room. "Sir, I have a private detective here to see you regarding the Gemma Bassil case; says he needs to speak with you." She listened intently for a few seconds. "Sure thing," she said and hung up. "Take a seat, he'll be with you in a minute."

Lucas looked around and sat on an old hard wooden bench against the far wall. It looked as if it had been donated by a church.

It was about twenty minutes before Inspector Connolly came bustling into the foyer and showed Lucas into his office. Inspector Connolly stood just on six feet, was thick-set, and had greying brown hair. On first impression his appearance was perfect, his uniform immaculate, but when the subject of Gemma came up his eyes started darting evasively.

Lucas needed to dig a little deeper.

"I need to see the case file on Gemma Bassil."

"We don't release police files," Inspector Connolly snapped. "Not without a court order."

"So, you won't provide me with any information?"

"No, we consider the case closed."

"What can you tell me about the seven other mysterious deaths in Picton?" Lucas asked, changing tack.

"There's nothing mysterious about them. I'll grant you, some were unusual, but the cases all came to logical conclusions."

"You don't find seven suicides over the last two years a lot for Picton?" Lucas questioned.

"I don't know where you're getting your information from, but out of the nine deaths, including Gemma and Paige, four were ruled suicide and five were ruled accidents."

"And what did you rule Gemma's?"

"It was suicide."

"What about the four missing girls, what information do you have on them?"

"Not enough; they're missing persons. We're following up all leads, but we've had very little to go on. No sightings. I have detectives working on every one of them," Connolly said.

"Ya don't think they're related?" Lucas asked.

"No; do you?"

"I think they're very similar, so it's possible," Lucas answered.

"I'm sure my detectives will make a connection, if there is one," Connolly said.

Lucas was getting stonewalled at every turn. He had to try a different approach.

"Look, I get where you're coming from. I used to be on the force. Nothing worse than when a relative keeps arguing with the outcome. Let me help you out here . . . Give me some information from the crime scene. Mrs Bassil won't stop hassling you if my investigation ends in an open finding."

Lucas had given him the old 'help me, help you' argument. Connolly was considering it. He had gone quiet, and was rocking back on his chair, fiddling with his pen as if it was helping him think.

"Giving me zip doesn't allow me to come to a conclusion," Lucas added, trying desperately to push him over the line.

"All right, I'll show you the file, full access to the photos and coroner's findings, on the condition that in your report to family, you acknowledge the assistance my office provided you with the investigation," Connolly instructed.

Lucas agreed, but if the information showed that Gemma's death had just been brushed over, he would have no trouble in detailing the police incompetence.

A few moments later, Connolly returned to his office with a full folder under his arm. On the tab read one word: 'Bassil'.

"Follow me into interview room one. You can take as long as you like to read through it. If you have any questions, well, you know where I am," Connolly said.

Lucas was surprised he had gone from no access, to full access, unsupervised.

He opened the file.

Everything looked to have been done professionally. This was not what Lucas was expecting at all. The death had been reported by hotel management. Isabella had been listed specifically as the person who'd called in. Her statement was attached.

She had entered the room as usual around noon to perform housekeeping duties, whereupon she found the deceased in the bath. She immediately called the police and ambulance.

Lucas looked at the photos. Gemma had a wash cloth over her face. Could that have been left there by the killer, a sign of remorse? Possibly, unlikely: more likely she was trying to relax in a hot bath.

Photos were taken of her feet and the radio that lay in the bottom of the tub. The photo clearly showed the cord of the radio caught under Gemma's heel.

It was as he'd tested previously. Maybe her leg had been out of the bath and when she'd pulled it back in, it had caught the cord of the radio and dragged the radio with it.

With her eyes covered by the face washer, she might not have known the immediate danger she was in.

There were no signs of force, no bruises, no trauma. She hadn't been raped. There was nothing to point to murder, that was for sure. Based on all the evidence Lucas had now seen, he would have deemed her death accidental.

How had they arrived at suicide?

He read through the attached reports.

The radio had been tested. It had been ruled the cause of the electrocution and had damage consistent with being submerged while active. They had even had the radio tested for DNA. Two sets were found, Gemma's and Isabella's. Isabella was questioned about her DNA being present and the answer supplied—that her DNA would be on every radio in every room as she did most of the housekeeping—was ruled reasonable, so she was removed as the one and only possible suspect.

The report then listed the items tested.

Made sense, Lucas thought. Every box had been ticked before Isabella had been ruled out.

The police had even documented a report from Gemma's psychologist which provided a list of medications and her current mental health state. 'Severely Depressed. On desipramine nortriptyline.' She had also been prescribed cyclobenzaprine for back pain since the car accident.

The toxicology report showed elevated levels of desipramine nortriptyline plus a large amount of alcohol, with blood alcohol concentration of.13.

She was seriously drunk, Lucas thought.

He read down further.

Finally, there was the medical examiner's report.

Lucas skipped to the conclusion.

'Due to the high level of prescription drugs and alcohol in the deceased's system, combined with the fact that it took a conscious effort to pull the radio into the bath, and the deceased's predetermined metal instability, death therefore more likely than not was a pre-planned suicide and not an accidental misadventure.'

Lucas closed the file. While he might have favoured accidental death over suicide, he could see how the ME had drawn his conclusion.

Really, only Gemma knew what her intent was.

Lucas leaned on the door of Connolly's office where he was talking on the phone. He noticed Lucas and indicated for him to wait a moment.

"What can I help you with?" Connolly asked after hanging up.

"I'm done. Thank you for your time. I just have one more question. It relates to the accident that killed Paige. Do you recall that car crash?"

"Yes, I know all about it. How does that relate to the suicide of Miss Bassil?" Connolly asked.

"I'm trying to track down a couple of journals and a phone that belonged to Gemma. I know the phone was lost during their first trip here."

"Everything we found was handed back to the next of kin after the accident."

"What happened to the car?" Lucas asked.

"From memory they didn't want to pay for it to be towed back to Melbourne, so I sent it to the wreckers. It was a write-off. No good to anyone. I doubt it would still be there. Compacted by now, I would suggest," Connolly added.

"I'll go check it out," Lucas said.

"The wreckers are on the way to Tahmoor, just off Old Gully Road."

Lucas thanked Connolly for his time again and decided to head out to the wreckers, hoping he would have time before his lunch appointment.

* * *

The road was dusty, poorly maintained and with the gravel build-up on the sides, it would be easy to skid off into a tree and not be discovered in this remote area for some time.

He snapped the thoughts of his crushed dying body out of his head and focused on the road ahead.

Glimmering, a mountain of metal rose out of the dust ahead. The wreckage yard was enormous; Lucas was heading into a sea of disused, mangled cars, trucks and buses.

A metal chain-link fence bordered the wreckage yard surrounded by neighbouring forest. The gates were open, so Lucas drove in and headed towards an old school portable that had been converted into the office.

The heat had picked up, as had the north wind, and the previously mild day was now unbearable.

The wind blew the dust up around his ankles and he had turn away to avoid getting grit in his eyes.

"Whatya looking for?" a man asked. He was a big guy wearing a blue singlet and matching shorts, clearly a country Aussie, Lucas thought.

"I'm looking for a car," Lucas said.

"We've got thousands of them, none working, but thousands of them." The man laughed.

"It's a particular car."

"Always is, a particular car, a particular part."

The desk was swamped in paperwork and invoice books. Behind him there were hooks holding orders. The office seemed very disorganised.

"It's a blue 2010 Ford Focus I'm after."

"Lots ten to fourteen," the man said.

"Ya have four lots of 2010 Fords?"

"No, I have fourteen lots of Fords but post 2000 are in ten to fourteen," he said. "Take what you need off the car and bring it back here to pay."

"I don't need any parts."

The man stopped shuffling papers and looked at him, somewhat confused. "What do you need then?" he asked.

"I'm looking for some belongings that were left in a car."

"Nothin' in the cars. They're clean when they come here."

"Do you mind if I go have a look?"

"Sure, knock yourself out." The man waved him out of his office. "Just be aware there are a lot of snakes and spiders out there, especially browns. They're all over the place out here; I often find them curled up in boots or under motors, etc."

Lucas acknowledged the proprietor's advice before leaving the shaded office for the heat.

A path was carved out between lots, nothing special, just gravel and dirt, but it was better than walking on the grass. There were wooden signs along the way for different lots. Lucas followed the directions to lot ten.

Every lot he passed was full of cars. Some were stacked on top of others. Some had been compacted by a machine he assumed was somewhere on site.

By the time Lucas arrived at lot ten, he was drenched in sweat. The back of his shirt was all wet.

There were blue Fords scattered over all four lots. Lucas wandered randomly from blue car to blue car, sometimes through the grass, being vigilant for snakes.

Some cars had the rego plates still intact, while others had none, which meant he might need to check the serial numbers. He was looking for a write-off.

He'd been in the yard for a bit over an hour before he located the car he was after. It was sitting in the far back corner near the post-and-wire fence. Lucas could see straightaway why it was a write-off; the front driver's side had been badly crushed.

Lucas guessed it had hit a big tree. Now he knew why Paige hadn't survived. No one would have.

Lucas climbed in from the passenger side. The rear door had already been removed. He opened the console. Inside was a scrap of paper, with the words 'Redbank Range Tunnel after midnight' written in pencil.

It confirmed he had the right vehicle.

The back seat and floor were empty. The glove box contained half a pack of Tic Tacs, a service manual and a can of So deodorant. Lucas sprayed a little on himself. It had a strong, enticing musk smell.

Lucas then knelt down beside the car. He slid the seat back and looked under it. The heat inside the car was intense.

Struggling to see under the seat, Lucas contorted his body to get a look, but it was futile, nothing there, no phone, no diaries. Lucas uncurled himself and stepped away from the car. Next, the boot, and apart from an old tartan picnic blanket and accompanying cane basket, it too was empty.

Only one more place to search; the driver's side. Being so badly crumpled it was tough to access. Lucas returned to the passenger side and slid across the back floor towards the driver's side. The nearer he got the narrower the floor became. The front seat was a buckled mess, and half of it had been cut. Lucas assumed this was the work of Fire and Rescue, trying to remove Paige from the car.

Defying the laws of physics, Lucas managed to wedge himself onto the passenger side floor. Under the front seat was a black rectangular object. It was the phone.

Lucas had to wiggle the phone out from under the front seat track, which was easier than he thought. By the time Lucas was out of the car he was covered in sweat, his shirt almost see-through, but he felt a sense of triumph.

It was an iPhone; what model he wasn't exactly sure. All he knew was it was one of the early ones, with the wide charger.

He held down the power key to see if it would power up. It remained lifeless. Hell, the thing might not even work now when charged.

He headed back to his car, and as he passed the office stopped in to offer the man $50 for the phone. Instead, he ended up parting with $100. Still, it was better than applying for a court order to claim the phone.

A hundred was the cheapest and easiest way out. Lucas wished he had just lied and said he hadn't found anything, but for some reason he couldn't lie; it just wasn't in his nature.

* * *

Lucas arrived back in town at 11.45 and although his shirt had dried on the drive back, he stopped in at the local chemist for some deodorant to freshen up. He looked for a phone charger, but they didn't sell them.

Arriving first at the café, he took the liberty of ordering himself a tea and a bottle of water. Walking around the junk yard had really dried him out.

He had finished his tea and almost half the water before Megan Lupia arrived and sat opposite him.

Lucas ordered her a coffee. A skinny latté to be exact.

"You look hot and bothered," she said.

"I've been out, gallivanting around."

"How did you sleep after the incident in the tunnel?" she asked.

"I had some bad dreams, or visions, I'm not sure which."

"Visions?"

"Well, I dreamt I heard the bath running, and then I thought I saw blood running out of my eyes when I looked in the mirror. Clearly none of that happened, so I guess it was a dream," Lucas said. "Let me ask you, can you communicate with the dead?"

"No, I'm not a medium like John Edwards. But I can feel their presence."

"Have you ever seen ghosts?" Lucas asked.

"I've seen ghosts here in town. At each place on my tour I've personally seen a ghost; that's why I started the tour," Megan said.

"Have you ever seen the thing Talia and I saw last night?"

"No, I haven't, although many on my tour have claimed to have seen a creature lurking in the tunnel. Up until now, none had reported it interacting with them."

It was 12.25 when Megan asked if Lucas had heard from Talia.

"No, I haven't. She had an appointment this morning apparently, that's all I know," Lucas said.

Megan pulled out her phone and called. There was no answer, so she left a message.

"The thing you saw in the tunnel last night; can you tell me more about it?" Megan asked.

"The more time that passes the less real it feels. I really don't know what I saw except it was some sort of man in a hat. It changed shape and tried to prevent us leaving that tunnel. It spoke, saying something that sounded like 'soon', but I can't be sure," Lucas said.

"I definitely think it was something demonic. I wish I'd been able to see it," Megan said.

"This thing you wouldn't ever want to see. It was evil. Whatever it is, it's best to keep away from it. I wouldn't be sending any more people into that tunnel," Lucas said.

"The tunnel is why they come, and as long as no one gets hurt, I'll keep taking them there."

"Try Talia again," Lucas suggested, unwilling to argue.

Megan did. This time she didn't bother to leave a message. "Voicemail again," she said.

"Well, without Talia, I don't know how much more I can add."

"Yes, it's a shame; I wonder what happened to her?" Megan questioned.

"Maybe call the hotel room to see if she's checked out?" Lucas suggested.

She called the Picton Inn. "Talia Baxter's room please."

The phone rang out before returning to reception.

"Has she checked out?" Megan asked.

"No, she left early this morning after breakfast, but I haven't seen her since," they said.

"So, you expect her to return?" Megan asked.

"Yes, she needs to check out."

Megan turned to Lucas. "They say she went out this morning and hasn't come back. Maybe she got caught up at the meeting."

"Maybe," Lucas replied. "Do ya know where I could get a charger for an iPhone? It's an old style one."

"Maybe try the electronics section at Kmart. Otherwise you need to go to Thirlmere. They have a Dick Smith store there."

Lucas stood up, paid for the drinks and offered to contact Megan as soon as he had made contact with Talia.

Megan said she would ring him if she heard from Talia first.

Lucas was lucky. He found a charger for Gemma's old phone at the local Kmart. The battery symbol came on, which was a good sign and as he waited for it to charge, he wondered if he would find any little piece of information that could be helpful.

The phone finally fired up.

Lucas was desperate to see the photos; the selfies and whatever else it contained. He was right; they had taken photos.

The first photo was taken at the pub. Paige was at the bar talking to the bigger of the two Brown brothers, Dave, if he recalled correctly.

The second photo was later in the evening based on the time stamp and it was a selfie, similar to the one he had watched Ellie take yesterday.

The third was of the green gate and the Redbank Range Tunnel.

The fourth and final photo showed their blue Ford in the background and over to the right appeared the front corner of a red truck; looked to be a Ford F100, possibly early 90s model, but he wasn't sure.

Lucas scrolled through the diary pages, but found nothing, no notes, no appointments. He clicked the Facebook app, but the page no longer existed.

Maybe someone had been tampering with Paige's car? Someone else had been there for sure. Maybe the red truck was significant?

Lucas took the business card he had been given by Talia and called her office number.

"I'm after Talia please," Lucas said.

"I'm sorry; she is out of the office at the moment. Would you like me to take a message for you?" the receptionist asked.

"I've called her mobile, but she hasn't returned my calls and I'm just wondering if you've heard from her?"

"Let me check." The phone went on to its usual hold music.

A few seconds later a male voice replaced the receptionist. "Can I help you?"

"I was waiting on the receptionist. She was trying to locate Talia."

"May I ask who I'm speaking with?"

Lucas gave his details.

"My name is Earl Johnson, I am Editor in Chief here at *The Australian*. We too are concerned about her whereabouts. She was in Picton, working on a story. She believed all the deaths and the missing girls in the area were connected. She hasn't checked in at all today."

"Is it unusual for her not to check in?"

"It's unheard of, especially when I leave a message," Earl replied.

"I take it then you're just as concerned for her safety as I am?"

"Extremely concerned. It's only been five hours, but she told me she was following up a lead that might connect everything. Did she tell you where she was going?" Earl asked.

"No, just that she had a lead to follow up. Tell you what, I'll ring the local inspector and see if he can help. I also know people in homicide. I'll get her phone traced—it might give us a location at least. What sort of car does she drive?"

"It's a silver Toyota Prius hatchback. I'll get you the rego number." Lucas heard the phone being placed on the desk.

A minute later Earl was back on the phone reeling off the rego number.

"In the meantime, if you hear from her, will you call me to let me know she's all right?" Lucas requested.

"Will do, thank you. Keep us updated," Earl replied.

Lucas hung up the phone and wrote down Earl's name next to the details of Talia's car on the pad provided.

Even though it had been only a few hours since contact, the fact that she hadn't spoken to her boss was concerning. Staying in touch with the office when you're an investigative journalist is of paramount importance, Lucas thought.

His gut told him something was terribly wrong, but common sense kept providing rational answers. Maybe her phone died? Maybe she hadn't got the messages because the phone service was so patchy out here. Or maybe her car broke down and she was stranded somewhere.

Then he remembered the nine unusual deaths and the four missing girls she was investigating, and his gut kicked in again.

Something was amiss. Lucas picked up the phone again and got on the line to Inspector Connolly.

The desk sergeant recognised him and put him straight through.

"Connolly."

"Inspector, it's Lucas Taylor," he said, sounding panicked.

"What can I help you with now?" the inspector answered in a tone that was less than helpful.

Hearing the frustration in his response, Lucas apologised before he began. "Sorry to bother you, but an investigative journalist has gone missing and I was wondering if you could keep an eye out for her."

"How long has she been missing?"

"Five hours," Lucas replied.

"Five hours is hardly missing. You know the drill. She has to be missing for twenty-four before I can even open a missing person's file. Give me a call back tomorrow," Connolly replied.

"Wait," Lucas begged. When he realised Connolly was still there, he began again. "I'm not asking you to open a missing person's case, I just think she might have broken down somewhere. If you could get your guys to keep an eye out it would be helpful." He passed on the details provided by Earl.

"Okay, we'll keep an eye out. Do you know where she was going?" Connolly asked.

"No, just that she was following up a lead on the missing girls. She believes their disappearances were linked."

"They are not linked. I've had staff working on them for years. Can't find anything that links them, except that they're all missing."

Lucas didn't want to start an argument about his policing methods, so he held his tongue. Connolly hung up, promising to call him as soon as he had any information.

Immediately, the hotel phone rang, startling Lucas. Calming himself, he answered the phone. "Hello?" He hoped it would be Earl, calling with good news.

"Lucas, it's Jake. I've done some research on the missing girls."

"What have you found?" Lucas asked.

"I've found a lot of angry parents who feel they're being dismissed by the police. It's as if they're not making any effort to look for these girls."

"Inspector Connolly just told me himself that the cases are not related."

"How can they get away with thinking that?"

"The police are claiming there is nothing to connect them," Lucas explained. Before Jake could reply, Lucas spoke again, blurting out, "I'm glad you called. The investigative journalist who told me about the missing girls has now gone missing herself."

"Talia? Seriously?"

"Seriously. She was supposed to turn up to lunch with me and the ghost tour operator, Megan Lupia, but Talia didn't show. I haven't been able to get hold of her and neither has her work. Everyone is worried about her."

"Why were you having lunch with the tour operator?" Jake asked.

"She wanted details about last night's tour, after we had calmed down."

"What do you think you saw in the tunnel?"

"A fucking evil ghost."

Jake didn't comment further. He didn't believe in ghosts and the only evil he knew was in the monsters he chased. "Do you have any idea where Talia was going?" he asked.

"Nup. She wouldn't say. Just that she was going to see a couple of locals and they didn't know she was coming yet."

"A couple? Did she mean husband and wife?" Jake asked.

"Doubt it. I think she meant two people. Her comment to me was she was going to meet a couple of locals."

'A couple of locals that don't know I am coming.' It repeated in his head. He had even warned her.

What had she walked into? His fears intensified.

"You there? Hello, Lucas!" Jake called.

"Sorry. I was thinking. I'm worried what she's stumbled into." He tapped the bedside table with the end of his pen like a drummer from the 80s as thoughts raced through his head.

"Jake, could you do me a favour and run her credit cards and phone? We might be able to find her that way."

"Sure, but it'll take me some time. I'll need to get Monique to do it for me. I don't have the authority anymore. I'll call you as soon as I get something," Jake replied. "Anything else to report?"

"Back on Gemma . . . I found her iPhone. It was jammed in the car under the crumpled driver's seat. There were a couple of photos on it and one was of particular interest. It was time-stamped just before the accident. It showed a red vehicle near their car. It looks like a Ford F100 but it's hard to tell. The photo only captures the front corner of the vehicle," Lucas said.

"So, someone else was at the tunnel with them?"

"Looks that way."

"Do you think the tunnel could be the place they went to communicate with the dead?" Jake asked

"It's possible. There's a lot of energy in that tunnel. I don't know if seeing ghosts is the same as communicating with the dead, though. Even if they did come up here to try and contact her father the first time, Gemma didn't do that on the second visit. She died the first night."

"Don't ask me why, but I think the two visits are linked. There had to be a reason she came back. We need to know what that was," Jake said.

"What do you think it was?"

"I don't know; maybe she was depressed and wanted to die at the place Paige met her fate."

Lucas thought about it for a while, before answering with a very unconvincing, "Perhaps. I need to try and find out what she did between arriving here and hopping into that bath. All I know to this point is she arrived early afternoon, got a prescription filled, had dinner at the bistro, and was found in the bath the next day."

"Filling in the gaps of that Friday is key," Jake agreed.

"Every time I answer one question, more questions are raised. I just need to continue the process. Like any investigation, all the clues will lead to the answer," Lucas said hopefully.

"The evidence never lies," Jake returned.

"Let me follow up a couple of these new developments. I'll get back to you as soon as I find out anything new."

"Okay, Lucas. I'll get onto Talia's phone and the credit card usage."

Lucas placed the hotel phone back in its cradle. He sat on the bed, notepad and pen in hand, and wrote himself a list.

Red Truck F100?

Gemma's Friday afternoon?

Talia?

He was starting to get the impression that all these little things were pieces to a bigger puzzle.

Chapter 25

Melbourne December 2016

Jake didn't even hang the phone up, he just clicked the receiver and dialled again.

Monique answered in her usual 'head of homicide' way. "Monique."

"Monique, it's Jake."

"You wanna come back yet?"

"Not yet," Jake said.

At least he hadn't said 'No'. It sounded like he was considering it.

"I need your help," Jake continued.

"Sure; what do you need?"

"I need you to run a credit card and a phone number. As you know, we're investigating a suicide in Picton. Talia Baxter from *The Australian* was also looking into some missing girls there, and well, she's now gone missing."

"I know Talia. Why do you think she's missing? No one has opened a missing person's file on her. How long has it been?" Monique asked.

"Only a few hours, but her boss is concerned," Jake said.

"It's a bit premature to do a phone and card check after just a few hours, don't you think, Jake?"

"I agree, but Lucas was supposed to meet her, and she didn't show. He thinks something is wrong and I trust his judgement."

"You got Lucas working for you too?" Monique asked.

"Just on contract," Jake said.

"He was a great cop, almost as good as you. I trust his judgement too. You'd better give me the details."

Jake gave her the phone number; the credit card she would obtain from the bank on her own.

Jake expected that Monique would get back to him within the hour. While he was waiting, he walked back out into the lounge and found Hayley unpacking Indiana's day-care bag.

Indiana sat on her play mat playing with all the colourful toys hanging from the rainbow bar criss-crossing the mat.

Hayley looked amazing today, although, come to think of it, he thought she looked amazing every day. He'd loved her from the instant he had met her; it was love at first sight.

"Hey you," she said, hooking her arms around his shoulders and dragging him in for a kiss. He was bigger than her by a fair margin, so she had to stand on tippy-toes and he had to stoop.

"I think I might need to go to Picton, to help Lucas," Jake said after their lips finally parted.

"Why? What do you mean . . . help Lucas?"

"There's more to follow up than we first thought. I'll be away two or three days maybe. Your mum could come to stay and help you out with Indy."

"I'll be fine. It's no problem. It's what you have to do. When will you be leaving?"

"Not till the morning. How about we go out for dinner tonight?"

"That would be great." She smiled, and added, "Maybe tonight we could get an early night, if you know what I mean?" Still holding him, she kissed him again. This time it was long and passionate. Both of them wanted it to last forever.

* * *

Jake had finished packing for his trip the next day when Monique rang back.

"I've done the searches. The credit card hasn't been used since yesterday. Her last purchase was $98 to a company called Lupia Tours. I looked it up; it's the ghost tour company," Monique said.

"Lucas went on that tour with her. Anything on the phone?" Jake asked.

"Nothing concrete, I'm afraid. There have been no outgoing calls since yesterday. We even triangulated her last known call. At 9.30 this morning she received a call from her work. It went unanswered, but the cell tower it came from was just outside Picton on the corner of the Old Hume Highway and Mount Hercules Road," Monique said.

Jake jotted down the details. "What about the later calls?"

"There has been no more communication with that tower or any tower since 9.30, which means it's switched off, dead battery or . . ."

Jake butted in " . . . or the sim has been smashed."

"Exactly," Monique said.

"It doesn't necessarily mean that something bad has happened," Jake said.

"You've been in homicide long enough, Jake. You know that when someone is taken or killed nowadays the perp always destroys the phone."

"I know, I'm just saying, it could be other things."

"We're opening a missing person's file for Talia. Get things moving as quickly as possible," Monique said. "We've already put out an APB on her car. It's a silver Toyota Prius." She reeled off the rego.

"I'll be heading up there myself in the morning so call me if you get anything more," Jake said.

"Always," Monique agreed.

Jake dialled Lucas's room number to relay Monique's info.

* * *

Picton December 2016

Lucas hung up from Jake and immediately wanted to go to the Old Hume Highway and Mount Hercules Road to the phone tower to see if Talia's car had broken down nearby. He knew the chances of finding anything were slim, but he had nothing else to do.

He drove out of town, heading back the exact way he had come.

The T-intersection appeared out of nowhere and if he had blinked he would have missed it. He turned right and headed up the hill towards the horizon. Farmhouses were scattered. He had hit farmland now. There was one house on the right corner, one on the left halfway up the hill, and a third home on the right set far back from the road on the hilltop.

The dry open paddocks reminded him of his childhood; of visiting his grandparents on their farm. He used to roam it from sunrise to sunset, playing with his brothers and cousins. Their land wasn't as barren as this. Their farm was more treed, with more places to play hide and seek and build forts.

Just past the house on the corner, he saw the telecommunications tower, the owners having leased part of their land to the phone company. Lucas imagined the owners had been well compensated for it.

He hoped to find Talia's Prius, but there were no cars anywhere in sight. He continued his drive up the side road towards the top of the hill.

He looked down the other side of the road; nothing there either. Maybe she hadn't taken this road, but had headed further out of town, back towards Sydney.

Just as his thoughts had begun to explore other possibilities, something caught his eye; a red truck behind a barn on the hill. Even though he couldn't be sure, he thought maybe it was a Ford F100. The design of the vehicle was distinctive.

He turned onto the potholed dirt drive and followed it up the hill to a large garage. Lucas guessed it would hold six or eight cars. As he drew closer to it, he realised his estimation was way off; it resembled a hangar rather than a garage. The brakes on his car squeaked from the dust as he stopped just below the garage.

Directly in front of him was the shed. To his right and further up the hill was the farmhouse, with a barn behind that. In the distance a tractor moved back and forth across the horizon.

He stepped out of the car, his black leather shoes now covered in dust.

His sunglasses shielded his eyes from the rising dust whipped up by the wind. He could see a large heavy-set man working away in the garage. As he approached him he recognised him; Dave Brown.

Suspicion ran through him. All his internal sirens were going off. When he had spoken to Anthony in the bistro, he was told they hadn't been with the girls before the crash, but he now doubted their story.

"Excuse me?"

The man in the shed who was stooped over the workbench tinkering with something mechanical turned and stood up straight. He towered over Lucas.

"Hey," he said offhandedly.

"Sorry to bother you, but I was just wondering if you've seen a silver Prius broken down around here earlier today?"

"No, sorry mate, been working in here all day. Haven't seen anyone," Dave answered.

Lucas introduced himself as a private detective and apologised for being rude.

"I spoke with your brother the other night at the bistro. I was asking him about the night the two girls, Gemma and Paige, had the car accident. Do you remember that at all?"

"No, not really. I was pretty drunk in the bistro that night; I heard about the crash after. You never miss out on gossip in a small town," was the reply.

"Gemma said she thought someone was tampering with their car, and they were being followed before the accident, apparently by someone in a red Ford F100."

Dave was wiping the grease off his hands with an old flannelette shirt that had now become a rag. "What's that got to do with me?" He sounded annoyed.

"I notice you have a red Ford F100 parked up behind your hay shed."

"Oh that. It was my dad's. We've been trying to rebuild it since he died."

"Anthony told me that your dad had retired."

"He says that sometimes. He's still pretty devastated by his passing. Being the older one, I think he had a stronger relationship with Dad than I did," Dave said.

"So, you're rebuilding the Ford. Does it go?" Lucas asked.

"Come and I'll show you, then you'll understand it can't be the same one," Dave said. He led Lucas out of the shed and up the hill towards the barn.

"How long have you guys lived here?" Lucas asked.

"All our lives. Dad owned this place since before we were born." Dave's huge frame cast a large shadow over Lucas, momentarily blocking out the sun.

The barn ran across the top of the property east to west. They reached the barn and turned down the far side. Lucas saw Dave had tucked the greasy towel into the back of the pants.

The F100 was red, old and slightly rusted but didn't look as if it needed restoration.

"So, this is her," Dave began. "She needs a lot of work." He lifted the bonnet, showing an empty engine bay. "See what I mean?"

Lucas saw the big hole.

"No motor, no go." Dave laughed.

"Unless you're Fred Flintstone," Lucas quipped. Privately, he thought that Dave was probably strong enough to pick up the truck and run with it.

"There's the engine over there," Dave said, pointing to a pile of tyres and spare parts resting against the side of the barn. "Over there in the milk crate is the carburettor."

Lucas looked further up the garage wall to the milk crate, which had a large metal box sitting inside it. Behind it were a few old number plates. One in particular drew Lucas's attention. The first three letters read REX-7 and even though he couldn't see the rest of the plate, he was confident it was the letters of Peta Reid's red Laser. Lucas didn't believe in coincidences.

Lucas realised he had been staring at the plate for a few seconds; probably a few seconds too long. "That's one big carburettor," he said, turning back towards Dave.

Dave was right there, just feet way. His demeanour had changed, and he was looking at Lucas suspiciously.

Lucas wondered if Dave had realised his sudden insight.

"Don't think I don't know what you're doing here," Dave said.

Lucas immediately felt uneasy. The investigator in him put the pieces together in a second; the Brown brothers were involved. Somehow, they were responsible for the missing girls. Why the hell had he left his Beretta in the car? he asked himself. Now he needed to get the hell out of there. He had to play super dumb.

As good a street fighter as Lucas was, he knew he wouldn't be able to compete with Dave's sheer bulk. Dave looked as if he would literally be able to tear him apart, limb from limb. He had to bluff his way to safety.

"I don't know what you mean. I was just looking for a friend who was having car trouble," Lucas bluffed.

The giant didn't say anything, just stared.

The silence was concerning. He had always been told, don't worry about the guys that are threatening and mouthing off; they usually aren't capable of carrying out their threats. However, always be wary of the quiet ones, they're the dangerous ones.

For the first time since leaving the police force, Lucas seriously feared for his safety.

He stepped away from the truck and turned to go, saying calmly, "I'll try the other neighbours; see if they've seen her."

Before he could get any further, Dave stepped into him and punched him in the chest and stomach twice. They were fairly soft punches for such a large guy.

If this is the way he fights, I'm in with a chance, Lucas thought.

Lucas kicked him back in the chest, as hard as he would kick in a door when he was on the force. The big man staggered backwards. As he regained his balance, Lucas brought his hands up ready to fight.

Then Lucas saw it; a long thin screwdriver.

He hadn't even seen Dave grab the screwdriver. Where had it come from?

Lucas looked down at his shirt, which was now covered in blood. Everything seemed to instantly slow down once he realised he'd been stabbed.

He looked up towards his attacker, who seemed to be enjoying Lucas's current state way too much. In fact, Lucas swore this was exciting him.

Lucas stepped away and attempted to make his way to his car. He only made it a few metres before his breathing became shallow and he began to cough. He could taste blood. Gasping for air, he staggered forward a little more before falling to his knees, face first into the dust.

* * *

Anthony had seen Dave talking to the investigator and noted his brother was now standing over the body on the ground. He stopped the tractor, turned off the spray unit and made his way towards his brother. Dave was still standing behind the investigator's body.

"What the hell are you doing?" Anthony asked.

"He knew," Dave said.

"How do you know that?"

"He saw the licence plate; he stood there staring at it as if recalling the number."

"That doesn't mean he knew. What if someone else knew he was coming here?"

"He would have worked it out eventually. I had no choice," Dave said flatly.

Anthony glared at him. "If anyone comes sniffing around he was never here, you understand?"

Dave stood there transfixed, still holding the screwdriver so tightly his knuckles had turned white.

Blood had dried along the screwdriver and on his hand, but a final drip fell from the screwdriver.

"Get inside, now. Hat Man will be here soon. We don't want to disturb him while he feeds."

The brothers, cowering inside, watched as Hat Man appeared out of thin air, took hold of the investigator's stunned soul and consumed him head first. The investigator didn't even move. He just stood there staring at his corpse in bewilderment.

Neither of the brothers made a sound. Once Hat Man had eaten and left, Anthony slapped his brother hard across the back of the head. "Fuck, you're an idiot. That's why we don't kill them here. I told you that last time. We don't need that thing coming to us. If we kill them in the tunnel, we can leave while it feeds. Now, take him and bury him behind the hay shed. Make it deep, you hear me?" Anthony shouted.

Dave didn't answer. Instead he headed outside to do as he was told. Anthony followed.

Dave heaved the investigator off the dirt drive and hoisted him over his shoulder. Blood now dripped down the front and back of Dave's overalls. The investigator's lifeless face had blood and dust encrusted on it.

Dave expected the investigator to be heavier dead, yet he seemed to carry him with ease.

Anthony searched the investigator's pockets for the keys to his Mazda which he found in his right pants pocket.

After sliding the driver's seat back a little, he drove the car into the hay shed so it couldn't be seen. Anthony made sure he wiped it clean before he got out.

Dave laid the investigator's body out next to the milk crate and junk pile, while he dug the hole. Anthony joined him and started digging.

The dead investigator's phone rang. Dave and Anthony stopped their digging and quickly searched the body for the phone. By the time they found it in the breast pocket, the call had gone to message bank.

"Before you take the chip out, find out who was calling," Anthony instructed his brother.

"Some bloke named Jake," Dave said.

Dave took the iPhone and went searching through his tool box for a pin to eject the chip. A paper clip would do, he thought, although finding one of them in his tool box was highly unlikely. Dave ended up settling on a small piece of wire. He pushed in the wire and out popped the chip holder. Dave took the chip, placed it into the back of the truck's tray and smashed it into pieces with his hammer.

He then rejoined his brother digging the grave.

It took them about forty minutes to dig the hole. Dave scattered the pieces of the phone on top of the body the way a relative would place a rose or a picture onto a deceased after they had been lowered into their final resting place.

Once the body was completely covered, Dave merely patted down the soil, scraping some loose dirt and grass on top to disguise the grave.

"I'll go call Dad and tell him what's happened. Then I'll put a couple of steaks on the BBQ. All this digging's made me hungry," Anthony said.

"What about the girl?" Dave asked.

"We'll have to move her soon, don't want anyone else snooping around . . . tomorrow perhaps. Till then, we make sure she's well cared for." Anthony wiped the sweat from his face with his sleeve, leant the shovel up against the truck and headed indoors.

Chapter 26

In-Between December 2016

I hardly paid attention to my body where I lay in the hospital bed in the world below. Every time I looked down at it, I was drawn to my name on the wall above the bed. Brodie Foxx. The admission date was printed underneath, but I'd lost track of how long I had been lying there.

I always watched and waited for Jake to come and visit. I missed him a lot. I have no doubt that part of the reason he left the force was the fact that I got shot. I don't think he ever got over taking the vest, even though I had insisted.

He came in to see me a lot earlier than usual this day. It would have been 5 in the morning. He read me the trivia as per our usual ritual. He answered most of the questions correctly. He didn't really need my input anyway.

He told me about how my NBA team was doing, which was terrible as usual. He then told me about the Knicks, and how their season had started to derail so soon after it had begun.

"I've got to go away for a few days, or maybe a week," Jake said.

This comment got my immediate attention.

"Hayley said she'll come in and see you while I'm gone." His head dropped. He looked worried, a little upset.

I wondered what was wrong with him. Something was obviously troubling him.

"I need to go to Picton Town to find out what happened to Gemma."

He had told me about the case previously, and how Lucas had gone to investigate it further.

"Lucas doesn't think it was suicide. He thinks it was more of an accident if anything, but he's far from convinced. Since being up there he's uncovered a lot of unexplained disappearances and deaths. I'm going to help him try and put all this to bed once and for all."

Jake sat as if he was waiting for my response even though he knew one wasn't coming. It seemed he was hoping that talking about his latest case would magically wake me.

Of course, it didn't.

Jake slid a book out from under his newspaper. It was a journal. He turned towards the back of the book.

The front cover was plain except for something written in Texta.

Jake found the page he was looking for and began reading. It was as if he was reading me a bedtime story.

"This entry was from the day before she left for her first trip to Picton Town. It's the last entry we have before the accident and the last entry we can find. We don't know where any subsequent diaries are."

Thursday 3rd of July 2014

Tomorrow we're heading to Picton for a girls' weekend away. Paige is really excited to go to a town that might have ghosts. I'm not so sure I want to go anymore. For some reason it doesn't feel right. I don't even like horror movies. Since your passing, it just seems all too real, too close to home. Maybe it's because it's still raw. You know I love Paige, but she just seems to think going there will bring back the bubbly, happy Gemma. I don't know if that girl will ever be back. The world just isn't as bright since you left.

I miss you more than anything.

I never used to believe in ghosts or even in an afterlife, but with Paige showing me all these ghost stories—I'm not sure what to believe.

Paige says that Picton is a spiritual hub and that because it seems to have so much paranormal activity the chances are high that we might be able to communicate with you . . . summon you, so to speak. Apparently, there is a tunnel up there where you can talk to the dead.

I'm not sure that's something I want, but Paige says it will do me good. Maybe she is right. I don't know.

Maybe we'll get to speak to you. I would love the chance to tell you how much I love you.

If not, let's hope you can see these diary entries, from wherever you are. Love you Dad. Miss you.

"So, what do you think?" Jake asked me.

Of course, I gave no response.

He went on as if I had answered. "I agree. Sounds like she went to see a ghost to prove to herself there is an afterlife; prove that her dad was in a better place."

I could tell as the words left his mouth that he wondered where I was, for I was neither dead nor alive. I appeared to be a vegetable, a lifeless body lying in the bed. Except my spirit was somewhere else, not in heaven, not on earth. I was in the in-between apparently, waiting to finally let go of earth, I assumed.

The white door behind me shook as if it was about to fly off its invisible hinges. I was even more terrified of it than I had been before. Yet for some unknown reason I was still drawn to it. I could feel some magnetic force pulling me towards the door.

I turned away from the door and focused back on Jake. He had stopped at the doorway of my room and turned to me before leaving.

"I love you mate. If anything happens to me. I'll see you in the clearing at the end of the path."

He was quoting Stephen King, from our favourite series *The Dark Tower*.

As he left the room, the door shook again. For a brief second, I thought I heard a muffled scream from far beyond it.

Maybe the door leads to the clearing? I thought.

Maybe once I stepped through the door there was no coming back, no visiting earth again.

* * *

Melbourne December 2016

Jake stopped by his office after the hospital visit to finish some paperwork on a new case. He was keen to get on the road but was not looking forward to the ten-hour drive ahead.

By the time he got through the city traffic congestion, it was already nearing 10 o'clock. Jake had already placed another call to Lucas; his mobile was going straight to voicemail. Jake even tried his hotel room, which just rang out. He was becoming more concerned. Something was wrong.

He drove until about 2 o'clock before stopping in Gundagai for lunch. The town was small and charming. The pub food was pretty good too. He had heard of this town but had never actually been there before.

He placed another call to Lucas. Again, it went to voicemail. That was now three unanswered calls, including the one yesterday.

Jake reached the outskirts of Picton just before 6.30 pm, which wasn't too bad considering the delays and the stop for lunch. Even though he had eaten only four hours before, he was hungry again, which was pretty standard for him.

He saw a sign that read Dream Catcher B&B, although he couldn't see any establishment from the road. As he headed into the narrow hairpin bend and up the hill, all the hairs on his arms stood up. His neck and arms had come alive, and his hunger seemed to turn to nausea, the feeling coming deep from the pit of his stomach. A cold shiver ran across his shoulders. It felt as if he was coming down with food poisoning. Maybe the food in Gundagai wasn't so crash-hot after all. But as suddenly as it had come, the sensation disappeared. Was his body trying to tell him something? During his years on the force he'd had a similar feeling once before. It was during a raid on a drug house. Everything was going well until he found himself on the wrong end of a shotgun.

Jake had only stared at the barrel for a split second, but it was long enough to realise he was about to die.

On that occasion, the gun had backfired, taking the drug-dealing hand of its owner with it.

Jake often wondered if in that split second, he'd had an out-of-body experience, not that he would ever admit it to anyone.

Was this the same?

Was his soul trying to warn him?

A loud thudding noise suddenly came from the left-hand side of the car as if the front tyre had exploded. Shaken back to reality by the noise, Jake became aware that he had drifted to the side of the road and hit the sleeper bumps, as he called them. They were designed to make a loud noise, loud enough to wake a sleeping driver on a long trip.

They certainly worked, Jake thought. He had lost concentration and had drifted into dangerous territory.

He immediately focused back on the road and the traffic in front of him, refreshing himself with water he had on board.

The township of Picton really surprised him. It was a lot more modern than he had imagined. As he headed towards the hotel, he occasionally saw an old heritage building surrounded by new additions. The town clearly had tried to retain its past and its history.

Despite his body's earlier possible warning signs, the town appealed to him.

* * *

Picton December 2016

Jake pulled into the hotel car park. Most of the other cars were old and didn't look like what a private detective would drive.

Jake removed his bag from the boot and headed through the door marked 'Reception'. It was a dimly lit area with a small chest-high counter located beside the stairs.

"Welcome, sir," the middle-aged lady said from behind the counter.

"I've a booking under Detective Miller," Jake said. He wasn't yet used to not calling himself detective. It was an old habit that was proving hard to break.

"Ah yes, here we are," the lady said after fiddling about on her keyboard. She placed two cards in a folder on the counter in front of him.

"You here on holiday, or business?" she asked.

"Business, I'm afraid."

"We don't get many detectives around these parts. I hope it's nothing serious?"

"Just looking into a possible suicide. Nothing too exciting," Jake said.

"What a coincidence. We had a PI up here for a few days looking into a suicide as well."

"Would it have been Lucas Taylor?" Jake asked, knowing full well Lucas was staying there.

"Is he a friend of yours?" she asked.

"Colleague, actually."

"I'm not supposed to give out information on other guests but as you're a police detective, I think it's okay?"

Jake nodded, indicating it was okay to talk about him.

"Yes, it was Lucas who stayed in the room next door to the one I just gave you. He was a bit of a strange character. He asked me for a radio, so he could run some tests— seemed weird to me, but I just did as he asked."

"You're talking as if he's already left."

"He checked out yesterday."

"Checked out?" Jake questioned.

"Yesterday afternoon," she clarified.

Jake stood there tapping the hotel cards against the counter, reassessing whether he should check in at all.

Where had Lucas gone?

Why hadn't he called him back?

"I've his room tab receipt if you want to see it," the lady offered.

Jake looked at the receipt; paid at 4.18 pm.

He'd paid for some chips, three bottles of Coke and a charge for a lost card.

"What's this lost card charge?" Jake asked.

"He lost one of his key cards," she said.

"How did he pay?"

"PayPass."

Jake wasn't sure what had happened to Lucas, but he knew this wasn't right. Something had happened.

"Can I have the same room Lucas was in?"

"No problem," she said.

She took the cards back off the counter and reissued ones for the room Lucas had occupied. "What is it with you guys? It's the same room the girl killed herself in. I don't know what you're expecting to find in there. It's just a room, same as all the others. I'm sorry, there's still only one card. I haven't had time to re-magnetise a new one yet."

"There's only one of me so I'll be okay with just one. By the way, did Lucas say anything when he checked out?"

The lady stood looking at the ceiling, as if she was trying to remember the exact conversation. "No, nothing really. He just thanked me for his stay. I didn't get to speak to him very often. He was always out."

"What do you know about the girl?" Jake asked.

"Only what I told your friend. She seemed nice. I had met her before when she came here the first time— the time they had that terrible car accident. You know about that?"

Jake nodded.

"When she came, she had dinner and a few drinks in the bistro. The next morning, I went into the room to clean it as I do for all my guests and found her dead in the tub. It was horrific!"

"You found her?" Jake asked, surprised.

"It was horrific to see her like that, I really don't like talking about it," she said, looking to the floor.

"Okay, thanks for your help," Jake said.

"No problem, Detective, just up the stairs. By the way, my name is Isabella. If you need anything, just let me know."

Chapter 27

Picton December 2016

Talia had spent two days captive in the large metal box, unsure of her fate. She thought her prison was a shipping container or something similar. It was hard to know exactly. She wasn't sure why they were keeping her alive. She thought of rape but dismissed it almost instantly because after two days, they hadn't even touched her.

Maybe it was a human trafficking syndicate. She had investigated some in the past; they definitely existed. Usually they involved small children of twelve and under.

Something didn't add up; if they were going to kill her why hadn't they done it already? The longer she was held captive, the higher the risk of her captors getting caught. Maybe they were waiting for the interest in her disappearance to die down before they killed her.

The only thing she knew now was the brothers were responsible for the four missing girls. This room was proof of that. She didn't know what had happened to the girls. She guessed she would find out their fate because it would soon become her own.

She had to get out of this box.

Talia stood up from her brown, woollen blanket and foam makeshift bed. There was no handle on the door, no instrument she could use to facilitate an escape. There were air vents above square grates. If she could get to them, she might be able to fit through them. At a guess, the roof of the container was a couple of metres above her head. There was no way she could reach the grates. At the other end of the box there was a small bucket. This was her toilet.

Talia walked end to end looking for any break in the metal, even just a glimpse of the outside world. Was she still on the farm? Or had they moved her to a different location after they'd knocked her out? She couldn't be sure. There were no cracks, no gap to see out through. She reached the bucket at the far end of the box. It had been emptied yesterday, but it still smelt disgusting. She headed back to her blanket and sat back down in the corner.

The blanket looked fresh and was free of dust. The mattress was free of stains and discolouration; in fact, it was near new. Whatever they had done with the girls, they hadn't killed them in here. Talia sat back down on the mattress, legs crossed, back against the metal wall, to consider her predicament.

She sat staring upwards at the vents, trying to imagine herself up there squeezing through. She would fit. She knew she would. She shook her head, closed her eyes and her inner self screamed, *there is no way up, so think of something else, you stupid bitch.*

She banged the back of her head against the wall in frustration. She drew her legs up and placed her head on her crossed arms, like a six-year-old. Then she noticed it. At first, she thought it was just a scratch. Then she realised it was more.

On the opposite wall, lettering was scratched into the metal. It looked at first like initials, then she realised it was a message, a simple message.

PR was scratched on the first line, and below that, what looked like a date: *4/7/14.*

PR? Talia racked her brains for a few seconds before the answer came to her. Peta Reid, one of the missing girls, had been here. She had been reported missing on 5 July 2014, so it made sense that she could have been here on the 4th.

They had held her here too.

Maybe others had been held here also.

The thought of whatever had happened to them happening to her, sent her mind racing.

Somehow, she had to get out of here!

Chapter 28

Picton December 2016

Jake stood in the doorway of the room that only twenty-four hours before, had been occupied by Lucas Taylor. The place was bare. It was as if Lucas had never set foot in it. The bed was made, a chocolate mint sat upon each pillow, and the room was clean and tidy, spotless, in fact.

Jake rested his luggage against the mirrored wardrobe door before sitting on the bed.

He dialled Lucas's number. It went straight to message bank; didn't even ring this time.

So, this was what it felt like being on the other end of a missing person's case, Jake thought. He had to switch into detective mode, otherwise it might be too late for Lucas too. If it wasn't already.

Jake removed his jacket and placed it at the foot of the bed before going to the bathroom. It wasn't a big room. Vanity. Bath/shower and a toilet. Jake's focus was immediately drawn to the power point above the vanity. Lucas had run tests on the radio and while he had said it was highly unlikely to have been the cause of Gemma's death, it was possible, but he hadn't believed it was suicide. So why had he now disappeared? What had he stumbled upon?

Jake knew Lucas was following up on Talia's disappearance. Had he found her? Had what happened to Talia happened to Lucas too?

Many puzzling questions ran through Jake's mind as he paced up and down the room.

"What do we know?" he mumbled to himself to focus his thoughts.

Talia had suggested a serial killer was working the area.

Talia had been going to see 'a couple of locals' about the disappearances.

Lucas was more concerned about Talia's whereabouts than with Gemma's case.

Did the other disappearances have something to do with Gemma's death? Had Lucas found a connection?

Jake stopped mid-step at the foot of the bed. What did Lucas know that he didn't?

He needed to find out who Lucas had called, and who might have called him just before he disappeared.

Jake sat on the bed and called Monique.

"Monique, it's Jake. I need you to run a trace on Lucas's phone."

"What, why?"

"He's missing."

"What do you mean, missing?" Monique asked disbelievingly.

"I spoke to him yesterday afternoon and relayed the information you gave me relating to Talia. I haven't been able to get onto him since and when I arrived in Picton this afternoon, he'd checked out," Jake answered. His response was rushed, as if he was trying to get all the information out at once.

"Slow down, Jake. Did the hotel management say where he was going?"

"No, he didn't say. Apparently, he just paid his bill and left," Jake replied.

"He never called you to tell you what he was doing?" Monique asked.

"No, the last time I spoke to him I gave him the trace information on Talia's phone and her car details. I'm thinking something else came up since which has sent him off in another direction."

"I'll get the trace done on his phone, as soon as possible," Monique replied.

"Thanks. Can you also give me his vehicle details? I have no idea what he's driving these days."

"Consider it done."

Jake removed his laptop from the bag resting against the mirror. He needed to speak to the lady who ran the ghost tours. She was the only one Jake knew of who had spoken to both Lucas and Talia.

Jake searched 'Picton Tunnel Tours'. The page loaded several articles and dozens of pictures of Picton, in particular of the tunnel.

In the middle of the page was a name he recognised. Megan Lupia.

Chapter 29

Picton December 2016

Despite the disgusting odour of the bucket, Talia managed to remove its handle. She tried not to let the destiny of any of the other girls enter her mind. No matter what had happened, she couldn't help them now and she certainly wouldn't be able to save anyone else from suffering the same fate if she too perished.

She took the end of the metal handle and began to carve into the container. She wasn't going to settle for initials; she was going to make sure that if anyone ever found this place, they would know who had been here.

She began with her name followed by her date of birth followed by the previous day's date. Talia's next priority was to set about figuring a way out of here. There had to be an answer.

Still wearing her watch, she knew it was over twenty-four hours since she had been taken. By now, her work mates and family would be worried. Alarms would have been raised, maybe bank accounts checked. Phone records would be investigated.

But no one knew she had been coming here.

Earl had always told her never to go chasing a lead without telling someone where she was going. It was a rule. The most important one, and she had ignored it. Now look at the consequences, she thought.

The container was beginning to cool as the afternoon progressed towards sunset. Soon she would need her blanket. In the early hours of the morning, it was cold.

She heard a noise from outside. She couldn't decipher exactly what it was. She tried to imagine what the sound could be.

Was it the latch on a gate? It had to be, Talia thought. Then a second sound came, this one directly outside the box. She guessed one of the brothers was unlocking the door. There were three locks in total, she now recalled.

The door opened outwards. The shorter of the two brothers entered. He was so bulky he almost filled the whole doorway.

In one hand he had two bottles of water. In the other he had a bowl. She couldn't see what was in it from where she was sitting on her mattress.

She just hoped it was food; she was starving.

"Got some grub for you." He placed it on the floor in front of her. The food looked disgusting. At first, she couldn't even make out what it was. She must have frowned in disgust.

"You one of those vegie chicks, are you?" the brother asked.

"No."

"You better eat up. There's nothing else till morning," the brother said.

Talia remembered hearing something similar from her stepmother when she was a child. "If you don't finish your dinner now, you can have it for breakfast," she used to say.

Talia realised the brother was still standing in front of her.

"Sorry, I just wasn't sure what it was," Talia apologised.

"I'm sorry I didn't include a menu," the brother said sarcastically.

He dropped the water to the floor. "It's beef stir-fry, don't you eat that in the city?"

Talia saw a change in his eyes; his anger was growing. For a second, she was expecting the back of his hand, but no slap came.

"Thank you," Talia said, trying to defuse the situation before he erupted. "Why are you keeping me here? Why don't you just let me go?"

"You came here asking what happened to the other girls, so we'll show you," he said flatly.

Talia didn't respond. She didn't know what his answer meant, but she knew it wouldn't be pleasant.

He closed the door behind him and began reapplying the locks.

As soon as he closed the door, Talia hit her stop-watch and left it running until she heard the sound she thought was a gate latch. Twenty-three seconds total.

She would note the time that it took and test him again in the morning.

The food didn't taste as bad as it looked. Even though he'd called it a stir-fry, it was more meat and gravy on rice. There was very little in the way of vegetables; a couple of pieces of capsicum and two sprigs of broccoli, but that was it.

It didn't matter at this point; she was so hungry.

While eating, Talia sat staring at the bucket, the final destination for the food she was putting into her mouth. Suddenly, she came up with her escape plan.

Chapter 30

Picton December 2016

Jake had managed to get hold of Megan Lupia. He had dealt with mediums before. His thoughts on them had changed; he had gone from sceptic to true believer. Beliefs change when they save your life, he thought.

They met at Picton Café. It was a busy establishment, yet it retained the feel of a relaxed country café. The walls were a lemony yellow, and the floors were old polished hardwood. The tables and chairs were made of a light-coloured timber, with yellow cushions. Each table had a silver triangle in one corner which displayed the table number.

Jake ordered a coffee for himself and a chai for Megan.

"Mr Miller, you said on the phone you think Lucas is missing?" she said.

"Yes. Well, I'm not sure, but I can't get in contact with him. He told me you had lunch together yesterday. I'm trying to find out what happened after that which led to him checking out," Jake answered.

"Well, I don't know how much help I'll be, Mr Miller," Megan said.

"Please, call me, Jake."

She nodded.

"How did Lucas seem at lunch?" Jake asked.

"He was very distracted, and I know he was worried about Talia. We were supposed to all meet for lunch, but she didn't show," Megan answered.

"When did you last see Talia?" Jake asked.

"The night before at the tunnel. She was really shaken up by what she had seen in the tunnel. In fact, they both were, so Lucas drove her back to her motel. When we made the date, it was meant to be a morning coffee to catch up, but she said she had an appointment, so we made it lunch. I'll be honest with you, after Lucas left me yesterday, I rang Talia's motel. I thought for a second he might have done something to her. After all, he was the one who drove her back to the motel."

She paused, then continued, "I know most of the townsfolk, so I rang her motel and asked if they had seen her since last night. They said they had seen her in the restaurant for breakfast, and she'd headed out straight after that, so I knew she was alive and well in the morning."

Megan had finished her tea, so Jake offered her another. She declined at first, but Jake suggested joining him in some scones as well. She smiled and accepted.

"So, where do you think she went?" Jake asked.

"Maybe after the appointment she just left town. She had a hell of fright in the tunnel the night before. Over the years, I've seen a lot of people suffer all kinds of scares here in Picton and leave because of them. This place isn't for those who are afraid of the next world and whatever lies beyond," Megan said.

Jake made a note of the time of Talia's last sighting. "Lucas told me that Talia was here following up four missing girls and numerous bizarre deaths. Do you know about any of those cases?" Jake asked.

"I can't explain the four missing girls, except to say they didn't disappear from here. As for the unexplained deaths, they are what they are, some suicides, some accidents, and some . . ." she paused as if to change what she was about to say, "some more paranormal," she finished.

"What do you mean; more paranormal?"

"Picton is a beautiful country town and most people will come here for a few days, see the graveyard and go on a ghost tour and never see anything scary. They go home happy and they tell their family, oh, it was a bit eerie, but that's the extent of their thoughts on Picton. Others pass through not noticing anything different about Picton than any other small town across Australia.

"Then, there are the few, like me, who have what my mum used to call 'the power'. The people with the power can see the dead. Those who haven't moved on, haven't crossed. Some of these people have seen the town's ghosts walking in the cemetery, standing in the hotel window and even the girl who tried to out-run the train in the tunnel."

"I don't see how the paranormal could have anything to do with these deaths."

"People have reported they have felt an entity trying to strangle them in their sleep by a ghost that walks the hotel. Some have seen and been chased by the lady in the tunnel. Some think the ghosts are evil."

"You think these evil ghosts actually kill people?" Jake questioned.

"No, Mr Miller. I think it's possible that the ghosts feed off the person's insecurities, their past fears, and maybe by the time the ghosts are done, the people no longer want to live. If they survive, they leave, and that's what I suspect happened to the girl and your friend. They both escaped from here while they still could."

Megan picked a warm scone from the plate and began to pile on the jam, followed by the freshly whipped cream.

Jake asked, "What did they say they saw in the tunnel that had you so interested?"

"When they came out, they both claimed to have encountered the 'Hat Man'. The way they described it, it seems they had met a demonic spirit. Something that wanted to hurt them," Megan mumbled, as she finished her scone.

"Hat Man?" Jake questioned. He recalled Lucas mentioning it briefly over the phone at some point.

"I used to think Hat Man was a myth, something the crazy old Pastor Elijah Dwyer made up. Until some people on another tour saw him," Megan said.

All this talk of demonic spirits, ghosts strangling people and crazy priests was getting a bit much for Jake. But he had to find out what the hell was going on in this town.

Ignoring his better judgement, Jake asked the question he'd rather have left unsaid. "Where do I find this pastor?"

"He lives in the chapel next to the graveyard, with his granddaughter. I wouldn't bother trying to visit, they're hermits."

Jake frowned, imagining a big fat priest eating pizza while lying on a bed watching daytime TV. All hermits he had heard about were hugely obese.

Jake knew he needed to speak to this pastor.

Megan checked her watch.

"I'll be able to find the pastor on my own, so if you need to get going, please feel free," Jake said.

"Thank you, I have to prepare for my next tour. Maybe you'd like to come along?" Megan asked.

"I'll keep it in mind. See how the investigation goes."

"You're always welcome. Please keep me up to date on the investigation. If I hear anything around the traps, I'll give you a call."

Jake watched as Megan exited the café. As soon as she stepped out the door, the sunglasses went on and her sunhat followed. It was as if Megan had celebrity status. Maybe in this town, the lady who could see ghosts was the closest thing the town had to a celebrity.

Jake paid the bill and headed out. The worry about Lucas continued. Where was he?

Jake walked down the street, heading towards the cemetery. He guessed it was the only one in town.

He slowed from a brisk walk to a stroll as he approached the sign which read 'St Mark's'. As he walked along the fence-line that abutted the footpath, he could see a girl sitting at a red and yellow plastic table. She had some paper in front of her, and a cup of crayons to her right. She looked about six years old and had beautiful blonde hair, with a pink ribbon tied in a bow on each pigtail.

From where he was standing he couldn't see what she was drawing. As he moved closer, like a teacher looking over his students' shoulders, he saw the girl had drawn a moon on the left corner of the page. On the ground were rocks of some sort. The top of the page and around the moon had been coloured in a dark grey, or black, Jake assumed to reflect the darkness of night.

Jake stepped a little closer. Due to his height advantage he could see the right side of the page, where three people were drawn, the largest wearing a wide-brimmed hat and standing on the other side of the fence.

Jake leant on the fence as he watched the girl draw, not hearing a man approach until he spoke. "Are you one of those lolly guys?" the old man asked.

Jake turned, unsure if the comment was directed at him.

"I'm looking for the pastor who used to live here."

"Seems to me you were stalking the girl," the man said.

Jake now understood the lolly comment. "Not at all. I'm a detective." Jake pulled out his private detective identification. "I'm here to speak to the pastor."

"I'm afraid he no longer lives here. This is a private residence. The church no longer owns the chapel. It's my house now," the old man said. He turned to the child. "Olly— inside."

The girl with the ribbons in her blonde hair quickly packed up her drawing materials and headed inside. She didn't turn to look at either the old man or Jake.

"Are you the pastor?" Jake persisted.

"The pastor is dead. I'm afraid he died long ago."

The old man moved away from the fence and followed the girl into the chapel.

"You can't just ignore me," Jake called as the man neared the entrance. "I'm a private detective."

"I don't care. Get a warrant," the old man snapped back.

Jake stood on the path wondering what the old man had to hide. He watched as the man disappeared inside and the old wooden door slammed shut.

Chapter 31

Picton February 1944

Elijah laid the bible softly on the pew. He walked a few paces and laid another at the other end of the pew. He zig-zagged between rows from the front of the church to the back and then he did the opposite on the other side.

He met his father who was preparing the altar at the front. He had filled the tray of little cups with wine. The bread was cut up and placed on a second tray.

There was always the same number of bread pieces and a large chalice that his father would later fill with wine to serve his parishioners.

Tommy bustled in through the front door of St Mark's Church.

"Pa, can I go fishing with Adam at Stonequarry Creek this afternoon?" he asked enthusiastically.

Tommy, who had turned twelve in the winter, was Pastor Joseph Dwyer's elder son. There were only two years between Elijah and Tommy, but the boys were very different. Though they were both good boys, they liked very different things. Elijah was an inside boy, a reader, who loved to help his father at church. Occasionally, Joseph would find Elijah in his room wearing his collar, holding the bible and giving a sermon to his three stuffed toy bears. Tommy, on the other hand, was always outside either fishing, climbing trees or building a fort. He was always respectful and behaved himself in church, but he wasn't as religious as his brother.

"Sure, as long as you're back and cleaned up into your Sunday best before the evening service starts," Joseph said.

Elijah, who was busy arranging the candles, didn't see the nod of suggestion his dad gave Tommy or the sour pout on Tommy's face when he realised his dad expected him to take his younger brother with him.

Tommy's pout evaporated as he asked his brother if he would like to join him. "Hey Elijah, would you like to come down to the lake with me and Adam?"

"Adam and me," his father corrected him.

"Would you like to come down to the creek with Adam and me this afternoon to do some fishing?" Tommy asked.

"No thanks," Elijah said, too busy with the candles to even face his brother.

Tommy shrugged to his father, as if to say, 'I tried.' He turned to leave.

His father held up his palm. "Son, I think you should go. I can finish up here."

Elijah looked up at his smiling dad, who had placed his hand on his shoulder.

"Are you sure?" Elijah asked.

"Go," his father insisted. As the boys turned to leave, he added, "Boys, no roughhousing. No mischief; you hear?"

"Yes, Pa," Elijah answered immediately.

Tommy remained quiet.

"Did you hear me, Tommy?"

"Yes Pa. Sorry," he added, as an afterthought.

"Boys, don't go playing in that tunnel, or on the old disused pile of sleepers."

This time they both answered. They also knew the reason their pa had banned them from entering the tunnel. Townsfolk considered it cursed. Both boys had heard the stories at school. Neither was game to find out for themselves.

Tommy and Elijah called in at home so Tommy could collect his fishing rods and bait. He had spent some of Saturday morning digging up the back yard, gathering fresh worms in an old jam jar ready for the fishing trip. Elijah, who wasn't that keen on fishing, decided to take a book. There was nothing better than sitting under the shade of a tree and reading. He picked up his copy of *The Hobbit*, not a new release, but new to him. While he was waiting for Tommy, he quickly made some sandwiches. His mum even gave him some slices of lemon cake, wrapped inside a tea towel. Lemon cake was rare with the war still going on. Finally, Elijah filled their canteens with water and they were ready to go.

The boys headed off with the morning sun at their backs. It was about half an hour's walk to the lake, but the spot that Tommy had in mind was a little further.

"Are we there yet?" Elijah asked.

"It's just a little further," Tommy said.

"Why can't we fish here?"

"Because we're meeting Adam and his sister Becca under the bridge."

"Dad said not to go to the tunnel."

"We aren't, we're going to the creek under the bridge."

Elijah knew his dad wouldn't be happy had he known they were going to be fishing this close to the tunnel. Elijah also knew why Tommy hadn't said anything to Pa about Becca. He was smitten with her; had been since the fifth grade. Now they were both in high school and Becca had begun to blossom. He was sure his brother had taken note.

Elijah could see the two figures in the distance.

Both were wearing hats. Adam's was a straw hat similar to the ones the brothers were wearing. Becca had on a girl's sun hat with a floppy brim. Adam was wearing shorts, shirt and boots while Becca was dressed in a light blue knee-length summer dress with a white blouse underneath, and black summer sandals on her feet. Adam was a year older than Tommy, while Becca was younger by a few months.

Adam had already cast his line and was sitting on the bank with his feet dangling in the water. His boots and socks sat next to a knapsack behind him. He too had a jar of worms at his side.

"You caught anything yet?" Tommy asked.

"Nah," Adam said.

The spot they had chosen was flat, lightly grassed, and the bridge above provided enough shade from the summer sun. At the rear of the grassed area stood two silver birch trees.

Elijah quietly made his way to one of those trees and found himself a comfortable nook. He undid the strap of his knapsack and removed his book. He had never heard of hobbits or read about wizards before. As he turned the cover and began to read, he wondered if his dad would approve.

Tommy had forgotten his brother was even there. All his attention was on Becca. Even though he was making idle chatter with Adam and baiting his rod, his focus was on Becca. He studied everything she did, how she played and pulled the grass beside her, how her lips looked when she pursed them to blow the pollen off the wild fairy flowers.

Tommy glanced over to her again as he threw his first line into the water.

She smiled at him, blushing a little. Tommy loved her smile, as it revealed her dimples. A gust of wind blew across the creek sending Becca's hair across her face. She simply flicked her head in the opposite direction and her blonde hair went back into place.

Nothing flustered her, Tommy thought.

"Do you want to have a go?" Tommy asked her.

She smiled, revealing dimples again. "You'll need to show me how," she said softly.

Her hair blew over her face again, and this time she gave a little giggle. It was a giggle that Tommy immediately loved.

Tommy passed her the rod. At first, she held it incorrectly.

Adam laughed. Her face blushed with embarrassment.

"You're such a dunce." Her brother chuckled.

Tommy took hold of her hand. A spark ran up his arm as his fingers touched hers. He moved her hands to the correct position, placing her right index finger under the rod, ensuring it rested against the line. The touch of her skin sent his heart racing.

His eyes met hers. He could have looked at those eyes for hours if he had the chance. They were ocean blue and mesmerising. She softly licked her lips.

Maybe she wanted to kiss him. He had thought about kissing her many times; maybe now was the right time.

"You fishing, or just going to stand there looking at each other all day?" her brother mocked.

"Thanks, I have it now," Becca said, pulling her hands away.

Tommy dragged a spare handline out of his gear and baited the hook, which he had brought in case Elijah wanted to fish.

Tommy cast his line into the water, sat on a small grass patch on the bank, looked over to Becca and smiled.

She smiled back.

Fishing was slow. No one was catching anything. Tommy and Becca remained on the bank chatting about general stuff that kids their age talked about. There was only one thing they never discussed and that was the war. Their talking was full of the usual awkward pauses when teens sometimes don't know what to say.

"What do you want to do when you're older?" Becca asked.

"A detective," Tommy said swiftly. "You?"

"A teacher," she said, smiling.

Her answer sent Tommy's thoughts to something completely unexpected— the tunnel. Were the rumours true?

He turned his head. High on the hill in the distance the tunnel's dark mouth over his left shoulder stared back, as if it were alive and somehow calling him, whispering in his ear, "Come to me." A shiver ran through him.

Tommy recalled the day he had first heard the myth about the creature they called the Hat Man. It had become folklore amongst the students of Picton Primary. The myth had only grown over the last twenty-five years. By the time it reached Tommy's impressionable ears, the Hat Man had been responsible for Anne's death and her friends' as well. According to classmate Mark McGuire, Hat Man was able to breath fire from his mouth and put you in a trance with his eyes, and he was still haunting the tunnel.

Tommy, curious about Mark's Hat Man story, had raced straight to the church after school to see if it was true. His dad refused to discuss the validity of the story except to say it was based on a normal person who had done bad things. "Lost his way and now he is in jail paying for his sins."

Tommy was mesmerised by the darkness of the tunnel, still wondering if the Hat Man stories that Mark had told were true.

"Do you think he's real?" Becca asked. She must have noticed the direction of his gaze.

Tommy didn't answer. He was still deep in thought.

"Tommy?" Becca asked again.

"Huh?" he said, coming out of his trance.

"The Hat Man creature, do you think he's real?"

"Pa says it was just some guy who lost his way and now he's in jail," Tommy answered.

"Well, here's your chance to be a detective. We could go look and see for ourselves," Becca said excitedly.

She placed her rod on the bank and took Tommy by the hand, as a girlfriend would do. Sparks ran up his arm. Feelings of excitement and fear conflicted within his body.

"I don't think we should. Pa said to stay away," Tommy said.

"I thought you wanted to be a detective?" Becca questioned.

"Yeah, but Pa said we shouldn't go near the tunnel."

Becca ignored his pleas, pulling him up the hill by the hand.

He passed Elijah still nestled under his tree, his head in his book.

"Where you going?" Elijah asked.

"Up to the tunnel," Becca answered for Tommy.

"But Pa said—" Elijah was cut off mid-sentence by his brother.

"Don't be a baby. We'll be back soon," Tommy said, with an attitude Elijah didn't recognise.

Stunned, Elijah watched as Tommy and Becca walked hand in hand towards the tunnel.

They stood holding hands under the shadow of the tunnel's entrance. The heat had given way to a cool, if not cold, breeze from within the tunnel. Tommy noticed their arms had erupted in goose bumps.

Becca took the first steps inside the tunnel, but Tommy remained flatfooted on the outside. She pulled on his hand several times, yet he didn't budge.

"You, coming?" Becca asked with a smile that made the world disappear.

Tommy answered with his feet, stepping inside the darkness.

They walked deeper into the chill towards the alcove.

"This is where he pushed her," Tommy said.

"Well, he's not here anymore," Becca replied.

Tommy was busy scanning the tunnel for any sign of this mysterious Hat Man.

Becca placed her hand on his face. "It's okay. He's not here. We're alone. Do you like me, Tommy?" She stepped closer.

"Ye-ye-yes. Of course." He croaked and stuttered his answer.

"No one can see us here, Tommy. You can kiss me if you like." Becca smiled her world-stopping smile. He could only just see it in the dim light.

Tommy put his nerves aside, closed his eyes and leant in. The kiss was amazing, and like nothing he had ever experienced. He instantly wanted more. Her lips were soft and damp and tasted like strawberries. Her hair brushed against his face. He had never known feelings as wonderful as these before.

As he opened his eyes, his thoughts were instantly replaced by fear. Towering over Becca stood a faceless, shadowy man wearing a wide-brimmed hat and with eyes of blazing red.

Tommy screamed. Becca joined him seconds later. Her scream was so loud, it ricocheted off the tunnel walls and out into the open air. It reached both Elijah and Adam clearly.

Adam dropped his rod and ran towards the tunnel. Elijah stood up from his reading spot, dropping his book in the dirt, losing his place as it landed.

He stood motionless at the tree as he saw Adam run and then disappear into the tunnel.

Adam arrived in the tunnel to find both Becca and Tommy suspended in mid-air, three feet off the ground. Suspended in time and space—they were in a trance. Their eyes were wide open, fear on their faces, their hands still interlocked.

A thin, bony creature wearing a long coat and a hat stood behind them, transfixed, letting out a grumble, like a hungry dog.

Adam picked up several rocks that lay just inside the entrance, hurling them at the thing in the hat. The first rock flew high and to the left. The second one hit it right in the head, sending it backwards and Tommy and Becca sprawling to the ground.

Adam threw a third rock, this one bigger than the last two. It hit the 'man' in the right shoulder as it regained its balance. Hat Man shrugged and flew across the tunnel floor. Hovering inches above the ground, Hat Man was just feet from Adam's face. Adam wanted to back-pedal, but his feet refused to obey. Like Tommy and Becca, he was frozen to the spot.

Hat Man stood, eyes blazing. The two little holes that Adam thought was its nose flared and retracted every few seconds. Then as Hat Man grinned, yellow, jagged teeth appeared. A wretched smell came from its mouth. It was unfamiliar to Adam, but it was the worst thing he had ever smelt.

Hat Man raised his right hand, lifting it from down beside his leg, moving it into a throwing position. His arm was locked and loaded as if he was about to fling something at Adam, except his hand was empty. Behind him, a rock rose from the ground. It was bigger than all three of the rocks Adam had thrown. Hat Man swung his arm like a baseball pitcher. The rock flew through the air. It swung around Hat Man's shoulder. That was when Adam realised it was heading straight for him. His initial reaction was to try to duck and dive to the ground. Yet he couldn't move, no matter how hard he tried. The rock hit his forehead. Before he could react, he was sent flying backwards.

As he landed, he felt blood pour down his face. Through the dripping blood he watched as Tommy and Becca struggled to get up as if the spell over them had been broken.

"Run!" Adam screamed.

He repeated his instructions several times in the following seconds as he staggered out of the tunnel.

Hat Man followed him out into the sunlight.

He's coming for me, Adam thought, trying to run. His legs were not cooperating. They couldn't hold his weight and as his vision blurred with concussion and cascading blood, he couldn't seem to maintain his balance. Nothing was working. He dropped to the ground.

Adam wiped the blood from his face only to see Hat Man standing over him. Behind him he could see Becca and Tommy fleeing the tunnel. They veered towards the pile of sleepers stacked on the ridge.

Hide, Adam thought.

Hat Man's shadow was long and thin, just like the bony fingers that suddenly appeared out from under the coat. Adam was pulled up by the throat. He could feel the bones shifting against the side of his neck. The knuckles cracked and creaked as they moved.

Tommy and Becca scurried towards the sleepers, but Adam was no longer aware of where they were. His face remained inches from Hat Man's plain featureless face. Its snake-like nostrils continued to flare as if smelling the fear oozing out of Adam.

Adam felt as if he was about to be devoured.

He didn't realise until he felt the warm liquid against his leg, but he had begun to piss himself.

Bruises appeared under Hat Man's bony thumbs. Hat Man snarled again, displaying his horrible teeth. Adam felt his whole body shudder with fear.

Hat Man drew a deep breath, sucking up all the fear. When satisfied it had taken all Adam had to give, Hat Man squeezed its thin claws until Adam's neck snapped under the pressure. From his place near the sleepers, Tommy gasped as he heard Adam's neck crack. He could see Adam's head drop to one side, his eyes still wide open, his mouth agape as if about to speak.

Hat Man dropped Adam's body onto the dusty dry ground.

Tommy was ready to run again, but for some reason he needed to know what this thing, this Hat Man, was doing. It remained in the same spot staring at Adam's lifeless carcass; admiring its handiwork perhaps.

Before Tommy could work out what Hat Man was waiting for, it happened. Adam's soul rose, like the last smoke of an extinguished fire.

Adam clearly hadn't realised he was dead. He doesn't know what's happened, Tommy thought.

A bright beam of light appeared midway between Adam and the stack of sleepers where Tommy and Becca were crouched. The beam was brighter than any sunlight Tommy had ever witnessed.

Maybe it was the shock or the dry summer's day, or a combination of the two, but Tommy couldn't generate enough base in his voice to shout, so what should have been his call to run came out only as 'n' followed by a dry coughing fit.

Tommy's eyes captured the horror of Adam's soul fighting to reach the light.

Adam's soul had either reacted to his cry or was automatically drawn to the beam of light; either way it began to move. Hat Man reacted to the soul's movement, its bony claws leaping into action, slamming into the sides of Adam's soul somehow, disappearing into the translucent figure that was now Adam.

Once the claws were inserted, Adam's momentum towards the light ceased. Despite his struggling, he wasn't breaking free of Hat Man's hold. The light began to fade as quickly as it had arrived, then it vanished.

What Tommy saw next made him want his father and more importantly God's protection that he'd often spoken of. He tried to remember his prayers but they too, like his voice, had deserted him when he needed them most.

Hat Man lifted Adam's soul up and towards his mouth, then swallowed it.

"We need to run. Don't stop until we're clear of this place," Tommy told Becca.

She only nodded in agreement, still holding Tommy's hand.

They turned and sprinted down the bank, with the sleeper stack providing perfect cover. Elijah hadn't followed Adam. He'd chosen to stay behind and look after their belongings. At least that's what's he would tell Tommy when asked. The truth of it was that the scream that had sent Adam running to his sister's aid had the opposite effect on Elijah. Instead of filling him with adrenaline to run to battle, it had paralysed him with fear. He had interpreted the scream as not one of *help*, but as a warning to stay away.

Stay away he did. He remained under the shade of his reading tree, eyes transfixed on the hill in the distance. There was no sign of anyone since Adam had disappeared beyond its crest.

Elijah had been staring so long his eyes had begun to water.

Finally, movement came. It was Tommy and Becca running out from behind the sleeper pile back towards where they had been fishing. A huge rumble sounded behind them, which Becca first mistook for thunder. Tommy saw it first, tumbling behind him, chasing him. Somehow, the whole pile of sleepers had broken free and were hurtling towards them.

Tommy pulled Becca by the hand, and they darted to the left. The sleepers followed. One bounced behind them before lifting and hurling itself over their heads. Had it not been for Tommy's peripheral vision and exquisite timing in ducking, both would have been decapitated. Another sleeper rolled, edge to edge, accelerating along the ground as it chased the pair. Tommy expected the sleeper to bounce and fly through the air. Unfortunately for both of them he was wrong; it dived, staying just inches off the ground, taking their legs from under them.

As Tommy flew backwards through the air, he caught a glimpse of several other sleepers changing direction. It appeared as if they were alive. How could that be, Tommy thought.

He landed hard. With the fall, his connection to Becca was lost. Their hands separated for the first time since they had touched.

Tommy didn't see the second sleeper land on Becca, crushing her chest and killing her instantly, until he had stopped tumbling.

He sat there in disbelief, stunned. Time had stopped. All he could see was Becca's lifeless body crushed, almost split in two. The green grass on which she lay was covered in a widening pool of crimson.

Transfixed on Becca's now lifeless body, Tommy lost his desire for self-preservation. His fate had been sealed when Becca was hit; Tommy just didn't know it. Sleepers hurtled past him. One clipped his shoulder, another just missed his head, creating a swift gust of wind as it passed. Finally, a sleeper collected him. It struck him on the back of the head. There was nothing else for Tommy, until he rose.

Elijah had watched both Becca and his brother die. He stayed hidden behind the tree as the sleepers made their assault down the hill towards the creek bank. Only one sleeper gathered enough speed to reach the water itself. It was the first one that Tommy had managed to duck under.

With only one eye peering out from behind the tree trunk, Elijah saw something he would never forget. Two spirits rose as if called by Jesus himself. Becca was first, followed a few seconds later by Tommy. Both just hovered there looking at their own bodies.

A man stood at the top of the hill. He was tall, thin and wore a hat. Elijah thought about calling to him for help, but his gut told him to stay hidden.

The man didn't walk down the hill; instead, he glided. Elijah gasped, before clasping a hand over his mouth to stifle the scream and cowering back behind the tree's thick trunk.

Only managing a brief glance now and then, he saw what appeared to be the ghost of Tommy join that of Becca. Together, they ran off in the distance towards the creek. A bright light had appeared on the riverbank, brighter than any light Elijah had ever seen. He could even feel its heat from where he was standing. At first, he thought it was where Tommy and Becca were heading but they chose to ignore the light, instead continuing towards town.

By the time the light disappeared, the ghosts of Tommy and Becca were barely visible. Elijah remained hidden behind the tree. With the light gone, the heat had disappeared also. Suddenly Elijah felt very cold.

The tall man in the hat stopped the pursuit of Tommy and Becca once they had reached the bank. Now it was just standing there. Elijah hugged the tree, making sure every part of him was hidden.

When he dared to look from behind tree, the riverbank was empty. He scanned the hill for the man, but all that remained were the fallen sleepers and the crushed bodies of Tommy and Becca.

Elijah sprinted frantically back towards town, leaving the fishing gear where it lay and his book still at the base of the tree, pages fluttering in the wind.

When Elijah returned home, his face was ashen, sickly and drawn.

His mother immediately ran to his aid. "Elijah what's wrong? You look like death warmed up."

Elijah fell into her arms, mumbling incoherently. After realising Tommy wasn't in tow, she asked the whereabouts of his elder brother. His pa came running into the front yard at the cries of his wife. Elijah managed to tell his parents all he knew, including the mysterious 'man' he had seen after the sleeper collapse. The only part he omitted was the souls rising; that was just too bizarre.

"Where is Tommy?" his mum continued to ask.

"I think he's dead," Elijah replied.

His mum screamed. His pa comforted her in his arms. "Let's not jump to conclusions. I'll take the sergeant and we'll go and look," he said in a calm, forthright manner.

"Elijah says he's dead," she repeated.

"I'm sure he's mistaken, he's probably just injured," Pa said. "I told you boys to stay away from those sleepers because they're dangerous."

When Pa arrived back in the late afternoon, he too was ashen. Elijah stood at the window watching his dad tell his mother what he had known all along. Tommy was dead.

His mother fell to the ground. Her screams filled the afternoon air. That terrible sound was now etched in Elijah's memory.

His pa knelt beside her. Elijah and his parents were never the same after that horrendous day.

Chapter 32

Picton December 2016

Jake arrived back at his hotel after spending the afternoon driving around the town. He had been to all the places he knew Lucas had been; the wreckers and the Redbank Range Tunnel . . . only he hadn't stepped foot past the green gate. That whole place freaked him out for some reason.

He also walked amongst the tombstones, next to the chapel. It was quiet and peaceful. Nothing about it made him feel uneasy. He felt no evil presence amongst the dead, that was for sure.

It was nearing dinner when he walked up the steps of the hotel entrance to be greeted again by Isabella. Jake wondered if she had any other staff, or if she did everything herself.

"Any news?" Isabella asked.

Jake stopped at the foot of the stairs to answer her. He didn't want to come across as rude. "No, I'm afraid not."

"Well, let me know if there's anything you need."

"Will do. While I'm here, were there any calls for me? My mobile doesn't get any service around town."

"It's a bit of a dead spot for reception, this place. Let me check." Isabella shuffled through some papers on her desk, and about twenty seconds later was able to answer his question. "Yes, a Monique called," she said, holding a yellow Post-It note.

So that was the high-tech system run here in Picton. Yellow Post-It notes. Jake doubted if everyone got their messages. He took his out of politeness and began to head for his room.

"Is Monique your girlfriend?" Isabella asked.

Jake again stopped mid-step. "No, she's a work colleague."

"Does she have any information on your missing friend?"

"I'll ring her and find out," Jake said, ending the conversation regardless of Isabella's intentions.

After speaking to Monique, the only new information Jake had to go on was about Lucas's phone. According to Monique's search, the last time his phone had pinged was off the same tower that Talia's phone had last registered.

It was a coincidence Jake couldn't ignore. What had they stumbled upon?

Whatever Talia had found, Jake now thought it was highly likely that Lucas had found it too.

Although hungry, Jake decided dinner would wait. He needed to go to the phone tower and see what he could find.

Isabella was still at the desk as he left the hotel.

"What did you find out?" she called.

Ignoring her, Jake continued on his way.

Upon his arrival at the tower, located at the corner of Old Hume Highway and Mount Hercules Road, Jake expected to find something; a broken-down car perhaps. There was nothing. Nothing but open spaces, bare paddocks and old farmhouses with the occasional shed.

He stood beside his car and looked across the wide-open fields abutting the highway. A house set approximately two hundred metres down from the corner was visible. Up the side road he could just make out another farmhouse, high on the hill, with the sun setting behind it. On the other side of the side street, perhaps a little closer to him, was a third farmhouse.

On the lower side of the highway were two long driveways, side by side. The only thing separating them was a pair of mailboxes. One read *Marsh*, the other *Forrest*. The driveways veered off in different directions. Jake could see the Forrest farmhouse down deep in the gully on his right.

Jake looked for the farmhouse on the left, but it was hidden from the road. As it was meal time it was likely the owners would be home.

Jake enquired, but neither the Forrests nor the Marshes had seen anything suspicious. No broken-down cars. Neither of them had seen Talia or Lucas either.

Jake headed over to the other side of the highway. He started with the house just down from the corner, followed by the one up the hill on the left. Again, neither of the owners had seen anything, or anyone.

So far, he had door-knocked the immediate area, without a single lead. The only remaining house was the one on the hill. After that he would have to door-knock along the highway until he reached the next tower.

Out of all the farms he had visited so far, this was by far the biggest. It had large sheds and a large barn, although the house was relatively small. Jake could see a large tractor sitting on the hilltop.

Jake made his way up the dusty drive and headed over to the house on his left. The steps were half rotten and a little dangerous, so Jake side-stepped those spots. The front door was made of timber; the house was weatherboard with paint peeling off, obviously affected by the sun.

Jake felt the floor shake as someone approached to answer his knock. The door swung open and Jake was staring at the neck of a hulking man in overalls. The overalls were covered in blood, the sight of which shook Jake a little.

The man seemed to realise his appearance had shocked his visitor. "I'm sorry about the blood; I had to butcher a lamb today. Gives us meat for a month. I haven't had time to clean up yet."

Jake introduced himself and showed his badge, as he had done at the four previous homes. The big guy introduced himself as Dave Brown. The name sounded familiar, but he couldn't quite place it yet.

Jake shook his hand and even though Jake was strong, he felt this guy was about to crush every bone in his hand.

Jake asked the same questions as at the other four residences. "Have you seen this woman or this man around here in the last couple of days?" Jake showed pictures on his phone of Lucas and Talia.

Dave said he hadn't seen either of them. Then he frowned. "Wait a minute, show me a photo of that guy again."

Jake swiped back through his phone.

"Yeah, I saw that guy. He was talking to my brother in the pub. He wanted to know about that girl who killed herself. Then he was asking about the ghost tours."

"When was that?" Jake asked.

"About two or three nights ago, I think. But I'd have to check with my brother."

"Is he home?"

"No, sorry; he's gone to the market. He'll be back tomorrow night."

"You sure you haven't seen these two around here?"

"Positive."

Jake described their vehicles to Dave. "Have you seen either of these?"

"No. Sorry." He grinned. "Maybe he got scared of the ghosts and left town. It happens a lot around here."

"What do you know about the ghosts?"

"They're a crock of shit, spread about by that crazy lady who runs the tour company. She makes hundreds of thousands a year from telling people about ghosts," Dave said dismissively.

"What do you know about the Hat Man?" Jake asked.

"That's just hearsay. Apparently, a hundred years ago this town had three freak deaths. Two of them ended up being identified as murders by a man who worked in the hospital. He killed a nurse, if I recall. Anyway, it turned out he'd been stalking other townspeople in a long coat and a big hat. I believe that's the legend of the Hat Man. The rest is embellishment by that tour lady."

"Megan?" Jake confirmed.

"Yep, that's her. Would you like to come in? I'm cooking some of the lamb now, and there's plenty to go around."

Although Jake loved lamb, the sight of a blood-soaked Dave put him off.

The man should have cleaned up before preparing food. "I'd better get going, thanks. More houses to visit. Please call me when your brother gets back." Jake handed Dave his card.

Jake headed north up the highway. It was about three kilometres before he saw another tower. There were eight houses on the high side and nine on the low. Jake door-knocked every house; all but three occupants were home. None had seen anything of Lucas or Talia or their vehicles.

It was dead-ends all round.

By the time Jake arrived back at the hotel, it was 9 and he was past hungry. He would settle for something small, maybe just some hot chips; definitely not meat, not tonight.

Jake rang reception to see if he could order some chips. Isabella was still on duty. She advised him room service ran until 10. He was in luck. He placed his order.

"Do you want a burger with that?" she asked.

"No thank you," Jake responded quickly.

"Be about ten minutes," Isabella finished, before hanging up.

The chips were beer-battered, thick-cut and came with tubs of herb mayo and tomato sauce. They were delightful.

Jake had an accompanying Coke and rang Hayley while he finished off the last few chips.

Indiana was well and truly asleep, and Hayley was spending the night reading. Since Indiana's birth, she hadn't had a lot of time for it. The older Indiana became, the more time she seemed to gain.

Jake told her of his dead-end with Lucas, and Hayley provided a listening ear as she always did but offered no solution in this case.

Jake watched TV for an hour or so, trying to clear his mind.

Sleep took him before he could think any more about the case.

* * *

He woke suddenly to the sound of running water. Where the hell was he? Where was the noise coming from?

From the bathroom, his mind acknowledged. The rushing water sound had now changed to a slow drip.

Switching on the light, Jake noticed steam rising from under the bathroom door as if someone was having a hot shower or running a bath.

Jake got up abruptly. The bedside drawers had been opened. The cabinet drawers under the TV were also open. The steam had reached his bed. Jake could even feel the dampness of the steam against his arms.

Someone was in his room. Jake reached for his gun, a Glock that lay on the bedside table. The feel of the metal gun in his hand made him feel safer, yet the steam and the dripping sound terrified him. He looked over at the alarm clock to gauge the time. The clock was flashing midnight. He glanced at the wall clock; it also showed midnight. This didn't seem real. It seemed much later.

He stood barefoot on the carpet, his feet by now covered by the steam. With his gun by his side, he headed towards the steam and whoever was in the bathroom. The carpet felt damper the closer he got to the bathroom. As he reached the door, the carpet became wet; he could feel the water flow between his toes.

Jake thought about giving a verbal warning to whoever was on the other side of the door, as he would have done in his days on the force. Yet he thought it better to have the advantage of surprise.

The door was slightly ajar, so Jake flung it open to reveal the intruder.

He stood back from the door, his gun positioned by his cheek, both hands clasped around the grip, finger on the trigger, always ready for what he might encounter.

He stepped into the bathroom, arms now extended, gun at the ready. Jake fully expected to find someone, but the room was empty.

Water washed over his feet, overflowing from the bath, yet the taps were turned off. His immediate thoughts reverted to the ghost stories Megan had told him in the diner.

'A nurse is thought to haunt the hotel,' he remembered her saying. Jake made his way over to the bath, ready to release the water. He placed his Glock on the sink and leant over the bath. The water was hot, steam rising from the top.

Could this be the work of the ghost he'd been warned about? Before he knew it, Jake was overpowered and forced into the hot water by the body of a dead girl. Its flesh was blue and rotting. Arms came flailing up from under the water and dragged him under. Chunks of her slimy flesh fell off in the struggle.

Quickly and forcefully, Jake ripped himself free and scrambled to his feet. His gun was back in his hand ready to fire at whatever had grabbed him. Instantly the girl was gone. Had the girl in the tub been Gemma Bassil?

How was that possible? She was dead.

Had he just seen the ghost of the person they were investigating?

Jake double-checked the bath. Not only was the girl gone, the water had also vanished. The steam had dissipated. Jake triple-checked the bath. The corpse was gone. Everything was as it had been hours earlier. The bathroom floor was no longer wet. The carpet was now bone dry!

Had he imagined the whole thing? Was the vision of Gemma just a figment of his tired and overworked imagination?

Jake didn't know any longer. What he experienced had felt real enough—but was it?

Jake sat on his bed, every light in the room on. TV on. His knees were bent up, folded in. He crossed his arms and rested his head on them, with his Glock still gripped firmly in his right hand.

His body so badly wanted sleep, and it took all of his will to stay awake. He tried watching the TV just to keep himself alert. Only infomercials were showing, and the demonstration of a magical non-stick pot provided no help with his battle to stay awake.

Jake's eyes closed briefly before he forced them open again.

His eyes were back on the TV. He looked up at the wall clock. It still said midnight, although it must have been at least twenty minutes since he'd first looked at it.

The clock radio still flashed 12.00. Jake hadn't bothered to reset it and he wasn't going to.

The lady demonstrating a magic pot on the commercial showed the finished product of the scrambled eggs she had baked. "Light fluffy and delicious," she said. They looked delicious, Jake thought. He wondered if Hayley would have liked a magic pot, maybe. Jake even considered buying one, then realised that was exactly what the infomercial was hoping for, tired people like himself giving in when they weren't thinking straight.

Jake's eyes closed again. This time he succumbed to the need for sleep. He had lost his battle to stay awake.

Jake dreamt of a door, a bright, white door, shaking on its hinges. He and the door were surrounded by darkness. The floor began to vibrate. The whistle of a train sounded to his left, deep in the darkness. The floor beneath his feet began to rock and shake, and the train whistle sounded again. It was much closer this time.

A strong beam of light broke the darkness. At first, Jake thought it was a lighthouse beam. The light hit the side of his face, instantly blinding him. Jake stood back from the shaking door, shielded his eyes with his palm and looked directly into the light. It was a train and it was coming straight for him. The blackness around him gave up its secret. He was in a tunnel and Jake suspected which one. The only way to avoid being hit by the train was to go through the shaking white door. Jake dived for the handle as fast as his reflexes would allow. He pulled hard, but the door remained closed. He pulled again. The train was gaining ground quickly. Still nothing. Jake pushed and then pulled. The train was now almost upon him. From the corner of his eye he saw an alcove off the side of the tracks. Jake dived into the alcove expecting the train to whistle past soon after. Yet it was still in the distance.

Jake gathered himself.

The first thing Jake saw were two flaming red circles. They moved in unison towards him. Jake reached for his gun, whipping it from his belt and gripping it firmly by his side.

"Freeze!" Jake called.

The fiery dots continued to advance upon him.

Jake repeated his call, yet it went unheeded.

The tall man stepped forward, with eyes ablaze. Jake looked at his face yet couldn't see his mouth or nose. The man was wearing a wide-brimmed hat and a long jacket.

Out of the jacket appeared long bony hands, which pushed Jake in the chest, sending him flying backwards.

Jake fired his gun as his feet left the ground. "Soon," the Hat Man called, as Jake flew back into the path of the train.

Jake braced for impact, but nothing happened.

Suddenly he woke. He lurched his head up from his folded arms. The reflex action sent a sharp pain down the back of his neck and into his spine. Jake was breathing frantically, deep heavy breaths, his whole chest heaving. Sweat soaked his back.

The room was in complete darkness.

Power must have gone out, was Jake's immediate thought. He looked to where the clock radio usually sat but there was nothing. Jake was surprised there was no flashing lights; maybe the battery backup was faulty, he guessed.

Jake stretched out with his left hand and fumbled about the top of the bedside table trying to locate his mobile. His palm and fingertips padded the top of the table. He reached for his clock radio, but the tabletop was empty. Jake continued to pad down the table and finally the tips of his fingers touched the protective rubber casing of his phone. He clasped it and dragged it towards him.

Jake couldn't hear or see anything, but he could feel a presence. It was as if someone was watching him. His nose twitched. A foul smell hit him. It was a smell he had smelt once before. It was burning flesh.

Jake flicked the torch on his iPhone on. It lit up the bedside table. His clock radio was gone. He shone his phone around the room from the front door back towards his bed. There was nothing visible at first until it revealed a girl who was standing at the foot of his bed.

It was Gemma, naked and soaking, and staring at Jake, the light from his phone revealing her face. It had no expression. She closed her eyes, turned and walked away.

Jake watched her disappear into the bathroom.

Subconsciously, Jake had been holding his breath. Finally, he took a breath.

His heart was beating rapidly. It was going so fast he could hardly breathe. He sucked in air through his nose.

Jake crept to his feet, desperately trying not to make a sound. Unfortunately, his body was too big for that to be a possibility. When he stood up, the bed let out a creak that was only amplified by the still of the night.

Jake made his way quietly to the edge of the bathroom door. His feet standing on wet carpet for the second time tonight, Jake peered into the bathroom. Gemma's decomposing corpse was sitting quietly in the bath. She placed a washcloth over her face.

Music began to play on the clock radio that had relocated itself to the side of the vanity. It was resting delicately on the side. Jake noted it wasn't even plugged in. Jake didn't recognise the song playing immediately, but he was sure it was one of Katy Perry's hits.

A dark figure brushed past Jake. It was moving slowly. Jake tried to make out what or who it was but all he could be sure of, was that it was a human shape. Jake held his breath as the dark shape paused in the bathroom looking over the bath. The radio played on.

Without warning, the black shape threw the radio into the bath where Gemma was lying. Gemma's body shook, twitching and convulsing violently. Her legs buckled. Her body fell silent, motionless. The dark thing that had thrown the radio turned and left the room.

Jake was trying to process what he had just witnessed when the lights and the TV returned to life. The room was suddenly bright again. The clock radio had reset and was now showing 5.30 am.

Jake wondered who or what the other ghost was.

What was this whole night about?

Who was the dark figure? Was it the man from his dream?

Jake was totally confused.

Sleep for him was out of the question. There was no way he could sleep now after what he had just seen.

Chapter 33

Picton December 2016

Overnight, the container had cooled considerably. The humidity that had made the box nearly unbearable during the day was replaced by cold night air. It had cooled so much that Talia was shivering. The skimpy blanket was totally inadequate.

Talia had been woken by movement and talking outside her box about 6 am. It was the brothers. Their voices were unmistakable.

Breakfast was due in half an hour, if yesterday's schedule was anything to go by. Considering they ran a farm, Talia expected they would remain true to their schedule.

She lay there listening to them talking, trying to make out individual words, yet it all came through muffled. She could hear them moving around outside and listened patiently for that gate latch. As soon as she heard it, the count began. *One cat and dog, two cat and dog*. By the time she got to *twenty-four cat and dog*, the door opened.

The timing was within one second of yesterday's count.

Now she could plan.

Talia was sitting on her mattress like a good little girl waiting to be fed her breakfast.

This time it was the shorter and older brother who brought in the food. He'd been in the fields on the tractor when the younger brother had kidnapped her. He didn't seem to object to his brother's decision.

He placed a tray of food along with a fresh bottle of water on the floor of the shipping container and left without saying a word.

Talia looked at the plate. Vegemite on toast. She was starving, and she doubted two small pieces of toast would do much to ease her rumbling stomach.

Talia kept looking at the ceiling grates, but they were too high up. Even if she stood on the upturned bucket, she wouldn't reach them. She would be short by at least half a metre. There had to be another way to escape this prison.

Then the idea came to her.

Next time one of them came, she would be ready with the bucket in hand.

She thought her best chance would be to empty the contents of the now nearly full bucket, her toilet, on whichever brother came in next. While he was turning away from the flying crap (as anyone would do) she would then turn her bucket into a weapon, striking him repeatedly on the head.

It was hard metal, and swung with enough power it could do serious damage to someone's head.

Talia still had no idea why they had taken her or the other girls. To be sold as sex slaves, or tortured, or worse? She wasn't going to wait to find out. At the next opportunity she would have to make a run for it.

Where would she go? She couldn't just run without purpose or without any idea about where she was running.

She needed to see outside just to get her bearings.

Her toast was cold, and too thick with Vegemite for her liking, yet this wasn't the time to be picky about her food.

The water was cold and refreshing, yet it would only stay that way for a short time before the container heated up again in the summer sun.

Chapter 34

Picton December 2016

Jake didn't care that it was only 7.45 am. He had been up for hours and he was done waiting.

He dialled Megan's number. The phone rang a few times before switching over to voicemail. Jake clicked the receiver and dialled again. It rang a few times before switching over to voicemail once more.

"Fuck!" Jake screamed.

Megan was probably still asleep. Maybe she'd had a late night showing more ghosts on the tour.

He dialled again, and it rang twice before an angry and tired Megan answered.

"Hello?" she slurred.

"Megan, it's Jake. We need to talk."

"What's this about?"

"I'll tell you when I see you. Too much to get into over the phone," Jake replied.

"Give me thirty. I'll meet you at the coffee shop."

"Okay, thanks." Jake hung up and headed to the coffee shop immediately. He wanted to be waiting there when Megan arrived.

Jake waved her over as Megan entered the coffee shop.

"Sorry about my appearance. I rushed out." Megan sounded anxious.

Jake, who couldn't care less about appearance, especially his own during a criminal investigation, answered quickly and professionally, "You look great. I think I saw her," he added.

"Saw who?"

"Gemma Bassil," Jake answered. "Well, her ghost at least."

"What do you mean? What happened?"

Jake went through the details of the night before, from start to finish. "Why do think she visited me?"

"I think she was trying to communicate with you," Megan replied.

"Okay. But who do you think the other ghost was?"

"The one that pushed the radio into the bath?"

"Yes. Who was that?"

"I think it was Gemma too. She was trying to show you what happened."

"What do you mean . . . *Gemma too*?"

"Spirits are not like humans. They can do many things. I think she was showing you how she died. You said the clock radio was suddenly in the bathroom, she was in the bath and music was playing. I think she was showing you exactly what happened."

"If she was showing me her murder, why wouldn't she show me who it was?" Jake asked.

"Maybe she doesn't know who it was, only that it happened," Megan offered.

"Sounds crazy."

"Well, does what happened last night look like the crime scene photos?" Megan asked.

"I haven't seen them."

"I suggest you go and find out. Then you'll know. Spirits don't tend to visit people for fun. Usually they have a reason."

"Why don't spirits go to heaven?" Jake asked, looking away.

"You're not a spiritual man, are you, Jake?" Megan guessed.

"No, I've seen too much evil to believe in God."

"In my opinion, some spirits get stuck between their life on earth and wherever they're going. Until they can find peace, they're stuck here. That's why Gemma still haunts that room. Once she comes to terms with her death, she will move on. That's my theory anyhow. Oh, and I do believe good people go to heaven." She got up. "I have to go, but let me know how you fare with the crime scene photos."

She put on her yellow woollen cardigan which she had hung over the back of the chair.

Jake reached out and took her hand. "Wait, I have something else."

"Mr Miller, I really need to be going."

"I saw the Hat Man. He came to me in a dream."

"I really don't have time to listen to your dreams. Maybe we could catch up later."

"I don't think it was a real dream. I have marks; three lines like burns, where he touched me in my dream." He sat looking up at Megan's face. She had instantly become pale and she reached for her chair and sank into it.

"Did you speak to the pastor?" she asked.

"No, the old guy I spoke to said the pastor had moved out."

"The old guy *is* the pastor," Megan replied. "You need to speak to him."

"Why? What does he know about Hat Man?"

"He thinks Hat Man is the devil and killed his whole family. Speak to him." She sighed. "I really can't help you when it comes to Hat Man. A couple of people on my tours, along with your friend and Talia, are the only ones I know who have ever seen him. The rest is a myth that has been around this town for a hundred years." Megan stood for a second time. "I really have to go. I'm late for an appointment. Speak to the pastor and look at the crime scene photos and we can chat again."

Jake nodded and watched her leave. Then he jumped on his phone.

No service. He would have to go back to the hotel.

* * *

Jake returned to find the hotel reception unattended.

By the time he reached the top of the stairs, Isabella was just leaving his room.

"Just making up your room. Is there anything I can get for you?" she asked.

"No, I'm fine, thank you," Jake replied.

The room looked clean. The bed was made, and there were fresh towels in the bathroom, but one thing puzzled Jake. She had no cleaning equipment, and no trolley full of dirty linen with her. Oh well, maybe she'd already done that and had just come back to finish off a few things.

He headed for the phone sitting on the desk at the end of the bed and dialled Monique. While he waited for the phone to connect, he pulled up the chair that sat at the desk. The phone connected to an automated receptionist. "If you know the extension number, please enter it now, otherwise hold for reception," the robotic voice stated.

Jake entered Monique's four-digit number and waited again. He picked up the pen sitting on the pad to his right. That was when he noticed it. At first it was almost invisible, but the harder he looked the clearer it became. There were indentations on the notepad. Someone, maybe Lucas, had written himself a note.

All Jake needed was a pencil to bring it to life. He searched the desk drawer. There were 'with compliments' slips, local restaurant menus, some promotional matches, and resting against the back of the drawer, a grey lead pencil.

Jake glided the edge of the pencil across the indented words. Three lines appeared.

Red Truck F100?

Gemma's Friday afternoon?

Talia?

"Hello?" a voice from the phone said. "Is anyone there?"

Jake stopped staring at the inscribed page. "Monique, it's Jake," he mumbled, still trying to think what the note meant.

"I was about to have this call traced, Jake," Monique said.

"Having stalker issues again?"

"No more than usual," Monique said.

Jake wondered how many crazies the top cop would attract. He had attracted a few in his time and he was only a detective.

"Monique, could I bother you with a few requests?" He'd originally rung wanting help with the crime scene photos, but since he'd discovered the note he had two other searches to be done.

"What do you need?" she said.

"Who do I speak to about getting a hold of the crime scene photos for Gemma Bassil's death?"

"Inspector Mike Connolly. He's based in Thirlmere, just outside Picton. Tell him you worked for me. He'll give you whatever you need."

"Will do, thanks," Jake said.

"What else do you need?"

"Could you find out if any calls were made from this room on Friday the 14th of August 2014?" Jake reeled off the direct line of the room. He waited while Monique scribbled it down at the other end. "Finally, I need to know if there are any red Ford F100s registered around here."

"Okay. But that could take some time. I'll get back to you as soon as I can," Monique said.

Jake was desperate to look at the photos of a deceased Gemma, before the images of the night before faded from his memory. It would be first on his 'to do' list.

But the leads Lucas was following up had also piqued his curiosity. Lucas had said the phone he had found at the wreckers had a photo of a red Ford F100. Had he subsequently located it?

* * *

Thirlmere December 2016

Jake arrived in Thirlmere just before 1 pm. He walked up the steps leading to the police station as if he owned it. In some ways he still felt a part of the police force, even though he had left months ago.

"Inspector Connolly?" Jake asked the officer at the counter.

"You are?" the officer queried.

"Det—" Jake, stopped himself. "Jake Miller. I'm a private detective."

"Is it regarding something in particular, Mr Miller?"

"Gemma Bassil."

"One moment." The officer disappeared through a door behind the counter.

Jake turned to sit on a bench, before realising there was a guy sleeping across it.

Jake had seen it many times before; guys would usually hide out in the police foyer when they had someone chasing them, wanting to do them harm. Usually it was someone who had slept with someone they shouldn't have.

Jake stood against the wall, folded his arms and waited.

The officer returned. "The inspector will be with you shortly."

"Thank you." Jake waved an arm in appreciation.

The man on the bench suddenly sat upright. He looked around, got his bearings and then gave a sigh of relief when he saw the officer behind the desk.

Jake assumed he'd had a bad dream, or his situation had hit him when he'd woken. "Can I please speak to the detective?" the man asked.

"Sir, you have been told to go home," the officer said calmly.

"But he said he'd kill me! Why won't you help me?" the man asked.

Jake had noticed him looking over his shoulder several times since approaching the desk. Whoever had scared him had done a good job.

"Sir, we've spoken to the man in question. He denies ever threatening you. Unfortunately, our hands are tied until he does something, or threatens you in front of witnesses."

"So, he has to kill me before you will do something?" The man was now terrified and agitated.

"We need him to break the law, or to have proof of him breaking the law. As the detective said, go to the courthouse and apply for an intervention order."

The man thought about his options, took another quick glance over his shoulder and headed out of the police station.

Jake watched as the man paused on the steps outside the station, looked both ways and then sprinted off towards the parking lot.

"Mr Miller!" a male voice called.

Jake returned his attention to the counter.

The inspector stood in the doorway, his wide, stocky body blocking the entrance.

"Did Mrs Bassil hire a whole team of detectives?" he asked.

"Why do you ask that?" Jake said.

"I spoke to a PI about Gemma only a couple of days ago, or maybe you're his replacement? The other guy didn't seem to have much of a clue."

"Lucas is part of my team," Jake said, ignoring his dig at Lucas's ability.

"So how can I help you?" the inspector asked.

"I'd like to see the crime scene photos, please."

"Can't Lucas guide you on that? After all, he's seen them."

Jake didn't want to tell him Lucas was missing as well. At least not until he had heard back from Monique. "Lucas could have taken photos of the crime scene with his phone, but he didn't. He did the right thing. Just one quick look and then I'm out of your hair," Jake offered.

Inspector Connolly knew Jake was right. Lucas could have taken copies of the crime scene; obviously he hadn't. "Come through," the inspector motioned, waving Jake towards him.

The inspector took Jake to the same room he had taken Lucas. He placed the large file on the desk. "Just let me know when you're done."

"Thanks."

Jake was surprised at how helpful the inspector was being. Maybe that was the difference between country police and city police. City police were often more guarded and less friendly. He wondered what Lucas's impressions of the inspector were. He had dealt with the country police more often, and maybe he saw them differently.

Jake sifted through the file, report after report. The police pathologist's initial report was followed by a second and independent pathologist's report.

He flicked through all the statements and the list of the deceased's belongings.

Then he came across the photos. The first was of Gemma in the bath. Exactly as in his dream, the room was steamy, and the radio was at the bottom of the bath. The body was in the same position as the ghost of Gemma had displayed.

Megan was right. It was a re-enactment. This meant one thing. She hadn't killed herself. Based on his vision, she had been murdered. Someone had thrown the radio into the bath. But who? Why?

Jake wondered if she'd met someone while she was in Picton with Paige. A relationship that had gone bad, maybe?

It was a line of enquiry he would need to follow up further.

Jake left the file on the desk. On his way out, he thanked Inspector Connolly for his assistance.

Driving back, those two questions occupied his thoughts. Who? Why?

Jake knew the answer lay in 'why'. If he found out why she was murdered, he would find out who had killed her.

* * *

Isabella greeted him at hotel reception as usual. "I have some messages for you, Mr Miller," she said, waving more yellow Post-It notes above her head. "A lady named Monique called. She's rung twice. She's not very patient. Seems bossy."

Even if Jake wanted to answer there wasn't a break in Isabella's one-way conversation. "It's as if she didn't think I had given you the message. I told her you were out."

"She's bossy, all right," Jake answered.

He went to retrieve the messages, but Isabella wasn't ready to part with them quite yet.

"It's a good thing you didn't get tangled up with her. You would regret it for the rest of your life. Believe me," Isabella said. Her expression went from one of happiness to one of anger and spite, as if she had once been told she was impatient and overbearing herself. "She wouldn't even tell me what it was about. I think she assumed I must be Picton's Queen of Gossip."

"She's a police officer. She wouldn't be able to tell you. It would be confidential," Jake said.

"Don't you think I can keep confidential information?"

Jake didn't want to get into the whole meaning of that with Isabella because he knew it would be futile. Instead, he humoured her, just to end the conversation. "I'm sure you can. I'll let her know."

Jake didn't even close the door to his room. The urgency to speak to Monique was buzzing through his body. She had called twice; she must have something of interest.

He looked at his mobile. It showed no missed calls or messages, yet he was sure she had tried his mobile. How did people in this town survive without mobile coverage?

The phone rang only once before Monique answered.

"Hi Jake, I found some interesting stuff."

"Go on."

"We traced the phone from the hotel. There was a call on the Friday afternoon which, from what we can gather, was only minutes after Gemma checked in."

"Who did she call?" Jake asked.

"Inspector Connolly."

"The police department, do you mean?"

"No, Inspector Connolly on his direct number."

"Why would she call him?" Jake asked, frowning.

"No idea, but I think you need to find out."

"I agree."

"In regard to the red F100, I found four registered to addresses in the Picton area," Monique continued.

"How many actually in Picton?" Jake asked.

"Just the one. Registered to a Mr Brown, last registered in 2012. Hasn't been registered since."

Brown? Suddenly, Jake remembered the name. Lucas had mentioned he had spoken to the Brown boys.

"It's registered to an address at 12-16 Mount Hercules Road," Monique said.

Jake knew that was where they lived, right next to the tower . . . the tower where both Lucas's and Talia's phones had last registered. It was a coincidence too big to ignore, and a great place to start.

Jake decided to keep his revelation to himself, for now anyway. "I'm going to check out that address. It's just near the tower. If that's a dead-end, then I'll try the others," Jake said.

"Do you want me to call for backup?" Monique asked.

"No, I'll be fine. I'm going to wait until later tonight."

"You always did like doing things under the cover of darkness." Monique laughed.

"You still know me," Jake joked. "How long was Gemma's call to Connolly, by the way?"

"Brief, one minute and forty-two seconds."

"Enough time to make an appointment or maybe ask a question or two but nothing of substance."

"Sounds about right."

Jake thought of telling Monique about the dream but dismissed the idea almost instantly. He trusted Monique, but trust only gave you so much credit. He didn't have enough credit for such a crazy story.

"I have a meeting I need to get to. Now, promise me you won't go doing anything stupid?"

"I promise," Jake said.

It was a promise he couldn't guarantee he'd keep. He had done some crazy things before.

Chapter 35

Talia had pissed and shat everything she had in her into that disgusting metal bucket. She had even vomited because of the smell. The only bad thing was, she had vomited away from the bucket and not into it.

Now all she had to do was wait. Lunch had come and gone. It was getting late in the afternoon; the prison box had even begun to cool down.

Talia had moved her bedding from the usual spot in the top right corner to just in front of the door. She was hoping it would disorient him, just briefly—a second or two was all she needed.

She had gone over the plan in her head a thousand times, and it seemed like each time a new 'what if' arose.

What if she dumped the bucket on him, and couldn't get past the door?

What if the gate he came through locked automatically each time? She would be trapped.

What if she got past the gate and sprinted off the farm and couldn't find anyone to help her? Then she would be recaptured.

The 'what ifs' stopped running through her head when she heard the gate opening.

She started counting *one cat and dog, two cat and dog*. She knew she was behind by one or two seconds. She tried to keep counting steadily in her head while she positioned herself to the right of the door, bucket in hand.

Talia had reached twenty-one in her head when the younger brother stepped inside.

Her plan of disorienting the man by moving the bed had seemed to work. As soon as he entered, he stopped. He stood with her meal in one hand, two fresh bottles of water in the other, staring at the empty bed lying in front of him instead of the far-right corner, as he was used to.

Talia wasted no time in throwing the contents of the bucket over her stationary target.

Poo and piss flew from the bucket, hitting him in the face. Her aim couldn't have been better if she had rehearsed it. Large chunks hit him in the face; Talia swore she saw a piece of crap hit him right in the eye.

Talia charged at the burly man, swinging the bucket as he tried to shield his face.

Instinctively, he dropped what he was carrying, and raised his hands to his face, leaving her dinner to fall to the floor amongst the remains of the bucket.

The bucket connected with the back of the man's skull. Dave staggered a little and the bucket flew out of her hands as it collected him on the right side of his head.

The momentum sent Talia sprawling out through the door.

She landed firmly and unceremoniously in the dirt. She fought the pain that shot through her ankles and hips and got to her feet swiftly. Her right knee caved in a little and sent a sharp pain up her leg when she took her first step.

Talia saw her captor lying face down in the excrement, motionless, and assumed he was knocked out, not dead. She also knew he wouldn't stay that way for long.

A padlock hung from the open door.

Talia frantically removed the padlock and flung the door shut. As it was closing, she could see the brother stirring.

He was coming to.

She hurried to thread the padlock back through the handle. In her panic, she fumbled with it and it fell from her grasp to the ground.

She could hear the brother try and get to his feet. He moaned loudly, probably still unsure what had happened.

Talia quickly swept her fingers over the dirt, looping the fumbled lock with one of her fingers. There was a loud thud followed by another "Arrgh." She assumed he had fallen to his knees or his belly, unable to stand due to his concussion and still unsteady on his feet.

She took the metal lock and threaded it through the loop under the handle, then pressed her fingers and thumb together hard. The click that followed was the most fantastic sound she had ever heard. The man now locked inside the box began to hammer on the door with his fists.

Talia's adrenaline took over. She bolted through the gate.

It was freedom or nothing!

Without looking back, Talia could hear the metal door of the container being bashed behind her. The gate led her to a dusty path covered by a few loose stones. She had arrived at the back of the farmhouse.

She knew instantly she was still on the farm where she'd been captured.

She could see the garage to the right and beyond it, a driveway to the road, directly in front of her.

Her car was nowhere to be seen—not that she had the keys anyway.

She poked her head out and looked down the drive. She couldn't see the other brother.

She looked to her right. Over her shoulder, high on the horizon, a tractor was working in the fields. It was the other brother. She could see his big frame sitting in the cabin. She doubted he could see her. If she could make it to the garage, it would provide cover for her dash to the road.

Wasting no time, Talia took a deep breath and darted out from behind the house. She ran as fast as she could.

She felt exposed the whole time before reaching the garage where she dived for cover. Once hidden by the garage, she stopped to regain her breath. She needed to prepare herself for another sprint, a longer one out in the open with nowhere to hide until she reached the shrubbery of the neighbour's driveway.

She peeked out from behind the garage to get a fix on the tractor. It was still sitting on the horizon. The brother was still there. He was looking down at something in the cabin.

Anthony Brown couldn't hear anything over the noise of his tractor, but he had seen everything. He saw movement from the back of the house as the girl sprinted across the dusty drive and hid behind the garage.

How had she escaped?

Where the fuck was Dave?

He had to get her back before she made it to the neighbour's place.

He climbed down from the tractor, picking the rifle up from the floor. It would be a tough shot from here but one he would have to make. He couldn't kill her either; that would defeat the whole purpose of taking her in the first place.

He loaded his .308 magazine. It held four cartridges, and he had to slide the bolt in between shots, so for tasks like this it proved cumbersome. At this distance it would test his accuracy.

He clicked the magazine into the bottom of the rifle, lifted and slid the bolt back, and watched as the first bullet loaded into the chamber.

Anthony tucked the butt of the gun firmly under his chin and looked through the scope.

As she neared the letterbox, she would be fully exposed. It would be his best chance to make the shot. Every step she took after that would make his shot harder.

In the right-hand corner of the scope was his letterbox. In the middle sitting right between the cross hairs was the space between the gates. She would soon be on target.

Talia sprinted as fast as she could go. The first run had tired her. Consequently, her second run wasn't as quick as she had hoped. She saw the gate directly in front of her. It was open, and the green letterbox sat atop the right-hand fence post.

She passed the letterbox and, in an instant, was running along the road itself. The surface was loose, the gravel uneven and slippery, and if she wasn't careful she could lose her footing. Before she had time to tell herself not to jinx herself, she was sprawled out on the road, face and palms in the dirt. She got up and as she did so, an excruciating pain shot up her left leg. She noticed blood pouring down her jeans, too much blood for a scraped knee, she thought.

Still deeply concerned the brothers weren't far behind, she quickly raised the leg of her jeans to discover a wound, in fact a hole. She had been shot in the calf. Panicking, she looked around, but couldn't see either brother. How had she been shot? She had heard no sound other than the tractor.

Frantically she sought out the tractor. It appeared empty. The driver was gone. She quickly scanned the horizon, and a loud bang echoed nearby. A puff of dust hit the ground beside her.

She couldn't tell where the shots were coming from, but someone was shooting at her. Must be Anthony.

It didn't matter, she thought. If she stayed a moment longer, he would hit her again. She had heard once that if you were being shot at, to run in a diagonal pattern. It made it harder for the shooter to aim than if you were running in a straight line.

She stood up. The pain in her calf was horrendous. She took a deep breath and ran as best she could. Even though it was more like a hobble she was at least moving, and she made sure to change directions, although her injured leg prevented her from making much progress.

Anthony was now standing leaning on the fence post, cigarette in mouth, rifle in hand.

"You going to give up now? Or do I have to kill you where you stand?" Anthony asked.

Talia turned and looked how far she had to go to reach the neighbours. She began to cry. She felt utterly defeated.

"Just leave me alone," she sobbed.

"I can't do that, I'm afraid. You know too much," Anthony replied.

"Then just kill me!" Talia screamed.

"We will, soon enough."

Talia had asked for it, but when she heard his words, fear overpowered her body and she began to shake.

Without a word, Anthony approached her, picked her up one-handed and hauled her over his shoulder, and headed back to the farmhouse.

"You know how hard that shot was?" Anthony asked as he walked.

Chapter 36

Picton December 2016

Jake had so far done as he had promised Monique, which was to wait for dark.

As much as he wanted to go to the Browns' farm and keep them under surveillance, he knew sitting in front of their house in broad daylight would be indiscreet. Jake also knew if they had the slightest inclination that they were under surveillance, they would go to ground and if anything was happening, it would stop and possibly never be uncovered.

Darkness was his only option.

In the meantime, he had decided to keep an eye on the church. Dining across the road from it was the perfect cover.

Jake sat down at a table near the window.

The waitress came to offer Jake some bread and take his drinks order. As usual he didn't order any alcohol, only a ginger ale.

"That looks like a beautiful building. Is it still used as a church?" Jake asked the waitress.

"No, unfortunately, it's such a shame."

"Who lives there now?" Jake enquired.

"The same pastor who used to preach there. He bought the house and the church from the ministry after a family tragedy. He has basically been a shut-in ever since."

"That sounds horrible. I thought I saw him there with a young girl the other day?"

"Yes, That's his granddaughter, Olly, poor thing. Never knew her parents. They were killed in a horrific accident on the outskirts of Picton when she was born after her mum had died." She no longer looked cheery.

"Sorry, I shouldn't have asked."

"No, it's okay. Just one of the sad events in Picton's history."

She left to get his ginger ale and returned ready to take his main order.

"I don't want to upset you any further, but do you know why he became a hermit?" Jake asked.

"It's no problem," she said, placing a glass with three ice cubes in front of him and an open bottle of ginger ale on the table. "He's . . . how would you say . . . a self-imposed shut-in. I guess."

"Self-imposed?"

"Ever since the accident, he believes the devil is out to get him. He has lost any faith he had. It's so sad."

Jake half smiled, a sad smile, unsure what to say.

"Now, what can I get you?" the waitress asked. She had purposely changed the subject. It was obviously upsetting her.

"I can't decide between the roast and the fettuccine. What would you recommend?"

"I'd go with the roast lamb. It's fresh off the farm, local too."

Jake remembered the brother at the farm covered in lamb's blood. It instantly put him off the roast.

"I think I'll go the pasta. Maybe I'll get the roast next time."

She took the order and left Jake to finish his bread.

Jake hoped he hadn't upset her by not accepting her recommendation, yet he feared he had. Can't please everyone, he thought.

No one entered or left the church the whole time Jake was sitting eating.

In fact, there looked to be no movement at all.

I need to talk to this pastor again, Jake decided.

Chapter 37

Picton December 2016

They had never come to check on her at this time of night. Usually, 6 o'clock dinner time was the last visit for the day. Something was going on.

Both brothers were standing in the doorway, one behind the other.

When the brother had carried her back to the box, he had checked the injury to her leg. She was lucky it had only put a gash at the edge of her calf. Anthony stitched up the wound as best he could. There was no pain relief for Talia. She had passed out. When she came around, she noticed Anthony had wrapped her leg in a fresh bandage. She couldn't understand why he had gone to the effort to stitch and dress the wound when they clearly said their plan was to kill her.

"Get up!" the bigger brother said.

Dave looked as if he had copped the worst of the bucket. He had a large patch across his forehead. She assumed he too had needed stitches. She hoped it was the case anyhow.

Both the brothers had gloves on. That's not a good sign, Talia thought.

"Follow us," the brother commanded.

She did as she was asked. She walked slowly through the gate she had earlier sprinted through. She stepped off the gravelled dirt path and followed them onto the porch of the house. It felt as if every board was rotten underfoot and could give way at any time. The house looked old and dishevelled. She couldn't decide if it needed a paint or a bulldozer. She was leaning towards bulldozer.

One brother walked in front of her while the other followed, to prevent her escape.

Her car was waiting for her, yet she had no idea where she was going. Were they letting her go?

Talia stood on the cracked porch steps that seemed in far worse condition than the porch boards themselves. The middle step had given way altogether.

In front of her car was a white ute. It wasn't the red F100 she had come to the farm asking about.

"Get in the driver's seat of your car." The smaller brother pulled the gun from his waistband and waved it at her vehicle. "I'll be sitting in the back. You will do exactly as you're told, do you understand?"

Talia knew that the consequences of not doing as she was told would be a bullet in her back. She had begun to think the brothers were not going to kill her. Instead, she felt it was likely she would be sold into a prostitution slave house, hidden somewhere nearby. She suspected that all the deaths she had been investigating were elaborate cover-ups for killings when the slave house had no further use for the victims.

It was the only thing that made sense to her. What else could they be doing? Why keep her for days only to kill her? What purpose did that serve?

The country road was dark, other than her headlights. The taillights of the younger brother's old ute in front of her was the only other light she could see. The brothers made sure to take back roads, anything to avoid the main roads. When the ute braked, Talia had no idea where on earth she was, and she guessed that was the way the brothers wanted it.

"Get out," the voice behind her said.

She stepped out. She was in a turning circle, one that looked as if it had been made by occasional use, rather than design. As dark as it was, she could tell she was in in the middle of bushland somewhere. She began to rethink her whole prostitution theory. This was how Ivan Milat had killed. Panic shot through her body.

He stood behind her, gun pointed at her back. "Open the boot," he ordered.

She complied.

"Take the rope."

She scanned the floor of the boot. She didn't recall carrying any rope. The spare wheel was there, and her bag, but that was all. Then she looked to the left and saw a bundle of rope on the floor. The brothers had placed it there. The rope had a noose tied in one end. They were going to hang her; make it look like another suicide, she thought.

Dave had joined them at the back of her vehicle. "Follow him," Anthony said.

Dave led the way. He walked off into the darkness, with only his dimly lit torch beam to guide him.

Despite the lack of light, Talia recognised where she was. She was standing on the far side of the Redbank Range Tunnel. They had parked on the overgrown disused railway tracks on the other side of the tunnel. She looked down and could see the dense gully below, about a twenty-metre drop. Was this where they were going to hang her—leave her dangling from the track over Stonequarry Creek?

"Take her into the tunnel. He'll come for her," Anthony said.

Dave continued to lead the way.

He entered the Redbank Range Tunnel.

Talia stopped, paralysed in fear. Anthony must have kept walking because suddenly she felt the gun press into the small of her back.

"I can't go in. Please don't make me," she whined, shaking her head.

"Keep going," Anthony replied, jabbing her with the gun and pushing her towards the tunnel.

Talia shuffled slowly forward. Anthony could see her delaying tactics and shoved her forward violently. Talia fell to her knees. She could see the over-grown sleepers and caught a glimpse of the creek below.

Jump for it, a voice in her head called. Although it would mean certain death.

But at least it would be at your own hands, not due to these scum. You would control your fate . . .

Yes! Talia agreed. Why give them the satisfaction? If I'm going to go, I'll go out my way.

She took a deep breath and prepared to jump to her death.

Do it, do it now.

She had taken two steps towards the edge and was about to push off when she realised the voice she was hearing was not her own. She didn't know whose it was, but she was suddenly sure she didn't want to die tonight.

A hand grabbed her sweater before her brain had corrected her course. "Don't even think about it," Dave said.

The tunnel towered over her head like the giant clown-mouth at Luna Park. She was pushed through the entrance by the constant prodding of the gun in her back. She went from being pushed to being dragged by her shirt. She could feel her heels digging in the dirt.

The tunnel felt as if it had closed behind her. The temperature dropped, and the night sounds were instantly silenced. Talia felt an unwelcome pres-ence; the same one she had experienced last time she was in the tunnel.

On that occasion she had come in contact with Hat Man.

A jolt of fear shot up her spine. Her body was sending off signals every way it knew how. Sweat poured from her forehead, her hands trembled, the hairs on her arms stood up. Alarm bells were ringing.

Talia knew she was in trouble.

"Scat!" Anthony called out from behind her.

"We have one for you," Dave, the brother in front, added.

From the alcove on the right, the faceless being she had seen a few nights before glided out into the tunnel. Its coat was hovering just above the ground. It made no sound as it glided to a halt.

It stood there silently, with burning, fiery-red eyes staring at them.

Chapter 38

Picton December 2016

With his car hidden behind a windbreak of pine trees in a far back paddock, Jake entered the Browns' farm property from the back. It had become a habit, perhaps a bad one.

Jake wanted to see if the red F100 was here and if it was operational.

The cows in the back paddock were quiet, hardly stirring as Jake crept past. The house was in darkness except for a small glimmer of light shining from the front. Jake assumed it was the porch light.

There was a large shipping container at the back of the property. Jake guessed the owners were using it to store farming equipment or stock feed. He was surprised to find it had a small door, just big enough for a person to enter.

The door was damaged and buckled as though it had come in contact with an angry bull, and a big one at that. Jake stepped over the twisted metal door that lay half off its hinges. He noted several unlocked padlocks on the ground, as well as one still bolted to the middle lock. This was definitely not a storage shed. Jake knew the second he stepped inside that it had been used to keep someone captive, and whoever it was, appeared to have broken out. Lucas, he thought. He would be strong enough to get out of here. By the look of the door, it had been bent and kicked in until he got free. Jake noticed blood on the floor and then a trail to a bucket. Maybe Lucas had ambushed his captor.

Jake couldn't be sure. He didn't have time to investigate the scene further now. He needed to find the F100 if it was here, before the brothers returned home. Jake headed out from the container and into a large storage shed, one of several he had seen on the property.

A large tractor and a plough were stored there. Behind were hay bales stacked from the floor to the rafters. At the rear of the shed, Jake could see a large mezzanine area.

There appeared to be car-like shapes stored under tarps. Jake manoeuvred his way through the machinery and headed towards the tarps. He lifted the cover off the first vehicle. He could tell by the shape it was too small to be a F100, but curiosity got the better of him. It was a dark blue Toyota RAV4. A 'P' plate stared back at him from the back window. Jake pressed his face up against the window. Inside was clean except for a few scraps of paper. Looked like a girl's car, Jake thought. This car had been here a while, judging from the flat tyres.

Jake replaced the tarp and wiped the dust from his face and hands. He removed the tarp from the second car. This one, a Mazda, had been reversed in and the plates had been removed. The tarp had very little dust on it compared to the RAV4. Jake again tried to look in through the window. This car was a mess. There were folders and notes thrown all over the place. Someone had been rummaging through it.

Jake opened the car door and was greeted by a chiming sound and a bright interior light. The car battery was still functioning. This car hadn't been here long at all.

Jake scooped up the papers and sat on the seat, closing the door to silence the annoying chime.

After flicking through several pieces of paper, he came across something he recognised, a brochure detailing *Ghost Tours in Picton*. It had Megan's company logo. Whoever owned this car had met Megan, as her card was attached.

Jake opened the glove box. He was hoping to find some registration papers or owner's manual; something that would identify the owner of the vehicle.

He found the manual resting under some papers. The name on the inside cover stopped Jake in his tracks.

Mr L. Taylor. Lucas's car.

Where the hell was Lucas?

Jake searched the rest of the car and found a loaded Beretta under the passenger seat. Lucas had obviously thought he wasn't in any danger if he had left his gun in the car.

Jake placed the Beretta back under the seat, deciding it was best not to remove evidence from the crime scene.

Jake had to see if Lucas was here also.

There was another shed at the front of the driveway and Jake headed there next. He paused at the corner of the tractor shed and double-checked if the house was still in darkness. It was.

He made his way down the driveway towards the front of the house. His search had taken him in a wide arc, from the storage container up to the large shed and now back down to a second garage. If the F100 wasn't here, the only other place it could be was in the shed in the lower paddock at the front of the property. That was unless the owners were out driving it.

Jake arrived at the front of the garage. The door was closed. It was a large heavy sliding door, padlocked and chained. He wasted no time in deciding what to do, simply pulling out his Glock and shooting at the padlock. The bullet almost ricocheted back at him. Luckily, it didn't hit him. Jake dragged the chain off the door and pushed the door slowly ajar, just enough to slip through.

This shed was pitch black. There were no gaps in the roof to allow the moonlight to filter through. Here, he would need his torch.

Jake grabbed for his phone and even though he had no service the torch function still worked.

There were more cars in this garage, including the mysterious red Ford F100.

Now Jake needed to see if this thing was still in working condition.

Chapter 39

Picton December 2016

Talia was so fixated on the burning eyes of Hat Man, she didn't notice Anthony slip the rope over her head. The eyes of the beast kept her mesmerised even as the noose tightened. It wasn't until she began to gasp for air that she finally realised what was happening to her.

A smirk began to appear on Hat Man's face where previously it had been expressionless. Talia thought she even captured a glimpse of some teeth but couldn't be sure in the darkness without her glasses.

The rope tightened against her throat. Talia clawed at it, desperately trying to get her fingers between the rope and her throat, anything to gain oxygen. It was no use. There was no way to create some space. The air supply in her lungs was quickly running out and the more she struggled to breathe, the more she panicked and the more she panicked, the faster the air was depleted.

Talia pushed back against her attacker, slamming her head back into his chest.

Anthony, who had hold of the rope, hadn't expected this much fight out of such a little package. The force on the back of her head almost sent him stumbling backwards, but Talia was no match for someone with such a large frame and solid legs.

Before she could muster a second push, she was shoved forward, with what felt like a boot to her lower back. The rope cut into her throat.

Talia suffered a quick secondary push to her left knee. She again figured it was his boot doing the damage. This time she fell to the ground, her knees grinding into the gravel as she landed, tearing away both material and flesh. The rope burnt and cut into her neck once more, cutting the final air from her windpipe. Her vision went hazy before she blacked out.

The rope then loosened, and a sudden rush of oxygen brought her back to consciousness in a spluttering gasping mess. When her vision returned she could see Hat Man was now closer.

Once more, the rope was pulled tight and the foot pushed against her back.

Her vision began to fade again as the choking continued.

The last thing Talia saw before blacking out again was Hat Man calmly approaching, his fiery-red eyes glowing in the dark.

Talia didn't realise she had died until she was standing over her own body.

Her body was slumped in the tunnel, the noose around her neck. Anthony was holding the other end of the rope. He had removed his foot from her back.

Talia stepped away and stood against the inside wall of the tunnel, watching the brothers haul her body along the ground with her heels dragging in the gravel.

After a few metres, Dave scooped her up and placed her limp body over his shoulder.

She screamed but nothing came out.

Hat Man stood staring at her not more than two metres away. He was grinning at her; she could see his jagged yellow teeth.

"Come," he called, his voice dark and hollow.

"He will come for you if you don't go. You don't have a choice; you're his now," Dave said as he turned to exit the tunnel, still carrying her body over his shoulder.

"What does he want with me?" Talia asked.

"He wants your soul. He collects them," Dave replied.

Anthony came up and grabbed Dave by the shirt. "Come on, we have to leave. We can't be here," Anthony said, dragging him towards the exit as he spoke.

"Go to him. It will be easier that way," Dave added as they left the tunnel.

Talia stood against the wall staring as the red-eyed monster approached. Its arms were outstretched, its fingers, bony and thin, protruded from the long jacket.

Talia tried to back away but there was nowhere to go. She was trapped.

The men had left the tunnel, although she could still feel their presence outside. Hat Man moved metres in an instant by floating across the ground. This thing was no 'man'; Talia was sure of that. A smell of sulphur floated with him. It was strong and overpowering. His breath was rancid. Even though she was dead, Talia still had her senses.

"What do you want with me?" Talia asked.

"Your soul," Hat Man replied.

His bony fingers clawed down on her shoulders. She turned away, desperately trying to remove herself from his grasp. She kicked him, but her leg appeared to go through him. How could that be? How could he hold her if when she touched him, she went through him?

Hat Man opened his mouth wide, and his jaw appeared to dislocate like that of an anaconda. The rancid smell escaped from it and a strong wind rushed in from behind Talia, as if an invisible train was bearing down on them both.

Hat Man's mouth was like a vacuum and Talia could feel herself being sucked into it. She was being eaten. Her hair was being sucked into his mouth, then her eyes, into the dark abyss. After that, everything went numb for Talia.

* * *

The brothers had hung Talia's body from the old disused railway tracks, dangled at the end of the rope between the tracks and the bottom of the ravine.

Her vehicle lay abandoned not far away.

They piled into their white ute and were ready to leave, when Dave froze with the keys in his fingers. As he fumbled to place them in the ignition, they slipped from his grasp and fell to the floor.

Anthony, who was also frozen in fear, slapped his brother. "Hurry up. Let's get out of here," he pleaded.

"I'm trying," Dave replied. His big hands and thumbs suddenly seemed way too cumbersome to handle and operate the delicate keys quickly and with any precision.

After more fumbling, Dave managed to start the engine. "Do I run him over?" Dave yelled.

"Go straight over him, if you have to," Anthony replied.

"We took too long in the tunnel," Dave shrieked.

Dave shifted into gear and dropped the clutch. The wheels spun on the loose gravel and the old metal rail, before gaining some traction on a sleeper. The ute went sideways first, before sling-shotting forward and fishtailing as it approached Hat Man.

The ute went straight through Hat Man. He passed through the ute as if he was smoke, arms stretched out, his hands clawing both the brothers across the chest as he went.

"Soon," Hat Man said in a cold, rough voice.

Dave looked in the rear-vision mirror and Anthony turned to see Hat Man standing behind the ute.

"Is he still standing there?" Dave whispered.

"Yep. It's like we didn't even hit him," Anthony replied.

Anthony returned his gaze to meet his brother's. Dave's eyes darted back to the track in front of him.

"Your shoulder looks burnt," Anthony said.

Dave quickly looked down, taking his eyes off the road momentarily to see his shirt had been burnt in three horizontal lines. He assumed his skin had suffered the same fate.

"You've been burnt too," Dave pointed out, returning his eyes to the road.

Anthony looked at his own chest. He had the three same horizontal burns as his brother.

"What do you think he meant by 'soon?'" Dave asked.

"Maybe he wants to be fed again, soon."

"Maybe he's becoming hungrier?" Dave offered.

"Maybe he wants to eat us next," Anthony wailed.

"Why would he, when we're supplying him with innocent souls for him to devour?" Dave questioned.

"I don't know. He's the devil. How do I know how his mind works? If we just keep doing what we're doing, we'll be okay. I'm sure of it." Anthony tried to sound convincing.

Dave gave a final glance in the rear-view mirror. Hat Man was still there, his fiery-red eyes looking back at the ute as it drove away.

Talia's lifeless body swung in the mild night breeze, halfway between the bottom of the creek and the tracks.

Hat Man's appetite satisfied, he returned to the tunnel.

Chapter 40

Melbourne December 2016

I stood in the in-between looking down at my lifeless body and the white door at my back. The door had been shaking more and more over the past few days, as if it was calling me. Maybe I had overstayed my welcome in the in-between; maybe it was my time to move on.

It shook violently behind me once more and this time I didn't think it was ever going to stop.

Whether the door led to Heaven or hell, I had resigned myself to my fate. Whatever was beyond the door I was ready to accept.

I summoned up enough courage just to touch the silver knob, but I doubted I would be able to convince myself to turn it. The knob shook in my hand and the quiver went through my palm and travelled up my arm and into my shoulder.

I took a deep breath and turned the knob. The shaking instantly stopped. The door swung away from my hand, opening inwards. Only darkness greeted me.

"Hello?" I called. I had no idea what I was doing.

No answer came. No sound of any kind.

"I was told you wanted to see me? Hello?" I repeated.

"You need to help Jake," a soft female voice replied.

I couldn't see who had spoken. I only knew the voice had come from within the darkness.

"Why, what will happen?" I asked cautiously.

"Go to him, before it's too late."

I stepped into the darkness of the room. A young lady greeted me. Her face was disfigured. Her long brown hair was torn from the right side of her face. Her right eyeball was missing; the cheek below was torn away. Four of her teeth were showing through the gaping hole.

"Your friend is in danger. Only you, with faith, can save him," she said.

"In danger from whom?" I asked.

"I cannot speak his name here."

"Who are you?" I asked.

"I am Paige," she replied.

It dawned on me it really was Paige. The same girl who had died in the car accident, related to the suicide case that Jake was investigating.

"I don't understand. Why is Jake in danger?"

"The whole town is in danger. He comes for them all."

"Who? Who is coming?" I asked.

The disfigured woman moved closer and took both my hands in hers.

A vision of a tall man in a hat with fiery-red eyes stood before me. I could smell him. He had no face, no nose, no mouth. He was just red eyes with a blank face.

"Who is it?" I asked.

"The locals call him Hat Man," Paige answered.

"Why don't you stop him?" I asked.

"I have already crossed, and this is as far as I can come. Once you cross, you can't go back."

"How did you get here?" I asked.

Once again, she took my hands and a vision came into my head. While I saw the pictures, I could also hear her talking to me as if she was narrating the scene for me.

"We were at the Redbank Range Tunnel looking for ghosts. We had decided to go by ourselves. We thought we would have a better chance of a sighting without the tour crowd," she began, and as she spoke, I could see Paige and another girl, whom Paige had told me was her best friend, Gemma. They were strolling through a dark tunnel, late at night. They seemed to be in the middle of nowhere. I couldn't see a road or any signs.

"Where are you?" I wondered aloud.

"Picton New South Wales," Paige answered.

I had heard of it before. As the vision continued, Hat Man appeared from nowhere. I watched as the girls ran in terror, desperately trying to escape the tunnel. The Hat Man chasing them didn't seem to change speed and didn't seem to care if he didn't catch them. He chased them anyway.

I watched as the women ran. They sprinted for several hundred metres. I could see they were clearly exhausted and running on adrenaline. By the time they reached their blue Ford, Gemma was gasping for air.

Paige got in and started the car. Hat Man had reached the end of the tunnel where the darkness finished and the outside world began. He stepped out and continued after them.

Gemma was busy trying to get service on her phone without any luck. Paige threw the car into drive and jumped on the pedal. The wheels spun before gaining traction and they rocketed down the dirt track. They would have only been two hundred metres down the road when they saw a Ford F100 parked on the opposite side of the road.

Paige pulled over. "Quick, take a photo," she told Gemma.

"Why?"

"Maybe it's the creep's car; quick, get the number plate," Paige urged.

"Move up a little. I can't quite get it."

I saw Gemma click away. I was so immersed in what was happening with the girls I had almost forgotten where I was. It was strange watching these two girls having a conversation. They appeared so full of life, yet now they were both dead.

As Paige jerked the car forward she screamed, and Gemma dropped the phone in fright. It tumbled down the driver's side seat and disappeared.

"Shit!" Gemma cried.

Paige hit the accelerator hard. The car was moving again.

"Did you see those guys?" she asked Gemma.

Gemma nodded. "Yeah, I saw them."

"They were dragging a woman into the scrub. Maybe a kidnapping!" Paige yelled, amazed her friend had missed it.

By this time, Paige had swerved, and the back tyres sent the car drifting across the loose dirt that had built up on the edge of the road. Instantly, the car jerked and whipped back in a sideways drift. Paige tried furiously to correct it, but it only made matters worse.

The car slammed into a large gum tree, crushing the driver's side, sending shattered glass flying over Paige. Her head hit the tree, killing her instantly, then it bounced off the steering wheel and was whipped wildly back and forth into the broken window, glass fragments tearing at her face each time. Finally, when she landed, her head was mangled and torn, resting on her shoulder.

Gemma's head jerked forward, only restricted by her belt, which burnt into her chest. The force of the impact fractured three of her ribs, and broke her collarbone and her right arm and leg.

Even though Paige was dead, I could still see everything that was happening. It was as if I was Paige's spirit, watching over the crash site.

Gemma's breathing was shallow.

A pair of boots appeared at Gemma's upside-down window. A large hand reached in and cut the belt holding Gemma.

"Dave, someone's coming. We can't take her," a voice from the scrub called.

The boots vanished.

Doors slammed further up the road. "There's a car down there," a middle-aged man called out.

Paige let go of my hands and the vision fell away.

"You need to go back," Paige said.

"How do I get back? I'm stuck here."

"You haven't crossed yet. You're not like me. Let me help you." Paige placed her hands on my chest. Immediately, I felt an electric current through her palms; her hands were like resuscitation paddles. I felt every inch of the shock. Every kilowatt ran around my body and ended up in my back teeth.

I was jolted back to life and opened my eyes. I was no longer in the in-between. I was back in my body and it hurt like a motherfucker.

Chapter 41

Picton December 2016

The F100 was unlocked, and Jake lifted the hood.

He was no expert on cars, but he could tell this car wasn't operational. No motor, no go. There were several different makes and models of cars in the shed. Jake counted five others, none of them particularly valuable or rare.

Jake shone his phone torch around, checking the rego labels. Some were current, some missing.

Maybe the Brown boys were making money on the side from stolen vehicles. They wouldn't be the first farmers who were habitual car thieves. At the far end of the shed was an office door, more like one in a panelbeater's workshop than in a farmer's shed.

He tried the doorknob. The door was locked.

Jake took a step back and kicked the door in. The lock shattered. Pieces flew off into the darkness. The door swung back hard, tearing off the top hinge as the momentum carried it back.

Jake entered the room and tried to scan the contents. He realised he hadn't stepped into a thieves' workshop but had stumbled upon something far worse.

The shipping container now made sense. He had found a pair of potential killers; not only were they very active, but also extremely experienced.

The wall of the room displayed drivers' licences, locks of hair, and polaroid photos of girls taken captive. There was a collection of earrings, necklaces, hair ties, and other personal belongings. Trophies, Jake thought.

There were even mobile phones sitting on a wooden shelf.

Jake looked at them and imagined the girls in their last desperate moments at the hands of these men.

Trophies.

Reminders of their dominance and control.

Trophies, to relive their experiences.

Jake had no idea how many girls they had captured or killed, but he guessed up to seven based on the number of cars. He was sure that given enough time, these cars would be linked to victims. After seeing Lucas's car,

Jake realised the likelihood was that he too had come off second best, had fallen victim to the brothers.

If he was still alive, he may have been kept in the container. But that was damaged and empty. If he wasn't there, where would he be?

Where did serial killers usually keep their victims? Jake reflected on past cases. Some had kept their captives in boxes, sheds and even underground huts, but the ones who held their victims for a while generally kept them in their home somewhere.

Perhaps they had lured Lucas into the house and jumped him?

Maybe he was still there?

Now was as good a time as any to check it out.

Jake made his way back through the cars and headed out into the night. The moon was now providing enough light, so Jake didn't need his phone torch to make out where he was going.

He leant against the shed door and tried to close it, but it had come off its track. He left it slightly ajar. The chain remained on the ground, the padlock dangling from the handle.

Heading for the house, Jake crossed the dirt driveway and walked cautiously to the house. He stepped onto the veranda and tried the front door, but it was locked. It took him a few seconds to pick it and gain entry.

The front door opened directly into the lounge and the first thing that greeted Jake was the glass-eyed stuffed deer's head, mounted on the far wall above the fireplace. It had an expression of innocence about it.

On each side of the fireplace were wall-mounted bookshelves that went from the floor almost to the celling. They held an assortment of books, magazines and some old thick encyclopaedias.

To the left was a kitchen with an open sitting area. There was no sign of Lucas. Jake was about to head through the lounge when a horrible thought crossed his mind. That day he had met the brother covered in blood . . . what if it had been Lucas's blood, not a lamb's at all?

Jake almost vomited at the thought.

He didn't want his mind to think its next thought, but it was too late. The thought had already formed in his mind.

What if Lucas was cut up and in the freezer?

It was a thought he didn't want but one he couldn't ignore, considering what else he'd found so far.

The kitchen resembled something you would expect to find in an abandoned house. The tiles were falling from the wall in rows, the floor lino was ripped, and the oven was rusted and missing the door.

There were two freezers in the kitchen. One was the fridge freezer, the other was a large chest freezer. Big enough to store a dismembered body, Jake assessed.

Jake opened the fridge freezer first. He was surprised to find just two food items, a cheap brand of frozen pizza, and some choc-chip ice cream.

His stomach lurched as he placed his hands on the lid of the chest freezer. Lifting the lid, he envisaged finding Lucas's severed head with dismembered body parts underneath.

He hadn't seen Lucas in a few years, and this was not how he wanted their reunion to be.

His heart was racing.

A puff of chilled air rose as Jake lifted the freezer lid up above his head. He shivered.

At first, all he could see were red lumps in bags, covered with shaved ice. Clumps of ice were wedged in the corners. It looked as if the freezer had never been defrosted.

Jake removed his pistol and started digging through the ice with the barrel.

It was hard to make out what kind of meat was in the bags as they were all covered in ice, frozen solid and stuck to one another.

He couldn't immediately retrieve any single bags to make a closer inspection.

All the while, at the back of his mind, Jake wondered when the owners would return home. Would he hear them if they did? He hoped so.

Finally, Jake managed to scrape away enough of the ice covering to get a good look at one of the bags. It was chicken. He could tell by the colour of the meat. He scraped and dug at the ice at the other end of the chest. He tugged at a bag wedged in the far corner. After a few minutes of digging and rocking it back and forth it came loose, bringing the bag below with it. The top bag could have been meat, although Jake couldn't be sure exactly what cut. His guess was some type of lamb and by the shape of the bone, he thought it was probably chops.

The bag below clearly contained human remains; bright-red, polished nails were visible through the plastic. Jake could count five fingers.

Jake gasped, almost dropping the bag. Whoever the hand belonged to had been in there for some time. Lucas had been missing only a few days, so he might still be alive.

Another horrific thought ran though Jake's mind. What if Lucas wasn't in the freezer, because he was still being dismembered in the bathroom? That was usually where it happened, in the tub. The blood was easy to contain and easier to drain away, but most of all, it was easiest to clean up.

The floorboards groaned as Jake made his way through the lounge, peering out of the dust-covered window for any signs of a car or the boys.

Nothing, only darkness.

Jake continued his way past the bookcase, and down the narrow hall. The bathroom was much like the kitchen, falling apart, with tiles missing. One of the vanity cupboard doors had fallen off while the other had a hinge missing, leaving it hanging at right angles.

A shower curtain was drawn across the bath. It was a combo bath-shower, like the ones in cheap by-the-hour motels whose main clients were whores and johns.

Jake didn't hesitate in swiping the curtain aside, revealing only a few shampoo bottles and white tiles. Yet the emptiness didn't answer the question of Lucas's whereabouts.

Jake knelt and shone his torch in the bottom of the tub. The drain looked clean; no signs of dried blood. He scanned the wall tiles; nothing.

The tiles on the floor beside the tub, however, appeared to have specks of red. It was dried blood, Jake thought. They had been cleaned but as with many killers, their cleaning of the grout lacked diligence.

His battery was running low, so he tapped on the power save mode and turned off his flashlight. He noticed he had one bar of service. It was the only time, apart from when he'd been standing directly under the tower on the main road, that he'd had any service.

He needed to call for backup, before the boys returned.

Jake removed Inspector Connolly's card while he still had battery, to tell him what was going on.

The connection was choppy. It was breaking up, as Jake listened to the ringing on the other end.

The line cleared.

"Inspector Connolly."

Jake spoke quickly while the line was clear, being careful not to move at all.

"It's Jake Miller here. I've found signs of serial murders at the Browns' farm in Picton." Jake waited for a response.

Nothing came.

"Inspector Connolly, are you there?"

"Sorry, the phone dropped out, I only heard you say signs of murder," came the reply.

Jake wasn't sure if this phone connection was strong enough to get the information across. He repeated himself.

"I know of the Brown boys, Jake. Don't go anywhere. Stay there. I'm on my way."

"I need you and your guys to put out an arrest warrant on the two boys. I think they've been working together. Get your forensics here to process the crime scene. There is evidence all over the place, cars, victims' trophies, body parts, blood," Jake said.

"Of course. Where are the Brown boys now?" Inspector Connolly asked.

The phone crackled a little as the inspector spoke, but Jake managed to make out what was being said.

"They're out, I have no idea where they are."

"Jake, are you armed? Can you defend yourself if they return?"

"I have my Glock on me, and my shotgun in the boot of my car, at the rear of the property."

"Just stay hidden. I'll be there within fifteen minutes."

Jake was about to thank him, but the line disconnected.

Jake's battery had five per cent remaining now. The service bar of a few seconds ago was gone.

He thought it best to hide in one of the sheds until the inspector arrived.

He was on his way back past the bookcase in the lounge when something familiar caught his eye. It was two thin gold-spined books, the same gold spines he had seen in Gemma's room. Jake tugged one of the books out. The gold binding led to a diamond black and white front. It was exactly the same as Gemma's diary.

Turning the cover, he recognised the writing. It was another volume of Gemma's diary. There was no doubt about it.

Thursday 3th August

Dear Dad

I hope I'm doing the right thing? I've decided to go back to Picton and make a statement to the police about what I saw just before the accident.

I know what I saw was real, both with the man in the hat and the men dragging the girl into the bushes. The doctors have said I suffered severe head trauma and the memories may not be real. I have been told it could be a movie I saw once and now my mind is replaying it as if it happened to me.

It feels real. I remember seeing Paige, next to me driving. I remember seeing the red ute and trying to take a photo of it. It must be real. I don't have my phone anymore, so I can't check.

I remember seeing Paige lying there next to me, her face torn, blood everywhere. All those things are real so why would the girl being dragged be any different?

I am so confused Dad.

I wish you were here to help me.

I wonder every day what happened to that girl?

Is she dead?

If I give my statement, then they can at least investigate it and maybe they'll find out what happened.

I gave my statement to a police station. Apparently, they sent it on.

You always told me to do the right thing. I am sure this is the right thing.

Jake flicked the page.

Friday August 14th

Dear Dad

Coming back here brought so many memories; well at least I think they are mine.

I'm staying in the same room that Paige and I stayed in a few months ago. It's a bit creepy being back here, but not because of the so-called ghosts. I think that's just a way for the town to make money.

I rang Inspector Connolly. He is coming tomorrow morning to take my statement. He said he never received my statement from the Victorian office.

I have just had dinner in the bistro. It wasn't very good either I might add.

It's been a long drive, so I am quite tired and my back is hurting from the long drive, so I am going to take a bath and get an early night.

Really glad I'm doing this; it will put my conscience to rest.

As always lots of love

Gemma xxxx

To end up here, there was only one way that could have happened. Somehow, between that entry and the one the next morning, one or both of the Brown boys had been in her hotel room.

One or both of them had probably killed her and made it look like a suicide. They'd done a pretty good job of it too.

But now their secret was about to come out and soon they would face justice.

Jake only had one question.

Why had Inspector Connolly never mentioned the planned meeting with Gemma for the following morning?

Considering Gemma was found dead in the bathtub the following morning, it was probably just an oversight.

Jake placed the gold-bound diary down the back of his pants and added the other one from the shelf. This was one lot of evidence he was taking with him.

No sooner had he tucked his shirt back into his pants than lights flashed across the front of the house.

Too soon to be the inspector, Jake thought.

He crept to the window and peered out.

He heard a vehicle pull up. Doors opening and closing.

Fuck, it was the brothers! Jake could hear them talking but couldn't hear the exact words. He thought he made out the word 'shed'.

The taller of the two headed towards the house while the smaller one ran towards the garage. He had met the taller one previously. Dave, if he remembered correctly.

The other man was standing at the front of that steel sliding door holding the chain with the open padlock dangling from it.

"Fuck, fuck, fuck!" Jake swore under his breath. He knew his mistake instantly. The door being left open had set off alarm bells with the brothers.

Next thing Jake knew, the house shook as the large brother ran up onto the porch. Jake ducked down under the windowsill. The only cover he had was some dusty old La-Z-Boy recliner which barely covered him. Better than nothing, Jake thought.

He'd removed his Glock without even realising. If this was going to turn into a gun fight, he was ready.

Jake was sitting on the floor, his back up against the wall and his knees drawn up so none of his body protruded from behind the recliner. He listened for the door.

He had to wait. Surprise was his only advantage and considering there were two of them, he needed every advantage he could get.

The door opened. Jake felt the cool night air across the top of his head.

Then he clearly heard, "Dave, come here!" from across the drive.

Jake heard Dave sigh heavily and close the door behind him.

The house shook again as Dave leapt off the porch and headed towards his brother.

The room fell silent.

Jake waited five, maybe ten seconds, before he dared to peek out the window again.

He saw the brothers both standing at the front of the steel door, looking at the chain. One had a torch trained on the garage. They both walked inside.

Jake thought through his options. The first was to run for his car, but he didn't want the inspector getting ambushed.

He peeked again. They were back now in front of the garage. Both men were looking for the intruder. Jake knew he had to move from the lounge before one, or both, of them returned to the house. He was a sitting duck if he stayed here.

He moved as quietly as he could, staying low and heading back towards the bedrooms, worried that the house groaning and creaking would give up his presence. He was only halfway down the hall when he heard the front door open for a second time.

Instantly he slowed his movement, trying desperately not to make a sound. He wasn't where he wanted to be. He had hoped to be hiding in one of the bedrooms by now.

Their voices were loud.

"Someone's been here," one of the brothers said. Jake thought it must be the other brother.

"We have to find them," Dave replied angrily.

"Dad will be pissed if he finds out we haven't dumped the belongings," the other replied.

"We won't tell him. Will we?" Dave suggested.

Silence.

"Anthony, we won't tell him, will we?" Dave repeated emphatically.

Anthony only grunted in agreement.

So, they are both here, Jake thought. Anthony and Dave Brown, the serial killing brothers.

"You check the house. I'll check the other shed. Whoever it is, kill them. They already know too much," Anthony said.

Jake heard drawers open and the unmistakable sound of weapons being loaded. He peeked out the bedroom window, and while his view of the drive and the gate wasn't as clear as from the lounge room, any car lights should light up the night and the house.

There was nothing, only darkness.

Jake twisted his head, trying to get a view of the main road. He couldn't see much and more importantly he couldn't see lights.

"Fucking hurry up!" Jake muttered.

He could hear Dave searching the house from room to room, switching lights on as he entered, followed by the opening of wardrobe doors. Jake even thought he heard him getting down on all fours; probably checking under the beds.

Jake had made it all the way to the last bedroom on the right. He hadn't counted how many rooms were bedrooms, only that he had passed three other doors before he'd reached the room where he had taken refuge. The window was located at the far side of the room. The door to this room opened against the foot of the bed. Opposite the bed was a double wardrobe with timber doors. On each side of the bed was a two-drawer bedside table. The one on the near side had a lamp sitting on top.

The first thing Jake needed to do was remove the globe. He needed to stay in the darkness. Every advantage was critical.

Dave's search had moved to a room two down from where Jake was. He was getting closer. Jake had to move now. He pulled himself out from between the bed and the window. There was only just enough room, so he didn't hit the wall or move the bed. The light globe was screwed into an open opaque glass fitting, decorated with butterflies and birds. Luckily for Jake he could access the globe without removing the fitting. It was a simple and quick job.

Jake knelt on the bed and reached up so his fingers touched the bulb. The bed sighed as he stretched to grasp it. Jake froze, listening for sounds of Dave suddenly stopping his search and heading towards him.

Dave hadn't heard the bed. Had he been a room closer Jake doubted he would have been as lucky.

The bulb came out with a slight push and half a turn, and the bed creaked again when Jake removed his knee.

This time Jake heard Dave's footsteps stop instantly.

Jake rolled across to the other side of the bed towards the bedroom door and braced himself for a soft landing. He backed up against the wall behind the door. When the door opened it would help conceal him. Jake placed the bulb on the floor just inside the door, hoping Dave would kick it or better still, step on it. He just wanted Dave to be looking down when he entered, if only for an instant. It would give Jake enough time to strike.

Jake stilled his breathing and flipped his gun around so he was holding his Glock in the reverse position, butt up. His eyes were intent on the door handle, watching for the slightest movement.

The handle jiggled before turning and the door suddenly swung in on Jake. He waited, frozen, breathless, calm. Dave's large frame appeared, and he scanned the room for what had caused the noise earlier. Jake watched as a big hand curled around the door, and he knew the man was ready to check behind it. Jake heard him as he took another step forward. His step was heavy on the wonky timber floor beneath the threadbare carpet.

Crunch. The globe shattered under his hefty weight.

Jake knew that was his time to strike.

Jake knew the human mind well. Dave did what any person does when they step on something that breaks; they immediately look to investigate what they have just broken.

Looking down exposed Dave's cerebellum. Jake aimed for the middle of the back of his head and whipped the butt of his pistol down hard. He hoped the hard whack would disrupt his balance and movement long enough to bring Dave down quietly.

The hit was hard enough to cause big Dave to stumble forward before he fell to the floor. Jake was surprised at how quickly he'd fallen for such a big guy. His body thudded face first into the carpet. Jake watched as Dave tried to steady himself before succumbing to the effects of the blow and losing consciousness.

He wouldn't be out for long. Jake now needed something to tie him up with before he regained consciousness. He no longer owned handcuffs, as he had handed them in with his badge and gun. Jake was going to cut the cord of the lamp but decided to check the bedside drawer first. The top drawer only held some pornographic tapes and a few loose condoms.

Jake riffled through the second drawer. It resembled his kitchen drawer at home, containing AA batteries, rubber bands, a pencil, and some packing tape. Jake grabbed the tape. He wasted no time in binding Dave, taping his feet and his wrists, and tying his wrists together with the cord from the lamp. Lastly Jake taped his mouth, not just across the face but right around his head, three times.

Jake dragged his hostage back to the lounge, ready for Anthony.

Dave moaned before he woke. His head was hurting, and he didn't remember what had happened exactly. His breathing was laboured. He couldn't move his hands or his feet.

It took him a minute to realise he was lying in his own lounge room, flat on his stomach facing the front door. He could see the beam from his brother's torch bobbing about outside, as he went to and fro across the front of the house. Finally, he watched the torch jump around as his brother took the stairs to the front porch, before switching it off as he entered the house.

"Dave, what the . . . Who the hell are you?" Anthony asked, pointing his pistol straight at Jake.

Chapter 42

Melbourne December 2016

I didn't know what day it was, or even what year. I had no clue how long I had lain in that hospital bed. My body was considerably thinner. Any previous muscle definition had wasted away, and I could tell I had severe muscle atrophy as soon as I tried to lift my hand. My arm felt as if it weighed a ton. There was no way I would be able to help Jake in this condition. I thought about trying to stand but gave up on that idea when I couldn't even raise my right foot off the bed.

"I can't help you or Jake like this. What do you expect me to do?" I asked the empty room.

Without warning, a sharp pain drove through me, from the soles of my feet to the tips my ears. I couldn't see anything, but it felt like electricity flowing through my body.

I tried to lift my foot again and this time, it cleared the bed easily and I had the strength to hold it elevated in mid-air.

Had Paige somehow fixed me?

Possibly.

I tried to stand up. My legs were still a little like spaghetti, but I managed to stand after about ten minutes of trying. Mind you, I was exhausted already, and I hadn't gone anywhere. Once I was standing, I walked, holding onto the bed. Pain shot up my leg. This pain was different from the electricity that had flowed through my body earlier. With my limited medical knowledge, I thought it was most likely to be the beginning of a blood clot and I worried it would eventually travel from my leg to my brain and I would die where I stood. I had heard many stories about people who had gone on long-haul flights and five minutes after disembarking at their destination, they had died in the terminal. This was caused by the clot forming on the flight with such little movement of the legs, and then shifting as soon as movement resumed. Sometimes the clot went to the brain, sometimes to the heart. Both were likely to be fatal.

It took about thirty minutes of stumbling and near falls before I felt half comfortable on my feet. The whole time I was worried a nurse would walk in and try to stop me.

If what Paige had shown me was real, Jake was in danger. He was in NSW in a place called Picton. It rang a bell, deep in the back of my mind, yet I didn't know why. I had a vague recollection that I had discussed it with Jake at some point, but I couldn't remember any more than that. I looked in my side table. In the bottom cupboard was a blue bag with my belongings; wallet, shoes and some clothes. I rifled through the bag. My suit pants and shoes were there, but my jacket and shirt were missing.

I remembered being shot in the chest as I was running to the mansion. I looked down at my chest. The wound had now healed but the scar was still prominent. The blood-soaked shirt and jacket I had been wearing had probably been tossed out when I'd arrived in the ER.

I put my pants and shoes on, although they looked stupid without socks. I left the hospital gown on and tucked it into my pants. I imagined it looked rather odd, but my appearance was my last concern. I placed the wallet in my back pocket and headed out of the room.

The nurses' station on my ward was empty, luckily. The last thing I wanted was people knowing I was up and about. They would never let me leave. I scooted past the desk and headed down the hall and out of the ward.

The halls on the ground floor were all green, making me feel I was still in my dream. I followed all the exit signs.

By the time I was halfway down the third corridor, my walking had improved although there was pain in both my calves. As I passed a sign saying, 'Lung Function Centre', a nurse stopped me.

"Are you all right, sir?" she asked me.

She must have noticed my strange gait, and the hospital gown tucked into my pants.

"Just going outside for a smoke," I replied.

"You will have to go out through that door. The main doors are locked. You do realise it's past 11 pm, don't you?"

I tried to pretend I did. It explained why the place was almost empty.

Her helpful look turned to disgust and with a frown, she snapped, "You're in a hospital. Don't you think it's time to give up the smokes?" and she stormed off.

I must have looked like a stroke patient. Hell, I felt like one with only half my body working properly.

The night air was still warm so I assumed it was summer, but I didn't know if it was the same year. Had I missed Christmas? Part of me remembered seeing people from above, but was that real? Paige was real, I was sure of that, wasn't I?

I wasn't sure of anything. Everything seemed so scrambled.

What if I headed to Picton for no reason? What would I do then, drive back home?

I supposed so. I couldn't risk Jake being in trouble and me not going. I had to find out.

I headed for the car park, all four storeys of it. I needed a to steal a car; preferably an older one. The newer ones had too many security devices; older ones were easier to enter and easier to hot-wire.

On the third level I found a Holden Commodore. I looked around and found I was alone. In the middle pillar of the car park was a fire extinguisher cabinet. I thought about breaking the car window with my elbow, but the notion was followed by a vision of me bleeding to death on the way to Picton. I opened the cabinet. Just what I needed, an extinguisher. I took it back to the Commodore and rammed it into the back window. The glass shattered. The car had no alarm.

Nothing sounded my entry.

I opened the glove box and released the boot. I needed tools.

In the boot next to the spare tyre was a red toolbox. I flicked the lid, and there were several screwdrivers, pliers, spanners, some electrical tape, and a flare.

I took the whole box with me and sat in the driver's seat. I was hoping I could just break the ignition with the screwdriver. Usually, the lock had to be drilled out first. I hit the spanner against the end of the screwdriver, hearing the pins and springs break. Like magic, it started.

Maybe I should have been a car thief.

I didn't bother stopping at the boom gates. I was sure by the morning they would realise someone had broken out.

I had no GPS, no phone and absolutely no idea how to get to Picton.

The only thing I did know was that NSW was north of Melbourne and the best way to get there was by following the Hume Highway.

It was a good place to start.

I headed on the western ring-road towards the airport. By the time I reached the Hume Highway, a fuel light had flashed up on the dash. The car I had stolen was running low on fuel.

I had my wallet, but I had no idea if any of the cards in there were still valid. If I'd been in a coma for years, they might have expired. I searched my wallet for cash. I found a hundred tucked away behind my badge insert. I remembered always hiding one there for emergencies. If this wasn't an emergency, nothing was. It was enough to get to Picton. I hoped.

I stopped at the next service station. Everything looked the same, so perhaps I hadn't been out of action that long at all.

I went to fill the car only to realise I had to pay first. (After 11 pm they didn't allow people to gas up without first paying.)

I walked in and paid for $50 worth of petrol.

The pain in my leg seemed worse.

I began to fill my tank.

A red Toyota with two blonde girls in it pulled up. Both looked dressed for a night out. Ready to party.

They took one look at me and started giggling. One girl filled up while the other talked to her through the passenger window, taking selfies at the same time.

"I'm going in to get some smokes; do you want anything?" the blonde girl in the dark blue dress asked.

"No, I'm fine," the girl in the passenger seat replied. Then she took a second look at me and decided it was best to go with her friend.

"Wait— I'll get a drink," she called out.

The girl in blue replaced the pump back in the bowser and they both walked inside.

I noticed a phone sitting on the middle console of the girls' car. I looked up. The girls were still in the shop, walking between aisles. They were now getting more than smokes and a drink.

I pulled on the door handle of their Toyota, opened it, and took the phone and the charger attached.

I now had a GPS.

The first thing I noticed when I thumbed through the phone to find the GPS was the date. I had been in a coma for eleven months. A year of my life gone, vanished. The time in the in-between had seemed only hours. I had done some long stints in hospital before, but this was a record.

I placed the stolen phone in the centre console of my stolen car, so I could see the screen while I drove. Before today, I had never stolen anything in my life. Now I had become a serial offender.

Chapter 43

Picton December 2016

"I'm Detective Miller and you're both under arrest. Put your gun down," Jake ordered.

Jake had his Glock pointed at Anthony while he had Dave's gun pointed straight at the back of Dave's head.

"How do you figure that? I don't put my gun down for anyone," Anthony replied.

Anthony's demeanour was extremely calm, totally unflustered. He didn't seem to care that his brother was being held hostage or that they had been caught.

This really concerned Jake.

"The police are on their way," Jake said. "Put your gun down!"

"I could legally kill you now. You're in my house, you have a gun to my brother's head and a gun on me. Nothing stops me from ending you right here," Anthony said.

"I suppose you're used to killing people, aren't you? I know about the girls," Jake replied.

"Killing people is no different from killing a pig or a lamb; just different-tasting meat," Anthony said.

Where the fuck's the backup? Jake thought.

Dave began to muffle a scream, so Jake dug his boot toe into his back to quieten him.

"What did you do with my partner?" Jake asked.

"Don't know who you're talking about."

"You have his car in your shed. Where is he?"

"My brother took care of him. Turned him into pig food, I think." Anthony smirked.

Jake had met some callous killers before, but this guy was clearly disturbed.

"Maybe take the tape off my brother's mouth and you can ask him yourself?" Anthony suggested.

"I doubt that's going to happen."

Jake wondered if he would have to fire first to get out of this. "Why did you kill the girl in the bathtub?" he asked.

"We didn't."

"Don't lie to me."

"There's so much going on here. You're out of your depth, copper," Anthony said. "You'll be dead soon, so it won't matter, but I'll make sure you meet him before you go."

"Meet who?"

"You'll find out, very soon."

Jake wondered why Anthony would deny killing Gemma when he was so quick to admit his brother had done something to Lucas. It was something that Jake couldn't answer yet, but he was sure when the police arrived he would find the evidence.

Dave tried to get up. Jake again dug him in the back with the toe of his boot.

Out of the corner of his eye, he saw headlights and heard the cop's cruiser pull to a stop.

Connolly walked up the stairs calling out to Jake. Then he walked in, fist over fist, one hand holding his torch, the other holding his gun.

"All right son. Put your gun down!" he said to Anthony.

Anthony placed it on the floor next to him.

Connolly put his torch away and pushed Anthony against the wall before collecting his gun from the floor.

"Stay there," he instructed Anthony. He turned to Jake. "What's going on here?"

"They've been killing girls, and I think they killed my partner. Go look in the shed; there are cars and trophies from the victims everywhere. There's even a hand in the freezer." Jake was controlled, firm and emotionless in stating the case to Connolly.

Connolly flicked the light in the lounge on.

Jake kept his eyes on Anthony who was now leaning against the wall with his palms pressed against the plaster.

Jake's eyes had trouble adjusting to the light after spending so long sitting in the dark.

Items that had only been shadowy objects previously now came to life. The fireplace showed its character. The books now had identities. Stephen King novels were there, as were some by Lee Child. There were even some books on Ted Bundy that Jake remembered Brodie having read.

Jake looked back from the bookcase to Anthony and Connolly.

Then Jake saw it, sitting on the far wall to the left of the bookcase. Suddenly his stomach churned, and terror gripped him. He realised he was in big trouble.

Jake just hoped Connolly hadn't caught him looking.

"You search the house, Jake?" Connolly asked.

"Only the freezer and the outside sheds." He indicated Anthony. "Aren't you going to cuff him?"

"He isn't going anywhere," Connolly said calmly. "I'll call the office for backup. You can get going. I'll handle it from here."

"I'm not going anywhere, until the homicide department arrives," Jake said.

"You're no longer a cop, Jake, you can't call the shots."

"Sorry, can't do it. I'm not going anywhere until they're locked up," Jake said firmly.

He stood, his left foot still firmly resting against Dave's back. "Cuff him."

Connolly sighed, then walked over to the wall where Anthony was leaning. He tapped Anthony on the back. As Anthony turned, Connolly handed him back his gun.

"It's a shame, Jake, I genuinely liked you, but you just couldn't keep your nose out of our business." He nodded to Anthony. "Kill him."

Anthony stepped forward, gun at the ready.

Jake had dragged Dave to his knees and was crouched behind him.

Dave was his shield.

Jake had nowhere to go. It was either make a stand here or die. He pressed his gun hard against Dave's head. "I'll kill him, I swear."

Connolly didn't seem fazed by Jake's threat. "I'll save you the trouble, Jake." He drew his own gun and fired three shots into Dave, instantly ending any leverage Jake might have had.

Jake waited to feel the bullets enter him after they had passed through Dave. None did. His shield was too thick-set. After all, he was the size of a tree. Probably grew up on a diet of meat and potatoes.

Jake wasted no time. Immediately he returned fire. His first shot was aimed at Anthony. It clipped his arm before straying wide, hitting the wall that Anthony had been leaning against minutes earlier. The second of his shots was dead on target, hitting Connolly just under his police name badge.

In the academy, they called that shot centre mass. It was where Jake had aimed, and it was where he'd hit.

"He'll come for all of us now," Connolly spluttered.

Jake didn't understand what that meant. He didn't give the comment the attention it deserved.

Anthony didn't hang around long enough to see Connolly hit the floor and gargle his last breath. Instead he decided his best course of action would be to hightail it out the back door.

Jake had no idea where Anthony had gone, only that it was out the back and into the darkness.

He ducked down behind the kitchen bench to try and establish a visual on Anthony, but in the pitch black with the lights on behind him, it was impossible.

The lights began to flicker before going out. At first Jake's immediate thought was that Anthony had cut off the power, until he heard the scream behind him.

He would have sworn under oath that the scream belonged to a dead man. It was Dave's voice. Jake swung around, startled, finger on the trigger. He was on his haunches with his back against the kitchen cupboards looking into the lounge room.

Jake could see Dave's body was still lying there motionless. How could it be him? But it was. He was sure of it.

A silhouetted figure appeared out of thin air as if it had arisen from the body.

It's Dave, Jake thought in bewilderment, but it wasn't, not really. It was more like a transparent aura. A ghost.

Whatever it was, it just stood there staring down at the body. It then took three big steps back from the corner of the room.

It saw Jake staring at it, but it seemed more concerned with something else. It turned back towards the corner of the room, before moving away again. It stepped further back towards Jake.

Jake smelt it before he saw it. Its eyes were transfixing, but it was the hat that he noticed first.

It appeared out of the dark corner of the room. Jake stood to get a better look.

Whatever it was, it wore a wide-brimmed hat and had fiery-red eyes. It frightened Jake more than anything had ever scared him before.

Jake didn't think the thing had noticed him.

It seemed focused on the transparent Dave. Jake noticed its long arms that suddenly withdrew from its coat. Its hands were long and had thin fingers like rake forks.

Jake stood in dismay at what he was seeing. He watched the shadowy Hat Man insert his claw-like bony fingers into the silhouetted figure of Dave. Then its blank face, where nothing had been seconds earlier, opened up like an anaconda's mouth for a meal. But instead of swallowing what Jake now believed was Dave's soul, it inhaled him, head first.

Jake's trepidation escalated as he watched the big brother's soul get sucked into this Hat Man, before his very eyes. It was like watching a vacuum suck up dust.

Jake stepped back towards the rear door that Anthony had just used, being careful not to draw its attention. Yet it had hearing like a deer. Its head whipped around. Its eyes fixed on Jake. Jake noticed they looked even deeper, brighter. Whatever it was, it was feeding on the souls of the dead and feeding seemed to make it stronger.

The Hat thing rushed at Jake, and it was only metres away. Had Connolly's soul not risen at that instant, Jake was sure it would have come for him.

The second Connolly's spirit rose, it became transfixed on the silhouette that seemed to be frozen over his own corpse. Jake wondered if this was the soul realising that the body in which it was once housed was now dead.

Whatever it was, the silhouette seemed stunned. It just stood there. Connolly hadn't even registered Hat Man's presence.

Connolly's spirit turned to Jake. "When it comes for me, run."

Hat Man, as if being lured by Connolly's spirit, left Jake, floating instantly to Connolly.

"We don't get the light for what we have done," Connolly said, apparently resigned to his fate.

Jake didn't understand what he was talking about and he didn't want to stick around to find out.

Where had Anthony gone? His attention had been so taken by this thing that he'd briefly forgotten there was a killer on the loose.

Hat Man had no sooner put his claws straight into Connolly's throat than glass went shattering over Jake's back. Jake felt a bullet whiz past his cheek, yet he saw it as it hit the Hat Man. It glowed orange as it flew through his shadow and hit the wall on the far side of the lounge.

Hat Man turned and hissed at Jake like a tormented cat. Yellow jagged teeth appeared in a mouth that hadn't previously existed.

Jake wasn't sure who Anthony was shooting at, but he suspected it wasn't Hat Man. He decided to take Connolly's advice and sprint for the back door. Three more shots rang out. Glass smashed with each shot, and one of the shots even collected two cups that had been left on the sink. The shots followed Jake's path.

Anthony was aiming for him, all right. The shots seemed to be coming from behind the container at the rear. It sounded like rifle shots, rather than a handgun.

Jake dived out the back door, taking cover behind an old rusted water tank. He looked for the slightest movement but in the darkness, he could see very little, only outlines.

Jake heard the crunching of rock underfoot, followed by a flutter of steps, but the sound came and went so quickly it was hard to gauge exactly where it was coming from.

Off to his right, movement caught his eye, then more bullets thudded into the house behind him.

Jake crouched tighter into the curve of the tank to protect himself.

He knew where Anthony was heading; the barn where they had Lucas's car. Jake assumed he planned to hide amongst the farming machinery and the hay, waiting to cut him down. That was what Jake would do if the positions were reversed.

Jake ran to the barn and kicked the door ajar, holding it for a few seconds with his foot, keeping his body and head out of harm's way. Jake knew the tractor was to his right, Lucas's car was under cover in the middle and to his left was some type of cropping farming machinery. Jake tried to imagine where Anthony would hide. Between the cars, crouched in the darkness, or maybe up in the mezzanine, hiding in the hay, for height advantage.

Jake hoped Anthony would think the same. He was a killer and a good one at that, one with plenty of experience. An experienced killer would use the mezzanine, Jake confirmed with himself.

The barn was darker than outside. The glow of the moonlight was eclipsed by the barn roof. If he was in here, Anthony would have noticed the door open and the light enter.

Jake dived behind the grille of Lucas's covered Mazda. The barn door swung shut behind him, enclosing him in darkness. Flickers of light filtered in through gaps and cracks in the roof. They helped visibility slightly.

Jake closed his eyes, trying to help them adjust to the darkness. He closed one eye and lay on his belly. He slid under Lucas's car on elbow and knees like an army soldier.

The fit was tight. For a second, Jake wondered if he would get stuck. There was only about two centimetres' clearance.

He could see a pair of feet on the mezzanine floor, but he was too far under the car to see the mezzanine itself. Jake crawled forward. His head was close to the rear bumper, and the chrome almost grazed the back of his head as he lifted it to look up.

Now he could see the mezzanine floor, and it was covered in hay bales.

Jake cursed to himself.

Anthony was probably sitting on one of the bales, finger on the trigger, just waiting for a clean shot. The hay was stacked four bales wide, and there was a small space between each stack, easily wide enough to slide a rifle barrel into.

There was no way to tell where Anthony was. It was the perfect hiding spot. As soon as Jake got out from under this car, he would come under fire immediately.

Anthony had all the advantage, and Jake couldn't get to a position that would give him a shot. Then he thought maybe he could move Anthony.

Jake scooted backwards to the front of the car. He slid out. He was back behind the front bumper bar. He headed to the passenger side door, only because it was off centre from one of the four spaces between the hay bales, and it would make any shot more difficult than the driver's side, which was directly in front of one of the spaces between the bales. Jake opened the passenger door. Instantly, the chime sounded and a shot rang out.

A bullet shattered the door window, sending glass fragments flying in all directions. Jake felt bits hit him in the ear, nose and cheek. A second bullet grazed his right forearm. The force of the bullet flung his hand backwards, jarring his shoulder, at the same time sending his Glock flying off into the darkness.

He dived onto the car floor, keeping as low as possible, his legs hanging out the open door.

Jake expected to see the keys hanging from the steering column. There was nothing there. He noticed a button on the passenger side of the car. It had keyless entry; the only problem was that the keys needed to be in the car.

Jake remembered seeing a set of keys when he'd found the folder with Megan's contact details. He couldn't remember exactly where. He lifted the console as another bullet shattered the back window and thudded into the back of the passenger seat.

Jake put his head down under the dash. He saw the handle of Lucas's Beretta, then recalled that he'd seen the keys in the under-dash coin holder.

Jake retrieved the Beretta and crawled further into the vehicle, his arse now curled over the middle console.

Three more shots rang out. One flew high, skimming the dash, then piercing a hole in the front window. Jake felt the second one slam into the back of the driver's seat headrest. The third shot hit just above the glove box, causing the airbag to deploy. Jake pushed his hand down on the brake, using his other hand to push the button. The Mazda started instantly. The engine was quiet.

Jake slipped the car into reverse before removing his hand from the brake and exchanging it for the accelerator. He pushed hard. The car jerked at first before hurtling backwards.

Jake listened for the car hitting the beam; soon enough, the loud crack came. He expected the mezzanine to come crashing down with it. But it held steady, though it sagged a little when it lost its front support, and a few hay bales toppled off, landing on the bonnet of the Mazda.

Jake hit the brake and flicked the car back into drive. Pulling on the wheel, he turned it hard right. He needed to take out the other front support of the mezzanine. He pushed hard on the pedal, and the back wheels spun on what Jake suspected was loose hay, before they got traction and the car lurched forward. Using the reversing camera, Jake lined up the pole with the middle of the boot.

The upright snapped more easily than he'd expected, perhaps because it had been weakened by the loss of the other support, and the mezzanine came crashing down. Jake could see Anthony bounce off the boot and land hard on the hay-covered floor of the barn. Seconds later, a bale toppled on top of him. Jake wasted no time in putting the car back into reverse. He slammed the pedal down to the floor, and the car went straight back over Anthony as if he was a speed hump. The Mazda bounced up before it hit the ground.

For the first time, Jake lifted his head and looked out the front windshield. He flicked on the headlights. Only the driver's side headlight worked; the other must have been damaged either by a bullet or by hitting the mezzanine. The light was enough for Jake to see Anthony, still alive, badly injured, but not yet dead.

Anthony got to his knees. His legs looked shattered, and his body resembled a large tree stump surrounded by hay. He pulled his rifle from the hay next to him and put it to his shoulder.

As Jake sat in the driver's seat, Anthony fired.

Jake ducked as two bullets pierced the windscreen.

He wanted to return fire, but his gun was in the hay somewhere, and the Beretta was sitting under the passenger seat out of reach..

Jake ducked his head as Anthony fired again. He pushed his foot down hard on the pedal. He didn't lift his head until he heard the car rattle over Anthony. Driving over Anthony's crushed body, he thought he deserved no less after what they had done to Lucas and all the others.

The brake lights provided enough light for Jake to see Anthony's spirit rise from his corpse, followed by the smell of sulphur. Then he saw Him stepping out of the shadows as if he had been there all along, watching the battle. Perhaps he had been.

The Hat Man with fiery-red eyes aglow swept past the cropping machine and floated through the front of the Mazda, pausing near Jake. Its head turned. A smile appeared on the previously blank face, now only centimetres from Jake's own face. Its teeth, jagged, sharp and yellow, were now visible.

"Soon," it said as a waft of foul odour floated into Jake's face. Then out of nowhere a bony hand with long claw-like nails dangling from the tips of the fingers appeared and swiped Jake's face though the shattered window.

Jake felt the nails on his cheek before he even saw the hand move.

This thing will kill me if I stay, Jake told himself. He needed to leave, yet he remained frozen in the seat.

Jake could see in the rear-vision mirror that Anthony's spirit had realised he was dead.

Hat Man, still grinning at Jake, turned its head. It had a choice either to feed or to go after Jake. It was one or the other.

It chose to go to feed. As it flew to Anthony, Jake reversed the car a little, before driving the battered vehicle straight though the barn doors, sending wood flying as he exited.

He sped back to town, away from that thing. Whatever it was, it was pure fucking evil.

Chapter 44

Victoria December 2016

I'd been travelling for just over an hour. My legs were cramping, and I had a nagging pain in my calves. Whatever was happening couldn't be normal.

I tried to ignore the strange sensation at the back of my mind and press on, but the pain nagged at me.

This isn't right, Brodie, you need medical attention, my mind persisted. "Yeah, yeah," I answered myself and continued, ignoring my own advice. Although I didn't want to admit it even to myself, I was worried.

I didn't understand how I could be tired, after all I had been asleep for eleven months. Yet after an hour's driving, I was close to exhaustion.

"You can rest soon," I said to myself. "Keep going."

My body didn't want to obey. My eyes were feeling heavier by the second. It was as if someone was hanging off them, trying to pull them down like window shutters.

White lines passed by swiftly, and the occasional set of headlights travelling in the opposite direction kept waking me, but then there were seconds of darkness. I was drifting off.

I put the driver's window down. The chill of the outside wind hit me in the face and refreshed me, but the effects didn't last long.

I needed to sleep, if only for a few minutes.

It had to be soon, before the car chose a tree to rest against.

'Maygar's Hill Winery 2k.'

A sign appeared off to my right. If I pulled off there, I could at least sleep in the car.

The winery was large, with hill upon hill of potentially award-winning vines waiting to be harvested at exactly the right time. Wineries meant years of hard work, money and sweat, all of it coming down to the day of picking which would spell either success or failure.

The homestead was small in comparison to several accommodation cottages scattered across the property, perhaps for weddings or special occasions.

I thought the cottages would suit wine drinkers who overindulged on sunny Saturday afternoons and decided to stay the night rather than driving intoxicated.

I parked the car just outside the entrance gates, turned off the lights and locked the doors. It was almost 1 am by this time.

Chapter 45

Picton December 2016

Jake had one more arrest to make before he left this God-forsaken place once and for all.

He parked Lucas's mangled car diagonally across the entrance of the hotel. The car moaned as he switched off the engine and climbed out.

Glass fell to the ground when he shut the door and headed into the hotel. The reception was unattended, which wasn't a surprise for that hour of the night.

With his bloodstained hand, Jake tapped the little bell on the counter three times. Isabella was nowhere to be seen. In his other hand, below the counter and resting against his leg, was Lucas's Beretta.

Jake suspected she had been tipped off. Maybe Connolly had warned her.

"Isabella!" Jake called out.

She poked out her head from her office door down the hall, past the reception area.

"Oh Detective, you woke me. What's wrong?" she asked.

Maybe she hadn't been tipped off after all. As Jake couldn't see her hands, he wondered if she might be armed, ready to open fire.

"Can you come out here? I have some news I really need to talk to you about," Jake said as calmly as possible.

"Can't you talk to me from there? I'm in my pyjamas."

She wasn't moving. As he still couldn't see her hands, the alarm bells rang.

Obviously having noticed Lucas's car parked across the entry to her hotel, Isabella asked, "What happened to your car?"

"Had an accident."

Jake knew she could see his blood-soaked hand, yet she didn't ask if he was okay.

She had been tipped off.

Jake drew his gun above the counter and aimed it straight at her. "Show me your hands."

At first, it appeared as if she was going to obey.

That was until she stepped out into the hall and flung open her pink polka-dot dressing gown, revealing her own gun. It was a shotgun and at this range, it would be devastating.

Jake reflexes were quicker, and he managed to get a shot off before she did, but it went high, sailing into the wall behind her.

"What did you do to my boys? You fucker!" Isabella called out before firing her shotgun. The shot tore apart half of her front counter, sending splinters of wood flying in all directions.

Jake, who had dived behind the wall, timed his return fire perfectly. As soon as the shot went off, he fired two more quick shots, knowing she would have to pump her gun to reload.

The first clipped her right hand (pure luck, Jake thought), while the second bullet hit her right shoulder. Her shotgun tumbled to the floor. Isabella staggered backwards. Jake took the opportunity to rush at her.

He took her like a rugby player making a try-saving tackle, hitting her hard and fast.

He heard a bone break beneath him, not his, maybe her hip or leg.

"You cocksucker!" she cried.

Jake stood up, dragging her by the gown as he kicked the shotgun away, sending it sliding back towards the entrance.

She spat at Jake as he dragged her up. Isabella stood with ease, and Jake wondered what he had heard break; something, he was sure of it.

He took the cord of her gown and bound her hands together. It would hold until he could find something more suitable. Isabella looked fine; nothing broken apart from her hand and maybe her shoulder. Maybe she had a cracked rib?

Jake sat her down on the bottom step of her hotel stairs.

"You know, your boys and your husband are dead," Jake said without sympathy.

"He wasn't my husband."

"Boyfriend then? I saw the family photo at the boys' house."

Isabella nodded. "My house," she clarified.

"Well, either way, they're all dead."

Jake drew out from the back of his pants the journals he'd found at the house.

"Which one of them killed Gemma? I know one did, because I found these in the house."

"Neither of them," came the reply.

"So, it was Connolly then?

"No."

"Don't lie to me."

"I killed the slut. She was going to tell on my boys," she replied.

Jake realised she was telling the truth. She had no reason not to.

"What happened?"

"I told you, the slut was going to dob on my boys."

"I want to know everything," Jake said.

"When she and her slutty friend had the accident a few months earlier, she saw the boys heading into the tunnel with some food for Hat Man."

"By food, you mean a human?" Jake asked. "Hat Man, is that the thing that lives in the tunnel?"

She nodded. "If we fed him, he kept away from us. Sometimes we wouldn't see it for months."

"What happened when Gemma came back?" Jake asked.

"She made a call to Connolly, to tell him she had seen two boys chasing a girl the night of the accident. She named my sons. Apparently, the boys chasing the girl caused the accident. I had to get rid of her. Connolly was going to kill her the next day, but when I heard her having a bath in her room, I let myself in. There she was, lying in the bath, face washer over her face and radio playing on the vanity. So, I pushed it. She didn't even know I was there. It was easy to cover up. It looked like an accident." Isabella grinned. "She still haunts this place, especially that room. I have lost a lot of business because of that bitch."

Jake just wanted to slap her smug, remorseless face. "The other night I saw her in the room."

"Most people do when they stay in there," Isabella replied.

"Why didn't the Hat Man take her, after you killed her? If she haunts here, then she didn't get eaten?" Jake asked.

"I don't know. My only guess is, it was feeding somewhere else. Look, I don't know all the ins and outs of that thing. The boys once told me sometimes when the Hat Man takes them, their soul splits. I guess a part of it is consumed and a part of it stays here." Isabella looked around as if Gemma's spirit was watching.

"I take it she didn't go towards the light either?" Jake said grimly.

"She didn't accept that she was dead. She just stood staring at herself in the bath."

"Why kill her? I'm sure Connolly could have covered it up."

"He'd dismissed her calls several times. She even made a statement to police in Victoria. It was sent to Connolly to investigate and he covered it up, yet she wouldn't let it go."

So, they had killed Gemma because she'd been rattling the wrong cage.

"What about Lucas, your boys kill him?" Jake asked.

"Yeah, he was nosey, like that reporter mole, come around here asking all sorts of fucking questions, wanting to examine this and that. Do fucking tests on the radio, like a dog with a bone he was. Well, he followed that bone all the way to his grave." She spat, as if spitting on his grave.

Jake stood stunned, trying to control his rage. "What happened to his stuff?"

"Took what was valuable, dumped the rest."

There was no empathy in her, no emotion, no soul, just evil, Jake thought.

"I'm taking you to Thirlmere Police Station," he stated. He walked her out to the car. Putting her in the back seat of a Mazda with her hands tied behind her back only with a dressing gown cord was not an ideal way to transport a criminal, but what other choice did he have?

He thought about ringing the station and getting them out here, but he didn't know who else she knew. People could disappear on the way back to the lockup, especially in a town like this. It would be a lot harder to cover up this crime once he was back at the station.

Jake headed off into the darkness, one headlight showing the way.

"Did he come for the boys?" Isabella asked from the back seat.

"Who?"

"You know who I'm talking about, the one that did that to your face."

Jake touched the side of his cheek, checking it in the mirror. The three horizontal scratches were still there. They were red and painful, just like a burn.

"Yes, he came for them, but I don't think he's a man," Jake replied.

"He is no man. This thing is the devil," Isabella snapped.

"There is no such thing."

"You saw him for yourself and you still doubt the devil exists? Did you see it feed?"

Jake nodded.

"That's not human. You're a marked man."

"What do you mean, 'marked'?" Jake asked.

"Those burns on your face are his mark. He'll come for you. When he comes for you, there's no escape." She laughed. "He's coming for you!" she repeated, laughing louder.

"Shut up!" Jake shouted.

Jake passed the sign, 'Thank you for visiting Picton', then passed the last petrol station in town.

Seconds later he saw a sign saying, 'Welcome to Picton Population 4721'.

Jake blinked twice. What the fuck just happened?

He looked over to the other side of the road. The service station he'd just passed on his right was now on his left. He was heading back into Picton. He'd been spun around. But how?

"I told you, you're marked. He won't let you leave," Isabella reiterated.

"Let me out, he's coming for you. Let me out, you prick!" Isabella kicked the seat like a spoilt child.

"You're staying with me and if he comes for me then he will come for you too," Jake retorted.

He drove the car over the median strip and onto the other side of the road. The tyres squealed and screeched as he turned the car around again.

For the second time in a minute, he passed the sign and the service station. A thick white fog rolled in suddenly, out of nowhere. The only other time Jake had seen something as bizarre was in San Francisco near the Golden Gate Bridge. With one headlight out, his visibility was severely restricted.

Only fifty metres past the service station, Jake saw him. He was hovering in the middle of the road.

Part of Jake wanted to drive straight over him, but the marks on his face started burning a little more, as if to provide a warning.

Jake hit the brakes hard. He heard Isabella's forehead hit the back of the front passenger seat. The tyres gripped and then gave and gripped again. The car shuddered to a stop.

Jake sat there staring at Hat Man. Less than twenty metres away, it hovered against a backdrop of a thick blanket of white fog.

Jake had seen how fast Hat Man could move. He was getting out of here.

"I told you he was coming for you. There's no escape!" Isabella screamed. "Please let me out. He'll kill us both."

"I've already told you, you're staying with me. If he comes for me, then he'll come for you too," Jake promised.

"You bastard pig!" Isabella wailed in despair.

Jake took a side street and headed back into town. If this really was the devil, then there was only one person who could help him, and he was locked inside the church.

* * *

At the church, Jake dragged Isabella out of the car and knocked on the door. A light inside flickered on before a peephole opened. The elderly man's face appeared behind an iron grille of the church door.

"I told you to leave me alone," the old man said.

"I need your help, Father. I have seen him. Help me stop him," Jake begged. He looked over his shoulder, terrified that the Hat Man was standing behind him.

"You've been marked," Pastor Elijah Dwyer said, noticing Jake's red cheek.

Jake touched his cheek. It felt hotter than before.

"Who's she?" Pastor Dwyer asked, peering at Isabella.

"Isabella Brown."

Pastor Elijah Dwyer stood there looking at her, dissatisfied with Jake's response.

"She tried to kill me. Let us in, and I'll tell you the story," Jake said.

Pastor Dwyer closed the peep door. It felt like an eternity before the door swung open.

"Please keep your voices low; my granddaughter is asleep," Pastor Dwyer said.

He led them into a small chapel. There were disused pews stacked each side of what would have been the aisle, and at the end of the room was a raised area which Jake assumed would have once been the altar. Now the chapel was being used as a sitting room. There were two small couches on each side of the room, and a rug on the original timber floors. And the original altar had been converted into a makeshift play area for the girl.

The pastor offered Jake a rare smile.

"I heard you abandoned your religion?"

"People talk. I don't pay any attention to it," Pastor Dwyer replied.

"I didn't introduce myself. I'm Jake Miller. I'm a detective, I mean I was a detective," Jake corrected. He didn't believe in God, but he didn't want to begin a habit of lying in church. "I'm a private investigator now. Can you tell me about the Hat Man?"

"Well, firstly, its name is Scat. I believe it's a demon, summoned from hell. I don't necessarily think it has a gender," Father Dwyer explained.

"Summoned by whom? How did it get here?" Jake asked.

"A hundred years ago when my father, Pastor Joseph Dwyer, worked in this very church he was told by a nurse that she and her two friends had performed a séance, and soon after the Hat Man was seen around town. All three people who performed the séance died in unusual circumstances."

"What sort of circumstances?"

"The man shot himself, the nurse was crushed to death in the morgue by a cadaver's bed and the third was hit by a train in the Redbank Range Tunnel."

"They don't sound too unusual, apart from the morgue episode," Jake replied.

"The train wasn't even due. It arrived at the station forty minutes late."

Jake was unsure how to answer. In the end, he remained silent.

Pastor Dwyer continued, "People have disappeared from all over these parts, not just here in Picton but from neighbouring towns too. Sometimes there are two or three accidents and then nothing for years. Then in 1944, the Hat Man directly affected our family. My older brother Tommy was killed. I still remember it as if it was yesterday."

"You don't think it was an accident?" Jake questioned.

"It was no accident. I was there. I have seen the Hat Man myself."

"Did the Hat Man get Tommy?"

"No, he and Becca ran away. He saved their souls. I wish I could say the same for Becca's brother; he wasn't so lucky."

"Why didn't the Hat Man take you?"

"I hid behind a tree like a coward," Pastor Dwyer replied, looking at the floor in shame. "Some nights I see Tommy and Becca running through the tombstones," Pastor Dwyer added, diverting the subject from his cowardliness.

He shuffled in his seat, looking sore and uncomfortable.

"You, okay?" Jake asked.

"Just old. I am eighty-eight years old. My joints tend to freeze up if I sit still too long."

"What happened after Tommy died?" Jake asked.

"For the first few months, Homicide looked for the man in the hat, but no one was ever found. They thought it was a paedophile who had tried to abduct Tommy and Becca." Tears rolled down his face. Even though the memories were decades old, they were still raw to the pastor. "Life went on as normal for a few years, although nothing was normal any more. Pa lost some of his belief in God. Not that he said so, but I could see it in the way he conducted his Sunday sermons, the way he prepared for church. Then when Mum passed in 1953, Pa began to drink. He became an alcoholic. In 1961, he was found hanging off the Redbank Range Bridge."

Just past the tunnel, Jake thought.

Jake knew that it couldn't have been the brothers. It was before their time. He wondered if Hat Man had had something to do with it.

"Sounds to me like the Hat Man got inside his head!" Isabella chimed in.

Pastor Dwyer scowled at her.

"Do you think it was the Hat Man?"

"I think the grief my mother suffered caused the cancer that killed her. And I think he filled my father with enough darkness that his only option was at the end of a rope."

"So, is that why you don't go out into the town?" Jake asked.

"No, after Pa passed I ran the church here until November 2010. It's strange how the worst days of your life seem to present the most vivid memories. All you want to do is forget them, but somehow, they get burnt inside somewhere deep and they never leave.

"It was a cold morning, a lot of fog and mist around, and I was always nervous when my son drove long distances but that morning, I was exceptionally nervous. My son Richard and my daughter-in-law, Kate, were setting off to visit her family. She was eight months pregnant. It was a joyous time.

Being so far away, she had missed out on all the little things that go with pregnancy, especially when it's the first grandchild for both families."

Pastor Dwyer closed his eyes and took a breath.

Jake could feel that what was coming next was hard for the pastor to say.

"Until, until . . ." His voice began to falter, as if a lump was forming in his throat. The pastor crossed himself and said some type of blessing or prayer in Latin that Jake was unfamiliar with.

Jake looked over at Isabella who had sat her frumpy frame down in the pew in the next aisle. Her look had gone from contempt to fear and panic. She must have known the story that was coming.

"Until the accident." Pastor Dwyer turned away from Jake as he spoke, instead choosing to look at the cross of Jesus hanging on the wall. Jake thought he was either seeking comfort or assigning blame.

"A truck careered onto the wrong side of the road, colliding with my family's car. All three of them were killed. The only survivor was Olivia, whom they managed to deliver after my daughter-in-law died. I have raised her since birth. I am all she has known: this place is all she has known."

"You think the Hat Man had something to do with that accident?" Jake questioned.

"After they left for their trip, I was walking in the grounds when I saw him standing at the other side of the river, mist at his feet. Those fiery-red eyes stared at me. When I looked again he was gone. Does that answer your question?"

Jake nodded, and the pastor shuffled in his seat again.

"How does being a shut-in help you?" Jake asked.

"This is a house of God, and the Hat Man or the demon or whatever he is, is prohibited from setting foot on this soil. It's holy."

"Can we defeat it?" Jake asked.

"I don't see how," Pastor Dwyer replied. "I hear that bullets go straight through it."

"I saw that happen tonight. They have no effect. I think when someone dies, and it feeds, it gets stronger," Jake replied. "What about some holy water and a crucifix, would they protect me?"

"Maybe a little." Pastor Dwyer sounded doubtful.

"If it was summoned here, could we perform an exorcism to kill it?"

"An exorcism is only if the demon has taken over someone's body. This demon is in its own form. We could try to cleanse the tunnel where it hides, but my faith isn't strong enough to cast out a demon. It has taken quite a battering over recent years. I can't help you any further; I'm sorry."

"Pastor, we need you. The town needs you."

"I'm sorry," he repeated.

Jake frowned. "Tell me, Pastor. How come the Hat Man never killed this evil bitch and her family?" he asked, turning towards Isabella.

Isabella answered with a one-finger salute, which Jake thought was inappropriate considering they were standing in a house of God. He turned his attention from her back to Pastor Dwyer, who didn't react at all.

"Evil doesn't kill evil, so while they were committing their evil acts, it left them alone. Once they were dead, their souls were food just like everyone else's," Father Dwyer said.

Jake examined the small, old church; the place the pastor had called home for the last six years. How could you live in such small confines without venturing outside?

His eyes took in the wooden cross below the three arched, stained-glass windows, and he said, "Pastor, come with me. We will defeat this thing together."

The pastor stepped away, distancing himself from Jake.

Jake shook his head in disappointment.

"I can't. I am sorry."

"Pastor, we need you. The town needs you. Is this how you want your granddaughter to live? Only going outside in the daytime and not leaving the grounds of the church?"

"If it stops her from being taken, then it's how it must be."

Jake removed Lucas's Beretta and began unloading the bullets. "Well, I'm not going to hide here. I would rather die on my feet than live the rest of my life on my knees like you. Hiding in a church is not living."

Pastor Dwyer looked at him and bowed his head, and Jake knew he was bowing it in shame.

Jake took the handful of shells from the magazine and began dipping them into the holy water in the font, ensuring that the firing pin end remained dry. The last thing he wanted was a misfire.

He took a blue Disney water bottle he had spotted earlier from one of the pews. It was clearly the granddaughter's. Bubbles reached the surface as Jake dunked the bottle in the font of holy water. It filled fast.

Holding the bottle in his left hand, Jake took the sacred cross from the wall below the stained-glass windows.

"You can't take those things; they are not yours," Pastor Dwyer said.

"I am taking them, Pastor. It's not open for discussion. I need a bible. Are you going to give me one, or do I have to steal that too?"

Without a word, the pastor handed him a bible.

Jake took the bible, nodded in appreciation and then grabbed Isabella by the wrist and yanked her down the aisle in front of him.

"A word of advice. He will be at his strongest at night, especially seeing he has just fed," the pastor's voice echoed down the aisle.

Jake stopped in his tracks. "Are you saying we should wait until morning?"

"I would, but I am not you. The Hat Man lives in the tunnel only because it's dark. Demons hide in the shadows during the day."

"Any other advice you might want to give me?" Jake said.

"Well, you look as if you're ready to hunt a vampire. Demons are different from vampires, you know. You can't just kill it by putting a wooden stake through its heart; you need to perform a cleansing ritual."

"Don't you have to be a priest to do that?" Jake enquired.

"No. Anyone can kill a demon. You must remember the demon is not a human spirit; it is a dark entity that shapes itself into human form to fit in. The Hat Man, as you call it, is from hell itself, and only belief in God and love of God can remove him. You show him fear, then he grows stronger. You show him you have faith, and you can banish him from earth."

"Sounds easy." Jake's only problem was, he didn't believe in God.

"He will eat you up," Isabella cackled.

Jake ignored her.

"We'll leave in the morning then," he instructed Isabella.

The pastor attended to Isabella's hand, applying a fresh bandage that covered all but her fingers. Jake tied her feet to take pressure off her hand.

While Isabella slept on one of the couches, Jake sat opposite, waiting for the night to end.

Chapter 46

Melbourne December 2016

I don't know whether it was the pain in my legs or the stranger bashing on my window with his flashlight that woke me.

"You can't stay here!" he shouted into the glass.

I waved and nodded and started the car with my screwdriver. My left leg had been stretched over the passenger seat. It was protesting loudly in pain. I raised the pants leg.

Tender, hot, red, and pulsating. Most likely, clot-ridden.

Soon the clots would likely travel north to my brain and either give me a stroke or kill me.

"Just a few more hours and you can do what you want with me," I told my leg.

My attention returned to Jake.

I didn't know how he needed my help, only that he did.

The vision I had been shown was clear. Jake was trapped in a tunnel, with a man, a thing, a man in a hat—something from another dimension, something from hell.

After re-entering the highway, I continued north, north towards Jake, towards trouble; perhaps, towards my death.

The drive was quiet, the low hum of the motor broken only by the occasional road train.

A word came into my head. "Soon," spoken by a low, gruff voice I didn't recognise. The voice was how I imagined a troll under a bridge would sound.

It sounded mean, mad, evil.

Chapter 47

Picton December 2016

Jake had spent the hours between 12 am and 2 am hovering over a candle, reading bible scriptures, looking for anything that might be helpful. Nothing stood out. He wasn't expecting a chapter on how to banish a demon, but he was hoping for something.

He was about to turn in himself, when he caught Olly peeking out from the side of the altar. Quietly Jake moved towards her. She was hugging a stuffed faded bear.

"What's your bear's name?" Jake whispered.

"Teddy," she mumbled.

"He's beautiful."

She held the bear out. "Cuddle you," she said.

Jake took Teddy and gave him a hug. At that moment, he realised how lucky he was.

"Let's get you back to bed." Jake picked her up and she held the bear tightly.

He walked down a hall past the altar and through a small kitchen, behind which were two small rooms.

The girl's name was written on her bedroom door in colourful wooden letters. Jake pushed open the door that was slightly ajar. Her room had just a few toys, a bed and a lamp. Her walls were covered with her own drawings. Every drawing depicted the Hat Man. She must have seen him. Jake was about to ask her more when he realised she had fallen asleep on his shoulder.

He tucked her into bed with Teddy wedged tightly under her chin.

"Everything all right?" a voice from the door said.

"She came out. I just put her back to bed; didn't think you were awake."

"I'm a light sleeper. You are good with her."

"I take it she has seen the Hat Man?" Jake whispered, eyes fixed on Olly's wall.

"Unfortunately, she has."

Jake could see the sorrow in the pastor's eyes as he left the room.

"You have children?" Pastor Dwyer asked

"A baby girl," Jake replied. "What do I say to get rid of him?" Jake asked humbly.

"Just keep it simple. Something like, 'in the name of the Father, the Son and the Holy Spirit, I banish you from this earth," Pastor Dwyer offered.

Jake turned back towards the lounge. He needed sleep before the morning.

"Most importantly, Jake, you need to believe in what you're saying."

Jake paused a moment, before continuing without a reply.

As dawn finally broke, a dense, ominous fog began rolling into town like a billion cotton balls.

Isabella remained asleep. She had snored the whole night. Jake decided not to wake her until he was ready to leave. The less he had to deal with her the better.

Normally, as it rose in the sky, the sun burnt off the fog yet half an hour later, it lingered, appearing thicker, denser, even more ominous than before.

Jake suspected today wasn't going to be any ordinary day.

He woke Isabella. Pastor Dwyer let them freshen up in his residence at the back of the church. Jake only saw the kitchen and the bathroom, both of which were small but neat. The pastor provided toast and juice for breakfast. Jake sat opposite Isabella as she ate, after which he decided to re-tie her hands but untied her feet so she would be able to walk. This time, he used some rope the pastor had lying around. He checked that she was secure and that her circulation wasn't restricted.

With holy water, cross and bible all stacked in a Dora the Explorer backpack, Jake and Isabella took their first steps outside the church in over twelve hours.

The air was crisp and clean, the wind warm. The fog swirled around Jake and Isabella's feet and seconds later, he couldn't see his shoes. By the time they reached the path, away from the sanctuary of the church, the outside world had vanished. Pausing at the gate, Jake looked both ways as if checking for traffic, except it wasn't cars he was afraid of, it was Hat Man.

"He could be waiting for us in the fog and we would never know," he mused aloud.

"You're going to kill us both," Isabella said.

His legs still trembling, Jake forced himself through the gate. Isabella kicked up a fuss, as he knew she would. He pulled hard on her tied hands, almost dragging her along.

Lucas's car was parked outside the front fence at a right angle, with the left tyre over the curb. The car seats were damp from the cool night air. As Jake sat down, he felt the wetness seep into his pants.

"Oh shit, me fucking pants are wet now," Isabella's obnoxious voice came from behind him.

He ignored her. He planned on ignoring her for the rest of her life. She was nothing but a low-life serial killer to him.

The hunk of damaged metal that once was Lucas's car started with the first push of the ignition button. The motor was still quiet, yet when the car moved it sounded as if every part of it was being tortured. If the car could speak, Jake had no doubt it would cry out in pain.

He headed south towards the end of town, turning right at a closed and now disused road. The fog was still thick, still eerie, making driving difficult.

When he arrived at the end of the road, Jake was confronted by a green gate blocking the road. The sign on it read: 'Road closed. Tunnel closed. Entry prohibited'.

The fog had cleared a little as if it was making a path for him.

Jake exited the car, a damp patch from the seat now evident on his pants. Gravel and dirt crunched beneath his shoes as he walked around the car.

He removed Isabella from the car. At first, she resisted, trying to hook her legs around the seat in front of her to avoid being dragged out.

Jake was strong; much too strong for Isabella. In the end she fell out of the car, landing her fat rear in the gravel.

"I am not going in there. No fucking way!"

The south side entrance to the tunnel stood a hundred metres away. Although it was just a structure, to Jake it seemed to have a personality, a demeanour, an attitude, a cold and unwelcoming presence.

Jake stared and gulped.

Isabella refused to walk forward.

Jake dragged her. Stones gouged her knees and she let out a cry of anguish. It took another few paces before her knees become so sore she gave up her fight and found her feet.

"You know he'll kill us both," Isabella murmured from behind.

"Shut up," Jake responded instantly.

He didn't want to hear her chatter, not now, not ever.

"He'll take our souls," she added. She dropped to her knees, begging for Jake to let her go.

Jake, ignoring her protests, only pulled on the rope harder. He could hear her dragging in the gravel for a few seconds, before she gathered her feet under her and decided to walk again.

They arrived at the entrance to the tunnel.

It was cold, almost icy, five to seven degrees less than the outside temperature. It was as if they were about to walk into a fridge.

Jake took a breath and stepped into the darkness.

His legs of jelly nearly failed him.

As he walked into the tunnel, the world outside began to disappear and when Jake looked back, the outside world shimmered and glistened as if it were a different dimension. Jake felt like an animal trapped inside a zoo enclosure; he could see the outside world but couldn't get there.

Jake and Isabella both moved forward with trepidation, Jake waiting for the second when the mysterious Hat Man would appear. He removed the bottle of holy water from the pack and began to splash it about. Sprinkles of it hit the walls, and the dirt floor in front of him. Jake was using it like weed-killer, yet they were alone.

"In the name of the Father, the Son and the Holy Spirit, I banish you," Jake repeated over and over, as they walked deeper into the tunnel.

Jake swirled the bottle. It was a little over half full as he approached the tunnel's alcove, midway along.

Jake sprayed each wall with it and repeated his cleansing speech, except this time he added a second line.

"In the name of Jesus Christ, I banish you."

Jake reached the end of the tunnel. He stepped out into the daylight and immediately felt warmer.

Isabella was walking so close behind, she trod on his heels a few times as they made their way through the tunnel.

"It's worked. He's gone. We can leave now," she said.

Jake paid little attention to her ramblings. His focus was on the car that was parked at the edge of the ravine.

Jake began his walk towards the vehicle, but before he could reach it, a dangling rope caught his attention in his peripheral vision.

It was tied to one of the disused tracks that led over the edge of the ravine.

Jake lay on his belly and looked over the precipice, his shirt and slacks becoming soiled.

Something was dangling at the end of the rope; a body, a girl's body.

Jake wondered if it was that of the reporter Lucas had spoken of.

The dead body was swinging in the breeze.

Jake thought about pulling her up but decided against it. Something about this whole place didn't seem right. He felt as if he was being watched.

Jake examined the vehicle without opening the door. He checked the seating position, which was in close to the wheel, far too close for one of the Brown brothers to have been driving, unless they'd readjusted it afterwards.

"Your boys do this?" Jake said to Isabella.

She didn't offer any excuse, just nodded in the affirmative.

Jake now knew where the Brown brothers had been last night; they were here, feeding him.

Jake headed back into the tunnel, pushing Isabella forward in front of him.

At first, she resisted, until Jake threatened to use his gun by placing his hand on his holster inside his jacket.

Isabella begrudgingly entered the tunnel for the second time that morning.

Jake followed closely.

Again, the sudden and dramatic drop in temperature was noticeable.

As they passed the alcove again, Jake noticed Isabella turned her head away.

Jake on the other hand, felt compelled to look in case he saw the mysterious Hat Man.

Instead, he saw empty space, nothing but darkness and shadows.

Jake stared at the shadows for a moment, looking for any movement.

Nothing.

He moved on.

He was three or four paces past the alcove when he first smelt it.

It was a faint, subtle smell at first, then stronger. The smell was unmistakeably that of sulphur.

A tidal wave of fear struck Jake, a sensation stronger than he had ever felt before. It was the fear of impending doom.

He was here. Somewhere in the darkness, Hat Man was here.

* * *

New South Wales December 2016

As the darkness made way for morning and the sun appeared on the horizon, the throbbing pain in my leg had become a strong constant ache. The pain suggested a possible deep-vein thrombosis. If that was the case, it would lead to a stroke and potentially to my death.

I even talked aloud to myself, so I could check my speech wasn't slurring. The last thing I wanted was to have a stroke while driving. I imagined myself having a head-on collision with a truck.

I didn't say anything in particular; just random words. Boot and shoe and tape and gun. Fucker and bitch usually came out when the pain in my leg flared.

I realised I should have stayed in hospital. Whatever was wrong with my leg would probably kill me if I didn't get medical attention soon.

I wondered why Paige would wake me from my coma and direct me to come here, only to let me die.

Why wouldn't she help me? I wondered.

I knew she was watching me from the in-between.

"Paige, help me," I called.

Of course, there was no answer.

Maybe she couldn't help me.

Maybe she could only watch.

I drove on.

* * *

Picton December 2016

Isabella got a whiff of the sulphur too. She screamed and began to sprint for the tunnel's entrance. She wanted out.

The fiery-red eyes of the Hat Man appeared before her and he stood blocking her path. To get out, Isabella would have to go through him. With her hands still tied, she ran, half-crouched over.

With her head down, she ran straight towards Hat Man and at the last second, she managed to avoid his outstretched arms.

Jake watched Isabella fly past Hat Man, then suddenly, he saw her levitating against the roof of the tunnel. With one wave of his arm, Hat Man dragged her along the roof and back towards Jake. She was only metres in front of him when Hat Man swung his arm in a downward direction.

Isabella went from floating against the roof to being slammed into the dirty, rocky ground.

Her crumpled, torn body lay slumped and bleeding on the tunnel floor.

Jake gasped at what he had just witnessed. The thing had moved her without even laying a finger on her. He had telekinetic powers.

Jake shuffled forward cautiously.

He aimed the bottle and squeezed it. Water spurted like a bullet. The water splashed onto Hat Man's chest. Steam rose in a puff. Jake expected to hear a scream or some form of anguish. Instead, there was nothing.

Just silence.

Jake took the cross and recited his banishing call.

"In the name of the Father, the Son and the Holy Spirit, I banish you from earth."

Hat Man stood motionless.

The words had no effect.

As Jake crept closer, a devious smile spread across Hat Man's face. His yellow teeth shone in the darkness. His fiery-red eyes narrowed and dimmed, as Jake stepped ever closer.

"Jesus Christ demands you exit this earth," Jake said, spraying more water from his bottle. It landed just in front of Hat Man's feet and evaporated into a small puff of steam.

As soon as the words 'Jesus Christ' left Jake's lips, Hat Man hissed and growled.

The Lord's name in combination with the water had an effect.

"Jesus Christ banishes you from this earth," Jake repeated.

Hat Man hissed and reared, arms and long bony hands poised as if readying himself for battle.

Jake squirted more water. It was running low now, with only a quarter of the bottle left. Shouldn't have wasted it in the entrance, he thought.

He stepped closer. Jake was doing all the moving. Hat Man was just hovering. Jake began to feel he was walking into a trap.

They stood about five metres apart, like duelling gunslingers from the Wild West.

Jake stared.

Hat Man stared back.

Jake was set upon. He was so transfixed by Hat Man he failed to notice Isabella.

She came at him hard and before he knew it, her arms were wrapped around his neck and her fingers were scratching and clawing at his face.

The first thing Jake noticed were that her eyes had rolled back so all he could see were the whites. Her face was criss-crossed in cuts from being dragged across the tunnel roof.

He struggled to keep her off him, with a cross in one hand and the bottle of holy water in the other. Jake raised his forearm to try and fend her off, but she had gained strength.

She was stronger than she had ever been. She was chanting continuously in a dull monotone.

"Satanas qui laetificat juventutem meam. Veni, omnipotens aeterne diabolus! Diabolus, custodiam!"

Jake had no idea what she was saying although he recognised 'Diabolus' as the word for devil.

Jake fell backwards under Isabella's immense force. She swiped at his face. Jake held up the cross, pressing it against her forehead. Smoke poured out, flesh burnt, yet she did not let up. She swung again wildly, this time collecting both the cross and the bottle of water, sending them flying off into the darkness of the tunnel.

The chanting didn't stop. She repeated the same words over and over again.

And she kept scratching, clawing, biting. It was as if she had turned into a zombie from some post-apocalyptic movie. With his free hand, Jake tried to fend her off again. With one arm under her throat and the other on her forehead, he could feel the heat where the cross had burnt her forehead radiate into his palm.

Her hands wrapped around his throat and began to squeeze. Jake still couldn't push her back. She was too strong. He was losing this battle fast.

He had to do something quickly before she killed him.

Jake kneed her in the crotch. She didn't even flinch.

He used his forearm to clip Isabella in the chin again, but it had no effect. He did it several times. Nothing.

Jake thought if he had hit anyone else like that, he would have knocked them out, but not this bitch. Apart from a bloody mouth, she was unrelenting.

Jake was really struggling to breathe. He could feel the oxygen being squeezed out of his body. He felt as if his eyeballs were about to pop out of his skull.

Bloody saliva from the bitch's mouth dripped on his face as she pushed down harder on his throat. The parts of the tunnel he could see went black as he faded in and out of consciousness. The more he struggled to breathe, the less oxygen he took in and the closer he came to suffocating.

Her chanting face faded into darkness and then a few seconds later it reappeared, eyes still all-white, mouth still moving to the chant, salivating.

As if in an entirely other world, Jake heard a distant voice. "In the name of the Father, the Son and the Holy Spirit and in the name of our Lord and Saviour, Jesus Christ, I condemn you back to hell!" the voice shouted.

Jake blacked out again.

When he woke, the thing on top of him that had been Isabella was smouldering from her back. Her grip had loosened. Jake gasped for air while he could.

Realising her grip had weakened, Jake took advantage of the opportunity and head-butted her strong and hard, hitting her flush on the nose.

For the first time, his attack had an impact on her.

Isabella rolled off him, and the chanting stopped.

Jake reached for his Beretta, aimed at her chest and fired.

He slowly regained his feet and stumbled on the rocky cobblestones of the tunnel's surface.

He could see Pastor Elijah Dwyer dousing Hat Man in holy water.

He had come. Maybe he still believed in his faith after all, Jake thought.

As he splashed water on the Hat Man, Isabella burnt. Jake realised Hat Man was controlling Isabella. When he burnt, she burnt.

Jake's eyes darted into the darkness, searching for his water bottle. He located it, but it was now empty.

The only holy water Jake had left was on the tips of eleven bullets remaining in his Beretta.

"Pastor, step away!" Jake yelled.

The instruction echoed through the tunnel and by the second echo, Jake had fired three shots at Hat Man's chest.

Jake saw a burst of steam explode where every bullet landed. Every explosion was followed by a high-pitched shriek.

He had hurt it.

Jake was sure it was working.

He fired again, another group of three.

Again, the puffs of steam rose, and the cries followed.

Hat Man turned to face Pastor Elijah Dwyer. It was the first time Jake had seen him move since he'd appeared.

He floated swiftly towards the pastor across the tunnel floor.

"Pastor, you don't have the faith to banish me. You wear the collar of faith, but it has left your soul. I can smell your fear!" Hat Man bellowed.

It was the first time Jake had heard Hat Man speak more than one word. His voice was gruff, almost monstrous.

Ignoring, Hat Man's words, Pastor Elijah continued his cleansing ritual, flicking more holy water towards the creature.

Despite smouldering from the holy water, Hat Man bore down on the pastor, hissing at him like a cobra about to strike.

"Where is your God now?" Hat Man growled.

Pastor Dwyer continued as if what Hat Man was saying had no effect on him. Raising the hand in which he held the cross, he pressed it hard into Hat Man's head, sending the wide-brimmed hat flying into the tunnel. The horns on Hat Man's head were now visible.

The cross burnt, and smoke poured from Hat Man's skin. But Hat Man was gripping the pastor around the throat. Although the pastor tried to back away, Hat Man's grip was too strong.

It spoke again, "Your God won't come. He won't save you. He didn't save your wife or your son. I have their souls, and they belong to me now."

The pastor squirted his remaining water all over the face of the now hatless demon. Its skin steamed before melting away like an ice cream left in the sun.

"In the name of . . ." the pastor began.

Hat Man struck in one quick motion, so fast the pastor didn't even see him move. His bony claws wrapped around the clergyman's throat, and the nails drew blood as they squeezed. Pastor Dwyer could feel his larynx being crushed so tightly he could neither speak nor breathe.

"See? No God," Hat Man boasted.

Pastor Dwyer pushed harder on the cross. Hat Man removed the cross from his head with his other claw. As it caught fire, he held it, crushing the flaming cross to dust.

A burnt outline remained imprinted on his forehead, but it seemed to have had little impact, Jake thought, as he watched them.

Isabella looked dead. Jake thought about checking for a pulse but decided against it. He thought she had probably been killed when Hat Man had thrown her to the ground.

Jake had five shots left. He hoped it would be enough, or he too would end up dead. Or worse, consumed by Hat Man.

Chapter 48

Picton December 2016

I had found some Panadol in the centre console. I took four, twice the recommended dose. The pain in my leg eased momentarily, but I knew the problem remained.

I passed a sign, on my left. It read 'Welcome to Picton'.

It was the sign Paige had shown me in the vision.

A thick fog descended the instant I entered the town, engulfing the car.

I slowed down. My radio went from having crystal-clear reception to static. I switched stations. All static.

I looked at the phone I had taken. The GPS had begun to lag, and the directions had stopped. The green line I was following had ended abruptly.

'No Service' showed in the top corner. That would explain the GPS also stopping.

Perhaps the phone's owner had contacted her service provider and reported it stolen, and it had been disconnected.

Surely if I headed into town, a local would be able to tell me where the tunnel was.

Had I not been driving so slowly, I would have missed it.

'Tunnel closed to Public. Do not Enter'.

I pulled the car into a gravel side road, which I followed for approximately a hundred metres before I spotted a car which was bullet-ridden, blood-smeared and heavily damaged.

I dragged myself out to inspect the abandoned vehicle. As soon as I applied any pressure, the pain instantly returned to my leg.

This place looked so familiar. This was it, I was sure of it.

I saw a wide, gravelled path from the car leading to a tunnel off in the distance. It looked like an old train line. Although I couldn't see any tracks, some of the old sleepers were still there.

Across the gravel walkway was a green gate. It reiterated the sign at the highway. I ignored it and dragged my throbbing, swollen leg over it. Pain shot through my body like a lightning bolt.

Fog lingered each side of the path, creating a runway to the tunnel. It was enticing me, encouraging me to enter.

I was only metres out from the entrance when I heard gunshots ring out from within, followed by muffled voices.

I headed cautiously into the darkness, leg throbbing, pain intensifying.

* * *

Jake was down to his remaining three bullets.

The pastor appeared to be losing the battle. His cross had been destroyed, his holy water was spent and the Hat Man, into whom Jake had unloaded several bullets laced with holy water, had only temporarily been halted before returning to full strength.

The cleansing wasn't working. Something was wrong.

Hat Man held Pastor Dwyer in one outstretched arm. "Did you ever wonder what happened to your father? Before you die, I think you should know," he said demonically.

His grip around the pastor's throat was so tight he couldn't even nod in response.

"I told him to hang himself from the bridge. He was so weak, so disappointed in your God, that he did as I said. Did your God come and save him? No. He just left him swinging at the end of the rope. What you don't know is, I killed your mother too. I put that cancer in her. Once she was gone, your father was easy to break. I'm sure he would have been asking where his precious God was. First his son, then his wife; his faith was shattered."

The pastor's eyes bulged; his face was red with anger. This thing had killed his whole family and now it was going to kill him.

"Don't worry, Pastor, your family is waiting for you. You will join them in my kingdom."

Without another word, Hat Man slit Pastor Dwyer's throat with one of his long nails. Blood sprayed all over Hat Man. The pastor collapsed to the floor, desperately trying to cover his throat with his hands, but it was to no avail. He couldn't stem the tide of blood.

"I missed your brother all those years ago, but I won't miss you and I won't miss Olly."

The pastor, who couldn't reply, lay slumped on the ground staring at him, his eyes full of fear.

His body began to convulse. It twitched two or three times, then went still.

Now he will come for me, Jake expected. His hand gripped the gun even tighter. Three shots left, he reminded himself. If I get down to one and I'm still no closer to ending this thing, then I'll bite it myself. There is no way I am letting this thing end me.

Hat Man stood over the body . . .

Waiting.

Then Jake realised he was waiting to feed.

The apparition of Pastor Elijah Dwyer rose. As it did so, a blinding, white light appeared between Jake and the pastor's body. Jake shielded his eyes. He could just make out the pastor's spirit travelling towards the light. Then he saw Hat Man stick its bony claws into the spirit, preventing it from moving forward.

Hat Man's mouth opened like an anaconda's and began to suck in the pastor's spirit. Jake had seen this before, at the Browns' house, and it wasn't something he wanted to witness again, but he was transfixed, unable to look away. He stood immobilised, fixated on this thing from another world.

Then Jake heard his name being called in the distance.

* * *

As I made my way deeper into the tunnel, I could make out what appeared to be a tall man eating the feet of a second man. It was bizarre. Beyond, I could see an extremely bright beam stretching from the tunnel celling to the floor. There stood Jake, transfixed by the shadowy figures.

"Jake!" I called again.

He was in a trance, staring out into the tunnel, at the horned man and what appeared to be a disappearing shadow or apparition.

I repeated the call for Jake three times. No response.

By the time I had approached the horned man, he had finished digesting whatever it was he was eating. Whatever this thing was, it scared me just to look at it. A feeling of dread came over my body.

This must be the evil that Paige had told me about. The thing looked like the devil itself.

It turned its head. Its eyes of bright blazing red bore down on me. It was as if they had direct access into my soul. I felt he knew everything about me just by looking at me.

A sudden fear raced through my body, a fear I hadn't experienced in a long time. It was the same fear I'd felt when I'd had my heart operation at the age of eight.

It was a horrible feeling, one I didn't want to experience again.

As I cautiously approached the horned man, it fled, or so I thought. When I looked again to see where it had gone, it was over standing in front of Jake.

It had travelled ten metres in a second.

It now had Jake by the throat, its long bony hands holding him tight, squeezing.

It pulled Jake in close. His feet were swinging in mid-air. The thing drew in a breath as if it was trying to smell his soul.

Nostril-like holes had appeared on the creature's face. In and out they moved as it sniffed.

How strong this thing must be to be holding Jake off the ground with one hand!

As I passed the lifeless pastor, I saw a small bible had fallen from his pocket. I collected it, though bending down sent bolts of pain firing up my leg. On the cover was a cross.

Jake was doing his best to fight off the thing.

"God didn't save the pastor. God won't save you. Your soul will be mine!" the demon bellowed.

Its breath smelt of death, a smell I knew Jake also recognised immediately. It was rancid.

I took the bible and slammed it into the shadowy horned man's back and pushed as hard as my body would allow.

The horned man hissed and snarled, trying to reach behind him.

Fire erupted where the bible touched. Smoke poured from him.

Then it happened. First, I felt my vision go blurry. Not now! I thought. Please, just give me a few more minutes.

I tried to talk but no sound came out. I felt my face droop; I had no control over my mouth.

I was having a stroke. The clot had finally reached my brain.

Then my legs went.

Down I went. I had instantly become a sprawling useless heap.

I was paralysed down my right-hand side. The stroke had hit hard. Although I could see and hear, I couldn't move.

I was about to die, and the last thing I would see was this devil-like creature killing my best friend.

The horned man had transformed from a human shape to a half-snake half-human creature. It had hands, a torso and a head, yet its legs had transformed into a serpent-like tail.

It turned and faced me. Its snake tail coiled around my motionless body and it began to squeeze. I felt my ribs crush. I felt my clotted leg burst and break.

I heard Jake scream in the background. My eyes shifted from the hovering serpent devil to Jake. A woman, fat and ugly and covered in blood, was on his back and she was clawing at his face.

Jake was doing his best to fight her off.

The deceased pastor, who had been lifeless only moments ago, joined her in attacking Jake's face. His head was hanging backwards, eyes facing the ceiling. His head bounced so much as he moved that I was waiting for it to fall off.

The air was being choked out of me. Every time I tried to breathe, I could feel the serpent tighten its grip.

"How is the heart going, has God fixed that for you yet?" Its breath stank as the words came out of its mouth. "Look at what God gave you. You have never had any faith. God wrecked your life; you could have been anything, but you were given a raw deal."

I could see jagged yellow vampire teeth as it spoke. The thing smelt me with its flared nostrils.

"I had already killed you once. But I am happy to kill you again," the thing said viciously.

I had no time to consider what he was talking about.

It squeezed harder; I couldn't breathe. It was killing me.

I didn't realise immediately that I had died. I guessed that either it had choked the life out of me or a bigger clot had hit my heart. There was no real feeling. No pain. I just drifted away. I had always feared death, wondering how it would end. I was glad I was with Jake.

I only realised my fate when I saw my body lying on the tunnel floor. My eyes were wide open, fixed on Jake.

When my soul rose, the serpent-horned-man turned to face me, as if being called to me. Within seconds it had grabbed me, inserting a claw in each shoulder. This was the real demon, stripped away from its human form.

I grabbed at its claw with my right hand, trying to release the grip. Then I realised my sprit could move.

A bright light appeared off to my right. I knew the light was for me; a reward for being good on earth.

The serpent opened its mouth, ready to consume me.

"Jake, shoot it!" I called out.

My voice sounded soft. I was worried it didn't exist any longer, and Jake wouldn't hear it.

Jake had thrown the pastor against the tunnel wall. Freeing his gun hand, he raised his weapon and fired at the back of the serpent. The demon screamed and hissed, turning its head a full one hundred and eighty degrees, trying to see what had hurt it.

With it distracted, I pulled towards the light.

"You know . . . you're right, I never had faith. Faith is for those who haven't seen the afterlife. I have seen it twice now, and I know there is a God. I'll show you he exists."

I found strength I had never had as a human being and it felt good. I pulled the serpent closer and closer to the light. I was going to go into the light and it was coming with me.

The serpent's head spun back to me, its eyes burning through me. It hissed, unlocking its jaw, and its claws dug in deeper. The grip tightened.

"Again!" I called out.

Jake fired again.

The serpent reared in pain, hissed and spun its head back to Jake. After the shot rang out, the pastor and the woman increased their ferocity upon Jake.

Jake had blood pouring down his face from where they had clawed him. He looked as if he had been attacked by a wild bear or a large feral cat. The fat woman was now going for his eyes. She was on his back digging her thumbs into his eyes.

I pulled, fast and hard, digging my heels into the tunnel floor for leverage. I was now only two steps away from the beam of bright, golden light.

The serpent turned its attention back to me. I could smell the stench of death from its belly as the jaw opened over the top of my head.

It was wet and slimy, and smelt putrid.

"Again!" I cried out.

I couldn't see Jake anymore. The serpent's mouth was down over my eyes.

I could hear him slamming something against the wall of the tunnel. My guess was the lady who was on his back.

"It's my last shot!" Jake called out.

I felt the thing's mouth touch the tops of my ears, then go over the lobes.

Everything was dark and muffled.

The deeper it took me, the louder the screaming was. At first, I thought it was coming from the outside, from Jake.

Then I realised it was coming from within. The screaming was all the past souls it had devoured. All were screaming in eternal hell and I was about to join them.

I could feel my feet begin to lift off the ground.

"Shoot!" I screamed.

I heard a distant gunshot that sounded a galaxy away, yet I knew it was only a few metres.

I slipped out of the serpent's mouth. Only its claws were hanging onto me.

I felt it rear up and whip around in pain, towards Jake.

I grabbed it around the waist and pulled one more time.

I could feel the warmth from the beam as I stepped closer to it.

I was closer now.

I pulled again as hard as I could manage.

Finally, I stepped into the light.

I heard an ear-piercing scream like I had never heard before. The serpent combusted, it seemed. Thousands of tiny ashes fell over my face, covering my spirit.

Hundreds of little glimmers of light shot up the beam. I guessed these were all the souls taken by the serpent.

Jake was watching me. Both the pastor and the woman had fallen silent the moment the serpent had turned to ash.

My body, lying in the corner, remained lifeless.

Surrounded by light, I waved to Jake.

He waved back.

Then I was gone.

* * *

Jake sat silently in the cold dark tunnel. He had just witnessed what appeared to be hundreds of stolen souls head into the light.

They were free.

Wiping the blood from his face, he got up and headed out of the tunnel. The sun was brighter than he had ever seen it, so bright it hurt his eyes. The sky was blue and cloudless.

Jake's phone sounded, indicating messages waiting in his voicemail. It was the first time since he had been at the Browns' farm that anything had come through. Jake removed it from his pocket; his service bar was full.

Jake rang the Thirlmere Police Department, followed by a call to Monique. He explained everything. He knew he sounded like a lunatic, but he told them the truth as he knew it.

Monique had called the Department of Social Services to attend the church and collect Olly until a foster home could be found for her.

Jake's wounds were only superficial; bruises plus a few claw marks where fingernails had dug in, the type you would expect from a brawl. Nothing more.

Two ambulances and four police patrol cars arrived. The paramedics requested Jake accompany them to the hospital. He refused. Instead, he insisted one of the uniformed officers take him to St Mark's Church.

He found Olly sitting on the altar step waiting for her grandfather to return. In her hands she was grasping a letter.

Jake knelt in front of her. "Hi Olly, do you remember me?"

She nodded but did not speak.

"Are you waiting for your grandpa?"

"Yes."

Jake looked at the officer. He was watching Jake, but he didn't offer any advice.

Jake had never done a death knock to a six-year-old.

"He can't come back, Olly," Jake said.

She began to cry.

"May I see the letter?" Jake said, seeing it was addressed to him.

It was a simple note.

This is my last will and testament. Should I die I would like all my posses-sions and the house sold with the proceeds placed in trust for Olly Dwyer, until she turns 21.

As she has no living relatives I would like her to reside with Detective Miller. Should he be unable to have her, a suitable foster home approved by Detective Miller should be found.

"Olly, would you like to come and live with me?"

Still crying, she nodded.

Jake didn't need to ask Hayley; she would never say no to an abandoned child. Jake had no doubt she would love her as her own.

Both of them would.

Chapter 49

In-between December 2016

I watched from the in-between, but only for a few days.

The last time I saw Jake was at my funeral. He gave the eulogy and performed much better than I would have done had our roles been reversed.

It was tough on him.

In the time between the events of the tunnel and my funeral, Jake applied for adoption papers and was accepted to adopt Olly.

His family had grown. He now had two beautiful daughters to care for.

Paige took me by the hand.

"We can go now," she said.

"What happens to the others, like Gemma? When do they come?"

"You have freed them. When they are ready, they will cross. They are not ready yet."

We turned and walked into the light.

www.ingramcontent.com/pod-product-compliance
Lightning Source LLC
Chambersburg PA
CBHW070727120726
47910CB00001B/10